2010

Guide To Literary Agents®

includes a 1-year online subscription to
Guide To Literary Agents on WritersMarket.com

WritersMarket.com
WHERE & HOW TO SELL WHAT YOU WRITE

THE ULTIMATE MARKET RESEARCH TOOL FOR WRITERS

To register your *2010 Guide To Literary Agents* book and START YOUR 1-YEAR ONLINE GENRE ONLY SUBSCRIPTION, scratch off the block below to reveal your activation code, then go to www.WritersMarket.com. Click on "Sign Up Now" and enter your contact information and activation code. It's that easy!

UPDATED MARKET LISTINGS FOR YOUR INTEREST AREA

EASY-TO-USE SEARCHABLE DATABASE

DAILY UPDATES

RECORD KEEPING TOOLS

INDUSTRY NEWS

PROFESSIONAL TIPS AND ADVICE

Your purchase of *Guide To Literary Agents* gives you access to updated listings related to this genre of writing. For just $9.99, you can upgrade your subscription and get access to listings from all of our best-selling Market books. Visit www.WritersMarket.com for more information.

2010 19TH ANNUAL EDITION

GUIDE TO LITERARY AGENTS®

Chuck Sambuchino, Editor

WRITER'S DIGEST BOOKS
CINCINNATI, OH

Publisher & Editorial Director, Writing Communities: Jane Friedman
Managing Editor, Writer's Digest Market Books: Alice Pope

Guide to Literary Agents Web site:www.guidetoliteraryagents.com
Writer's Market Web site: www.writersmarket.com
Writer's Digest Web site: www.writersdigest.com

Distributed in Canada by Fraser Direct
100 Armstrong Avenue
Georgetown, ON, Canada L7G 5S4 Tel: (905) 877-4411

Distributed in the U.K. and Europe by David & Charles
Brunel House, Newton Abbot, Devon, TQ12 4PU, England
Tel: (+44) 1626 323200, Fax: (+44) 1626 323319
E-mail: postmaster@davidandcharles.co.uk

Distributed in Australia by Capricorn Link
P.O. Box 704, Windsor, NSW 2756 Australia
Tel: (02) 4577-3555
ISSN: 1078-6945
ISBN-13: 978-1-58297-586-3
ISBN-10: 1-58297-586-8

Cover design by Claudean Wheeler
Production coordinated by Greg Nock
Illustrations©Dominique Bruneton/PaintoAlto

Attention Booksellers: This is an annual directory of F+W Media, Inc.
Return deadline for this edition is December 31, 2010.

Contents

RESOURCES

INDEXES

From the Editor

Each year, I make an effort to attend a handful of writers' conferences and retreats. In all, I've attended around 30 different events during my time at Writer's Digest Books. (You may have met me at one such conference—perhaps we're friends!) Sure, airline delays and flaky hotel thermostats can get to me once in a while, but it's all worth it. By traveling the country, meeting writers in person, and listening to their questions, I get a unique and comprehensive perspective of one big thing: what writers want to know. Because that's what it all comes down to, right?

With that in mind, I give you the *2010 Guide to Literary Agents*. You already know you need a literary agent to break out, so we've listed tons of agencies—experienced and new, large and boutique—to help writers snag a rep who can sell their work. We've continued to break down agencies into individual agents so you can see each rep's personal tastes. All listings are updated and verified, naturally—and we've got writers' conferences galore listed in the back section.

Want more? You got it. Agent Mollie Glick shows examples of query letters that worked and examines why they broke out of the slush pile (page 30); agent Cricket Freeman lays out the sections of a nonfiction book proposal (page 42); and agent Paul S. Levine falls back on his legal knowledge to explain the essentials of copyright and protecting your work (page 56). Everything else you need to know about the road to publishing success is also spelled out in this book's instructional articles.

And regarding the ever-changing state of the publishing industry in this technological age, we've got you covered there, too. The publishing world is changing—quickly—and writers must stay on top of how the submissions game is played. To help you get a leg up, we've called in some pros to help. Check out new articles on social networking and blogs (page 66), how *not* to get an agent (page 76), and what makes an agent consider taking on a self-published book (page 79).

As always, stay in touch with me at www.guidetoliteraryagents.com/blog. Also, please continue to pass along success stories, improvement ideas and news from the ever-changing agent world. In the meantime, good luck—and maybe I'll see you at a writers' conference this year!

Chuck Sambuchino
literaryagent@fwmedia.com

How to Use This Book

Searching for a literary agent can be overwhelming, whether you've just finished your first book or you have several publishing credits on your résumé. More than likely, you're eager to start pursuing agents and anxious to see your name on the spine of a book. But before you go directly to the listings of agencies in this book, take time to familiarize yourself with the way agents work and how you should approach them. By doing so, you will be more prepared for your search and ultimately save yourself effort and unnecessary grief.

Read the articles

This book begins with feature articles that explain how to prepare for representation, offer strategies for contacting agents, and provide perspectives on the author/agent relationship. The articles are organized into three sections appropriate for each stage of the search process: **Getting Started**, **Contacting Agents** and **Sealing the Deal**. You may want to start by reading through each article, and then refer back to relevant articles during each stage of your search.

Since there are many ways to make that initial contact with an agent, we've also provided a section called **Perspectives**. These personal accounts from agents and published authors offer information and inspiration for any writer hoping to find representation.

Decide what you're looking for

A literary agent will present your work directly to editors or producers. It's the agent's job to get her client's work published or sold and to negotiate a fair contract. In the **Literary Agents** section, we list each agent's contact information and explain what type of work the agency represents as well as how to submit your work for consideration.

For face-to-face contact, many writers prefer to meet agents at **Conferences**. By doing so, writers can assess an agent's personality, attend workshops and have the chance to get more feedback on their work than they get by mailing submissions and waiting for a response. The conferences section is divided into regions, and lists only those conferences agents and/or editors attend. In many cases, private consultations are available, and agents attend with the hope of finding new clients to represent.

Utilize the extras

Aside from the articles and listings, the book offers a section of **Resources**. If you come across a term with which you aren't familiar, check out the Resources section for a quick explanation. Also, note the gray tabs along the edge of each page. The tabs block off each section so they are easier to flip to as you conduct your search.

Frequently Asked Questions

1. **Why do you include agents who are not seeking new clients?** Some agents ask that their listings indicate they are currently closed to new clients. We include them so writers know the agents exist and know not to contact them at this time.

2. **Why do you exclude fee-charging agents?** We have received a number of complaints in the past regarding fees, and therefore have chosen to list only those agents who do not charge fees.

3. **Why are some agents not listed in *Guide to Literary Agents*?** Some agents may not have responded to our requests for information. We have taken others out of the book after receiving very serious complaints about them.

4. **Do I need more than one agent if I write in different genres?** It depends. If you have written in one genre and want to switch to a new style of writing, ask your agent if she is willing to represent you in your new endeavor. Most agents will continue to represent clients no matter what genre they choose to write. Occasionally, an agent may feel she has no knowledge of a certain genre and will recommend an appropriate agent to her client. Regardless, you should always talk to your agent about any potential career move.

5. **Why don't you list more foreign agents?** Most American agents have relationships with foreign co-agents in other countries. It is more common for an American agent to work with a co-agent to sell a client's book abroad than for a writer to work directly with a foreign agent. We do, however, list agents in the United Kingdom, Australia, Canada and other countries who sell to publishers both internationally and in the United States. If you decide to query a foreign agent, make sure they represent American writers (if you're American). Some may request to only receive submissions from Canadians, for example, or UK residents.

6. **Do agents ever contact a self-published writer?** If a self-published author attracts the attention of the media or if his book sells extremely well, an agent might approach the author in hopes of representing him.

7. **Why won't the agent I queried return my material?** An agent may not answer your query or return your manuscript for several reasons. Perhaps you did not include a self-addressed, stamped envelope (SASE). Many agents will discard a submission without a SASE. Or, the agent may have moved. To avoid using expired addresses, use the most current edition of *Guide to Literary Agents* or access the information online at www.WritersMarket.com. Another possibility is that the agent is swamped with submissions. Agents can be overwhelmed with queries, especially if the agent has recently spoken at a conference or has been featured in an article or book. Also, some agents specify in their listing that they never return materials of any kind.

Finally—and perhaps most importantly—are the Indexes in the back of the book. These can serve as an incredibly helpful way to start your search because they categorize the listings according to different criteria. For example, you can look for literary agents by name or according to their specialties (fiction/nonfiction genres). Similarly, you can search for script agents by name or according to format (e.g., plays/sitcoms). Plus, there is a **General Index** that lists every agent and conference in the book.

Listing Policy and Complaint Procedure

Listings in *Guide to Literary Agents* are compiled from detailed questionnaires, phone interviews and information provided by agents. The industry is volatile, and agencies change frequently. We rely on our readers for information on their dealings with agents and changes in policies or fees that differ from what has been reported to the editor of this book. Write to us (*Guide to Literary Agents*, 4700 E. Galbraith Road, Cincinnati, OH 45236) or e-mail us (literaryagent@fwpubs.com) if you have new information, questions or problems dealing with the agencies listed.

Listings are published free of charge and are not advertisements. Although the information is as accurate as possible, the listings are not endorsed or guaranteed by the editor or publisher of *Guide to Literary Agents*. If you feel you have not been treated fairly by an agent or representative listed in *Guide to Literary Agents*, we advise you to take the following steps:

- First try to contact the agency. Sometimes one phone call, letter or e-mail can clear up the matter. Politely relate your concern.
- Document all your correspondence with the agency. When you write to us with a complaint, provide the name of your manuscript, the date of your first contact with the agency and the nature of your subsequent correspondence.

We will keep your letter on file and attempt to contact the agency. The number, frequency and severity of complaints will be considered when deciding whether or not to delete an agency's listing from the next edition.

Guide to Literary Agents reserves the right to exclude any agency for any reason.

GETTING STARTED

Do I Need an Agent?

Preparing for Representation

A writer's job is to write. A literary agent's job is to find publishers for her clients' books. Because publishing houses receive more and more unsolicited manuscripts each year, securing an agent is becoming increasingly necessary. Finding an eager and reputable agent can be a difficult task. Even the most patient writer can become frustrated or disillusioned. As a writer seeking agent representation, you should prepare yourself before starting your search. Learn when to approach agents, as well as what to expect from an author/agent relationship. Beyond selling manuscripts, an agent must keep track of the ever-changing industry, writers' royalty statements, fluctuating reading habits—and the list goes on.

So, once again, you face the question: Do I need an agent? The answer, much more often than not, is yes.

WHAT CAN AN AGENT DO FOR YOU?

For starters, today's competitive marketplace can be difficult to break into, especially for unpublished writers. Many larger publishing houses will only look at manuscripts from agents—and rightfully so, as they would be inundated with unsatisfactory writing if they did not. In fact, approximately 80 percent of books published by the major houses are acquired through agents.

But an agent's job isn't just getting your book through a publisher's door. The following describes the various jobs agents do for their clients, many of which would be difficult for a writer to do without outside help.

Agents know editors' tastes and needs

An agent possesses information on a complex web of publishing houses and a multitude of editors to ensure her clients' manuscripts are placed in the right hands. This knowledge is gathered through relationships she cultivates with acquisition editors—the people who decide which books to present to their publisher for possible publication. Through her industry connections, an agent becomes aware of the specializations of publishing houses and their imprints, knowing that one publisher only wants contemporary romances while another is interested solely in nonfiction books about the military. By networking with editors, an agent also learns more specialized information—which editor is looking for a crafty Agatha-Christie-style mystery for the fall catalog, for example.

Agents track changes in publishing

Being attentive to constant market changes and shifting trends is another major requirement of an agent. An agent understands what it may mean for clients when publisher A merges

To-Do List for Fiction Writers

1. **Finish your novel** or short story collection. An agent can do nothing for fiction without a finished product.
2. **Revise your novel.** Have other writers offer criticism to ensure your manuscript is as polished as possible.
3. **Proofread.** Don't ruin a potential relationship with an agent by submitting work that contains typos or poor grammar.
4. **Publish** short stories or novel excerpts in literary journals, proving to potential agents that editors see quality in your writing.
5. **Research** to find the agents of writers whose works you admire or are similar to yours.
6. **Use the indexes in the back of this book** to construct a list of agents who are open to new writers and looking for your type of fiction (e.g., literary, romance, mystery).
7. **Rank your list.** Use the listings in this book to determine the agents most suitable for you and your work and to eliminate inappropriate agencies.
8. **Write your synopsis.** Completing this step will help you write your query letter and be prepared for when agents contact you.
9. **Write your query letter.** As an agent's first impression of you, this brief letter should be polished and to the point.
10. **Read about the business** of agents so you are knowledgeable and prepared to act on any offer. Start by reading this book's articles section completely.

with publisher B and when an editor from house C moves to house D. Or what it means when readers—and therefore editors—are no longer interested in Westerns, but instead can't get their hands on enough suspense novels.

Agents get your manuscript read faster

Although it may seem like an extra step to send your manuscript to an agent instead of directly to a publishing house, the truth is an agent can prevent writers from wasting months sending manuscripts that end up in the wrong place or buried in someone's slush pile. Editors rely on agents to save them time as well. With little time to sift through the hundreds of unsolicited submissions arriving weekly in the mail, an editor is naturally going to prefer a work that has already been approved by a qualified reader (i.e., the agent) that knows the editor's preferences. For this reason, many of the larger publishers accept agented submissions only.

Agents understand contracts

When publishers write contracts, they are primarily interested in their own bottom line rather than the best interests of the author. Writers unfamiliar with contractual language may

To-Do List for Nonfiction Writers

1. **Formulate a concrete idea** for your book. Sketch a brief outline making sure you have enough material for an entire book-length manuscript.
2. **Research** works on similar topics to understand the competition and determine how your book is unique.
3. **Write sample chapters.** This step should indicate how much time you will need to finish and if your writing needs editorial help.
4. **Publish** completed chapters in journals and/or magazines. This validates your work to agents and provides writing samples for later in the process.
5. **Polish your outline** so you can refer to it while drafting a query letter and you're prepared when agents contact you.
6. **Brainstorm** three to four subject categories that best describe your material.
7. **Use the indexes in this book** to find agents interested in at least two of your subject areas and who are looking for new clients.
8. **Rank your list.** Narrow your list further by reading the listings of agencies you found in the indexes, and organize the list according to your preferences. Research agent Web sites to be even more selective.
9. **Write your query.** Give an agent an excellent first impression by professionally and succinctly describing your premise and your experience.
10. **Read about the business** of agents so you're knowledgeable and prepared to act on any offer. Start by reading this book's articles section completely.

find themselves bound to a publisher with whom they no longer want to work. Or, they may find themselves tied to a publisher who prevents them from getting royalties on their first book until subsequent books are written. Agents use their experiences and knowledge to negotiate a contract that benefits the writer while still respecting the publisher's needs. After all, more money for the author will almost always mean more money for the agent—another reason they're on your side.

Agents negotiate–and exploit–subsidiary rights

Beyond publication, a savvy agent keeps in mind other opportunities for your manuscript. If your agent believes your book will also be successful as an audio book, a Book-of-the-Month Club selection or even a blockbuster movie, she will take these options into consideration when shopping your manuscript. These additional opportunities for writers are called subsidiary rights. Part of an agent's job is to keep track of the strengths and weaknesses of different publishers' subsidiary rights offices to determine the deposition of these rights regarding your work. After the contract is negotiated, the agent will seek additional moneymaking opportunities for the rights she kept for her client.

Agents get escalators

An escalator is a bonus that an agent can negotiate as part of the book contract. It is commonly given when a book appears on a bestseller list or if a client appears on a popular television show. For example, a publisher might give a writer a $30,000 bonus if he is picked for a book club. Both the agent and the editor know such media attention will sell more books, and the agent negotiates an escalator to ensure the writer benefits from this increase in sales.

Agents track payments

Since an agent only receives payment when the publisher pays the writer, it's in the agent's best interest to make sure the writer is paid on schedule. Some publishing houses are notorious for late payments. Having an agent distances you from any conflict regarding payment and allows you to spend your time writing instead of making phone calls.

Agents are advocates

Besides standing up for your right to be paid on time, agents can ensure your book gets a better cover design, more attention from the publisher's marketing department or other benefits you may not know to ask for during the publishing process. An agent can also provide advice during each step of the process, as well as guidance about your long-term writing career.

ARE YOU READY FOR AN AGENT?

Now that you know what an agent is capable of, ask yourself if you and your work are at a stage where you need an agent. Look at the To-Do Lists for fiction and nonfiction writers on pages 6 and 7, and judge how prepared you are for contacting an agent. Have you spent enough time researching or polishing your manuscript? Does your nonfiction book proposal include everything it should? Is your novel completely finished and thoroughly revised? Sending an agent an incomplete project not only wastes your time, but also may turn off the agent in the process. Literary agents are not magicians, and they can't solve your personal problems. An agent will not be your banker, CPA, social secretary or therapist. Instead, agents will endeavor to sell your book because that's how they earn their living.

Moreover, your material may not be appropriate for an agent. Most agents do not represent poetry, magazine articles, short stories, or material suitable for academic or small presses; the agents' commission does not justify spending time submitting these types of works. Those agents who do take on such material generally represent authors on larger projects first, and then adopt the smaller items as a favor to the client.

If you strongly believe your work is ready to be placed with an agent, make sure you're personally ready to be represented. In other words, consider the direction in which your writing career is headed. Besides skillful writers, agencies want clients with the ability to produce more than one book. Most agents will say they represent careers, not books.

WHEN DON'T YOU NEED AN AGENT?

Although there are many reasons to work with an agent, an author can benefit from submitting his own work directly to a book publisher. For example, if your writing focuses on a very specific area, you may want to work with a small or specialized press. These houses are usually open to receiving material directly from writers. Small presses can often give more attention to a writer than a large house can, providing editorial help, marketing expertise and other advice directly to the writer.

Academic books or specialized nonfiction books (such as a book about the history of Rhode Island) are good bets if you're not with an agent. Beware, though, as you will now be responsible for negotiating all parts of your contract and payment. If you choose this path, it's wise to use a lawyer or entertainment attorney to review all contracts. If a lawyer specializes in intellectual property, he can help a writer with contract negotiations. Instead of giving the lawyer a commission, the lawyer is paid for his time only.

And, of course, some people prefer working independently instead of relying on others to do their work. If you're one of these people, it's probably better to shop your own work instead of constantly butting heads with an agent. Let's say you manage to sign with one of the few literary agents who represent short story collections. If the collection gets shopped around to publishers for several months and no one bites, your agent may suggest retooling the work into a novel or novella(s). Agents suggest changes—some bigger than others--and not all writers think their work is malleable. It's all a matter of what you're writing and how you feel about it.

Agents Tell All

Expert Answers to Some Common (and Not So Common) Questions

There are some common questions writers ask time and time again. A handful of the mot common ones are answered below by several professional literary agents.

ON QUERIES & PITCHING

What are the most common problems you see in a query letter from an unknown author?

First, mistakes in grammar, spelling, word usage, or sentence structure. Anything like that is going to put me right off. Second, not saying what the book is about right away. I am only able to spend a minute at most reading your query letter—tell me exactly what I should know immediately because I may not read all the way to the end. Third, being boring or unoriginal—writers don't seem to realize how many query letters we read in a day or a week; we've seen everything and are looking, more than anything, for our attention to be caught, to be taken by surprise. Be surprising!

— **Ellen Pepus** *is the co-founder of Signature Literary*

Let's say you're looking through the slush pile at query letters. What are common things/elements you see in a query letter that don't need to be in there?

If your query letter is more than one page long, there are things in there that are superfluous. The most common unnecessary addition is a description of the writer's family/personal life if the book is not a memoir. Some personal background is good, but I would much prefer to know about the amazing novel you wrote. The personal information can come later. The other most common misstep is listing weak qualifications for writing the book. What I mean by that is when someone says "I have a daughter so I am qualified to write this very general book about how to raise daughters." In today's very crowded book market, you must have a strong platform to write nonfiction.

— **Abigail Koons** *is a literary agent with The Park Literary Group.*

ON FICTION

With literary fiction, what do you look for? What gets you to keep reading?

With literary fiction, I often look for a track record of previous publications. If you've been published in *Tin House* or *McSweeney's* or *GlimmerTrain*, I want to know. It tells me that the writer is in fact committed to their craft and building an audience out there in the journals. But if you have a good story and are a brilliant writer, I wouldn't mind if you lived in a cave in the Ozarks. For the record, I have yet to sign anyone who lives in a cave in the Ozarks.

— **Michelle Brower** *is a literary agent with Wendy Sherman Associates*

Can you throw out a few things that you believe are integral to a good suspense genre book?

These suggestions come to mind:

1. **Learn the formula** by reading and studying this genre. (Of course, you won't let your readers know you're following a formula). Analyze your favorite book to see how the writer adds suspense, to the book in general and individual scenes.
2. **Your central problem** or issue must be serious enough to engage readers' attention. What's at stake? Don't go overboard (like saving the earth from giant insects), but make sure your protagonist faces a life-changing threat. Make it personal for the hero.
3. **You'll need a sympathetic protagonist**, complete with flaws, quirks, and a reason for us to care what happens to her.
4. **Have a great ending** in mind before you start the book.
5. **Your bad guys should be interesting**, entertaining, and smart. Don't use cardboard villains. The hero should be fully tested by his adversaries.

— **Sammie Justesen** *is the founder of Northern Lights Literary Services*

If you were speaking to someone who was sitting down to write a romance book but had never done so before, what would you tell them about the necessities of how to write?

The word count would range from 50K to about 100K. There is a formula to write a good romance. The hero must be a man the reader would like to date and the heroine should be the type of girl that is bigger than life that the reader would like to be like. They should meet, overcome obstacles and in the end get together. There are dozens of different kind of romances—the author could join the Romance Writers of America for support and get into critique groups. All my published authors have critique groups.

— **Mary Sue Seymour** *is the founder of The Seymour Agency*

How does a writer know she's writing women's fiction, as opposed to literary fiction?

I think I have a fairly good definition of women's fiction. These are not simply stories with female characters but stories that tell us the female journey. Women's fiction is a way for women to learn and grow and to relate to others what it is to be a woman. When I think of literary fiction, the emphasis is placed more on the telling of a good story instead of making the female journey the centerpiece.

— **Scott Eagan** *is the founder of Greyhaus Literary*

ON NONFICTION

At a recent event, I met a writer who was also a scholar. She was writing a nonfiction book (and knew her subject inside out), but she seemed to have very little concept of platform. When you meet with someone like that—some who has superior knowledge but no marketing ideas—what are some basic helpful things you would tell them to do?

Build your base. I've given workshops at writers' conferences about establishing an author platform, and it all boils down to one basic concept: Develop a significant following before you go out with your nonfiction book. If you build it, they (publishers) will come. Think about that word platform. What does it mean? If you are standing on a physical platform, it gives you greater visibility. And that's what it's all about: visibility. How visible are you to the world? That's what determines your level of platform. Someone with real platform is the "go to" person in their area of expertise. If a reporter from the *New York Times* is doing a story on what you know about most, they will want to go to you for an interview first. But if you don't make yourself known to the world as the expert in your field, then how will the *NYT* know to reach out to you? RuPaul used to say, "If you don't love yourself, how the hell else is anybody else gonna love you?" I'm not saying be egotistical. I'm just saying, know your strengths, and learn to toot your own horn. Get out there. Make as many connections as you possibly can. We live in a celebrity-driven world. Love it or hate it, either way we all have to live with it. So, celebrate what you have to offer, and if it's genuine and enough people respond to it, then you will become a celebrity in your own right. Get out there and prove to the world that you are the be-all and end-all when it comes to what you know about most. Publishers don't expect you to be as big as Oprah, or Martha, or the Donald, but they do expect you to be the next Oprah, or Martha, or the next Donald in your own field.

— **Jeffery McGraw** *is a literary agent with The August Agency*

Your bio says you seek "travel narrative nonfiction." Can you help define this category for writers?

Travel and adventure narrative nonfiction is the type of book that takes you away to another place. It is often a memoir, but can be a journalistic story of a particular event or even a collection of essays. The key here is that it tells an interesting and engaging story. It is also very important these days that the story is fresh and new—you'd be surprised at how many people have had the exact same experience with the rickshaw in Bangkok that you had. Some recent successful examples of this genre are Jon Krakauer's *Into Thin Air*, Elizabeth Gilbert's *Eat, Pray, Love*, and most things by Paul Theroux and Bill Bryson.

— **Abigail Koons** *is a literary agent with The Park Literary Group*

It seems like if someone wanted to write about cooking or politics or history, it's all been done before. That said, what stands out for you in a proposal? What are you looking for immediately to draw you into a project?

There are several factors that can help a book's ultimate prospects: great writing, great platform, or great information, and ideally all three. For narrative works, the writing should be gorgeous, not just functional. For practical works, the information should be insightful, comprehensive and preferably new. And for any work of nonfiction, the author's platform is enormously important.

— **Ted Weinstein** *is the founder of Ted Weinstein Literary*

ON CHILDREN'S

Can you give us some 101 tips on writing children's nonfiction?

You can write about almost anything when it comes to children's nonfiction, even if it's been done before. But you need to come at the subject from a different angle. If there is already a book on tomatoes and how they grow, then try writing about tomatoes from a cultural angle. There are a ton of books on slavery, but not many on slaves in Haiti during the Haitian Revolution (is there even one? There's an idea—someone take it and query me!). Another thing to always consider is your audience. Kids already have textbooks at school, so you shouldn't write your book like one. Come at the subject in a way that kids can relate to and find interesting. Humor is always a useful tool in nonfiction for kids.

— **Joanna Stampfel-Volpe** *is a literary agent at Nancy Coffey Literary & Media Representation*

Where are writers going wrong in picture book submissions?

Rhyming! So many writers think picture books need to rhyme. There are some editors who won't even look at books in rhyme, and a lot more who are extremely wary of them, so it limits an agent on where it can go and the likelihood of it selling. It's also particularly hard to execute perfectly. Aside from rhyming, I see way too many picture books about a family pet or bedtime.

— **Kelly Sonnack** *is a literary agent at the Andrea Brown Literary Agency*

ON EVERYTHING ELSE

Can you throw out some examples so writers can get a feel for what constitutes a "pop culture" work?

I think of "pop culture" as anything that's an up-to-the minute trend. For example, playing off of our current economic situation I sold a book called *Bitches on a Budget* to NAL. It's a smart, witty (sometimes snarky) guide for women to who want to survive a recession in style. I'm also interested in blog culture, fashion, style, film, and entertainment.

— **Alanna Ramirez** *is a literary agent at Trident Media Group*

To a writer looking for an agent, can you offer any advice about something we haven't discussed?

Above all, remember the following:

1. You will be rejected.
2. You will be rejected.
3. When you're at the stage of catching an agent's eye, your query letter is as important as anything. Polish that baby!
4. Your first 10 pages hold your fate. Forward momentum is critical. It's not fair, but you have to give an agent a reason to turn the page. Know that you are one of 100 queries he or she will read that day. You don't have the luxury to meander.
5. Give them exactly what they ask for. If they ask for a one-page synopsis, don't give them a page and a half. If they ask for the submission to be sent as a Microsoft Word attachment, don't send a submission in the body of the e-mail. I know that agents seem like a disgruntled bunch with classic Napoleon complexes, but I assure you that we are diehard fans of writing who want to contribute to the world of books.
6. Do not call if you haven't heard back from an agent after a week, or even a month. I wish it weren't true, but it takes time to get through submissions. If you haven't heard back in a few months, then drop a polite e-mail, but after that, you have to let it go, which is why...
7. You should send out simultaneous submissions. There is no reason you should be expected to wait on an agent before you send your work to other agents. It's simply not fair. Do not hesitate to send out submissions to as many agents as possible. What's the worst that could happen? More than one agent is interested in your work. Call me crazy and unethical, but I am willing to bet this is a problem any writer without representation would welcome.
8. Your writing is worthwhile. Do not listen to the skeptics. They are just jealous because you've found something in this world that you're passionate about.
9. Oh yeah, you will be rejected.

— **Paul Lamb** *is a literary agent with Reece Halsey North*

To a writer looking for an agent, can you offer advice about something we haven't discussed?

It still surprises me how many writers are angry or defensive when agents reject their work. It's a wasted opportunity. We invest countless hours reading book proposals and giving each proposal careful thought. We have firsthand knowledge of what's selling (or easy to sell) and what's not. Rather than firing off a counter-response (which has probably never convinced an agent in the history of agenting), authors should use the opportunity to find out why they were rejected and improve their future chances of success. It is not rude to ask for more detailed feedback following a rejection, as long as the request is polite. We may be able to give advice or point out character, dialogue, pacing, pitch, or structural issues that you might have missed. It could also lead to a referral or a request to resubmit.

— **Brandi Bowles** *is a literary agent at Howard Morhaim Literary*

GETTING STARTED

Assessing Credibility

The Scoop on Researching Agents

Many people wouldn't buy a used car without at least checking the odometer, and savvy shoppers would consult the blue books, take a test drive and even ask for a mechanic's opinion. Much like the savvy car shopper, you want to obtain the best possible agent for your writing, so you should do some research on the business of agents before sending out query letters. Understanding how agents operate will help you find an agent appropriate for your work, as well as alert you about the types of agents to avoid.

Many writers take for granted that any agent who expresses interest in their work is trustworthy. They'll sign a contract before asking any questions and simply hope everything will turn out all right. We often receive complaints from writers regarding agents after they have lost money or have work bound by contract to an ineffective agent. If writers put the same amount of effort into researching agents as they did writing their manuscripts, they would save themselves unnecessary grief.

The best way to educate yourself is to read all you can about agents and other authors. Organizations such as the Association of Authors' Representatives (AAR; www.aar-online.org), the National Writers Union (NWU; www.nwu.org), American Society of Journalists and Authors (ASJA; www.asja.org) and Poets & Writers, Inc. (www.pw.org), all have informational material on finding and working with an agent.

Publishers Weekly (www.publishersweekly.com) covers publishing news affecting agents and others in the publishing industry. The Publishers Lunch newsletter (www.publishersmarketplace.com) comes free via e-mail every workday and offers news on agents and editors, job postings, recent book sales and more.

Even the Internet has a wide range of sites where you can learn basic information about preparing for your initial contact, as well as specific details on individual agents. You can also find online forums and listservs, which keep authors connected and allow them to share experiences they've had with different editors and agents. Keep in mind, however, that not everything printed on the Web is solid fact; you may come across the site of a writer who is bitter because an agent rejected his manuscript. Your best bet is to use the Internet to supplement your other research.

Once you've established what your resources are, it's time to see which agents meet your criteria. Below are some of the key items to pay attention to when researching agents.

LEVEL OF EXPERIENCE

Through your research, you will discover the need to be wary of some agents. Anybody can go to the neighborhood copy center and order business cards that say "literary agent," but that title doesn't mean she can sell your book. She may lack the proper connections with others in the publishing industry, and an agent's reputation with editors can be a major strength or weakness.

Agents who have been in the business awhile have a large number of contacts and carry the most clout with editors. They know the ins and the outs of the industry and are often able to take more calculated risks. However, veteran agents can be too busy to take on new clients or might not have the time to help develop the author. Newer agents, on the other hand, may be hungrier, as well as more open to unpublished writers. They probably have a smaller client list and are able to invest the extra effort to make your book a success.

If it's a new agent without a track record, be aware that you're taking more of a risk signing with her than with a more established agent. However, even a new agent should not be new to publishing. Many agents were editors before they were agents, or they worked at an agency as an assistant. This experience is crucial for making contacts in the publishing industry and learning about rights and contracts. The majority of listings in this book explain how long the agent has been in business, as well as what she did before becoming an agent. You could also ask the agent to name a few editors off the top of her head who she thinks may be interested in your work and why they sprang to mind. Has she sold to them before? Do they publish books in your genre?

If an agent has no contacts in the business, she has no more clout than you do. Without publishing prowess, she's just an expensive mailing service. Anyone can make photocopies, slide them into an envelope and address them to "Editor." Unfortunately, without a contact name and a familiar return address on the envelope, or a phone call from a trusted colleague letting an editor know a wonderful submission is on its way, your work will land in the slush pile with all the other submissions that don't have representation. You can do your own mailings with higher priority than such an agent could.

PAST SALES

Agents should be willing to discuss their recent sales with you: how many, what type of books and to what publishers. Keep in mind, though, that some agents consider this information confidential. If an agent does give you a list of recent sales, you can call the publishers' contracts department to ensure the sale was actually made by that agent. While it's true that even top agents are not able to sell every book they represent, an inexperienced agent who proposes too many inappropriate submissions will quickly lose her standing with editors.

You can also find out details of recent sales on your own. Nearly all of the listings in this book offer the titles and authors of books with which the agent has worked. Some of them also note to which publishing house the book was sold. Again, you can call the publisher and affirm the sale. If you don't have the publisher's information, simply go to your local library or bookstore to see if they carry the book. Consider checking to see if it's available on Web sites like Amazon.com, too. You may want to be wary of the agent if her books are nowhere to be found or are only available through the publisher's Web site. Distribution is a crucial component to getting published, and you want to make sure the agent has worked with competent publishers.

TYPES OF FEES

Becoming knowledgeable about the different types of fees agents may charge is vital to conducting effective research. Most agents make their living from the commissions they receive after selling their clients' books, and these are the agents we've listed. Be sure to ask about any expenses you don't understand so you have a clear grasp of what you're paying for. Described below are some types of fees you may encounter in your research.

Office fees

Occasionally, an agent will charge for the cost of photocopies, postage and long-distance phone calls made on your behalf. This is acceptable, so long as she keeps an itemized account of the expenses and you've agreed on a ceiling cost. The agent should only ask for office expenses after agreeing to represent the writer. These expenses should be discussed up front, and the writer should receive a statement accounting for them. This money is sometimes returned to the author upon sale of the manuscript. Be wary if there is an up-front fee amounting to hundreds of dollars, which is excessive.

Reading fees

Agencies that charge reading fees often do so to cover the cost of additional readers or the time spent reading that could have been spent selling. Agents also claim that charging reading fees cuts down on the number of submissions they receive. This practice can save the agent time and may allow her to consider each manuscript more extensively. Whether such promises are kept depends upon the honesty of the agency. You may pay a fee and never receive a response from the agent, or you may pay someone who never submits your manuscript to publishers.

Officially, the Association of Authors' Representatives' (AAR) Canon of Ethics prohibits members from directly or indirectly charging a reading fee, and the Writers Guild of America (WGA) does not allow WGA signatory agencies to charge a reading fee to WGA members, as stated in the WGA's Artists' Manager Basic Agreement. A signatory may charge you a fee if you are not a member, but most signatory agencies do not charge a reading fee as an across-the-board policy.

Warning Signs! Beware of . . .

Important

- Excessive typos or poor grammar in an agent's correspondence.
- A form letter accepting you as a client and praising generic things about your book that could apply to any book. A good agent doesn't take on a new client very often, so when she does, it's a special occasion that warrants a personal note or phone call.
- Unprofessional contracts that ask you for money up front, contain clauses you haven't discussed or are covered with amateur clip-art or silly borders.
- Rudeness when you inquire about any points you're unsure of. Don't employ any business partner who doesn't treat you with respect.
- Pressure, by way of threats, bullying or bribes. A good agent is not desperate to represent more clients. She invites worthy authors but leaves the final decision up to them.
- Promises of publication. No agent can guarantee you a sale. Not even the top agents sell everything they choose to represent. They can only send your work to the most appropriate places, have it read with priority and negotiate you a better contract if a sale does happen.
- A print-on-demand book contract or any contract offering you no advance. You can sell your own book to an e-publisher any time you wish without an agent's help. An agent should pursue traditional publishing routes with respectable advances.

Reading fees vary from $25 to $500 or more. The fee is usually nonrefundable, but sometimes agents agree to refund the money if they take on a writer as a client, or if they sell the writer's manuscript. Keep in mind, however, that payment of a reading fee does not ensure representation.

No literary agents who charge reading fees are listed in this book. It's too risky of an option for writers, plus nonfee-charging agents have a stronger incentive to sell your work. After all, they don't make a dime until they make a sale. If you find that a literary agent listed in this book charges a reading fee, please contact the editor at literaryagent@fwpubs.com.

Critique fees

Sometimes a manuscript will interest an agent, but the agent will point out areas requiring further development and offer to critique it for an additional fee. Like reading fees, payment of a critique fee does not ensure representation. When deciding if you will benefit from having someone critique your manuscript, keep in mind that the quality and quantity of comments varies from agent to agent. The critique's usefulness will depend on the agent's knowledge of the market. Also be aware that agents who spend a significant portion of their time commenting on manuscripts will have less time to actively market work they already represent.

In other cases, the agent may suggest an editor who understands your subject matter or genre and has some experience getting manuscripts into shape. Occasionally, if your story is exceptional or your ideas and credentials are marketable but your writing needs help, you will work with a ghostwriter or co-author who will share a percentage of your commission, or work with you at an agreed upon cost per hour.

An agent may refer you to editors she knows, or you may choose an editor in your area. Many editors do freelance work and would be happy to help you with your writing project. Of course, before entering into an agreement, make sure you know what you'll be getting for your money. Ask the editor for writing samples, references or critiques he's done in the past. Make sure you feel comfortable working with him before you give him your business.

An honest agent will not make any money for referring you to an editor. We strongly advise writers not to use critiquing services offered through an agency. Instead, try hiring a freelance editor or joining a writer's group until your work is ready to be submitted to agents who don't charge fees.

GETTING STARTED

Revisions and Self-Editing

Get Your Work Ready for Submission

by James Scott Bell

Submitting a novel without rewriting is like playing hockey naked. You're just not equipped to put your best, um, face on things. And sooner rather than later, a well-placed puck is going to hit you where it hurts most. That puck is editors' and agents' built-in prejudice against weak material. They are tuned to say No. That's why you rewrite. You want to take out all those No reasons.

Rewriting is one of the most important—if the not the most important—parts of writing. In that first draft you've completed is plenty of gold, but also plenty of waste that needs excising. So it's time to get to work.

THE TIME TO REVISE

So you have a completed manuscript. This is a crucial time. What you must avoid is any temptation to stop and do wholesale revisions before you have read the entire manuscript once.

Think of this process as Google Earth. You want to get a complete overview of your "earth." Your novel. Your story as a whole. You can spin the earth a little here and there to get a better view, but stay up top. You'll tag a few places to visit later, to zoom in on. That'll be the nuts and bolts of revision.

First, it's essential to give yourself a break from the first draft. At least two weeks. During this "cooling phase," try to forget about your book completely. Then try to read the manuscript through in a couple of sittings—three or four at the most. What you want to create is the feeling of being a fresh reader, getting into this book for the first time.

Don't stop to make changes at this point. You may jot a few things down, notes to yourself and the like, but keep going to get the overall impression of the book. Too many writers just sit down and read a manuscript page by page, making changes as they come up. Big or small, each item is dealt with the moment it's seen. Much better is to go from large to small. To start with the most crucial aspects and work your way down to the final step, which is The Polish.

MAKING BIG-PICTURE REVISIONS

When it comes to revision, I've found that most writers need a systematic approach. Think of this, then, as your ultimate revision checklist. Apply these questions to every manuscript you write.

JAMES SCOTT BELL is a novelist and writer. This article excerpted with permission from *Write Great Fiction: Revision and Self-Editing* (Writer's Digest Books).

Lead Character

- Is my Lead worth following for a whole novel? Why?
- How can I make my Lead "jump off the page" more?
- Do my characters sufficiently contrast? Are they interesting enough on their own

Will readers bond to my Lead because he:
. . . cares for someone other than himself?
. . . is funny, irreverent, or a rebel with a cause?
. . . is competent at something?
. . . is an underdog facing long odds without giving up?
. . . has a dream or desire readers can relate to?
. . . has undeserved misfortune, but doesn't whine about it?. . . is in jeopardy or danger?

Opposition Character

- Is the opposition character just as fully realized as the Lead?
- Is his behavior justified (in his own mind)?
- Are you being "fair" with the opposition?
- Is he as strong or (preferably) stronger than the Lead, in terms of ability to win the fight?

Plot

- Is there any point where a reader might feel like putting the book down?
- Does the plot feel forced or unnatural?
- Is the story out of balance? Too much action? Too much reaction?

The Opening

- Do I open with some part of the story engine running? Or am I spending too much time warming up?
- How do my opening pages conform to Hitchcock's axiom ("A good story is life with the dull parts taken out")? What is the story world I'm trying to present?
- What mood descriptions bring that story world to life for the reader?
- What is the tone of my novel going to be? Are the descriptions consistent with that mood?
- What happens in Act I that's going to compel the reader to keep reading? What danger to the lead? Is there enough conflict in the setup to run through the whole book?
- Do I deepen character relationships? Why should the reader care what's happening? Have I justified the final battle or final choice that will wrap things up at the end? Is there a sense of death (physical, professional, or psychological) that overhangs?
- Is there a strong adhesive keeping the characters together (such as moral or professional duty, physical location, or other reasons characters can't just walk away)?

Endings

- Are there loose threads left dangling? (You must either resolve these in a way that doesn't distract from the main plotline, or go back and snip them out.)
- Do I give a feeling of resonance? (The best endings leave a sense of something beyond the confines of the book covers.)
- Will the readers feel the way I want them to feel?

Scenes

- Is there conflict or tension in every scene?
- Do I establish a viewpoint character?
- If the scene is action, is the objective clear?
- If the scene is reaction, is the emotion clear?

Exposition

- Do I have large chunks of information dumped in one spot?
- Is my exposition doing double duty? Cut out any exposition that doesn't also add to the mood or tone of your novel.

Voice, Style, & Point of View

- Are there sections where the style seems forced or stilted? (Try reading it out loud. Hearing it will often help identify places to be cut or modified.)
- Is the POV consistent in every scene?
- If writing in first person, can the character see and feel what it is I describe?
- If writing in third person, do I slip into the thoughts of other characters rather than sticking to the POV character in the scene? Do I describe something the character can't see or feel?

Setting & Description

- Have I brought the setting to life for the reader?
- Does the setting operate as a "character"?
- Are my descriptions of places and people too generic?
- Are my descriptions doing "double duty" by adding to the mood or tone?

Dialogue

- Can I put in non-sequiturs, or answer a question with a question, and so on?
- Can I change some attributions—he said, she said—to action beats?
- Does my dialogue have conflict or tension, even between allies?

Theme

- Do I know what my theme is?
- Has a different theme emerged in the writing? Am I fighting it?
- Have I woven in thematic elements naturally?
- Have I avoided "the lecture"?

THE POLISH

Now, before you send off the manuscript, give it one more going over. This won't take long in comparison, but it will add that extra sparkle that could make all the difference.

Chapter Openings

- Can you begin a little further in?
- Does the opening grab? Have a hint of conflict or action?
- Do most of your chapters begin the same way? Vary them.

Chapter Endings

- Do most of your chapters end the same way? Vary them.
- Can you end the chapter earlier? How does it feel? If it's better, use it.

Dialogue

- Is there plenty of "white space" in your dialogue exchanges?
- Can you cut any words to make the dialogue tighter?

Word Search

- Do a word search for those repeated words and phrases you tend to overuse, then modify them accordingly.

- Look for overuse of the words "very," "really," and "suddenly."
- Adverbs are usually not necessary, and the emotion you're trying to clarify can be better shown through action.

Big Moments

- Identify five big moments in your manuscript. After each moment, make a list of 10 ways you can heighten that moment, make it more intense, and give it more juice.

WHAT THE PROCESS LOOKS LIKE

Below are two versions of a section from my novel, *Sins of the Fathers*. The first is my original. The second shows a little of the thinking process that goes into self-editing.

Original Version

First came the children.

In Lindy's dream they were running and screaming, dozens of them, in some sunlit field. A billowing surge of terrified kids, boys and girls, some in baseball garb, others in variegated ragtag clothes that gave the impression of a Dickens novel run amok.

What was behind them, what was causing the terror, was something dark, unseen. In the hovering over visions that only dreams afford, Lindy sought desperately the source of the fear.

There was a black forest behind the field, like you'd see in fairy tales. Or nightmares.

She moved toward the forest, knowing who it was, who was in there, and she'd meet him coming out. It would be Darren DiCinni, and he would have a gun, and in the dream she kept low to avoid being shot herself.

Moving closer and closer now, the screams of the scattering children fading behind her. Without having to look behind she knew that a raft of cops was pulling up to the scene.

She wondered if she was going to warn DiCinni, or was she just going to look at him?

Would he say anything to her, or she to him?

The dark forest had the kind of trees that come alive at night, with gnarly arms and knotted trunks. It was the place where the bad things lived.

Lindy didn't want to go in, but she couldn't stop herself.

That's when the dark figure started to materialize, from deep within the forest, and he was running toward her.

Edited Version

First came the children.

In Lindy's dream they were running and screaming, dozens of them, in some sunlit field. A billowing surge of terrified kids, boys and girls, some in baseball garb, others in variegated ragtag clothes that gave the impression of a Dickens novel run amok.

~~What was behind them, what was causing the terror, was something dark, unseen.~~ [Weak sentence structure. Rethink. Check "dark." I use it a lot!] ~~In the hovering over visions~~ [Confusing.] that only dreams afford, Lindy sought desperately the source of the fear.

~~There was~~ [Sentences starting with "There" are generally weak. Rethink.] a black forest behind the field, like you'd see [Using "you" in this way can be effective in some places, but overuse is not good. Rethink.] in fairy tales. Or nightmares.

She moved toward the forest, ~~knowing who it was, who was in there~~, [Awkward.] and she'd meet him coming out. I~~t would be Darren DiCinni, and he would have a~~

~~gun, and in the dream she kept low to avoid being shot herself~~. [See if I can strengthen this dramatic image.]

Moving closer and closer now, the screams of the scattering children fading behind her. Without having to look behind she knew that a raft of cops was pulling up to the scene.

~~She wondered if she was going to warn DiCinni, or was she just going to look at him?~~ [Tighten.]

Would he say anything to her, or she to him?

~~The dark forest had the kind of trees that come alive at night, with gnarly arms and knotted trunks. It was the place where the bad things lived.~~ [Rethink. There's "dark" again.]

Lindy didn't want to go in, but she couldn't stop herself.

~~That's when~~ [Unneeded verbiage.] the dark figure started to materialize, from deep within the forest, and ~~he~~ [How do we know it's he?] was running toward her.

LEARNING TO BE A REAL WRITER

Self-editing is the ability to know what makes fiction work. You learn to be your own guide so you may, as Renni Browne and Dave King put it in *Self-Editing for Fiction Writers*, "See your manuscript the way an editor might see it-to do for yourself what a publishing house editor once might have done."

By self-editing exercises and revising your work, you'll be operating on all cylinders. This is how you become a real writer. Cutting, shaping, adding, subtracting, working it, making it better, that's what real writing is all about. This is how unpublished writers become published.

Avenues to an Agent

Getting Your Foot in the Door

Once your work is prepared and you have a solid understanding of how literary agents operate, the time is right to contact an agent. Your initial contact determines the agent's first impression of you, so you want to be professional and brief.

Again, research plays an important role in getting an agent's attention. You want to show the agent you've done your homework. Read the listings in this book to learn agents' areas of interest, check out agents' Web sites to learn more details on how they do business, and find out the names of some of their clients. If there is an author whose book is similar to yours, call the author's publisher. Someone in the contracts department can tell you the name of the agent who sold the title, provided an agent was used. Contact that agent, and impress her with your knowledge of the agency.

Finding an agent can often be as difficult as finding a publisher. Nevertheless, there are four ways to maximize your chances of finding the right agent: submit a query letter or proposal; obtain a referral from someone who knows the agent; meet the agent in person at a writers' conference; or attract the agent's attention with your own published writing.

SUBMISSIONS

The most common way to contact an agent is through a query letter or a proposal package. Most agents will accept unsolicited queries. Some will also look at outlines and sample chapters. Almost none want unsolicited complete manuscripts. Check the "How to Contact" subhead in each listing to learn exactly how an agent prefers to be solicited.

Agents agree to be listed in directories such as *Guide to Literary Agents* to indicate what they want to see and how they wish to receive submissions from writers. As you start to query agents, make sure you follow their individual submission directions. This, too, shows an agent you've done your research.

Like publishers, agencies have specialties. Some are only interested in novel-length works. Others are open to a variety of subjects and may actually have member agents within the company who specialize in only a handful of the topics covered by the entire agency.

Before querying any agent, first consult the Agent Specialties Indexes in the back of this book for your manuscript's subject, and identify those agents who handle what you write. Then, read the agents' listings to see which are appropriate for you and your work.

REFERRALS

The best way to get your foot in an agent's door is through a referral from one of her clients, an editor or another agent she has worked with in the past. Since agents trust their clients, they'll usually read referred work before over-the-transom submissions. If you are friends with anyone in the publishing business who has connections with agents, ask politely for a referral. However, don't be offended if another writer will not share the name of his agent.

Communication Etiquette

Via Mail

- Address the agent formally and make sure her name is spelled correctly.
- Double-check the agency's address.
- Include a SASE.
- Use a clear font and standard paragraph formatting.
- A short handwritten thank-you note can be appropriate if the agent helped you at a conference or if she provided editorial feedback along with your rejection.
- Don't include any extraneous materials.
- Don't try to set yourself apart by using fancy stationery. Standard paper and envelopes are preferable.

Via E-mail

- Address the agent as you would in a paper letter–be formal.
- If it's not listed on the Web site, call the company to get the appropriate agent's e-mail address.
- Include a meaningful subject line.
- Keep your emotions in check: Resist the temptation to send an angry response after being rejected, or to send a long, mushy note after being accepted. Keep your e-mails businesslike.
- Don't type in all caps or all lower case. Use proper punctuation and pay attention to grammar and spelling.
- Don't overuse humor—it can be easily misinterpreted.
- Don't e-mail about trivial things.

On the Phone

- Be polite: Ask if she has time to talk, or set up a time to call in advance.
- Get over your "phone phobia." Practice your conversation beforehand if necessary.
- Resist the urge to follow up with an agent too quickly. Give her time to review your material.
- Never make your first contact over the phone unless the agent calls you first or requests you do so in her submission guidelines.
- Don't demand information from her immediately. Your phone call is interrupting her busy day and she should be given time to respond to your needs.
- Don't call to get information you could otherwise obtain from the Internet or other resources.
- Don't have your spouse, secretary, best friend or parent call for you.

In Person

- Be clear and concise.
- Shake the agent's hand and greet her with your name.
- Be yourself, but be professional.
- Maintain eye contact.
- Don't monopolize her time. Either ask a brief question or ask if you can contact her later (via phone/mail/e-mail) with a more in-depth question.
- Don't get too nervous–agents are human!

CONFERENCES

Going to a conference is your best bet for meeting an agent in person. Many conferences invite agents to give a speech or simply be available for meetings with authors, and agents view conferences as a way to find writers. Often agents set aside time for one-on-one discussions with writers, and occasionally they may even look at material writers bring to the conference. These critiques may cost an extra fee, but if an agent is impressed with you and your work, she'll ask to see writing samples after the conference. When you send your query, be sure to mention the specific conference where you met and that she asked to see your work.

When you're face to face with an agent, it's an important time to be friendly, prepared and professional. Always wait for the agent to invite you to send work to them. Saying "I'll send it to your office tomorrow" before they've offered to read it comes off wrong. Don't bring sample chapters or a copy of your manuscript unless you've got a professional critique arranged beforehand. Agents will almost never take writers' work home (they don't have the suitcase space), and writers nervously asking agents to take a look at their work and provide some advice could be considered gauche.

Remember, at these conferences, agents' time is very valuable—as is yours. If you discover that agent who's high on your list recently stopped handling your genre, don't hunt her down and try to convince her to take it on again. Thank the agent for her time and move on to your next target.

If you plan to pitch agents, practice your speech-and make sure you have a pitch that clocks in at less than one minute. Also have versions of your pitch for 2-minute pitches and 3-minute pitches, depending on the conference. Keep your in-person pitch simple and exciting-letting the agent become interested and ask the follow-up questions.

Because this is an effective way to connect with agents, we've asked agents to indicate in their listings which conferences they regularly attend. We've also included a section of Conferences, starting on page xxx, where you can find more information about a particular event.

PUBLISHING CREDITS

Some agents read magazines or journals to find writers to represent. If you have had an outstanding piece published in a periodical, an agent wanting to represent you may make contact. In such cases, make sure the agent has read your work. Some agents send form letters to writers, and such representatives often make their living entirely from charging reading fees and not from commissions on sales.

However, many reputable and respected agents do contact potential clients in this way. For them, you already possess attributes of a good client: You have publishing credits and an editor has validated your work. To receive a letter from a reputable agent who has read your material and wants to represent you is an honor.

Occasionally, writers who have self-published or who have had their work published electronically may attract an agent's attention, especially if the self-published book has sold well or received a lot of positive reviews.

Recently, writers have been posting their work on the Internet with the hope of attracting an agent's eye. With all the submissions most agents receive, they probably have little time to peruse writers' Web sites. Nevertheless, there are agents who do consider the Internet a resource for finding fresh voices.

Start Your Story Right

What Agents Don't Want to See in Chapter 1

by Chuck Sambuchino

Ask any literary agent what they're looking for in a first chapter and they'll all say the same thing: "Good writing that hooks me in." Agents appreciate the same elements of good writing that readers do. They want action; they want compelling characters and a reason to read on; they want to see your voice come through in the work and feel an immediate connection with your writing style.

Sure, the fact that agents look for great writing and a unique voice is nothing new. But, for as much as you know about what agents want to see in chapter one, what about all those things they don't want to see? Obvious mistakes such as grammatical errors and awkward writing aside, writers need to be conscious of chapter one clichés and agent pet peeves—either of which, when included in your writing, can sink a manuscript and send a form rejection letter your way.

Have you ever begun a story with a character waking up from a dream? Or opened chapter one with a line of salacious dialogue? Both clichés! Chances are, you've started a story with a cliché or touched on a pet peeve (or many!) in your writing and you don't even know it—and nothing turns an agent off like what agent Cricket Freeman of the August Agency calls "nerve-gangling, major turn-off, ugly-as-sin, nails-on-the-blackboard pet peeves."

To help compile a grand list of these poisonous chapter one no-no's, dozens of established literary agents (and even one editor) were more than happy to chime in and vent about everything that they can't stand to see in that all-important first chapter. Here's what they had to say.

DESCRIPTION

"I dislike endless 'laundry list' character descriptions. For example: 'She had eyes the color of a summer sky and long blonde hair that fell in ringlets past her shoulders. Her petite nose was the perfect size for her heart-shaped face. Her azure dress—with the empire waist and long, tight sleeves—sported tiny pearl buttons down the bodice and ivory lace peeked out of the hem in front, blah, blah, blah.' Who cares! Work it into the story."

— **Laurie McLean**, *Larsen/Pomada, Literary Agents*

"Slow writing with a lot of description will put me off very quickly. I personally like a first chapter that moves quickly and draws me in so I'm immediately hooked and want to read more."

— **Andrea Hurst**, *Andrea Hurst & Associates Literary Management*

CHUCK SAMBUCHINO is the editor of *Guide to Literary Agents* (www.guidetoliteraryagents.com/blog) and *Screenwriter's & Playwright's Market* (both Writer's Digest Books). He is a former staffer on *Writer's Digest* and a frequent presenter at writers' conferences.

"Avoid any description of the weather."
— **Denise Marcil**, *Denise Marcil Literary Agency*

VOICE AND POINT-OF-VIEW

"A pet peeve of mine is ragged, fuzzy point-of-view. How can a reader follow what's happening? I also dislike beginning with a killer's POV. Who would want to be in such an ugly place? I feel like a nasty voyeur."
— **Cricket Freeman**, *The August Agency*

"An opening that's predictable will not hook me in. If the average person could have come up with the characters and situations, I'll pass. I'm looking for a unique outlook, voice, or character and situation."
— **Debbie Carter,** *Muse Literary Management*

"Avoid the opening line is 'My name is...,' introducing the narrator to the reader so blatantly. There are far better ways in chapter one to establish an instant connection between narrator and reader."
— **Michelle Andelman**, *Lynn C. Franklin Associates*

"I hate seeing a 'run-down list:' Names, hair color, eye color, height, even weight sometimes. Another thing that bothers me: Over-describing the scenery or area where the story starts. Usually a manuscript can lose the first 3-5 chapters and start there. I also don't like having a character immediately tell me how much he/she hates the world for whatever reason. In other words, tell me your issues on politics, the environment, etc. through your character. That is a real turn off."
— **Miriam Hees** *editor, Blooming Tree Press*

"I hate reading purple prose, taking the time to set up—to describe something so beautifully and that has nothing to do with the actual story. I also hate when an author starts something and then says '(the main character) would find out later.' I hate gratuitous sex and violence anywhere in the manuscript. If it is not crucial to the story then I don't want to see it in there, in any chapters."
— **Cherry Weiner**, *Cherry Weiner Literary*

"I recently read a ms when the second line was something like, 'Let me tell you this, Dear Reader...' What do you think of that?"
— **Sheree Bykofsky**, *Sheree Bykofsky Literary*

ACTION (OR LACK THEREOF)

"I don't really like 'First day of school' beginnings, or the 'From the beginning of time,' or 'Once upon a time' starts. Specifically, I dislike a chapter one where nothing happens."
— **Jessica Regel**, *Jean V. Naggar Literary Agency*

"'The Weather' is always a problem—the author feels he has to set up the scene and tell us who the characters are, etc. I like starting a story *in media res*."
— **Elizabeth Pomada**, *Larsen/Pomada, Literary Agents*

"I want to feel as if I'm in the hands of a master storyteller, and starting a story with long, flowery, overly-descriptive sentences (kind of like this one) makes the writer seem amateurish and the story contrived. Of course, an equally jarring beginning can be nearly as off-putting, and I hesitate to read on if I'm feeling disoriented by the fifth page. I enjoy when writers can find a good balance between exposition and mystery. Too much accounting always ruins the mystery of a novel, and the unknown is what propels us to read further. It is what keeps me up at night saying, 'Just one more chapter, then I'll go to sleep.' If everything is explained away in the first chapter; I'm probably putting the book down and going to sleep."

— **Peter Miller**, *Peter Miller Literary*

"Characters that are moving around doing little things, but essentially nothing. Washing dishes & thinking, staring out the window & thinking, tying shoes, thinking ... Authors often do this to transmit information, but the result is action in a literal sense but no real energy in a narrative sense. The best rule of thumb is always to start the story where the story starts."

— **Dan Lazar**, *Writers House*

CLICHÉS AND FALSE BEGINNINGS

"I hate it when a book begins with an adventure that turns out to be a dream at the end of the chapter."

— **Mollie Glick**, *Jean V. Naggar Literary Agency*

"Anything cliché such as 'It was a dark and stormy night' will turn me off. I hate when a narrator or author addresses the reader (e.g., 'Gentle reader')."

— **Jennie Dunham**, *Dunham Literary*

"Sometimes a reasonably good writer will create an interesting character and describe him in a compelling way, but then he'll turn out to be some unimportant bit player. I also don't want to read about anyone sleeping, dreaming, waking up or staring at anything. Other annoying, unoriginal things I see too often: some young person going home to a small town for a funeral, someone getting a phone call about a death, a description of a psycho lurking in the shadows, or a terrorist planting a bomb."

— **Ellen Pepus**, *Signature Literary Agency*

"I don't like it when the main character dies at the end of chapter one. Why did I just spend all this time with this character? I feel cheated."

— **Cricket Freeman**, *The August Agency*

"1. Squinting into the sunlight with a hangover in a crime novel. Good grief—been done a million times. 2. A sci-fi novel that spends the first two pages describing the strange landscape. 3. A trite statement ('Get with the program' or 'Houston, we have a problem' or 'You go girl' or 'Earth to Michael' or 'Are we all on the same page?'), said by a weenie sales guy, usually in the opening paragraph. 4. A rape scene in a Christian novel, especially in the first chapter. 5. 'Years later, Monica would look back and laugh...' 6. 'The [adjective] [adjective] sun rose in the [adjective] [adjective] sky, shedding its [adjective] light across the [adjective] [adjective] [adjective] land.'"

— **Chip MacGregor**, *MacGregor Literary*

"A cheesy 'hook' drives me nuts. I know that they say 'Open with a hook!'—something to grab the reader. While that's true, there's a fine line between a hook that's intriguing and a hook that's just silly. An example of a silly hook would be opening with a line of overtly sexual dialogue. Or opening with a hook that's just too convoluted to be truly interesting."

— **Dan Lazar**, *Writers House*

"Here are things I can't stand: Cliché openings in Fantasy can include an opening scene set in a battle (and my peeve is that I don't know any of the characters yet so why should I care about this battle) or with a pastoral scene where the protagonist is gathering herbs (I didn't realize how common this is). Opening chapters where a main protagonist is in the middle of a bodily function (jerking off, vomiting, peeing, or what have you) is usually a firm NO right from the get-go. Gross. Long prologues that often don't have anything to do with the story. So common in Fantasy again. Opening scenes that our all dialogue without any context. I could probably go on..."

— **Kristin Nelson**, *Nelson Literary*

CHARACTERS AND BACKSTORY

"I don't like descriptions of the characters where writers make the characters seem too perfect. Heroines (and heroes) who are described physically as being virtually unflawed come across as unrelatable and boring. No 'flowing, windswept golden locks'; no 'eyes as blue as the sky'; no 'willowy, perfect figures.'"

— **Laura Bradford**, *Bradford Literary Agency*

"Don't use inauthentic dialogue to tell the reader who the characters are, instead of showing who the characters are."

— **Jennifer Cayea**, *Avenue A Literary*

"Many writers express the character's backstory before they get to the plot. Good writers will go back and cut that stuff out and get right to the plot. The character's backstory stays with them—it's in their DNA—even after the cut. To paraphrase Bruno Bettelheim: 'The more the character in a fairy tale is described, the less the audience will identify with him ... The less the character is characterized and described the more likely the reader is to identify with him.'"

— **Adam Chromy**, *Artists and Artisans*

"I'm really turned off by a protagonist named Isabelle who goes by 'Izzy.' No. Really. I am. I'm also turned off when a writer feels the need to fill in all the backstory before starting the story; a story that opens on the protagonist's mental reflection of their situation is (usually) a red flag."

— **Stephany Evans**, *FinePrint Literary Management*

"One of the biggest problems I encounter is the 'information dump' in the first few pages, where the author is trying to tell us everything we supposedly need to know to understand the story. Getting to know characters in a story is like getting to know people in real life. You find out their personality and details of their life over time."

— **Rachelle Gardner**, *Wordserve Literary*

(AND FINALLY...) PROLOGUES

"Most of us hate prologues—just make the first chapter relevant and well written."

— **Andrea Brown**, *Andrea Brown Literary Agency*

"Prologues are usually a lazy way to give backstory chunks to the reader and can be handled with more finesse throughout the story. Damn the prologue, full speed ahead!"

— **Laurie McLean**, *Larsen/Pomada, Literary Agents*

Write a Killer Query Letter

How to Hook an Agent

by Mollie Glick

At conferences, I often meet worried writers who think they've got to be well connected in order to find an agent—thinking that agents don't pay any attention to query letters. But the truth is that I've found some of my favorite clients through unsolicited queries, and almost every agency I know has someone on staff whose job it is to sort through the queries and let their higher-ups know if they spot one that looks promising. The trick is to write a query letter strong enough to catch that person's attention.

A good query letter accomplishes two things: It makes an agent want to read your book, and it makes it easy for them to contact you to request sample material. Sounds pretty easy, right? Well, if you follow the following guidelines, it can be.

PROFESSIONALISM

The first thing to think about when you sit down to write a query letter is that, in a lot of ways, it's similar to writing a cover letter for a job application. You're addressing your letter to a person who's never met you before, and who sorts through hundreds of such letters a day. This crucial first contact is your chance to demonstrate that you're smart, professional, and interesting. The way to convey those traits is through the tone and content of your letter. The tone should be professional, specific and engaging—never general, overly familiar or abrasive. Make sure your letter is well written and grammatically correct. And make sure to include all of your contact information, including your mailing address, phone number and e-mail address.

These suggestions may sound obvious, but you'd be surprised how many letters I get that leave out vital contact information, start out with "Hi Mollie—" instead of "Dear Ms. Glick:", or include unprofessional phrases such as, "You'll probably just throw this letter out like the other agents have." Occasionally, I get a letter written in a lighter, more humorous tone, and that's OK—as long as the letter reflects the kind of book the author is querying me about (i.e., a humorous nonfiction book or funny novel) and it still includes all the information I need to know. But if in doubt, stick with a professional tone, and include a one- or two-line quote from the book to give the agent a taste of its voice.

Like a cover letter, your query letter should be no longer than a page. It should include your contact information, a salutation, a paragraph describing your book, and a paragraph explaining why you're the perfect person to write that book. Lets take a closer look at each of these components.

MOLLIE GLICK is a literary agent with Foundry Literary + Media in New York.

CONTACT INFORMATION

To be perfectly honest, it doesn't really matter where you include the information on a snail mail query; it just matters that the information is complete and easily located. That said, you can't go wrong by putting your contact information at the top of a letter, centered.

What's more important to note is that the location of your contact information in e-mail correspondence is very important. Whereas a snail mail letter would have your information (as well as the agent's address) at the top, an e-query should include your information at the bottom, following your signature. The reasoning is simple. When an agent opens up your e-mail, they only see part of the letter in the e-mail window. It's most effective if we can just jump into the meat of the query rather than scrolling down past ten lines. (See the e-query example on Page 35.)

THE SALUTATION

You should address the agent by his/her last name, or at the very least as "Dear Agent"—never by their first name unless you've met them previously in person and they've invited you to do so. At the start of your letter, feel free to explain why you've chosen to query this particular agent (i.e., "I read on the Writer's Digest Web site that you're particularly interested in acquiring smart, funny women's fiction," or "I noticed that you represent both Greg Olear and Ames Holbrook and thought you would be an excellent fit for my humorous political memoir"). If you were referred by a current client or an editor, or recently heard the author speak at a conference, this is also a good place to mention it.

If the agent has a name such as Chris or Pat and you're unsure of the gender, feel free to use the rep's full name: "Dear Pat Richardson:".

ABOUT THE BOOK

This is the trickiest part of the query letter—your chance to summarize, in one paragraph, what your book is about and who it will appeal to. Before you sit down to write this paragraph, you might want to start by developing a hook or "elevator pitch." This is a one- or two-sentence description that sums up what you're hoping to achieve—the kind of thing you'd say to a Hollywood exec if you bumped into them on an elevator and had 30 seconds to get them interested in your project.

One approach to an elevator pitch is to capture the theme of the novel. For example, if you were my author, Dorothy Hearst, pitching her first novel, *Promise of the Wolves*, you might say: "*Promise of the Wolves* is a debut novel that tells the story of the first wolves who became dogs, from the wolf's point of view."

Another approach is to give a brief summary of the plot. So if you were Brenda Janowitz, pitching *Jack with a Twist*, you could write something like "When NY attorney Brooke Miller lands her first big case, and finds out that her opposing attorney is her fiancé, Jack, she realizes that she's going to have to decide between the case of her life and actually having a life."

If you're writing a nonfiction book, you might lead with your audience. For example, you might say something like "Over the past year, more than 10,000 new cases of autism have been diagnosed, and parents are hungry for information about dealing with this devastating diagnosis."

An elevator pitch is a good way to start off your About the Book paragraph, immediately grabbing the attention of the agent, but whether you're writing fiction or nonfiction, it's also a good idea to make a case in this paragraph that there's going to be a large, appreciative audience for your book. One way to do that is to compare your book to other books that have already been successfully published. For example, if you were my client Ellen Bryson pitching her fiction debut, you might say something like this: "A historical novel set in the Barnum and Bailey Museum in New York at the turn of the century, *Hungry* will appeal to fans of Sara Gruen's *Water for Elephants* and Elizabeth McCracken's *The Giant's House.*" Just make sure you don't overreach by saying you're the next Dan Brown, J.K. Rowling or Elizabeth Gilbert. No agent wants to hear that you've got the next *Da Vinci Code, Harry Potter*, or *The Secret*. Make sure you've earned any comparisons you make and that they're not the same two "hot" books everyone else in the world is using as comparisons.

If you're writing nonfiction, you could also make an argument for the timeliness and relevance of your subject. For example, nonfiction writer John Park's query for *The Last Farmer* starts out with the following paragraph:

"Five years ago, no one in America was talking about farmers, and most of us were blissfully ignorant about the origins of our food. Sure, the occasional bestseller like *Fast Food Nation* lifted a section of the veil from time to time, but agriculture itself was not a sexy subject. That's about to change. With the price of food escalating to record heights, increasing concern over the safety of genetically modified foods, the terrifyingly rapid spread of E. coli outbreaks, and new research into ethanol as an alternative to oil, farming is about to move into the mainstream. Last month there were more news stories about farmers than there were about Britney Spears, and recently even magazines like *Vanity Fair* and *New York Magazine* have featured articles about farmers. Books such as Paul Roberts's *The End of Food* and Michael Pollan's *The Omnivore's Dilemma* have piqued the public's interest in learning more about the origins of the food they eat, but the real story is just beginning to surface."

ABOUT THE AUTHOR

In addition to introducing your book, your query letter should also introduce you. Agents aren't interested in hearing your full life history, but we do want to know who you are in relation to the project you're submitting. Why are you uniquely qualified to write the book you're writing? Do you have academic credentials (and MFA or journalism degree, PhD or MD) in a related subject? Did you have a real-life experience that your book is based upon? What's your publishing history? Have you ever been written about in national publications, or been interviewed on TV or on the radio? The term "platform" gets bandied about quite frequently in publishing, and it can be confusing, but it really means two things: 1) Why do you have the particular expertise to write on a certain subject, and 2) do you have the media connections to get attention for your book? It's more important for a nonfiction author to prove that he's got a strong platform, but if you're a fiction author who went to a great MFA program or has published articles on a topic related to your novel, there's no harm in saying so.

RESEARCHING AGENTS

Once you've written your query letter, the next step is to do some research into the best agents to approach, and whether those agents prefer to be queried via e-mail or via snail mail. If you're querying a bunch of agents at once ("simultaneous submissions"), take extra care not to mix up the names and addresses of agents you're querying; and if you're sending your letters out via e-mail, make sure to send each of them individually. You'd be amazed how many letters I get with my address but another agent's name in the salutation, and how many e-mail queries get sent out with every agent in town CC'd.

It may take a few weeks for you to hear back from agents (and you should check their Web sites to get a sense of whether they respond to all queries received, or just the ones they're interested in) but if you've done a good job with your query letter, and your project is viable, your query letter will have done its job and you'll soon receive requests for sample material—usually a "partial." If your letter is really good, your agent may later cull from it in his/her pitch letter, and your editor will pull lines from it for your back cover copy. But first things first, you've got to catch an agent's eye. So get cracking on those elevator pitches ... and don't forget to check your spelling!

More Query Tips

What Works Best

- Taking a polite, professional tone.
- Including multiple forms of contact information.
- Mentioning why you chose to query a particular agent.
- If you've got a connection, were referred by a client, or met the agent at a conference, make sure to point that out early in your letter.
- Developing a killer "elevator pitch" based on theme, plot, or importance of your topic.
- Making a case for the book's built-in audience.
- Don't try to set yourself apart by using fancy stationery. Standard paper and envelopes are preferable.
- Showing why your expertise and media contacts make you the best author for your project.
- Including blurbs or references from established, well-respected authors.

What Doesn't

- Querying an agent who doesn't handle the kind of book you're writing.
- Overly familiar, aggressive, or incorrect salutations.
- Pitching more than one book at a time.
- Overreaching with your comparisons.
- Outlining the full plot of your book—save it for your synopsis, if the agent has indicated that she'd like to see one. Your query should not give away the ending, for example.
- Querying agents about incomplete novels. (While it's preferable to query with an unfinished nonfiction project, as long as you've written a proposal, novels should be finished before you start contacting agents.)
- Including personal information that isn't related to the topic of your book.
- Telling your agent that your writers group, your congregants, or your mother's next-door neighbor's cockerspaniel loved your book.

Good Query Example #1

An entertaining but professional tone

Full contact information

Demonstrating that you have researched and handpicked this agent

A quick, catchy hook or "elevator pitch"

An author bio that demonstrates your platform and why you're the right author for this project

Short and simple.

Signature

Dr. Doreen Orion
123 Author Road
Alberquerque, NM 21290
DoreenOrion@email.com
(212)345-2345

April 5, 2006

Dear Ms. Glick:

I am a psychiatrist, published author, and expert for the national media seeking representation for my memoir titled, *Queen of the Road: The True Tale of 47 States, 22,000 Miles, 200 Shoes, 2 Cats, 1 Poodle, a Husband, and a Bus with a Will of Its Own*. Because you are interested in unique voices, I thought we might be a good match.

When Tim first announced he wanted to "chuck it all" and travel around the country in a converted bus for a year, I gave this profound and potentially life-altering notion all the thoughtful (1) consideration it deserved. "Why can't you be like a normal husband with a midlife crisis and have an affair or buy a Corvette?" I asked, adding, "I will never, ever, EVER live on a bus." What do you get when you cram married shrinks—one in a midlife crisis, the other his materialistic, wise-cracking wife—two cats who hate each other and a Standard Poodle who loves licking them all, into a bus for a year? *Queen of the Road* is a memoir of my dysfunctional, multi-species family's travels to and travails in the 49 continental states. (Tim insisted on seeing them all, despite my assurances that there were a few we could skip.)

As a psychiatrist, award-winning author (*I Know You Really Love Me*, Macmillan/Dell) and frequent media expert on psychiatric topics, (including *Larry King*, GMA, *48 Hours, The New York Times* and *People Magazine*), my life has centered on introspection, analysis and storytelling. Yet, I count among my greatest accomplishments that last year, our bus was featured as the centerfold of *Bus Conversions Magazine*, thus fulfilling my life-long ambition of becoming a Miss September. The story of our year-long adventure is already garnering interest in the media and has been mentioned in AMA News (circulation 250,000, and this journal of the American Medical Association has already agreed to review the book with an author interview when it comes out), *Woman's Day, Quick and Simple*, Match.com and *Best Life Magazine*. An upcoming *Parade Magazine* article on the growing phenomenon of mid-life career breaks (who knew I was a trend setter?) will include a photo of Tim and me, along with our story. My blog of our trip has also been mentioned in Andy Serwer's *Street Life* ecolumn *(Fortune Magazine)*. I hope you are interested in seeing the proposal and if so, would be most happy to send it to you via e-mail or snail mail.

Best wishes,

Doreen Orion

Good Query Example #2

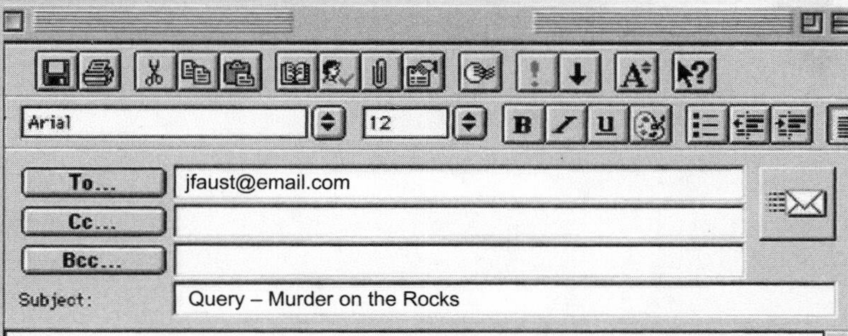

To: jfaust@email.com

Subject: Query – Murder on the Rocks

Dear Ms. Faust:

I enjoyed meeting you at the conference in Austin ❷ this past weekend. As I mentioned, I have had my eye on BookEnds ❷ for quite some time; when I discovered you would be at the conference, I knew I had to attend. We met during the final pitch session and discussed how the series I am working on might fit in with your current line of mystery series ❼. Per your request, I have enclosed a synopsis and first three chapters of *Murder on the Rocks*, and ❸ 80,000-word cozy mystery that was a finalist in this year's Writers' League of Texas manuscript contest and includes several bed-and-breakfast recipes.

Thirty-eight-year-old Natalie Barnes has quit her job, sold her house and gambled everything she has on the Gray Whale Inn on Cranberry Island, Maine. But she's barely fired up the stove when portly developer Bernard Katz rolls into town and starts mowing through her morning glory muffins ❹. Natalie needs the booking, but Katz is hard to stomach—especially when he unveils his plan to build an oversized golf resort on top of the endangered tern colony next door. When the town board approves the new development not only do the terns face extinction, but Natalie's Inn might just follow along. Just when Natalie thinks she can't face more trouble, she discovers Katz's body at the base of the cliff and becomes the number one suspect in the police's search for a murderer. If Natalie doesn't find the killer fast she stands to lose everything—maybe even her life.

I am a former pubic relations writer, a graduate of Rice University, a member of the Writers' League of Texas ❺, and founder of the Austin Mystery Writers critique group. I have spent many summers in fishing communities in Maine and Newfoundland, and escape to Maine as often as possible. The second Gray Whale Inn mystery, Dead and Berried, is currently in the computer.

If you would like to see the manuscript, I can send it via e-mail or snail mail. Thank you for your time and attention; I look forward to hearing from you soon. ❻

Sincerely,

Karen Swartz MacInerney ❶
123 Author Lane
Writerville, CA
(323) 555-0000
Karen@email.com

Query critique provided by Jessica Faust of BookEnds, LLC.

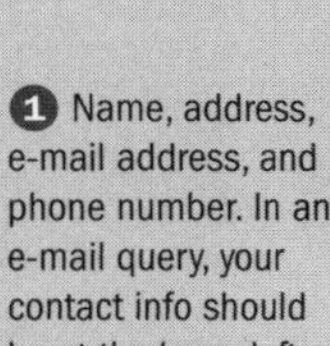

❶ Name, address, e-mail address, and phone number. In an e-mail query, your contact info should be at the lower left.

❷ Notes the personal connection and a reason to querying this agent.

❸ The word count is right there with the standards for cozy mysteries. Also, her description fits her genre.

❹ Establishes voice and a feeling for the book.

❺ Impressive credentials. She's obviously been writing for a while and I really like the addition of her summers in Maine. I think it's a personal touch, but one that's perfectly related to the book.

❻ Polite wrap up; offers to send more.

❼ You would usually want to pitch only one book, but Karen knew that I liked to handle mystery series, so this worked well in her case.

Good Query Example #3

Mary Timmins
Writer Blvd.
Los Angeles, CA
(323) 555-0000
marytwriter@email.com

October 31, 2008
Steven T. Murray, Editor-in-Chief
Fjord Press
P.O. Box 16349
Seattle, WA 98116

Dear Mr. Murray:

Plenty Good Room concerns the emotional struggles a thirteen-year-old African-American boy endures when his mother declares that he must leave his native Harlem and move down south (Florida) to live with a father he has never known. The three stages of the story show the young man's life: His time in New York and the events that subsequently lead to his mother's insistence that the father shoulder the remaining responsibility of rearing him; the not so clear-cut path he takes to become part of his father's life; and his life with father and the ultimate unraveling of a dream he thought had come true.

The story is written entirely from the viewpoint of the teen protagonist (a la *Catcher in the Rye*) and is a first-person account replete with emotion and stingingly blunt dialogue. Despite the age of the protagonist, *Plenty Good Room* is not a children's book. The language is contemporary and often raw and unrelenting. The book is, however, a timely expose on a young black male growing up in a single-parent home where the parent is too young, too inexperienced, and too poor to adequately parent and where the father is not at all involved.

I have enclosed to the first twenty pages of my thirteen-chapter manuscript. Please notify me if you are interested in reviewing the complete text. Thank you for your consideration.

Sincerely,

Teresa McClain

Encl.: SASE (6)

1" margin

Addressed to a specific editor

The query jumps right into the pitch, which is perfectly acceptable.

Good that she gives a clear idea of the overall structure of the novel.

Single-spaced text

Effective pitch thus far shows map of the novel.

Signature

Details enclosures.

Query critique provided by Lauren Mosko, former editor of *Novel & Short Story Writer's Market.*

Bad Query Example

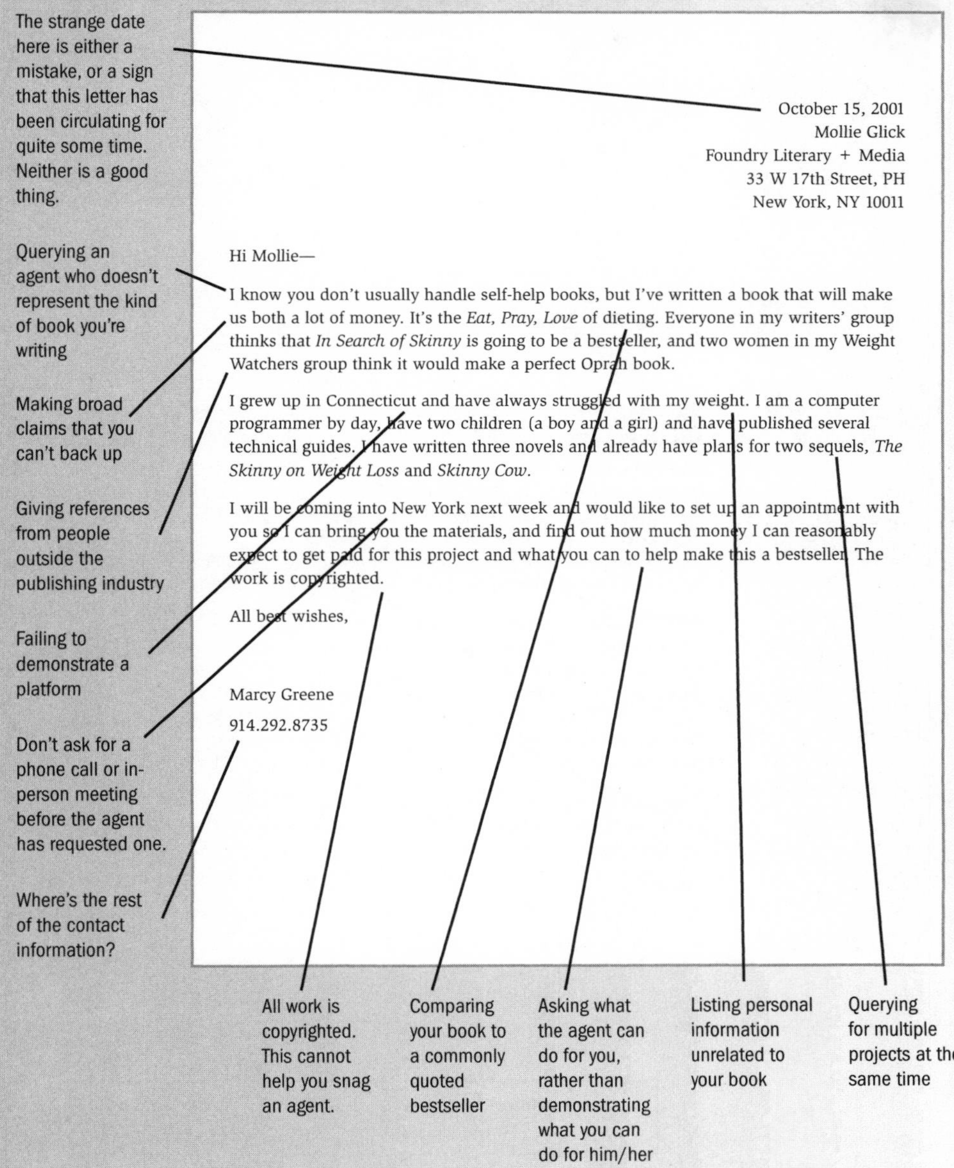

October 15, 2001
Mollie Glick
Foundry Literary + Media
33 W 17th Street, PH
New York, NY 10011

Hi Mollie—

I know you don't usually handle self-help books, but I've written a book that will make us both a lot of money. It's the *Eat, Pray, Love* of dieting. Everyone in my writers' group thinks that *In Search of Skinny* is going to be a bestseller, and two women in my Weight Watchers group think it would make a perfect Oprah book.

I grew up in Connecticut and have always struggled with my weight. I am a computer programmer by day, have two children (a boy and a girl) and have published several technical guides. I have written three novels and already have plans for two sequels, *The Skinny on Weight Loss* and *Skinny Cow*.

I will be coming into New York next week and would like to set up an appointment with you so I can bring you the materials, and find out how much money I can reasonably expect to get paid for this project and what you can to help make this a bestseller. The work is copyrighted.

All best wishes,

Marcy Greene
914.292.8735

CONTACTING AGENTS

Wheeling and Dealing

Make the Most Out of a Writers' Conference

by Chuck Sambuchino

Writing is a solitary task. It means a lot of time sitting at the computer, researching facts online, checking your e-mail, and staring at that first chapter you've rewritten 18 times but still doesn't seem to work. If you want to be a writer, you're going to spend plenty of time alone, but at the same time, you need to understand the importance of networking and making friends who are fellow scribes. That's where writers' conferences come in.

Conferences are your rare and invaluable opportunities to simply get out there-to mingle, network, have fun, and meet new contacts that can help further your career. There are plenty of conferences all across the country and beyond. Now you just need to know how to maximize a conference's worth, and you'll be all set.

CONFERENCES: THE BASICS

Conferences are events where writers gather to meet one another and celebrate the craft and business of writing. Attendees listen to authors and publishing professionals who present on various topics of interest. Each day is filled with sessions regarding all aspects of writing, and attendees will likely have a choice of which sessions to attend. For example, you can attend the "Query Letter Writing" session versus other panels on "The Secrets of Mystery Writing" and "The Secrets of Successful Book Proposals" held at the same time. To find out what speakers and sessions will be included, check the event's official Web site or e-mail the coordinator.

Since they usually take place during a weekend, you may have to clear your Friday schedule to see all speakers. Also, conferences are not to be confused with retreats, which are longer outings that include a lot of writing assignments. Retreats typically have small attendance and cost more because of the personal attention.

Some conferences are longstanding, while others are brand new. Most are not out to make money-and few could, even if they wanted to. A regional writers group usually organizes them, and the organizers are likely all volunteers. For example, the Southeast Mystery Writers of America hosts Killer Nashville, while the Space Coast Writers' Guild organizes the Space Coast Writers' Conference in Cocoa Beach.

CHUCK SAMBUCHINO is the editor of *Guide to Literary Agents* (www.guidetoliteraryagents.com/blog) and *Screenwriter's & Playwright's Market* (both Writer's Digest Books). He is a former staffer on *Writer's Digest* and a frequent presenter at writers' conferences.

HOW DO YOU FIND CONFERENCES?

Conferences are all over the place. With approximately 200 per year in the U.S., you can find them in practically every state and area of the country-and then there are even more in Canada. Some areas are hotspots, such as New York, Texas and California, whereas other states may not have a lot of choices, but still have at least one annual event nearby.

To find a conference, you can use print directories, online directories or simply a search engine. This book—*Guide to Literary Agents*—lists a whole smorgasbord of conferences in its back section, while GLA's sister publications, such as *Children's Writer's & Illustrator's Market*, will list conferences specific to the book's target readers. Also, conferences advertise in magazines (such as *Writer's Digest*) and are featured in writing-related newsletters, such as Absolute Write and Writer Gazette. Subscribe to free newsletters to get conference alerts along with plenty of other helpful info.

Helpful online directories exist-especially for genre fiction writers. Look online for the Web sites of the Romance Writers of America, the Mystery Writers of America, or the Society of Children's Book Writers and Illustrators, and you will find lists of upcoming conferences that are great value to scribes of those categories.

Another option is to simply use Google. The results are usually incomplete, but helpful enough. Try searching for "writers conference (month and year)" and see what comes up. You won't find a ton of gatherings that way, but searches will provide a few promising leads. Since conferences sometimes pop up out of nowhere without a whole lot of hubbub, this can be a good way to find newer events.

No matter where you find a conference listing, you will want to immediate check out the conference Web site, where updated lists of speakers, time, dates and registration forms can be found.

WHO WILL YOU MEET?

Perhaps the most valuable aspect of a conference is writers' ability to meet the power players and decision makers in the publishing world. In addition, they can make contacts and form partnerships with their fellow writers. Here are three different types of people you will meet.

Peers and writers

This is where the schmoozing comes in. Besides classes and presentations, there are usually dinners as well as meet-and-greet opportunities, not to mention simply banding together at night and hitting the hotel lobby or nearby bar to relax and talk. Perhaps you didn't even know the regional writers' group in charge existed, and may be able get involved with the organization.

Editors

As an editor myself, I spend a lot of time at conferences meeting with writers one-on-one and essentially answering any and all questions that they have for me. Editors specialize in presenting sessions and workshops, teaching everything from craft and characters to book proposal writing and the basics of agents.

Agents

Perhaps the biggest draw, agents attend conferences for a specific reason: to find potential clients. They are bombarded with pitches and request writing samples from those attendees who dazzle them with a good idea or pitch. Short of an excellent referral, conferences are the best way to snag an agent, so take advantage of meeting one. (I found my literary agent at a conference. Trust me: They work.)

Usually it works like this: You will schedule a short amount of time to pitch your idea to an agent. Your "elevator pitch" should be relatively short, and then there's some time for the agent to ask questions. If the agent is interested in seeing some of your work, she will pass you a business card and request a "partial" (a sample of the manuscript, such as the first 30 pages or the first three chapters). If the agent is not interested, she will say so. When an agent requests your manuscript, you can send it in and put "Requested Material" on the envelope (or in the e-mail) so it gets past the slush pile.

While there are designated times to pitch agents, it should be said that agents are usually ready for pitches at all times from all sides. However, beware crossing the line into "annoying." Don't pitch agents in the restroom. Don't interrupt them if they're having a conversation. If an agent is sitting down with fellow agents and trying, for a brief moment, not to talk business, don't hover around waiting for eye contact so you can step in and pitch.

The simple fact that you're at a conference shows that you're dedicated and professional. That in itself is enough to get agents' attention. Though writers still find in-person pitching quite nerve-wracking, the good news is that agents are not the mean stereotypes you may have in mind. They are almost all friendly booklovers like you.

HOW TO MAXIMIZE THE VALUE

If you want to make the most out of a conference, you have to stay busy and get involved. Go to presentations; hang out at late-night fiction readings; and make sure to stay for the whole shebang. Sign up for pitch slams and meet the power players in attendance. A little face time can pay off down the line. If you're involved with the sponsoring organization, offer to volunteer. If you pick up an agent from the airport, for example, that's plenty of one-on-one time in the car to slip in a pitch or two.

Make sure you schmooze. When you sit down at the dinner banquet, ask people what they're working on. Networking can be as simple as "I'll pass your name on to so-and-so, and I'd be appreciative if you could give me a referral to such-and-such." If you don't have business cards, make some basic ones just so others can know your contact info.

An unfortunate truth about conferences is that they can be a hit on the wallet. Some are affordable ($100-200) while others not so much ($700+). It all depends on how long the conference is, what is included, the price the conference paid to fly in speakers, etc. I've spoken at conferences where the crowd gathered at a Days Inn, and another where the event was hosted in a posh San Francisco hotel. Can you guess which event cost more? In addition to the basic conference cost, you have to budget money for "extras." Sometimes, the little things at a conference, such as 10-minute pitch sessions with agents or an editor's personal critique of your work, will mean an additional cost. If you want to truly make the most of a conference, you will need to indulge in some extras. When all is said and done, you may have to take a day off work and spend a chunk of money on costs and hotels. Think of it as an annual writing vacation for you and budget money early in the year. If you gain contacts that lead to writing assignments down the line, the conference will pay for itself before you know it!

KNOW WHICH ONE IS RIGHT FOR YOU

With so many to choose from, how can you know which one is the best investment? Obviously, proximity will play a factor, as we can't all afford a ticket to the Maui Writers' Conference. Look for events in your area and start from there. Some locations, such as Tennessee and Colorado, have a surprisingly large number of gatherings each year.

Ask yourself: "What do I want to get out of this?" Is it simply to recharge your batteries and get motivated? Because a general goal like that can be accomplished by most conferences. Do you have a polished and ready manuscript that needs an agent? Look for conferences with not only agents in attendance, but agents (or acquiring editors, as they function basically the same) in attendance that handle your specific area of work, be it science fiction, medical nonfiction, or whatever else.

Conferences usually have either a general focus on all subjects of writing, or a more narrow purpose. With some looking, you can find conferences devoted to screenwriting, playwriting, romance, mysteries, fantasy, science fiction, medical thrillers, and more.

GET OUT THERE!

Now that you know the ins and outs of a writers' conference, all that's left is for you to hunt down an event and sign up for 2008 or 2009. Going to a gathering and pitching agents may seem intimidating, especially if you're going alone, but the payoff is definitely worth it, and you're likely to make several friends who can ensure you don't go to a conference alone again. At the very least, you'll get some tips on how to start the befuddling first chapter that never seems to click.

CONTACTING AGENTS

Nonfiction Book Proposals

Make Your Proposal Stand Out

by Cricket Freeman

Remembering then: Authors, agents, publishers. Fine books, superior contracts, impressive sales. Authors become authorities. Simple.

Grasping now: Authorities become authors. Mediagenic authors. Celebrity authors. Namebrand authors. Über agents. Corporate agencies. Conglomerate buyouts. Publishing mergers. Restructurings. Layoffs. Mega-publishers. Micro-presses. Book trailers. Author platforms. RSS feeds. BookScan. Kindle. Facebook. MySpace. YouTube. Blogs. Podcasts. Twitter. The bottomline.

Not so simple anymore.

It's a new world of publishing out there, Kiddo. So, how can you stand out in all the noise? Because when it comes down to it, as editors flip through submissions from agents, all their questions boil down to just two: 1) Will this book enhance our profit and reputation? and 2) Can this writer do it?

How can you best answer those questions?

LAYING THE GROUNDWORK

You've toiled over your manuscript. You've rewritten it dozens of times, making sure every sentence is the *right* sentence—every metaphor, every image, every word is *right*. You've checked the spelling. Twice. You're ready to send it off to agents.

Are you? Better than 90 percent of submissions to agents are rejected at first glance. Why? Are there that many bad manuscripts? Are they sent to the wrong agent? Certainly, but most bite the dust because the writers submitted *too soon*. They lacked something. Submitting a manuscript, proposal, or even a query letter before you're ready is a waste of your time and the agent's. You may as well send it to Monkey Island at the Zoo.

No matter what type of nonfiction book you've written, if you're proposing your book for publication you must show you're prepared.

PUBLISHING TODAY

Several million words ago, I started out as a writer—eager to see my name on a book jacket, words flowing faster than I could type. I studied literary guides, read books on style, subscribed to *Writer's Digest*, saved pennies to trek to writers' conferences near and far, and

CRICKET FREEMAN has hustled in publishing for decades, as writer, editor, publisher, designer, publicist, agent. She and her intrepid partner, Jeffery McGraw, operate The August Agency from offices in New York and Florida. Would you like her to take you by the hand and help you compile each detail of your submission package? She swears a workbook is coming soon...

chatted up every writer who crossed my path till their eyes glazed over. Like any professional, I studied the art, the craft, the business. I grew rhino hide from rejection letters and got paid in magazines, steak dinners, river cruises, coffee mugs, yellow paint, and enough dollars to keep baloney sandwiches on the table most of the time. Eventually I was a career writer with credits I no longer counted. Creativity carried joy on its shoulders.

Opportunity knocked, bearing a persistent paycheck and an editor-in-chief's desk at a magazine—a full-color, trade slick. (Did I mention dental?) I spent long days tweaking ads; overseeing staff, design, and production; and cranking out 1,100 sparkling words a day—every word for the magazine, not a damn one for myself. I imploded.

However, the writer who emerged had a wiser view of publishing. I was a market-savvy writing machine.

Opportunity swirled around me again and the writer-turned-editor-turned-better-writer turned into a literary agent. I attacked the avalanche of 50+ queries a day and I found myself looking at things differently yet again. But my perspective hadn't changed, publishing had.

Year after year the industry seemed to slip deeper into the new American business model: Bigger = Better. Conglomorate takeovers and Corporate Mother drove profit margins. Beancounters ruled. The result? Good manuscripts alone could no longer secure the golden fleece of a book deal. Publishers demanded writers go outside beautiful words and prove the profitability potential for their projects.

REACHING THE TOP 10 PERCENT

Today's publishing marketplace is a far cry from that romanticized in movies. Agents simply cannot sell an unknown writer's *idea* for a nonfiction book. For an agent to sell a book to a major publisher it requires:

1. A fresh idea to spark interest
2. A catchy title and concept to grab attention
3. A distinctive author's voice to hold that attention
4. The expertise to back up the concept
5. The skill to execute it
6. The capacity to promote it
7. The ability to present it with enough passion so editors can see the first six elements and grasp the vision.

Many people have the first element. Some have the second, third, fourth, fifth, and maybe the sixth. But a very rare few have the last. Bring all seven to the table and you'll jump to the top 10 percent of submissions.

UNDERSTANDING EDITORS

Imagine an editor is considering two submissions by first-time writers. Both books are equally well written, suited for his house, and he'd be proud publishing either. But he only has budget for one.

Reviewing one he sees a tight synopsis, a descriptive table of contents, and a short author bio. Promising. Reviewing the other he sees those things, but also a colorful author with blurbs from known writers, who knows her competition, is connected to her target market, provides several versatile outlines, plus plans for self-promotion. Valuable. A professional writer on a firm career path.

Which author would you rather be?

Or, look at it this way: Suppose you wanted to open a bakery, would you waltz into a bank, plop a box of your wonderful donuts on the banker's desk, assuming he'll hand over a hundred grand? Nah, you know Mr. Banker wants more than a yummy crueller; he wants facts and figures to reassure his board. Well, publishers are no different.

Editors look at the big picture—past a good read. They look at things like audience, relevance, sales climate, marketing possibilities, sales history of similar books, current trends, the author's professionalism, and, of course, potential profits. Give more info than expected and you deliver a welcomed baker's dozen. If you've fleshed out an idea and written a great book, now is the time to take command. Steer the next stage of its production, shape each section, and create a terrific submission package.

SECTION ONE: INTRODUCING YOU AND YOUR BOOK

1. Title Page

Besides a dynamic title, have you included your contact info for agents at the lower right-hand corner of the page? Later, your agent's info will replace yours.

2. Contents Page

Have you listed all the elements of the proposal, including page numbers?

3. Good Words

Do you have any endorsements from recognizable names? Could you write the blurbs for them? If you have one or more in hand, you're more valuable.

SECTION TWO: PRESENTING YOUR BOOK IN DETAIL

4-7. Outlines

Can you provide a synopsis, summary, overview, or outline so agents can grasp the concept of your book quickly and fully? Over the years, based on publishers' needs, I developed the Quick View, Overview, Broad View, and Full View. These wide-ranging descriptions increase the versatility, thus the profitability, of your book.

Now let's look at each of these.

4. Quick View

Can you develop an on-the-money pitch in 25 words or fewer? It's the single most important thing you can do—sparking a chain of enthusiasm for your book.

From your opening sentence, you want agents to promptly wrap their minds around the concept of your book. A few years ago at a conference, I overheard a novelist deliver a precise pitch to the agent next to me. He put up his hand. "Stop!" The writer, taken aback, started to sweat. The agent extended his business card. "That's enough. Send it to me." As the perplexed writer got up, a smile eased into her face as she realized how easy it could be—if you're prepared.

The Quick View is a provocative 30-second view of your book you use to pitch your book to agents, your agent uses to pitch your book to editors, editors to pitch to editorial committees, book reps to pitch to retail booksellers, and booksellers use to excite readers. Once you perfect it, you'll want to lead off all query letters, proposals, discussions, and book signings with this handy tool. Look to movie listings for examples of this unique style of compressed writing.

5. Overview

Can you expand your Quick View, filling in the picture for a comprehensive understanding of the project and clearly showing payoffs to readers?

Just 100-200 words, the Overview works well as paperback back cover copy, in shorter review copy, as catalog copy, in press releases, and on promo items like postcards and posters, so look to those items for inspiration. A widespread use is when agents or editors ask, "Tell me more..."

6. Broad View

Can you provide 250-500 words to bring in features, facets, and themes, expanding your description with broad, sweeping strokes?

7. Full View

Can you outline your book in detail, showing how it's organized? Several pages—about 1,000 words—is sufficient. Often the Full View is expressed as a Table of Contents with a 25-word Quick View describing each chapter.

The Full View is used to determine you know how to fully cover the topic, to show you can tell a satisfying story with the necessary elements and pacing, by reviewers with no time to read the entire book, and during production by the sales or art departments. Supplying a comprehensive Full View boosts trust in you, thus increasing your value.

8. Graphics

Could charts, graphs, photos, maps, etc. enrich your reader's experience? If so, include a short description and a sample.

9. Excerpts

Are your most magnificent passages or most insightful comments buried deep within your book? Including a tasty tidbit can whet an agent's appetite for more. In selecting which paragraphs to select, consider they're used in press kits, longer jacket copy, and longer reviews.

SECTION THREE: SUPPORTING YOUR BOOK

10. Target Audience

Can you identify your readers?

You may say, "Isn't that the publisher's job?" but think about it: If you help the publisher distinguish your book buyers, then the higher the projected sales, and *ka-ching*—the value of your book goes up.

Once you identify your exact audience, perhaps several overlapping groups, supply statistics to measure them, such as how many subscribe to special-interest publications, attend conferences and conventions, visit special Web sites, buy similar products, are part of a certain segment of the population, etc. Show you know who your audience is and how to reach them.

11. Like-Minded Books

Can you compare your book to others, showing how it differs, what benefits it brings that others do not, and how it's relevant now? Agents and editors often jump immediately to the competition section, then decide whether to continue reading. It all boils down to this: Before you can expect publishers to lay out money to produce your book, you must show them:

- There's a market for it.
- There's a hole in that market.
- Your book can fill this existing hole better than any other.

Use a narrative style or bulleted lists, charts, tables, whatever complements your book.

Draw conclusions and voice opinions, but never trash the competition. Some should be published by a major house, reflecting a large target market. Throw figures out there. List comparable books, making sure to include as much info as you can, such as author, publisher, publishing date, formats, foreign or audio editions, or even Amazon sales rankings—whatever you can garner to illustrate the need for your book.

12. About the Author

Can you appear fascinating, informed, captivating, wise, compelling, authoritative, and intriguing? A bio has one purpose: to attract readers—starting with agents, then editors, and ultimately, readers pondering whether to drop $20 on what you have to say.

When surveyed, readers admitted the #1 reason they buy a book is the author. Readers don't want to know what you've done, *they want to know who you are*. So don't you dare give them a gagging grocery list of names of schools, towns, spouses, kids, or cats. *Blah, blah, blah.* You owe readers more than that.

Bios are used by agents, editors, librarians, reviewers, booksellers, and talkshow hosts to promote your book. Try several multipurpose versions, slanted for different audiences, of 50, 100, and 250 words. You can easily drop an intriguing author's photo right into it, too.

13. Author-Driven Promotion

Do you picture your publisher sending you on a lobster-and-limos, 20-city booksigning tour? Fact is, even career authors are rarely given the Big Celebrity Treatment. Publishers look for writers who are *already connected* to their target audience in some way. How can you show your ability to jump in and connect with readers? Can you compose a comprehensive, multi-strategy marketing plan to reach that target audience you know so well?

Having a platform, a place from which to reach your audience, is essential for writers of nonfiction. But it's now adventageous for writers of creative nonfiction and memoir, as well, as publishers' publicity budgets shrink to peanuts. Create an author Web site, generate Web buzz, and plan your own mini book tours to cities where friends, college roommates, and relatives will put you up.

Publishers *are* willing to do a lot for authors and build on your efforts, if you show them:

- You understand promotion produces sales
- You can reach your target audience
- You can work hand-in-hand with them
- You're energetic, resourceful, and show initiative.

In fact, one author told me her publisher was so impressed by her publicity plans they upped her print run from 5,000 to 50,000!

14. Beyond One Book

How could you expand this book? Come up with a short list of potential spin-off projects. Developing the book into a series is the most common. But what about subsidiary rights, foreign sales, workshops, products? Describe each one with a Quick View. These possibilities may never see the light of day, but it shows you have vision, versatility, and room to grow. Author careers are built on thinking down the line.

15. Sample Chapters

What's needed? Chapter 1, plus any two other chapters is sufficient to show your style, approach, capability, reach, and voice, usually 15-50 pages.

CLOSING THOUGHTS

Four things should guide you: presentation, profitability, platform, and professionalism.

Remember you have *only one* shot at an agent with each project. There are no do-overs. You need a crackerjack proposal. Why? Agents are tough. Editors are tougher. Readers are the toughest of all. Is it worth it? Oh, hell, yes. It'll launch you into the top 10 percent.

Synopsis Writing

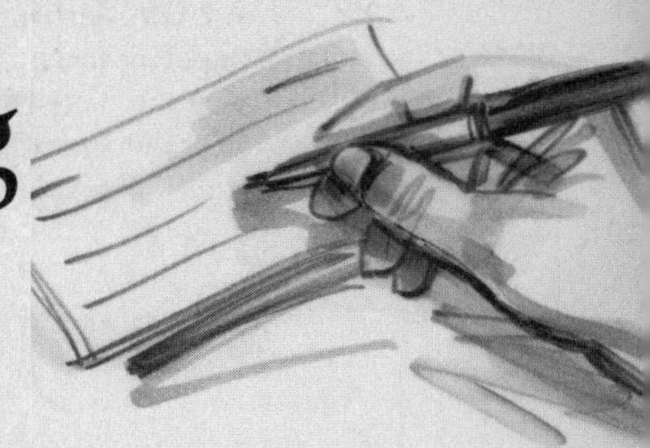

Summing Up Your Novel For an Agent

by Pam McCutcheon

It's no secret: Most novelists hate writing synopses-but if you want to sell your work, a synopsis is a vital part of the sales package. Since many agents initially ask for just the first few chapters of your work, it's not enough to have scintillating prose with well-drawn characters and an intriguing idea; the editor must also be convinced you can sustain the story for the full length of the novel.

To do this, you need a well-written summary that explains your entire story from beginning to end. If you're unpublished, editors want to ensure your story ends appropriately; and if you *are* published, the synopsis may be all the editor sees. Once the editor falls in love with your story, she may use the synopsis to sell your story at the buying meeting, to write the back cover blurb, and/or to give the cover artist some idea of what your story is about. So you must make your synopsis shine as brightly as your manuscript.

Unfortunately, once you've written a 400-page book, it's tough to know how to condense it down to eight or 10 pages-or worse, one or two. Here are a few tips to help you figure out what to put in-and what to leave out.

Use the correct format. This is the same format you would use in writing your manuscript: one-inch margins, double-spacing, ragged right margin, white paper, etc. Write the synopsis in third person, present tense, no matter what your manuscript is written in.

Watch your length. Most editors and agents have a distinct preference for what they want to see, and it often varies from one person to another in the same literary agency. The rule used to be to have approximately one page of synopsis for every 30-50 pages of text. That makes for a six- to 12-page synopsis when you're finished. Lately, though, agents are requesting shorter and shorter synopses-even as short as one or two pages. To be safe, draft up a "long synopsis" as well as a "short synopsis." To discover an agent's specific preference, research their submission guidelines using this book, the Internet, or call and ask—then give them the length they ask for. If you're uncertain how many pages to send, err on the short side.

Know your target market. Make sure you know how your story fits within your targeted genre. There are certain expectations for each, and you need to ensure these are met in your synopsis or you run the risk of being rejected. For example, in a romance, you must show the development of the relationship. For a mystery, you need to show the clues, red herrings, and suspects. For a fantasy, we need to know the rules of the world you have set

PAM MCCUTCHEON is an award-winning fiction author and popular writing instructor who has published two how-to books for writers: *Writing the Fiction Synopsis: A Step by Step Approach* and *The Writer's Brainstorming Kit: Thinking in New Directions* (with Michael Waite). She lives in Colorado.

up, and so on. I can hear some of you saying, "Duh!" but surprisingly, many writers leave out these elements. They get so caught up in the external plot that they forget to show these all-important genre expectations.

Make the characters interesting and sympathetic. Summing up the plot is crucial, but don't concentrate so much on the plot that the characters don't come alive. Show us the major characters' goals (what they want), motivations (why they want it) and conflicts (why they can't have it). Then at the end, show if they achieved their goals or not, and how they've grown as a result of the story. That will help your readers care about what happens to them. Try to briefly show us the characters' emotions on their journey.

Use transitions. Don't tell your story with a series of unconnected declarative sentences: "She yelled. He retaliated. They left." It makes for disjointed reading and interrupts the smooth flow of the story. Sometimes, writers who use transitions with ease and skill in their manuscripts somehow still fail to use them in their synopses. The objective is to make your synopsis flow as easily as your manuscript-to make the story so interesting that the reader will continue reading without a hitch from beginning to end. So, connect those ideas from one sentence or one paragraph to the next to show how each plot point and character change are related to one another and affect what comes next. Even if you have to use such phrases as "Meanwhile, back at the ranch . . ." or "What Harold didn't realize was . . .", it's worth it to make your story read smoothly.

Keep your tone consistent. Don't use widely varying moods in the synopsis; it does nothing but confuse the reader. For example, don't start off describing a horrible, angst-filled character background, and then segue into a humorous romp. It leaves the agent baffled, wondering what kind of story it really is. Make sure your tone is consistent throughout the synopsis-and that it matches the tone of your novel.

Keep the authorial voice silent. Don't insert comments in the synopsis that address the agent directly to ensure she "gets it," such as "The conflict is . . ." or "At this point in the story . . ." Talking directly to the reader jerks her out of the flow of the story. Also avoid telling the agent the story is heartrending, humorous, exciting, etc. If you tell the agent how to feel, you run the risk of offending her. Quite literally, the agent will be the judge of whether your story makes her feel the way you intended.

Leave out irrelevant details. Don't get so caught up in the minutia of your intricate plot, fascinating research, historical period, or speculative world that the synopsis is stuffed with irrelevant details and characters. In the synopsis, we don't really need to know how a spinning wheel works or what a minor character looks like-unless it's necessary for understanding the plot or the major character(s). Save the details for the story itself-and include them there only if they're relevant.

Keep names to a minimum. Don't refer to all of your 20-plus characters by name. In a short synopsis, that's a lot of names to remember. Just mention the names of the key protagonist(s) and antagonist(s). Don't mention secondary characters by name unless they show up several times in the synopsis. Instead, refer to them by function or relationship: the cab driver, the housekeeper, Sarah's daughter, Joel's boss, etc. It will make it a lot easier for your readers to follow.

Use dialogue sparingly. The problem with including or using dialogue in the synopsis is that you are usually slowing down to telling the story word by precious word, which makes the pacing very erratic and takes up a lot of unnecessary space in the synopsis. Instead, summarize the gist of the conversation and move on.

Make the ending complete. Make sure you explain key character motivations (why they do the things they do) and tie up loose ends of plot and character development. Never commit the unpardonable sin of telling the agent she has to read the whole story to find out how it ends-unless you want an immediate rejection. Instead, at the end, show the resolution of the main characters' goals and conflicts, and the resolution of the plot. If you're unsure if anything is missing, give your synopsis to someone who knows nothing about your story and ask him to tell you if he has any unanswered questions after reading it.

Final advice. Remember that the synopsis is a summary of the story told in narrative form, as if you were relating it to a friend over a cup of coffee. Though some of the minor formatting details may vary from one person to person, if you just tell your story and follow the tips above, you should have a winning synopsis.

Play the Field

Don't Pounce on the First Agent You Hear About

by Roberta Beach Jacobson

I remember my mother advising me to play the field when I was a teen. "Why kiss the first boy you meet?" she asked me. "See who's out there."

Such advice also applies to hunting for a literary agent. You'll waste precious time if you zero in on just one, or sign a contract with the first rep that shows the slightest interest. Teaming up with a literary agent is a long-term collaboration, and you don't want to sell yourself short or limit your options.

SIMULTANEOUS SUBMISSIONS

Sending out simultaneous submissions to several or many agents is the norm, so don't think that you have to simply query one agent at a time. By this point you know that there is great value in personalizing and researching your submissions, rather than sending out a blanket query or proposal to many agents. Naturally, this is true. However, just as bad as contacting too many agents is contacting too few. Don't spread your efforts too thin, but don't put all your eggs in one basket.

It's tempting to focus all your efforts on one—or a few—specific reps. Maybe it's because you visited their Facebook page and saw they love dogs; maybe it's because you met them at a conference and everything just "clicked"; and maybe it's because they recently said in an interview that they're looking for paranormal horror YA books and you just happen to be writing a paranormal horror YA book. These are good reasons to target a specific agent, but no reason is good enough to solely target a specific agent.

Another reason a writer may be hooked up on an agent is their location. It's a misconception to think that you have to find a "local" agent that you can meet before signing with. Don't sweat the miles. Case in point: I live in Greece, but my agent is located in Boston.

Go ahead and put that "perfect" agent's name on your list, but cast your net out into the agent sea. It may take up to several months for an agent to respond to a query and partial submission (sample pages), and it can be very frustrating to wait five months only to get a form rejection after everything is said and done. Rather than querying one, break your list up into groups of five, and query a block at a time—starting with your "ideal" choices.

Do note that there is a difference between exclusively submitting queries versus the complete manuscript. It's expected and encouraged for writers to contact numerous agents with the initial query letter, but later in the process, some agents may request an exclusive peek when reviewing the full work—your complete manuscript. If you do agree to this

ROBERTA BEACH JACOBSON is an author and humorist. She recently co-authored *Almost Perfect: Disabled Pets and the People Who Love Them* (Enspirio House, Word Forge Books)

exclusivity, you will be unable to send the full story to any other agents who wish to consider it, so make sure that you agree upon a determined window of time for such an agreement (for example, one month).

FINDING YOUR TOP CHOICES

After studying agent listings and visiting countless agency Web sites, I advanced my personal agent search from general to specific by asking 11 author friends who write in my genre (pets) about their agent experiences.

All offered me bits of advice on how to proceed and a few even gave me referrals to their agents who represent nonfiction pet titles. Andrea Campbell, an author and e-teacher for online classes on how to write book proposals, also recommended "a concentrated effort to network with other professionals in your field, (so) you can build camaraderie to such an extent that you can ask for feedback and input in a discreet way."

Campbell's point about discretion is an important one. I didn't contact my 11 writer buddies via public forums. I didn't rely on a group e-mail either. I wrote each a personal request. Knowing how busy the writers are, I kept my messages brief. Afterwards, I thanked all for being generous enough with their time to help me in my search for an agent.

Let me interject that finding the right agent match isn't something done on a rainy Saturday afternoon. It's not as easy as it might sound and takes considerable legwork on the part of an author. I cringe when someone discovers an agent's name on the acknowledgments page of some book and immediately chases after that agent—totally unprepared. (Remember: Why kiss the first boy you meet? See who else is out there.)

THE OFFER: IS SHE RIGHT FOR YOU?

The "interview" need not be a face-to-face fancy luncheon, or even a friendly chat over coffee. Perhaps it's nothing more than a simple telephone call.

Do your best to keep things positive. To prevent the agent from wondering if you've pulled names out of a hat, mention any clients of the agent whom you know or whose work you admire. Assemble a few questions to ask the potential agent, but keep in mind a conversation is a two-way street. The agent will certainly wish to hear more about you than your bubbly enthusiasm about your current manuscript. Don't be flustered. Be prepared.

Moreover, since a literary agent represents your entire career, don't be jolted by questions such as, "What's the next book you have planned after this one?" Or "Where do you see your writing career five years from now?"

Just as important as what she will ask you is what you will ask her. Inquire as to why she wants to represent you. What are her expectations? Can you review her agency agreement?

A MATCH MADE IN HEAVEN?

Very possibly, all will be rosy between you and your new agent. But personalities do clash; rifts form; all is not perfect in the publishing world. If things aren't working out, your agency agreement specifies how to break ties, be it a 30-day written notice or whatever. Breaking from a rep is typically a painful experience—all the more reason to do plenty of research upfront and make sure you're not too narrow in your choices. You'll thank yourself later.

Sign on the Dotted Line

Research Your Options and Beware of Scams

Once you've received an offer of representation, you must determine if the agent is right for you. As flattering as any offer may be, you need to be confident that you are going to work well with the agent and that she is going to work hard to sell your manuscript.

EVALUATE THE OFFER

You need to know what to expect once you enter into a business relationship. You should know how much editorial input to expect from your agent, how often she gives updates about where your manuscript has been and who has seen it, and what subsidiary rights the agent represents.

More importantly, you should know when you will be paid. The publisher will send your advance and any subsequent royalty checks directly to the agent. After deducting her commission-usually 10 to 15 percent-your agent will send you the remaining balance. Most agents charge a higher commission of 20 to 25 percent when using a co-agent for foreign, dramatic or other specialized rights. As you enter into a relationship with an agent, have her explain her specific commission rates and payment policy.

Some agents offer written contracts and some do not. If your prospective agent does not, at least ask for a "memorandum of understanding" that details the basic relationship of expenses and commissions. If your agent does offer a contract, be sure to read it carefully, and keep a copy for yourself. Since contracts can be confusing, you may want to have a lawyer or knowledgeable writer friend check it out before signing anything.

The National Writers Union (NWU) has drafted a Preferred Literary Agent Agreement and a pamphlet, *Understand the Author-Agent Relationship*, which is available to members. The union suggests clauses that delineate such issues as:

- the scope of representation (One work? One work with the right of refusal on the next? All work completed in the coming year? All work completed until the agreement is terminated?)
- the extension of authority to the agent to negotiate on behalf of the author
- compensation for the agent and any co-agent, if used
- manner and time frame for forwarding monies received by the agent on behalf of the client
- termination clause, allowing client to give about 30 days to terminate the agreement
- the effect of termination on concluded agreements as well as ongoing negotiations
- arbitration in the event of a dispute between agent and client.

If you have any concerns about the agency's practices, ask the agent about them before you sign. Once an agent is interested in representing you, she should be willing to address any questions or concerns that you have. If the agent is rude or unresponsive, or tries to tell

What Should I Ask?

The following is a list of topics the Association of Authors' Representatives suggests authors discuss with literary agents who have offered to represent them. Please bear in mind that most agents are not going to be willing to spend time answering these questions unless they have already read your material and wish to represent you.

1. Are you a member of the Association of Authors' Representatives or do you adhere to their basic canon of ethics?
2. How long have you been in business as an agent?
3. Do you have specialists at your agency who handle movie and television rights? Foreign rights?
4. Do you have subagents or corresponding agents in Hollywood and overseas?
5. Who in your agency will actually be handling my work? Will the other staff members be familiar with my work and the status of my business at your agency?
6. Will you oversee or at least keep me apprised of the work that your agency is doing on my behalf?
7. Do you issue an agent/author agreement? May I review the language of the agency clause that appears in contracts you negotiate for your clients?
8. How do you keep your clients informed of your activities on their behalf?
9. Do you consult with your clients on any and all offers?
10. What are your commission rates? What are your procedures and time frames for processing and disbursing client funds? Do you keep different bank accounts separating author funds from agency revenue? What are your policies about charging clients for expenses incurred by your agency?
11. When you issue 1099 tax forms at the end of each year, do you also furnish clients–upon request–with a detailed account of their financial activity, such as gross income, commissions and other deductions and net income for the past year?
12. In the event of your death or disability, what provisions exist for my continued representation?
13. If we should part company, what is your policy about handling any unsold subsidiary rights to my work?

you that the information is confidential or classified, the agent is uncommunicative at best and, at worst, is already trying to hide something from you.

AVOID GETTING SCAMMED

The number of literary agents in the country, as well as the world, is increasing. This is because each year, aspiring authors compose an increasing number of manuscripts, while publishing houses continue to merge and become more selective as well as less open to working directly with writers. With literary agents providing the crucial link between writers and publishers, it's no wonder dozens of new agencies sprout up each year in the United States alone.

While more agencies may seem like a good thing, writers who seek to pair up with a successful agent must beware when navigating the murky waters of the Internet. Because agents are such a valuable part of the process, many unethical persons are floating around the online publishing world, ready to take advantage of uninformed writers who desperately want to see their work in print.

To protect yourself, you must familiarize yourself with common agent red flags and keep your radar up for any other warning signs. First of all, it can't be stressed enough that you should never pay agents any fees just so they consider your work. Only small fees (such as postage and copying) are acceptable—and those miniscule costs are administered *after* the agent has contacted you and signed you as a client.

A typical scam goes something like this: You send your work to an agency and they reply with what seems like a form letter or e-mail, telling you they love your story. At some point, they ask for money, saying it has to do with distribution, production, submissions, analysis or promotion. By that point, you're so happy with the prospect of finding an agent (you probably already told family and friends) that you nervously hand over the money. Game over. You've just been scammed. Your work may indeed end up in print, but you're likely getting very little if any money. To be a successful author, publishers must pay you to write; you must never pay them.

When a deal seems too good to be true, it likely is. If you want to learn more about a particular agent, look at her Web site. If she doesn't have a Web site (some small agents do not), look in this book to see if she has legitimate sales in the industry. Google her name: You'll likely find a dozen writers just like you discussing this agent on an Internet forum asking questions such as "Does anyone know anything about agent so-and-so?" These writer-oriented Web sites exist so writers like you can meet similar persons and discuss their good/bad experiences with publications, agents and publishing houses.

Protect yourself from scams by getting questions answered before you make any deals. When an abundance of research material is not available, you must be cautious. Ask around, ask questions and never pay upfront fees.

If you've been scammed

If you have trouble with your agent and you've already tried to resolve it to no avail, it may be time to call for help. Please alert the writing community to protect others. If you find agents online, in directories or in this book who aren't living up to their promises or are charging you money when they're listed as non-fee-charging agents, please let the Web master or editor of the publication know. Sometimes they can intervene for an author, and if no solution can be found, they can at the very least remove a listing from their directory so that no other authors will be scammed in the future. All efforts are made to keep scam artists out, but in a world where agencies are frequently bought and sold, a reputation can change overnight.

If you have complaints about any business, consider contacting The Federal Trade Commission, The Council of Better Business Bureaus or your state's attorney general. (For full details, see Reporting a Complaint below). Legal action may seem like a drastic step, but sometimes people do it. You can file a suit with the attorney general and try to find other writers who want to sue for fraud with you. The Science Fiction & Fantasy Writers of America's Web site offers sound advice on recourse you can take in these situations. For more details, visit www.sfwa.org/beware/.

If you live in the same state as your agent, it may be possible to settle the case in small claims court. This is a viable option for collecting smaller damages and a way to avoid lawyer fees. The jurisdiction of the small claims court includes cases in which the claim is $5,000 or less. (This varies from state to state, but should still cover the amount for which you're suing.) Keep in mind that suing takes a lot of effort and time. You'll have to research all the necessary legal steps. If you have lawyers in the family, that could be a huge benefit if they agree to help you organize the case, but legal assistance is not necessary.

Above all, if you've been scammed, don't waste time blaming yourself. It's not your fault if someone lies to you. Respect in the literary world is built on reputation, and word gets around about agents who scam, cheat, lie and steal. Editors ignore their submissions and writers avoid them. Without clients or buyers, a swindling agent will find her business collapsing.

Meanwhile, you'll keep writing and believing in yourself. One day, you'll see your work in print, and you'll tell everyone what a rough road it was to get there, but how you wouldn't trade it for anything in the world.

Reporting a Complaint

If you feel you've been cheated or misrepresented, or you're trying to prevent a scam, the following resources should be of help.

- The Federal Trade Commission, Bureau of Consumer Protection. While the FTC won't resolve individual consumer problems, it does depend on your complaints to help them investigate fraud, and your speaking up may even lead to law enforcement action. Visit www.ftc.gov.
- Volunteer Lawyers for the Arts is a group of volunteers from the legal profession who assist with questions of law pertaining to the arts. Visit www.vlany.org.
- The Council of Better Business Bureau is the organization to contact if you have a complaint or if you want to investigate a publisher, literary agent or other business related to writing and writers. Contact your local BBB or visit www.bbb.org.
- Your state's attorney general. Don't know your attorney general's name? Go to www.attorneygeneral.gov. This site provides a wealth of contact information, including a complete list of links to each state's attorney general Web site.

Copyright

What You Need to Know to Protect Your Work

by Paul S. Levine

My old boss at the first law firm I worked for called the Copyright Act the greatest piece of self-help legislation ever enacted by Congress. And he was absolutely right. Unlike a trademark, which protects the name of goods or services, and unlike a patent, which protects inventions, you have a copyright in your work at the moment of its creation. You don't have to apply to a government agency and wait an interminable length of time for the agency to process your application and decide whether your product name is "worthy" enough to be given a trademark, or whether your invention is "unique" enough to be given a patent. The moment you put your finger to keyboard or pen to paper, you have a copyright in the work which you create. The way the Copyright Act puts it is: "Copyright inheres in a work at the moment of its creation." Bet you never thought you would read (and even understand) a word like "inheres" in this publication, huh?

Note that the word "copyright" should never, ever be used as a verb or adverb; it is a noun, and a noun only. One does not copyright a book, or a script, or anything else for that matter. You *have* a copyright in you work as soon as you create it.

REGISTERING YOUR WORK

You can register your work for copyright with the Copyright Office in Washington, D.C. If you do so within a 90 days of publication of your work, or prior to the actual infringement of your work (i.e., *before* someone actually rips you off) you get two *huge* benefits of the Copyright Act you wouldn't otherwise get: statutory damages and attorney's fees (both explained further below). Download a Form TX from the Copyright Office Web site and send it in, together with one copy of your unpublished manuscript and a check for $45. Do you *need* to do this? No. Do you *want* to do this? Yes.

When you begin circulating copies of your manuscript to potential agents or to potential publishers, keep in mind that you do *not* have to place a copyright notice on the title page of your manuscript (the "©" symbol, the year of creation, and your full legal name) in order to get these benefits, however. Publishing professionals know that everything is protected, whether it's registered or not.

PAUL S. LEVINE is a literary agent and publishing and intellectual property attorney based in Venice, CA who has been representing writers for over 27 years. Visit his websites at www.paulslevine.com and www.paulslevinelit.com.

HELP FROM PUBLISHERS

Once your book is published, per a standard provision in most publishing contracts, the publisher will usually agree to register the book copyright in *your name*—with you listed as the "Author" of the book and as the "Owner" of the copyright in the book. Make sure the publisher does this within 90 days of publication of the book, so that you get those two aforementioned bonus benefits from the Copyright Act. The publisher will do so by sending the same Form TX mentioned earlier, together with its check for $45 (the publisher will pay the fee this time!) to the Copyright Office, but this time it will send two copies of the published book—one goes to the Copyright Office for its records, and one goes to the Library of Congress. Some of the most fun you will ever have as a published author is to travel to Washington, D.C., go to the Library of Congress, and check your book out of the library!

INFRINGEMENT

The two benefits I repeatedly speak of are extremely important should you ever have to file a copyright infringement lawsuit against someone. The first is the right to collect "statutory damages," instead of having to prove your "actual damages." If this is your first book, and you don't have a track record of previous deals so that you can argue to a jury that, for example, "If I hadn't been ripped off, I would have gotten what I got last time from my publisher plus 10 percent," then electing statutory damages instead of having to prove actual damages will be a godsend for you. They can range from $250 in the case of "innocent" infringement (someone unintentionally, without malice, rips you off) to $250,000 for willful, knowing infringement (think pirated DVDs of a movie currently in theaters being sold in Times Square).

The other benefit is that the defendant may be liable to pay your attorneys fees. Normally, in a typical civil suit in the United States, each side pays his or her own lawyer, regardless of who wins or who loses the case. But, if you register your work for copyright within ninety (90) days of its publication or prior to the date of infringement, you can get attorneys fees and costs added onto the judgment you get against the defendant. The reverse is also true, however—if you *lose* your claim for copyright infringement, the defendant can get a judgment against you for all of the attorneys fees he or she has had to pay to a lawyer to defend himself or herself against your claim.

CAN YOU PROTECT IDEAS?

Copyright protects "original works of authorship"—"original" in the sense that it originates with you, and you haven't ripped off anyone else in order to create it, and "original" in the sense that it has some modicum of originality to it—that it is something more than a mere list of names and numbers for example—that it has at least a little bit of originality, or creativity, to it.

The original work of authorship must be "fixed in a tangible medium of expression"—it must be able to be perceived with the senses. Until recently, for example, choreography wasn't protected by copyright, because it wasn't "recorded" in a way which could be seen, but now that a system of recording it has been invented (similar to the way musical notes are "recorded" on sheet music), choreography can indeed be protected by copyright.

Copyright protects the expression of an idea, not the idea itself. For example, the idea of a play or movie where a boy meets a girl, but both sets of parents are against the boy and the girl getting together (think *Romeo and Juliet*, but also think *West Side Story*) is not protected by copyright (or by anything else for that matter). If Shakespeare were alive at the time *West Side Story* was released, he could not have sued the studio or anyone else involved with the movie for copyright infringement, because all that was "taken" from his play is the basic idea. If, however, characters, plot, theme, lines of dialogue, settings, etc., are "taken" from one work and incorporated in another, there may be a claim of copyright infringement.

More Ways to Protect Yourself

By Chuck Sambuchino

I've said it before and I'll say it again. Agents and editors don't steal ideas. Writers steal ideas.

If you're sending work out to legitimate pros, you have little to fear. If they like your idea, they'll hire you for the job. The chance of you work getting stolen is infinitesimal. Writers, on the other hand, *will* steal your ideas, and there are some basic things you can do to protect yourself.

- **Don't post stuff on the Internet.** Let's say you blog and say, "Today I thought of a funny new idea for a novel. It's about two guys who habitually crash weddings to bed women, but find themselves falling for girls at one particular high-profile reception." There's nothing you can do to protect that idea. It's out in the open, and it's fair game to any writer.
- **Trust your writing peers.** Eventually, you're going to have to give the work to a friend or writing peer who can give you feedback. You should be working with people who are honest, intelligent, and—naturally—trustworthy.
- **Just trust your gut.** If you go to a writers' conference and get asked to pitch in front of everybody, and you don't want to do it, then don't.

BOOK PROPOSALS

Because copyright protects the expression of an idea and not the idea itself, book proposals are not protected by copyright—only the actual full-length manuscript of your nonfiction book (e.g., the actual methods for losing weight, and the way you tell people how to do so, and not merely the idea of eating a low-carbohydrate diet) is protected by copyright. So, don't register your book proposal for copyright, because you're not gaining anything by doing so. Wait until your manuscript is completely written, and *then* go ahead and register it for copyright. And remember that the publisher will register it *again* (on your behalf) once your book is actually published.

A CLAIM WITH MERIT

A claim for copyright infringement must satisfy two essential elements: "access" and "substantial similarity." The claimant must prove that the infringer had access to his or her work—sometimes no easy task. The "chain of custody" doesn't have to be direct, however; your giving your manuscript to your Aunt Martha for a quick read, who then decides to give it to her hairdresser, because she just "knows" how much she will enjoy it, who then gives it to … you get the idea. As long as every link in the chain is established, culminating with the infringer getting your manuscript so that he or she can rip it off, you have proven the element of access.

And, even if the claimant proves that infringer had access to the work, the claimant must also prove (i.e., make a judge or jury believe) that the infringing work is *substantially* (not just somewhat) similar to the claimant's work—that whole scenes, lines of dialogue, characters and character description, etc., are too close for comfort—that the similarities are so striking that it is virtually impossible to chalk it up to mere coincidence. This, too, is not an easy burden to meet. In twenty-seven plus years of law practice, I've only seen two cases where the claim had merit.

DRASTIC MEASURES

The Copyright Act has some extraordinary remedies that are sometimes granted at the *very beginning* of the case—when it is first filed. These remedies are granted if the judge decides that the case has merit, and are granted without the defendant being given much of an opportunity to respond (probably unconstitutional, but nobody has successfully challenged these extraordinary remedies on those grounds). The remedies include injunctive relief, stopping the further sale of the infringing work and requiring all copies of the infringing work to be recalled from retail outlets where it might be available; seizure orders, requiring the U.S. Marshal to seize all infringing copies of the work from wherever they may be located (warehouses, etc.), and also seize the "means of manufacturing" those infringing copies (printing presses, DVD duplicators, etc.) and the business records associated with those infringing copies (this used to be file cabinets full of files, but now are usually computer "hard" drives); orders requiring that all of the defendant's bank accounts be "frozen," so that no monies go in or out of them for the duration of the lawsuit;, and orders allowing what is called "expedited discovery," so that depositions can be taken, for example, to determine the location(s) of the infringing copies or the bank(s) where the defendant maintains his account(s).

Some of the most fun I've had as a copyright lawyer is to "ride along" with the U.S. Marshals on one of their "seizure raids"—they burst into the warehouse where the infringing copies are located with their guns drawn, line everybody in the warehouse up against the wall, and then turn to me (after holstering their guns) and ask me to identify all the infringing copies, which they then haul away (along with the printing presses, computer hard drives, and anything else they feel like taking. Couldn't ask for a better time—now *that's* why I listened to my Jewish mother and went to law school!

Copyright Q&A: 7 Quick Questions

By Chuck Sambuchino

1. *Can you continue writing someone else's fiction series?*

   Essentially, no.

2. *If you mail yourself a copy of the manuscript but never open the package, is that equivalent to a copyright?*

   What you're talking about is sometimes called "poor man's copyright," and no, it does not work.

3. *How long does a copyright last?*

   Till 70 years after the creator's death. Note that works written prior to 1978 to do not adhere to current copyright laws.

4. *Can I use song lyrics in my manuscript?*

   That's tricky. Technically, no, but publishers will likely help you secure any necessary permissions and decide "fair use."

5. *What's the difference between slander and libel?*

   Slander is spoken, while libel is in print.

6. *What restrictions exist on using the names of professional sports teams or real people, etc.?*

   You won't catch grief for writing neutral or positive words about real people, places and things. Beware negative or defamatory remarks.

7. *If someone sends me an e-mail or post card, can I publish what the sender has written?*

   No. Correspondence sent to you, whether through postal mail or e-mail, is copyrighted.

SEALING THE DEAL

Improve Your Book Contract

Nine Negotiating Tips

Even if you're working with an agent, it's crucial to understand the legal provisions associated with book contracts. After all, you're the one ultimately responsible for signing off on the terms set forth by the deal. Below are nine clauses found in typical book contracts. Reading the explanation of each clause, along with the negotiating tips, will help clarify what you are agreeing to as the book's author.

1. Grant of Rights

The Grant of Rights clause transfers ownership rights in, and therefore control over, certain parts of the work from the author to the publisher. Although it's necessary and appropriate to grant some exclusive rights (e.g., the right to print, publish and sell print-book editions), don't assign or transfer your copyright and use discretion when granting rights in languages other than English and territories other than the United States, its territories and Canada. Also, limit the publication formats granted to those that your publisher is capable of exploiting adequately.

- Never transfer or assign your copyright or "all rights" in the work to your publisher.
- Limit the languages, territories and formats in which your publisher is granted rights.

2. Subsidiary Rights

Subsidiary rights are uses that your publisher may make of your manuscript other than issuing its own hardcover or paperback print book editions. Print-related subsidiary rights include book club and paperback reprint editions, publication of selections, condensations or abridgments in anthologies and textbooks and first and second serial rights (i.e., publication in newspapers or magazines either before or after publication of the hardcover book). Subsidiary rights not related to print include motion picture, television, stage, audio, animation, merchandising and electronic rights.

Subsidiary rights may be directly exploited by your publisher or licensed to third parties. Your publisher will share licensing fees with you in proportion to the ratios set forth in your contract. You should receive at least 50 percent of the licensing proceeds.

- Consider reserving rights outside the traditional grant of primary print book publishing rights, especially if you have an agent.
- Beware of any overly inclusive language, such as "in any format now known or hereafter developed," used to describe the scope of the subsidiary rights granted.
- Make sure you are fairly compensated for any subsidiary rights granted. Reputable publishers will pay you at least 50 percent of the proceeds earned from licensing certain categories of rights, much higher for others.

3. Delivery and Acceptance

Most contracts stipulate that the publisher is only obligated to accept, pay for and publish a manuscript that is "satisfactory to the publisher in form and content." It may be difficult to negotiate a more favorable, objective provision, but you should try. Otherwise, the decision as to whether your manuscript is satisfactory, and therefore publishable, will be left to the subjective discretion of your publisher.

- If you cannot do better, indicate that an acceptable manuscript is one which your publisher deems editorially satisfactory.
- Obligate your publisher to assist you in editing a second corrected draft before ultimately rejecting your manuscript.
- Negotiate a nonrefundable advance or insert a clause that would allow you to repay the advance on a rejected book from re-sale proceeds paid by a second publisher.

4. Publication

Including a publication deadline in your contract will obligate your publisher to actually publish your book in a timely fashion. Be sure that the amount of time between the delivery of the manuscript and the publication of the book isn't longer than industry standard.

- Make sure you're entitled to terminate the contract, regain all rights granted and keep the advance if your publisher fails to publish on or before the deadline.
- Carefully limit the conditions under which your publisher is allowed to delay publication.

5. Copyright

Current copyright law doesn't require authors to formally register their copyright in order to secure copyright protection. Copyright automatically arises in written works created in or after 1978. However, registration with the Copyright Office is a prerequisite to infringement lawsuits and important benefits accrue when a work is registered within three months of initial publication.

- Require your publisher to register your book's copyright within three months of initial publication.
- As previously discussed in Grant of Rights, don't allow your publisher to register copyright in its own name.

6. Advance

An advance against royalties is money that your publisher will pay you prior to publication and subsequently deduct from your share of royalty earnings. Most publishers will pay, but might not initially offer, an advance based on a formula which projects the first year's income.

- Bargain for as large an advance as possible. A larger advance gives your publisher greater incentive to publicize and promote your work.
- Research past advances paid by your publisher in industry publications such as *Publishers Weekly*.

7. Royalties

You should earn royalties for sales of your book that are in line with industry standards. For example, many authors are paid 10 percent of the retail price of the book on the first 5,000 copies sold, 12.5 percent of the retail price on the next 5,000 copies sold, and 15 percent of the retail price on all copies sold thereafter.

- Base your royalties on the suggested retail list price of the book, not on net sales income earned by your publisher. Net-based royalties are lower than list-based royalties of the same percentage, and they allow your publisher room to offer special deals or write off bad debt without paying you money on the books sold.

- Limit your publisher's ability to sell copies of your book at deep discounts—quantity discount sales of more than 50 percent—or as remainders.
- Limit your publisher's ability to reduce the percentage of royalties paid for export, book club, mail order and other special sales.

8. Accounting and Payments

Your accounting clause should establish the frequency with which you should expect to receive statements accounting for your royalty earnings and subsidiary rights licensing proceeds. If you are owed money in any given accounting period, the statement should be accompanied by a check.

- Insist on at least a bi-annual accounting.
- Limit your publisher's ability to withhold a reserve against returns of your book from earnings that are otherwise owed to you.
- Include an audit clause in your contract which gives you or your representative the right to examine the sales records kept by the publisher in connection with your work.

9. Out of Print

Your publisher should only have the exclusive rights to your work while it is actively marketing and selling your book (i.e., while your book is "in print'"). An out-of-print clause will allow you to terminate the contract and regain all rights granted to your publisher after the book stops earning money.

It is crucial to actually define the print status of your book in the contract. Stipulate that your work is in print only when copies are available for sale in the United States in an English language hardcover or paperback edition issued by the publisher and listed in its catalog. Otherwise, your book should be considered out of print and all rights should revert to you.

- Don't allow the existence of electronic and print-on-demand editions to render your book in print. Alternatively, establish a floor above which a certain amount of royalties must be earned or copies must be sold during each accounting period for your book to be considered in print. Once sales or earnings fall below this floor, your book should be deemed out of print and rights should revert to you.
- Stipulate that as soon as your book is out of print, all rights will automatically revert to you regardless of whether or not your book has earned out the advance.

SEALING THE DEAL

The Next Steps

So You Have an Agent–Now What?

by Chuck Sambuchino

In this book, we've told you all about contacting and securing agents. Details on everything from writing to pitching to getting the most out of your subsidiary rights are included in these pages. But should your hard work and passion pay off in a signed deal with a big-shot agent, the journey isn't over. Now it's time to learn what lies in store after the papers are signed.

LET YOUR AGENT WORK

In the time leading up to signing a contract, you may have bantered around plenty with your agent—realizing you both love the New York Yankees and Kung Pao Chicken. But don't let this camaraderie allow you to forget that the relationship is a business one first and foremost. Does this mean you can't small talk occasionally and ask your agent how her children are doing? No. But don't call every day complaining about the traffic and your neighbor's habit of mowing his lawn before the sun comes up.

Your agent is going to read your work again (and again . . .) and likely suggest possible changes to the manuscript. "When you sign with an agent, you should go over next steps, and talk about what the agent expects from you," says Sorche Fairbank, principal of the Fairbank Literary Agency. "This can vary with each author-agent relationship, and on the type of book project. We (at the Fairbank agency) are fairly hands-on with shaping and polishing a proposal or manuscript, and there often is quite a bit of work to be done before we and the author feel it's ready to send out.

"If you have a nonfiction project, there is certain to be some final tweaking of the proposal and sample chapter(s)," Fairbank says. "If you have a novel, then I hope you would be... taking any agent advice on tightening and polishing it. Go through it one more time and weed out extraneous words, overused pet words and phrases, and stock descriptions."

KEEP WRITING

If you're not working with your agent on rewrites and revisions, it's your responsibility to continue creating. One challenge is over—another begins. As your agent is trying hard to sell your work and bring home a nice paycheck, you're expected to keep churning out material for her to sell. Keep her informed of what you're working on and when it'll be ready.

Stay passionate. Once you've convinced yourself that your first book was not a fluke,

CHUCK SAMBUCHINO is the editor of *Guide to Literary Agents* (www.guidetoliteraryagents.com/blog) and *Screenwriter's & Playwright's Market* (both Writer's Digest Books). He is a former staffer on *Writer's Digest* and a frequent presenter at writers' conferences.

you've convinced yourself that you're a capable writer—and a capable writer needs to keep writing and always have material to sell. Always be considering new projects and working on new things, but give preference to the first work that got you a contract. Rewrites and revisions--wanted by agents and editors alike—will likely take months and become somewhat tedious, but all that frustration will melt away when you have that first hardcover book in your hands.

SELLING THE BOOK

When the book is as perfect as can be, it's time for your agent to start shopping it to her publishing contacts. During this process, she'll likely keep you abreast of all rejections. Don't take these to heart--instead, learn from each one, especially those with editors who have kindly given a specific reason as to why they don't want the book. "When the project is being shopped around, discuss rejections with your agent. There may be patterns that point to a fixable weak spot," Fairbank says.

Your book may be bought in a pre-empt. That's when a publishing house tries to beat other potential buyers to your work and offers a solid price in the hopes of securing your book early and avoiding a bidding war. An actual bidding war—or "auction"—happens when a work is so stunningly marvelous that every house in town wants it bad enough to compete against each other, offering different perks such as a large advance and guaranteed ad dollars. Traditionally, the best deal (read: most money and enthusiasm) wins and signs. After the auction was finished for Elizabeth Kostova's *The Historian*, her advance was a cool $2 million. (Note: First-time novelists will likely get an advance of $20,000 to $60,000, but hey, anything can happen!)

Your agent will submit the work to publishers (either exclusively or simultaneously, depending on her opinion) and hold a private auction if need be to secure the best deal possible. Fairbank says it's important for writers to relax during the auction process and not call every 30 minutes for an update. "In an auction, everything should go through the agent, but writers may be called upon to do a few things," she says. "I have had some cases where it made sense to bring the author around to meet with the various interested houses, usually to drive home the author's expertise and promotability. In every instance, it increased the size of the offers. There have also been times where a particular house asked for more specifics on something, and I needed my author ready to respond ASAP."

PROMOTE YOURSELF

Besides continuing to write and revise, the most important thing a writer needs to focus on is promotion. It's likely your work will not have the benefit of countless publicists setting up interviews for you. How you want to promote your work is up to you.

According to Regina Brooks, president of Serendipity Literary Agency, "It's always a great time to research who you might want on your team once the book is published (e.g., publicists, Web developers, graphic artists, etc.). Often times, authors wait until the last minute to start researching these options. The more lead time a publicist has to think about your project, the better. This is also an ideal time to attend conferences to network and workshops to tighten your writing skills."

GO WITH THE FLOW

An agent's job is to agent. That means knowing which people are buying what, and where they're headed if a move is in the works. Throughout the editing process, you'll work hand-in-hand with your agent and editor to revise and polish the manuscript. But let's say the editor makes the not-so-uncommon decision to switch jobs or switch houses. Ideally, an agent will shepherd you through the change.

"It happens more often than we'd like," says Brooks. "When it does, you hope that someone in-house will be as excited about the project as the acquiring editor initially was, but there's no guarantee." Fairbank agrees: "The most important thing the author and agent can do in that case is take a deep breath, pick up the phone, and wholeheartedly welcome the new editor to the book team. Once they have their feet under them and have reviewed your work, ask them what they think, and listen to any questions or comments they may have."

In addition to switching editors at publishing houses, a writer must concern himself with the possibility of his agent hitting the lottery and quitting (or just quitting without hitting the lottery, which is more probable). To protect yourself, make sure that this scenario is clearly addressed in your contract with the agent. "It really depends on the initial written agreement between the agent and the author," says Brooks. "It's important that the agreement cover such situations in their termination language. This assures that all parties including the publishing company know how to proceed with royalty statements, notices, etc."

AND WHAT IF . . . ?

A difficult question that may come up is this: What should you do if you think your agent has given up on you, or isn't fulfilling her end of the bargain? (In other words, how do you get out? Can you get out?) First, consider that if an agent is trying and failing to sell your manuscript, then at least the trying part is there. It could just be an unfortunate instance where you and an agent both love a work but can't find anyone else who feels the same. This is no one's fault. As far as simply quitting an agent is concerned, you can't opt out of a contract until the contract says so.

A similar dilemma involves authors who have a satisfactory agent but want out in favor of one perceived to be better. If you already have an agent, but others are calling in hopes to work with you, the new agents likely don't know you already possess representation. Obviously, you need to tell them you are currently represented. That said, you most likely can't just switch agents because you're under contract. When the time comes when you can legally opt out of a contract (and you think your agent has had ample time to make a sale), consider your options then.

GET READY FOR YOUR RIDE

Hopefully, you'll never need to experience the difficulty and confusion of switching agents and/or editors. Hopefully, your work will smoothly find a house and then a large audience once it's published. Just remember that the smoother things go, the less excuses exist for you not to keep writing then promote the heck out of your work. Simply do what you do best (write) and continue to learn what you can about the publishing world. As Fairbank puts it so simply, "Be available, willing, and ready to help your agent."

PERSPECTIVES

Social Networking

The Ins and Outs of Blogs, Facebook and More

by Ron Hogan

If you aren't blogging now, and you don't plan on starting any time soon, there may come a time when an agent or a publicist says to you, "You have to get the word out about your book on the Internet—hey, you should start a blog!"

This is the worst possible reason to start a blog.

Remember that scene in *A Christmas Story* when Ralphie becomes totally absorbed in the coded message from his favorite radio show only to walk away in disgust when he finds out it's a "crummy commercial"? That's how online readers feel, and they can usually sniff out the marketing a lot sooner. If you want to establish an online presence that will help readers to discover you when you become a published author, now is the perfect time to start.

AN OUTLET FOR YOUR INTERESTS

You should blog for the same reason you want to write in the first place: There's something you want to say to the world, and you can't imagine not saying it. You should be writing from a position of *passionate authority*—that is, you should be writing about a subject into which you've fully immersed yourself and ready to share your enthusiasm with others. Once you get past the basic format—a series of posts, similar to short articles or journal entries, arranged in reverse chronological order so readers will see the most recent material first—it doesn't matter what you're writing about: A 13-year-old girl blogging about videogames can be just as passionate as a 25-year-old man sharing his favorite recipes, or a 40-year-old woman writing about the books she's reading.

I started my Web site, Beatrice.com, back in 1995 because I was working in an independent bookstore and realized the opportunity in interviewing writers during their book tours. I posted those Q&As irregularly for years until work commitments forced me to spend less time on my personal site; that's when I started posting short commentaries about the literary world every weekday.

You don't necessarily have to share a lot of your personal life in a blog, but you should be revealing a lot of your personality... and for those of you who are about to ask, "How's this supposed to help me sell books?" the answer is, it's not (assuming you even have a book to sell yet). If it's about "selling" anything to other people, *you* are the merchandise. Your blog, along with the other social networking platforms I'll mention shortly, is a way to establish that you are an interesting person who has something to say. Once people are convinced of that, it's a lot easier to for them to believe your book (if you have one) is worth reading.

RON HOGAN helps run GalleyCat online, www.mediabistro.com/galleycat.

POST FREQUENCY

So, if you do start blogging, how often should you do it? Some people are comfortable writing several posts a day, others find one thing to say each day, and others can get by waiting a week (or even longer) between posts. But *frequency* is, in the long run, not as important an issue as consistency. When blogs first became popular, readers would typically use their web browsers to view the actual pages for their favorite blogs at least once a day; if they noticed that a particular site hadn't been updated for a while, they would visit less frequently, perhaps even drop the blog from their checklist. Now that RSS (which stands for Really Simple Syndication) has made it possible for readers to be notified about new posts without having to visit the sites themselves, that isn't as much of an issue, but there's still the question of how to get new readers to subscribe to your RSS feed to begin with. Ultimately, readers choose to follow a blog because they know they can expect the author to say something interesting on a regular basis, so you'll want your most recent posts—the first things people will see when they visit your home page—to be as interesting as possible. Your prose doesn't have to be perfect; one of the great benefits of blogging is the way it allows your voice to develop as you go along. Just concentrate on finding a pace that allows you to write comfortably and confidently.

CONNECTING THROUGH OTHERS

If you choose not to start your own blog, you can still participate in the blogosphere by commenting on other people's posts. Impromptu communities often emerge from the comments sections of popular blogs, and the discussions can get lively. (During the last presidential election, for example, when the outcome was still in doubt, political sites like TalkingPointsMemo.com or LittleGreenFootballs.com became hangouts where supporters of one party could vent openly about the other's campaign tactics.) When taking part in comment threads, basic common sense and courtesy apply: Don't come in looking for a fight, and try to have something meaningful to say, instead of just posting "Me too!" or "Is not!"

Social networking sites build upon the basic sense of community that blog commenting can offer, intensifying and enriching it. For developing writers, social networks like GoodReads.com, Readerville.com, and Backspace (BKSP.org) provide a space to trade opinions on the books you're reading or talk through the problems in your latest manuscript. You can find similar discussion groups in broader social networks like Facebook, along with opportunities to pursue any number of other interests with like-minded people.

TO FRIEND OR NOT TO FRIEND?

Once you create a profile page on a social network, you'll find yourself getting friend requests from lots of people, many of whom you won't actually know. You'll have to decide for yourself how comfortable you are calling somebody a "friend" just because you both like Stephen King books, or organic gardening. You'll also find a lot of writers, including some very famous ones, on these networks. Before you ask someone you like if they'll be your friend, look at their profiles. Every writer has his or her own boundaries; if I get a friend request from somebody I don't know, I check to see if we have mutual friends in common, or if they've taken the trouble to write a personal note, before I decide whether to approve the request. Some authors prefer to keep their friend lists to an intimate, manageable level—if your literary idol turns you down (or doesn't even bother to reply), don't take it personally.

Concerned that all this blogging and commenting and making friends will cut into your creative time? Many writers find room in their schedules for both, but if you're feeling squeezed, or you just don't feel like you have much to say, it's perfectly okay to not spend time on blogs or social networks. An online presence may be increasingly important for a *published writer*, but your top priority, before and after publication, should be the *writing*—

and you can always get by with a simple home page that tells people what they need to know about you and your book. Remember: The point of writing online, wherever you choose to do it, is that you've got something you need to tell the rest of the world. If you sincerely believe a book is not just the best but the only way to share your story, then that's where you need to be. Either way, good luck!

YOUR STARTER BLOG

If you've never blogged before, Tumblr.com has a very simple interface. It was originally designed to be more of a "scrapbook" than a typical blog, so it has a very basic format, but it's all you need to write an entry, post a picture, embed a YouTube video, or link to one of your favorite Web sites. Some people recommend using a Tumblr blog "under the radar" as a starter project, like a practice writing journal you'd keep to yourself (or maybe show a few trusted friends). You can learn the format and see if you feel comfortable posting regularly—or if you even have that much you want to share with other people. If you realize blogging's not for you, you'll find out soon enough, and you can just scrap your account.

Many people find that Tumblr has all the blogging power they need. But you may want to do more—you might want to put more than one picture in a post, for example, or create a sidebar list of your favorite websites. There are several websites that can host a blog for you: WordPress.com and Blogspot.com offer free hosting, while Typepad.com has several pricing levels (and the most likely options for individual writers are still less than $9 a month). Each of these platforms has its advocates and detractors; check each out for yourself and see which feels right for you.

(The last two paragraphs assume you don't already have your own Web site, but if you do, and your technical literacy is strong, you might consider installing blogging software such as WordPress or Movable Type on your site. This can make it easier for you to design a blog that is visually consistent with your existing online presence.)

PERSPECTIVES

Getting the Word Out

Professional Advice from Publicists

If there's one thing writers know, it's that their work is never finished. You write a book, find an agent, attract a publisher, make revisions, and all the while you've got a million other ideas swarming around in your head for the next book. Just as agents can relieve an author's workload by dealing with contracts and business meetings, hiring an independent publicist can take some of the weight of promoting your book off your shoulders. You'll still be part of the process (and success), but the detailed work will be left to a professional. Below, three experts explain what you can expect from the publicist/author relationship.

Alice B. Acheson has been an independent publicist since 1981. She provides marketing, publicity and subsidiary rights campaigns (national and/or local) for publishers and authors of fiction and nonfiction.

Rod Mitchell has been a freelance literary publicist for more than 20 years.

Sherri Rosen opened her agency in 1997. She works with eclectic clients whose writing focuses on self-help, sex, spirituality, personal inspiration, etc.

At what stage in the publishing process should an author contact a publicist? Is it ever too late?

Alice B. Acheson: The earlier the better, so that marketing opportunities are not lost because of missed deadlines. However, the author should try to get the publishing house to commit to as much marketing as possible before contacting a freelance publicist. If the author and freelance publicist are solely responsible for the marketing, the publisher will have little vested interest. That said, six months prior to publication date would be a good benchmark. It is too late when the book is due next week.

Rod Mitchell: We prefer to launch campaigns 30 days in advance of release so we can send out galleys to reviewers, morning network shows and syndicated radio shows. Is it ever too late? This depends on a number of factors: Was a professional publicist on the scene previously? How well did the book sell in the first six months? Does the book have longevity, regardless of how long it has been released? We typically do not represent books that are over one year old unless the author is an expert in a field that would allow us to pitch him/her to news and talk programs.

Sherri Rosen: The author needs to contact the publicist at least six months in advance, mainly if the author is interested in having galleys sent out for book reviews to places that require the galleys three months before the publishing date of the book. Our philosophy is that it is never too late to contact a publicist to do publicity.

What personality traits and/or habits do you look for in potential clients?

Acheson: I look at how their philosophy, enthusiasm and personality compare with mine. Are they available to consult during my nine-to-five day and from a site where they can read and write notes? Do they work in a business-like manner? Are they willing to proceed according to a timeline, providing material in a timely fashion so that I don't have to burn the midnight oil to comply with a deadline? Are they willing to listen, learn and work together? They may not take my suggestion, but it should be a partnership (i.e., telling me why a suggestion is not appropriate, which might lead to another suggestion).

Mitchell: We migrate toward authors who have a friendly, positive and confident personality. We also like authors who are not afraid to express themselves with a commanding voice and presence. Talk and news shows prefer authors who have fascinating and thought-provoking points of views. We feign away from those who are arrogant or inflexible in their thought process.

Rosen: I look for someone who is easy to get along with and who is personable-in many cases an author who is a great self-promoter. This is a two-way street and both the author and I must work together to get the book out there.

What is the most critical thing an author should look for when hiring a publicist?

Acheson: Authors should look at the publicist's reputation and how long he/she has been in book publicity. Authors should also try to determine the publicist's dedication to their project. Will the book be handled routinely, or passed to someone in the firm with little experience? Contacts are not absolutely necessary, but the ability to find the appropriate contact is. For example, a publicist may never have worked on a bowling book and therefore has no contact with those magazines, but she should quickly be able to ferret out those who will make an impact.

Mitchell: Nothing beats experience, and a publicist with experience promoting books similar to the author's book is an added bonus. An author should want a publicist who has a well-rounded background in pitching print and electronic media all over the country (not just locally or regionally), with an expansive contact list of major market and syndicated radio and television stations. (Ask the publicist how many contacts are in his/her database.) A publicist should be willing to provide references of both authors they've represented and those in the media who are willing to vouch for the publicist.

Rosen: Authors need to look at a publicist's experience and see whom the publicist has worked with. Has the publicist worked on the particular genre in the past? What were the results? Does the author like the publicist? Does the author feel as though the publicist takes personal interest in the author and the book? Is the publicist respectful to the author? Is the publicist good at following up with contacts?

What do publicists do that authors can't do on their own?

Acheson: Authors can't talk to book review editors because they haven't built up trust of judgment or a working relationship over the years, and don't know the rules under which they operate. The same is generally true about interviewers. The media, in general, doesn't want to talk to authors for three basic reasons: It is very difficult to say no to someone who has labored for years on a project; most authors don't understand how to pitch their book; and many don't know when to say thank you and hang up. By nature, most are writers, not marketers.

Rosen: Publicists can see a much bigger picture and view of how to proceed because they are coming into the project fresh, open and perhaps with ideas of thinking outside of the box.

Does it matter where a publicist is located?

Acheson: Since I live on an island far west of Seattle, my answer is pretty obvious. If the publicist has experience and contacts, location is not an issue. On the other hand, if it is truly a regional book, or one that will at least begin regionally, then the first choice should be someone whose prime experience is that region. And, if the author lives on the East Coast and is unavailable after 5 p.m., it doesn't make sense to hire a publicist on the West Coast, no matter how qualified he/she is. It would limit constructive conversation to hours between noon and 5 p.m., with lunch interrupting that time.

Mitchell: I live in Houston, Texas, and I can count on one hand the number of authors I have personally met over the past 20 years. It doesn't matter where you live; what matters is experience and a long working history with media contacts that are located across the country.

Rosen: I have lived out of town and in New York City, and I feel it is best to live in New York City. I am living in the center of one of the biggest arenas of publishing, and I have the opportunity to connect with people in the publishing world, as well as radio and television producers. I am also able to meet my clients, and personal touch is a very powerful tool in book publishing.

What are some things an author should expect a publicist to ask of them?

Acheson: One practical chore I always require of authors is filling out an extensive author questionnaire, which includes a request for a headshot. That form provides a wealth of marketing possibilities for future action.

Mitchell: Publicists should gather a biography (they should be able to assist in the writing of this bio), recent photographs and a copy of the book (for both reading and scanning for the press kit). They should also assist the author in preparing interview questions and talk points for interviews, and provide suggestions for appearances that are outside media (churches, schools, civic organizations, etc.).

Rosen: Publicists will often have the author contemplate on any contacts they may have and manifest a list. Authors may also have to stop by their local bookstores to introduce themselves.

What is the most important marketing tool these days?

Acheson: The Internet, and by that I mean e-mail and the ability to transfer information quickly, be it a promotion sheet, news that can be used to revitalize a pitch (e.g., inclusion on a best-seller list) or reiteration of something sent by mail and not received (saving the cost of sending a second book).

Mitchell: Bar none, the first and most important marketing tool is the Internet. Authors should ask the publicist if he can provide this service. Also, if the author is an expert on a particular topic, or has a particularly newsworthy story or idea disclosed in the book, the publicist should pitch national news desks with the author as a news contributor. Nothing grabs the public's attention more then an author who has a breakthrough piece of information or comments that will enhance a timely news story.

Most authors hear about book tours, radio interviews and book reviews. What are some of the more creative marketing options out there?

Acheson: Naturally, the options are driven by the book. For a book I worked on named Old Turtle, we painted a Volkswagen Beetle to look like Old Turtle, transported it in a trailer across the country, painted the trailer appropriately so that it became a traveling billboard, and two employees spoke to children about the themes of the book. Along the way, we collected "a million messages of peace" from the children for delivery to the United Nations—which later became another book.

Mitchell: In some cases publicists will contract with other freelancers who specialize in providing book tours, like BookTours.com in Boston.

Rosen: Perhaps a creative way to market a book would be through branding--connecting the author and/or the book with a particular store or product that is well known. Or, running a contest on the author's Web site, depending upon the type of book, and at the same time getting press on the contest.

What is the biggest misconception about publicists?

Acheson: That we are wealthy. Authors think publicists' fees are expensive, but they do not realize how labor intensive the work is. Every day we spend hours updating our databases so that our contacts' information is current. A book sent to the wrong person becomes a holiday gift from someone in the mailroom. Publicity, versus advertising, is free. Publicists are asking the media to donate time or space. When weighed against those costs, publicity is not expensive.

Mitchell: Authors think they can pay for their publicists with the royalties they receive from a publisher or distributor. Even if the author is self-published, the dollars they will see back are long in coming. Also, first-time authors have no idea how much a publicist charges—retainer fees run from $1,000-10,000 per month. Some publicists also charge on a per-venue basis, which means they only pay for the actual bookings (interviews and appearances) that the publicist delivers. This is often misleading, and the ultimate price an author will pay, especially if the publicist is well connected, could be $5,000-$10,000 per month. Most authors cannot afford services that run this high.

Rosen: That they take no for an answer. If one pitch doesn't work, then we try other ways to get the author in the door.

PERSPECTIVES

Leaping Into the Fray

A Writer's First Year with an Agent and Editor

by Therese Walsh

Gifts come in mysterious wrappings. One of the very best gifts I ever received came in the guise of a rejection letter from an agent back in 2004, after I'd spent two years working on my novel, *The Last Will of Moira Leahy*. Said agent wrote: "Your story is just too much a hybrid right now. My gut tells me you need to write something bigger and that eventually you will. Why not analyze ways to make this story something more?"

Though that agent didn't inevitably become my agent, her advice changed my life. After sulking over the mammoth undertaking it would be to rewrite *Moira*, I studied, then studied some more. I brainstormed ways to explode the story out while maintaining the heart. I experimented with voice, created new characters, thought through the interweaving of plotlines. The reshaping took an entire year. It was only then, elated with the story's fresh potential, that I began rebuilding the literary equivalents of bone and muscle and flesh around that well-preserved heart; I rewrote every word.

In the spring of 2008, I prepared to send the second complete incarnation of *Moira* out into the world—proud of its metamorphosis, but aware of one likely problem: It was still a hybrid, just a bigger one, with various parts women's fiction, psychological suspense, family saga, love story, mystery and magical realism. I knew that agents (and editors) like books to fit into simple classifications so they're easy to market and sell. I wondered if my cross-genre story would ever find a home. More than anything, I wanted *Moira* to find a publisher so that I could hold it one day, bound and covered, and show it to my children.

AGENT HUNTING: PART II

My first strategy was to look for agents who represented as many of the elements in *Moira* as possible, write a damn good query letter and call my story commercial fiction; I'd leave it to the experts to figure out what specific label it should be given, if any. I created a list of top-notch agents, began querying and received a few positive rejection letters that amounted to the same message: the story was intriguing but would be difficult to market because of the supernatural elements.

Plan B emerged. Since the magical realism reflected the heart of the story, I decided to focus on agents with both a love for this niche genre and established connections (read: sales) in it. I submitted again and right away had a request for the full manuscript from a highly respected agent, followed later by a half-hour phone conversation with him. He loved the suspense and the magical realism but didn't connect with the emotional aspects of the

THERESE WALSH is the founder of Writer Unboxed, a blog about craft and business of genre fiction, http://writerunboxed.com.

story; he suggested major revisions.

This marked a low point for me; part of me wondered if I'd wasted six years of my life on something unmarketable, if my instinct for story was intrinsically flawed, if I should give up the nonfiction writing that had long sustained my fiction habit and just get a 9-5 job already. A stronger side of me refused to give up, though, believing *Moira* was not only unique but sellable; I just needed to find the right person.

It was early June when it occurred to me that one of my blog partners at Writer Unboxed, Allison Winn Scotch, had an forthcoming book that contained a touch of magical realism (*Time of My Life*). Her agent, Elisabeth Weed, had recently started her own agency and had only a short résumé of fiction credits, but I knew Allison believed Elisabeth to be up-and-coming and very well connected in the industry. I shot Allison an e-mail to ask if she thought Elisabeth might be interested in more touch-of-magic tales. Allison asked Elisabeth if she could pass along my query. Elisabeth gave the green light. She asked for my query and I sent it.

Then a partial.

Then the full.

Elisabeth called a few days later, full of enthusiasm for the manuscript and eager to help me sell the story that had held my imagination captive for the better part of a decade. She encouraged me to ask as many questions as I had, and she answered all of them, but it was her answer to one question—"Do you think it will sell?"—that really impacted me.

"If this story doesn't sell, I'll lose my faith in publishing," she said.

There was no question in my mind; I'd found the perfect agent for *Moira*.

EMBRACING THE "BIG BOOK"

Several times during my interview with Elisabeth, she used the phrase "big book." This referred to more than the scope, as I was to learn. "Big book" meant she'd send it to senior editors, the heads of imprints, specific women she felt would respond to the story. "Big book" meant she wanted to send it to everyone at once, hoping for either an auction or a pre-emptive offer.

I had a difficult time wrapping my brain around these concepts, as she named names and outlined her plan, so I focused on her suggested editorial changes instead, reworking scenes, clarifying motivations and tweaking prose. By mid-July, we both felt *Moira* was ready to go and wanted to get the manuscript out before August—a known vacation month in the publishing industry. We worked on perfecting the cover letter: "Part psychological suspense, part love story, Therese Walsh's novel will appeal to readers of Keith Donohue's *The Stolen Child* and Jennifer Egan's *The Keep*."

On July 17, a Thursday, Elisabeth called her A-list editors to introduce and gauge their interest in *Moira*, then she e-mailed them the story. I was told that response times could range from twelve hours to one month, so I readied myself for a long wait. A mere four days later, we had an offer—and it was improved upon the day after that, following some negotiating over world rights. Shaye Areheart Books, an imprint of Random House, had offered a major two-book deal for *Moira*. My hard work and relentless belief in the story had been validated, though the deal also stunned me utterly.

I stammered to Elisabeth over the phone: "Never in my wildest…I never thought…I didn't realize…"

"*I* did," Elisabeth said.

We accepted the deal.

EDITING AND GROWING PAINS

Elisabeth, ever so wise. might also have guessed that my new editor, Sarah Knight, and I were both strong-willed women who wouldn't always agree. Still, Sarah was a great editor for *Moira*—because she truly loved the story and demanded as much of herself as she did of me. If my book sings today, it sings in part because she held the baton and encouraged its song.

It wasn't all easy, though.

Having written and published a good deal of nonfiction, I was well versed in deadline pressure, requests for revisions, and the other various demands of publishing. I mean—I'd worked at Rodale Press, once upon a time; I knew publishing. (You can see the next part coming, can't you?) Thing is, I'd never taken large-scale direction on anything remotely personal, let alone a six-year writing project, so I really had no business assuming the no-hurt-feelings nonfiction writer I'd been would show up to work when Sarah took pencil to hand and urged me to ready a scalpel for mine.

The hardest lump to take involved the title, which wasn't always *The Last Will of Moira Leahy*. A few days after the deal, Sarah mentioned concerns about the book's original title: *Unbounded*. She asked that I brainstorm new possibilities. The idea sapped me of joy and made me so anxious that the issue was tabled. It might seem a ridiculous, petty thing to worry over after such a great deal. The only thing I can liken it to is this: Imagine having a six-year-old child and being told his name didn't suit him and that from that day forward everyone would call him Stinking Cloud of Doom.

Following that, Sarah and I went to work on edits. I learned that I had a tendency to overuse certain words (check). A few sections required fleshing out while others needed pruning (check). Overall, the story needed another thousand words or so to reach an ideal length (check). The biggest overhaul to *Moira* came from some smart, open-ended questions Sarah asked about pacing issues in one section of the story and uneven tensions in another. I suggested a plot twist and character makeover, and she agreed that these revisions could solve the problems. The changes cut deep into the story, though, and affected more than I'd bargained for originally—and probably more than Sarah had bargained for, too. What followed was a lot of time at the computer and a few bloodless battles with Sarah over this and that. Ironically, the manuscript that had once been too lean became too fat, and so I was asked to trim smart while sanding every last rough sentence into shape. We even settled on a new title and—happy day—it wasn't Stinking Cloud of Doom.

A few days before Thanksgiving, I turned in my final draft, exhausted but knowing it was my best work. Sarah knew it, too. Her pride in the story we both loved was audible when we spoke, and I have to admit that it made mine surge, too. This particular editorial journey was finally at an end. I have to admit that, after six long years, it felt bittersweet.

AWAITING THE NEXT CHAPTER

The Last Will of Moira Leahy will be released in September of 2009. Before then, I'll see galleys and glimpse the cover; I'll work with publicity and develop a Web site—maybe even a book trailer. I'll hope for more foreign rights sales. Exciting, yes. But for now, since the knowledge of having written a "big book" has finally sunk in, and since I've finished the hard work of editing, I've circled back to my original, blissfully simple goal: Hold the book, bound and covered, and show it to my children. That sounds pretty darn good.

PERSPECTIVES

How Not to Get an Agent

10 Things You Should Never Do

by Jean Daigneau

You've finished your first manuscript (or your second or third)—so what's the next step you should take? Start preparations for a book tour? Nope. Search for the right publicist? Nope. Call your mom with the news? Maybe.

But really, if you're ready to venture into the world of publishing, the first thing to do is get an agent. Any serious writer knows agents can magically open doors that some of us only dream about. In a market as tight as the current one, however, even getting an agent can be challenging. Which means this is the time to really put your creativity to work—forget the rules, ignore the experts, and listen to what they're *not* telling you.

1. Watts a Few Typos Among Friends

Prior to submitting to an agent, you've no doubt read your manuscript until you could almost recite it verbatim. Why worry then about those last few thousand words you just revised? That's what spelling and grammar check tools are for. *Sew watts the wurst that mite hap pen if ewe have knot red yore man yew script won Moor thyme?* If an agent can't overlook a few mistakes, she's probably not very flexible or easy to get along with, right? Who wants to work with someone like that? Besides, isn't that an agent's job—to take an unpolished manuscript and turn it into a bestseller? Your job is to write. You may as well leave the editing to the experts.

2. Gimmicks, Gimmicks, Gimmicks

Cute sells. Think Beanie Babies and dyed baby chicks. (Okay, you probably weren't even born when people could buy baby chicks in a rainbow of colors, but they were cute.) So enhancing your manuscript with clip art will certainly add an interesting element. Or consider using colored stationery or perhaps an unusual font. Something like Bradley Hand ITC is definitely eye-catching. Remember, it's all about making it to the top of the slush pile, or at least getting an agent's attention.

Besides, agents are people driven by the same human emotions as the rest of us—mostly greed. What agent in his or her right mind would turn down chocolate? Or football tickets? Or cash? Okay, I'm just kidding about the cash, but don't think it can't work.

Anything that makes your submission stand out is worth trying. Steven Chudney, principal of the Steven Chudney Agency, will attest to that fact. "Twice I've received 8x10 glossies from prospective clients," he said. "*That* certainly told me a lot about their writing *and them.*"

JEAN DAIGNEAU is a writer and former Regional Advisor for the Northern Ohio Society of Children's Book Writers and Illustrators. Her work has been published in children's and adult magazines and craft and teacher reference books. She lives in Kent, Ohio.

See? From the hundreds of submissions he's received, which ones does he remember? The two authors who sent glossies. I told you gimmicks work.

3. No Time to Be Humble

One thing most successful people have is confidence. What better way to show it than by letting an agent know that your spouse, best friend, grandchildren, or fellow inmates all love your story? Any agent will be thrilled to know that you're the next Dr. Seuss, especially when you tell her that, while your manuscript may seem very similar to *How the Grinch Stole Christmas*, it's actually much better. So remember, you can't say enough about what a great writer you are. That agent will be so impressed with you she'll probably mention your approach during a conference presentation—as one of the most unforgettable she's encountered.

4. Show Off Your Best Feature

Relax. This has nothing to do with thong bathing suits (which is a good thing since some men don't look good in them anyway—and neither do some women). When an agent asks for the first three chapters and a synopsis, who says that's what you should send? Let's say your story really kicks into high gear in chapter five. By all means, send chapter five! Once an agent gets a taste for how talented you are, he'll be begging for the rest of your manuscript anyway.

Then, too, some agents change their submittal policies like my Uncle Jerome changes his underwear—once a week, whether he needs to or not. Just trying to keep those guidelines straight is a full-time job. Why bother? Writing is hard enough as it is.

5. One Size Fits All

Some so-called experts will say it's important to find out which agent is the best fit for your style of writing. Don't you believe it! Just because an agent doesn't rep a certain genre doesn't mean you shouldn't send it. After all, there are plenty of successful writers who have found their niche. If horror works for Stephen King, it stands to reason any agent will want your latest chiller. Once an agent reads it, she'll be more than delighted to change her entire business focus just to sign you up. Well, unless she's a loser. But then who wants to sign with an agent who would pass up the next Stephen King?

6. Cut to the Chase

We all know that agents are busy people. But, hey, you're busy, too. Why waste time waiting to hear back from an agent? The best thing to do if you don't get an answer right away is to pick up the phone. After all, any agent will appreciate the fact that he or she doesn't have to call you back. Is there such a thing as calling too often? I'd let the agent worry about that if I were you.

Serendipity Literary Agency founder Regina Brooks deals with her share of persistent authors all the time. "Some authors call and call again and often it's not just about the book project," she said. Brooks, however, has no complaints. "I always wanted to be a therapist. And since agents border on practicing law without a license when we review contracts, what's the harm in practicing psychiatry without one, too?" Should you ever sign with her, you'll be glad to know that her diagnoses are free. Well, only if you're committed. Or perhaps need to be.

7. Look Out For Numero Uno

Once you're lucky enough to have gotten to an agent who is interested in your work, this is your opportunity to question how she runs her business. You might not know everything there is about being an agent, but you certainly know what's best for you. Getting her to lower her commission rates is only a matter of telling her how outrageous they are. No amount of nitpicking is too much; when you get to this stage, it's all about you.

Then, too, you surely have some idea of what publisher you want handling your masterpiece and, therefore, where it should be sent. Don't be afraid to let an agent know exactly what you expect. And, once you're on your way to sealing the deal, you'll want to let her know that PR is her responsibility. After all, you've done the hard part; your work is done.

8. It's Never Too Early

But let's say you haven't finished your first novel yet. Contrary to what you might think, that makes you one of the lucky ones. Why bother even writing something if the chances of it getting published are so slim? If you sign up with an agent *before* you've finished your first novel, or even started it for that matter, think of the aggravation you'll save yourself. You can pitch your idea, an agent will fall in love with it, he'll give you plenty of direction on where to go with it, and you can write with the knowledge that an adoring public and an even more grateful agent are awaiting your every word.

9. Don't Overlook Any Opportunity

Fate, too, can sometimes play a part in your success in getting an agent. Say you're at a writers' conference and you happen to follow an agent to the bathroom and into the stall next to her. If you see a hand waving at you from underneath the divider, you, my friend, are golden. I'm not suggesting you shouldn't help a person in need. Just wrap the toilet paper around your manuscript and pass it on over—or in this case, under.

After all, agents go to conferences, retreats, and workshops to meet clients, right? As the author of a future *New York Times* bestseller, the only obstacle between you and instant fame and fortune is getting your manuscript into an agent's hands so she knows it, too. Once she does, chances are good she'll whip out a contract and sign you on the spot.

10. Draw Attention to Yourself

It's especially important during a tough publishing market to shed that high school wallflower persona and let the world know you're interested in finding an agent. It's all about getting the word out that you're available. Of course, for some of you, thoughts of high school and "being available" might conjure up different images—like your phone number on a few restroom walls. Which is okay, I guess, since you might pick up an agent that way. Or vice versa.

When it comes to getting noticed, children's author Cinda Chima shared this advice, gleaned from a conference she recently attended: "If you're unhappy with your agent, attend a writing conference with editors and agents and complain loudly to anyone who will listen about what an idiot your agent is. No doubt other agents will hear about it and know you're in the market and will contact you about representation." Chima, whose young adult Heir trilogy *did* make it onto the *New York Times* bestseller list, unfortunately did things the hard way. Prior to publication she wrote her manuscript to near perfection, then researched and queried agents until she found one that was a good fit. How that got her an agent, I'll never know. Some people are just lucky, I guess.

IN THE END

What happens, though, if you've tried all of these things and for some unknown reason, they haven't worked? My advice is simple—don't worry. Who says you need an agent in the first place? You don't really believe everything you read in *Guide to Literary Agents*, do you? Besides, between you and me, a person has to be pretty lame to read the kind of book that claims to give advice on something as simple as getting an agent. We both know you are way beyond that.

PERSPECTIVES

Self-Publishing and Agents

Here's Why Some Projects Interest Agents and Others Don't

by Chuck Sambuchino

Between subsidy publishers, vanity presses, print-on-demand companies, Lulu.com and other options, plenty of avenues exist for writers to see their work brought to life outside of the traditional publishing route. While writers young and old will argue all day about the benefits and downsides of self-publishing, one thing is fairly certain. It's very difficult for a self-published book to be available in bookstores all across the country and break out. That's why acquiring a literary agent to rep the book is seen as a logical step in the process.

As inspiring as it is to stare at that copy of *Eragon* on your bookshelves, know that getting an agent to take on a self-published book and take it to best-seller lists is no easy task. In fact, the odds are very slim. Some agents won't even consider your book, no matter what. The many that will consider it are already deluged in slush—so your submission better stand out. Before you send out any more queries (or worse, the whole book), keep reading to find out what agents said about what they look for—and what they absolutely must see—when considering to take on a self-published book.

FOR YOUR CONSIDERATION, MS. AGENT

Let's go straight to the good news: Many agents are open to representing self-published books and trying to see those books get a new contract. "Most agents will at least hear out an author with a self-published book to the same extent that they would hear out any query letter," says agent Stephany Evans, president of FinePrint Literary Management.

Make sure that, as always, you follow agency submission guidelines to a T. If the agency says "Query only," then don't send the book. Also be certain that the rep you're contacting does indeed handle works in your particular genre or category. (If you haven't defined what your work is—e.g., memoir, thriller—you need to identify it before starting the query process, or else you'll waste a lot of money sending out books.)

As you might expect, some agents, on the other hand, won't consider self-published works of any kind. Those closed to submissions include high-brow reps in the literary world with a full list of clients. And then there are just a small number of agents who pass on self-published books because they take pleasure of finding "fresh" projects. "A self-published book is already viewed as a 'used product.' There are so many great new manuscripts out there for editors to choose from, so why take on one that already has some community?" says Andrea Brown, founder of Andrea Brown Literary Agency.

CHUCK SAMBUCHINO is the editor of *Guide to Literary Agents* (www.guidetoliteraryagents.com/blog) and *Screenwriter's & Playwright's Market* (both Writer's Digest Books). He is a former staffer on *Writer's Digest* and a frequent presenter at writers' conferences.

Michelle Andelman, an associate agent at Brown's agency, echoes the same opinion: "I won't consider self-published books, because they deflate that great sense of 'discovery' for me. I always feel I can most enthusiastically champion something brand new to editors, who I think are eager to feel that sense of discovery as well."

MAKE YOUR PROJECT STAND OUT

When an author sends in a query for a novel, the *hook* is the crucial element. An agent wants to know what makes this particular book unique. Queries for self-published books have the disadvantage of immediately being scanned for not only a clever hook, but also a promising track record of sales.

In fact, your sales may be *the* most important factor in the query, because agents are looking for proof that the book has markets into which to tap. Concerning how many sales constitute a number impressive enough to attract attention, the answer varies greatly; however, a general rule of thumb would be to start querying after you've sold no fewer than 3,000 books. Another guideline to consider is that nonfiction sells easier than fiction. A lower number of sales for a novel would be somewhat equal to a higher number of nonfiction sales. Agent Adam Chromy of Artists and Artisans says he also weighs the number of books sold against how long the book has been available for purchase. "It's about momentum," he says. "If it's out two months and has sold 5,000 copies and it's getting press, that's great. If it's out for years, the number would have to be higher."

When Sharlene Martin, principal of Martin Literary Management, sits down to consider a self-published book, she's looking not only for sales information, but also for a mention that the author self-published by choice, not default by rejection of agents and editors on previous submission rounds. Agents are looking for authors who self-published *before* drowning in rejections who sold enough books to warrant the project a new life with traditional publishing.

Whether your work is fiction or nonfiction, agents will definitely be looking for a solid platform—meaning all the avenues you possess to sell/market your book to the identified markets of readers who will buy it. "A couple of aspects of a query letter for a self-published book will get me interested," says Jennie Dunham of Dunham Literary. "How much of an expert is the author? Really strong credentials help. Also, what type of platform does the author have? An author who can promote and sell a book is valuable."

If the writer's platform is good, and the book is on its way up (rather than fizzling out sales-wise), then your odds are improved. Agent Andrea Hurst, who founded an agency in Sacramento, came across a proposal from a self-published nonfiction author who had recently appeared on the Dr. Laura Show. Hurst signed the client and made a deal. Other writers have successfully signed with Hurst the same way, she says, though self-published books she reps may sometimes need an overhaul before a publisher's review. "We have taken on a few where we had the author add chapters, possibly change the title, and update it before it sold," she says.

In addition to detailing out your platform and how you intend to sell the book, include independent praise of your work. Awards, accolades, reviews, press and endorsements can all help stir the buzzstorm. Evans says she took on a self-published project when the book picked up several high-profile endorsements that helped trigger a few thousand sales. Diane Freed, another agent at FinePrint, noticed an article in a Maine newspaper about an award-winning self-published book written by a local librarian. The article was enough to get Freed's attention, and that librarian just signed a two-book deal with Freed's help.

RECOGNIZING A POSSIBLE DEAD END

Knowing that agents immediately look for sales, you may be tempted to head outside right this moment and peddle your wares at the nearest independent bookstore. But the flipside problem to not selling enough copies of your book is selling too many. Believe it or not, that's actually a bad thing. "There's a bit of a Catch-22 here," says Jessica Regel, agent at the Jean V. Naggar Literary Agency. "If they haven't sold very many copies and the book was just self-published, then you try to convince a mainstream publisher that the book hasn't hit its market yet, because it had no marketing/publicity. If the book has sold a good number of copies—let's say more than 10,000—then a publisher will worry that it has already hit its market, so you need to convince them that there is still an untapped audience out there."

For example, let's say you printed a book about the history of Mobile, Ala. After five months, you've sold several thousand copies—to local historians, community members, as well as your friends and relatives. Impressive, sure—but there isn't much of a point finding an agent or publisher, as you're probably close to maxing out your sales. Dunham agrees that very strong sales can be a deterrent: "I want to know that the author is off to a solid start. I also have to be convinced, however, that there's a wider audience beyond that," she says. "I've seen a couple of books where I felt there were strong sales, but then I felt like there wouldn't be many more."

Memoir is one of the most common categories where writers self-publish their work. With memoirs in particular, getting an agent to take on the book is a steep hill to climb, as there are just *too many* self-published memoirs out there to compete against. If writing the memoir gave you a new vigor for writing, then set the self-published book aside and start on a new book that you will take to agents first. Get the first book out of your system and keep writing. "I have only taking on a couple of self-published books and have sold almost all of them, but I will often look at a self-published author and see if we can't just let the self-pub book go and work on the next book in their career," says Chromy.

BATTLING (YET RECOGNIZING) THE STIGMA

Perhaps the biggest reason why the odds are against self-published books catching the eye of an agent is this: "Often they have not sold well, are not professionally edited, and have been out for quite a while," says Hurst.

Self-published books are constantly fighting against assumptions. Agents and editors will assume that the work was turned down by dozens (or hundreds) of people already—even if this is not the case. If your work is print-on-demand, they will assume it sold the average amount of copies: 75. They will assume the writing is below average and the author has no ability to market the work—even if these thoughts, too, are not the case. That's why your query letter that introduces the self-published book must squelch all misconceptions immediately—and that includes the assumption that you, the writer, will be difficult to work with. Books are changed and edited and some drastically reworked throughout the publishing process. Just because your literary fiction book has already sold 2,500 copies won't make it immune to major suggestions from agents and editors on how to rework it.

"I've found that a lot of self-published writers don't want to revise their books," says Debbie Carter of Muse Literary. "These projects can be a waste of time for agents and editors who are looking to develop new talent."

ADDRESSING PREVIOUS SELF-PUBLISHED BOOKS

If you've decided to go the route of letting your self-published book stay self-published and move on to Work No. 2, then how do you address your prior books when crafting that next query?

Previous self-published works can easily be found and analyzed if they have ISBN numbers. Nielson's BookScan allows the publishing industry to search sales records of books and authors. You must mention all your self-published books upfront in the interest of full disclosure. If you're worried because sales were weak, then include mentions of them at the bottom of the query letter in your "bio" paragraph. Don't even include the titles just yet.

This way, you're honest about your publishing past, but not drawing a whole lot of attention to it. If you mention your self-published books in the first line or two, the agent may stop reading simply because of the stigma. Let the agent see your pitch and get hooked. If they are interested enough, your bio details—including a list of any self-published books in your arsenal—should have little effect.

MARKETS

Literary Agents

Agents listed in this section generate 98-100 percent of their income from commission on sales. They do not charge for reading, critiquing or editing your manuscript or book proposal. It's the goal of an agent to find salable manuscripts: Her income depends on finding the best publisher for your manuscript. Since an agent's time is better spent meeting with editors, she will have little or no time to critique your writing. Agents who don't charge fees must be selective and often prefer to work with established authors, celebrities or those with professional credentials in a particular field. Some agents in this section may charge clients for office expenses such as photocopying, foreign postage, long-distance phone calls or express mail services. Make sure you have a clear understanding of what these expenses are before signing any agency agreement.

SUBHEADS

Each agency listing is broken down into subheads to make locating specific information easier. In the first section, you'll find contact information for each agency. You'll also learn if the agents within the agency belong to any professional organizations; membership in these organizations can tell you a lot about an agency. For example, members of the Association of Authors' Representatives (AAR) are prohibited from charging reading or evaluating fees. Additional information in this section includes the size of each agency, its willingness to work with new or unpublished writers, and its general areas of interest.

Member Agents: Agencies comprised of more than one agent list member agents and their individual specialties. This information will help you determine the appropriate person to whom you should send your query letter.

Represents: This section allows agencies to specify what nonfiction and fiction subjects they represent. Make sure you query only those agents who represent the type of material you write.

Look for the key icon (🔑) to quickly learn an agent's areas of specialization. In this portion of the listing, agents mention the specific subject areas they're currently seeking, as well as those subject areas they do not consider.

How to Contact: Most agents open to submissions prefer an initial query letter that briefly describes your work. While some agents may ask for an outline and a specific number of sample chapters, most don't. You should send these items only if the agent requests them. In this section, agents also mention if they accept queries by fax or e-mail, if they consider simultaneous submissions, and how they prefer to obtain new clients.

Recent Sales: To give you a sense of the types of material they represent, the agents list specific titles they've sold, as well as a sampling of clients' names. Note that some agents consider their client list confidential and may only share client names once they agree to represent you.

Terms: Provided here are details of an agent's commission, whether a contract is offered and for how long, and what additional office expenses you might have to pay if the agent agrees to represent you. Standard commissions range from 10-15 percent for domestic sales and 15-20 percent for foreign or dramatic sales (with the difference going to the co-agent who places the work).

Writers' Conferences: A great way to meet an agent is at a writers' conference. Here agents list the conferences they usually attend. For more information about a specific conference, check the Conferences section starting on page 239.

Tips: In this section, agents offer advice and additional instructions for writers.

SPECIAL INDEXES

Literary Agents Specialties Index: This index (page 285) organizes agencies according to the subjects they are interested in receiving. This index should help you compose a list of agents specializing in your areas. Cross-referencing categories and concentrating on agents interested in two or more aspects of your manuscript might increase your chances of success.

Agents Index: This index (page 341) provides a list of agents' names in alphabetical order, along with the name of the agency for which they work. Find the name of the person you would like to contact, and then check the agency listing.

General Index: This index (page 355) lists all agencies and conferences appearing in the book.

Quick Reference Icons

At the beginning of some listings, you will find one or more of the following symbols:

- N Agency new to this edition
- Canadian agency
- International agency
- Agency actively seeking clients
- Agency seeking both new and established writers
- Agency seeking mostly established writers through referrals
- Agency specializing in certain types of work
- Agency not currently seeking new clients

2M COMMUNICATIONS, LTD.

121 W. 27 St., #601, New York NY 10001. (212)741-1509. Fax: (212)691-4460. E-mail: morel@bookhaven.com. Website: www.2mcommunications.com. **Contact:** Madeleine Morel. Member of AAR. Represents 100 clients. 20% of clients are new/unpublished writers. Currently handles: nonfiction books 100%.

- Prior to becoming an agent, Ms. Morel worked at a publishing company.

Represents nonfiction books. **Considers these nonfiction areas:** biography, child, ethnic, health, history, self help, womens, music; cookbooks. This agency specializes in exclusively and non-exclusively representing professional ghostwriters and collaborators. This agency's writers have penned multiple bestsellers. They work closely with other leading literary agents and editors whose high-profile authors require confidential associations.

O‑ This agency specializes in exclusively and non-exclusively representing professional ghostwriters and collaborators. This agency's writers have penned multiple bestsellers. They work closely with other leading literary agents and editors whose high-profile authors require confidential associations. "Our primary interests are in the non-fiction market. We are especially skilled in the following areas: parenting, multi-cultural issues, memoir & personal growth, pop-culture, health & beauty, cooking, relationships & psychology, and business."

How to Contact Query with SASE. Submit outline, 3 sample chapters. Accepts simultaneous submissions. Responds in 1 week to queries. Responds in 1 month to mss. Obtains most new clients through recommendations from others, solicitations.

Terms Agent receives 15% commission on domestic sales. Agent receives 20% commission on foreign sales. Offers written contract, binding for 2 years. Charges clients for postage, photocopying, long-distance calls, faxes.

A+B WORKS

E-mail: amy@aplusbworks.com;literary@aplusbworks.com. Website: www.aplusbworks.com/. **Contact:** Amy Jameson.

- Prior to her current position, Ms. Jameson worked at Janklow & Nesbit Associates.

Represents nonfiction books, novels. **Considers these fiction areas:** young adult and middle grade fiction, women's fiction, and select narrative non-fiction.This agency specializes in middle grade and YA fiction, women's fiction and some adult nonfiction. We are only interested in established writers at this time. Does not want to receive thrillers or science fiction.

O‑ This agency specializes in middle grade and YA fiction, women's fiction and some adult nonfiction. We are only interested in established writers at this time. Does not want to receive thrillers or science fiction.

How to Contact Query with SASE. Query via e-mail only. Send queries to query@aplusbworks.com

DOMINICK ABEL LITERARY AGENCY, INC.

146 W. 82nd St., #1B, New York NY 10024. (212)877-0710. Fax: (212)595-3133. E-mail: agency@dalainc.com. Member of AAR. Represents 100 clients. Currently handles: nonfiction books adult, novels adult.

How to Contact Query via e-mail.

Terms Agent receives 15% commission on domestic sales. Agent receives 20% commission on foreign sales.

ABOUT WORDS AGENCY

885 Woodstock Road, Ste. 430-323, Roswell GA 30075. Website: agency.aboutwords.org. **Contact:** Susan Graham, Vicki Flier.Currently handles: nonfiction books 40%, novels 60%.

Represents Does not want true crime, religious market, poetry.

O‑ Does not want true crime, religious market, poetry.

Terms Agent receives 15% commission on domestic sales. Agent receives 20% commission on foreign sales. Offers written contract.

ACACIA HOUSE PUBLISHING SERVICES, LTD.

62 Chestnut Ave., Brantford ON N3T 4C2 Canada. (519)752-0978. **Contact:** (Ms.) Frances Hanna or Bill Hanna. Represents 100 clients. Currently handles: nonfiction books 30%, novels 70%.

- Ms. Hanna has been in the publishing business for 30 years, first in London as a fiction editor with Barrie & Jenkins and Pan Books, and as a senior editor with a packager of mainly illustrated books. She was condensed books editor for 6 years for *Reader's Digest* in Montreal and senior editor and foreign rights manager for William Collins & Sons (now HarperCollins) in Toronto. Mr. Hanna has more than 40 years of experience in the publishing business.

Member Agents Frances Hanna; Bill Hanna, vice president (self-help, modern history, military history).

Represents nonfiction books, novels. **Considers these nonfiction areas:** animals, biography, language, memoirs, military, music, nature, film, travel. **Considers these fiction areas:** adventure, detective, literary, mainstream, mystery, thriller. This agency specializes in contemporary fiction—literary or commercial. Actively seeking outstanding first novels with literary merit. Does not want to receive horror, occult or science fiction.

- This agency specializes in contemporary fiction—literary or commercial. Actively seeking outstanding first novels with literary merit. Does not want to receive horror, occult or science fiction.

How to Contact Query with outline, SASE. *No unsolicited mss.* No phone queries. Responds in 6 weeks to queries.

Terms Agent receives 15% commission on English language sales; 20% commission on dramatic sales; 25% commission on foreign sales. Charges clients for photocopying, postage, courier.

Recent Sales This agency prefers not to share information on specific sales.

Tips "We prefer that writers be previously published, with at least a few short stories or articles to their credit. Strongest consideration will be given to those with three or more published books. However, we would take on an unpublished writer of outstanding talent."

ADAMS LITERARY

7845 Colony Road C4, #215, Charlotte NC 28226. (704)542-1440. Fax: (704)542-1450. E-mail: info@adamsliterary.com. Website: www.adamsliterary.com. **Contact:** Tracey Adams, Josh Adams. Member of AAR. Other memberships include SCBWI.

Member Agents Tracey Adams; Josh Adams.

Represents Adams Literary is a full-service literary agency exclusively representing children's book authors and artists.

- Adams Literary is a full-service literary agency exclusively representing children's book authors and artists.

How to Contact "Guidelines are posted (and frequently updated) on our Web site."

BRET ADAMS LTD. AGENCY

448 W. 44th St., New York NY 10036. (212)765-5630. E-mail: literary@bretadamsltd.net. **Contact:** Bruce Ostler, Mark Orsini. Member of AAR. Currently handles: movie scripts, TV scripts, stage plays.

Represents movie, TV, feature, TV movie, theatrical stage play. Handles theatre/film and TV projects. No books.

- Handles theatre/film and TV projects. No books.

How to Contact Professional recommendation.

THE AGENCY GROUP, LLC

1880 Century Park E., Suite 711, Los Angeles CA 90068. (310)385-2800. E-mail: marcgerald@theagencygroup.com. Website: www.theagencygroup.com. **Contact:** Marc Gerald, Caroline Greeven. Represents 50 clients. 10% of clients are new/unpublished writers. Currently handles: nonfiction books 60%, novels 30%, multimedia 10%.

- Prior to becoming an agent, Mr. Gerald owned and ran an independent publishing and entertainment agency.

Member Agents Marc Gerald; Caroline Greeven; Sarah Stephens.

Represents nonfiction books, novels. **Considers these nonfiction areas:** anthropology, art, biography, business, child, cooking, ethnic, government, health, history, how to, humor, memoirs, money, music, nature, popular culture, psychology, self help, sports, true crime, interior design/decorating. "While we admire beautiful writing, we largely represent recording artists, celebrities, authors, and pop culture and style brands with established platforms. When we represent fiction, we work almost exclusively in genre and in areas of expertise. We tend to take a non-linear approach to content—many of our projects ultimately have a TV/film or digital component." This agency is only taking on new clients through referrals.

- "While we admire beautiful writing, we largely represent recording artists, celebrities, authors, and pop culture and style brands with established platforms. When we represent fiction, we work almost exclusively in genre and in areas of expertise. We tend to take a non-linear approach to content—many of our projects ultimately have a TV/film or digital component." This agency is only taking on new clients through referrals.

How to Contact Accepts simultaneous submissions. Responds in 1 month to queries. Responds in 3 months to mss. Obtains most new clients through recommendations from others.

Terms Agent receives 15% commission on domestic sales. Agent receives 20% commission on foreign sales. Offers written contract. Charges clients for office fees (only for mss that have been sold).

AGENTS INK!

P.O. Box 4956, Fresno CA 93744. (559)438-8289. **Contact:** Sydney H. Harriet, director. Other memberships include APA. Represents 20 clients. 70% of clients are new/unpublished writers. Currently handles:

nonfiction books 80%, novels 20%.

- Prior to opening his agency, Dr. Harriet was a psychologist, radio and television reporter, and professor of English.

Member Agents Sydney Harriet.

Represents nonfiction books, novels. **Considers these nonfiction areas:** animals, cooking, government, health, mind/body healing, history, language, psychology, science, self help, sociology, sports, medicine, psychology, foreign affairs; international topics. "This agency specializes in writers who have education experience in the business, legal and health professions. It is helpful if the writer is licensed, but not necessary. Prior nonfiction book publication is not necessary. For fiction, previously published fiction is a prerequisite for representation." Does not want to receive memoirs, autobiographies, stories about overcoming an illness, science fiction, fantasy, religious materials or children's books.

O‑ "This agency specializes in writers who have education experience in the business, legal and health professions. It is helpful if the writer is licensed, but not necessary. Prior nonfiction book publication is not necessary. For fiction, previously published fiction is a prerequisite for representation." Does not want to receive memoirs, autobiographies, stories about overcoming an illness, science fiction, fantasy, religious materials or children's books.

How to Contact Query with SASE. Other

Terms Agent receives 15% commission on domestic sales. Agent receives 20% commission on foreign sales. Offers written contract, binding for 6-12 months (negotiable).

Tips "Remember, query first. Do not call to pitch an idea. The only way we can judge the quality of your idea is to see how you write. Unsolicited manuscripts will not be read if they arrive without a SASE. Currently, we are receving more than 200 query letters and proposals each month. Send a complete proposal/manuscript only if requested. Ask yourself why someone would be compelled to buy your book. If you think the idea is unique, spend the time to create a query and then a proposal where every word counts. Fiction writers need to understand that craft is just as important as the idea. Once you finish your novel, put it away and let it percolate, then take it out and work on fine-tuning it some more. A novel is never finished until you stop working on it. We would love to represent more fiction writers and probably will when we read a manuscript that has gone through a dozen or more drafts. Because of rising costs, we no longer can respond to queries, proposals and/or complete manuscripts without receiving a return envelope and sufficient postage."

THE AHEARN AGENCY, INC.

2021 Pine St., New Orleans LA 70118. E-mail: pahearn@aol.com. Website: www.ahearnagency.com. **Contact:** Pamela G. Ahearn.Other memberships include MWA, RWA, ITW. Represents 35 clients. 20% of clients are new/unpublished writers. Currently handles: novels 100%.

- Prior to opening her agency, Ms. Ahearn was an agent for 8 years and an editor with Bantam Books.

Represents Considers these fiction areas: contemporary, glitz, psychic, adventure, detective, ethnic, family, feminist, historical, humor, literary, mainstream, mystery, regional, romance, thriller. "This agency specializes in historical romance and is also very interested in mysteries and suspense fiction. Does not want to receive category romance, science fiction or fantasy."

O‑ "This agency specializes in historical romance and is also very interested in mysteries and suspense fiction. Does not want to receive category romance, science fiction or fantasy."

How to Contact Query with SASE. Accepts simultaneous submissions. Responds in 8 weeks to queries. Responds in 10 weeks to mss. Obtains most new clients through recommendations from others, solicitations, conferences.

Terms Agent receives 15% commission on domestic sales. Agent receives 20% commission on foreign sales. Offers written contract, binding for 1 year; renewable by mutual consent.

Recent Sales *Red Chrysanthemum*, by Laura Rowland; *Only a Duke Will Do*, by Sabrina Jeffries; *The Alexandria Link*, by Steve Berry.

Writers Conferences Moonlight & Magnolias; RWA National Conference; Thriller Fest; Florida Romance Writers; Bouchercon; Malice Domestic.

Tips "Be professional! Always send in exactly what an agent/editor asks for—no more, no less. Keep query letters brief and to the point, giving your writing credentials and a very brief summary of your book. If one agent rejects you, keep trying—there are a lot of us out there!"

AITKEN ALEXANDER ASSOCIATES

18-21 Cavaye Place, London England SW10 9PT United Kingdom. (44)(207)373-8672. Fax: (44)(207)373-6002. E-mail: reception@aitkenalexander.co.uk. Website: www.aitkenalexander.co.uk. **Contact:** Submissions Department. Represents 300+ clients. 10% of clients are new/unpublished writers.

Member Agents Gillon Aitken, agent; Clare Alexander, agent; Andrew Kidd, agent; Lesley Thorne, film/television.

Represents nonfiction books, novels. **Considers these nonfiction areas:** current affairs, government, history, memoirs, popular culture. **Considers these fiction areas:** historical, literary. "We specialize in literary fiction and nonfiction."

"We specialize in literary fiction and nonfiction."

How to Contact Query with SASE. Submit synopsis, first 30 pages. Responds in 6-8 weeks to queries. Obtains most new clients through recommendations from others, solicitations.

Terms Agent receives 15% commission on domestic sales. Agent receives 20% commission on foreign sales. Offers written contract; 28-day notice must be given to terminate contract. Charges for photocopying and postage.

Recent Sales Sold 50 titles in the last year. *My Life With George*, by Judith Summers (Voice); *The Separate Heart*, by Simon Robinson (Bloomsbury); *The Fall of the House of Wittgenstein*, by Alexander Waugh (Bloomsbury); *Shakespeare's Life*, by Germane Greer (Picador); *Occupational Hazards*, by Rory Stewart.

Tips "Before submitting to us, we advise you to look at our existing client list to establish whether your work will be of interest. Equally, you should consider whether the material you have written is ready to submit to a literary agency. If you feel your work qualifies, then send us a letter introducing yourself. Keep it relevant to your writing (e.g., tell us about any previously published work, be it a short story or journalism; you may be studying or have completed a post-graduate qualification in creative writing; when it comes to nonfiction, we would want to know what qualifies you to write about the subject)."

ALIVE COMMUNICATIONS, INC.

7680 Goddard St., Suite 200, Colorado Springs CO 80920. (719)260-7080. Fax: (719)260-8223. E-mail: submissions@alivecom.com. Website: www.alivecom.com. Member of AAR. Other memberships include Authors Guild. Represents 100+ clients. 5% of clients are new/unpublished writers. Currently handles: nonfiction books 50%, novels 40%, juvenile books 10%.

Member Agents Rick Christian, president (blockbusters, bestsellers); Lee Hough (popular/commercial nonfiction and fiction, thoughtful spirituality, children's); Beth Jusino (thoughtful/inspirational nonfiction, women's fiction/nonfiction, popular/commercial nonfiction & fiction); Joel Kneedler popular/commercial nonfiction and fiction, thoughtful spirituality, children's).

Represents nonfiction books, novels, short story collections, novellas. **Considers these nonfiction areas:** biography, business, child, how to, memoirs, religion, self help, womens. **Considers these fiction areas:** contemporary, adventure, detective, family, historical, humor, literary, mainstream, mystery, religious, thriller. This agency specializes in fiction, Christian living, how-to and commercial nonfiction. Actively seeking inspirational, literary and mainstream fiction, and work from authors with established track records and platforms. Does not want to receive poetry, scripts or dark themes.

This agency specializes in fiction, Christian living, how-to and commercial nonfiction. Actively seeking inspirational, literary and mainstream fiction, and work from authors with established track records and platforms. Does not want to receive poetry, scripts or dark themes.

How to Contact Query via e-mail. "Be advised that this agency works primarily with well-established, bestselling, and career authors." Obtains most new clients through recommendations from others.

Terms Agent receives 15% commission on domestic sales. Offers written contract; 2-month notice must be given to terminate contract.

Recent Sales Sold 300+ titles in the last year. A spiritual memoir by Eugene Peterson (Viking); A biography of Rwandan president Paul Kagame, by Stephen Kinzaya (St. Martin's Press); *Ever After*, by Karen Klingsbury (Zondervan).

Tips Rewrite and polish until the words on the page shine. Endorsements and great connections may help, provided you can write with power and passion. Network with publishing professionals by making contacts, joining critique groups, and attending writers' conferences in order to make personal connections and to get feedback. Alive Communications, Inc., has established itself as a premiere literary agency. We serve an elite group of authors who are critically acclaimed and commercially successful in both Christian and general markets.

ALLEN O'SHEA LITERARY AGENCY

615 Westover Road, Stamford CT 06902. (203)359-9965. Fax: (203)357-9909. E-mail: marilyn@allenoshea.com. Website: www.allenoshea.com. **Contact:** Marilyn Allen. Represents 100 clients. 20% of clients are new/unpublished writers. Currently handles: nonfiction books 99%.

- Prior to becoming agents, both Ms. Allen and Ms. O'Shea held senior positions in publishing.

Member Agents Marilyn Allen; Coleen O'Shea.

Represents nonfiction books. **Considers these nonfiction areas:** biography, business, cooking, current affairs, health, history, how to, humor, military, money, popular culture, psychology, self help, sports, interior design/decorating. "This agency specializes in practical nonfiction including cooking, sports, business, pop culture, etc. We look for clients with strong marketing platforms and new ideas coupled with strong writing." Actively seeking narrative nonfiction, health and history writers. Does not want to receive fiction, memoirs, poetry, textbooks or children's.

"This agency specializes in practical nonfiction including cooking, sports, business, pop culture, etc. We look for clients with strong marketing platforms and new ideas coupled with strong writing." Actively seeking narrative nonfiction, health and history writers. Does not want to receive fiction, memoirs, poetry, textbooks or children's.

How to Contact Query with via e-mail or mail with SASE. Submit outline, author bio, marketing page. No phone or fax queries. Accepts simultaneous submissions. Responds in 1 week to queries. Responds in 1-2 months to mss. Obtains most new clients through recommendations from others, conferences.

Terms Agent receives 15% commission on domestic sales. Offers written contract, binding for 2 years; 1-month notice must be given to terminate contract. Charges for photocopying large mss, and overseas postage—"typically minimal costs."

Recent Sales Sold 45 titles in the last year. "This agency prefers not to share information about specific sales, but see our Web site."

Writers Conferences ASJA, Publicity Submit for Writers, Connecticut Authors and Publishers, Mark Victor Hansen Mega Book Conference.

Tips "Prepare a strong overview, with competition, marketing and bio. We will consider when your proposal is ready."

MIRIAM ALTSHULER LITERARY AGENCY

53 Old Post Road N., Red Hook NY 12571. (845)758-9408. Website: www.miriamaltshulerliteraryagency.com. **Contact:** Miriam Altshuler. Estab. 1994. Member of AAR. Represents 40 clients. Currently handles: nonfiction books 45%, novels 45%, story collections 5%, juvenile books 5%.

- Ms. Altshuler has been an agent since 1982.

Represents nonfiction books, novels, short story collections, juvenile. **Considers these nonfiction areas:** biography, ethnic, history, language, memoirs, multicultural, music, nature, popular culture, psychology, sociology, film, womens. **Considers these fiction areas:** literary, mainstream, multicultural, some selective children's books.literary commercial fiction and non-fiction. Does not want self-help, mystery, how-to, romance, horror, spiritual, fantasy, poetry, screenplays, science fiction or techno-thriller, western.

O→ literary commercial fiction and non-fiction. Does not want self-help, mystery, how-to, romance, horror, spiritual, fantasy, poetry, screenplays, science fiction or techno-thriller, western.

How to Contact Query with SASE. Submit contact info with e-mail address. Prefers to read materials exclusively. Accepts simultaneous submissions. Responds in 3 weeks to mss. Obtains most new clients through recommendations from others.

Terms Agent receives 15% commission on domestic sales. Agent receives 20% commission on foreign sales. Charges clients for overseas mailing, photocopies, overnight mail when requested by author.

Writers Conferences Bread Loaf Writers' Conference; Washington Independent Writers Conference; North Carolina Writers' Network Conference.

Tips See the Web site for specific submission details.

AMBASSADOR LITERARY AGENCY

P.O. Box 50358, Nashville TN 37205. (615)370-4700. E-mail: Wes@AmbassadorAgency.com. Website: www.AmbassadorAgency.com. **Contact:** Wes Yoder. Represents 25-30 clients. 10% of clients are new/unpublished writers. Currently handles: nonfiction books 95%, novels 5%.

- Prior to becoming an agent, Mr. Yoder founded a music artist agency in 1973; he established a speakers bureau division of the company in 1984.

Represents nonfiction books, novels. **Considers these nonfiction areas:** biography, child, current affairs, education, ethnic, government, health, history, how to, memoirs, money, popular culture, religion, self help, womens. **Considers these fiction areas:** adventure, ethnic, family, literary, mainstream, religious. "This agency specializes in religious market publishing and has excellent national media relationships, dealing primarily with A-level publishers. Actively seeking popular nonfiction themes, including the following: practical living; Christian spirituality; literary fiction. Does not want to receive short stories, children's books, screenplays or poetry."

O→ "This agency specializes in religious market publishing and has excellent national media relationships, dealing primarily with A-level publishers. Actively seeking popular nonfiction themes, including the following: practical living; Christian spirituality; literary fiction. Does not want to receive short stories, children's books, screenplays or poetry."

How to Contact Query with SASE. Submit proposal package, outline, synopsis, 6 sample chapters, author bio. Accepts simultaneous submissions. Responds in 2-4 weeks to queries. Obtains most new clients through recommendations from others.

Terms Agent receives 15% commission on domestic sales. Agent receives 20% commission on foreign sales. Offers written contract.

Recent Sales Sold 20 titles in the last year. *The Death and Life of Gabriel Phillips*, by Stephen Baldwin (Hachette); *Amazing Grace: William Wilberforce and the Heroic Campaign to End Slavery*, by Eric Mataxas (Harper San Francisco); *Life@The Next Level*, by Courtney McBath (Simon and Schuster); *Women, Take Charge of Your Money*, by Carolyn Castleberry (Random House/Multnomah).

MARCIA AMSTERDAM AGENCY

41 W. 82nd St., Suite 9A, New York NY 10024-5613. (212)873-4945. **Contact:** Marcia Amsterdam. Signatory of WGA. Currently handles: nonfiction books 15%, novels 70%, movie scripts 5%, TV scripts 10%.

- Prior to opening her agency, Ms. Amsterdam was an editor.

Represents novels, feature, sitcom. **Considers these fiction areas:** adventure, detective, horror, mainstream, mystery, romance (contemporary, historical), science, thriller, young. **Considers these script areas:** comedy, romantic comedy.

How to Contact Query with SASE. Responds in 1 month to queries.

Terms Agent receives 15% commission on domestic sales. Agent receives 20% commission on foreign sales. Agent receives 10% commission on film sales. Offers written contract, binding for 1 year. Charges clients for extra office expenses, foreign postage, copying, legal fees (when agreed upon).

Recent Sales *Hidden Child*, by Isaac Millman (FSG); *Lucky Leonardo*, by Jonathan Canter (Sourcebooks).

Tips "We are always looking for interesting literary voices."

BETSY AMSTER LITERARY ENTERPRISES

P.O. Box 27788, Los Angeles CA 90027-0788. **Contact:** Betsy Amster. Estab. 1992. Member of AAR. Represents more than 65 clients. 35% of clients are new/unpublished writers. Currently handles: nonfiction books 65%, novels 35%.

- Prior to opening her agency, Ms. Amster was an editor at Pantheon and Vintage for 10 years, and served as editorial director for the Globe Pequot Press for 2 years.

Represents nonfiction books, novels. **Considers these nonfiction areas:** art & design, biography, business, child guidance, cooking/nutrition, current affairs, ethnic, gardening, health/medicine, history, memoirs, money, parenting, popular culture, psychology, science/technology, self-help, sociology, travelogues, social issues, women's issues.**Considers these fiction areas:** ethnic, literary, quirky mysteries & thrillers, womens, high quality. "Actively seeking strong narrative nonfiction, particularly by journalists; outstanding literary fiction (the next Richard Ford or Jhumpa Lahiri); witty, intelligent commerical women's fiction (the next Elinor Lipman or Jennifer Weiner); mysteries that open new worlds to us; and high-profile self-help and psychology, preferably research based." Does not want to receive poetry, children's books, romances, Western, science fiction, action/adventure, screenplays, fantasy, techno thrillers, spy capers, apocalyptic scenarios, or political or religious arguments.

- O→ "Actively seeking strong narrative nonfiction, particularly by journalists; outstanding literary fiction (the next Richard Ford or Jhumpa Lahiri); witty, intelligent commerical women's fiction (the next Elinor Lipman or Jennifer Weiner); mysteries that open new worlds to us; and high-profile self-help and psychology, preferably research based." Does not want to receive poetry, children's books, romances, Western, science fiction, action/adventure, screenplays, fantasy, techno thrillers, spy capers, apocalyptic scenarios, or political or religious arguments.

How to Contact For adult titles: b.amster.assistant@gmail.com. Submissions for children's and teen titles: b.amster.kidsbooks@gmail.com. See submission requirements online at website. The requirements have changed. Accepts simultaneous submissions. Responds in 1 month to queries. Responds in 2 months to mss. Obtains most new clients through recommendations from others, solicitations, conferences.

Terms Agent receives 15% commission on domestic sales. Agent receives 20% commission on foreign sales. Offers written contract, binding for 1 year; 3-month notice must be given to terminate contract. Charges for photocopying, postage, long distance phone calls, messengers, galleys/books used in submissions to foreign and film agents and to magazines for first serial rights.

Writers Conferences Squaw Valley Writers' Workshop; San Diego State University Writers' Conference; UCLA Extension Writers' Program; The Loft Literary Center.

THE ANDERSON LITERARY AGENCY

435 Convent Ave., Suite 5, New York NY 10031. (212)234-0692. E-mail: gilescanderson@gmail.com. **Contact:** Giles Anderson.

Represents nonfiction books. Biography, Business/investing/finance, History, Religious, Mind/body/spirit, Science true crime, business, religion, science

- O→ Biography, Business/investing/finance, History, Religious, Mind/body/spirit, Science true crime, business, religion, science

How to Contact Send brief query via e-mail.

ANDERSON LITERARY MANAGEMENT, LLC

12 W. 19th St., New York NY 10011. (212)645-6045. Fax: (212)741-1936. E-mail: kathleen@andersonliterary.com; info@andersonliterary.com. Website: www.andersonliterary.com/. **Contact:** Kathleen Anderson.

Estab. 2006. Member of AAR. Represents 100+ clients. 20% of clients are new/unpublished writers. Currently handles: nonfiction books 50%, novels 50%.

Represents nonfiction books, novels, short story collections, juvenile. **Considers these nonfiction areas:** anthropology, art, biography, current affairs, education, ethnic, gay, government, history, memoirs, music, nature, psychology, womens. **Considers these fiction areas:** adventure, ethnic, family, feminist, gay, historical, literary, mystery, thriller, western, young adult, womens. "Specializes in adult and young adult literary and commercial fiction, narrative nonfiction, American and European history, literary journalism, nature and travel writing, memoir, and biography." Does not want to receive genre fantasy, sci-fi or romance.

- "Specializes in adult and young adult literary and commercial fiction, narrative nonfiction, American and European history, literary journalism, nature and travel writing, memoir, and biography." Does not want to receive genre fantasy, sci-fi or romance.

How to Contact Query with SASE. Submit synopsis, first 3 sample chapters, proposal (for nonfiction). Snail mail queries only. Accepts simultaneous submissions. Responds in 12 weeks to queries & to mss. Obtains most new clients through recommendations from others, solicitations, conferences.

Terms Agent receives 15% commission on domestic sales. Offers written contract.

Writers Conferences Squaw Valley Conference.

ANUBIS LITERARY AGENCY

7 Birdhaven Close Lighthorne Heath, Banbury Road, Warwick Warwickshire CV35 0BE United Kingdom. Phone/Fax: (44)(192)664-2588. E-mail: anubis.agency2@btopenworld.com. **Contact:** Steve Calcutt. Estab. 1994. Represents 15 clients. 50% of clients are new/unpublished writers. Currently handles: novels 100%.

- In addition to being an agent, Mr. Calcutt teaches creative writing and American history (U.S. Civil War) at Warwick University.

Represents novels. **Considers these fiction areas:** horror, mainstream, science fiction, dark fantasy. "Actively seeking horror fiction." Does not want to receive children's books, nonfiction, journalism or TV/film scripts.

- "Actively seeking horror fiction." Does not want to receive children's books, nonfiction, journalism or TV/film scripts.

How to Contact Query with proposal package. Send 50 pp. with one-page synopsis. Returns materials only with SASE/IRCs. Responds in 6 weeks to queries. Responds in 3 months to mss. Obtains most new clients through personal recommendation.

Terms Agent receives 15% commission on domestic sales. Agent receives 20% commission on foreign sales.

ARCADIA

31 Lake Place N., Danbury CT 06810. E-mail: arcadialit@sbcglobal.net. **Contact:** Victoria Gould Pryor. Member of AAR.

Represents nonfiction books, literary and commercial fiction. **Considers these nonfiction areas:** biography, business, current affairs, health, history, psychology, science, true crime, womens, investigative journalism; culture; classical music; life transforming self-help. "I'm a very hands-on agent, which is necessary in this competitive marketplace. I work with authors on revisions until whatever we present to publishers is as perfect as it can be. I represent talented, dedicated, intelligent and ambitious writers who are looking for a long-term relationship based on professional success and mutual respect." Does not want to receive science fiction/fantasy, horror, humor or children's/YA. "We are only able to read fiction submissions from previously published authors."

- "I'm a very hands-on agent, which is necessary in this competitive marketplace. I work with authors on revisions until whatever we present to publishers is as perfect as it can be. I represent talented, dedicated, intelligent and ambitious writers who are looking for a long-term relationship based on professional success and mutual respect." Does not want to receive science fiction/fantasy, horror, humor or children's/YA. "We are only able to read fiction submissions from previously published authors."

How to Contact Query with SASE. This agency accepts e-queries (no attachments).

EDWARD ARMSTRONG LITERARY AGENCY

fiction, PO Box 3343, Fayville MA 01745. (401)569-7099. **Contact:** Edward Armstrong.Currently handles: other 100% fiction.

- Prior to becoming an agent, Mr. Armstrong was a business professional specializing in quality and regulatory compliance.

Represents novels, short story collections, novellas. **Considers these fiction areas:** mainstream, romance, science, thriller, suspense.

- **This agency is not taking submissions at this time (5/3/07).** Please continue to check back. Does not want to receive nonfiction or textbooks.

How to Contact Query with SASE. Submit synopsis, 3 sample chapters, author bio. Accepts simultaneous submissions. Responds in 2-4 weeks to queries. Responds in 3 months to mss. Obtains most new clients through solicitations.
Terms Agent receives 5% commission on domestic sales. Agent receives 5% commission on foreign sales. This agency charges for photocopying and postage.

ARTISTS AND ARTISANS INC.

244 Madison Ave., Suite 334, New York NY 10016. Website: www.artistsandartisans.com. **Contact:** Adam Chromy and Jamie Brenner. Represents 70 clients. 80% of clients are new/unpublished writers. Currently handles: nonfiction books 50%, fiction 50%.
Member Agents Adam Chromy (fiction and narrative nonfiction); Jamie Brenner (thrillers, commercial and women's fiction, literary fiction, memoir, narrative nonfiction, books about pop culture/entertainment and YA).
Represents nonfiction books, novels. **Considers these nonfiction areas:** biography, business, child, cooking, current affairs, ethnic, health, how to, humor, language, memoirs, money, music, popular culture, religion, science, self help, sports, film, true crime, womens, fashion/style. **Considers these fiction areas:** confession, family, humor, literary, mainstream. "My education and experience in the business world ensure that my clients' enterprise as authors gets as much attention and care as their writing." Working journalists for nonfiction books. No scripts.

- "My education and experience in the business world ensure that my clients' enterprise as authors gets as much attention and care as their writing." Working journalists for nonfiction books. No scripts.

How to Contact Query with SASE. Accepts simultaneous submissions. Responds in 2 weeks to queries. Responds in 2 weeks to mss. Obtains most new clients through recommendations from others, solicitations, conferences.
Terms Agent receives 15% commission on domestic sales. Agent receives 25% commission on foreign sales. Offers written contract; 1-month notice must be given to terminate contract. "We only charge for extraordinary expenses (e.g., client requests check via FedEx instead of regular mail)."
Recent Sales *Keeping Time*, by Stacey McGlynn (Shaye Areheart); *House of Cards*, by David Ellis Dickerson (Penguin).
Writers Conferences ASJA Writers Conference.
Tips "Please make sure you are ready before approaching us or any other agent. If you write fiction, make sure it is the best work you can do and get objective criticism from a writing group. If you write nonfiction, make sure the proposal exhibits your best work and a comprehensive understanding of the market."

ROBERT ASTLE AND ASSOCIATES LITERARY MANAGEMENT, INC.

12 Desbrosses St., New York NY 10013. (212)277-8014. Fax: (212)226-7186. E-mail: robert@astleliterary.com. Website: www.astleliterary.com. **Contact:** Robert Astle.

- Prior to becoming an agent, Mr. Astle spent 25 years in theater.

Represents nonfiction books, novels. We are especially interested in receiving nonfiction projects with a wide range of topics, including narrative nonfiction, popular culture, arts and culture, theater and performance, sports, travel, celebrity, biography, politics, memoir, history, new media and multi-ethnic. We are actively seeking writers of literary fiction and commercial fiction—mysteries and suspense, thrillers, mainstream literary fiction, historical fiction, women's fiction, humor/satire and graphic novels. We will also seek writers in the genre of young audiences: middle grade and teen.

- We are especially interested in receiving nonfiction projects with a wide range of topics, including narrative nonfiction, popular culture, arts and culture, theater and performance, sports, travel, celebrity, biography, politics, memoir, history, new media and multi-ethnic. We are actively seeking writers of literary fiction and commercial fiction—mysteries and suspense, thrillers, mainstream literary fiction, historical fiction, women's fiction, humor/satire and graphic novels. We will also seek writers in the genre of young audiences: middle grade and teen.

How to Contact Use the online form to query. Specifications for nonfiction and fiction submissions are online. Obtains most new clients through recommendations from others, solicitations.
Tips Please read the submission guidelines carefully, and make sure your query letter is the best it can be.

THE AUGUST AGENCY, LLC

E-mail: submissions@augustagency.com. Website: www.augustagency.com. **Contact:** Cricket Freemain, Jeffery McGraw. Estab. 2004. Represents 25-40 clients. 50% of clients are new/unpublished writers. Currently handles: nonfiction books 75%, novels 20%, other 5% other.

- Before opening The August Agency, Ms. Freeman was a freelance writer, magazine editor and independent literary agent; Mr. McGraw worked as an editor for HarperCollins and publicity manager for Abrams.

Member Agents Jeffery McGraw (politics/current affairs, entertainment, business, psychology, self-help, narrative nonfiction, contemporary women's fiction, literary fiction); Cricket Freeman (mystery/crime fiction, chick lit, thrillers).

Represents nonfiction books, novels. **Considers these nonfiction areas:** interior design, biography, business, child guidance, cooking, current affairs, ethnic, gay, government, health, history, how to, humor, memoirs, military, money, music, pop culture, psychology, self help, sociology, sports, film, true crime, womens, inspirational. **Considers these fiction areas:** psychic, adventure, detective, ethnic, family, gay, historical, humor, literary, mainstream, mystery, thriller, smart chick lit (non-genre romance). "An array of fiction and nonfiction, with an emphasis in media (seasoned journalists receive special favor here), popular culture/entertainment, political science, diet/fitness, health, cookbooks, psychology, business, memoir, highly creative nonfiction, accessible literary fiction, women's fiction, and high-concept mysteries and thrillers. When it comes to nonfiction, we favor persuasive and prescriptive works with a...narrative command and...contemporary relevance. We like storytelling defined...by its extraordinary power to resonate universally on a deeply emotional level." Does not want academic textbooks, children's books, cozy mysteries, horror, poetry, science fiction/fantasy, short story collections, Westerns, screenplays, genre romance or previously self-published works.

- "An array of fiction and nonfiction, with an emphasis in media (seasoned journalists receive special favor here), popular culture/entertainment, political science, diet/fitness, health, cookbooks, psychology, business, memoir, highly creative nonfiction, accessible literary fiction, women's fiction, and high-concept mysteries and thrillers. When it comes to nonfiction, we favor persuasive and prescriptive works with a...narrative command and...contemporary relevance. We like storytelling defined...by its extraordinary power to resonate universally on a deeply emotional level." Does not want academic textbooks, children's books, cozy mysteries, horror, poetry, science fiction/fantasy, short story collections, Westerns, screenplays, genre romance or previously self-published works.

How to Contact Submit book summary (1-2 paragraphs), chapter outline (nonfiction only), first 1,000 words or first chapter, total page/word count, brief paragraph on why you have chosen to write the book. Send via e-mail only (no attachments). Responds in 2-3 weeks to queries if we are interested. Responds in 3 months to mss. Obtains most new clients through recommendations from others, solicitations, conferences.

Terms Agent receives 15% commission on domestic sales. Agent receives 20% commission on foreign sales. Offers written contract; 1-month notice must be given to terminate contract.

Writers Conferences Surrey International Writers' Conference; Southern California Writers' Conference; Naples Writers' Conference, et al.

AVENUE A LITERARY

419 Lafayette St., Second Floor, New York NY 10003. Fax: (212)228-6149. E-mail: submissions@avenuealiterary.com. Website: www.avenuealiterary.com. **Contact:** Jennifer Cayea. Represents 20 clients. 75% of clients are new/unpublished writers. Currently handles: nonfiction books 40%, novels 45%, story collections 5%, juvenile books 10%.

- Prior to opening her agency, Ms. Cayea was an agent and director of foreign rights for Nicholas Ellison, Inc., a division of Sanford J. Greenburger Associates. She was also an editor in the audio and large print divisions of Random House.

Represents nonfiction books, novels, short story collections, juvenile. **Considers these nonfiction areas:** cooking, current affairs, ethnic, health, history, memoirs, music, popular culture, self help, sports, theater/film. **Considers these fiction areas:** family, feminist, historical, literary, mainstream, thriller, young, women's/chick lit. "Our authors are dynamic and diverse. We seek strong new voices in fiction and nonfiction, and are fiercely dedicated to our authors."

- "Our authors are dynamic and diverse. We seek strong new voices in fiction and nonfiction, and are fiercely dedicated to our authors."

How to Contact Query via e-mail only. Submit synopsis, publishing history, author bio, full contact info. Paste info in e-mail body. No attachments. Accepts simultaneous submissions. Responds in 8 weeks to queries. Obtains most new clients through recommendations from others, solicitations, conferences.

Terms Agent receives 15% commission on domestic sales. Agent receives 15% commission on foreign sales. Offers written contract; 30-day notice must be given to terminate contract.

Tips "Build a résumé by publishing short stories if you are a fiction writer."

THE AXELROD AGENCY

55 Main St., P.O. Box 357, Chatham NY 12037. (518)392-2100. Fax: (518)392-2944. E-mail: steve@axelrodagency.com. **Contact:** Steven Axelrod. Member of AAR. Represents 15-20 clients. 1% of clients are new/unpublished writers. Currently handles: nonfiction books 5%, novels 95%.

- Prior to becoming an agent, Mr. Axelrod was a book club editor.

Represents nonfiction books, novels. **Considers these fiction areas:** mystery, romance, womens.

How to Contact Query with SASE. Accepts simultaneous submissions. Responds in 3 weeks to queries. Responds in 6 weeks to mss. Obtains most new clients through recommendations from others.
Terms Agent receives 15% commission on domestic sales. Agent receives 20% commission on foreign sales. No written contract.
Writers Conferences RWA National Conference.

BAKER'S MARK LITERARY AGENCY

P.O. Box 8382, Portland OR 97207. (503)432-8170. E-mail: info@bakersmark.com. Website: www.Bakersmark.com. **Contact:** Bernadette Baker-Baughman or Gretchen Stelter.Currently handles: nonfiction books 35%, novels 25%, 40% graphic novels.
Represents nonfiction books, novels, scholarly books, , graphic novels. **Considers these nonfiction areas:** anthropology, art, biography, business, ethnic, gay, how-to, humor, popular culture, true crime, women's issues, women's studies, comics/graphic novels. **Considers these fiction areas:** comic books, erotica, experimental, feminist, gay, historical, horror, literary, mainstream, mystery, thriller, young adult, urban fantasy, magical realism."Baker's Mark specializes in graphic novels and popular nonfiction with an extremely selective taste in commercial fiction." Actively seeking graphic novels, nonfiction, fiction (YA/Teen and magical realism in particular). Does not want to receive Westerns, poetry, sci-fi, novella, high fantasy, or children's picture books.

- "Baker's Mark specializes in graphic novels and popular nonfiction with an extremely selective taste in commercial fiction." Actively seeking graphic novels, nonfiction, fiction (YA/Teen and magical realism in particular). Does not want to receive Westerns, poetry, sci-fi, novella, high fantasy, or children's picture books.

How to Contact Query with SASE or e-mail. "If interested, we will request representative materials from you." Accepts simultaneous submissions. Obtains most new clients through recommendations from others, solicitations.
Terms Agent receives 15% commission on domestic sales. Agent receives 20% commission on foreign sales. Offers written contract, binding for 18 months; 30-day notice must be given to terminate contract.
Recent Sales *Never After*, by Dan Elconin (Simon Pulse); *Boilerplate: History's Mechanical Marvel,* by Paul Guinan and Anina Bennet (Abrams Image); *War Is Boring*, by David Axe with illustration by Matt Bors (New American Library); *The Choyster Generation*, by Amalia McGibbon, Claire Williams, and Lara Vogel (Seal Press).
Writers Conferences New York Comic Convention, BookExpo of America, San Diego Comic Con, Stumptown Comics Fest, Emerald City Comic Con.

BALKIN AGENCY, INC.

P.O. Box 222, Amherst MA 01004. Phone/Fax: (413)548-9835. E-mail: rick62838@crocker.com. **Contact:** Rick Balkin, president. Member of AAR. Represents 50 clients. 10% of clients are new/unpublished writers. Currently handles: nonfiction books 85%, scholarly books 5%, other 5% reference books .

- Prior to opening his agency, Mr. Balkin served as executive editor with Bobbs-Merrill Company.

Represents nonfiction books, scholarly. **Considers these nonfiction areas:** animals, anthropology, current affairs, health, history, how to, nature, popular culture, science, sociology, translation, biography. This agency specializes in adult nonfiction. Does not want to receive fiction, poetry, screenplays or computer books.

- This agency specializes in adult nonfiction. Does not want to receive fiction, poetry, screenplays or computer books.

How to Contact Query with SASE. Submit proposal package, outline. Responds in 1 week to queries. Responds in 2 weeks to mss. Obtains most new clients through recommendations from others.
Terms Agent receives 15% commission on domestic sales. Agent receives 20% commission on foreign sales. Offers written contract, binding for 1 year. This agency charges clients for photocopying and express or foreign mail.
Recent Sales Sold 30 titles in the last year. *The Many Faces of God* (W.W. Norton Co.); *A Perfect Mess*, by Eric Abrahamson and David H. Freedman (Little, Brown); *Note by Note: A Celebration of the Piano Lesson*, by Tricia Tunstall (Simon & Schuster).
Tips "I do not take on books described as bestsellers or potential bestsellers. Any nonfiction work that is either unique, paradigmatic, a contribution, truly witty, or a labor of love is grist for my mill."

THE PAULA BALZER AGENCY

55 Eastern Parkway, #5H, Brooklyn NY 11238. (347)787-4131. E-mail: info@pbliterary.com. Website: www.pbliterary.com. **Contact:** Paula Balzer. Member of AAR. Represents 35 clients. 50% of clients are new/unpublished writers. Currently handles: nonfiction books 50%, novels 50%.

- Prior to her current position, Ms. Balzer was with Carlisle & Company, as well as Sarah Lazin Books.

Represents nonfiction books, novels. **Considers these nonfiction areas:** biography, child, cooking, current affairs, education, gay, government, history, how to, humor, memoirs, popular culture, psychology, science, self help, womens. **Considers these fiction areas:** glitz, erotica, family, gay, historical, horror, humor, literary, mainstream, mystery, thriller, womens. Humor and popular culture.

O‑ Humor and popular culture.

How to Contact Query with email or by post with SASE. Submit proposal package, author bio, 50 sample pages. Responds in 3 weeks to queries. Responds in 4-6 weeks to mss. Obtains most new clients through recommendations from others.

Terms Agent receives 15% commission on domestic sales. Agent receives 20% commission on foreign sales. Offers written contract.

BARER LITERARY, LLC

270 Lafayette St., Suite 1504, New York NY 10012. Website: www.barerliterary.com. **Contact:** Julie Barer. Member of AAR.

Represents nonfiction books, novels, short story collections. **Considers these nonfiction areas:** biography, ethnic, history, memoirs, popular culture, womens. **Considers these fiction areas:** ethnic, family, historical, literary, mainstream. This agency no longer accepts young adult submissions.

O‑ This agency no longer accepts young adult submissions.

How to Contact Query with SASE.

Terms Agent receives 15% commission on domestic sales. Agent receives 20% commission on foreign sales. Offers written contract. Charges for photocopying and books ordered.

Recent Sales *The Unnamed*, by Joshua Ferris (Reagan Arthur Books); *Tunneling to the Center of the Earth*, by Kevin Wilson (Ecco Press); *A Disobedient Girl*, by Ru Freeman (Atria Books); *A Friend of the Family*, by Lauren Grodstein (Algonquin); *City of Veils*, by Zoe Ferraris (Little, Brown).

BAROR INTERNATIONAL, INC.

P.O. Box 868, Armonk NY 10504. E-mail: danny@barorint.com; heather@barorint.com. **Contact:** Danny Baror; Heather Baror.Represents 300 clients.

Represents "This agency represents authors and publishers in the international market. Currently representing all genres ranging from thrillers to science fiction/fantasy, self-help, spiritual, young adult, commercial fiction, and more."

O‑ "This agency represents authors and publishers in the international market. Currently representing all genres ranging from thrillers to science fiction/fantasy, self-help, spiritual, young adult, commercial fiction, and more."

Tips "No further information on this agency is available."

LORETTA BARRETT BOOKS, INC.

220 E. 23rd St., 11th Floor, New York NY 10010. (212)242-3420. Fax: (212)807-9579. E-mail: query@lorettabarrettbooks.com. Website: www.lorettabarrettbooks.com. **Contact:** Loretta A. Barrett, Nick Mullendore. Estab. 1990. Member of AAR. Currently handles: nonfiction books 50%, novels 50%.

- Prior to opening her agency, Ms. Barrett was vice president and executive editor at Doubleday and editor-in-chief of Anchor Books.

Member Agents Loretta A. Barrett; Nick Mullendore; Gabriel Davis.

Represents nonfiction books, novels. **Considers these nonfiction areas:** biography, child guidance, current affairs, ethnic, government, health/nutrition, history, memoirs, money, multicultural, nature, popular culture, psychology, religion, science, self help, sociology, spirituality, sports, womens, creative nonfiction. **Considers these fiction areas:** contemporary, psychic, adventure, detective, ethnic, family, historical, literary, mainstream, mystery, thriller. "The clients we represent include both fiction and non-fiction authors for the general adult trade market. The works they produce encompass a wide range of contemporary topics and themes including commercial thrillers, mysteries, romantic suspense, popular science, memoirs, narrative fiction and current affairs." No children's, juvenile, cookbooks, gardening, science fiction, fantasy novels, historical romance.

O‑ "The clients we represent include both fiction and non-fiction authors for the general adult trade market. The works they produce encompass a wide range of contemporary topics and themes including commercial thrillers, mysteries, romantic suspense, popular science, memoirs, narrative fiction and current affairs." No children's, juvenile, cookbooks, gardening, science fiction, fantasy novels, historical romance.

How to Contact See guidelines online. Use email or if by post, query with SASE. Accepts simultaneous submissions. Responds in 3-6 weeks to queries.

Terms Agent receives 15% commission on domestic sales. Agent receives 20% commission on foreign sales. Offers written contract. Charges clients for shipping and photocopying.

BARRON'S LITERARY MANAGEMENT

4615 Rockland Drive, Arlington TX 76016. E-mail: barronsliterary@sbcglobal.net. **Contact:** Adele Brooks, president.

Represents nonfiction books, novels. **Considers these nonfiction areas:** business, cooking, economics, finance, foods, government, health, history, medicine, nutrition, psychology, science, technology, true crime, business, investing, small business marketing, cook books, dating and relationships. **Considers these fiction areas:** action, adventure, detective, historical, horror, mystery, police, romance, science fiction, thriller, medical and political thrillers, historical, chick lit, contemporary suspense, paranormal. Barron's Literary Management is a small Dallas/Fort Worth-based agency with good contacts in New York and London. Actively seeking tightly written, fast moving fiction, as well as authors with a significant platform or subject area expertise for nonfiction book concepts.

- O→ Barron's Literary Management is a small Dallas/Fort Worth-based agency with good contacts in New York and London. Actively seeking tightly written, fast moving fiction, as well as authors with a significant platform or subject area expertise for nonfiction book concepts.

How to Contact Contact by e-mail initially. Send only a brief synopsis of your story or a proposal for nonfiction. Obtains most new clients through e-mail submissions.

Tips "I strongly favor a e-mail queries. Have your book tightly edited, polished and ready to be seen before contacting agents. I respond quickly and if interested may request an electronic or hard copy mailing."

LORELLA BELLI LITERARY AGENCY

54 Hartford House, 35 Tavistock Crescent, Notting Hill, London England W11 1AY United Kingdom. (44)(207)727-8547. Fax: (44)(870)787-4194. E-mail: info@lorellabelliagency.com. Website: www.lorellabelliagency.com. **Contact:** Lorella Belli. Other memberships include AAA.

Represents nonfiction books, novels. **Considers these nonfiction areas:** business, current affairs, history, science, self help, travel, womens, politics; food/wine; popular music; lifestyle. **Considers these fiction areas:** historical, literary, genre fiction; women's; crime. "We are interested in first-time novelists, journalists, multicultural and international writing, and books about Italy." Does not want children's books, fantasy, science fiction, screenplays, short stories, or poetry.

- O→ "We are interested in first-time novelists, journalists, multicultural and international writing, and books about Italy." Does not want children's books, fantasy, science fiction, screenplays, short stories, or poetry.

How to Contact For fiction, send query letter, first 3 chapters, synopsis, brief CV, SASE. For nonfiction, send query letter, full proposal, chapter outline, 2 sample chapters, SASE.

Terms Agent receives 15% commission on domestic sales. Agent receives 20% commission on foreign sales.

FAYE BENDER LITERARY AGENCY

fiction and non-fiction equally., 337 W. 76th St., #E1, New York NY 10023. E-mail: info@fbliterary.com. Website: www.fbliterary.com. **Contact:** Faye Bender. Estab. 2004. Member of AAR.

Represents nonfiction books, novels, juvenile. **Considers these nonfiction areas:** young, memoirs, popular culture, womens, narrative; health; biography; popular science. **Considers these fiction areas:** literary, young adult, middle-grade, women's; commercial. "I choose books based on the narrative voice and strength of writing. I work with previously published and first-time authors." Does not want to receive genre fiction (Western, romance, horror, fantasy, science fiction).

- O→ "I choose books based on the narrative voice and strength of writing. I work with previously published and first-time authors." Does not want to receive genre fiction (Western, romance, horror, fantasy, science fiction).

How to Contact Query with SASE and 10 sample pages via mail or e-mail. Guidelines online.

Tips "Please keep your letters to the point, include all relevant information, and have a bit of patience."

BENREY LITERARY

P.O. Box 812, Columbia MD 21044. (443)545-5620. Fax: (886)297-9483. E-mail: query@benreyliterary.com. Website: www.benreyliterary.com. **Contact:** Janet Benrey. Represents 35 clients. 20% of clients are new/unpublished writers. Currently handles: nonfiction books 50%, novels 50%.

- Prior to her current position, Ms. Benrey was with the Hartline Literary Agency.

Represents nonfiction books, novels, scholarly, narrow focus. **Considers these nonfiction areas:** how to, religion, self help, true crime. **Considers these fiction areas:** adventure, detective, family, literary, mainstream, mystery, religious, romance, thriller, womens. This agency's specialties include romance, women's fiction, mystery, true crime, thriller (secular and Christian), as well as Christian living, church resources, inspirational. Actively seeking women's fiction, romance, mystery, suspense, Christian living, church resources. Does not want to receive fantasy, science fiction, Christian speculative fiction, erotica or paranormal.

- O→ This agency's specialties include romance, women's fiction, mystery, true crime, thriller (secular and Christian), as well as Christian living, church resources, inspirational. Actively seeking women's fiction, romance, mystery, suspense, Christian living, church resources. Does not want to receive fantasy, science fiction, Christian speculative fiction, erotica or paranormal.

How to Contact Query via e-mail only. Submit proposal package, synopsis, 3 sample chapters, author bio.More submission details available online Accepts simultaneous submissions. Responds in 6 weeks to queries. Responds in 3 months to mss. Obtains most new clients through recommendations from others, solicitations, conferences.

Terms Agent receives 15% commission on domestic sales. Agent receives 20% commission on foreign sales. Offers written contract; 30-day notice must be given to terminate contract. We pass on the out-of-pocket costs of copying and shipping manuscripts for new clients until we have made their first sales.

Tips Understand the market as best you can. Attend conferences and network. Don't create a new genre.

MEREDITH BERNSTEIN LITERARY AGENCY

2095 Broadway, Suite 505, New York NY 10023. (212)799-1007. Fax: (212)799-1145. Member of AAR. Represents 85 clients. 20% of clients are new/unpublished writers. Currently handles: nonfiction books 50%, other 50% fiction.

- Prior to opening her agency, Ms. Bernstein served at another agency for 5 years.

Represents nonfiction books, novels. **Considers these fiction areas:** literary, mystery, romance, thriller, young adult. "This agency does not specialize. It is very eclectic."

O→ "This agency does not specialize. It is very eclectic."

How to Contact Query with SASE. Accepts simultaneous submissions. Obtains most new clients through recommendations from others, conferences, developing/packaging ideas.

Terms Agent receives 15% commission on domestic sales. Agent receives 20% commission on foreign sales. Charges clients $75 disbursement fee/year.

Recent Sales *House of Nighy* series, by P.C. Cast and Kristin Cast; *The No Cry Nap Solution*, by Elizabeth Pantrey, and *Following the Waters,* by David Carroll (2 McArthur Genius Award Winner).

Writers Conferences Southwest Writers' Conference; Rocky Mountain Fiction Writers' Colorado Gold; Pacific Northwest Writers' Conference; Willamette Writers' Conference; Surrey International Writers' Conference; San Diego State University Writers' Conference.

BIDNICK & COMPANY

E-mail: bidnick@comcast.net. Currently handles: nonfiction books 100%.

- Founding member of Collins Publishing. Vice President of HarperCollins, San Francisco.

Member Agents Carole Bidnick.

Represents nonfiction books. This agency specializes in cookbooks and narrative nonfiction.

O→ This agency specializes in cookbooks and narrative nonfiction.

How to Contact Send queries via e-mail only

VICKY BIJUR LITERARY AGENCY

333 West End Ave., Apt. 5B, New York NY 10023. E-mail: assistant@vickybijuragency.com. Member of AAR.

Represents nonfiction books, novels. **Considers these nonfiction areas:** cooking, government, health, history, psychology, psychiatry, science, self help, sociology, biography; child care/development; environmental studies; journalism; social sciences.

O→ Does not want science fiction, fantasy, horror, romance, poetry, children's or YA.

How to Contact Accepts e-mail queries.

DAVID BLACK LITERARY AGENCY

156 Fifth Ave., Suite 608, New York NY 10010-7002. (212)242-5080. Fax: (212)924-6609. **Contact:** David Black, owner. Member of AAR. Represents 150 clients. Currently handles: nonfiction books 90%, novels 10%.

Member Agents David Black; Susan Raihofer (general nonfiction, literary fiction); Gary Morris (commercial fiction, psychology); Joy E. Tutela (general nonfiction, literary fiction); Leigh Ann Eliseo; Linda Loewenthal (general nonfiction, health, science, psychology, narrative).

Represents nonfiction books, novels. **Considers these nonfiction areas:** biography, business, government, health, history, memoirs, military, money, multicultural, psychology, religion, sports, womens. **Considers these fiction areas:** literary, mainstream, commercial. This agency specializes in business, sports, politics, and novels. literary, mainstream/contemporary, commercial

O→ This agency specializes in business, sports, politics, and novels. literary, mainstream/contemporary, commercial

How to Contact Query with SASE, outline. Accepts simultaneous submissions. Responds in 2 months to queries.

Terms Agent receives 15% commission on domestic sales. Charges clients for photocopying and books purchased for sale of foreign rights.

BLACK ROSE WRITING

P.O. Box 1540, Castroville TX 78009. (210)232-1935. E-mail: creator@blackrosewriting.com. Website: www.blackrosewriting.com. **Contact:** Reagan Rothe.

- Prior to becoming an agent, Ms. Rothe was a writer and editor.

Represents nonfiction books, novels, short story collections, novellas, juvenile, movie, tv. **Considers these nonfiction areas:** crafts, biography, business, computers, cooking, how to, humor, sports, true crime. **Considers these fiction areas:** adventure, detective, fantasy, horror, humor, juvenile, mainstream, mystery, picture books, romance, science, sports, thriller, western, young adult. **Considers these script areas:** biography, comedy, detective, fantasy, horror, juvenile, mainstream, mystery, romantic comedy, romantic drama, science, sports, teen, thriller, western. Actively seeking fiction, novels and short story collections.

O→ Actively seeking fiction, novels and short story collections.

How to Contact Please view submission guidelines before contacting. Query with SASE. Submit synopsis, author bio. Accepts simultaneous submissions. Responds in 1 month to mss. Obtains most new clients through recommendations from others, solicitations, conferences.

Terms Agent receives 20% commission on domestic sales. Agent receives 30% commission on foreign sales.

Tips "Please visit our website for submission guidelines and information regarding Black Rose Writing. We are a new literary agency that values trust and loyalty. We will be happy to read anything you have written and will try our best to give a personal response for every submission. We can handle your writing and editing needs!"

BLEECKER STREET ASSOCIATES, INC.

532 LaGuardia Place, #617, New York NY 10012. (212)677-4492. Fax: (212)388-0001. E-mail: bleeckerst@hotmail.com. **Contact:** Agnes Birnbaum.Member of AAR. Other memberships include RWA, MWA. Represents 60 clients. 20% of clients are new/unpublished writers. Currently handles: nonfiction books 75%, novels 25%.

- Prior to becoming an agent, Ms. Birnbaum was a senior editor at Simon & Schuster, Dutton/Signet, and other publishing houses.

Represents nonfiction books, novels. **Considers these nonfiction areas:** newage, animals, biography, business, child, computers, cooking, current affairs, ethnic, government, health, history, how to, memoirs, military, money, nature, popular culture, psychology, religion, science, self help, sociology, sports, true crime, womens. **Considers these fiction areas:** ethnic, historical, literary, mystery, romance, thriller, womens. "We're very hands-on and accessible. We try to be truly creative in our submission approaches. We've had especially good luck with first-time authors." Does not want to receive science fiction, westerns, poetry, children's books, academic/scholarly/professional books, plays, scripts, or short stories.

O→ "We're very hands-on and accessible. We try to be truly creative in our submission approaches. We've had especially good luck with first-time authors." Does not want to receive science fiction, westerns, poetry, children's books, academic/scholarly/professional books, plays, scripts, or short stories.

How to Contact Query with SASE. No email, phone, or fax queries. Accepts simultaneous submissions. Responds in 2 weeks to queries. Responds in 1 month to mss. "Obtains most new clients through recommendations from others, solicitations, conferences, plus, I will approach someone with a letter if his/her work impresses me."

Terms Agent receives 15% commission on domestic sales. Agent receives 25% commission on foreign sales. Offers written contract; 1-month notice must be given to terminate contract. Charges for postage, long distance, fax, messengers, photocopies (not to exceed $200).

Recent Sales Sold 14 titles in the last year. *Following Sarah*, by Daniel Brown (Morrow); *Biology of the Brain*, by Paul Swingle (Rutgers University Press); *Santa Miracles*, by Brad and Sherry Steiger (Adams); *Surviving the College Search*, by Jennifer Delahunt (St. Martin's).

Tips "Keep query letters short and to the point; include only information pertaining to the book or background as a writer. Try to avoid superlatives in description. Work needs to stand on its own, so how much editing it may have received has no place in a query letter."

BLISS LITERARY AGENCY INTERNATIONAL, INC.

1601 N. Sepulveda Blvd, #389, Manhattan Beach CA 90266. E-mail: query@blissliterary.com. Website: www.blissliterary.com. **Contact:** Jenoyne Adams.

Member Agents Prior to her current position, Ms. Adams was with Levine Greenberg Literary Agency.

Represents nonfiction books, novels, juvenile, Willy Blackmore. **Considers these fiction areas:** literary, multicultural, commercial. "Middle grade, YA fiction and nonfiction, young reader? Bring it on. We are interested in developing and working on projects that run the gamut—fantasy, urban/edgy, serious, bling-blingy? SURE. We love it all." "I haven't found it yet, but with a deep appreciation for anime and martial arts flicks, we are looking for the perfect graphic novel."

- "Middle grade, YA fiction and nonfiction, young reader? Bring it on. We are interested in developing and working on projects that run the gamut—fantasy, urban/edgy, serious, bling-blingy? SURE. We love it all." "I haven't found it yet, but with a deep appreciation for anime and martial arts flicks, we are looking for the perfect graphic novel."

How to Contact Query via e-mail or snail mail. Send query, synopsis, one chapter, contact info. No attachments. Responds in 8 weeks to queries.

Tips "Non-query related matters can be addressed by e-mailing info@blissliterary.com."

REID BOATES LITERARY AGENCY

69 Cooks Crossroad, Pittstown NJ 08867. (908)797-8087. Fax: (908)788-3667. E-mail: reid.boates@gmail.com. **Contact:** Reid Boates. Represents 45 clients. 5% of clients are new/unpublished writers. Currently handles: nonfiction books 85%, novels 15%, story collections very rarely.

How to Contact No unsolicited queries of any kind. Obtains new clients by personal referral only.

Terms Agent receives 15% commission on domestic sales. Agent receives 20% commission on foreign sales.

Recent Sales Sold 15 titles in the last year. New sales include placements at HarperCollins, Wiley, Random House, and other major general-interest publishers.

BOND LITERARY AGENCY

4340 E Kentucky Ave, Suite 471, Denver CO 80246. **Contact:** Sandra Bond.

- Prior to her current position, Ms. Bond worked with agent Jody Rein.

Represents nonfiction books, novels. **Considers these nonfiction areas:** business, health, history, science, narrative nonfiction. **Considers these fiction areas:** literary, general fiction, mystery, juvenile fiction.

How to Contact Submit query by mail or e-mail (no attachments). "She will let you know if she is interested in seeing more material. No unsolicited manuscripts."

BOOK CENTS LITERARY AGENCY, LLC

2011 Quarrier Street, Charleston WV 25311. (304)347-2330, ext. 1105. E-mail: cwitthohn@hotmail.com. Website: www.bookcentsliteraryagency.com. **Contact:** Christine Witthohn, Judith Ann Miramontez.

Represents Actively seeking "single title romance (contemporary, romantic comedy, paranormal, mystery/suspense), women's lit (must have a strong hook), mainstream mystery/suspense, medical or legal fiction, literary fiction. For nonfiction, seeking women's issues/experiences, fun/quirky topics (particularly those of interest to women), cookbooks (fun, ethnic, etc.), gardening (herbs, plants, flowers, etc.), books with a "save-the-planet" theme, how-to books, travel and outdoor adventure." Does not want to receive category romance, erotica, inspirational, historical, sci-fi/fantasy, horror/dark thrillers, short stories/novella, children's picture books, poetry, screenplays.

- Actively seeking "single title romance (contemporary, romantic comedy, paranormal, mystery/suspense), women's lit (must have a strong hook), mainstream mystery/suspense, medical or legal fiction, literary fiction. For nonfiction, seeking women's issues/experiences, fun/quirky topics (particularly those of interest to women), cookbooks (fun, ethnic, etc.), gardening (herbs, plants, flowers, etc.), books with a "save-the-planet" theme, how-to books, travel and outdoor adventure." Does not want to receive category romance, erotica, inspirational, historical, sci-fi/fantasy, horror/dark thrillers, short stories/novella, children's picture books, poetry, screenplays.

How to Contact "We prefer and respond faster to e-mail queries and submissions."

BOOKENDS, LLC

136 Long Hill Rd., Gillette NJ 07933. Website: www.bookends-inc.com; bookendslitagency.blogspot.com. **Contact:** Jessica Faust, Jacky Sach, Kim Lionetti.Member of AAR. RWA, MWA Represents 50+ clients. 10% of clients are new/unpublished writers. Currently handles: nonfiction books 50%, novels 50%.

Member Agents Jessica Faust (fiction: romance, erotica, chick lit, women's fiction, mysterious and suspense; nonfiction: business, finance, career, parenting, psychology, women's issues, self-help, health, sex); Jacky Sach (mysteries, women's fiction, suspense, self-help, spirituality, alternative and mainstream health, business and career, addiction, chick-lit nonfiction); Kim Lionetti (women's fiction, mystery, true crime, pop science, pop culture, and all areas of romance).".

Represents nonfiction books, novels. **Considers these nonfiction areas:** newage, business, child, ethnic, gay, health, how to, money, psychology, religion, self help, sex, spirituality, true crime, womens. **Considers these fiction areas:** detective, cozies, mainstream, mystery, romance, thriller, womens, chick lit. "BookEnds is currently accepting queries from published and unpublished writers in the areas of romance (and all its sub-genres), erotica, mystery, suspense, women's fiction, and literary fiction. We also do a great deal of nonfiction in the areas of spirituality, new age, self-help, business, finance, health, pop science, psychology, relationships, parenting, pop culture, true crime, and general nonfiction." BookEnds does not want to receive children's books, screenplays, science fiction, poetry, or technical/military thrillers.

- "BookEnds is currently accepting queries from published and unpublished writers in the areas of romance (and all its sub-genres), erotica, mystery, suspense, women's fiction, and literary fiction. We also do a great deal of nonfiction in the areas of spirituality, new age, self-help, business, finance, health, pop science, psychology, relationships, parenting, pop culture, true crime, and general nonfiction." BookEnds does not want to receive children's books, screenplays, science fiction, poetry, or technical/military thrillers.

How to Contact Review Web site for guidelines, as they change.

BOOKS & SUCH LITERARY AGENCY

52 Mission Circle, Suite 122, PMB 170, Santa Rosa CA 95409. E-mail: representation@booksandsuch.biz. Website: www.booksandsuch.biz. **Contact:** Janet Kobobel Grant, Wendy Lawton, Etta Wilson, Rachel Zurakowski. Member of AAR. Member of CBA (associate), American Christian Fiction Writers. Represents 150 clients. 5% of clients are new/unpublished writers. Currently handles: nonfiction books 50%, novels 50%.

- Prior to becoming an agent, Ms. Grant was an editor for Zondervan and managing editor for *Focus on the Family*; Ms. Lawton was an author, sculptor and designer of porcelein dolls. Ms. Wilson emphasizes middle grade children's books. Ms. Zurakowski concentrates on material for 20-something or 30-something readers.

Represents nonfiction books, novels, juvenile books,. **Considers these nonfiction areas:** child, humor, religion, self help, womens. **Considers these fiction areas:** contemporary, family, historical, mainstream, religious, romance, African American adult. This agency specializes in general and inspirational fiction, romance, and in the Christian booksellers market. Actively seeking well-crafted material that presents Judeo-Christian values, if only subtly.

- This agency specializes in general and inspirational fiction, romance, and in the Christian booksellers market. Actively seeking well-crafted material that presents Judeo-Christian values, if only subtly.

How to Contact Query via e-mail only, no attachments. Accepts simultaneous submissions. Responds in 1 month to queries. Obtains most new clients through recommendations from others, conferences.

Terms Agent receives 15% commission on domestic sales. Agent receives 20% commission on foreign sales. Offers written contract; 2-month notice must be given to terminate contract. No additional charges.

Recent Sales Sold 105 titles in the last year. *Knit Together*, by Debbie Macomber (Faith Words); *The Lazarus Factor*, by Joanna Weaver (WaterBrook); *Moon Over Maui*, by Robin Jones Gunn (Howard Books); *Because I Said So* (Guideposts), by Dawn Meehan. Other clients include: Lori Copeland, Rene Gutteridge, Andy McGuire, Ed Gilbreath, BJ Hoff.

Writers Conferences Mount Hermon Christian Writers' Conference; Society of Childrens' Writers and Illustrators Conference; Writing for the Soul; American Christian Fiction Writers' Conference; San Francisco Writers' Conference.

Tips "The heart of our agency's motivation is to develop relationships with the authors we serve, to do what we can to shine the light of success on them, and to help be a caretaker of their gifts and time."

GEORGES BORCHARDT, INC.

136 E. 57th St., New York NY 10022. Member of AAR.

Member Agents Anne Borchardt; Georges Borchardt; Valerie Borchardt.

Represents This agency specializes in literary fiction and outstanding nonfiction.

- This agency specializes in literary fiction and outstanding nonfiction.

How to Contact *No unsolicited mss.* Obtains most new clients through recommendations from others.

Terms Agent receives 15% commission on domestic sales. Agent receives 20% commission on foreign sales. Offers written contract.

THE BARBARA BOVA LITERARY AGENCY

3951 Gulf Shore Blvd. No. PH 1-B, Naples FL 34103. (239)649-7263. Fax: (239)649-7263. E-mail: bovab4@aol.com. Website: www.barbarabovaliteraryagency.com. **Contact:** Barbara Bova, Michael Burke. Represents 30 clients. Currently handles: nonfiction books 20%, novels 80%.

Represents nonfiction books, novels. **Considers these nonfiction areas:** biography, history, science, self help, true crime, womens, social sciences. **Considers these fiction areas:** adventure, crime, detective, mystery, police, science fiction, suspense, thriller, women's, young adult, teen lit. This agency specializes in fiction and nonfiction, hard and soft science.

- This agency specializes in fiction and nonfiction, hard and soft science.

How to Contact Query through website Obtains most new clients through recommendations from

others.
Terms Agent receives 15% commission on domestic sales. Agent receives 20% commission on foreign sales. Charges clients for overseas postage, overseas calls, photocopying, shipping.
Recent Sales Sold 24 titles in the last year. *The Green Trap* and *The Aftermath*, by Ben Bova; *Empire and A War of Gifts*, by Orson Scott Card; *Radioman*, by Carol E. Hipperson.
Tips "We also handle foreign, movie, television, and audio rights."

BRADFORD LITERARY AGENCY

5694 Mission Center Road, #347, San Diego CA 92108. (619)521-1201. E-mail: laura@bradfordlit.com. Website: www.bradfordlit.com. **Contact:** Laura Bradford. Represents 50 clients. 20% of clients are new/unpublished writers. Currently handles: nonfiction books 10%, novels 90%.

- Ms. Bradford started with her first literary agency straight out of college and has 14 years of experience as a bookseller in parallel.

Represents nonfiction books, novels, novellas, within a single author's collection, anthology. **Considers these nonfiction areas:** business, child, current affairs, health, history, how to, memoirs, money, popular culture, psychology, self help, womens. **Considers these fiction areas:** adventure, detective, erotica, ethnic, historical, humor, mainstream, mystery, romance, thriller, psychic/supernatural.Actively seeking romance (including category), romantica, women's fiction, mystery, thrillers and young adult. Does not want to receive poetry, short stories, children's books (juvenile) or screenplays.

O→ Actively seeking romance (including category), romantica, women's fiction, mystery, thrillers and young adult. Does not want to receive poetry, short stories, children's books (juvenile) or screenplays.

How to Contact Query with SASE. Submit cover letter, first 30 pages of completed ms., synopsis and SASE. Send no attachments via e-mail; only send a query letter. Accepts simultaneous submissions. Responds in 10 weeks to queries. Responds in 10 weeks to mss. Obtains most new clients through solicitations.
Terms Agent receives 15% commission on domestic sales. Agent receives 20% commission on foreign sales. Offers written contract, non-binding for 2 years; 45-day notice must be given to terminate contract. Charges for photocopies, postage, extra copies of books for submissions.
Recent Sales Sold 52 titles in the last year. *Eternal Hunter*, by Cynthia Eden (Kensington Brava); *Coming Undone*, by Lauren Dane (Berkley Heat); *Wicked Enchantment*, by Anya Bast (Berkley Sensation); *The Salvation of Sarah*, by Beth Williamson (Kensingston Brava); *Dark Revenge*, by Juliana Stone (Avon); *The Ghost and the Goth*, by Stacey Kade (Hyperion); *Skin Game*, by Ava Gray (Berkley Sensation); *Taming the Cougar*, by Vonna Harper (Kensington Aphrodisia) and more.
Writers Conferences RWA National Conference; Romantic Times Booklovers Convention.

BRANDS-TO-BOOKS, INC.

419 Lafayette St., New York NY 10003. Website: www.brandstobooks.com. **Contact:** Robert Allen. 70% of clients are new/unpublished writers. Currently handles: nonfiction books 100%.

- Prior to co-founding Brands-to-Books, Mr. Allen was president and publisher of the Random House Audio Division; Ms. Spinelli was vice president/director of marketing for Ballantine Books.

Member Agents Kathleen Spinelli, kspinelli@brandstobooks.com (lifestyle, design, business, personal finance, health, pop culture, sports, travel, cooking, crafts, how-to, reference); Robert Allen, rallen@brandstobooks.com (business, motivation, psychology, how-to, pop culture, self-help/personal improvement, narrative nonfiction).
Represents nonfiction books, ghostwriters. **Considers these nonfiction areas:** crafts, interior, anthropology, art, biography, business, child, computers, cooking, current affairs, ethnic, gay, government, health, history, how to, humor, language, memoirs, money, music, photography, popular culture, psychology, self help, sports, film, books based from brands. "We concentrate on brand-name businesses, products, and personalities whose platform, passion, and appeal translate into successful publishing ventures. We offer more than literary representation--we provide clients a true marketing partner, pursuing and maximizing every opportunity for promotion and sales within the publishing process." "Actively seeking nonfiction proposals supported by strong media platforms and experienced ghostwriters--especially those who have worked with brands/personalities." Does not want fiction or poetry.

O→ "We concentrate on brand-name businesses, products, and personalities whose platform, passion, and appeal translate into successful publishing ventures. We offer more than literary representation--we provide clients a true marketing partner, pursuing and maximizing every opportunity for promotion and sales within the publishing process." "Actively seeking nonfiction proposals supported by strong media platforms and experienced ghostwriters--especially those who have worked with brands/personalities." Does not want fiction or poetry.

How to Contact E-Query with book overview, résumé/platform. Accepts simultaneous submissions. Responds in 3 weeks to queries. Obtains most new clients through recommendations from others, outreach to brand managers and the licensing industry.

Terms Agent receives 15% commission on domestic sales. Agent receives 20% commission on foreign sales. Offers written contract; 3-month written notice must be given to terminate contract. Charges for office expenses (copying, messengers, express mail).

Tips "In your query, clearly show your passion for the subject and why you are the best person to write this book. Establish your media experience and platform. Indicate you have done your market research and demonstrate how this book is different from what is already on the shelves."

BRANDT & HOCHMAN LITERARY AGENTS, INC.

1501 Broadway, Suite 2310, New York NY 10036. (212)840-5760. Fax: (212)840-5776. **Contact:** Gail Hochman. Member of AAR. Represents 200 clients.

Member Agents Carl Brandt; Gail Hochman; Marianne Merola; Charles Schlessiger; Bill Contardi; Joanne Brownstein.

Represents nonfiction books, novels, short story collections, juvenile, journalism. **Considers these nonfiction areas:** biography, current affairs, ethnic, government, history, womens. **Considers these fiction areas:** contemporary, ethnic, historical, literary, mainstream, mystery, romance, thriller, young adult.

How to Contact Submit through email or if by post, query with SASE. Accepts simultaneous submissions. Responds in 1 month to queries. Obtains most new clients through recommendations from others.

Terms Agent receives 15% commission on domestic sales. Agent receives 20% commission on foreign sales. Charges clients for ms duplication or other special expenses agreed to in advance.

Tips "Write a letter which will give the agent a sense of you as a professional writer--your long-term interests as well as a short description of the work at hand."

THE JOAN BRANDT AGENCY

788 Wesley Drive, Atlanta GA 30305-3933. (404)351-8877. **Contact:** Joan Brandt.

- Prior to her current position, Ms. Brandt was with Sterling Lord Literistic.

Represents nonfiction books, novels, short story collections. **Considers these nonfiction areas:** history, how-to, narrative, pop culture, true crime. **Considers these fiction areas:** detective/police/crime, family saga, historical, literary, mystery/suspense, thriller, womens.

How to Contact Query with SASE. Accepts simultaneous submissions.

Terms Agent receives 15% commission on domestic sales. Agent receives 20% commission on foreign sales. No written contract.

THE HELEN BRANN AGENCY, INC.

94 Curtis Road, Bridgewater CT 06752. Fax: (860)355-2572. Member of AAR.

How to Contact Query with SASE.

BARBARA BRAUN ASSOCIATES, INC.

151 West 19th St/, 4th floor, New York NY 10011. Fax: (212)604-9041. E-mail: bbasubmissions@gmail.com. Website: www.barbarabraunagency.com. **Contact:** Barbara Braun. Member of AAR.

Member Agents Barbara Braun; John F. Baker.

Represents nonfiction books, novels. **Considers these nonfiction areas:** We represent both literary and commercial and serious nonfiction, including psychology, biography, history, women's issues, social and political issues, cultural criticism, as well as art, architecture, film, photography, fashion and design. **Considers these fiction areas:** literary and commercial. "Our fiction is strong on women's stories, historical and multicultural stories, as well as mysteries and thrillers. We're interested in narrative nonfiction and books by journalists. We do not represent poetry, science fiction, fantasy, horror, or screenplays. Look online for more details."

- "Our fiction is strong on women's stories, historical and multicultural stories, as well as mysteries and thrillers. We're interested in narrative nonfiction and books by journalists. We do not represent poetry, science fiction, fantasy, horror, or screenplays. Look online for more details."

How to Contact Email submissions only marked "query" in subject line. Fiction submissions: One-page synopsis and two sample chapters. Nonfiction submissions: Send proposal with overview, chapter outline, author biography, 2 sample chapters and short profile of competition.

Terms Agent receives 15% commission on domestic sales. Agent receives 20% commission on foreign sales.

Tips " We are also active in selling motion picture rights to the books we represent, and work with various Hollywood agencies."

PAUL BRESNICK LITERARY AGENCY, LLC

115 W. 29th St., Third Floor, New York NY 10001. (212)239-3166. Fax: (212)239-3165. E-mail: paul@bresnickagency.com. **Contact:** Paul Bresnick.

- Prior to becoming an agent, Mr. Bresnick spent 25 years as a trade book editor.

Represents nonfiction books, novels. **Considers these nonfiction areas:** autobiography/memoir, biography, health, history, humor, memoirs, multicultural, popular culture, sports, travel, true crime, celebrity-branded books, narrative nonfiction, pop psychology, relationship issues. **Considers these fiction areas:** general fiction.

How to Contact For fiction, submit query/SASE and 2 chapters. For nonfiction, submit query/SASE with proposal

BRICK HOUSE LITERARY AGENTS

literary fiction and narrative non-fiction, 80 Fifth Ave., Suite 1101, New York NY 10011. Website: www.brickhouselit.com. **Contact:** Sally Wofford-Girand. Member of AAR.

Member Agents Sally Wofford-Girand; Jenni Ferrari-Adler; Melissa Sarver, assistant.

Represents nonfiction books, novels. **Considers these nonfiction areas:** ethnic, history, memoirs, womens, biography; science; natural history. **Considers these fiction areas:** literary. lifestyle, cookbooks, memoir, food writing, juvenile/general fiction Actively seeking history, memoir, women's issues, cultural studies, literary fiction and quality commerical fiction.

- O→ lifestyle, cookbooks, memoir, food writing, juvenile/general fiction Actively seeking history, memoir, women's issues, cultural studies, literary fiction and quality commerical fiction.

How to Contact "Email query letter (in body of email - not as attachment) and first page to either Sally or Jenni. We will ask to see more if interested and are sorry that we cannot respond to all queries."

M. COURTNEY BRIGGS

Derrick & Briggs, 100 N. Broadway Ave., 28th Floor, Oklahoma City OK 73102-8806. (405)235-1900. Fax: (405)235-1995. Website: www.derrickandbriggs.com.

- Prior to becoming an agent, Ms. Briggs was in subsidiary rights at Random House for 3 years; an associate agent and film rights associate with Curtis Brown, Ltd.; and an attorney for 16 years.

Represents nonfiction books, novels, juvenile. **Considers these nonfiction areas:** young adult. "I work primarily, but not exclusively, with children's book authors and illustrators. I will also consult or review a contract on an hourly basis." Actively seeking children's fiction, children's picture books (illustrations and text), young adult novels, fiction, nonfiction.

- O→ "I work primarily, but not exclusively, with children's book authors and illustrators. I will also consult or review a contract on an hourly basis." Actively seeking children's fiction, children's picture books (illustrations and text), young adult novels, fiction, nonfiction.

How to Contact Query with SASE. Only published authors should submit queries. Obtains most new clients through recommendations from others.

Terms Agent receives 15% commission on domestic sales. Agent receives 25% commission on foreign sales. Offers written contract; 60-day notice must be given to terminate contract.

Writers Conferences SCBWI Annual Winter Conference.

RICK BROADHEAD & ASSOCIATES LITERARY AGENCY

501-47 St. Clair Ave. W., Toronto ON M4V 3A5 Canada. (416)929-0516. Fax: (416)927-8732. E-mail: rba@rbaliterary.com. Website: www.rbaliterary.com. **Contact:** Rick Broadhead, president. Other memberships include Authors Guild. Represents 50 clients. 50%% of clients are new/unpublished writers. Currently handles: nonfiction books 100%.

- Prior to becoming an agent in 2002, Mr. Broadhead discovered his passion for books at a young age and co-authored his first bestseller at the age of 23. In addition to being one of the few literary agents with a business background, he has the rare distinction of having authored and co-authored more than 34 books.

Represents nonfiction books. **Considers these nonfiction areas:** crafts, animals, anthropology, biography, business, child, cooking, current affairs, government, health, history, how to, humor, memoirs, military, money, music, nature, popular culture, psychology, science, self help, sports, true crime, womens. "Rick Broadhead & Associates is an established literary agency that represents primarily nonfiction projects in a wide variety of genres. Priority is given to original, compelling proposals as well as proposals from experts in their fields who have a strong marketing platform. The agency represents American authors to American and foreign publishers in a wide variety of nonfiction genres, including narrative nonfiction, business, self-help, environment/conservation, history/politics, humor, sports, science, current affairs, health/medicine and pop culture. The agency is deliberately small, which allows clients to receive personalized service to maximize the success of their book projects and brands." Actively seeking compelling nonfiction proposals, especially narrative nonfiction (history, current affairs, business) from authors with relevant credentials and an established media platform (TV, radio, print exposure). Does not want to receive novels, television scripts, movie scripts, children's or poetry.

- O→ "Rick Broadhead & Associates is an established literary agency that represents primarily nonfiction projects in a wide variety of genres. Priority is given to original, compelling proposals as well as proposals from experts in their fields who have a strong marketing platform. The agency represents American authors to American and foreign publishers in a wide variety of nonfiction genres, including narrative nonfiction, business, self-help, environment/conservation, history/politics, humor, sports, science, current affairs, health/medicine and pop culture. The agency is deliberately small, which allows clients to receive personalized service to maximize the success of their book projects and brands." Actively seeking compelling nonfiction proposals, especially narrative nonfiction (history, current affairs, business) from authors with relevant credentials and an established media platform (TV, radio, print exposure). Does not want to receive novels, television scripts, movie scripts, children's or poetry.

How to Contact Query with SASE. Submit publishing history, author bio.E-mail queries preferred. Agency will reply only to projects of interest and request a full ms. Accepts simultaneous submissions. Obtains most new clients through recommendations from others, solicitations.

Terms Agent receives 15% commission on domestic sales. Agent receives 20% commission on foreign sales. Offers written contract. Charges for postage and photocopying expenses.

Tips "The agency has excellent relationships with New York publishers and editors and many of the agency's clients are American authors. The agency has negotiated many six-figure deals for its clients and has sold numerous unsolicited submissions to large publishers. We're good at what we do! E-mail queries are welcome."

CURTIS BROWN, LTD.

10 Astor Place, New York NY 10003-6935. (212)473-5400. Website: www.curtisbrown.com. Alternate address: Peter Ginsberg, president at CBSF, 1750 Montgomery St., San Francisco CA 94111. (415)954-8566. Member of AAR. Signatory of WGA.

Member Agents Ginger Clark; Katherine Fausset; Holly Frederick; Emilie Jacobson, senior vice president; Elizabeth Hardin; Ginger Knowlton, vice president; Timothy Knowlton, CEO; Laura Blake Peterson; Maureen Walters, senior vice president; Mitchell Waters. San Francisco Office: Nathan Bransford, Peter Ginsberg (President).

Represents nonfiction books, novels, short story collections, juvenile. **Considers these nonfiction areas:** agriculture horticulture, americana, crafts, interior, juvenile, New Age, young, animals, anthropology, art, biography, business, child, computers, cooking, current affairs, education, ethnic, gardening, gay, government, health, history, how to, humor, language, memoirs, military, money, multicultural, music, nature, philosophy, photography, popular culture, psychology, recreation, regional, religion, science, self help, sex, sociology, software, spirituality, sports, film, translation, travel, true crime, womens, creative nonfiction. **Considers these fiction areas:** contemporary, glitz, newage, psychic, adventure, comic, confession, detective, erotica, ethnic, experimental, family, fantasy, feminist, gay, gothic, hi lo, historical, horror, humor, juvenile, literary, mainstream, military, multicultural, multimedia, mystery, occult, picture books, plays, poetry, regional, religious, romance, science, short, spiritual, sports, thriller, translation, western, young, womens.

How to Contact Prefers to read materials exclusively. *No unsolicited mss.* Responds in 3 weeks to queries. Responds in 5 weeks to mss. Obtains most new clients through recommendations from others, solicitations, conferences.

Terms Offers written contract. Charges for some postage (overseas, etc.)

Recent Sales This agency prefers not to share information on specific sales.

MARIE BROWN ASSOCIATES, INC.

412 W. 154th St., New York NY 10032. (212)939-9725. Fax: (212)939-9728. E-mail: mbrownlit@aol.com. **Contact:** Marie Brown. Represents 60 clients. Currently handles: nonfiction books 75%, juvenile books 10%, other 15% other.

Member Agents Janell Walden Agyeman (Miami).

Represents nonfiction books, juvenile. **Considers these nonfiction areas:** juvenile, biography, business, ethnic, history, music, religion, womens. **Considers these fiction areas:** ethnic, juvenile, literary, mainstream. This agency specializes in multicultural and African-American writers.

O‑ This agency specializes in multicultural and African-American writers.

How to Contact Query with SASE. Prefers to read materials exclusively. Reports in 6-10 weeks on queries. Obtains most new clients through recommendations from others.

Terms Agent receives 15% commission on domestic sales. Agent receives 20% commission on foreign sales. Offers written contract.

CURTIS BROWN (AUST) PTY LTD

P.O. Box 19, Paddington NSW 2021 Australia. (61)(2)9361-6161. Fax: (61)(2)9360-3935. E-mail: info@curtisbrown.com.au. Website: www.curtisbrown.com.au. **Contact:** Submissions Department. Represents 350 clients. 10% of clients are new/unpublished writers. Currently handles: nonfiction books 30%, novels 30%, juvenile books 25%, scholarly books 5%, textbooks 5%, other 5% other.

- Prior to joining Curtis Brown, most of our agents worked in publishing or the film/theatre industries in Australia and the United Kingdom.

Member Agents Fiona Inglis, managing director; Fran Moore, agent/deputy managing director; Tara Wynne, agent; Pippa Masson, agent; Clare Forster, agent.

Represents nonfiction books, novels, novellas, juvenile. "We are the oldest and largest literary agency in Australia and we look after a wide variety of clients." No poetry, short stories, film scripts, picture books or translations.

O→ "We are the oldest and largest literary agency in Australia and we look after a wide variety of clients." No poetry, short stories, film scripts, picture books or translations.

How to Contact Submit 3 sample chapters, cover letter with biographical information, synopsis (2-3 pages), SASE

BROWNE & MILLER LITERARY ASSOCIATES

410 S. Michigan Ave., Suite 460, Chicago IL 60605-1465. (312)922-3063. E-mail: mail@browneandmiller.com. **Contact:** Danielle Egan-Miller. Member of AAR. Other memberships include RWA, MWA, Author's Guild. Represents 150 clients. 2%% of clients are new/unpublished writers. Currently handles: nonfiction books 25%, novels 75%.

Represents nonfiction books, novels. **Considers these nonfiction areas:** agriculture horticulture, crafts, animals, anthropology, biography, business, child, cooking, current affairs, ethnic, health, how to, humor, memoirs, money, nature, popular culture, psychology, religion, science, self help, sociology, sports, true crime, womens. **Considers these fiction areas:** glitz, detective, ethnic, family, historical, literary, mainstream, mystery, religious, romance, contemporary, gothic, historical, regency, sports, thriller, paranormal, erotica. We are partial to talented newcomers and experienced authors who are seeking hands-on career management, highly personal representation, and who are interested in being full partners in their books' successes. We are editorially focused and work closely with our authors through the whole publishing process, from proposal to after publication. Actively seeking highly commercial mainstream fiction and nonfiction. Does not represent poetry, short stories, plays, screenplays, articles, or children's books.

O→ We are partial to talented newcomers and experienced authors who are seeking hands-on career management, highly personal representation, and who are interested in being full partners in their books' successes. We are editorially focused and work closely with our authors through the whole publishing process, from proposal to after publication. Actively seeking highly commercial mainstream fiction and nonfiction. Does not represent poetry, short stories, plays, screenplays, articles, or children's books.

How to Contact Query with SASE. *No unsolicited mss.* Prefers to read material exclusively. Put submission in the subject line. Send no attachments. Responds in 6 weeks to queries. Obtains most new clients through referrals, queries by professional/marketable authors.

Terms Agent receives 15% commission on domestic sales. Agent receives 20% commission on foreign sales. Offers written contract, binding for 2 years. Charges clients for photocopying, overseas postage.

Writers Conferences BookExpo America; Frankfurt Book Fair; RWA National Conference; ICRS; London Book Fair; Bouchercon, regional writers conferences.

Tips "If interested in agency representation, be well informed."

PEMA BROWNE, LTD.

11 Tena Place, Valley Cottage NY 10989. E-mail: ppbltd@optonline.net. Website: www.pemabrowneltd.com. **Contact:** Pema Browne. Signatory of WGA. Other memberships include SCBWI, RWA. Represents 30 clients. Currently handles: nonfiction books 25%, novels 50% novels/romance, juvenile books 25%.

- Prior to opening her agency, Ms. Browne was an artist and art buyer.

Represents nonfiction books, novels, juvenile, reference books. **Considers these nonfiction areas:** juvenile, newage, business, child, cooking, ethnic, gay, health, how to, money, popular culture, psychology, religion, self help, spirituality, womens, reference. **Considers these fiction areas:** contemporary, glitz, adventure, feminist, gay, historical, juvenile, literary, mainstream, commercial, mystery, picture books, religious, romance, contemporary, gothic, historical, regency, young. "We are not accepting any new projects or authors until further notice."

O→ "We are not accepting any new projects or authors until further notice."

How to Contact Query with SASE. No attachments for e-mail.

Terms Agent receives 20% commission on domestic sales. Agent receives 20% commission on foreign sales.

Recent Sales *The Champion*, by Heather Grothaus (Kensington/Zebra); *The Highlander's Bride*, by Michele Peach (Kensington/Zebra); *The Daring Harriet Quimby*, by Suzanne Whitaker (Holiday House); *One Night to Be Sinful*, by Samantha Garver (Kensington); *Taming the Beast*, by Heather Grothaus (Kensington/Zebra); *Kisses Don't Lie*, by Alexis Darin (Kensington/Zebra).

Tips "We do not review manuscripts that have been sent out to publishers. If writing romance, be sure to receive guidelines from various romance publishers. In nonfiction, one must have credentials to lend credence to a proposal. Make sure of margins, double-space, and use clean, dark type."

BROWN LITERARY AGENCY

410 Seventh St. NW, Naples FL 34120. Website: www.brownliteraryagency.com. **Contact:** Roberta Brown. Member of AAR. Other memberships include RWA, Author's Guild. Represents 47 clients. 5% of clients are new/unpublished writers.

Represents novels. **Considers these fiction areas:** erotica, romance, single title and category, womens. This agency is selectively reading material at this time.

O→ This agency is selectively reading material at this time.

How to Contact Query via e-mail only. Response time varies. .

Terms Agent receives 15% commission on domestic sales. Agent receives 20% commission on foreign sales. Offers written contract; 30-day notice must be given to terminate contract.

Writers Conferences RWA National Conference.

Tips "Polish your manuscript. Be professional."

ANDREA BROWN LITERARY AGENCY, INC.

1076 Eagle Drive, Salinas CA 93905. E-mail: andrea@andreabrownlit.com. Website: www.andreabrownlit.com. **Contact:** Andrea Brown, president. 10% of clients are new/unpublished writers.

- Prior to opening her agency, Ms. Brown served as an editorial assistant at Random House and Dell Publishing and as an editor with Knopf.

Member Agents Andrea Brown; Laura Rennert (laura@andreabrownlit.com); Kelly Sonnack; Caryn Wiseman; Jennifer Rafe; Jennifer Laughran, associate agent; Jamie Weiss Chilton, associate agent, and Jennifer Mattson, associate agent.

Represents Juvenile nonfiction books, novels. **Considers these nonfiction areas:** juvenile nonfiction, memoirs, young adult, narrative. **Considers these fiction areas:** juvenile, literary, picture books, young adult, middle-grade, all juvenile genres.

How to Contact For picture books, submit complete ms, SASE. For fiction, submit short synopsis, SASE, first 3 chapters. For nonfiction, submit proposal, 1-2 sample chapters. For illustrations, submit 4-5 color samples (no originals). "We only accept queries via e-mail." Accepts simultaneous submissions. Obtains most new clients through referrals from editors, clients and agents. Check website for guidelines and information.

Terms Agent receives 15% commission on domestic sales. Agent receives 20% commission on foreign sales. Offers written contract.

Recent Sales *Chloe*, by Catherine Ryan Hyde (Knopf); Sasha Cohen Autobiography (HarperCollins); *The Five Ancestors*, by Jeff Stone (Random House); *Thirteen Reasons Why*, by Jay Asher (Penguin); *Identical*, by Ellen Hopkins (S&S)

Writers Conferences SCBWI; Asilomar; Maui Writers' Conference; Southwest Writers' Conference; San Diego State University Writers' Conference; Big Sur Children's Writing Workshop; William Saroyan Writers' Conference; Columbus Writers' Conference; Willamette Writers' Conference; La Jolla Writers' Conference; San Francisco Writers' Conference; Hilton Head Writers' Conference: Pacific Northwest Conference; Pikes Peak Conference.

TRACY BROWN LITERARY AGENCY

P.O. Box 88, Scarsdale NY 10583. (914)400-4147. Fax: (914)931-1746. E-mail: tracy@brownlit.com. **Contact:** Tracy Brown. Represents 35 clients. Currently handles: nonfiction books 75%, novels 25%.

- Prior to becoming an agent, Mr. Brown was a book editor for 25 years.

Represents nonfiction books, novels, anthologies. **Considers these nonfiction areas:** biography, cooking, current affairs, environment, foods, health, history, how-to, humor, medicine, memoirs, money, nature, personal improvement, popular culture, psychology, religious, self-help, sports, women's issues, women's studies. **Considers these fiction areas:** literary. Specializes in thorough involvement with clients' books at every stage of the process from writing to proposals to publication. Actively seeking serious nonfiction and fiction. Does not want to receive YA, sci-fi or romance.

O→ Specializes in thorough involvement with clients' books at every stage of the process from writing to proposals to publication. Actively seeking serious nonfiction and fiction. Does not want to receive YA, sci-fi or romance.

How to Contact Submit outline/proposal, synopsis, author bio. Accepts simultaneous submissions. Responds in 2 weeks to queries. Obtains most new clients through referrals.

Terms Agent receives 15% commission on domestic sales. Agent receives 20% commission on foreign sales. Offers written contract.

Recent Sales *Super in the City: A Novel*, by Daphne Uviller (Bantam); *Losing It*, by Jessica Valenti (Seal Press); *Jane Addams: A Life*, by Louise W. Knight (Norton).

THE BUKOWSKI AGENCY

14 Prince Author Ave., Suite 202, Toronto Ontario M5R 1A9 Canada. (416)928-6728. Fax: (416)963-9978. E-mail: assistant@thebukowskiagency.com; info@thebukowskiagency.com. Website: www.

thebukowskiagency.com. **Contact:** Denise Bukowski. Represents 70 clients.

- Prior to becoming an agent, Ms. Bukowski was a book editor.

Represents nonfiction books, novels. "The Bukowski Agency specializes in international literary fiction and up-market nonfiction for adults. Bukowski looks for Canadian writers whose work can be marketed in many media and territories, and who have the potential to make a living from their work." Actively seeking nonfiction and fiction works from Canadian writers. Does not want submissions from American authors, as well as genre fiction, poetry, children's literature, picture books, film scripts or television scripts.

O⁻ⁿ "The Bukowski Agency specializes in international literary fiction and up-market nonfiction for adults. Bukowski looks for Canadian writers whose work can be marketed in many media and territories, and who have the potential to make a living from their work." Actively seeking nonfiction and fiction works from Canadian writers. Does not want submissions from American authors, as well as genre fiction, poetry, children's literature, picture books, film scripts or television scripts.

How to Contact Query with SASE. Submit proposal package, outline/proposal, synopsis, publishing history, author bio.Send submissions by snail mail only. See online guidelines for nonfiction and fiction specifics. Responds in 6 weeks to queries.

SHEREE BYKOFSKY ASSOCIATES, INC.

PO Box 706, Brigantine NJ 08203. E-mail: submitbee@aol.com. Website: www.shereebee.com. **Contact:** Sheree Bykofsky. Member of AAR. Other memberships include ASJA, WNBA. Currently handles: nonfiction books 80%, novels 20%.

- Prior to opening her agency, Ms. Bykofsky served as executive editor of The Stonesong Press and managing editor of Chiron Press. She is also the author or co-author of more than 20 books, including *The Complete Idiot's Guide to Getting Published*. Ms. Bykofsky teaches publishing at NYU and SEAK, Inc.

Member Agents Janet Rosen, associate.

Represents nonfiction books, novels. **Considers these nonfiction areas:** americana, crafts, interior, newage, animals, art, biography, business, child, cooking, current affairs, education, ethnic, gardening, gay, government, health, history, how to, humor, language, memoirs, military, money, personal finance, multicultural, music, nature, philosophy, photography, popular culture, psychology, recreation, regional, religion, science, self help, sex, sociology, spirituality, sports, film, translation, travel, true crime, womens, anthropolgy; creative nonfiction. **Considers these fiction areas:** literary, mainstream, mystery. This agency specializes in popular reference nonfiction, commercial fiction with a literary quality, and mysteries. I have wide-ranging interests, but it really depends on quality of writing, originality, and how a particular project appeals to me (or not). I take on fiction when I completely love it - it doesn't matter what area or genre. Does not want to receive poetry, material for children, screenplays, westerns, horror, science fiction, or fantasy.

O⁻ⁿ This agency specializes in popular reference nonfiction, commercial fiction with a literary quality, and mysteries. I have wide-ranging interests, but it really depends on quality of writing, originality, and how a particular project appeals to me (or not). I take on fiction when I completely love it - it doesn't matter what area or genre. Does not want to receive poetry, material for children, screenplays, westerns, horror, science fiction, or fantasy.

How to Contact E-mail short queries to submitbee@aol.com. Please, no attachments, snail mail, or phone calls. Accepts simultaneous submissions. Responds in 3 weeks to queries with SASE. Responds in 1 month to requested mss. Obtains most new clients through recommendations from others.

Terms Agent receives 15% commission on domestic sales. Agent receives 20% commission on foreign sales. Offers written contract, binding for 1 year. Charges for postage, photocopying, fax.

Recent Sales *Red Sheep: The Search for my Inner Latina*, by Michele Carlo (Citadel/Kensington); *Bang the Keys: Four Steps to a Lifelong Writing Practice*, by Jill Dearman (Alpha, Penguin); *Signed, Your Student: Celebrities on the Teachers Who Made Them Who They Are Today*, by Holly Holbert (Kaplan); *The Five Ways We Grieve*, by Susan Berger (Trumpeter/Shambhala).

Writers Conferences ASJA Writers Conference; Asilomar; Florida Suncoast Writers' Conference; Whidbey Island Writers' Conference; Florida First Coast Writers' Festibal; Agents and Editors Conference; Columbus Writers' Conference; Southwest Writers' Conference; Willamette Writers' Conferece; Dorothy Canfield Fisher Conference; Maui Writers' Conference; Pacific Northwest Writers' Conference; IWWG.

Tips Read the agent listing carefully and comply with guidelines.

CYNTHIA CANNELL LITERARY AGENCY

833 Madison Ave., New York NY 10021. **Contact:** Cynthia Cannell. Member of AAR.

Represents Not accepting new clients at this time.

O⁻ⁿ Not accepting new clients at this time.

MARIA CARVAINIS AGENCY, INC.

1270 Avenue of the Americas, Suite 2320, New York NY 10019. (212)245-6365. Fax: (212)245-7196. E-mail: mca@mariacarvainisagency.com. **Contact:** Maria Carvainis, Donna Bagdasarian. Member of AAR. Signatory of WGA. Other memberships include Authors Guild, Women's Media Group, ABA, MWA, RWA. Represents 75 clients. 10%% of clients are new/unpublished writers. Currently handles: nonfiction books 35%, novels 65%.

- Prior to opening her agency, Ms. Carvainis spent more than 10 years in the publishing industry as a senior editor with Macmillan Publishing, Basic Books, Avon Books, and Crown Publishers. Ms. Carvainis has served as a member of the AAR Board of Directors and AAR Treasurer, as well as serving as chair of the AAR Contracts Committee. She presently serves on the AAR Royalty Committee. Ms. Bagdasarian began her career as an academic at Boston University, then spent 5 years with Addison Wesley Longman as an acquisitions editor before joining the William Morris Agency in 1998. She has represented a breadth of projects, ranging from literary fiction to celebrity memoir.

Member Agents Maria Carvainis, president/literary agent; Donna Bagdasarian, literary agent; June Renschler, literary associate/subsidiary rights manager; Jerome Murphy and Alex Slater, literary assistants.

Represents nonfiction books, novels. **Considers these nonfiction areas:** biography, business, history, memoirs, science, pop science, womens. **Considers these fiction areas:** historical, literary, mainstream, mystery, thriller, young, womens, middle grade. Does not want to receive science fiction or children's picture books.

O→ Does not want to receive science fiction or children's picture books.

How to Contact Query with SASE. to queries. Responds in up to 3 months to mss. Obtains most new clients through recommendations from others, conferences, query letters.

Terms Agent receives 15% commission on domestic sales. Agent receives 20% commission on foreign sales. Offers written contract. Charges clients for foreign postage and bulk copying.

Recent Sales *Simply Magic*, by Mary Balogh (Bantam Dell); *Save Your Own*, by Elizabeth Brink (Houghton Mifflin); *Richochet*, by Sandra Brown (Simon & Schuster); *The Marriage Wager*, by Candace Camp (Mira); *Jeb: America's Next Bush*, by S.V. Date (Penguin Group/Tarcher Imprint); *A Widow's Curse*, by Phillip DePoy (St. Martin's Press); *A Falconer's Voice*, by Tim Gallagher (Houghton Mifflin); *Into the Dark*, by Cindy Gerard (St. Martin's Press); *Picture Perfect*, by D. Anne Love (Simon & Schuster Children's Publishing). Other clients include Sue Erikson Bloland, David Bottoms, Pam Conrad, John Faunce, Samantha James, Lucy Lehrer, Dushan Zaric, and Jason Kosmas.

Writers Conferences BookExpo America; Frankfurt Book Fair; London Book Fair; Mystery Writers of America; Thrillerfest; Romance Writers of America.

CASTIGLIA LITERARY AGENCY

1155 Camino Del Mar, Suite 510, Del Mar CA 92014. (858)755-8761. Fax: (858)755-7063. Website: home.earthlink.net/~mwgconference/id22.html. Member of AAR. Other memberships include PEN. Represents 50 clients. Currently handles: nonfiction books 55%, novels 45%.

Member Agents Julie Castiglia; Winifred Golden; Sally Van Haitsma; Deborah Ritchken.

Represents nonfiction books, novels. **Considers these nonfiction areas:** animals, anthropology, biography, business, child, cooking, current affairs, ethnic, health, history, language, money, nature, psychology, religion, science, self help, womens. **Considers these fiction areas:** ethnic, literary, mainstream, mystery, womens. Does not want to receive horror, screenplays, poetry or academic nonfiction.

O→ Does not want to receive horror, screenplays, poetry or academic nonfiction.

How to Contact Query with SASE. Obtains most new clients through recommendations from others, solicitations, conferences.

Terms Agent receives 15% commission on domestic sales. Agent receives 25% commission on foreign sales. Offers written contract; 6-week notice must be given to terminate contract.

Recent Sales *Freefall*, by Reece Hirsch (Berkley/Penguin); *Wesley the Owl*, by Stacey O'Brien (Free Press/S&S); *Teardrops and Tiny Trailers*, by Douglas Keister (Gibbs Smith); *The Leisure Seeker*, by Michael Zadoorian (Morrow/HarperCollins); *Silverstein and Me*, by Marv Gold (Red Hen Press); *In Triumph's Wake*, by Julie Gelardi (St. Martin's Press); *Beautiful: The Life of Hedy Lamarr*, by Stephen Shearer (St. Martin's Press); *American Libre*, by Raul Ramos y Sanchez (Grand Central).

Writers Conferences Santa Barbara Writers' Conference; Southern California Writers' Conference; Surrey International Writers' Conference; San Diego State University Writers' Conference; Willamette Writers' Conference.

Tips "Be professional with submissions. Attend workshops and conferences before you approach an agent."

CHAMEIN CANTON AGENCY

E-mail: cantonsmithagency@cantonsmithagency.com. Website: www.cantonsmithagency.com. **Contact:** Eric Smith, senior partner (esmith@cantonsmithagency.com); Chamein Canton, partner (chamein@cantonsmithagency.com); Netta Beckford, associate (nettab@cantonsmithagency.com). Estab. 2001. Represents 28 clients. 100% of clients are new/unpublished writers.

- Prior to becoming agents, Mr. Smith was in advertising and bookstore retail; Ms. Canton was a writer and a paralegal.

Member Agents Chamein Canton, managing partner, chamein@cantonsmithagency (women's fiction, chick-lit, business, how to, fashion, romance, erotica, African American, Latina, women's issues, health, relationships, decorating, cookbooks, lifestyle, literary novels, astrology, numerology, New Age) Eric Smith, senior partner, ericsmith@cantonsmithagency.com (science fiction, sports, literature); James Weil, reviewer, jamesw@cantonsmithagency.com.

Represents nonfiction books, novels, juvenile, scholarly, textbooks, movie. **Considers these nonfiction areas:** art, business, child, cooking, education, ethnic, health, history, how to, humor, language, memoirs, military, music, photography, psychology, sports, translation, womens. **Considers these fiction areas:** fantasy, humor, juvenile, multicultural, romance, young, Latina fiction; chick lit; African-American fiction; entertainment. **Considers these script areas:** action, comedy, romantic comedy, romantic drama, science. "We specialize in helping new and established writers expand their marketing potential for prospective publishers. We are currently focusing on women's fiction (chick lit), Latina fiction, African American fiction, multicultural, romance, memoirs, humor and entertainment, in addition to more nonfiction titles (cooking, how to, fashion, home improvement, etc)."

- "We specialize in helping new and established writers expand their marketing potential for prospective publishers. We are currently focusing on women's fiction (chick lit), Latina fiction, African American fiction, multicultural, romance, memoirs, humor and entertainment, in addition to more nonfiction titles (cooking, how to, fashion, home improvement, etc)."

How to Contact Only accepts e-queries. Send a query with synopsis only--include title and genre in subject line. Accepts simultaneous submissions. Responds in 8-12 weeks to queries. Responds in 3-5 months to mss. Obtains most new clients through recommendations from others.

Terms Agent receives 15% commission on domestic sales. Agent receives 20% commission on foreign sales. Offers written contract; 2-month notice must be given to terminate contract.

Tips "Know your market. Agents, as well as publishers, are keenly interested in writers with their finger on the pulse of their market."

JANE CHELIUS LITERARY AGENCY

548 Second St., Brooklyn NY 11215. (718)499-0236. Fax: (718)832-7335. E-mail: queries@janechelius.com. Website: www.janechelius.com. Member of AAR.

Represents nonfiction books, novels. **Considers these nonfiction areas:** humor, womens, popular science; parenting; medicine; biography; natural history; narrative. **Considers these fiction areas:** literary, mystery, womens, men's adventure. Does not want to receive fantasy, science fiction, children's books, stage plays, screenplays, or poetry.

- Does not want to receive fantasy, science fiction, children's books, stage plays, screenplays, or poetry.

How to Contact Please see Web site for submission procedures.

ELYSE CHENEY LITERARY ASSOCIATES, LLC

270 Lafayette St., Suite 1504, New York NY 10012. Website: www.cheneyliterary.com. **Contact:** Elyse Cheney, Nicole Steen.

- Prior to her current position, Ms. Cheney was an agent with Sanford J. Greenburger Associates.

Represents nonfiction books, novels. **Considers these nonfiction areas:** biography, history, multicultural, sports, womens, narrative. **Considers these fiction areas:** historical, horror, literary, romance, thriller.

How to Contact Query this agency with a referral. Include SASE or IRC. No fax queries. Snail mail or e-mail (submissions@cheneyliterary.com) only.

Recent Sales *Moonwalking with Einstein: A Journey into Memory and the Mind*, by Joshua Foer; *The Coldest Winter Ever*, by Sister Souljah (Atria); *A Heartbreaking Work of Staggering Genius*, by Dave Eggers (Simon and Schuster).

THE CHOATE AGENCY, LLC

1320 Bolton Road, Pelham NY 10803. E-mail: mickey@thechoateagency.com. Website: www.thechoateagency.com. **Contact:** Mickey Choate. Member of AAR.

Represents nonfiction books, novels. **Considers these nonfiction areas:** history, memoirs, by journalists, military or political figures, biography; cookery/food; journalism; military science; narrative; politics; general science; wine/spirits. **Considers these fiction areas:** historical, mystery, thriller, select literary fiction.Does not want to receive chick lit, cozies or romance.

Does not want to receive chick lit, cozies or romance.

How to Contact Query with brief synopsis and bio. This agency prefers e-queries, but accepts snail mail queries with SASE.

THE CHUDNEY AGENCY

72 North State Road, Suite 501, Briarcliff Manor NY 10510. (914)488-5008. E-mail: steven@thechudneyagency.com. Website: www.thechudneyagency.com. **Contact:** Steven Chudney.Estab. 2001. Other memberships include SCBWI. 90% of clients are new/unpublished writers.

- Prior to becoming an agent, Mr. Chudney held various sales positions with major publishers.

Represents novels, juvenile. **Considers these nonfiction areas:** juvenile. **Considers these fiction areas:** historical, juvenile, literary, mystery, young. This agency specializes in children's and teens books, and wants to find authors who are illustrators as well. "At this time, the agency is only looking for Author/Illustrators (one individual), who can both write and illustrate wonderful picture books. The author/illustrator must really know and understand the prime audience's needs and wants--the child reader! Storylines should be engaging, fun, with a hint of a life lesson and cannot be longer than 800 words." Does not want to receive Board books or lift-the flap books, Fables, folklore, or traditional fairytales, Poetry or mood pieces, Stories for all ages (as these ultimately are too adult oriented), Message-driven stories that are heavy-handed, didactic or pedantic.

This agency specializes in children's and teens books, and wants to find authors who are illustrators as well. "At this time, the agency is only looking for Author/Illustrators (one individual), who can both write and illustrate wonderful picture books. The author/illustrator must really know and understand the prime audience's needs and wants--the child reader! Storylines should be engaging, fun, with a hint of a life lesson and cannot be longer than 800 words." Does not want to receive Board books or lift-the flap books, Fables, folklore, or traditional fairytales, Poetry or mood pieces, Stories for all ages (as these ultimately are too adult oriented), Message-driven stories that are heavy-handed, didactic or pedantic.

How to Contact Query with SASE. Submit proposal package, 4-6 sample chapters.For children's, submit full text and 3-5 illustrations. Accepts simultaneous submissions. Responds in 2-3 weeks to queries. Responds in 3-4 weeks to mss.

Terms Agent receives 15% commission on domestic sales. Agent receives 20% commission on foreign sales. Offers written contract, binding for 1 year; 30-day notice must be given to terminate contract.

Tips "If an agent has a Web site, review it carefully to make sure your material is appropriate for that agent. Read lots of books within the genre you are writing; work hard on your writing; don't follow trends—most likely, you'll be too late."

CINE/LIT REPRESENTATION

P.O. Box 802918, Santa Clarita CA 91380-2918. (661)513-0268. Fax: (661)513-0915. E-mail: cinelit@msn.com. **Contact:** Mary Alice Kier. Member of AAR.

Member Agents Mary Alice Kier; Anna Cottle.

Represents nonfiction books, novels. "Looking for non-fiction book: mainstream, thrillers, mysteries, supernatural, horror, narrative nonfiction, environmental, adventure, biography, travel and pop culture." Does not want to receive Westerns, sci-fi or romance.

"Looking for non-fiction book: mainstream, thrillers, mysteries, supernatural, horror, narrative nonfiction, environmental, adventure, biography, travel and pop culture." Does not want to receive Westerns, sci-fi or romance.

How to Contact Send query letter with SASE.

EDWARD B. CLAFLIN LITERARY AGENCY, LLC

128 High Ave., Suite #4, Nyack NY 10960. (845)358-1084. E-mail: edclaflin@aol.com. **Contact:** Edward Claflin. Represents 30 clients. 10% of clients are new/unpublished writers.

- Prior to opening his agency, Mr. Claflin worked at Banbury Books, Rodale and Prentice Hall Press. He is the co-author of 13 books.

Represents nonfiction books. **Considers these nonfiction areas:** business, cooking, current affairs, health, history, how to, military, money, psychology, sports. This agency specializes in consumer health, narrative history, psychology/self-help and business. Actively seeking compelling and authoritative nonfiction for specific readers. Does not want to receive fiction.

This agency specializes in consumer health, narrative history, psychology/self-help and business. Actively seeking compelling and authoritative nonfiction for specific readers. Does not want to receive fiction.

How to Contact Query with synopsis, bio, SASE or e-mail attachment in Word Responds in 1 month to queries. Obtains most new clients through recommendations from others.

Terms Agent receives 15% commission on domestic sales.

WM CLARK ASSOCIATES

186 Fifth Avenue, Second Floor, New York NY 10010. (212)675-2784. Fax: (646)349-1658. Website: www.wmclark.com. Member of AAR. 50% of clients are new/unpublished writers. Currently handles: nonfiction books 50%, novels 50%.

- Prior to opening WCA, Mr. Clark was an agent at the William Morris Agency.

Represents nonfiction books, novels. **Considers these nonfiction areas:** art, biography, current affairs, ethnic, history, memoirs, music, popular culture, religion, Eastern philosophy only, science, sociology, film, translation. **Considers these fiction areas:** contemporary, ethnic, historical, literary, mainstream, Southern fiction. "Building on a reputation for moving quickly and strategically on behalf of his clients, and offering individual focus and a global presence, William Clark practices an aggressive, innovative, and broad-ranged approach to the representation of content and the talent that creates it. His clients range from authors of first fiction and award-winning bestselling narrative nonfiction, to international authors in translation, musicians, and artists."

O‑ "Building on a reputation for moving quickly and strategically on behalf of his clients, and offering individual focus and a global presence, William Clark practices an aggressive, innovative, and broad-ranged approach to the representation of content and the talent that creates it. His clients range from authors of first fiction and award-winning bestselling narrative nonfiction, to international authors in translation, musicians, and artists."

How to Contact Accepts queries via online form only at www.wmclark.com/queryguidelines.html. Responds in 1-2 months to queries.

Terms Agent receives 15% commission on domestic sales. Agent receives 20% commission on foreign sales. Offers written contract.

Tips "WCA works on a reciprocal basis with Ed Victor Ltd. (UK) in representing select properties to the US market and vice versa. Translation rights are sold directly in the German, Italian, Spanish, Portuguese, Latin American, French, Dutch, and Scandinavian territories in association with Andrew Nurnberg Associates Ltd. (UK); through offices in China, Bulgaria, Czech Republic, Latvia, Poland, Hungary, and Russia; and through corresponding agents in Japan, Greece, Israel, Turkey, Korea, Taiwan, and Thailand."

COLCHIE AGENCY, GP

324 85th St., Brooklyn NY 11209. (718)921-7468. E-mail: ColchieLit@earthlink.net. **Contact:** Thomas or Elaine Colchie. Currently handles: other 100% fiction.

Represents novels. Does not want to receive nonfiction.

O‑ Does not want to receive nonfiction.

How to Contact This listing does not take or respond to unsolicited queries or submissions.

Recent Sales *The Angel's Game*, by Carlos Ruiz Zafon (Doubleday); *As Though She Were Sleeping*, by Elias Khoury (Archipelago); *The Philosopher's Kiss*, by Peter Prange (Scribner); *The Book of God and Physics*, by Enrique Joven (Morrow); *Child's Play*, by Carmen Posadas (Harper Collins).

FRANCES COLLIN, LITERARY AGENT

P.O. Box 33, Wayne PA 19087-0033. Website: www.francescollin.com. **Contact:** Sarah Yake, Associate. Member of AAR. Represents 90 clients. 1% of clients are new/unpublished writers. Currently handles: nonfiction books 50%, fiction 50%, .

Represents nonfiction books, fiction, young adult. "We are accepting almost no new clients unless recommended by publishing professionals or current clients." Does not want to receive cookbooks, craft books, poetry, screenplays, or books for young children.

O‑ "We are accepting almost no new clients unless recommended by publishing professionals or current clients." Does not want to receive cookbooks, craft books, poetry, screenplays, or books for young children.

How to Contact Query via e-mail describing project (text in the body of the e-mail only, no attachments) to queries@francescollins.com. "Please note that all queries are reviewed by both agents." No phone or fax queries. Accepts simultaneous submissions.

Terms Agent receives 15% commission on domestic sales. Agent receives 20% commission on foreign sales. Offers written contract.

DON CONGDON ASSOCIATES INC.

156 Fifth Ave., Suite 625, New York NY 10010-7002. (212)645-1229. Fax: (212)727-2688. E-mail: dca@doncongdon.com. **Contact:** Don Congdon, Michael Congdon, Susan Ramer, Cristina Concepcion, Maura Kye-Casella, Katie Kotchman, Katie Grimm. Member of AAR. Represents 100 clients. Currently handles: nonfiction books 60%, other 40% fiction.

Represents nonfiction books, fiction. **Considers these nonfiction areas:** anthropology, biography, child, cooking, current affairs, government, health, history, humor, language, memoirs, military, music, nature, popular culture, psychology, science, film, travel, true crime, womens, creative nonfiction.

Considers these fiction areas: adventure, detective, literary, mainstream, mystery, short, thriller, womens. Especially interested in narrative nonfiction and literary fiction.

O╤ Especially interested in narrative nonfiction and literary fiction.

How to Contact Query with SASE or via e-mail (no attachments). Responds in 3 weeks to queries. Responds in 1 month to mss. Obtains most new clients through recommendations from other authors.

Terms Agent receives 15% commission on domestic sales. Agent receives 19% commission on foreign sales. Charges client for extra shipping costs, photocopying, copyright fees, book purchases.

Tips "Writing a query letter with a self-addressed stamped envelope is a must. We cannot guarantee replies to foreign queries via standard mail. No phone calls. We never download attachments to e-mail queries for security reasons, so please copy and paste material into your e-mail."

CONNOR LITERARY AGENCY

2911 W. 71st St., Minneapolis MN 55423. (612)866-1486. E-mail: connoragency@aol.com. **Contact:** Marlene Connor Lynch. Represents 50 clients. 30% of clients are new/unpublished writers. Currently handles: nonfiction books 50%, novels 50%.

- Prior to opening her agency, Ms. Connor served at the Literary Guild of America, Simon & Schuster and Random House. She is author of *Welcome to the Family: Memories of the Past for a Bright Future* (Broadway Books) and *What is Cool: Understanding Black Manhood in America* (Crown).

Member Agents Marlene Connor Lynch (all categories with an emphasis on these nonfiction areas: Child guidance/parenting; cooking/foods/nutrition; crafts/hobbies; current affairs; ethnic/cultural interests; government/politics/law; health/medicine; how-to; humor/satire; interior design/decorating; language/literature/criticism; money/finance; photography; popular culture; self-help/personal improvement; women's issues/studies; relationships. Considers these fiction areas: historical; horror; literary; mainstream/contemporary; multicultural; thriller; women's; suspense); Deborah Coker (mainstream and literary fiction, multicultural fiction, children's books, humor, politics, memoirs, narrative nonfiction, true crime/investigative); Nichole L. Shields/Chicago (multicultural fiction and nonfiction with an emphasis on African-American literature, poetry and children's content); James L. Stroud, Jr (general fiction, nonfiction, fantasy, science fiction, mystery, political thought, vegan cooking and holistic lifestyle, celebrity bios and memoirs, popular culture, multicultural subjects.

Represents nonfiction books, novels. Actively seeking mysteries.

O╤ Actively seeking mysteries.

How to Contact Query with SASE. All unsolicited mss returned unopened. Obtains most new clients through recommendations from others, conferences, grapevine.

Terms Agent receives 15% commission on domestic sales. Agent receives 25% commission on foreign sales. Offers written contract, binding for 1 year.

Recent Sales *Beautiful Hair at Any Age*, by Lisa Akbari; *12 Months of Knitting*, by Joanne Yordanou; *The Warrior Path: Confessions of a Young Lord*, by Felipe Luciano.

Writers Conferences National Writers Union, Midwest Chapter; Agents, Agents, Agents; Texas Writers' Conference; Detroit Writers' Conference; Annual Gwendolyn Brooks Writers' Conference for Literature and Creative Writing, Wisconsin Writers' Festival.

Tips "Previously published writers are preferred; new writers with national exposure or potential to have national exposure from their own efforts preferred."

THE DOE COOVER AGENCY

P.O. Box 668, Winchester MA 01890. (781)721-6000. Fax: (781)721-6727. E-mail: info@doecooveragency.com. Website: doecooveragency.com. Represents more than 100 clients. Currently handles: nonfiction books 80%, novels 20%.

Member Agents Doe Coover (general nonfiction, cooking); Colleen Mohyde (literary and commercial fiction, general and narrative nonfiction); Amanda Lewis (children's books); Frances Kennedy, associate.

Represents Considers these nonfiction areas: biography, business, cooking, gardening, health, history, science, social issues, narrative nonfiction. **Considers these fiction areas:** literary, commercial. This agency specializes in nonfiction, particularly books on history, popular science, biography, social issues, and narrative nonfiction, as well as cooking, gardening, and literary and commercial fiction. Does not want romance, fantasy, science fiction, poetry or screenplays.

O╤ This agency specializes in nonfiction, particularly books on history, popular science, biography, social issues, and narrative nonfiction, as well as cooking, gardening, and literary and commercial fiction. Does not want romance, fantasy, science fiction, poetry or screenplays.

How to Contact Query with SASE. E-mail queries are acceptable. No unsolicited mss. Accepts simultaneous submissions. Obtains most new clients through recommendations from others, solicitations.

Terms Agent receives 15% commission on domestic sales. Agent receives 10% of original advance commission on foreign sales.

Recent Sales Sold 25-30 titles in the last year. *Jacques Pepin, the Best*, by Jacques Pepin (Houghton Mifflin Harcourt); *Stonewall Kitchen* series, by Jonathan King, Jim Stott, and Kathy Gunst (Chronicle Books); *Cooking for Isaiah*, by Silvana Nardone (Reader's Digest Books); *Lucille, A Memoir*, by Suzanne Berne (Algonquin Books); *Rosemary Kennedy: The Legacy of a Life*, by Kate Larson (Houghton Mifflin Harcourt); *The Book on Cool*, by Marianne Taylor (Running Press); *Everything I Know I Learned from Children's Books*, by Anita Silvey (Roaring Brook Press); *Mean Little Deaf Queer*, by Terry Galloway (Beacon Press); *Euphemania*, by Ralph Keyes (Little, Brown). Movie/TV MOW script(s) optioned/sold: A Crime in the Neighborhood, by Suzanne Berne, Mr. White's Confession, by Robert Clark. Other clients include: WGBH, New England Aquarium, Blue Balliett, David Allen, *Gourmet*, Deborah Madison, Rick Bayless, Adria Bernardi, Paula Poundstone.

CORNERSTONE LITERARY, INC.

4525 Wilshire Blvd., Ste. 208, Los Angeles CA 90010. (323)930-6037. Fax: (323)930-0407. E-mail: info@cornerstoneliterary.com. Website: www.cornerstoneliterary.com. **Contact:** Helen Breitwieser. Member of AAR. Other memberships include Author's Guild, MWA, RWA, PEN, Poets & Writers. Represents 40 clients. 30% of clients are new/unpublished writers.

- Prior to founding her own boutique agency, Ms. Breitwieser was a literary agent at The William Morris Agency.

Represents novels. **Considers these fiction areas:** glitz, detective, erotica, ethnic, family, historical, literary, mainstream, multicultural, mystery, romance, thriller, womens. "We are not taking new clients at this time. We do not respond to unsolicited e-mail inquiries. All unsolicited manuscripts will be returned unopened." Does not want to receive science fiction, Western, poetry, screenplays, fantasy, gay/lesbian, horror, self-help, psychology, business or diet.

O→ "We are not taking new clients at this time. We do not respond to unsolicited e-mail inquiries. All unsolicited manuscripts will be returned unopened." Does not want to receive science fiction, Western, poetry, screenplays, fantasy, gay/lesbian, horror, self-help, psychology, business or diet.

How to Contact Obtains most new clients through recommendations from others.

Terms Agent receives 15% commission on domestic sales. Agent receives 20% commission on foreign sales. Offers written contract, binding for 1 year; 2-month notice must be given to terminate contract.

CRAWFORD LITERARY AGENCY

92 Evans Road, Barnstead NH 03218. (603)269-5851. Fax: (603)269-2533. E-mail: crawfordlit@att.net. **Contact:** Susan Crawford. Winter Office: 3920 Bayside Rd., Fort Myers Beach FL 33931. (239)463-4651. Fax: (239)463-0125.

Represents nonfiction books, novels. This agency specializes in celebrity and/or media-based books and authors. Actively seeking action/adventure stories, medical thrillers, self-help, inspirational, how-to, and women's issues. No short stories, or poetry.

O→ This agency specializes in celebrity and/or media-based books and authors. Actively seeking action/adventure stories, medical thrillers, self-help, inspirational, how-to, and women's issues. No short stories, or poetry.

How to Contact Query with SASE. Accepts simultaneous submissions. Obtains most new clients through recommendations from others, solicitations, conferences.

Terms Agent receives 15% commission on domestic sales. Agent receives 20% commission on foreign sales. Offers written contract.

Recent Sales *The New Etiquette of Divorce*, by Tonja Weimer; *Partners in Crime*, by Julie Koca; *The Golden Temple*, by Mingmei Yip; *Untitled Memoir*, by John Travolta, *Final Finesse*, by Karna Bodman; *Skin Deep*, by Gary Braver.

Writers Conferences International Film & Television Workshops; Maui Writers Conference; Emerson College Conference; Suncoast Writers Conference; San Diego Writers Conference; Simmons College Writers Conference; Cape Cod Writers Conference; Writers Retreats on Maui Writers Alaskan Cruise; Western Caribbean Cruise and Fiji Island.

Tips "Keep learning to improve your craft. Attend conferences and network."

THE CREATIVE CULTURE, INC.

47 E. 19th St., Third Floor, New York NY 10003. (212)680-3510. Fax: (212)680-3509. Website: www.thecreativeculture.com. **Contact:** Debra Goldstein. Estab. 1998. Member of AAR.

- Prior to opening her agency, Ms. Goldstein and Ms. Gerwin were agents at the William Morris Agency; Ms. Naples was a senior editor at Simon & Schuster.

Member Agents Debra Goldstein (self-help, creativity, fitness, inspiration, lifestyle); Mary Ann Naples (health/nutrition, lifestyle, narrative nonfiction, practical nonfiction, literary fiction, animals/vegetarianism); Laura Nolan (literary fiction, parenting, self-help, psychology, women's studies, current affairs, science); Karen Gerwin; Matthew Elblonk (literary fiction, humor, pop culture, music and young adult. Interests also include commercial fiction, narrative non-fiction, science, and he is always on the lookout for something slightly quirky or absurd).

Represents nonfiction books, novels. Does not want to receive children's, poetry, screenplays or science fiction.

O→ Does not want to receive children's, poetry, screenplays or science fiction.

How to Contact Query with bio, book description, 5-7 sample pages (fiction only), SASE. We only reply if interested. Responds in 2 months to queries.

CREATIVE TRUST, INC.

5141 Virginia Way, Suite 320, Brentwood TN 37027. 615-297-5010. Fax: 615-297-5020. E-mail: info@creativetrust.com. Website: www.creativetrust.com/. Currently handles: novella Graphic Novels, movie scripts, multimedia, other Video Scripts.

Member Agents Dan Raines, President.

How to Contact "Creative Trust Literary Group does not accept unsolicited manuscripts or book proposals from unpublished authors. We do accept unsolicited inquiries from previously published authors under the following requisites: email inquiries only, which must not be accompanied by attachments of any kind. If we're interested, we'll e-mail you an invitation to submit additional materials and instructions on how to do so."

CRICHTON & ASSOCIATES

6940 Carroll Ave., Takoma Park MD 20912. (301)495-9663. Fax: (202)318-0050. E-mail: query@crichton-associates.com. Website: www.crichton-associates.com. **Contact:** Sha-Shana Crichton. 90% of clients are new/unpublished writers. Currently handles: nonfiction books 20%, novels 80%.

- Prior to becoming an agent, Ms. Crichton did commercial litigation for a major law firm.

Represents nonfiction books, novels. **Considers these nonfiction areas:** child, ethnic, gay, government, true crime, womens, Caribbean, Hispanic and Latin-American studies, African-American studies. **Considers these fiction areas:** ethnic, feminist, literary, mainstream, mystery, religious, romance. Actively seeking women's fiction, romance, and chick lit. Looking also for multicultural fiction and nonfiction. Does not want to receive poetry.

O→ Actively seeking women's fiction, romance, and chick lit. Looking also for multicultural fiction and nonfiction. Does not want to receive poetry.

How to Contact For fiction, include short synopsis and first 3 chapters with query. Send no e-attachments. For nonfiction, send a book proposal. Responds in 3-5 weeks to queries.

Terms Agent receives 15% commission on domestic sales. Agent receives 20% commission on foreign sales. Offers written contract, binding for 45 days. Only charges fees for postage and photocopying.

Recent Sales *Driven*, by Eve Kenin (Dorchester); *His Dark Prince*, by Eve Silver (Kensington); *Demon Kiss*, by Eve Silver (Warner); *Wish Club*, by Kim Strickland (Crown); *How to Salsa In a Sari*, by Dona Sakar (Kimani TRU); *My Soul Cries Out*, by Sherri Lewis (Urban Christian), *Dead Broke*, by Trista Russell (Simon & Schuster); *Give Me More*, by PJ Mellor (Kensington); *Spirit of our Ancestors*, by Natalie Robertson (Praeger). Other clients include Dirk Gibson, Kimberley White, Beverley Long, Jessica Trap, Altonya Washington, Ann Christopher.

Writers Conferences Silicon Valley RWA; BookExpo America.

THE MARY CUNNANE AGENCY

PO Box 336, Bermagui, NSW 2546, Australia. Website: www.cunnaneagency.com.

Member Agents Mary Cunnane: mary@cunnaneagency.com; Isobel Wightman: isobel@cunnaneagency.com.

Represents This agency does not work with North American authors.

O→ This agency does not work with North American authors.

RICHARD CURTIS ASSOCIATES, INC.

171 E. 74th St., New York NY 10021. (212)772-7363. Fax: (212)772-7393. Website: www.curtisagency.com. Signatory of WGA. Other memberships include RWA, MWA, SFWA. Represents 100 clients. 1% of clients are new/unpublished writers. Currently handles: nonfiction books 50%, other 50% genre fiction.

- Prior to opening his agency, Mr. Curtis was an agent with the Scott Meredith Literary Agency for seven years. He has also authored more than 50 published books.

Represents Considers these nonfiction areas: biography, business, health, history, science.

How to Contact Send 1-page query letter and no more than a 5-page synopsis. Don't send ms unless specifically requested. If requested, submission must be accompanied by a SASE. Responds in 6 weeks to queries.

Terms Agent receives 15% commission on domestic sales. Agent receives 25% commission on foreign sales. Offers written contract. Charges for photocopying, express mail, international freight, book orders.

Recent Sales Sold 100 titles in the last year. *Pendragon*, by DJ MacHale; *City at the End of Time*, by Greg Bear; *White Wicca, Black Curse*, by Kim Harrison; *Crave*, by Cynthia Bulik.

Writers Conferences SFWA Conference; HWA Conference; RWA National Conference.

JAMES R. CYPHER, THE CYPHER AGENCY

816 Wolcott Ave., Beacon NY 12508-4261. Phone/Fax: (845)831-5677. E-mail: jim@jimcypher.com. Website: www.jimcypher.com. **Contact:** James R. Cypher. Member of AAR. Other memberships include Authors Guild. Represents 23 clients. 56% of clients are new/unpublished writers. Currently handles: nonfiction books 100%.

- Prior to opening his agency, Mr. Cypher worked as a corporate public relations manager for a Fortune 500 multi-national computer company for 28 years.

Represents nonfiction books. **Considers these nonfiction areas:** current affairs, health, history, memoirs, popular culture, science, sports, NASCAR, golf, baseball, true crime, biography. This agent is semi-retired, and taking on few new clients. Does not want to receive humor, sewing, computer books, children's, gardening, cookbooks, spiritual, religious, or New Age topics.

O→ This agent is semi-retired, and taking on few new clients. Does not want to receive humor, sewing, computer books, children's, gardening, cookbooks, spiritual, religious, or New Age topics.

How to Contact Query with SASE. Submit proposal package. Accepts e-mail queries, though proposals should be sent snail mail with envelope/postage. Accepts simultaneous submissions. Responds in 2 weeks to queries. Responds in 6 weeks to mss. Obtains most new clients through recommendations from others, conferences, networking on online computer service.

Terms Agent receives 15% commission on domestic sales. Agent receives 20% commission on foreign sales. Offers written contract; 1-month notice must be given to terminate contract.

D4EO LITERARY AGENCY

7 Indian Valley Road, Weston CT 06883. (203)544-7180. Fax: (203)544-7160. E-mail: d4eo@optonline.net. **Contact:** Bob Diforio. Represents more than 100 clients. 50% of clients are new/unpublished writers. Currently handles: nonfiction books 70%, novels 25%, juvenile books 5%.

- Prior to opening his agency, Mr. Diforio was a publisher.

Represents nonfiction books, novels. **Considers these nonfiction areas:** juvenile, art, biography, business, child, current affairs, gay, health, history, how to, humor, memoirs, military, money, psychology, religion, science, self help, sports, true crime, womens. **Considers these fiction areas:** adventure, detective, erotica, historical, horror, humor, juvenile, literary, mainstream, mystery, picture books, romance, science, sports, thriller, western, young.

How to Contact Query with SASE. Accepts and prefers e-mail queries. Prefers to read material exclusively. Responds in 1 week to queries. Obtains most new clients through recommendations from others.

Terms Agent receives 15% commission on domestic sales. Agent receives 25% commission on foreign sales. Offers written contract, binding for 2 years; 60-day notice must be given to terminate contract. Charges for photocopying and submission postage.

LAURA DAIL LITERARY AGENCY, INC.

350 Seventh Ave., Suite 2003, New York NY 10010. (212)239-7477. Fax: (212)947-0460. E-mail: queries@ldlainc.com. Website: www.ldlainc.com. Member of AAR.

Member Agents Talia Rosenblatt Cohen; Laura Dail; Tamar Ellman.

Represents nonfiction books, novels. "Due to the volume of queries and manuscripts received, we apologize for not answering every e-mail and letter. Specializes in historical, literary and some young adult fiction, as well as both practical and idea-driven nonfiction."

O→ "Due to the volume of queries and manuscripts received, we apologize for not answering every e-mail and letter. Specializes in historical, literary and some young adult fiction, as well as both practical and idea-driven nonfiction."

How to Contact Query with SASE or e-mail. This agency prefers e-queries. Include the word "query" in the subject line.

DANIEL LITERARY GROUP

1701 Kingsbury Drive, Suite 100, Nashville TN 37215. (615)730-8207. E-mail: submissions@danielliterarygroup.com. Website: www.danielliterarygroup.com. **Contact:** Greg Daniel. Represents 45 clients. 30% of clients are new/unpublished writers. Currently handles: nonfiction books 85%, novels 15%.

- Prior to becoming an agent, Mr. Daniel spent 10 years in publishing - six at the executive level at Thomas Nelson Publishers.

Represents nonfiction books, novels. **Considers these nonfiction areas:** biography, business, child, current affairs, health, history, how to, humor, memoirs, nature, popular culture, religion, self help, sports, film, womens. **Considers these fiction areas:** contemporary, adventure, detective, family, historical, humor, literary, mainstream, mystery, religious, thriller, The agency currently accepts all fiction topics, except for children's, romance and sci-fi."We take pride in our ability to come alongside our authors and help strategize about where they want their writing to take them in both the near and long term. Forging close relationships with our authors, we help them with such critical factors as editorial refinement, branding, audience, and marketing." Nonfiction. The agency is open to submissions in almost every popular category of nonfiction, especially if authors are recognized experts in their fields. No screenplays, poetry or short stories.

"We take pride in our ability to come alongside our authors and help strategize about where they want their writing to take them in both the near and long term. Forging close relationships with our authors, we help them with such critical factors as editorial refinement, branding, audience, and marketing." Nonfiction. The agency is open to submissions in almost every popular category of nonfiction, especially if authors are recognized experts in their fields. No screenplays, poetry or short stories.

How to Contact Query via e-mail only. Submit publishing history, author bio, brief synopsis of work, key selling points. E-queries only. Send no attachments. For fiction, send first 5 pages pasted in e-mail. Responds in 2-3 weeks to queries.

CAROLINE DAVIDSON LITERARY AGENCY

5 Queen Anne's Gardens, London England W4 ITU United Kingdom. (44)(208)995-5768. Fax: (44) (208)994-2770. E-mail: caroline@cdla.co.uk. Website: www.cdla.co.uk. **Contact:** Caroline Davidson.

Represents nonfiction books, serious material only, novels. Does not consider autobiographies, chick lit, children's, crime, erotica, fantasy, horror, local history, murder mysteries, occult, self-help, short stories, sci-fi, thrillers, individual short stories, or memoir.

Does not consider autobiographies, chick lit, children's, crime, erotica, fantasy, horror, local history, murder mysteries, occult, self-help, short stories, sci-fi, thrillers, individual short stories, or memoir.

How to Contact Query with SASE. See website for additional details and what to include for fiction and nonfiction. Responds in 2 weeks to queries. Obtains most new clients through recommendations from others, solicitations.

Tips "Visit our Web site before submitting any work to us."

DAVIS WAGER LITERARY AGENCY

419 N. Larchmont Blvd., #317, Los Angeles CA 90004. (323)383-2974. E-mail: submissions@daviswager.com. Website: www.daviswager.com. **Contact:** Timothy Wager.

- Prior to his current position, Mr. Wager was with the Sandra Dijkstra Literary Agency, where he worked as a reader and associate agent.

Represents nonfiction books, novels. **Considers these fiction areas:** literary. Actively seeking: literary fiction and general-interest nonfiction.

Actively seeking: literary fiction and general-interest nonfiction.

How to Contact Query with SASE. Submit author bio, synopsis for fiction, book proposal or outline for nonfiction. Query via e-mail. No author queries by phone.

LIZA DAWSON ASSOCIATES

350 Seventh Ave., Ste. 2003, New York NY 10001. (212)465-9071. Fax: (212)947-0460. Website: www.lizadawsonassociates.com. Member of AAR. Other memberships include MWA, Women's Media Group. Represents 50+ clients. 15% of clients are new/unpublished writers. Currently handles: nonfiction books 60%, novels 40%.

- Prior to becoming an agent, Ms. Dawson was an editor for 20 years, spending 11 years at William Morrow as vice president and 2 years at Putnam as executive editor. Ms. Bladell was a senior editor at HarperCollins and Avon. Ms. Miller is an *Essence*-bestselling author and niche publisher. Ms. Olswanger is an author.

Member Agents Liza Dawson (plot-driven literary fiction, historicals, thrillers, suspense, parenting books, history, psychology (both popular and clinical), politics, narrative nonfiction and memoirs) Caitlin Blasdell (science fiction, fantasy (both adult and young adult), parenting, business, thrillers and women's fiction) Anna Olswanger (gift books for adults, young adult fiction and nonfiction, children's illustrated books, and Judaica) Havis Dawson (business books, how-to and practical books, spirituality, fantasy, Southern-culture fiction and military memoirs); David Austern (fiction and nonfiction, with an interest in young adult, pop culture, sports, and male-interest works).

Represents nonfiction books, novels, novels and gift books (Olswanger only). **Considers these nonfiction areas:** biography, health, history, memoirs, psychology, sociology, womens, politics; business; parenting. **Considers these fiction areas:** fantasy, Blasdell only, historical, literary, mystery, regional, science, Blasdell only, thriller, African-American (Miller only). "This agency specializes in readable literary fiction, thrillers, mainstream historicals, women's fiction, academics, historians, business, journalists and psychology."

- "This agency specializes in readable literary fiction, thrillers, mainstream historicals, women's fiction, academics, historians, business, journalists and psychology."

How to Contact Query only with SASE. Individual query e-mails are query[agentfirstname]@lizadawsonassociates.com. Responds in 3 weeks to queries. Responds in 6 weeks to mss. Obtains most new clients through recommendations from others, conferences.

Terms Agent receives 15% commission on domestic sales. Agent receives 20% commission on foreign sales. Offers written contract. Charges clients for photocopying and overseas postage.

THE JENNIFER DECHIARA LITERARY AGENCY

31 East 32nd St., Suite 300, New York NY 10016. (212)481-8484. E-mail: jenndec@aol.com. Website: www.jdlit.com. **Contact:** Jennifer DeChiara, Stephen Fraser. Represents 100 clients. 50% of clients are new/unpublished writers. Currently handles: nonfiction books 25%, novels 25%, juvenile books 50%.

- Prior to becoming an agent, Ms. DeChiara was a writing consultant, freelance editor at Simon & Schuster and Random House, and a ballerina and an actress.

Represents nonfiction books, novels, juvenile. **Considers these nonfiction areas:** crafts, interior, juvenile, biography, child, cooking, current affairs, education, ethnic, gay, government, health, history, how to, humor, language, memoirs, military, money, music, nature, photography, popular culture, psychology, science, self help, sociology, sports, film, true crime, womens, celebrity biography. **Considers these fiction areas:** confession, detective, ethnic, family, fantasy, feminist, gay, historical, horror, humor, juvenile, literary, mainstream, mystery, picture books, regional, sports, thriller, young, chick lit; psychic/supernatural; glitz. "We represent both children's and adult books in a wide range of ages and genres. We are a full-service agency and fulfill the potential of every book in every possible medium--stage, film, television, etc. We help writers every step of the way, from creating book ideas to editing and promotion. We are passionate about helping writers further their careers, but are just as eager to discover new talent, regardless of age or lack of prior publishing experience. This agency is committed to managing a writer's entire career. For us, it's not just about selling books, but about making dreams come true. We are especially attracted to the downtrodden, the discouraged, and the downright disgusted." Actively seeking literary fiction, chick lit, young adult fiction, self-help, pop culture, and celebrity biographies. Does not want westerns, poetry, or short stories.

- "We represent both children's and adult books in a wide range of ages and genres. We are a full-service agency and fulfill the potential of every book in every possible medium--stage, film, television, etc. We help writers every step of the way, from creating book ideas to editing and promotion. We are passionate about helping writers further their careers, but are just as eager to discover new talent, regardless of age or lack of prior publishing experience. This agency is committed to managing a writer's entire career. For us, it's not just about selling books, but about making dreams come true. We are especially attracted to the downtrodden, the discouraged, and the downright disgusted." Actively seeking literary fiction, chick lit, young adult fiction, self-help, pop culture, and celebrity biographies. Does not want westerns, poetry, or short stories.

How to Contact Query with SASE. Accepts simultaneous submissions. Responds in 3-6 months to queries. Responds in 3-6 months to mss. Obtains most new clients through recommendations from others, conferences, query letters.

Terms Agent receives 15% commission on domestic sales. Agent receives 20% commission on foreign sales. Offers written contract.

Recent Sales Sold over 100 titles in the past year. *The Chosen One*, by Carol Lynch Williams (St. Martin's Press); *The 30-Day Heartbreak Cure*, by Catherine Hickland (Simon & Schuster); *Naptime for Barney*, by Danny Sit (Sterling Publishing); *The Screwed-Up Life of Charlie the Second*, by Drew Ferguson (Kensington); *Heart of a Shepherd*, by Rosanne Parry (Random House); *Carolina Harmony*, by Marilyn Taylor McDowell (Random House); *Project Sweet Life*, by Brent Hartinger (HarperCollins). Movie/TV MOW scripts optioned/sold: *The Elf on the Shelf*, by Carol Aebersold and Chanda Bell (Waddell & Scorsese); *Heart of a Shepherd*, by Rosanne Parry (Tashtego Films); *Geography Club*, by Brent Hartinger (The Levy Leder Company). Other clients include Sylvia Browne, Matthew Kirby, Sonia Levitin, Susan Anderson, Michael Apostolina.

DEFIORE & CO.

47 E. 19th St., 3rd Floor, New York NY 10003. (212)925-7744. Fax: (212)925-9803. E-mail: info@defioreandco.com. Website: www.defioreandco.com. **Contact:** Lauren Gilchrist. Member of AAR. Represents 75 clients. 50% of clients are new/unpublished writers. Currently handles: nonfiction books 70%, novels 30%.

- Prior to becoming an agent, Mr. DeFiore was publisher of Villard Books (1997-1998), editor-in-chief of Hyperion (1992-1997), and editorial director of Delacorte Press (1988-1992).

Member Agents Brian DeFiore (popular nonfiction, business, pop culture, parenting, commercial fiction); Laurie Abkemeier (memoir, parenting, business, how-to/self-help, popular science).

Represents nonfiction books, novels. **Considers these nonfiction areas:** young, and middle grade, biography, business, child, cooking, money, multicultural, popular culture, psychology, religion, self help, sports. **Considers these fiction areas:** ethnic, literary, mainstream, mystery, thriller. "Please be advised that we are not considering children's picture books, poetry, adult science fiction and fantasy, romance, or dramatic projects at this time."

"Please be advised that we are not considering children's picture books, poetry, adult science fiction and fantasy, romance, or dramatic projects at this time."

How to Contact Query with SASE or e-mail to submissions@defioreandco.com. Accepts simultaneous submissions. Responds in 3 weeks to queries. Responds in 2 months to mss. Obtains most new clients through recommendations from others.

Terms Agent receives 15% commission on domestic sales. Agent receives 20% commission on foreign sales. Offers written contract; 10-day notice must be given to terminate contract. Charges clients for photocopying and overnight delivery (deducted only after a sale is made).

Writers Conferences Maui Writers Conference; Pacific Northwest Writers Conference; North Carolina Writers' Network Fall Conference.

JOELLE DELBOURGO ASSOCIATES, INC.

516 Bloomfield Ave., Suite 5, Montclair NJ 07042. (973)783-6800. Fax: (973)783-6802. E-mail: info@delbourgo.com. Website: www.delbourgo.com. **Contact:** Joelle Delbourgo, Molly Lyons. Represents more than 100 clients. Currently handles: nonfiction books 75%, novels 25%.

- Prior to becoming an agent, Ms. Delbourgo was an editor and senior publishing executive at HarperCollins and Random House.

Member Agents Joelle Delbourgo (parenting, self-help, psychology, business, serious nonfiction, narrative nonfiction, quality fiction); Molly Lyons (practical and narrative nonfiction, popular culture, memoir, quality fiction).

Represents nonfiction books, novels. **Considers these nonfiction areas:** biography, business, child, cooking, current affairs, education, ethnic, gay, government, health, history, how to, money, nature, popular culture, psychology, religion, science, self help, sociology, true crime, womens, New Age/metaphysics, interior design/decorating. **Considers these fiction areas:** historical, literary, mainstream, mystery. "We are former publishers and editors, with deep knowledge and an insider perspective. We have a reputation for individualized attention to clients, strategic management of authors' careers, and creating strong partnerships with publishers for our clients." Actively seeking history, narrative nonfiction, science/medicine, memoir, literary fiction, psychology, parenting, biographies, current affairs, politics, young adult fiction and nonfiction. Does not want to receive genre fiction or screenplays.

"We are former publishers and editors, with deep knowledge and an insider perspective. We have a reputation for individualized attention to clients, strategic management of authors' careers, and creating strong partnerships with publishers for our clients." Actively seeking history, narrative nonfiction, science/medicine, memoir, literary fiction, psychology, parenting, biographies, current affairs, politics, young adult fiction and nonfiction. Does not want to receive genre fiction or screenplays.

How to Contact Query with SASE. Accepts simultaneous submissions. Responds in 3 weeks to queries. Responds in 2 months to mss.

Terms Agent receives 15% commission on domestic sales. Agent receives 20% commission on foreign sales. Offers written contract. Charges clients for postage and photocopying.

Recent Sales *Amen, Amen*, by Abby Sher (Scribner/Simon & Schuster); *Talk to Me Like I'm Someone You Love*, by Nancy Dreyfus, PsyD (Tarcher/Penguin); *Sneaky Chef 4*, by Missy Chase Lapine (Running Press); *Lessons from the Fat-O-Sphere*, by Kate Harding and Marianne Kirby (Perigee/Penguin); *The Gift of Neurodiversity*, by Thomas Armstrong, MD (Da Capo); *Retirement Heist*, by Ellen E. Schultz (Portfolio); *Summer Shift*, by Lynn Bonasia (Touchstone Fireside).

Tips "Do your homework. Do not cold call. Read and follow submission guidelines before contacting us. Do not call to find out if we received your material. No e-mail queries. Treat agents with respect, as you would any other professional, such as a doctor, lawyer or financial advisor."

DH LITERARY, INC.

P.O. Box 805, Nyack NY 10960-0990. E-mail: dhendin@aol.com. **Contact:** David Hendin.Member of AAR. Represents 10 clients. Currently handles: nonfiction books 80%, novels 10%, scholarly books 10%.

- Prior to opening his agency, Mr. Hendin served as president and publisher for Pharos Books/World Almanac, as well as senior VP and COO at sister company United Feature Syndicate.

Represents "We are not accepting new clients. Please do not send queries or submissions."

"We are not accepting new clients. Please do not send queries or submissions."

Terms Agent receives 15% commission on domestic sales. Agent receives 20% commission on foreign sales. Offers written contract, binding for 1 year. Charges for out-of-pocket expenses for overseas postage specifically related to the sale.

Recent Sales *Miss Manners Guide to a Surprisingly Dignified Wedding*, by Judith and Jacobina Martin (Norton); *Killer Cuts*, by Elaine Viets (NAL/Signet); *The New Time Travelers*, by David Toomey (Norton).

DHS LITERARY, INC.

10711 Preston Road, Suite 100, Dallas TX 75230. (214)363-4422. Fax: (214)363-4423. Website: www.dhsliterary.com. **Contact:** David Hale Smith, president.Represents 35 clients. 15% of clients are new/unpublished writers. Currently handles: nonfiction books 60%, novels 40%.

- Prior to opening his agency, Mr. Smith was an agent at Dupree/Miller & Associates.

Represents nonfiction books, novels. **Considers these nonfiction areas:** biography, business, child, cooking, current affairs, ethnic, popular culture, sports, true crime. **Considers these fiction areas:** detective, ethnic, literary, mainstream, mystery, thriller, western. This agency is not actively seeking clients and usually takes clients on by referral only.

O→ This agency is not actively seeking clients and usually takes clients on by referral only.

How to Contact Only responds if interested. *No unsolicited mss.*

Terms Agent receives 15% commission on domestic sales. Agent receives 25% commission on foreign sales. Offers written contract; 10-day notice must be given to terminate contract. This agency charges for postage and photocopying.

Recent Sales Safer, by Sean Doolittle; Person of Interest, by Theresa Schwegel; Monday Morning Choices, by David Cottrell

Tips "Remember to be courteous and professional, and to treat marketing your work and approaching an agent as you would any formal business matter. If you have a referral, always query first via e-mail. Sorry, but we cannot respond to queries sent via mail, even with a SASE. Visit our Web site for more information."

SANDRA DIJKSTRA LITERARY AGENCY

1155 Camino del Mar, PMB 515, Del Mar CA 92014. (858)755-3115. Fax: (858)794-2822. E-mail: sdla@dijkstraagency.com. Website: www.dijkstraagency.com. Member of AAR. Other memberships include Authors Guild, PEN West, Poets and Editors, MWA. Represents 100+ clients. 30% of clients are new/unpublished writers. Currently handles: nonfiction books 50%, novels 45%, juvenile books 5%.

Represents nonfiction books, novels. **Considers these nonfiction areas:** americana, juvenile, animals, pets, anthropology, business, cooking, ethnic, gay, government, health, history, language, memoirs, military, money, nature, psychology, regional, religion, science, self help, sociology, travel, womens, Asian studies; art; accounting; biography; environmental studies; technology; transportation. **Considers these fiction areas:** erotica, ethnic, fantasy, juvenile, YA, middle grade, literary, mainstream, mystery, science, thriller, graphic novels. Does not want to receive Western, screenplays, short story collections or poetry.

O→ Does not want to receive Western, screenplays, short story collections or poetry.

How to Contact Submit for fiction, send brief synopsis and 50 sample pages double-spaced and single-sided, SASE. Does not accept e-mail queries. Responds in 6 weeks to queries. Obtains most new clients through recommendations from others, solicitations, conferences.

Terms Agent receives 15% commission on domestic sales. Agent receives 20% commission on foreign sales. Offers written contract. Charges clients for expenses for foreign postage and copying costs if a client requests a hard copy submission to publishers.

Tips Be professional and learn the standard procedures for submitting your work. Be a regular patron of bookstores, and study what kind of books are being published and will appear on the shelves next to yours. Read! Check out your local library and bookstores—you'll find lots of books on writing and the publishing industry that will help you. At conferences, ask published writers about their agents. Don't believe the myth that an agent has to be in New York to be successful. We've already disproved it!

THE JONATHAN DOLGER AGENCY

49 E. 96th St., Suite 9B, New York NY 10128. Fax: (212)369-7118. Member of AAR.

Represents nonfiction books, novels. **Considers these nonfiction areas:** biography, history, womens, cultural/social. **Considers these fiction areas:** womens, commercial.

How to Contact Query with SASE. No e-mail queries.

Terms Agent receives 15% commission on domestic sales. Agent receives 25% commission on foreign sales.

Tips "Writers must have been previously published if submitting fiction. We prefer to work with published/established authors, and work with a small number of new/previously unpublished writers."

DONADIO & OLSON, INC.

121 W. 27th St., Suite 704, New York NY 10001. (212)691-8077. Fax: (212)633-2837. E-mail: mail@

donadio.com. **Contact:** Neil Olson. Member of AAR.
Member Agents Neil Olson (no queries); Edward Hibbert (no queries); Carrie Howland (query via snail mail or e-mail).
Represents nonfiction books, novels. This agency represents mostly fiction, and is very selective.
O→ This agency represents mostly fiction, and is very selective.
How to Contact Query by snail mail is preferred; for e-mail use mail@donadio.com; only send submissions to open agents. Obtains most new clients through recommendations from others.

JANIS A. DONNAUD & ASSOCIATES, INC.

525 Broadway, Second Floor, New York NY 10012. (212)431-2664. Fax: (212)431-2667. E-mail: jdonnaud@aol.com; donnaudassociate@aol.com. **Contact:** Janis A. Donnaud. Member of AAR. Signatory of WGA. Represents 40 clients. 5% of clients are new/unpublished writers. Currently handles: nonfiction books 100%.

- Prior to opening her agency, Ms. Donnaud was vice president and associate publisher of Random House Adult Trade Group.

Represents nonfiction books. **Considers these nonfiction areas:** biography, child, cooking, current affairs, health, humor, psychology, pop, womens, lifestyle. This agency specializes in health, medical, cooking, humor, pop psychology, narrative nonfiction, biography, parenting, and current affairs. We give a lot of service and attention to clients. Does not want to receive "fiction, poetry, mysteries, juvenile books, romances, science fiction, young adult, religious or fantasy."
O→ This agency specializes in health, medical, cooking, humor, pop psychology, narrative nonfiction, biography, parenting, and current affairs. We give a lot of service and attention to clients. Does not want to receive "fiction, poetry, mysteries, juvenile books, romances, science fiction, young adult, religious or fantasy."
How to Contact Query with SASE. Submit description of book, 2-3 pages of sample material.Prefers to read materials exclusively. No phone calls. Responds in 1 month to queries. Responds in 1 month to mss. Obtains most new clients through recommendations from others.
Terms Agent receives 15% commission on domestic sales. Agent receives 20% commission on foreign sales. Agent receives 20% commission on film sales. Offers written contract; 1-month notice must be given to terminate contract. Charges clients for messengers, photocopying and purchase of books.
Recent Sales Paula Deen's *The Deen Family Cookbook*; Mark Lach's *If Only I Knew I Would Live This Long*.

JIM DONOVAN LITERARY

4515 Prentice St., Suite 109, Dallas TX 75206. E-mail: jdlqueries@sbcglobal.net. **Contact:** Melissa Shultz, agent. Represents 30 clients. 10% of clients are new/unpublished writers. Currently handles: nonfiction books 75%, novels 25%.
Member Agents Jim Donovan (history--particularly American, military and Western; biography; sports; popular reference; popular culture; fiction--literary, thrillers and mystery); Melissa Shultz (chick lit, parenting, women's issues, memoir).
Represents nonfiction books, novels. **Considers these nonfiction areas:** biography, business, child, current affairs, government, health, history, how to, memoirs, military, money, music, nature, popular culture, sports, true crime, womens. **Considers these fiction areas:** adventure, detective, literary, mainstream, mystery, thriller, womens. This agency specializes in commercial fiction and nonfiction. "Does not want to receive poetry, children's, short stories, inspirational or anything else not listed above."
O→ This agency specializes in commercial fiction and nonfiction. "Does not want to receive poetry, children's, short stories, inspirational or anything else not listed above."
How to Contact For nonfiction, send query letter and SASE. For fiction, send 3 sample chapters, synopsis, SASE. Responds to e-queries only if interested. Accepts simultaneous submissions. Responds in 3 weeks to queries. Responds in 1 month to mss. Obtains most new clients through recommendations from others.
Terms Agent receives 15% commission on domestic sales. Agent receives 20% commission on foreign sales. Offers written contract, binding for 1 year; 30-day notice must be given to terminate contract. This agency charges for things such as overnight delivery and manuscript copying. Charges are discussed beforehand.
Recent Sales Sold 27 titles in the last year. *Born to Be Hurt*, by Sam Staggs (St. Martin's Press); *To Hell on a Fast Horse*, by Mark Gardner (Morrow); *The Last Gunfight*, by Jeff Guinn (Simon and Schuster); *Resurrection*, by Jim Dent (St. Martin's Press)
Tips "Get published in short form--magazine reviews, journals, etc. first. This will increase your credibility considerably, and make it much easier to sell a full-length book."

DOYEN LITERARY SERVICES, INC.

1931 660th St., Newell IA 50568-7613. (712)272-3300. Website: www.barbaradoyen.com. **Contact:**

(Ms.) B.J. Doyen, president. Represents over 100 clients. 20% of clients are new/unpublished writers. Currently handles: nonfiction books 95%, novels 5%.

- Prior to opening her agency, Ms. Doyen worked as a published author, teacher, guest speaker, and wrote and appeared in her own weekly TV show airing in 7 states. She is also the co-author of *The Everything Guide to Writing a Book Proposal* (Adams 2005) and *The Everything Guide to Getting Published* (Adams 2006).

Represents nonfiction books, novels. **Considers these nonfiction areas:** agriculture horticulture, americana, crafts, interior, newage, young, animals, anthropology, art, biography, business, child, computers, cooking, current affairs, education, ethnic, gardening, government, health, history, how to, language, memoirs, military, money, multicultural, music, nature, philosophy, photography, popular culture, psychology, recreation, regional, religion, science, self help, sex, sociology, software, spirituality, film, travel, true crime, womens, creative nonfiction. **Considers these fiction areas:** family, historical, literary, mainstream. This agency specializes in nonfiction and occasionally handles mainstream fiction for adults. Actively seeking business, health, how-to, self-help--all kinds of adult nonfiction suitable for the major trade publishers. Does not want to receive pornography, children's books, or poetry.

O→ This agency specializes in nonfiction and occasionally handles mainstream fiction for adults. Actively seeking business, health, how-to, self-help--all kinds of adult nonfiction suitable for the major trade publishers. Does not want to receive pornography, children's books, or poetry.

How to Contact Query with SASE or "you can submit an e-mail via Web site as well. Include background info. Send no unsolicited samples. Accepts simultaneous submissions. Responds immediately to queries. Responds in 3 weeks to mss.

Terms Agent receives 15% commission on domestic sales. Agent receives 20% commission on foreign sales. Offers written contract, binding for 2 years.

Recent Sales *The Complete Idiot's Guide to Playing the Fiddle*, by Ellery Klein; *Healthy Aging for Dummies*, by Brent Agin, M.D. and Sharon Perkins, R.N.

Tips "Our authors receive personalized attention. We market aggressively, undeterred by rejection. We get the best possible publishing contracts. We are very interested in nonfiction book ideas at this time and will consider most topics. Many writers come to us from referrals, but we also get quite a few who initially approach us with query letters. Do not call us regarding queries. It is best if you do not collect editorial rejections prior to seeking an agent, but if you do, be upfront and honest about it. Do not submit your manuscript to more than 1 agent at a time--querying first can save you (and us) much time. We're open to established or beginning writers--just send us a terrific letter!"

DUNHAM LITERARY, INC.

156 Fifth Ave., Suite 625, New York NY 10010-7002. (212)929-0994. Website: www.dunhamlit.com. **Contact:** Jennie Dunham. Member of AAR. Represents 50 clients. 15% of clients are new/unpublished writers. Currently handles: nonfiction books 25%, novels 25%, juvenile books 50%.

- Prior to opening her agency, Ms. Dunham worked as a literary agent for Russell & Volkening. The Rhoda Weyr Agency is now a division of Dunham Literary, Inc.

Represents nonfiction books, novels, short story collections, juvenile. **Considers these nonfiction areas:** anthropology, biography, ethnic, government, health, history, language, nature, popular culture, psychology, science, womens. **Considers these fiction areas:** ethnic, juvenile, literary, mainstream, picture books, young.

How to Contact Query with SASE. Responds in 1 week to queries. Responds in 2 months to mss. Obtains most new clients through recommendations from others, solicitations.

Terms Agent receives 15% commission on domestic sales. Agent receives 20% commission on foreign sales.

Recent Sales *America the Beautiful*, by Robert Sabuda; Dahlia, by Barbara McClintock; *Living Dead Girl*, by Tod Goldberg; *In My Mother's House*, by Margaret McMulla; *Black Hawk Down*, by Mark Bowden; *Look Back All the Green Valley*, by Fred Chappell; *Under a Wing*, by Reeve Lindbergh; *I Am Madame X*, by Gioia Diliberto.

DUNOW, CARLSON, & LERNER AGENCY

27 W. 20th St., #1107, New York NY 10011. E-mail: mail@dclagency.com. Website: www.dclagency.com/. **Contact:** Jennifer Carlson, Henry Dunow, Betsy Lerner. Member of AAR.

Member Agents Jennifer Carlson (young adult and middle grade, some fiction and nonfiction); Henry Dunow (quality fiction - literary, historical, strongly written commercial - and with voice-driven nonfiction across a range of areas - narrative history, biography, memoir, current affairs, cultural trends and criticism, science, sports); Erin Hosier (nonfiction: popular culture, music, sociology and memoir); Betsy Lerner (nonfiction writers in the areas of psychology, history, cultural studies, biography, current events, business; fiction: literary, dark, funny, voice driven; Jeff Moores (quality contemporary fiction and literature, narrative nonfiction, memoir, politics, current affairs, journalism, graphic novels, gay & lesbian, popular culture and popular science).

Represents nonfiction books, novels, juvenile.

How to Contact Query with SASE or by e-mail to mail@dclagency.com. No attachments. Unable to respond to queries except when interested.

DUPREE/MILLER AND ASSOCIATES INC. LITERARY

100 Highland Park Village, Suite 350, Dallas TX 75205. (214)559-BOOK. Fax: (214)559-PAGE. Website: www.dupreemiller.com. **Contact:** Submissions Department.Other memberships include ABA. Represents 200 clients. 20% of clients are new/unpublished writers. Currently handles: nonfiction books 90%, novels 10%.

Member Agents Jan Miller, president/CEO; Shannon Miser-Marven, senior executive VP; Annabelle Baxter; Nena Madonia; Cheri Gillis.

Represents nonfiction books, novels, scholarly, syndicated, inspirational/spirituality. **Considers these nonfiction areas:** americana, crafts, interior, newage, animals, anthropology, art, biography, business, child, cooking, creative, current affairs, education, ethnic, gardening, government, health, history, how to, humor, language, memoirs, money, multicultural, music, nature, philosophy, photography, popular culture, psychology, recreation, regional, science, self help, sex, sociology, sports, film, translation, true crime, womens. **Considers these fiction areas:** glitz, psychic, adventure, detective, ethnic, experimental, family, feminist, historical, humor, literary, mainstream, mystery, picture books, religious, sports, thriller. This agency specializes in commercial fiction and nonfiction.

O⇁ This agency specializes in commercial fiction and nonfiction.

How to Contact Submit 1-page query, outline, SASE. Obtains most new clients through recommendations from others, conferences, lectures.

Terms Agent receives 15% commission on domestic sales. Offers written contract.

Writers Conferences Aspen Summer Words Literary Festival.

Tips If interested in agency representation, it is vital to have the material in the proper working format. As agents' policies differ, it is important to follow their guidelines. "The best advice I can give is to work on establishing a strong proposal that provides sample chapters, an overall synopsis (fairly detailed), and some biographical information on yourself. Do not send your proposal in pieces; it should be complete upon submission. Remember you are trying to sell your work, and it should be in its best condition."

DWYER & O'GRADY, INC.

Agents for Writers & Illustrators of Children's Books, P.O. Box 790, Cedar Key FL 32625-0790. (352)543-9307. Fax: (603)375-5373. Website: www.dwyerogrady.com. **Contact:** Elizabeth O'Grady. Other memberships include SCBWI. Represents 30 clients. Currently handles: juvenile books 100%.

- Prior to opening their agency, Mr. Dwyer and Ms. O'Grady were booksellers and publishers.

Member Agents Elizabeth O'Grady; Jeff Dwyer.

Represents juvenile. **Considers these nonfiction areas:** juvenile. **Considers these fiction areas:** juvenile, picture books, young. "We are not accepting new clients at this time. This agency represents only writers and illustrators of children's books." No juvenile books.

O⇁ "We are not accepting new clients at this time. This agency represents only writers and illustrators of children's books." No juvenile books.

How to Contact *No unsolicited mss.* Obtains most new clients through recommendations from others, Direct approach by agent to writer whose work they've read.

Terms Agent receives 15% commission on domestic sales. Agent receives 20% commission on foreign sales. Offers written contract; 1-month notice must be given to terminate contract. This agency charges clients for photocopying of longer mss or mutually agreed upon marketing expenses.

Writers Conferences BookExpo America; American Library Association Annual Conference; SCBWI.

Tips "This agency previously had an address in New Hampshire. Mail all materials to the new Florida address."

DYSTEL & GODERICH LITERARY MANAGEMENT

1 Union Square W., Suite 904, New York NY 10003. (212)627-9100. Fax: (212)627-9313. E-mail: miriam@dystel.com. Website: www.dystel.com. **Contact:** Miriam Goderich.Member of AAR. Represents 300 clients. 50% of clients are new/unpublished writers. Currently handles: nonfiction books 65%, novels 25%, other 10% cookbooks.

- Dystel & Goderich Literary Management recently acquired the client list of Bedford Book Works.

Member Agents Stacey Glick; Jane Dystel; Miriam Goderich; Michael Bourret; Jim McCarthy; Lauren Abramo; Adina Kahn.

Represents nonfiction books, novels, cookbooks. **Considers these nonfiction areas:** newage, animals, anthropology, biography, business, child, cooking, current affairs, education, ethnic, gay, government, health, history, humor, military, money, popular culture, psychology, religion, science, true crime, womens. **Considers these fiction areas:** adventure, detective, ethnic, family, gay, literary, mainstream, mystery, thriller. "This agency specializes in cookbooks and commercial and literary fiction and nonfiction."

O-- "This agency specializes in cookbooks and commercial and literary fiction and nonfiction."

How to Contact Query with SASE. See website for full guidelines. Accepts simultaneous submissions. Responds in 1 month to queries. Responds in 6 weeks to mss. Obtains most new clients through recommendations from others, solicitations, conferences.

Terms Agent receives 15% commission on domestic sales. Agent receives 19% commission on foreign sales. Offers written contract. Charges for photocopying. Galley charges and book charges from the publisher are passed on to the author.

Writers Conferences Whidbey Island Writers' Conference; Backspace Writers' Conference; Iowa Summer Writing Festival; Pacific Northwest Writers' Association; Pike's Peak Writers' Conference; Santa Barbara Writers' Conference; Harriette Austin Writers' Conference; Sandhills Writers' Conference; Denver Publishing Institute; Love Is Murder.

Tips "Work on sending professional, well-written queries that are concise and addressed to the specific agent the author is contacting. No dear Sirs/Madam."

TOBY EADY ASSOCIATES

Third Floor, 9 Orme Court, London England W2 4RL United Kingdom. (44)(207)792-0092. Fax: (44)(207)792-0879. E-mail: Jamie@tobyeady.demon.co.uk. Website: www.tobyeadyassociates.co.uk. **Contact:** Jamie Coleman. Represents 53 clients. 13% of clients are new/unpublished writers. Currently handles: nonfiction books 50%, novels 50%.

Member Agents Toby Eady (China, the Middle East, Africa, politics of a Swiftian nature); Laetitia Rutherford (fiction and nonfiction from around the world).

Represents nonfiction books, novels, short story collections, novellas, anthologies. **Considers these nonfiction areas:** art, cooking, current affairs, ethnic, government, health, history, memoirs, popular culture. **Considers these fiction areas:** adventure, confession, historical, literary, mainstream. "We handle fiction and nonfiction for adults and we specialize in China, the Middle East and Africa." Actively seeking "stories that demand to be heard." Does not want to receive poetry, screenplays or children's books.

O-- "We handle fiction and nonfiction for adults and we specialize in China, the Middle East and Africa." Actively seeking "stories that demand to be heard." Does not want to receive poetry, screenplays or children's books.

How to Contact Send the first 50 pages of your work, double-spaced and unbound, with a synopsis and a brief bio attn: Jamie Coleman. Accepts simultaneous submissions. Responds in 2 weeks to queries. Responds in 2 weeks to mss. Obtains most new clients through recommendations from others, solicitations, conferences.

Terms Agent receives 15% commission on domestic sales. Agent receives 20% commission on foreign sales. Offers written contract; 3-month notice must be given to terminate contract.

Writers Conferences City Lit; Winchester Writers' Festival.

Tips "Send submissions to this address: Jamie Coleman, Third Floor, 9 Orme Court, London W2 4RL."

EAMES LITERARY SERVICES

4117 Hillsboro Road, Suite 251, Nashville TN 37215. Fax: (615)463.9361. E-mail: info@eamesliterary.com; John@eamesliterary.com; Ahna@eamesliterary.com. Website: www.eamesliterary.com. **Contact:** John Eames.

Member Agents John Eames, Jonathan Rogers.

Represents nonfiction books, novels. **Considers these nonfiction areas:** young, memoirs, religion. **Considers these fiction areas:** religious, young. This agency specializes in the Christian marketplace. Actively seeking "adult and young adult fiction that sparks the imagination, illuminates some angle of truth about the human condition, causes the reader to view the world with fresh eyes, and supports a Christian perspective on life in all its complexities. Stories might be redemptive, or tragic. Characters might be noble, or flawed. Situations might be humorous, or dark. And many manuscripts might contain some combination of all of the above. We also seek adult and young adult nonfiction that is anecdotal as well as instructional, utilizes a 'show, don't tell' philosophy of writing, and offers a unique and biblically sound perspective on a given topic. If the submission is a nonfiction narrative (e.g., memoir), the work should follow most of the same recommendations for a work of fiction, as listed above. We look for proposals that are very well written and (especially for nonfiction) are from authors with an expansive platform and processing some literary notoriety."

O-- This agency specializes in the Christian marketplace. Actively seeking "adult and young adult fiction that sparks the imagination, illuminates some angle of truth about the human condition, causes the reader to view the world with fresh eyes, and supports a Christian perspective on life in all its complexities. Stories might be redemptive, or tragic. Characters might be noble, or flawed. Situations might be humorous, or dark. And many manuscripts might contain some combination of all of the above. We also seek adult and young adult nonfiction that is anecdotal as well as instructional, utilizes a 'show, don't tell' philosophy of writing, and offers a unique and biblically sound perspective on a given topic. If the submission is a nonfiction narrative (e.g., memoir), the work should follow most of the same recommendations for a work of fiction, as listed above. We look for proposals that are very well written and (especially for nonfiction) are from authors with an expansive platform and processing some literary notoriety."

EAST/WEST AGENCY

1158 26th St., Suite 462, Santa Monica CA 90403. (310)573-9303. Fax: (310)453-9008. E-mail: creativeideaz@roadrunner.com. **Contact:** Deborah Warren, founder.Other memberships include adheres to AAR canon of ethics. Represents 100 clients. 70% of clients are new/unpublished writers. Currently handles: nonfiction books 25%, juvenile books 75%.

Member Agents Deborah Warren; Lisa Rojany Buccieri; Susan B. Katz (writers/illustrators in the Latino market, representing Spanish-speaking clients).

Represents nonfiction books, juvenile. **Considers these nonfiction areas:** crafts, interior, juvenile, art, how to, humor, language, music, photography, popular culture, religion, self help. **Considers these fiction areas:** comic, ethnic, juvenile, picture books, young. "EWA is, purposefully, a niche agency, to facilitate hands-on, personalized service and attention to our authors, authorial illustrators, illustrators and their books. EWA provides career management for established and first time authors and our breadth of experience in many genres enables us to meet the demands of a diverse clientele. Understanding the in-depth process of acquisitions, sales and marketing helps Ms. Warren and her co-agents attain the stated goals for each of the agency's clients: to close the best possible deal with the best possible editor at the best possible publishing house." Actively seeking clients by referral only. This agency works with board books, illustrated picture books and bilingual (Spanish-speaking) authors frequently.

"EWA is, purposefully, a niche agency, to facilitate hands-on, personalized service and attention to our authors, authorial illustrators, illustrators and their books. EWA provides career management for established and first time authors and our breadth of experience in many genres enables us to meet the demands of a diverse clientele. Understanding the in-depth process of acquisitions, sales and marketing helps Ms. Warren and her co-agents attain the stated goals for each of the agency's clients: to close the best possible deal with the best possible editor at the best possible publishing house." Actively seeking clients by referral only. This agency works with board books, illustrated picture books and bilingual (Spanish-speaking) authors frequently.

How to Contact Query with SASE. Submit first 3 sample chapters, table of contents (2 pages or fewer), synopsis (1 page).For picture books, submit entire ms. For chapter books/novels. "Send submissions to CreativeIdeaz@roadrunner.com, or snail mail to Requested Materials, EWA, 1543 Sycamore Canyon Drive, Westlake Village, CA 91361. Submit the manuscript as a Word document in Courier, 12-point, double-spaced, with 1.20 inch margin on left, ragged right text, 25 lines per page, continuously paginated, with all your contact info on the first page. Include an SASE and a manila envelope with appropriate postage to expedite our response." Responds in 2 months to mss. Obtains most new clients through recommendations from others.

Terms Agent receives 15% commission on domestic sales. Agent receives 25% commission on foreign sales. Offers written contract; 30-day notice must be given to terminate contract. Charges for out-of-pocket expenses, such as postage and copying.

EBELING AND ASSOCIATES

P.O. Box 790267, Pala HI 96779. (808)579-6414. Fax: (808)579-9294. Website: www.ebelingagency.com. **Contact:** Michael Ebeling or Kristina Holmes. Represents 6 clients. 50% of clients are new/unpublished writers. Currently handles: nonfiction books 100%.

- Prior to becoming an agent, Mr. Ebeling established a career in the publishing industry through long-term author management. He has expertise in sales, platforms, publicity and marketing. Ms. Holmes joined the agency in 2005, and considers many types of projects. She is interested in books that take a stand, bring an issue to light or help readers.

Member Agents Michael Ebeling, ebothat@yahoo.com; Kristina Holmes, kristina@ebelingagency.com.

Represents nonfiction books. **Considers these nonfiction areas:** animals, anthropology, art, biography, business, child, computers, cooking, current affairs, education, ethnic, gay, government, health, history, how to, humor, memoirs, money, music, nature, photography, popular culture, psychology, religion, science, self help, sports, travel, womens, food/fitness. "We accept very few clients for representation. We represent nonfiction authors, most predominantly in the areas of business and self-help. We are very committed to our authors and their messages, which is a main reason we have such a high placement rate. We are always looking at new ways to help our authors gain the exposure they need to not only get published, but develop a successful literary career." Actively seeking well written nonfiction material with fresh perspectives written by writers with established platforms. Does not want to receive fiction.

"We accept very few clients for representation. We represent nonfiction authors, most predominantly in the areas of business and self-help. We are very committed to our authors and their messages, which is a main reason we have such a high placement rate. We are always looking at new ways to help our authors gain the exposure they need to not only get published, but develop a successful literary career." Actively seeking well written nonfiction material with fresh perspectives written by writers with established platforms. Does not want to receive fiction.

How to Contact E-mail query and proposal to either Michael or Kristina. E-queries only. Accepts simultaneous submissions. Responds in 2-4 weeks to queries. Obtains most new clients through recommendations from others, solicitations.

Terms Agent receives 15% commission on domestic sales. Agent receives 15% commission on foreign sales. Offers written contract; 60-day notice must be given to terminate contract. There is a charge for normal out-of-pocket fees, not to exceed $200 without client approval.

Writers Conferences BookExpo America; San Francisco Writers' Conference.

Tips "Approach agents when you're already building your platform, you have a well written book, you have a firm understanding of the publishing process, and have come up with a complete competitive proposal. Know the name of the agent you are contacting. You're essentially selling a business plan to the publisher. Make sure you've made a convincing pitch throughout your proposal, as ultimately, publishers are taking a financial risk by investing in your project."

ANNE EDELSTEIN LITERARY AGENCY

20 W. 22nd St., Suite 1603, New York NY 10010. (212)414-4923. Fax: (212)414-2930. E-mail: info@aeliterary.com. Website: www.aeliterary.com. Member of AAR.

Member Agents Anne Edelstein; Krista Ingebretson.

Represents nonfiction books, Fiction. **Considers these nonfiction areas:** narrative history, memoirs, psychology, religion. **Considers these fiction areas:** literary. This agency specializes in fiction and narrative nonfiction.

O→ This agency specializes in fiction and narrative nonfiction.

How to Contact Query with SASE; submit 25 sample pages.

Recent Sales *Confessions of a Buddhist Athlete*, by Stephen Batchelor (Spiegel & Grau); *April & Oliver*, by Tess Callahan (Doubleday).

EDUCATIONAL DESIGN SERVICES, LLC

5750 Bou Ave., Suite 1508, Bethesda MD MD 20852. (301)881-8611. E-mail: blinder@educationaldesignservices.com. Website: www.educationaldesignservices.com. **Contact:** Bertram L. Linder, president. Represents 14 clients. 95% of clients are new/unpublished writers. Currently handles: other 100% textbooks and professional materials for education.

- Prior to becoming an agent, Mr. Linder was an author and a teacher.

Member Agents Bertram Linder (textbooks and professional materials for education).

Represents scholarly, textbooks. "We are one of the few agencies that specialize exclusively in materials for the education market. We handle text materials for grades preK-12, text materials for college/university use, and materials for professionals in the field of education, staff development and education policy." Does not want to receive children's fiction and nonfiction, or picture books.

O→ "We are one of the few agencies that specialize exclusively in materials for the education market. We handle text materials for grades preK-12, text materials for college/university use, and materials for professionals in the field of education, staff development and education policy." Does not want to receive children's fiction and nonfiction, or picture books.

How to Contact Query with SASE. Submit proposal package, outline, outline/proposal, 2-3 sample chapters, SASE. . Accepts simultaneous submissions. Responds in 3-4 weeks to queries. Responds in 3-4 weeks to mss. Obtains most new clients through recommendations from others, solicitations, conferences.

Terms Agent receives 15% commission on domestic sales. Agent receives 25% commission on foreign sales. Offers written contract; 30 days notice must be given to terminate contract. Charges clients for extraordinary expenses in postage and shipping, as well as long distance telephone calls.

Recent Sales Sold 4 titles in the last year. *No Parent Left Behind*, by P. Petrosino and L. Spiegel (Rowman & Littlefield Education); *Preparing for the 8th Grade Test in Social Studies*, by E. Farran and A. Paci (Amsco Book Company); *Teaching Test-Taking Skills*, by G. Durham (Rowman & Littlefield Education); *Teacher's Quick Guide to Communicating*, by G. Sundem (Corwin Press).

JUDITH EHRLICH LITERARY MANAGEMENT, LLC

880 Third Ave., Eighth Floor, New York NY 10022. (646)505-1570. E-mail: jehrlich@JudithEhrlichLiterary.com. Website: www.judithehrlichliterary.com. Other memberships include Author's Guild, the American Society of Journalists and Authors.

- Prior to her current position, Ms. Ehrlich was an award-winning journalist; she is the co-author of *The New Crowd: The Changing of the Jewish Guard on Wall Street* (Little, Brown). Emmanuelle Alspaugh was an agent at Wendy Sherman Associates and an editor at Fodor's, the travel division of Random House.

Member Agents Judith Ehrlich, jehrlich@judithehrlichliterary.com; Emmanuelle Alspaugh, ealspaugh@judithehrlichliterary.com (romance in most subgenres, especially historical and paranormal, women's fiction, memoir, narrative nonfiction, and select how-to's. Sophia Seidner is currently taking new clients only by referral for both fiction and nonfiction; Martha Hoffman currently looking only at proposals in history and historical fiction.

Represents nonfiction books, novels. "Special areas of interest include compelling narrative nonfiction, outstanding biographies and memoirs, lifestyle books, works that reflect our changing culture, women's issues, psychology, science, social issues, current events, parenting, health, history, business, and prescriptive books offering fresh information and advice." Does not want to receive children's or young adult books, novellas, poetry, textbooks, plays or screenplays.

- "Special areas of interest include compelling narrative nonfiction, outstanding biographies and memoirs, lifestyle books, works that reflect our changing culture, women's issues, psychology, science, social issues, current events, parenting, health, history, business, and prescriptive books offering fresh information and advice." Does not want to receive children's or young adult books, novellas, poetry, textbooks, plays or screenplays.

How to Contact Query with SASE. Queries should include a synopsis and some sample pages. Send e-queries to jehrlich@judithehrlichliterary.com. The agency will respond only if interested

Recent Sales Fiction: *Breaking the Bank*, by Yona Zeldis McDonough (Pocket); *Sinful Surrender*, by Beverley Kendall (Kensington); Nonfiction: *Strategic Learning: How to be Smarter Than Your Competition and Turn Key Insights Into Competitive Advantage*, by William Pieterson (Wiley); *Paris Under Water: How the City of Light Survived the Great Flood of 1910*, by Jeffrey Jackson (Palgrave Macmillan); *When Growth Stalls: How It Happens, Why You're Stuck & What to Do About It*, by Steve McKee (Jossey-Bass); *I'm Smarter Than My Boss. Now What?* by Diane Garnick (Bloomberg Press).

THE LISA EKUS GROUP, LLC

57 North St., Hatfield MA 01038. (413)247-9325. Fax: (413)247-9873. E-mail: LisaEkus@lisaekus.com. Website: www.lisaekus.com. **Contact:** Lisa Ekus-Saffer. Member of AAR.

Represents nonfiction books. **Considers these nonfiction areas:** cooking, occasionally health/well-being and women's issues.

How to Contact Submit a one-page query via e-mail or submit your complete hard copy proposal with title page, proposal contents, concept, bio, marketing, TOC, etc. Include SASE for the return of materials.

Recent Sales Please see the regularly updated client listing on website.

Tips "Please do not call. No phone queries."

ETHAN ELLENBERG LITERARY AGENCY

548 Broadway, #5-E, New York NY 10012. (212)431-4554. Fax: (212)941-4652. E-mail: agent@ethanellenberg.com. Website: ethanellenberg.com/. **Contact:** Ethan Ellenberg. Represents 80 clients. 10% of clients are new/unpublished writers. Currently handles: nonfiction books 25%, novels 75%.

- Prior to opening his agency, Mr. Ellenberg was contracts manager of Berkley/Jove and associate contracts manager for Bantam.

Represents nonfiction books, novels, children's books. **Considers these nonfiction areas:** current affairs, health, history, military, science, narrative, biography. This agency specializes in commercial fiction—especially thrillers, romance/women's, and specialized nonfiction. We also do a lot of children's books. Actively seeking commercial fiction as noted above—romance/fiction for women, science fiction and fantasy, thrillers, suspense and mysteries. Our other two main areas of interest are children's books and narrative nonfiction. We are actively seeking clients, follow the directions on our Web site. Does not want to receive poetry, short stories, Western's, autobiographies or screenplays.

- This agency specializes in commercial fiction—especially thrillers, romance/women's, and specialized nonfiction. We also do a lot of children's books. Actively seeking commercial fiction as noted above—romance/fiction for women, science fiction and fantasy, thrillers, suspense and mysteries. Our other two main areas of interest are children's books and narrative nonfiction. We are actively seeking clients, follow the directions on our Web site. Does not want to receive poetry, short stories, Western's, autobiographies or screenplays.

How to Contact For fiction, send introductory letter, outline, first 3 chapters, SASE. For nonfiction, send query letter, proposal, 1 sample chapter, SASE. For children's books, send introductory letter, up to 3 picture book mss, outline, first 3 chapters, SASE. Accepts simultaneous submissions. Responds in 4-6 weeks to mss.

Terms Agent receives 15% commission on domestic sales. Agent receives 10% commission on foreign sales. Offers written contract. Charges clients (with their consent) for direct expenses limited to photocopying and postage.

Writers Conferences RWA National Conference; Novelists, Inc.; and other regional conferences.

Tips We do consider new material from unsolicited authors. Write a good, clear letter with a succinct description of your book. We prefer the first 3 chapters when we consider fiction. For all submissions, you must include a SASE or the material will be discarded. It's always hard to break in, but talent will find a home. Check our Web site for complete submission guidelines. We continue to see natural storytellers and nonfiction writers with important books.

THE NICHOLAS ELLISON AGENCY

Affiliated with Sanford J. Greenburger Associates, 55 Fifth Ave., 15th Floor, New York NY 10003. (212)206-5600. Fax: (212)463-8718. E-mail: nellison@sga.com. Website: www.greenburger.com. **Contact:** Nicholas Ellison. Represents 70 clients. Currently handles: nonfiction books 50%, novels 50%.

- Prior to becoming an agent, Mr. Ellison was an editor at Minerva Editions and Harper & Row, and editor-in-chief at Delacorte.

Member Agents Nicholas Ellison; Sarah Dickman.
Represents nonfiction books, novels. **Considers these fiction areas:** literary, mainstream.
How to Contact Query with SASE. Responds in 6 weeks to queries.
Terms Agent receives 15% commission on domestic sales. Agent receives 20% commission on foreign sales.

ANN ELMO AGENCY, INC.

60 E. 42nd St., New York NY 10165. (212)661-2880. Fax: (212)661-2883. **Contact:** Lettie Lee. Member of AAR. Other memberships include Authors Guild.
Member Agents Lettie Lee; Mari Cronin (plays); A.L. Abecassis (nonfiction).
Represents nonfiction books, novels. **Considers these nonfiction areas:** biography, current affairs, health, history, how to, popular culture, science. **Considers these fiction areas:** ethnic, family, mainstream, romance, contemporary, gothic, historical, regency, thriller, womens.
How to Contact Only accepts mailed queries with SASE. Do not send full ms unless requested. Responds in 3 months to queries. Obtains most new clients through recommendations from others.
Terms Agent receives 15% commission on domestic sales. Agent receives 20% commission on foreign sales. Offers written contract.
Tips "Query first, and only when asked send a double-spaced, readable manuscript. Include a SASE, of course."

THE ELAINE P. ENGLISH LITERARY AGENCY

4710 41st St. NW, Suite D, Washington DC 20016. (202)362-5190. Fax: (202)362-5192. E-mail: elaine@elaineenglish.com; kvn.mcadams@yahoo.com. Website: www.elaineenglish.com. **Contact:** Elaine English.Kevin McAdams, Executive V.P., 400 East 11th St., # 7, New York, NY 10009 Member of AAR. Represents 20 clients. 25% of clients are new/unpublished writers. Currently handles: novels 100%.

- Ms. English has been working in publishing for more than 20 years. She is also an attorney specializing in media and publishing law.

Represents novels. **Considers these fiction areas:** historical, multicultural, mystery, romance, single title, historical, contemporary, romantic, suspense, chick lit, erotic, thriller, general women's fiction. The agency is slowly but steadily acquiring in all mentioned areas. Actively seeking women's fiction, including single-title romances. Does not want to receive any science fiction, time travel, children's, or young adult.

O→ Actively seeking women's fiction, including single-title romances. Does not want to receive any science fiction, time travel, children's, or young adult.

How to Contact Prefers e-queries sent to queries@elaineenglish.com. If requested, submit synopsis, first 3 chapters, SASE. Responds in 4-8 weeks to queries; 3 months to requested submissions Obtains most new clients through recommendations from others, conferences, submissions.
Terms Agent receives 15% commission on domestic sales. Agent receives 20% commission on foreign sales. Offers written contract; 30-day notice must be given to terminate contract. Charges only for copying and postage; generally taken from proceeds.
Recent Sales Sourcebooks, Tor, Harlequin
Writers Conferences RWA National Conference; Novelists, Inc.; Malice Domestic; Washington Romance Writers Retreat, among others.

THE EPSTEIN LITERARY AGENCY

P.O. Box 356, Avon MA 02368. (781)718-4025. E-mail: kate@epsteinliterary.com. Website: www.epsteinliterary.com. **Contact:** Kate Epstein. Member of AAR. Represents 30 clients. 70% of clients are new/unpublished writers. Currently handles: nonfiction books 100%.

- Prior to opening her literary agency, Ms. Epstein was an acquisitions editor at Adams Media.

Represents nonfiction books. **Considers these nonfiction areas:** animals, biography, business, crafts, current affairs, health, hobbies, humor, memoirs, popular culture, psychology, sociology, travel. "My background as an editor means that I'm extremely good at selling to them. It also means I'm a careful and thorough line editor. I'm particularly skilled at hardening concepts to make them sellable and proposing the logical follow-up for any book. Most of my list is practical nonfiction, and I have a particular affinity for pets." Actively seeking commercial nonfiction for adults. Does not want scholarly works.

- "My background as an editor means that I'm extremely good at selling to them. It also means I'm a careful and thorough line editor. I'm particularly skilled at hardening concepts to make them sellable and proposing the logical follow-up for any book. Most of my list is practical nonfiction, and I have a particular affinity for pets." Actively seeking commercial nonfiction for adults. Does not want scholarly works.

How to Contact Query via e-mail (no attachments). Accepts simultaneous submissions. Responds in 2 months to queries. Obtains most new clients through solicitations.

Terms Agent receives 15% commission on domestic sales. Agent receives 20% commission on foreign sales. Offers written contract; 30-day notice must be given to terminate contract.

Recent Sales *Nervous Breakdowns and Psychopathic Killers: The Writer's Guide to Psychology*, by Carolyin Kaufman, Psy.D. (Quilldriver); *Crossing the Gates of Alaska: One Man and Two Dogs 600 Miles Off the Map*, by Dave Metz (Citadel); *Eagle Walker*, by Jeffery Guidry (William Morrow).

FELICIA ETH LITERARY REPRESENTATION

555 Bryant St., Suite 350, Palo Alto CA 94301-1700. (650)375-1276. Fax: (650)401-8892. E-mail: feliciaeth@aol.com. **Contact:** Felicia Eth. Member of AAR. Represents 25-35 clients. Currently handles: nonfiction books 85%, novels 15% adult.

Represents nonfiction books, novels. **Considers these nonfiction areas:** animals, anthropology, biography, business, child, current affairs, ethnic, government, health, history, nature, popular culture, psychology, science, sociology, true crime, womens. **Considers these fiction areas:** literary, mainstream. This agency specializes in high-quality fiction (preferably mainstream/contemporary) and provocative, intelligent, and thoughtful nonfiction on a wide array of commercial subjects.

- This agency specializes in high-quality fiction (preferably mainstream/contemporary) and provocative, intelligent, and thoughtful nonfiction on a wide array of commercial subjects.

How to Contact Query with SASE. Accepts simultaneous submissions. Responds in 3 weeks to queries. Responds in 4-6 weeks to mss.

Terms Agent receives 15% commission on domestic sales. Agent receives 20% commission on foreign sales. Agent receives 20% commission on film sales. Charges clients for photocopying and express mail service.

Recent Sales Sold 70-10 titles in the last year. *Bumper Sticker Philosophy*, by Jack Bowen (Random House); *Boys Adrift*, by Leonard Sax (Basic Books); *A War Reporter*, by Barbara Quick (HarperCollins); Pantry, by Anna Badkhen (Free Press/S&S).

Writers Conferences "Wide Array - from Squaw Valley to Mills College."

Tips "For nonfiction, established expertise is certainly a plus--as is magazine publication--though not a prerequisite. I am highly dedicated to those projects I represent, but highly selective in what I choose."

MARY EVANS INC.

242 E. Fifth St., New York NY 10003. (212)979-0880. Fax: (212)979-5344. Website: www.maryevansinc.com. Member of AAR.

Member Agents Mary Evans (no unsolicited queries); Devin McIntyre, devin@maryevansinc.com (commericial and literary fiction, narrative nonfiction, pop culture, graphic novels, multicultural, pop science, sports, food).

Represents nonfiction books, novels.

How to Contact Query with SASE. Query with SASE. Query by snail mail. Non-query correspondence can be sent to info(at)maryevansinc.com. Obtains most new clients through recommendations from others, solicitations.

FAIRBANK LITERARY REPRESENTATION

199 Mount Auburn St., Suite 1, Cambridge MA 02138-4809. (617)576-0030. Fax: (617)576-0030. E-mail: queries@fairbankliterary.com. Website: www.fairbankliterary.com. **Contact:** Sorche Fairbank. Member of AAR. Represents 45 clients. 20% of clients are new/unpublished writers. Currently handles: nonfiction books 60%, novels 22%, story collections 3%, other 15% illustrated.

Member Agents Sorche Fairbank (narrative nonfiction, commercial and literary fiction, memoir, food and wine); Matthew Frederick (scout for sports nonfiction, architecture, design).

Represents nonfiction books, novels, short story collections. **Considers these nonfiction areas:** agriculture horticulture, crafts, interior, art, biography, cooking, current affairs, ethnic, gay, government, how to, memoirs, nature, photography, popular culture, science, sociology, sports, true crime, womens. **Considers these fiction areas:** adventure, feminist, gay, literary, mainstream, mystery, sports, thriller, womens, Southern voices. "I have a small agency in Harvard Square, where I tend to gravitate toward literary fiction and narrative nonfiction, with a strong interest in women's issues and women's voices, international voices, class and race issues, and projects that simply teach me something new about the greater world and society around us. We have a good reputation for working closely and developmentally with our authors and love what we do." Actively seeking literary fiction, international and culturally diverse voices, narrative nonfiction, topical subjects (politics, current affairs), history, sports, architecture/design and pop culture. Does not want to receive romance, poetry, science fiction, young adult or children's works.

O→ "I have a small agency in Harvard Square, where I tend to gravitate toward literary fiction and narrative nonfiction, with a strong interest in women's issues and women's voices, international voices, class and race issues, and projects that simply teach me something new about the greater world and society around us. We have a good reputation for working closely and developmentally with our authors and love what we do." Actively seeking literary fiction, international and culturally diverse voices, narrative nonfiction, topical subjects (politics, current affairs), history, sports, architecture/design and pop culture. Does not want to receive romance, poetry, science fiction, young adult or children's works.

How to Contact Query with SASE. Submit author bio. Accepts simultaneous submissions. Responds in 6 weeks to queries. Responds in 10 weeks to mss. Obtains most new clients through recommendations from others, solicitations, conferences, ideas generated in-house.

Terms Agent receives 15% commission on domestic sales. Agent receives 20% commission on foreign sales. Offers written contract, binding for 12 months; 45-day notice must be given to terminate contract.

Writers Conferences San Francisco Writers' Conference, Muse and the Marketplace/Grub Street Conference, Washington Independent Writers' Conference, Murder in the Grove, Surrey International Writers' Conference.

Tips "Be professional from the very first contact. There shouldn't be a single typo or grammatical flub in your query. Have a reason for contacting me about your project other than I was the next name listed on some Web site. Please do not use form query software! Believe me, we can get a dozen or so a day that look identical—we know when you are using a form. Show me that you know your audience—and your competition. Have the writing and/or proposal at the very, very best it can be before starting the querying process. Don't assume that if someone likes it enough they'll 'fix' it. The biggest mistake new writers make is starting the querying process before they—and the work—are ready. Take your time and do it right."

FARBER LITERARY AGENCY, INC.

14 E. 75th St., #2E, New York NY 10021. (212)861-7075. Fax: (212)861-7076. E-mail: farberlit@aol.com. Website: www.donaldfarber.com. **Contact:** Ann Farber, Dr. Seth Farber. Represents 40 clients. 50% of clients are new/unpublished writers. Currently handles: nonfiction books 25%, novels 35%, scholarly books 15%, stage plays 25%.

Member Agents Ann Farber (novels); Seth Farber (plays, scholarly books, novels); Donald C. Farber (attorney, all entertainment media).

Represents nonfiction books, novels, juvenile, textbooks, stage plays. **Considers these nonfiction areas:** child, cooking, music, psychology, film. **Considers these fiction areas:** adventure, humor, juvenile, literary, mainstream, mystery, thriller, young.

How to Contact Submit outline, 3 sample chapters, SASE. .Prefers to read materials exclusively. Responds in 1 month to queries. Responds in 2 months to mss. Obtains most new clients through recommendations from others.

Terms Agent receives 15% commission on domestic sales. Agent receives 20% commission on foreign sales. Offers written contract, binding for 1 year. Client must furnish copies of ms, treatments, and any other items for submission.

Tips "Our attorney, Donald C. Farber, is the author of many books. His services are available to the agency's clients as part of the agency service at no additional charge."

FARRIS LITERARY AGENCY, INC.

P.O. Box 570069, Dallas TX 75357. (972)203-8804. E-mail: farris1@airmail.net. Website: www.farrisliterary.com. **Contact:** Mike Farris, Susan Morgan Farris. Represents 30 clients. 60% of clients are new/unpublished writers. Currently handles: nonfiction books 40, novels 60.

- Both Mr. Farris and Ms. Farris are attorneys.

Represents nonfiction books, novels. **Considers these nonfiction areas:** biography, business, child, cooking, current affairs, government, health, history, how to, humor, memoirs, military, music, popular culture, religion, self help, sports, womens. **Considers these fiction areas:** adventure, detective, historical, humor, mainstream, mystery, religious, romance, sports, thriller, western. "We specialize in both fiction and nonfiction books. We are particularly interested in discovering unpublished authors. We adhere to AAR guidelines." Does not want to receive science fiction, fantasy, gay and lesbian, erotica, young adult or children's.

O→ "We specialize in both fiction and nonfiction books. We are particularly interested in discovering unpublished authors. We adhere to AAR guidelines." Does not want to receive science fiction, fantasy, gay and lesbian, erotica, young adult or children's.

How to Contact Query with SASE or by e-mail. Accepts simultaneous submissions. Responds in 2-3 weeks to queries. Responds in 4-8 weeks to mss. Obtains most new clients through recommendations from others, solicitations, conferences.

Terms Agent receives 15% commission on domestic sales. Agent receives 20% commission on foreign sales. Offers written contract; 30-day notice must be given to terminate contract. Charges clients for postage and photocopying.

Recent Sales Sold 4 titles in the last year. *The Show Must Go On*, by Doug Snauffer (McFarland); *The Yard Dog*, plus a second untitled in the series, by Sheldon Russell (St. Martin's Press).

Writers Conferences Oklahoma Writers Federation Conference; The Screenwriting Conference in Santa Fe; Pikes Peak Writers Conference; Women Writing the West Annual Conference.

THE FIELDING AGENCY, LLC

269 S. Beverly Drive, No. 341, Beverly Hills CA 90212. (323)461-4791. E-mail: wlee@fieldingagency.com; query@fieldingagency.com. Website: www.fieldingagency.com. **Contact:** Whitney Lee.Currently handles: nonfiction books 25%, novels 35%, juvenile books 35%, other 5% other.

- Prior to her current position, Ms. Lee worked at other agencies in different capacities.

Represents nonfiction books, novels, short story collections, juvenile. **Considers these nonfiction areas:** crafts, interior, juvenile, animals, anthropology, art, biography, business, child, cooking, current affairs, education, ethnic, gay, government, health, history, how to, humor, language, memoirs, military, money, nature, popular culture, psychology, science, self help, sociology, sports, translation, true crime, womens. **Considers these fiction areas:** glitz, adventure, comic, detective, ethnic, family, fantasy, feminist, gay, historical, horror, humor, juvenile, literary, mainstream, mystery, picture books, romance, thriller, young, womens. "We specialize in representing books published abroad and have strong relationships with foreign co-agents and publishers. For books we represent in the U.S., we have to be head-over-heels passionate about it because we are involved every step of the way." Does not want to receive scripts for TV or film.

O→ "We specialize in representing books published abroad and have strong relationships with foreign co-agents and publishers. For books we represent in the U.S., we have to be head-over-heels passionate about it because we are involved every step of the way." Does not want to receive scripts for TV or film.

How to Contact Query with SASE. Submit synopsis, author bio. Accepts queries by e-mail and snail mail. Accepts simultaneous submissions. Obtains most new clients through recommendations from others.

Terms Agent receives 15% commission on domestic sales. Agent receives 20% commission on foreign sales. Offers written contract, binding for 9-12 months.

Writers Conferences London Book Fair; Frankfurt Book Fair.

DIANA FINCH LITERARY AGENCY

116 W. 23rd St., Suite 500, New York NY 10011. (646)375-2081. E-mail: diana.finch@verizon.net. **Contact:** Diana Finch.Member of AAR. Represents 40 clients. 20% of clients are new/unpublished writers. Currently handles: nonfiction books 65%, novels 25%, juvenile books 5%, multimedia 5%.

- Prior to opening her agency, Ms. Finch worked at Ellen Levine Literary Agency for 18 years.

Represents nonfiction books, novels, scholarly. **Considers these nonfiction areas:** juvenile, biography, business, child, computers, current affairs, ethnic, government, health, history, how to, humor, memoirs, military, money, music, nature, photography, popular culture, psychology, science, self help, sports, film, translation, true crime, womens. **Considers these fiction areas:** adventure, detective, ethnic, historical, literary, mainstream, thriller, young. Actively seeking narrative nonfiction, popular science, and health topics. "Does not want romance, mysteries, or children's picture books."

O→ Actively seeking narrative nonfiction, popular science, and health topics. "Does not want romance, mysteries, or children's picture books."

How to Contact Query with SASE or via e-mail (no attachments). Accepts simultaneous submissions. Obtains most new clients through recommendations from others.

Terms Agent receives 15% commission on domestic sales. Agent receives 20% commission on foreign sales. Offers written contract. "I charge for photocopying, overseas postage, galleys, and books purchased, and try to recap these costs from earnings received for a client, rather than charging outright."

Recent Sales *Genetic Rounds* by Robert Marion, M.D. (Kaplan); *Honeymoon In Tehran* by Azadeh Moaveni (Random House); *Darwin Slept Here* by Eric Simons (Overlook); *The Tyranny of Oil* by Antonia Juhasz (HarperCollins); *Stalin's Children* by Owen Matthews (Bloomsbury); *Radiant Days* by Michael Fitzgerald (Shoemaker & Hoard); *The Queen's Soprano* by Carol Dines (Harcourt Young Adult); *What To Say to a Porcupine* by Richard Gallagher (Amacom).

Tips "Do as much research as you can on agents before you query. Have someone critique your query letter before you send it. It should be only 1 page and describe your book clearly—and why you are writing it—but also demonstrate creativity and a sense of your writing style."

FINEPRINT LITERARY MANAGEMENT

240 West 35th St., Suite 500, New York NY 10001. (212)279-1282. E-mail: stephany@fineprintlit.com. Website: www.fineprintlit.com. Member of AAR.

Member Agents Peter Rubie, CEO (nonfiction interests include narrative nonfiction, popular science, spirituality, history, biography, pop culture, business, technology, parenting, health, self help, music, and food; fiction interests include literate thrillers, crime fiction, science fiction and fantasy, military fiction and literary fiction); Stephany Evans, president (nonfiction interests include health and wellness - especially women's health, spirituality, lifestyle, home renovating/decorating, entertaining, food and wine, popular reference, and narrative nonfiction; fiction interests include stories with a strong and interesting female protagonist, both literary and upmarket commercial — including chick lit, romance, mystery, and light suspense); June Clark (nonfiction: entertainment, self-help, parenting, reference/how-to books, teen books, food and wine, style/beauty, and prescriptive business titles); Diane Freed (nonfiction: health/fitness, women's issues, memoir, baby boomer trends, parenting, popular culture, self-help, humor, young adult, and topics of New England regional interest); Meredith Hays (both fiction and nonfiction: commercial and literary; she is interested in sophisticated women's fiction such as urban chick lit, pop culture, lifestyle, animals, and absorbing nonfiction accounts); Janet Reid (mysteries and offbeat literary fiction); Amy Tipton (edgy fiction - gritty and urban, women's fiction, nonfiction/memoir, and YA); Colleen Lindsay.

Represents nonfiction books, novels. **Considers these nonfiction areas:** interior, young, business, child, cooking, government, health, history, how to, humor, memoirs, music, psychology, science, self help, spirituality, true crime, womens, narrative nonfiction, popular science. **Considers these fiction areas:** detective, fantasy, literary, military, mystery, romance, science, young, womens.

How to Contact Query with SASE. Submit synopsis and first two chapters for fiction; proposal for nonfiction. Do not send attachments or manuscripts without a request. Obtains most new clients through recommendations from others, solicitations.

Terms Agent receives 15% commission on domestic sales. Agent receives 20% commission on foreign sales.

FIREBRAND LITERARY

285 West Broadway, Suite 520, New York NY 10013. (212)334-0025. Fax: (347)689-4762. E-mail: info@firebrandliterary.com. Website: www.firebrandliterary.com. **Contact:** Nadia Cornier Represents 30 clients. 50% of clients are new/unpublished writers. Currently handles: nonfiction books 10%, novels 85%, novella 5%.

- Before becoming an agent, Ms. Cornier started her own publicity firm and currently channels her interest and skill in marketing into her work with authors.

Member Agents Nadia Cornier, nadia@firebrandliterary.com (young adult, adult commercial, adult genre romance, nonfiction, some middle grade); Stacia Decker; Danielle Chiotti; Chris Richman; Michael Stearns.

Represents nonfiction books, novels, novellas, juvenile. **Considers these nonfiction areas:** juvenile, business, how to, humor, language, money. **Considers these fiction areas:** erotica, fantasy, historical, juvenile, literary, mainstream, romance, young, womens. "Firebrand endeavors to be a perfect fit for a few authors rather than a good fit for every author—we do so by working with our writers with editing and marketing direction alongside the usual responsibilities of selling their properties. Most of all, we want the author to be excited about what they're doing and what they're writing. While we in turn want to be excited to work with them. That kind of enthusiasm is contagious and we feel it is an important foundation to have when it comes to pitching an author's ideas not only to publishers and the industry, but to the world." Does not want to receive children's books, screenplays, poetry or anything about terrorists.

"Firebrand endeavors to be a perfect fit for a few authors rather than a good fit for every author—we do so by working with our writers with editing and marketing direction alongside the usual responsibilities of selling their properties. Most of all, we want the author to be excited about what they're doing and what they're writing. While we in turn want to be excited to work with them. That kind of enthusiasm is contagious and we feel it is an important foundation to have when it comes to pitching an author's ideas not only to publishers and the industry, but to the world." Does not want to receive children's books, screenplays, poetry or anything about terrorists.

How to Contact This agency prefers its submissions made through the Web site form. See the site for all details. Send ms only by request. Accepts simultaneous submissions. Responds in 2 weeks to queries. Responds in 2 months to mss. Obtains most new clients through recommendations from others, solicitations.

Terms Agent receives 15% commission on domestic sales. Agent receives 20% commission on foreign

sales. Offers written contract; 30-day notice must be given to terminate contract.

Tips "Send a short query letter and let the work stand on its own."

JAMES FITZGERALD AGENCY

80 E. 11th St., Suite 301, New York NY (212)308-1122. E-mail: submissions@jfitzagency.com. Website: www.jfitzagency.com. **Contact:** James Fitzgerald.

- Prior to his current position, Mr. Fitzgerald was an editor at St. Martin's Press, Doubleday, and the New York Times.

Member Agents James Fitzgerald.

Represents nonfiction books, novels. Does not want to receive poetry or screenplays.

O→ Does not want to receive poetry or screenplays.

How to Contact Query with SASE. Submit proposal package, outline/proposal, publishing history, author bio, overview.

Recent Sales *Gimme Something Better: The Profound, Progressive, and Occasionally Pointless History of Punk in the Bay Area*, by Jack Boulware and Silke Tudor (Viking/Penguin); *Black Dogs: The Possibly True Story of Classic Rock's Greatest Robbery*, by Jason Buhrmester (Three Rivers/Crown); *Theo Gray's Med Science: Experiments You Can Do at Home—But Probably Shouldn't* (Black Dog and Loenthal).

Tips "As an agency, we primarily represent books that reflect the popular culture of today being in the forms of fiction, nonfiction, graphic and packaged books. Please submit all information in English, even if your manuscript is in Spanish."

FLAMING STAR LITERARY ENTERPRISES

320 Riverside Drive, New York NY 10025. E-mail: flamingstarlit@aol.com; janvall@aol.com. Website: flamingstarlit.com for Joseph Vallely; www.janisvallely.com for Janis Vallely. **Contact:** Joseph B. Vallely, Janis C. Vallely. Represents 100 clients. 25% of clients are new/unpublished writers. Currently handles: nonfiction books 100%.

- Prior to opening the agency, Mr. Vallely served as national sales manager for Dell; Ms. Vallely was vice president of Doubleday.

Represents nonfiction books. **Considers these nonfiction areas:** current affairs, government, health, memoirs, psychology, self help, sports. This agency specializes in upscale commercial nonfiction.

O→ This agency specializes in upscale commercial nonfiction.

How to Contact E-mail only (no attachments). Responds in week to mss. Obtains most new clients through recommendations from others, solicitations.

Terms Agent receives 15% commission on domestic sales. Agent receives 20% commission on foreign sales. Offers written contract. Charges clients for photocopying and postage only.

Recent Sales *His and Hers*, by Daniel Monti and Anthony Bazzan (Collins).

FLANNERY LITERARY

1155 S. Washington St., Suite 202, Naperville IL 60540. (630)428-2682. Fax: (630)428-2683. E-mail: FlanLit@aol.com. **Contact:** Jennifer Flannery. Represents 40 clients. 50% of clients are new/unpublished writers. Currently handles: juvenile books 100%.

Represents This agency specializes in children's and young adult fiction and nonfiction. It also accepts picture books.

O→ This agency specializes in children's and young adult fiction and nonfiction. It also accepts picture books.

How to Contact Query with SASE. No fax or e-mail queries. Responds in 2 weeks to queries. Responds in 1 month to mss. Obtains most new clients through recommendations from others, submissions.

Terms Agent receives 15% commission on domestic sales. Agent receives 20% commission on foreign sales. Offers written contract, binding for life of book in print; 1-month notice must be given to terminate contract.

Tips "Write an engrossing, succinct query describing your work. We are always looking for a fresh new voice."

PETER FLEMING AGENCY

P.O. Box 458, Pacific Palisades CA 90272. (310)454-1373. E-mail: peterfleming@earthlink.net. **Contact:** Peter Fleming. Currently handles: nonfiction books 100%.

Represents This agency specializes in nonfiction books that unearth innovative and uncomfortable truths with bestseller potential. "Greatly interested in journalists in the free press (the Internet)."

O→ This agency specializes in nonfiction books that unearth innovative and uncomfortable truths with bestseller potential. "Greatly interested in journalists in the free press (the Internet)."

How to Contact Query with SASE. Obtains most new clients through a different, one-of-a-kind idea for a book often backed by the writer's experience in that area of expertise.

Terms Agent receives 15% commission on domestic sales. Agent receives 25% commission on foreign

sales. Offers written contract, binding for 1 year. Charges clients only those fees agreed to in writing.
Recent Sales *Stop Foreclosure*, by Lloyd Segol; *Rulers of Evil*, by F. Tupper Saussy (HarperCollins); *Why Is It Always About You-Saving Yourself from the Narcissists in Your Life*, by Sandy Hotchkiss (Free Press)
Tips "You can begin by starting your own blog."

FLETCHER & COMPANY

78 Fifth Ave., 3rd Floor, New York NY 10011. (212)614-0778. Fax: (212)614-0728. E-mail: mail@fletcherparry.com. Website: www.fletcherandco.com. **Contact:** Christy Fletcher. Member of AAR.
Represents nonfiction books, novels. **Considers these nonfiction areas:** current affairs, history, memoirs, sports, travel, African American; narrative; science; biography; business; health; lifestyle. **Considers these fiction areas:** literary, young, commercial. Does not want genre fiction.

O→ Does not want genre fiction.

How to Contact Query with SASE or e-mail. No attachments. Responds in 6 weeks to queries.

THE FOLEY LITERARY AGENCY

34 E. 38th St., New York NY 10016-2508. (212)686-6930. **Contact:** Joan Foley, Joseph Foley.Represents 10 clients. Currently handles: nonfiction books 75%, novels 25%.
Represents nonfiction books, novels.
How to Contact Query with letter, brief outline, SASE. Responds promptly to queries. Obtains most new clients through recommendations from others (rarely taking on new clients).
Terms Agent receives 10% commission on domestic sales. Agent receives 15% commission on foreign sales.

FOLIO LITERARY MANAGEMENT, LLC

505 Eighth Ave., Suite 603, New York NY 10018. Website: www.foliolit.com. Alternate address: 1627 K St. NW, Suite 1200, Washington DC 20006. Member of AAR. Represents 100+ clients.

- Prior to creating Folio Literary Management, Mr. Hoffman worked for several years at another agency; Mr. Kleinman was an agent at Graybill & English; Ms. Wheeler was an agent at Creative Media Agency; Ms. Fine was an agent at Vigliano Associates and Trident Media Group; Ms. Cartwright-Niumata was an editor at Simon & Schuster, HarperCollins, and Avalon Books; Ms. Becker worked as a copywriter, journalist and author.

Member Agents Scott Hoffman; Jeff Kleinman; Paige Wheeler; Celeste Fine; Erin Cartwright-Niumata, Laney K. Becker; Rachel Vater (fantasy, young adult, women's fiction).
Represents nonfiction books, novels, short story collections. **Considers these nonfiction areas:** animals, equestrian, business, child, history, how to, humor, memoirs, military, nature, popular culture, psychology, religion, science, self help, womens, narrative nonfiction; art; espionage; biography; crime; politics; health/fitness; lifestyle; relationship; culture; cookbooks.**Considers these fiction areas:** erotica, fantasy, literary, mystery, religious, romance, science, thriller, psychological, young, womens, Southern; legal; edgy crime.
How to Contact Query via e-mail only (no attachments). Read agent bios online for specific submission guidelines. Responds in 1 month to queries.
Tips "Please do not submit simultaneously to more than one agent at Folio. If you're not sure which of us is exactly right for your book, don't worry. We work closely as a team, and if one of our agents gets a query that might be more appropriate for someone else, we'll always pass it along. Keep in mind, however, that although we do work closely together, we are all individuals, with specific tastes and preferences – as well as our own unique working styles. So it's important that you check each agent's bio page for clear directions as to how to submit, as well as when to expect feedback."

FOUNDRY LITERARY + MEDIA

33 West 17th St., PH, New York NY 10011. (212)929-5064. Fax: (212)929-5471. Website: www.foundrymedia.com.
Member Agents Peter H. McGuigan (smart, offbeat nonfiction, particularly works of narrative nonfiction on pop culture, niche history, biography, music and science; fiction interests include commercial and literary, across all genres, especially first-time writers); Yfat Reiss Gendell (favors nonfiction books focusing on all manners of prescriptive: how-to, science, health and well-being, memoirs, adventure, travel stories and lighter titles appropriate for the gift trade genre. Yfat also looks for commercial fiction highlighting the full range of women's experiences - young and old - and also seeks science fiction, thrillers and historical fiction); Stéphanie Abou (In fiction and nonfiction alike, Stéphanie is always on the lookout for authors who are accomplished storytellers with their own distinctive voice, who develop memorable characters, and who are able to create psychological conflict with their narrative. She is an across-the-board fiction lover, attracted to both literary and smart upmarket commercial fiction. In nonfiction she leans towards projects that tackle big topics with an unusual approach. Pop

culture, health, science, parenting, women's and multicultural issues are of special interest); Chris Park (memoirs, narrative nonfiction, Christian nonfiction and character-driven fiction).
Represents Considers these nonfiction areas: biography, child, health, memoirs, multicultural, music, popular culture, science. **Considers these fiction areas:** literary, religious.
How to Contact Query with SASE. Should be addressed to one agent only. Submit synopsis, 3 sample chapters, author bio, For nonfiction, submit query, proposal, sample chapter, TOC, bio. Put submisssions on your snail mail submission.

FOX CHASE AGENCY, INC.

701 Lee Road, Suite 102, Chesterbrook Corporate Center, Chesterbrook PA 19087. Member of AAR.
Member Agents A.L. Hart; Jo C. Hart.
Represents nonfiction books, novels.
How to Contact Query with SASE.

FOX LITERARY

168 Second Ave., PMB 180, New York NY 10003. (212)710-5907. E-mail: submissions@foxliterary.com. Website: www.foxliterary.com.
Represents Considers these fiction areas: erotica, fantasy, literary, romance, science, historical romance. Does not want to receive screenplays, poetry, category Westerns, horror, Christian/inspirational, or children's picture books.

- Does not want to receive screenplays, poetry, category Westerns, horror, Christian/inspirational, or children's picture books.

How to Contact E-mail query and first five pages in body of e-mail. E-mail queries preferred.

LYNN C. FRANKLIN ASSOCIATES, LTD.

1350 Broadway, Suite 2015, New York NY 10018. (212)868-6311. Fax: (212)868-6312. **Contact:** Lynn Franklin, Claudia Nys, Michelle Andelman. Other memberships include PEN America. Represents 30-35 clients. 50% of clients are new/unpublished writers. Currently handles: nonfiction books 90%, novels 10%.
Represents nonfiction books, novels. **Considers these nonfiction areas:** newage, biography, current affairs, health, history, memoirs, psychology, religion, self help, spirituality. **Considers these fiction areas:** literary, mainstream, commercial; juvenile, middle-grade, and young adult. "This agency specializes in general nonfiction with a special interest in self-help, biography/memoir, alternative health, and spirituality."

- "This agency specializes in general nonfiction with a special interest in self-help, biography/memoir, alternative health, and spirituality."

How to Contact Query via e-mail to agency@franklinandsiegal.com. No unsolicited mss. No attachments. For nonfiction, query letter with short outline and synopsis. For fiction, query letter with short synopsis and a maximum of 10 sample pages (in the body of the e-mail). Please indicate "query adult" or "query children's) in the subject line. Accepts simultaneous submissions. Responds in 2 weeks to queries. Responds in 6 weeks to mss. Obtains most new clients through recommendations from others, solicitations.
Terms Agent receives 15% commission on domestic sales. Agent receives 20% commission on foreign sales. Offers written contract. 100% of business is derived from commissions on ms. sales. Charges clients for postage, photocopying, long distance telephone (if significant).
Recent Sales *Made for Goodness*, by Archbishop Desmond Tutu and Reverend Mpho Tutu (HarperOne); *God Is Not a Christian*, by John Allen with an Introduction by Archbishop Desmond Tutu (HarperOne); *The Power of Your Child's Imagination*, by Charlotte Reznick (Perigee); *My Guantanamo Diary*, by Mahvish Khan (Public Affairs); *The 100 Year Die*t, by Susan Yager-Berkowitz (Rodale).

JEANNE FREDERICKS LITERARY AGENCY, INC.

221 Benedict Hill Road, New Canaan CT 06840. (203)972-3011. Fax: (203)972-3011. E-mail: jeanne.fredericks@gmail.com. Website: jeannefredericks.com/. **Contact:** Jeanne Fredericks.Member of AAR. Other memberships include Authors Guild. Represents 90 clients. 10% of clients are new/unpublished writers. Currently handles: nonfiction books 100%.

- Prior to opening her agency, Ms. Fredericks was an agent and acting director with the Susan P. Urstadt, Inc. Agency.

Represents nonfiction books. **Considers these nonfiction areas:** animals, autobiography, biography, child guidance, cooking, decorating, finance, foods, gardening, health, history, how-to, interior design, medicine, money, nature, nutrition, parenting, personal improvement, photography, psychology, self-help, sports (not spectator sports), women's issues. This agency specializes in quality adult nonfiction by authorities in their fields. Does not want to receive children's books or fiction.

- This agency specializes in quality adult nonfiction by authorities in their fields. Does not want to receive children's books or fiction.

How to Contact Query first with SASE, then send outline/proposal, 1-2 sample chapters, SASE. Accepts simultaneous submissions. Responds in 3-5 weeks to queries. Responds in 2-4 months to mss. Obtains most new clients through recommendations from others, solicitations, conferences.

Terms Agent receives 15% commission on domestic sales. Agent receives 25% commission on foreign sales with co-agent Offers written contract, binding for 9 months; 2-month notice must be given to terminate contract. Charges client for photocopying of whole proposals and mss, overseas postage, priority mail, express mail services.

Recent Sales *The Green Market Baking Book*, by Laura Martin (Sterling); *Tales of the Seven Seas*, by Dennis Powers (Taylor); *the Monopoly® Guide to Real Estate*, by Carolyn Janik (Sterling); *The Generosity Plan*, by Kathy LeMay (Beyond Words/Atria); *Canadian Vegetable Gardening*, by Doug Green (Cool Springs).

Writers Conferences Connecticut Authors and Publishers Association-University Conference; ASJA Writers' Conference; BookExpo America; Garden Writers' Association Annual Symposium; Harvard Medical School CME Course in Publishing.

Tips "Be sure to research competition for your work and be able to justify why there's a need for your book. I enjoy building an author's career, particularly if he/she is professional, hardworking, and courteous. Aside from 17 years of agenting experience, I've had 10 years of editorial experience in adult trade book publishing that enables me to help an author polish a proposal so that it's more appealing to prospective editors. My MBA in marketing also distinguishes me from other agents."

GRACE FREEDSON'S PUBLISHING NETWORK

375 North Broadway, Suite 102, Jericho NY 11753. (516)931-7757. Fax: (516)931-7759. E-mail: gfreedson@worldnet.att.net. **Contact:** Grace Freedson.Represents 100 clients. 10% of clients are new/unpublished writers. Currently handles: nonfiction books 90%, juvenile books 10%.

- Prior to becoming an agent, Ms. Freedson was a managing editor and director of acquisition for Barron's Educational Series.

Represents nonfiction books, juvenile. **Considers these nonfiction areas:** animals, business, cooking, current affairs, education, health, history, how to, humor, money, nature, popular culture, psychology, science, self help, sports, craft/hobbies. "In addition to representing many qualified authors, I work with publishers as a packager of unique projects—mostly series." Does not want to receive fiction.

- O→ "In addition to representing many qualified authors, I work with publishers as a packager of unique projects—mostly series." Does not want to receive fiction.

How to Contact Query with SASE. Submit synopsis, SASE. . Responds in 2-6 weeks to queries. Obtains most new clients through recommendations from others.

Terms Agent receives 15% commission on domestic sales. Offers written contract; 30-day notice must be given to terminate contract.

Recent Sales Sold 50 titles in the last year. *The Total Brain Workout*, by Marcel Danes (Harlequin); *When Numbers Don't Lie*, by Kaiser Fung (McGraw-Hill); *Image as a Second Language*, by Lizandra Vega (Anacom); *Pay Dirt*, by John Tullock (Adams Media); *Social Cruelty*, by Carl Pickhardt (Sourcebooks).

Writers Conferences BookExpo of America.

Tips "At this point, I am only reviewing proposals on nonfiction topics by credentialed authors with platforms."

FRESH BOOKS LITERARY AGENCY

231 Diana St., Placerville CA 95667. E-mail: matt@fresh-books.com. Website: www.fresh-books.com. **Contact:** Matt Wagner.Represents 30+ clients. 5% of clients are new/unpublished writers. Currently handles: nonfiction books 95%, multimedia 5%.

- Prior to becoming an agent, Mr. Wagner was with Waterside Productions for 15 years.

Represents nonfiction books. **Considers these nonfiction areas:** crafts, animals, anthropology, art, business, child, computers, cooking, current affairs, education, ethnic, gay, government, health, history, how to, humor, military, money, music, nature, photography, popular culture, psychology, science, sports. "I specialize in tech and how-to. I love working with books and authors, and I've repped many of my clients for upwards of 15 years now." Actively seeking popular science, natural history, adventure, how-to, business, education and reference. Does not want to receive fiction, children's books or poetry.

- O→ "I specialize in tech and how-to. I love working with books and authors, and I've repped many of my clients for upwards of 15 years now." Actively seeking popular science, natural history, adventure, how-to, business, education and reference. Does not want to receive fiction, children's books or poetry.

How to Contact Query with SASE. No phone calls. Accepts simultaneous submissions. Responds in 1-4 weeks to queries. Responds in 1-4 weeks to mss. Obtains most new clients through recommendations from others.

Terms Agent receives 15% commission on domestic sales. Agent receives 20% commission on foreign

sales.

Recent Sales *The Myth of Multitaking: How Doing It All Gets Nothing Done* (Jossey-Bass); *Wilderness Survival for Dummies* (Wiley); and *The Zombie Combat Manual* (Berkley).

Tips "Do your research. Find out what sorts of books and authors an agent represents. Go to conferences. Make friends with other writers—most of my clients come from referrals."

SARAH JANE FREYMANN LITERARY AGENCY

59 W. 71st St., Suite 9B, New York NY 10023. (212)362-9277. E-mail: sarah@sarahjanefreymann.com; Submissions@SarahJaneFreymann.com. Website: www.sarahjanefreymann.com. **Contact:** Sarah Jane Freymann, Steve Schwartz. Represents 100 clients. 20% of clients are new/unpublished writers. Currently handles: nonfiction books 75%, novels 23%, juvenile books 2%.

Member Agents Sarah Jane Freymann; Steve Schwartz, steve@sarahjanefreymann.com (historical novels, thrillers, crime, sports, humor, food, travel); Katharine Sands.

Represents nonfiction books, novels, illustrated books. **Considers these nonfiction areas:** interior, animals, anthropology, art, biography, business, child, cooking, current affairs, ethnic, health, history, memoirs, narrative, nature, psychology, religion, self help, womens, lifestyle. **Considers these fiction areas:** ethnic, literary, mainstream.

How to Contact Query with SASE. Responds in 2 weeks to queries. Responds in 6 weeks to mss. Obtains most new clients through recommendations from others.

Terms Agent receives 15% commission on domestic sales. Agent receives 20% commission on foreign sales. Offers written contract. Charges clients for long distance, overseas postage, photocopying. 100% of business is derived from commissions on ms sales.

Recent Sales *How to Make Love to a Plastic Cup: And Other Things I Learned While Trying to Knock Up My Wife*, by Greg Wolfe (Harper Collins); *I Want to Be Left Behind: Rapture Here on Earth*, by Brenda Peterson (a Merloyd Lawrence Book); *That Bird Has My Name: The Autobiography of an Innocent Man on Death Row*, by Jarvis Jay Masters with an Introduction by Pema Chodrun (HarperOne); *Perfect One-Dish Meals*, by Pam Anderson (Houghton Mifflin); *Souls of the Sky: The Essence of Birds*, by Sy Montgomery (Simon & Schuster); *Emptying the Nest: Launching Your Reluctant Young Adult*, by Dr. Brad Sachs (Macmillan); *Tossed & Found*, by Linda and John Meyers (Steward, Tabori & Chang).

Tips "I love fresh, new, passionate works by authors who love what they are doing and have both natural talent and carefully honed skill."

FREDRICA S. FRIEDMAN AND CO., INC.

136 E. 57th St., 14th Floor, New York NY 10022. (212)829-9600. Fax: (212)829-9669. E-mail: info@fredricafriedman.com; submissions@fredricafriedman.com. Website: www.fredricafriedman.com/. **Contact:** Ms. Chandler Smith. Represents 75+ clients. 50% of clients are new/unpublished writers. Currently handles: nonfiction books 95%, novels 5%.

Represents nonfiction books, novels, anthologies. **Considers these nonfiction areas:** art, biography, business, child, cooking, current affairs, education, ethnic, gay, government, health, history, how to, humor, language, memoirs, money, music, photography, popular culture, psychology, self help, sociology, film, true crime, womens, interior design/decorating. **Considers these fiction areas:** literary. "We represent a select group of outstanding nonfiction and fiction writers. We are particularly interested in helping writers expand their readership and develop their careers." Does not want poetry, plays, screenplays, children's books, sci-fi/fantasy, or horror.

- "We represent a select group of outstanding nonfiction and fiction writers. We are particularly interested in helping writers expand their readership and develop their careers." Does not want poetry, plays, screenplays, children's books, sci-fi/fantasy, or horror.

How to Contact Submit e-query, synopsis. Accepts simultaneous submissions. Responds in 4-6 weeks to queries. Responds in 4-6 weeks to mss. Obtains most new clients through recommendations from others.

Terms Agent receives 15% commission on domestic sales. Agent receives 25% commission on foreign sales. Offers written contract. Charges for photocopying and messenger/shipping fees for proposals.

Recent Sales *A World of Lies: The Crime and Consequences of Bernie Madoff*, by Diana B. Henriques (Times Books/Holt); *Polemic and Memoir: The Nixon Years*, by Patrick J. Buchanan (St. Martin's Press); *Angry Fat Girls: Five Women, Five Hundred Pounds, and a Year of Losing It...Again*, by Frances Kuffel (Berkley/Penguin); *Life With My Sister Madonna*, by Christopher Ciccone with Wendy Leigh (Simon & Schuster Spotlight); *The World Is Curved: Hidden Dangers to the Global Economy*, by David Smick (Portfolio/Penguin); *Going to See the Elephant*, by Rodes Fishburne (Delacorte/Random House); *Seducing the Boys Club: Uncensored Tactics from a Woman at the Top*, by Nina DiSesa (Ballantine/Random House); *The Girl from Foreign: A Search for Shipwrecked Ancestors, Forgotten Histories, and a Sense of Home*, by Sadia Shepard (The Penguin Press).

Tips "Spell the agent's name correctly on your query letter."

THE FRIEDRICH AGENCY

136 East 57th St., 18th Floor, New York NY 10022. Website: www.friedrichagency.com. **Contact:** Molly Friedrich. Member of AAR. Represents 50+ clients.

- Prior to her current position, Ms. Friedrich was an agent at the Aaron Priest Literary Agency.

Member Agents Molly Friedrich, Founder and Agent (open to queries); Paul Cirone, Foreign Rights Director and Agent(open to queries); Lucy Carson, assistant.

Represents full-length fiction and nonfiction.

How to Contact Query with SASE by mail, or e-mail.

Recent Sales *Vanished* by Joseph Finder, *T is for Trespass* by Sue Grafton, *Look Again* by Lisa Scottoline, *Olive Kitteridge* by Elizabeth Strout. Other clients include Frank McCourt, Jane Smiley, Esmeralda Santiago, Terry McMillan, Cathy Schine, and more.

FULL CIRCLE LITERARY, LLC

7676 Hazard Center Dr., Suite 500, San Diego CA 92108. E-mail: submissions@fullcircleliterary.com. Website: www.fullcircleliterary.com. **Contact:** Lilly Ghahremani, Stefanie Von Borstel. Represents 55 clients. 60% of clients are new/unpublished writers. Currently handles: nonfiction books 70%, novels 10%, juvenile books 20%.

- Before forming Full Circle, Ms. Von Borstel worked in both marketing and editorial capacities at Penguin and Harcourt; Ms. Ghahremani received her law degree from UCLA, and has experience in representing authors on legal affairs.

Member Agents Lilly Ghahremani (young adult, pop culture, crafts, "green" living, narrative nonfiction, business, relationships, Middle Eastern interest, multicultural); Stefanie Von Borstel (Latino interest, crafts, parenting, wedding/relationships, how-to, self help, middle grade/teen fiction/YA, green living, multicultural/bilingual picture books).

Represents nonfiction books, juvenile. **Considers these nonfiction areas:** animals, biography, business, child guidance, crafts, cultural interests, current affairs, ethnic, how-to, juvenile nonfiction, parenting, personal improvement, popular culture, self-help, women's issues, women's studies. **Considers these fiction areas:** ethnic, literary, young adult. "Our full-service boutique agency, representing a range of nonfiction and children's books (limited fiction), provides a one-stop resource for authors. Our extensive experience in the realms of law and marketing provide Full Circle clients with a unique edge." "Actively seeking nonfiction by authors with a unique and strong platform, projects that offer new and diverse viewpoints, and literature with a global or multicultural perspective. We are particularly interested in books with a Latino or Middle Eastern angle and books related to pop culture." Does not want to receive "screenplays, poetry, commercial fiction or genre fiction (horror, thriller, mystery, Western, sci-fi, fantasy, romance, historical fiction)."

- "Our full-service boutique agency, representing a range of nonfiction and children's books (limited fiction), provides a one-stop resource for authors. Our extensive experience in the realms of law and marketing provide Full Circle clients with a unique edge." "Actively seeking nonfiction by authors with a unique and strong platform, projects that offer new and diverse viewpoints, and literature with a global or multicultural perspective. We are particularly interested in books with a Latino or Middle Eastern angle and books related to pop culture." Does not want to receive "screenplays, poetry, commercial fiction or genre fiction (horror, thriller, mystery, Western, sci-fi, fantasy, romance, historical fiction)."

How to Contact Agency accepts e-queries. See Web site for fiction guidelines, as they are in flux. For nonfiction, send full proposal Accepts simultaneous submissions. Responds in 1-2 weeks to queries. Responds in 4-6 weeks to mss. Obtains most new clients through recommendations from others, solicitations, conferences.

Terms Agent receives 15% commission on domestic sales. Agent receives 20% commission on foreign sales. Offers written contract; up to 30-day notice must be given to terminate contract. Charges for copying and postage.

Tips "Put your best foot forward. Contact us when you simply can't make your project any better on your own, and please be sure your work fits with what the agent you're approaching represents. Little things count, so copyedit your work. Join a writing group and attend conferences to get objective and constructive feedback before submitting. Be active about building your platform as an author before, during, and after publication. Remember this is a business and your agent is a business partner."

NANCY GALLT LITERARY AGENCY

273 Charlton Ave., South Orange NJ 07079. (973)761-6358. Fax: (973)761-6318. E-mail: ngallt@aol.com. **Contact:** Nancy Gallt. Represents 40 clients. 30% of clients are new/unpublished writers. Currently handles: juvenile books 100%.

- Prior to opening her agency, Ms. Gallt was subsidiary rights director of the children's book division at Morrow, Harper and Viking.

Member Agents Nancy Gallt, Craig Virden.

Represents juvenile. I only handle children's books. Actively seeking middle-grade and young adult novels. Does not want to receive rhyming picture book texts.

- I only handle children's books. Actively seeking middle-grade and young adult novels. Does not want to receive rhyming picture book texts.

How to Contact Query with 3 sample chapters, SASE. If an author wants the ms returned, include a large SASE. Accepts simultaneous submissions. Responds in 3 months to queries. Responds in 3 months to mss. Obtains most new clients through recommendations from others, solicitations.

Terms Agent receives 15% commission on domestic sales. Agent receives 20% commission on foreign sales. Offers written contract; 30-day notice must be given to terminate contract.

Recent Sales Sold 50 titles in the last year. Percy Jackson series, by Rick Riordan (Hyperion); A-Z Mysteries Super-Edition, by Ron Roy (Random House Books for Young Readers); *Little Gnome* (Simon & Schuster); *The Story of My Bat Mitzvah*, by Nora Raleigh Baskin.

Tips A book stands on its own, so a submission should be as close to perfect as the author can make it.

THE GARAMOND AGENCY, INC.

12 Horton St., Newburyport MA 01950. E-mail: query@garamondagency.com. Website: www.garamondagency.com. Other memberships include Author's Guild.

Member Agents Lisa Adams; David Miller.

Represents nonfiction books. **Considers these nonfiction areas:** business, government, history, psychology, science, social science, narrative nonfiction. "We work closely with our authors through each stage of the publishing process, first in developing their books and then in presenting themselves and their ideas effectively to publishers and to readers. We represent our clients throughout the world in all languages, media, and territories through an extensive network of subagents." No proposals for children's or young adult books, fiction, poetry, or memoir.

- "We work closely with our authors through each stage of the publishing process, first in developing their books and then in presenting themselves and their ideas effectively to publishers and to readers. We represent our clients throughout the world in all languages, media, and territories through an extensive network of subagents." No proposals for children's or young adult books, fiction, poetry, or memoir.

How to Contact See Web site.

Recent Sales *The Breakthrough Imperative*, by Mark Gottfredson and Steven Schaubert (HarperCollins); *Loneliness*, by John Capioppo and William Patrick (Norton); T*he Virtue of Vice*, by Arthur Brooks (Basic). See web site for other clients.

Tips "Query us first if you have any questions about whether we are the right agency for your work."

MAX GARTENBERG LITERARY AGENCY

912 N. Pennsylvania Ave., Yardley PA 19067. (215)295-9230. Website: www.maxgartenberg.com. **Contact:** Anne Devlin.Represents 50 clients. 5% of clients are new/unpublished writers. Currently handles: nonfiction books 90%, novels 10%.

Member Agents Max Gartenberg, president, (biography, environment, and narrative nonfiction); Anne G. Devlin, agent, agdevlin@aol.com (politics, current events, women's issues, health, commercial fiction, sports, popular culture, and humor).

Represents nonfiction books, novels. **Considers these nonfiction areas:** agriculture horticulture, animals, art, biography, child, current affairs, health, history, money, music, nature, psychology, science, self help, sports, film, true crime, womens.

How to Contact Query with SASE. Send queries via snail mail. Accepts simultaneous submissions. Responds in 2 weeks to queries. Responds in 6 weeks to mss. Obtains most new clients through recommendations from others, following up on good query letters.

Terms Agent receives 15% commission on domestic sales. Agent receives 20% commission on foreign sales.

Recent Sales *What Patients Taught Me*, by Audrey Young, MD (Sasquatch Books); U*northodox Warfare: The Chinese Experience*, by Ralph D. Sawyer (Westview Press); *Encyclopedia of Earthquakes and Volcanoes*, by Alexander E. Gates (Facts on File); *Homebirth in the Hospital*, by Stacey Kerr, MD (Sentient Publications).

Tips "We have recently expanded to allow more access for new writers."

DON GASTWIRTH & ASSOCIATES

265 College St., New Haven CT 06510. (203)562-7600. Fax: (203)562-4300. E-mail: Donlit@snet.net. **Contact:** Don Gastwirth. Signatory of WGA. Represents 26 clients. 10% of clients are new/unpublished writers. Currently handles: nonfiction books 30%, scholarly books 60%, other 10% other.

- Prior to becoming an agent, Mr. Gastwirth was an entertainment lawyer and law professor.

Represents nonfiction books, scholarly. **Considers these nonfiction areas:** business, current affairs, history, military, money, music, nature, popular culture, psychology, translation, true crime. **Considers**

these fiction areas: mystery, thriller. This is a selective agency and is rarely open to new clients that do not come through a referral.

O→ This is a selective agency and is rarely open to new clients that do not come through a referral.

How to Contact Query with SASE.

Terms Agent receives 15% commission on domestic sales. Agent receives 10% commission on foreign sales.

GELFMAN SCHNEIDER LITERARY AGENTS, INC.

250 W. 57th St., Suite 2122, New York NY 10107. (212)245-1993. Fax: (212)245-8678. E-mail: mail@gelfmanschneider.com. **Contact:** Jane Gelfman, Deborah Schneider. Member of AAR. Represents 300+ clients. 10% of clients are new/unpublished writers.

Represents nonfiction books, novels. **Considers these fiction areas:** literary, mainstream, mystery, womens. Does not want to receive romance, science fiction, westerns, or children's books.

O→ Does not want to receive romance, science fiction, westerns, or children's books.

How to Contact Query with SASE. Send queries via snail mail only. Responds in 1 month to queries. Responds in 2 months to mss.

Terms Agent receives 15% commission on domestic sales. Agent receives 20% commission on foreign sales. Agent receives 15% commission on film sales. Offers written contract. Charges clients for photocopying and messengers/couriers.

THE GERNERT COMPANY

136 East 57th St., 18th Floor, New York NY 10022. (212)838-7777. Fax: (212)838-6020. E-mail: info@thegernertco.com. **Contact:** Sarah Burnes.

- Prior to her current position, Ms. Burnes was with Burnes & Clegg, Inc.

Member Agents Sarah Burnes, sburnes@thegernertco.com (commercial fiction, adventure and true story); Stephanie Cabot (literary fiction, commercial fiction, historical fiction); Chris Parris-Lamb, clamb@thegernertco.com.

Represents nonfiction books, novels.

How to Contact Query with SASE. E-query with cover letter and first sample chapter. Queries should be addressed to a specific agent via the email subject line. See company Web site for more instructions. Obtains most new clients through recommendations from others, solicitations.

Recent Sales *House of Joy*, by Sarah-Kate Lynch (Plume); *Mudbound*, by Hillary Jordan (Algonquin); *The Reluctant Diplomat: Peter Paul Rubens and His Secret Mission to Save Europe from Itself*, by Mark Lamster (Talese).

BARRY GOLDBLATT LITERARY, LLC

320 Seventh Ave., #266, Brooklyn NY 11215. Fax: (718)360-5453. Website: www.bgliterary.com/contactme.html. **Contact:** Barry Goldblatt, Joe Monti, Beth Fleisher. Member of AAR.

Represents juvenile books. **Considers these fiction areas:** picture books, young adult, middle grade, all genres.

How to Contact E-mail queries query@bgliterary.com, and include the first five pages and a synopsis of the novel pasted into the text of the e-mail. No attachments or links.

Recent Sales *The Infernal Devices* trilogy, by Cassandra Clare (McElderry Books); *Kat by Moonlight* trilogy, by Stephanie Burgis (Atheneum Books), *Giving Up a Ghost*, by Samantha Schutz (Scholastic).

FRANCES GOLDIN LITERARY AGENCY, INC.

57 E. 11th St., Suite 5B, New York NY 10003. (212)777-0047. Fax: (212)228-1660. E-mail: agency@goldinlit.com. Website: www.goldinlit.com. Member of AAR. Represents over 100 clients.

Member Agents Frances Goldin, principal/agent; Ellen Geiger, agent (commercial and literary fiction and nonfiction, cutting-edge topics of all kinds); Matt McGowan, agent/rights director (innovative works of fiction and nonfiction); Sam Stoloff, agent (literary fiction, memoir, history, accessible sociology and philosophy, cultural studies, serious journalism, narrative and topical nonfiction with a progressive orientation); Josie Schoel, agent/office manager (literary fiction and nonfiction).

Represents nonfiction books, novels. "We are hands on and we work intensively with clients on proposal and manuscript development." Does not want anything that is racist, sexist, agist, homophobic, or pornographic. No screenplays, children's books, art books, cookbooks, business books, diet books, self-help, or genre fiction.

O→ "We are hands on and we work intensively with clients on proposal and manuscript development." Does not want anything that is racist, sexist, agist, homophobic, or pornographic. No screenplays, children's books, art books, cookbooks, business books, diet books, self-help, or genre fiction.

How to Contact Query with SASE. No unsolicited mss or work previously submitted to publishers. Prefers hard-copy queries. If querying by e-mail, put word "query" in subject line. Responds in 6 weeks to queries.

THE SUSAN GOLOMB LITERARY AGENCY

875 Avenue of the Americas, Suite 2302, New York NY 10001. Fax: (212)239-9503. E-mail: susan@sgolombagency.com. **Contact:** Susan Golomb. Represents 100 clients. 20% of clients are new/unpublished writers. Currently handles: nonfiction books 50%, novels 40%, story collections 10%.

Represents nonfiction books, novels, short story collections, novellas. **Considers these nonfiction areas:** animals, anthropology, biography, business, current affairs, government, health, history, memoirs, military, money, nature, popular culture, psychology, science, sociology, womens. **Considers these fiction areas:** ethnic, historical, humor, literary, mainstream, thriller, young, women's/chick lit. "We specialize in literary and upmarket fiction and nonfiction that is original, vibrant and of excellent quality and craft. Nonfiction should be edifying, paradigm-shifting, fresh and entertaining." Actively seeking writers with strong voices. Does not want to receive genre fiction.

O→ "We specialize in literary and upmarket fiction and nonfiction that is original, vibrant and of excellent quality and craft. Nonfiction should be edifying, paradigm-shifting, fresh and entertaining." Actively seeking writers with strong voices. Does not want to receive genre fiction.

How to Contact Query with SASE. Submit outline/proposal, synopsis, 1 sample chapters, author bio, SASE. .Query via mail or e-mail. Responds in 2 week to queries. Responds in 8 weeks to mss. Obtains most new clients through recommendations from others, solicitations.

Terms Agent receives 15% commission on domestic sales. Agent receives 20% commission on foreign sales. Offers written contract.

Recent Sales Sold 20 titles in the last year. *Sunnyside*, by Glen David Gold (Knopf); *How to Buy a Love of Reading*, by Tanya Egan Gibson (Dutton); *Telex From Cuba*, by Rachel Kushner (Scribner); *The Imperfectionists*, by Tom Rachman (Dial).

GOODMAN ASSOCIATES

500 West End Ave., New York NY 10024-4317. (212)873-4806. Member of AAR.

Represents Accepting new clients by recommendation only.

O→ Accepting new clients by recommendation only.

IRENE GOODMAN LITERARY AGENCY

27 W. 24th Street, Suite 700B, New York NY 10010. E-mail: queries@irenegoodman.com. Website: www.irenegoodman.com. **Contact:** Irene Goodman, Miriam Kriss. Member of AAR.

Member Agents Irene Goodman; Miriam Kriss; Barbara Poelle; Jon Sternfeld (intelligent literary fiction, high-end modern fiction; nonfiction and narrative nonfiction dealing with social, cultural and historical issues; an occasional memoir and current affairs book).

Represents nonfiction books, novels. **Considers these nonfiction areas:** history, parenting, social issues, francophilia, anglophilia, Judaica, lifestyles, cooking, memoir. **Considers these fiction areas:** historical, literary, mystery, romance, thriller, young, womens, chick lit; modern urban fantasies. "Specializes in the finest in commercial fiction and nonfiction. We have a strong background in women's voices, including mysteries, romance, women's fiction, thrillers, suspense, and chick lit. Historical fiction is one of Irene's particular passions and Miriam is fanatical about modern urban fantasies. We are also very interested in young adult fiction, both literary and those with an edgy, chick-litty voice. In nonfiction, Irene is looking for topics on narrative history, social issues and trends, education, Judaica, Francophilia, Anglophilia, other cultures, animals, food, crafts, and memoir."

O→ "Specializes in the finest in commercial fiction and nonfiction. We have a strong background in women's voices, including mysteries, romance, women's fiction, thrillers, suspense, and chick lit. Historical fiction is one of Irene's particular passions and Miriam is fanatical about modern urban fantasies. We are also very interested in young adult fiction, both literary and those with an edgy, chick-litty voice. In nonfiction, Irene is looking for topics on narrative history, social issues and trends, education, Judaica, Francophilia, Anglophilia, other cultures, animals, food, crafts, and memoir."

How to Contact Query with SASE. Submit synopsis, first 10 pages.E-mail queries only! See the Web site submission page. No e-mail attachments. Responds in 2 months to queries.

Recent Sales *Beg for Mercy*, by Toni Andrews; *The Devil Inside*, by Jenna Black; *Hooking Up or Holding Out*, by Jamie Callan; *Seducing the Spy*, by Celeste Bradley.

Tips "We are receiving an unprecedented amount of e-mail queries. If you find that the mailbox is full, please try again in two weeks. E-mail queries to our personal addresses will not be answered."

GOUMEN & SMIRNOVA LITERARY AGENCY

Nauki pr., 19/2 fl. 293, St. Petersburg 195220 Russia. E-mail: info@gs-agency.com. Website: www.gs-agency.com. **Contact:** Julia Goumen, Natalia Smirnova. Represents 20 clients. 10% of clients are new/unpublished writers. Currently handles: nonfiction books 10%, novels 80%, story collections 5%, juvenile books 5%.

- Prior to becoming agents, both Ms. Goumen and Ms. Smirnova worked as foreign rights managers with an established Russian publisher selling translation rights for literary fiction.

Member Agents Julia Goumen (translation rights, Russian language rights, film rights); Natalia Smirnova (translation rights, Russian language rights, film rights).

Represents nonfiction books, novels, short story collections, novellas, movie, tv, tv movie, sitcom. **Considers these nonfiction areas:** biography, current affairs, ethnic, humor, memoirs, music. **Considers these fiction areas:** adventure, experimental, family, historical, horror, literary, mainstream, mystery, romance, thriller, young, womens. **Considers these script areas:** action, comedy, detective, family, mainstream, romantic comedy, romantic drama, teen, thriller. "We are the first full-service agency in Russia, representing our authors in book publishing, film, television, and other areas. We are also the first agency, representing Russian authors worldwide, based in Russia. The agency also represents international authors, agents and publishers in Russia. Our philosophy is to provide an individual approach to each author, finding the right publisher both at home and across international cultural and linguistic borders, developing original marketing and promotional strategies for each title." Actively seeking manuscripts written in Russian, both literary and commercial; and foreign publishers and agents with the high-profile fiction and general nonfiction—represent in Russia. Does not want to receive unpublished manuscripts in languages other then Russian, or any information irrelevant to our activity.

- "We are the first full-service agency in Russia, representing our authors in book publishing, film, television, and other areas. We are also the first agency, representing Russian authors worldwide, based in Russia. The agency also represents international authors, agents and publishers in Russia. Our philosophy is to provide an individual approach to each author, finding the right publisher both at home and across international cultural and linguistic borders, developing original marketing and promotional strategies for each title." Actively seeking manuscripts written in Russian, both literary and commercial; and foreign publishers and agents with the high-profile fiction and general nonfiction—represent in Russia. Does not want to receive unpublished manuscripts in languages other then Russian, or any information irrelevant to our activity.

How to Contact Query with SASE. Submit synopsis, author bio. Accepts simultaneous submissions. Responds in 14 days to mss. Obtains most new clients through recommendations from others, solicitations.

Terms Agent receives 20% commission on domestic sales. Agent receives 20% commission on foreign sales. Offers written contract, binding for 1 year; 2-month notice must be given to terminate contract.

GRAHAM MAW LITERARY AGENCY

19 Thornhill Square, London England N1 1BJ United Kingdom. (44)(207)812-9937. E-mail: enquiries@grahammawagency.com. Website: www.grahammawagency.com. Represents 20 clients. 30% of clients are new/unpublished writers. Currently handles: nonfiction books 100%.

- Prior to opening her agency, Ms. Graham Maw was a publishing director at HarperCollins and worked in rights, publicity and editorial. She has ghostwritten several nonfiction books, which gives her an insider's knowledge of both the publishing industry and the pleasures and pitfalls of authorships. Ms. Christie has a background in advertising and journalism.

Member Agents Jane Graham Maw; Jennifer Christie.

Represents nonfiction books. **Considers these nonfiction areas:** biography, child, cooking, health, how to, memoirs, popular culture, psychology, self help. "We aim to make the publishing process easier and smoother for authors. We work hard to ensure that publishing proposals are watertight before submission. We aim for collaborative relationships with publishers so that we provide the right books to the right editor at the right time. We represent ghostwriters as well as authors." Actively seeking work from UK writers only. Does not want to receive fiction, poetry, plays or e-mail submissions.

- "We aim to make the publishing process easier and smoother for authors. We work hard to ensure that publishing proposals are watertight before submission. We aim for collaborative relationships with publishers so that we provide the right books to the right editor at the right time. We represent ghostwriters as well as authors." Actively seeking work from UK writers only. Does not want to receive fiction, poetry, plays or e-mail submissions.

How to Contact Query with synopsis, chapter outline, bio, SASE. Responds in 2 weeks to queries. Obtains most new clients through recommendations from others.

Terms Agent receives 15% commission on domestic sales. Agent receives 20% commission on foreign sales. Offers written contract; 30-day notice must be given to terminate contract.

Writers Conferences London Book Fair, Frankfurt Book Fair.

Tips "UK clients only!"

ASHLEY GRAYSON LITERARY AGENCY

1342 W. 18th St., San Pedro CA 90732. Fax: (310)514-1148. E-mail: graysonagent@earthlink.net. Website: www.graysonagency.com/blog. Member of AAR. Represents 100 clients. 5% of clients are new/unpublished writers. Currently handles: nonfiction books 20%, novels 50%, juvenile books 30%.

Member Agents Ashley Grayson (fantasy, mystery, thrillers, young adult); Carolyn Grayson (chick lit, mystery, children's, nonfiction, women's fiction, romance, thrillers); Denise Dumars (mind/body/spirit, women's fiction, dark fantasy/horror); Lois Winston (women's fiction, chick lit, mystery).

Represents nonfiction books, novels. **Considers these nonfiction areas:** business, computers, history, popular culture, science, self help, sports, true crime, mind/body/spirit; health; lifestyle. **Considers these fiction areas:** fantasy, juvenile, multicultural, mystery, romance, science, young, womens, chick lit. "We prefer to work with published (traditional print), established authors. We will give first consideration to authors who come recommended to us by our clients or other publishing professionals. We accept a very small number of new, previously unpublished authors."

> O→ "We prefer to work with published (traditional print), established authors. We will give first consideration to authors who come recommended to us by our clients or other publishing professionals. We accept a very small number of new, previously unpublished authors."

How to Contact As of early 2008, the agency was only open to fiction authors with publishing credits (no self-published). For nonfiction, only writers with great platforms will be considered.

Terms Agent receives 15% commission on domestic sales. Agent receives 20% commission on foreign sales.

SANFORD J. GREENBURGER ASSOCIATES, INC.

55 Fifth Ave., New York NY 10003. (212)206-5600. Fax: (212)463-8718. E-mail: queryHL@sjga.com. Website: www.greenburger.com. Member of AAR. Represents 500 clients.

Member Agents Heide Lange; Faith Hamlin; Dan Mandel; Matthew Bialer; Jeremy Katz; Tricia Davey, Courtney Miller-Callihan, Michael Harriot.

Represents nonfiction books, novels. **Considers these nonfiction areas:** agriculture horticulture, americana, crafts, interior, juvenile, newage, young, animals, anthropology, art, biography, business, child, computers, cooking, current affairs, education, ethnic, gardening, gay, government, health, history, how to, humor, language, memoirs, military, money, multicultural, music, nature, philosophy, photography, popular culture, psychology, recreation, regional, religion, science, self help, sex, sociology, software, sports, film, translation, travel, true crime, womens. **Considers these fiction areas:** glitz, psychic, adventure, detective, ethnic, family, feminist, gay, historical, humor, literary, mainstream, mystery, regional, sports, thriller. No romances or Westerns.

> O→ No romances or Westerns.

How to Contact Submit query, first 3 chapters, synopsis, brief bio, SASE. Accepts simultaneous submissions. Responds in 2 months to queries and mss. Responds to mss. Obtains most new clients through recommendations from others.

Terms Agent receives 15% commission on domestic sales. Agent receives 20% commission on foreign sales. Charges for photocopying and books for foreign and subsidiary rights submissions.

THE GREENHOUSE LITERARY AGENCY

11308 Lapham Drive, Oakton VA 22124. E-mail: submissions@greenhouseliterary.com. Website: www.greenhouseliterary.com. **Contact:** Sarah Davies. Other memberships include SCBWI. Represents 8 clients. 100% of clients are new/unpublished writers. Currently handles: juvenile books 100%.

- Prior to becoming an agent, Ms. Davies was the publishing director of Macmillan Children's Books in London.

Represents juvenile. **Considers these fiction areas:** juvenile, young. "We exclusively represents authors writing fiction for children and teens. The agency has offices in both the USA and UK, and Sarah Davies (who is British) personally represents authors to both markets. The agency's commission structure reflects this – taking 15% for sales to both US and UK, thus treating both as 'domestic' market." All genres of children's and YA fiction - ages 5+. Does not want to receive nonfiction, poetry, picture books (text or illustration) or work aimed at adults.

> O→ "We exclusively represents authors writing fiction for children and teens. The agency has offices in both the USA and UK, and Sarah Davies (who is British) personally represents authors to both markets. The agency's commission structure reflects this – taking 15% for sales to both US and UK, thus treating both as 'domestic' market." All genres of children's and YA fiction - ages 5+. Does not want to receive nonfiction, poetry, picture books (text or illustration) or work aimed at adults.

How to Contact E-queries only as per guidelines given on Web site. Query should contain one-paragraph synopsis, one-paragraph bio, up to 5 sample pages pasted into e-mail. Replies to submissions in which agency is interested. Responds in 6-8 weeks to requested full manuscripts. Responds in 6 week to queries. Obtains most new clients through recommendations from others, solicitations, conferences.

Terms Agent receives 15% commission on domestic sales. Agent receives 25% commission on foreign sales. Offers written contract. This agency charges for copies for overseas submissions.

Writers Conferences Bologna Children's Book Fair, SCBWI conferences, BookExpo America.

Tips "Before submitting material, authors should read the Greenhouse's 'Top 10 Tips for Authors of Children's Fiction,' which can be found on our Web site."

KATHRYN GREEN LITERARY AGENCY, LLC

250 West 57th St., Suite 2302, New York NY 10107. (212)245-2445. Fax: (212)245-2040. E-mail: query@kgreenagency.com. **Contact:** Kathy Green.Other memberships include Women's Media Group. Represents approximately 20 clients. 50% of clients are new/unpublished writers. Currently handles: nonfiction books 50%, novels 25%, juvenile books 25%.

- Prior to becoming an agent, Ms. Green was a book and magazine editor.

Represents nonfiction books, novels, short story collections, juvenile, middle grade and young adult only). **Considers these nonfiction areas:** biography, business, child, cooking, current affairs, education, history, how to, humor, memoirs, popular culture, psychology, self help, sports, true crime, womens, juvenile. **Considers these fiction areas:** detective, family, historical, humor, juvenile, middle grade and young adult only, literary, mainstream, mystery, romance, thriller, young, women's. Keeping the client list small means that writers receive my full attention throughout the process of getting their project published. Does not want to receive science fiction or fantasy.

O┳ Keeping the client list small means that writers receive my full attention throughout the process of getting their project published. Does not want to receive science fiction or fantasy.

How to Contact Query with SASE. Query first. Send no samples unless requested. Accepts simultaneous submissions. Responds in 1-2 months to mss. Obtains most new clients through recommendations from others, solicitations, conferences.

Terms Agent receives 15% commission on domestic sales. Agent receives 20% commission on foreign sales. No written contract.

Recent Sales The Touch Series, by Laurie Stolarz; *An Island in the Pines*, by Donigan Merritt; *How Do You Light a Fart*, by Bobby Mercer; *Creepiosity*, by David Bickel; *Hidden Facets*, by Alan Orloff; *Don't Stalk the Admissions Officer*, by Risa Lewak

Tips "This agency offers a written agreement."

🌐 GREGORY & CO. AUTHORS' AGENTS

3 Barb Mews, Hammersmith, London W6 7PA England. (44)(207)610-4676. Fax: (44)(207)610-4686. E-mail: info@gregoryandcompany.co.uk. Website: www.gregoryandcompany.co.uk. **Contact:** Jane Gregory. Other memberships include AAA. Represents 60 clients. Currently handles: nonfiction books 10%, novels 90%.

Represents nonfiction books, novels. **Considers these nonfiction areas:** biography, history. **Considers these fiction areas:** detective, historical, literary, mainstream, thriller, contemporary women's fiction. As a British agency, we do not generally take on American authors. Actively seeking well-written, accessible modern novels. Does not want to receive horror, science fiction, fantasy, mind/body/spirit, children's books, screenplays, plays, short stories or poetry.

O┳ As a British agency, we do not generally take on American authors. Actively seeking well-written, accessible modern novels. Does not want to receive horror, science fiction, fantasy, mind/body/spirit, children's books, screenplays, plays, short stories or poetry.

How to Contact Query with SASE. Submit outline, first 10 pages by email or post, publishing history, author bio. Send submissions to Jane Gregory, submissions editor. Accepts simultaneous submissions. Returns materials only with SASE. Obtains most new clients through recommendations from others, conferences.

Terms Agent receives 15% commission on domestic sales. Agent receives 20% commission on foreign sales. Offers written contract; 1-month notice must be given to terminate contract. Charges clients for photocopying of whole typescripts and copies of book for submissions.

Recent Sales *Ritual*, by Mo Hader (Bantam UK/Grove Atlantic); *A Darker Domain*, by Val McDermid (HarperCollins UK); *The Chameleon's Shadow*, by Minette Walters (Macmillan UK/Knopf Inc); *Stratton's War*, by Laura Wilson (Orion UK/St. Martin's).

Writers Conferences CWA Conference; Bouchercon.

BLANCHE C. GREGORY, INC.

2 Tudor City Place, New York NY 10017. (212)697-0828. E-mail: info@bcgliteraryagency.com. Website: www.bcgliteraryagency.com. Member of AAR.

Represents nonfiction books, novels, juvenile. This agency specializes in adult fiction and nonfiction; children's literature is also considered. Does not want to receive screenplays, stage plays or teleplays.

O┳ This agency specializes in adult fiction and nonfiction; children's literature is also considered. Does not want to receive screenplays, stage plays or teleplays.

How to Contact Submit query, brief synopsis, bio, SASE. No e-mail queries. Obtains most new clients through recommendations from others.

GREGORY LITERARY AGENCY, LLC

Birmingham AL 35242. (205)799-0380. Fax: (205)278-8572. E-mail: gregoryliteraryagency@yahoo.com. **Contact:** Steven P. Gregory.Currently handles: nonfiction books 50%, novels 50%.

- Prior to becoming an agent, Mr. Gregory was an attorney.

Represents nonfiction books, novels. **Considers these nonfiction areas:** newage, biography, current affairs, ethnic, government, memoirs, military, money, religion, sports. **Considers these fiction areas:** glitz, adventure, detective, ethnic, literary, mainstream, mystery, sports, thriller, womens. Actively seeking mainstream fiction, mystery/thriller, memoir, biography, African-American fiction/nonfiction, military history, money/finance/economics, law/government/politics, economics/current affairs, New Age/Buddhist. Does not want children's, science fiction, cookbooks, how-to, general nonfiction, humor or religious/inspirational.

O→ Actively seeking mainstream fiction, mystery/thriller, memoir, biography, African-American fiction/nonfiction, military history, money/finance/economics, law/government/politics, economics/current affairs, New Age/Buddhist. Does not want children's, science fiction, cookbooks, how-to, general nonfiction, humor or religious/inspirational.

How to Contact Query with SASE. Send no unsolicited mss of any kind. Accepts simultaneous submissions. Responds in 1 month to queries. Responds in 2 months to mss. Obtains most new clients through recommendations from others, solicitations.

Terms Agent receives 15% commission on domestic sales. Agent receives 20% commission on foreign sales. Offers written contract. This agency charges for postage, overnight delivery and travel; costs are charged against advance after sales.

Tips "Write the best book you can then polish and edit the final version. Do not waste money on a 'professional editor.' Edit the manuscript yourself. If you write in first person, the narrator must exhibit a compelling and unique voice. My agency strongly prefers to receive queries and requested samples by e-mail and by pdf attachments."

JILL GRINBERG LITERARY AGENCY

244 Fifth Ave., Floor 11, New York NY 10011. (212)620-5883. Fax: (212)627-4725. E-mail: info@grinbergliterary.com. Website: www.grinbergliterary.com.

- Prior to her current position, Ms. Grinberg was at Anderson Grinberg Literary Management.

Member Agents Jill Grinberg; Kirsten Wolf (foreign rights).

Represents nonfiction books, novels. **Considers these nonfiction areas:** biography, business, current affairs, government, health, history, multicultural, psychology, science, spirituality, travel, womens. **Considers these fiction areas:** fantasy, historical, romance, science, young, womens, literary fiction, commercial fiction, children's, middle grade.

How to Contact Query with SASE. Submit Send a proposal and author bio for nonfiction; send a query, synopsis and the first 50 pages for fiction.

Tips "We prefer submissions by mail."

JILL GROSJEAN LITERARY AGENCY

1390 Millstone Road, Sag Harbor NY 11963-2214. (631)725-7419. Fax: (631)725-8632. E-mail: jill6981@aol.com. **Contact:** Jill Grosjean. Represents 40 clients. 100% of clients are new/unpublished writers. Currently handles: novels 100%.

- Prior to becoming an agent, Ms. Grosjean was manager of an independent bookstore. She has also worked in publishing and advertising.

Represents novels. **Considers these fiction areas:** historical, literary, mainstream, mystery, regional, romance. This agency offers some editorial assistance (i.e., line-by-line edits). Actively seeking literary novels and mysteries.

O→ This agency offers some editorial assistance (i.e., line-by-line edits). Actively seeking literary novels and mysteries.

How to Contact E-mail queries only, no attachments. No cold calls, please. Accepts simultaneous submissions. Responds in 1 week to queries. Responds in 1 month to mss. Obtains most new clients through recommendations from others, solicitations.

Terms Agent receives 15% commission on domestic sales. Agent receives 20% commission on foreign sales. No written contract. Charges clients for photocopying and mailing expenses.

Recent Sales *Single Thread* and *Thread of Truth*, by Marie Bostwick (Kensington); *Greasing the Pinata* and *Jump*, by Tim Maleeny (Poison Pen Press); *Black Widow Agency* and *Spun Tales*, by Felicia Donovan; *Shame and No Idea*, by Greg Garrett, David C. Cook; *The Reluctant Journey* of David Conners; *The Summer the Wind Whispered My Name*, by Don Locke; *Cyber Crime Fighters*, by Felicia Donovan and Kristyn Bernier.

Writers Conferences Book Passage's Mystery Writers' Conference; Agents and Editors Conference; Texas Writers' and Agents' Conference.

LAURA GROSS LITERARY AGENCY

P.O. Box 610326, Newton Highlands MA 02461. (617)964-2977. Fax: (617)964-3023. E-mail: query@lauragrossliteraryagency.com. **Contact:** Laura Gross.Represents 30 clients. Currently handles: nonfiction books 40%, novels 50%, scholarly books 10%.

- Prior to becoming an agent, Ms. Gross was an editor.

Represents nonfiction books, novels. **Considers these nonfiction areas:** biography, current affairs, ethnic, government, health, history, memoirs, popular culture, psychology, sports, women's issues, women's studies. **Considers these fiction areas:** historical, literary, mainstream, mystery, thriller.

How to Contact Query with SASE. Submit author bio. Responds in several days to queries. Obtains most new clients through recommendations from others.

Terms Agent receives 15% commission on domestic sales. Agent receives 20% commission on foreign sales. Offers written contract.

REECE HALSEY NORTH/PARIS/NEW YORK

98 Main St., #704, Tiburon CA 94920. Fax: (415)789-9177. E-mail: info@reecehalseynorth.com. Website: www.reecehalseynorth.com. **Contact:** Kimberley Cameron. Member of AAR. 30% of clients are new/unpublished writers. Currently handles: other 50% fiction, 50% nonfiction.

- The Reece Halsey Agency has had an illustrious client list of established writers, including the estate of Aldous Huxley, and has represented Upton Sinclair, William Faulkner, and Henry Miller.

Member Agents Kimberley Cameron, Elizabeth Evans; April Eberhardt, Amy Burkhardt.

Represents nonfiction and fiction. **Considers these nonfiction areas:** biography, current affairs, history, language, popular culture, science, true crime, women's issues, women's studies. **Considers these fiction areas:** contemporary, adventure, detective, ethnic, family, historical, horror, literary, mainstream, mystery, science, thriller, women's fiction. We are looking for a unique and heartfelt voice that conveys a universal truth.

O→ We are looking for a unique and heartfelt voice that conveys a universal truth.

How to Contact Query via e-mail with first 50 pages of novel. Responds in 3-6 weeks to queries. Responds in 1 month to mss. Obtains most new clients through recommendations from others, solicitations.

Terms Agent receives 15% commission on domestic sales. Agent receives 10% commission on film sales. Offers written contract, binding for 1 year.

Writers Conferences Maui Writers Conference; Aspen Summer Words Literary Festival; Willamette Writers Conference, numerous others.

Tips "Please send a polite, well-written query to info@reecehalseynorth.com."

HALSTON FREEMAN LITERARY AGENCY, INC.

140 Broadway, 46th Floor, New York NY 10005. E-mail: queryhalstonfreemanliterary@hotmail.com. **Contact:** Molly Freeman, Betty Halston.Currently handles: nonfiction books 65%, novels 35%.

- Prior to becoming an agent, Ms. Halston was a marketing and promotion director for a local cable affiliate; Ms. Freeman was a television film editor and ad agency copywriter.

Member Agents Molly Freeman, Betty Halston.

Represents nonfiction books, novels. **Considers these nonfiction areas:** agriculture horticulture, newage, biography, business, child, current affairs, ethnic, gay, government, health, history, how to, humor, memoirs, psychology, self help, true crime, womens. **Considers these fiction areas:** adventure, detective, ethnic, feminist, historical, horror, humor, literary, mainstream, mystery, romance, science, thriller, western, womens. "We are a hands-on agency specializing in quality nonfiction and fiction. As a new agency, it is imperative that we develop relationships with good writers who are smart, hardworking and understand what's required of them to promote their books." Does not want to receive children's books, textbooks or poetry. Send no e-mail attachments.

O→ "We are a hands-on agency specializing in quality nonfiction and fiction. As a new agency, it is imperative that we develop relationships with good writers who are smart, hardworking and understand what's required of them to promote their books." Does not want to receive children's books, textbooks or poetry. Send no e-mail attachments.

How to Contact Query with SASE. For nonfiction, include sample chapters, synopsis, platform, bio and competitive titles. For fiction, include synopsis, bio and three sample chapters. No e-mail attachments. Accepts simultaneous submissions. Responds in 2-6 weeks to queries. Responds in 1-2 months to mss. Obtains most new clients through recommendations from others, solicitations, conferences.

Terms Agent receives 15% commission on domestic sales. Agent receives 20% commission on foreign sales. This agency charges clients for copying and postage directly related to the project.

HALYARD LITERARY AGENCY

Chicago IL E-mail: submissions@halyardagency.com; agrayson@halyardagency.com (general info). Website: www.halyardagency.com. **Contact:** Alaina Grayson.

Member Agents Alaina Grayson.

Represents nonfiction books, novels. **Considers these nonfiction areas:** biography, history, science. **Considers these fiction areas:** fantasy, historical, juvenile, science, young, general, paranormal. Based out of Chicago, Halyard Literary Agency is a new agency on the lookout for authors who have the same passion for innovation that we do. Halyard is small, but provides assistance through every stage of book production. We're dedicated to building relationships with our authors, not just for one book or one year, but throughout their publishing life.

⊶ Based out of Chicago, Halyard Literary Agency is a new agency on the lookout for authors who have the same passion for innovation that we do. Halyard is small, but provides assistance through every stage of book production. We're dedicated to building relationships with our authors, not just for one book or one year, but throughout their publishing life.

How to Contact Query with SASE. E-mail queries only to submissions@halyardagency.com. Send requested materials as e-mail attachments only if requested from query.

THE MITCHELL J. HAMILBURG AGENCY

149 S. Barrington Ave., #732, Los Angeles CA 90049-2930. (310)471-4024. Fax: (310)471-9588. **Contact:** Michael Hamilburg. Signatory of WGA. Represents 70 clients. Currently handles: nonfiction books 70%, novels 30%.

Represents nonfiction books, novels. **Considers these nonfiction areas:** anthropology, biography, business, child, cooking, current affairs, education, government, health, history, memoirs, military, money, psychology, recreation, regional, self help, sex, sociology, spirituality, sports, travel, womens, creative nonfiction; romance; architecture; inspirational; true crime. **Considers these fiction areas:** glitz, New Age, adventure, experimental, feminist, humor, military, mystery, occult, regional, religious, romance, sports, thriller, crime; mainstream; psychic.

How to Contact Query with outline, 2 sample chapters, SASE. Responds in 1 month to mss. Obtains most new clients through recommendations from others, conferences, personal search.

Terms Agent receives 10-15% commission on domestic sales.

THE JOY HARRIS LITERARY AGENCY, INC.

156 Fifth Ave., Suite 617, New York NY 10010. (212)924-6269. Fax: (212)924-6609. **Contact:** Joy Harris. Member of AAR. Represents more than 100 clients. Currently handles: nonfiction books 50%, novels 50%.

Represents nonfiction books, novels. **Considers these fiction areas:** glitz, ethnic, experimental, family, feminist, gay, hi lo, historical, humor, literary, mainstream, multicultural, multimedia, mystery, regional, short, spiritual, translation, young, womens. No screenplays.

⊶ No screenplays.

How to Contact Query with sample chapter, outline/proposal, SASE. Accepts simultaneous submissions. Responds in 2 months to queries. Obtains most new clients through recommendations from clients and editors.

Terms Agent receives 15% commission on domestic sales. Agent receives 20% commission on foreign sales. Charges clients for some office expenses.

HARTLINE LITERARY AGENCY

123 Queenston Dr., Pittsburgh PA 15235-5429. (412)829-2483. Fax: (412)829-2432. E-mail: joyce@hartlineliterary.com. Website: www.hartlineliterary.com. **Contact:** Joyce A. Hart.Represents 40 clients. 20% of clients are new/unpublished writers. Currently handles: nonfiction books 40%, novels 60%.

Member Agents Joyce A. Hart, principal agent; Terry Burns; Tamela Hancock Murray; Diana Flegal.

Represents nonfiction books, novels. **Considers these nonfiction areas:** business, child, cooking, money, religion, self help, womens. **Considers these fiction areas:** contemporary, adventure, family, historical, literary, mystery, amateur sleuth, cozy, regional, religious, romance, contemporary, gothic, historical, regency, thriller. This agency specializes in the Christian bookseller market. Actively seeking adult fiction, self-help, nutritional books, devotional, and business. Does not want to receive erotica, gay/lesbian, fantasy, horror, etc.

⊶ This agency specializes in the Christian bookseller market. Actively seeking adult fiction, self-help, nutritional books, devotional, and business. Does not want to receive erotica, gay/lesbian, fantasy, horror, etc.

How to Contact Submit summary/outline, author bio, 3 sample chapters. Accepts simultaneous submissions. Responds in 2 months to queries. Responds in 3 months to mss. Obtains most new clients through recommendations from others.

Terms Agent receives 15% commission on domestic sales. Offers written contract.

Recent Sales *Aurora, An American Experience in Quilt, Community and Craft*, and *A Flickering Light*, by Jane Kirkpatrick (Waterbrook Multnomah); *Oprah Doesn't Know My Name*, by Jane Kirkpatric (Zondervan); *Paper Roses, Scattered Petals, and Summer Rains*, by Amanda Cabot (Revell Books); *Blood Ransom*, by Lisa Harris (Zondervan); *I Don't Want a Divorce*, by David Clark (Revell Books); *Love Finds You in Hope, Kansas*, by Pamela Griffin (Summerside Press); *Journey to the Well*, by Diana Wallis Taylor (Revell Books); *Paper Bag Christmas, The Nine Lessons*, by Kevin Milne (Center Street); *When Your Aging Parent Needs Care*, by Arrington & Atchley (Harvest House); *Katie at Sixteen*, by Kim Vogel

Sawyer (Zondervan); *A Promise of Spring*, by Kim Vogel Sawyer (Bethany House); *The Big 5-OH!*, by Sandra Bricker (Abingdon Press); *A Silent Terror & A Silent Stalker*, by Lynette Eason (Steeple Hill); *Extreme Devotion series*, by Kathi Macias (New Hope Publishers); *On the Wings of the Storm*, by Tamira Barley (Whitaker House); *Tribute*, by Graham Garrison (Kregel Publications); *The Birth to Five Book*, by Brenda Nixon (Revell Books); *Fat to Skinny Fast and Easy*, by Doug Varrieur (Sterling Publishers); *No Strings Attached*, by Lorre Lough (Whitaker House); *Love Finds You in Hershey, PA*, by Cerella Seachrist (Summerside Press)

ANTONY HARWOOD LIMITED

103 Walton St., Oxford OX2 6EB England. +44 01865 559 615. Fax: +44 01865 310 660. E-mail: mail@antonyharwood.com. Website: www.antonyharwood.com. **Contact:** Antony Harwood, James Macdonald Lockhart.Represents 52 clients.

- Prior to starting this agency, Mr. Harwood and Mr. Lockhart worked at publishing houses and other literary agencies.

Represents nonfiction books, novels. **Considers these nonfiction areas:** agriculture horticulture, americana, animals, anthropology, art, biography, business, child, computers, cooking, creative, current affairs, education, ethnic, gardening, gay, government, health, history, how to, humor, language, memoirs, military, money, multicultural, music, nature, philosophy, photography, popular culture, psychology, recreation, regional, religion, science, self help, sex, sociology, software, spirituality, sports, film, translation, travel, true crime, womens. **Considers these fiction areas:** adventure, comic, confession, detective, erotica, ethnic, experimental, family, fantasy, feminist, gay, gothic, hi lo, historical, horror, humor, literary, mainstream, military, multicultural, multimedia, mystery, occult, picture books, plays, regional, religious, romance, science, spiritual, sports, thriller, translation, western, young. "We accept every genre of fiction and nonfiction except for children's fiction for readers ages 10 and younger." No poetry or screenplays.

"We accept every genre of fiction and nonfiction except for children's fiction for readers ages 10 and younger." No poetry or screenplays.

How to Contact Submit outline, 2-3 sample chapters via e-mail in a Word or RTF format or postal mail (include SASE or IRC). Responds in 2 months to queries.

Terms Agent receives 15% commission on domestic sales. Agent receives 20% commission on foreign sales.

JOHN HAWKINS & ASSOCIATES, INC.

71 W. 23rd St., Suite 1600, New York NY 10010. (212)807-7040. Fax: (212)807-9555. E-mail: jha@jhalit.com. Website: www.jhalit.com. **Contact:** Moses Cardona (moses@jhalit.com). Member of AAR. Represents over 100 clients. 5-10% of clients are new/unpublished writers. Currently handles: nonfiction books 40%, novels 40%, juvenile books 20%.

Member Agents Moses Cardona.

Represents nonfiction books, novels, young adult. **Considers these nonfiction areas:** agriculture horticulture, americana, interior, young, anthropology, art, biography, business, current affairs, education, ethnic, gardening, gay, government, health, history, how to, language, memoirs, money, multicultural, nature, philosophy, popular culture, psychology, recreation, science, self help, sex, sociology, software, film, travel, true crime, music, creative nonfiction. **Considers these fiction areas:** glitz, psychic, adventure, detective, ethnic, experimental, family, feminist, gay, gothic, hi lo, historical, literary, mainstream, military, multicultural, multimedia, mystery, religious, short, sports, thriller, translation, western, young, womens.

How to Contact Submit query, proposal package, outline, SASE. Accepts simultaneous submissions. Responds in 1 month to queries. Obtains most new clients through recommendations from others.

Terms Agent receives 15% commission on domestic sales. Agent receives 20% commission on foreign sales. Charges clients for photocopying.

Recent Sales *Financial Lives of Poets*, by Jess Walter; *Urgent Care*, by CJ Lyons, *National Suicide*, by Martin Gross.

HEACOCK LITERARY AGENCY, INC.

West Coast Office, 507 Grand Blvd., P.O. Box 226, Cloudcroft NM 88317. E-mail: catt@heacockliteraryagency.com; tom@heacockliteraryagency.com. Website: www.heacockliteraryagency.com. **Contact:** Catt LeBaigue. 1020 Hollywood Way #439, Burbank, CA 91505 Member of AAR. Other memberships include SCBWI.

- Prior to becoming an agent, Ms. LeBaigue spent 18 years with Sony Pictures and Warner Bros.

Member Agents Rosalie Grace Heacock Thompson (semi-retired, no queries at this time); Catt LeBaigue (juvenile fiction, adult nonfiction including arts, crafts, anthropolgy, astronomy, nature studies, ecology, body/mind/spirit, humanities, self-help).

Represents nonfiction books, juvenile. **Considers these nonfiction areas:** hiking.

How to Contact Query with SASE. E-mail queries only. No unsolicited manuscripts. No e-mail

attachments. Obtains most new clients through recommendations from others, solicitations.
Terms Offers written contract.
Tips Take time to write an informative e-query letter expressing your book idea, the market for it, your qualifications to write the book, the 'hook' that would make a potential reader buy the book.

HELEN HELLER AGENCY INC.

892 Avenue Road, Toronto Ontario M5P 2K6 Canada. (416)489-0396. E-mail: info@helenhelleragency.com. Website: www.helenhelleragency.com. **Contact:** Helen Heller.Represents 30+ clients.

- Prior to her current position, Ms. Heller worked for Cassell & Co. (England), was an editor for Harlequin Books, a senior editor for Avon Books, and editor-in-chief for Fitzhenry & Whiteside.

Member Agents Helen Heller, helen@helenhelleragency.com; Daphne Hart, daphne.hart@sympatico.ca; Sarah Heller, sarah@helenhelleragency.com.
Represents nonfiction books, novels. Actively seeking adult fiction and nonfiction (excluding children's literature, screenplays or genre fiction). Does not want to receive children's literature, screenplays or genre fiction such as fantasy and science fiction.

O→ Actively seeking adult fiction and nonfiction (excluding children's literature, screenplays or genre fiction). Does not want to receive children's literature, screenplays or genre fiction such as fantasy and science fiction.

How to Contact Query with SASE. Submit synopsis, publishing history, author bio. Obtains most new clients through recommendations from others, solicitations.
Recent Sales Break on Through, by Jill Murray (Doubleday Canada); Womankind: Faces of Change Around the World, by Donna Nebenzahl (Raincoast Books); One Dead Indian: The Premier, The Police, and the Ipperwash Crisis, by Peter Edwards (McClelland & Stewart); a full list of deals is available online.
Tips "Whether you are an author searching for an agent, or whether an agent has approached you, it is in your best interest to first find out who the agent represents, what publishing houses has that agent sold to recently and what foreign sales have been made. You should be able to go to the bookstore, or search online and find the books the agent refers to. Many authors acknowledge their agents in the front or back or their books."

RICHARD HENSHAW GROUP

22 West 23rd St., Fifth Floor, New York NY 10010. (212)414-1172. Fax: (212)414-1182. E-mail: submissions@henshaw.com. Website: www.rich.henshaw.com. **Contact:** Rich Henshaw.Member of AAR. Other memberships include SinC, MWA, HWA, SFWA, RWA. Represents 35 clients. 20% of clients are new/unpublished writers. Currently handles: nonfiction books 35%, novels 65%.

- Prior to opening his agency, Mr. Henshaw served as an agent with Richard Curtis Associates, Inc.

Represents nonfiction books, novels. **Considers these nonfiction areas:** newage, animals, biography, business, child, computers, cooking, current affairs, gay, government, health, how to, humor, military, money, music, nature, popular culture, psychology, science, self help, sociology, sports, true crime, womens. **Considers these fiction areas:** glitz, psychic, adventure, detective, ethnic, family, fantasy, historical, horror, humor, literary, mainstream, mystery, romance, science, sports, thriller. This agency specializes in thrillers, mysteries, science fiction, fantasy and horror.

O→ This agency specializes in thrillers, mysteries, science fiction, fantasy and horror.

How to Contact Query with SASE. Responds in 3 weeks to queries. Responds in 6 weeks to mss. Obtains most new clients through recommendations from others, solicitations, conferences.
Terms Agent receives 15% commission on domestic sales. Agent receives 20% commission on foreign sales. No written contract. Charges clients for photocopying and book orders.
Recent Sales Kate Shugak mystery by Dana Stabenow; Wind River mystery by Margaret Coel; Diving Into the Wreck series by Kristine Kathryn Rusch; History of the World series, by Susan Wise Bauer; Maiden Lane series by Elizabeth Hoyt.
Tips "While we do not have any reason to believe that our submission guidelines will change in the near future, writers can find up-to-date submission policy information on our Web site. Always include a SASE with correct return postage."

THE JEFF HERMAN AGENCY, LLC

P.O. Box 1522, Stockbridge MA 01262. (413)298-0077. Fax: (413)298-8188. E-mail: jeff@jeffherman.com. Website: www.jeffherman.com. **Contact:** Jeffrey H. Herman. Represents 100 clients. 10% of clients are new/unpublished writers. Currently handles: nonfiction books 85%, scholarly books 5%, textbooks 5%.

- Prior to opening his agency, Mr. Herman served as a public relations executive.

Member Agents Deborah Levine, vice president (nonfiction book doctor); Jeff Herman.
Represents nonfiction books. **Considers these nonfiction areas:** business, government, health, recovery issues, history, how to, self help, spirituality, popular reference; technology; popular psychology. This

agency specializes in adult nonfiction.

O→ This agency specializes in adult nonfiction.

How to Contact Query with SASE. Accepts simultaneous submissions.

Terms Agent receives 15% commission on domestic sales. Offers written contract. Charges clients for copying and postage.

Recent Sales Sold 35 titles in the last year. This agency prefers not to share information on specific sales.

HIDDEN VALUE GROUP

1240 E. Ontario Ave., Ste. 102-148, Corona CA 92881. (951)549-8891. Fax: (951)549-8891. E-mail: bookquery@hiddenvaluegroup.com. Website: www.hiddenvaluegroup.com. **Contact:** Nancy Jernigan. Represents 55 clients. 10% of clients are new/unpublished writers.

Member Agents Jeff Jernigan, jjernigan@hiddenvaluegroup.com (men's nonfiction, fiction, Bible studies/curriculum, marriage and family); Nancy Jernigan, njernigan@hiddenvaluegroup.com (nonfiction, women's issues, inspiration, marriage and family, fiction).

Represents nonfiction books, novels, juvenile. **Considers these nonfiction areas:** juvenile, biography, business, child, history, how to, language, memoirs, money, psychology, religion, self help, womens. **Considers these fiction areas:** adventure, detective, fantasy, literary, religious, thriller, western, womens. "The Hidden Value Group specializes in helping authors throughout their publishing career. We believe that every author has a special message to be heard and we specialize in getting that message out." Actively seeking established fiction authors, and authors who are focusing on women's issues. Does not want to receive poetry or short stories.

O→ "The Hidden Value Group specializes in helping authors throughout their publishing career. We believe that every author has a special message to be heard and we specialize in getting that message out." Actively seeking established fiction authors, and authors who are focusing on women's issues. Does not want to receive poetry or short stories.

How to Contact Query with SASE. Submit synopsis, 3 sample chapters, author bio. Accepts queries to bookquery@hiddenvaluegroup.com. No fax queries. Accepts simultaneous submissions. Responds in 1 month to queries. Responds in 1 month to mss. Obtains most new clients through recommendations from others, solicitations.

Terms Agent receives 15% commission on domestic sales. Agent receives 15% commission on foreign sales. Offers written contract.

Writers Conferences Glorieta Christian Writers' Conference; CLASS Publishing Conference.

FREDERICK HILL BONNIE NADELL, INC.

1842 Union St., San Francisco CA 94123. (415)921-2910. Fax: (415)921-2802. Represents 100 clients.

Member Agents Bonnie Nadell; Elise Proulx, associate.

Represents nonfiction books, novels. **Considers these nonfiction areas:** current affairs, health, history, language, nature, popular culture, science, biography; government/politics, narrative. **Considers these fiction areas:** literary, mainstream.

How to Contact Query with SASE. Keep your query to one page. Send via snail mail. Accepts simultaneous submissions.

Terms Agent receives 15% commission on domestic sales. Agent receives 20% commission on foreign sales. Agent receives 15% commission on film sales. Charges clients for photocopying and foreign mailings.

HILL MEDIA

1155 Camino Del Mar, #530, Del Mar CA 92014. (858)259-2595. Fax: (858)259-2777. **Contact:** Julie Hill. Represents 50 clients. 20% of clients are new/unpublished writers. Currently handles: nonfiction books 90%, story collections 5%, other 5% books that accompany films.

Member Agents Julie Hill, agent/publicist; Anette Farrell, agent.

Represents nonfiction books, short story collections, anthologies. **Considers these nonfiction areas:** interior, New Age, art, biography, cooking, ethnic, health, history, how to, language, memoirs, music, popular culture, psychology, religion, self help, womens. "Check your ego at the door. If we love your book, we mean it. If we are so-so, we also mean that. If we cannot place it, we tell you ASAP." Actively seeking nonfiction: travel, health, media tie-ins. Does not want to receive horror, juvenile, sci-fi, thrillers or autobiographies of any kind.

O→ "Check your ego at the door. If we love your book, we mean it. If we are so-so, we also mean that. If we cannot place it, we tell you ASAP." Actively seeking nonfiction: travel, health, media tie-ins. Does not want to receive horror, juvenile, sci-fi, thrillers or autobiographies of any kind.

How to Contact Query with SASE. Submit outline/proposal, SASE. .Send all submissions via snail mail. Never send a complete ms unless requested. Accepts simultaneous submissions. Responds in 4-6 weeks to queries. Obtains most new clients through recommendations from others, solicitations, conferences.

Recent Sales TV: *Cracking Up*, from the book *The Happy Neurotic*, to GRBTV. Travel: multiple titles to

Frommers (Wiley) for kids travel and theme parks guides, by Laura Lea Miller, Barnes and Noble travel bestsellers. Falcon (Globe Pequot) hiking guides *Best Easy Day Hikes to Long Island*, and others by Susan Finch. *Elvis for Dummies*, by Susie Doll, Ph.D. (Wiley, 2009); *Publish This Book*, by Stephen Markley (Sourcebooks, Fall 2009); *Return to Naples*, by Robert Zweig, Ph.D. (Barricade Books), currently under consideration for film; *A Blessing in Disguise, Life Lesson by Today's Greatest Teachers*, by Andrea Joy Cohen M.D. (Berkley Books/Penguin).

HOPKINS LITERARY ASSOCIATES

2117 Buffalo Rd., Suite 327, Rochester NY 14624-1507. (585)352-6268. **Contact:** Pam Hopkins. Member of AAR. Other memberships include RWA. Represents 30 clients. 5% of clients are new/unpublished writers. Currently handles: novels 100%.

Represents novels. **Considers these fiction areas:** romance, historical, contemporary, category, womens. This agency specializes in women's fiction, particularly historical, contemporary, and category romance, as well as mainstream work.

- This agency specializes in women's fiction, particularly historical, contemporary, and category romance, as well as mainstream work.

How to Contact Submit outline, 3 sample chapters. Accepts simultaneous submissions. Responds in 2 weeks to queries. Responds in 1 month to mss. Obtains most new clients through recommendations from others, solicitations, conferences.

Terms Agent receives 15% commission on domestic sales. Agent receives 20% commission on foreign sales. No written contract.

Recent Sales Sold 50 titles in the last year. *The Wilting Bloom Series*, by Madeline Hunter (Berkley); *The Dead Travel Fast*, by Deanna Raybourn; *Baggage Claim*, by Tanya Michna (NAL).

Writers Conferences RWA National Conference.

HORNFISCHER LITERARY MANAGEMENT

P.O. Box 50544, Austin TX 78763. E-mail: queries@hornfischerlit.com. Website: www.hornfischerlit.com. **Contact:** James D. Hornfischer, president.Represents 45 clients. 10% of clients are new/unpublished writers. Currently handles: nonfiction books 100%.

- Prior to opening his agency, Mr. Hornfischer was an agent with Literary Group International and held editorial positions at HarperCollins and McGraw-Hill. "My New York editorial background working with a variety of bestselling authors, such as Erma Bombeck, Jared Diamond, and Erica Jong, is useful in this regard. In 14 years as an agent, I've handled twelve *New York Times* nonfiction bestsellers, including two No. 1's."

Represents nonfiction books. **Considers these nonfiction areas:** anthropology, biography, business, child, current affairs, government, health, history, how to, humor, memoirs, military, money, multicultural, nature, popular culture, psychology, religion, science, self help, sociology, sports, true crime. Actively seeking the best work of terrific writers. Does not want poetry or genre fiction.

- Actively seeking the best work of terrific writers. Does not want poetry or genre fiction.

How to Contact Submit proposal package, outline, 2 sample chapters. Accepts simultaneous submissions. Responds in 8 weeks to queries. Obtains most new clients through referrals from clients, reading books and magazines, pursuing ideas with New York editors.

Terms Agent receives 15% commission on domestic sales. Agent receives 25% commission on foreign sales. Offers written contract. Reasonable expenses deducted from proceeds after book is sold.

Recent Sales *The Next 100 Years*, by George Friedman (Doubleday), see this agency's website for more sales information.

Tips "When you query agents and send out proposals, present yourself as someone who's in command of his material and comfortable in his own skin. Too many writers have a palpable sense of anxiety and insecurity. Take a deep breath and realize that - if you're good - someone in the publishing world will want you."

ANDREA HURST LITERARY MANAGEMENT

P.O. Box 19010, Sacramento CA 95819. E-mail: (agentfirstname)@andreahurst.com. Website: www.andreahurst.com. **Contact:** Andrea Hurst, Judy Mikalonis, Amberly Finarelli. Represents 50+ clients. 50% of clients are new/unpublished writers. Currently handles: nonfiction books 75%, novels 10%, juvenile books 15%.

- Prior to becoming an agent, Ms. Hurst was an acquisitions editor as well as a freelance editor and published writer; Ms. Mikalonis was in marketing and branding consulting.

Member Agents Andrea Hurst, andrea@andreahurst.com (nonfiction—including personal growth, health and wellness, science, business, parenting, relationships, women's issues, animals, spirituality, women's issues, metaphysical, psychological, cookbooks and self help; fiction interests include adult fiction); Judy Mikalonis, judy@andreahurst.com (YA fiction, Christian fiction, Christian nonfiction); Amberly Finarelli amberly@andreahurst.com (Nonfiction: humor/gift books, crafts, how-to, Relationships/advice, Self-help, psychology, Travel writing, Narrative nonfiction. Fiction: Commercial women's fiction, Comic and cozy mysteries, Literary fiction with a focus on the arts, culture, and/or history, Contemporary young adult.

Represents nonfiction books, novels, juvenile. **Considers these nonfiction areas:** crafts, interior, juvenile, newage, animals, art, biography, business, child, cooking, education, health, how to, humor, memoirs, military, money, music, nature, photography, popular culture, psychology, religion, science, self help, sociology, true crime, womens, gift books. **Considers these fiction areas:** psychic, juvenile, literary, mainstream, religious, romance, thriller, young, womens. We work directly with our signed authors to help them polish their work and their platform for optimum marketability. Our staff is always available to answer phone calls and e-mails from our authors and we stay with a project until we have exhausted all publishing avenues. Actively seeking well written nonfiction by authors with a strong platform; superbly crafted fiction with depth that touches the mind and heart and all of our listed subjects. Does not want to receive sci-fi, mystery, horror, Western, poetry or screenplays.

- We work directly with our signed authors to help them polish their work and their platform for optimum marketability. Our staff is always available to answer phone calls and e-mails from our authors and we stay with a project until we have exhausted all publishing avenues. Actively seeking well written nonfiction by authors with a strong platform; superbly crafted fiction with depth that touches the mind and heart and all of our listed subjects. Does not want to receive sci-fi, mystery, horror, Western, poetry or screenplays.

How to Contact Query with SASE. Submit outline/proposal, synopsis, 2 sample chapters, author bio. Accepts simultaneous submissions. Obtains most new clients through recommendations from others, solicitations, conferences.

Terms Agent receives 15% commission on domestic sales. Agent receives 20% commission on foreign sales. Offers written contract, binding for 6 to 12 months; 30-day notice must be given to terminate contract. This agency charges for postage.

Recent Sales *Faith, Hope and Healing*, by Dr. Bernie Siegel (Rodale); *Code Name: Polar Ice*, by Jean-Michel Cousteau and James Fraioli (Gibbs Smith); *How to Host a Killer Party*, by Penny Warner (Berkley/Penguin); *Tame Your Terrible Office Tyrant (TOT)*, by Lynn Taylor (Wiley); *Imagine Life with a Well-Behaved Dog*, by Julie Bjelland (St. Martin's Press); *Dr. Laura's Wholesome Junk Food*, by Laura Trice (Running Press).

Writers Conferences San Francisco Writers' Conference; Willamette Writers' Conference; PNWA; Whidbey Island Writers Conference.

Tips "Do your homework and submit a professional package. Get to know the agent you are submitting to by researching their Web site or meeting them at a conference. Perfect your craft: Write well and edit ruthlessly over and over again before submitting to an agent. Be realistic: Understand that publishing is a business and be prepared to prove why your book is marketable and how you will market it on your own. Be Persistent!"

INKWELL MANAGEMENT, LLC

521 Fifth Ave., 26th Floor, New York NY 10175. (212)922-3500. Fax: (212)922-0535. E-mail: info@inkwellmanagement.com. Website: www.inkwellmanagement.com. Represents 500 clients. Currently handles: nonfiction books 60%, novels 40%.

Member Agents Michael Carlisle; Richard Pine; Kimberly Witherspoon; George Lucas; Catherine Drayton; David Forrer; Susan Arellano; Alexis Hurley; Patricia Burke, Susan Hobson; Nat Jacks; Ethan Bassoff, Julie Schilder, Libby O'Neill; Elisa Petrini, Mairead Duffy.

Represents nonfiction books, novels.

How to Contact Query with SASE or via e-mail to submissions@inkwellmanagement.com Obtains most new clients through recommendations from others.

Terms Agent receives 15% commission on domestic sales. Agent receives 20% commission on foreign sales. Offers written contract.

Tips "We will not read manuscripts before receiving a letter of inquiry."

INTERNATIONAL CREATIVE MANAGEMENT

825 Eighth Ave., New York NY 10019. (212)556-5600. Website: www.icmtalent.com. **Contact:** Literary Department.Member of AAR. Signatory of WGA.

Member Agents Lisa Bankoff, lbankoff@icmtalent.com (fiction interests include: literary fiction, family saga, historical fiction, offbeat/quirky; nonfiction interests include: history, biography, memoirs, narrative); Patrick Herold, pherold@icmtalent.com; Jennifer Joel, jjoel@icmtalent.com (fiction interests include: literary fiction, commercial fiction, historical fiction, thrillers/suspense; nonfiction interests include: history, sports, art, adventure/true story, pop culture); Esther Newberg; Sloan Harris; Amanda Binky Urban; Heather Schroder; Kristine Dahl; Andrea Barzvi, abarzvi@icmtalent.com (fiction interests include: chick lit, commercial fiction, women's fiction, thrillers/suspense; nonfiction interests include: sports, celebrity, self-help, dating/relationships, women's issues, pop culture, health and fitness); Tina

Dubois Wexler, twexler@icmtalent.com (literary fiction, chick lit, young adult, middle grade, memoir, narrative nonfiction); Kate Lee, klee@icmtalent.com (mystery, commercial fiction, short stories, memoir, dating/relationships, pop culture, humor, journalism).

Represents nonfiction books, novels. "We do not accept unsolicited submissions."

O→ "We do not accept unsolicited submissions."

How to Contact Query with SASE. Send queries via snail mail and include an SASE. Target a specific agent. Obtains most new clients through recommendations from others.

Terms Agent receives 15% commission on domestic sales. Agent receives 20% commission on foreign sales.

INTERNATIONAL LITERARY ARTS

RR 5, Box 5391 A, Moscow PA 18444. E-mail: query@InternationalLiteraryArts.com. Website: www.InternationalLiteraryArts.com. **Contact:** Pamela K. Brodowsky.

- Prior to her current position, Ms. Fazio worked at Prentice Hall, Random House, M.E. Sharpe and Baker & Taylor; Ms. Brodowsky is a public speaker, as well as the author of *Secrets of Successful Query Letters* and *Bulletproof Book Proposals*.

Member Agents Pamela K. Brodowsky; Evelyn Fazio.

Represents nonfiction books, movie. **Considers these nonfiction areas:** biography, business, cooking, current affairs, health, history, humor, money, science, self help, sports, travel, reference, parenting, lifestyle. "ILA is a full service literary property agency representing authors in all areas of nonfiction across the creative spectrum. The agency is committed to the clients it represents and to the publishers with whom we match our talent. Our goal is to provide for our publishers talented authors with long-term career goals. Our mission is to create the continuance of the discovery of new talent and thriving careers for our represented clients." No longer accepting fiction.

O→ "ILA is a full service literary property agency representing authors in all areas of nonfiction across the creative spectrum. The agency is committed to the clients it represents and to the publishers with whom we match our talent. Our goal is to provide for our publishers talented authors with long-term career goals. Our mission is to create the continuance of the discovery of new talent and thriving careers for our represented clients." No longer accepting fiction.

How to Contact Query with SASE. For nonfiction, send an e-mail cover letter, contact info, proposal and sample chapter. Send no e-attachments. Responds in 4-6 weeks to queries.

Writers Conferences BookExpo America.

Tips "If you are inquiring about a nonfiction book project, please address your material to the attention of the Book Department. For screenplays, please address your material to the attention of the Motion Picture Department. Due to the enormous amount of submissions we receive, we will only respond to queries that we feel are a good fit for our agency."

INTERNATIONAL TRANSACTIONS, INC.

P.O. Box 97, Gila NM 88038-0097. (845)373-9696. Fax: (845)373-7868. E-mail: info@intltrans.com. Website: www.intltrans.com. **Contact:** Peter Riva. Represents 40+ clients. 10% of clients are new/unpublished writers. Currently handles: nonfiction books 60%, novels 25%, story collections 5%, juvenile books 5%, scholarly books 5%.

Member Agents Peter Riva (nonfiction, fiction, illustrated; television and movie rights placement); Sandra Riva (fiction, juvenile, biographies); JoAnn Collins (fiction, women's fiction, medical fiction).

Represents nonfiction books, novels, short story collections, juvenile, scholarly, illustrated books, anthologies. **Considers these nonfiction areas:** anthropology, art, biography, computers, cooking, current affairs, ethnic, gay, government, health, history, humor, language, memoirs, military, music, nature, photography, science, self help, sports, translation, true crime, womens. **Considers these fiction areas:** adventure, detective, erotica, experimental, feminist, gay, historical, humor, literary, mainstream, mystery, spiritual, sports, thriller, young adult, women's/chick lit. "We specialize in large and small projects, helping qualified authors perfect material for publication." Actively seeking intelligent, well-written innovative material that breaks new ground. Does not want to receive material influenced by TV (too much dialogue); a rehash of previous successful novels' themes or poorly prepared material.

O→ "We specialize in large and small projects, helping qualified authors perfect material for publication." Actively seeking intelligent, well-written innovative material that breaks new ground. Does not want to receive material influenced by TV (too much dialogue); a rehash of previous successful novels' themes or poorly prepared material.

How to Contact First, e-query with an outline or synopsis. E-queries only!. Responds in 3 weeks to queries. Responds in 5 weeks to mss. Obtains most new clients through recommendations from others, solicitations.

Terms Agent receives 15% (25% on illustrated books) commission on domestic sales. Agent receives 20% commission on foreign sales. Offers written contract; 120-day notice must be given to terminate contract.

Tips 'Book'—a published work of literature. That last word is the key. Not a string of words, not a book of (TV or film) 'scenes,' and never a stream of consciousness unfathomable by anyone outside of the writer's coterie. A writer should only begin to get 'interested in getting an agent' if the work is polished, literate and ready to be presented to a publishing house. Anything less is either asking for a quick rejection or is a thinly disguised plea for creative assistance—which is often given but never fiscally sound for the agents involved. Writers, even published authors, have difficulty in being objective about their own work. Friends and family are of no assistance in that process either. Writers should attempt to get their work read by the most unlikely and stern critic as part of the editing process, months before any agent is approached.

JABBERWOCKY LITERARY AGENCY

P.O. Box 4558, Sunnyside NY 11104-0558. (718)392-5985. Website: www.awfulagent.com. **Contact:** Joshua Bilmes. Other memberships include SFWA. Represents 40 clients. 15% of clients are new/unpublished writers. Currently handles: nonfiction books 15%, novels 75%, scholarly books 5%, other 5% other.

Member Agents Joshua Bilmes; Eddie Schneider.

Represents nonfiction books, novels, scholarly. **Considers these nonfiction areas:** biography, business, cooking, current affairs, film, gay, government, health, history, humor, language, money, nature, popular culture, science, sociology, sports, young adult. **Considers these fiction areas:** contemporary, glitz, psychic, adventure, detective, ethnic, family, fantasy, gay, historical, horror, humor, literary, mainstream, regional, science, sports, thriller. This agency represents quite a lot of genre fiction and is actively seeking to increase the amount of nonfiction projects. It does not handle children's or picture books. Book-length material only--no poetry, articles, or short fiction.

- This agency represents quite a lot of genre fiction and is actively seeking to increase the amount of nonfiction projects. It does not handle children's or picture books. Book-length material only--no poetry, articles, or short fiction.

How to Contact Query with SASE. Do not send mss unless requested. Accepts simultaneous submissions. Responds in 3 weeks to queries. Obtains most new clients through solicitations, recommendation by current clients.

Terms Agent receives 15% commission on domestic sales. Agent receives 20% commission on foreign sales. Offers written contract, binding for 1 year. Charges clients for book purchases, photocopying, international book/ms mailing.

Recent Sales Sold 30 US and 100 foreign titles in the last year. *Dead and Gone*, by Charlaine Harris; *The Enchantment Emporium*, by Tanya Huff; *Underground*, by Kat Richardson; *The Alcatraz and Warbreakers series*, by Brandon Sanderson. Other clients include Elizabeth Moon, Simon Green, Tobias Bucknell, Peter V. Brett, Jack Campbell.

Writers Conferences Malice Domestic (May 2009); World Sci-Fi Convention (August 2008); World Fantasy Convention (October 2009); full schedule on Web site.

Tips "In approaching with a query, the most important things to us are your credits and your biographical background to the extent it's relevant to your work. I (and most agents) will ignore the adjectives you may choose to describe your own work."

JAMES PETER ASSOCIATES, INC.

P.O. Box 358, New Canaan CT 06840. (203)972-1070. E-mail: gene_brissie@msn.com. **Contact:** Gene Brissie. Represents 75 individual and 6 corporate clients. 15% of clients are new/unpublished writers. Currently handles: nonfiction books 100%.

Represents nonfiction books. **Considers these nonfiction areas:** anthropology, art, biography, business, child, current affairs, ethnic, gay, government, health, history, language, memoirs, political, business, military, money, music, popular culture, psychology, self help, film, travel, womens. "We are especially interested in general, trade and reference nonfiction." Does not want to receive children's/young adult books, poetry or fiction.

- "We are especially interested in general, trade and reference nonfiction." Does not want to receive children's/young adult books, poetry or fiction.

How to Contact Submit proposal package, outline, SASE. Prefers to read materials exclusively. Responds in 1 month to queries. Obtains most new clients through recommendations from others, solicitations, contact with people who are doing interesting things.

Terms Agent receives 15% commission on domestic sales. Agent receives 20% commission on foreign sales. Offers written contract.

JANKLOW & NESBIT ASSOCIATES

445 Park Ave., New York NY 10022. (212)421-1700. Fax: (212)980-3671. **Contact:** Morton L. Janklow, Lynn Nesbit.

Represents Does not want to receive unsolicited submissions or queries.

- Does not want to receive unsolicited submissions or queries.

How to Contact Obtains most new clients through recommendations from others.

J DE S ASSOCIATES, INC.

9 Shagbark Road, Wilson Point, South Norwalk CT 06854. (203)838-7571. **Contact:** Jacques de Spoelberch. Represents 50 clients. Currently handles: nonfiction books 50%, novels 50%.

- Prior to opening his agency, Mr. de Spoelberch was an editor with Houghton Mifflin.

Represents nonfiction books, novels. **Considers these nonfiction areas:** biography, business, cultural interests, current affairs, economics, ethnic, government, health, history, law, medicine, metaphysics, military, New Age, personal improvement, politics, self-help, sociology, sports, translation. **Considers these fiction areas:** crime, detective, frontier, historical, juvenile, literary, mainstream, mystery, New Age, police, suspense, westerns, young adult.

How to Contact Query with SASE. Responds in 2 months to queries. Obtains most new clients through Recommendations from authors and other clients.

Terms Agent receives 15% commission on domestic sales. Agent receives 20% commission on foreign sales. Charges clients for foreign postage and photocopying.

JET LITERARY ASSOCIATES

2570 Camino San Patricio, Santa Fe NM 87505. (505)474-9139. Fax: (505)474-9139. E-mail: etp@jetliterary.com. Website: www.jetliterary.com. **Contact:** Liz Trupin-Pulli. Represents 75 clients. 35% of clients are new/unpublished writers.

Member Agents Liz Trupin-Pulli (adult and YA fiction/nonfiction; romance, mysteries, parenting); Jim Trupin (adult fiction/nonfiction, military history, pop culture); Jessica Trupin, associate agent based in Seattle (adult fiction and nonfiction, children's and young adult, memoir, pop culture.

Represents nonfiction books, novels, short story collections. **Considers these nonfiction areas:** biography, business, child, current affairs, ethnic, gay, government, humor, memoirs, military, popular culture, sports, true crime, womens. **Considers these fiction areas:** adventure, detective, erotica, ethnic, gay, glitz, historical, humor, lesbian, literary, mainstream, mystery, romance, thriller. JET was founded in New York in 1975, so we bring a wealth of knowledge and contacts, as well as quite a bit of expertise to our representation of writers. Actively seeking women's fiction, mysteries and narrative nonfiction. Does not want to receive sci-fi, fantasy, horror, poetry, children's or religious.

- JET was founded in New York in 1975, so we bring a wealth of knowledge and contacts, as well as quite a bit of expertise to our representation of writers. Actively seeking women's fiction, mysteries and narrative nonfiction. Does not want to receive sci-fi, fantasy, horror, poetry, children's or religious.

How to Contact An e-query is preferred; if sending by snail mail, include an SASE. Responds in 1 week to queries. Responds in 8 weeks to mss. Obtains most new clients through recommendations from others, solicitations, conferences.

Terms Agent receives 15% commission on domestic sales. Agent receives 10% commission on foreign sales. Offers written contract, binding for 3 years. This agency charges for reimbursement of mailing and any photocopying.

Recent Sales Sold 25 titles in 2008. *Target Patton*, by Robert K. Wilcox (Regnery 2008); *Mom-In-chief*, by Jamie Woolf (Wiley, 2009); *Midnight Man*, by Charlotte Mede (Kensington, 2008); *Dangerous Games*, by Charlotte Mede (Kensington, 2009); *So You Think You Can Spell!*, by David Grambs and Ellen Levine (Perigee, 2009); *Cut, Drop & Die*, by Joanna Campbell Slan (Midnight Ink, 2009).

Writers Conferences Hillerman Mystery and Suspense Conference, Florida Writers Association Conference.

Tips "Do not write 'cute' queries—stick to a straightforward message that includes the title and what your book is about, why you are suited to write this particular book, and what you have written in the past (if anything), along with a bit of a bio."

CAREN JOHNSON LITERARY AGENCY

132 East 43rd St., No. 216, New York NY 10017. Fax: (718)228-8785. E-mail: caren@johnsonlitagency.com. Website: www.johnsonlitagency.com. **Contact:** Caren Johnson Estesen, Elana Roth. Represents 20 clients. 50% of clients are new/unpublished writers. Currently handles: nonfiction books 35%, juvenile books 35%, romance/women's fiction 30%.

- Prior to her current position, Ms. Johnson was with Firebrand Literary and the Peter Rubie Agency.

Member Agents Caren Johnson Estesen, Elana Roth, Rachel Downes.

Represents nonfiction books, novels. **Considers these nonfiction areas:** history, popular culture, science, women's studies, social science. **Considers these fiction areas:** detective, erotica, ethnic, romance, young adult, middle grade, women's fiction. Does not want to receive poetry, plays or screenplays/scripts. Elana Roth will consider picture books but is very selective of what she takes on.

- Does not want to receive poetry, plays or screenplays/scripts. Elana Roth will consider picture books but is very selective of what she takes on.

How to Contact Query via e-mail only, "directing your query to the appropriate person; responds in 12 weeks to all materials sent. Accepts simultaneous submissions. Responds in 4-6 weeks to queries. Responds in 6-8 weeks to mss. Obtains most new clients through recommendations from others.

Terms Agent receives 15% commission on domestic sales. Agent receives 20% commission on foreign sales. Offers written contract; 30-day notice must be given to terminate contract. This agency charges for postage and photocopying, though the author is consulted before any charges are incurred.

Recent Sales Check our website for our most recent sales. Clients include: A. E. Roman, Kelley St. John, Anna J. Evans, Stacey Jay, Karen Anders, Marlene Wagman-Geller, Stephanie Kuehnert, Kelsey Timmerman, Pam Bachorz, Darren Farrell, L. Faye Hughes

Writers Conferences RWA National; BookExpo America; SCBWI.

KELLER MEDIA INC.

23852 West Pacific Coast Hwy., Suite 701, Malibu CA 90265. (310)857-6828. Fax: (310)857-6373. E-mail: query@KellerMedia.com. Website: www.KellerMedia.com. **Contact:** Wendy Keller, senior agent. Other memberships include National Speakers Association. 25% of clients are new/unpublished writers. Currently handles: nonfiction books 100%.

- Prior to becoming an agent, Ms. Keller was an award-winning journalist and worked for PR Newswire and several newspapers.

Represents nonfiction books, scholarly. **Considers these nonfiction areas:** biography, business, current affairs, finance, health, history, money, nature, politics, psychology, science, self-help, sociology, spirituality, women's issues. "We focus a great deal of attention on authors who want to also become paid professional speakers, and speakers who want to become authors." Actively seeking nonfiction by highly credible experts, who have or want a significant platform in media, academia, politics, paid professional speaking, syndicated columns or regular appearances on radio/TV. Does not want (and absolutely will not respond to) to fiction, scripts, teleplays, poetry, juvenile, anything Christian, picture books, illustrated books, first-person stories of mental or physical illness, wrongful incarceration, or abduction by aliens, books channeled by aliens, demons, or dead celebrities (I wish I was kidding!).

O━ "We focus a great deal of attention on authors who want to also become paid professional speakers, and speakers who want to become authors." Actively seeking nonfiction by highly credible experts, who have or want a significant platform in media, academia, politics, paid professional speaking, syndicated columns or regular appearances on radio/TV. Does not want (and absolutely will not respond to) to fiction, scripts, teleplays, poetry, juvenile, anything Christian, picture books, illustrated books, first-person stories of mental or physical illness, wrongful incarceration, or abduction by aliens, books channeled by aliens, demons, or dead celebrities (I wish I was kidding!).

How to Contact E-mail queries strongly preferred. Make sure to include your credentials and a good overview of the proposed book. Do not send attachments; just a simple, succinct e-mail. Accepts simultaneous submissions. Responds in 7 days to queries. Responds in 2 weeks to mss. Obtains most new clients through recommendations from others.

Terms Agent receives 15% commission on domestic sales. Agent receives 20% commission on foreign sales.

Tips "Don't send a query to any agent unless you're certain they handle the type of book you're writing. 90% of rejections happen because what we're offered doesn't fit our established, advertised, printed, touted and shouted guidelines. Be organized! Have your proposal in order. Never make apologies for 'bad writing' or sloppy content—get it right before you waste your one shot with us. Have something new, different or interesting to say and be ready to dedicate your whole heart to marketing it to the world."

NATASHA KERN LITERARY AGENCY

P.O. Box 1069, White Salmon WA 98672. (509)493-3803. E-mail: queries@natashakern.com. Website: www.natashakern.com. **Contact:** Natasha Kern. Other memberships include RWA, MWA, SinC.

- Prior to opening her agency, Ms. Kern worked as an editor and publicist for Simon & Schuster, Bantam, and Ballantine. This agency has sold more than 700 books.

Represents Considers these nonfiction areas: animals, child, current affairs, ethnic, gardening, health, nature, popular culture, psychology, religion, self help, spirituality, womens, investigative journalism. "This agency specializes in commercial fiction and nonfiction for adults. We are a full-service agency." Does not represent sports, true crime, scholarly works, coffee table books, war memoirs, software, scripts, literary fiction, photography, poetry, short stories, children's, horror, fantasy, genre science fiction, stage plays, or traditional westerns.

O━ "This agency specializes in commercial fiction and nonfiction for adults. We are a full-service agency." Does not represent sports, true crime, scholarly works, coffee table books, war memoirs, software, scripts, literary fiction, photography, poetry, short stories, children's, horror, fantasy, genre science fiction, stage plays, or traditional westerns.

How to Contact See submission instructions online. Send query to queries@natashakern.com. "We do not accept queries by snail mail or phone." Accepts simultaneous submissions. Responds in 3 weeks to queries.
Terms Agent receives 15% commission on domestic sales. Agent receives 20% commission on foreign sales. Agent receives 15% commission on film sales.
Recent Sales Sold 43 titles in the last year. *China Dolls*, by Michelle Yu and Blossom Kan (St. Martin's); *Bastard Tongues*, by Derek Bickerton (Farrar Strauss); *Bone Rattler*, by Eliot Pattison; *Wicked Pleasure*, by Nina Bangs (Berkley); *Inviting God In*, by David Aaron (Shambhala); *Unlawful Contact*, by Pamela Clare (Berkley); *Dead End Dating*, by Kimberly Raye (Ballantine); *A Scent of Roses*, by Nikki Arana (Baker Book House); *The Sexiest Man Alive*, by Diana Holquist (Warner Books).
Writers Conferences RWA National Conference; MWA National Conference; ACFW Conference; and many regional conferences.
Tips "Your chances of being accepted for representation will be greatly enhanced by going to our website first. Our idea of a dream client is someone who participates in a mutually respectful business relationship, is clear about needs and goals, and communicates about career planning. If we know what you need and want, we can help you achieve it. A dream client has a storytelling gift, a commitment to a writing career, a desire to learn and grow, and a passion for excellence. We want clients who are expressing their own unique voice and truly have something of their own to communicate. This client understands that many people have to work together for a book to succeed and that everything in publishing takes far longer than one imagines. Trust and communication are truly essential."

LOUISE B. KETZ AGENCY

414 E. 78th St., Suite 1B, New York NY 10075. (212)249-0668. E-mail: ketzagency@aol.com. **Contact:** Louise B. Ketz. Represents 25 clients. 15% of clients are new/unpublished writers. Currently handles: nonfiction books 100%.
Represents nonfiction books. **Considers these nonfiction areas:** business, current affairs, history, military, science, sports, economics. This agency specializes in science, history and reference.
- This agency specializes in science, history and reference.

How to Contact Query with SASE. Submit outline, 1 sample chapter, author bio (with qualifications for authorship of work). Responds in 6 weeks to mss. Obtains most new clients through recommendations from others, idea development.
Terms Agent receives 15% commission on domestic sales.

VIRGINIA KIDD AGENCY, INC.

538 E. Harford St., P.O. Box 278, Milford PA 18337. (570)296-6205. Fax: (570)296-7266. Website: www.vk-agency.com. Other memberships include SFWA, SFRA. Represents 80 clients.
Member Agents Christine Cohen.
Represents novels. **Considers these fiction areas:** fantasy, historical, mystery, science, womens, speculative; mainstream. This agency specializes in science fiction and fantasy.
- This agency specializes in science fiction and fantasy.

How to Contact Query with SASE. Submit synopsis (1-3 pages), cover letter, first chapter, SASE. Snail mail queries only. Responds in 6 weeks to queries.
Terms Agent receives 15% commission on domestic sales. Agent receives 20-25% commission on foreign sales. Agent receives 20% commission on film sales. Offers written contract; 2-month notice must be given to terminate contract. Charges clients occasionally for extraordinary expenses.
Recent Sales *Sagramanda*, by Alan Dean Foster (Pyr); *Incredible Good Fortune*, by Ursula K. Le Guin (Shambhala); *The Wizard and Soldier of Sidon*, by Gene Wolfe (Tor); *Voices and Powers*, by Ursula K. Le Guin (Harcourt); *Galileo's Children*, by Gardner Dozois (Pyr); *The Light Years Beneath My Feet* and *Running From the Deity*, by Alan Dean Foster (Del Ray); *Chasing Fire*, by Michelle Welch. Other clients include Eleanor Arnason, Ted Chiang, Jack Skillingstead, Daryl Gregory, Patricia Briggs, and the estates for James Tiptree, Jr., Murray Leinster, E.E. "Doc" Smith, R. A. Lafferty.
Tips "If you have a completed novel that is of extraordinary quality, please send us a query."

KIRCHOFF/WOHLBERG, INC., AUTHORS' REPRESENTATION DIVISION

866 United Nations Plaza, #525, New York NY 10017. (212)644-2020. Fax: (212)223-4387. E-mail: tradeinfo@kirchoffwohlberg.com. **Contact:** Liza Pulitzer Voges. Member of AAR. Other memberships include AAP, Society of Illustrators, SPAR, Bookbuilders of Boston, New York Bookbinders' Guild, AIGA. Represents 50 clients. 10% of clients are new/unpublished writers. Currently handles: nonfiction books 5%, novels 25%, other 5% young adult.
- Kirchoff/Wohlberg has been in business for over 60 years.

Represents This agency specializes in only juvenile through young adult trade books.
- This agency specializes in only juvenile through young adult trade books.

How to Contact *Is not currently accepting unsolicted mss.* Accepts simultaneous submissions. Responds in 1 month to queries. Responds in 2 months to mss. Obtains most new clients through recommendations from authors, illustrators, and editors.

Terms Offers written contract, binding for at least 1 year. Agent receives standard commission, depending upon whether it is an author only, illustrator only, or an author/illustrator book.

KLEINWORKS AGENCY

2814 Brooks Ave., # 635, Missoula MT 59801. E-mail: judyklein@kleinworks.com. Website: www.kleinworks.com. **Contact:** Judy Klein. Represents 10 clients. Currently handles: nonfiction books 60%, novels 40%.

- Prior to becoming an agent, Ms. Klein spent a dozen years with Farrar, Straus & Giroux; she also held the position of editor-in-chief at The Literary Guild Book Club and at Booksonline.com.

Represents nonfiction books, novels. **Considers these nonfiction areas:** biography, business, health, how to, memoirs, money, nature, popular culture, self help. **Considers these fiction areas:** ethnic, experimental, humor, literary. "Kleinworks Agency may be geographically removed from the red-hot center of New York publishing, but our credentials and connections keep us close to New York's best publishers and editors. As a publishing veteran with two decades of book experience, intimate knowledge of the industry and expertise in domestic and international negotiations, I provide my clients with an edge in getting their books published well. Kleinworks offers dedicated services to a very small, select group of writers and publishers so that we can guarantee spirited and undivided attention."

O→ "Kleinworks Agency may be geographically removed from the red-hot center of New York publishing, but our credentials and connections keep us close to New York's best publishers and editors. As a publishing veteran with two decades of book experience, intimate knowledge of the industry and expertise in domestic and international negotiations, I provide my clients with an edge in getting their books published well. Kleinworks offers dedicated services to a very small, select group of writers and publishers so that we can guarantee spirited and undivided attention."

How to Contact Query with SASE. Submit proposal package, outline/proposal, synopsis, author bio, sample chapters. No phone queries. Accepts simultaneous submissions. Responds in 4 weeks to queries. Responds in 1-2 months to mss. Obtains most new clients through recommendations from others.

Terms Agent receives 15% commission on domestic sales. Agent receives 20% commission on foreign sales. Offers written contract, binding for optional, for 1 year; 3-month notice must be given to terminate contract. Charges for postage and photocopying fees after six months.

Writers Conferences Montana Festival of the Book, Yellowstone Nature Writers' Field Conference.

HARVEY KLINGER, INC.

300 W. 55th St., Suite 11V, New York NY 10019. (212)581-7068. E-mail: queries@harveyklinger.com. Website: www.harveyklinger.com. **Contact:** Harvey Klinger Member of AAR. Represents 100 clients. 25% of clients are new/unpublished writers. Currently handles: nonfiction books 50%, novels 50%.

Member Agents David Dunton (popular culture, music-related books, literary fiction, young adult, fiction, and memoirs); Sara Crowe (children's and young adult authors, adult fiction and nonfiction, foreign rights sales); Andrea Somberg (literary fiction, commercial fiction, romance, sci-fi/fantasy, mysteries/thrillers, young adult, middle grade, quality narrative nonfiction, popular culture, how-to, self-help, humor, interior design, cookbooks, health/fitness).

Represents nonfiction books, novels. **Considers these nonfiction areas:** biography, cooking, health, psychology, science, self help, spirituality, sports, true crime, womens. **Considers these fiction areas:** glitz, adventure, detective, family, literary, mainstream, mystery, thriller. This agency specializes in big, mainstream, contemporary fiction and nonfiction.

O→ This agency specializes in big, mainstream, contemporary fiction and nonfiction.

How to Contact Query with SASE. No phone or fax queries. Don't send unsolicited manuscripts or e-mail attachments. Responds in 2 months to queries and mss. Obtains most new clients through recommendations from others.

Terms Agent receives 15% commission on domestic sales. Agent receives 25% commission on foreign sales. Offers written contract. Charges for photocopying mss and overseas postage for mss.

Recent Sales *Woman of a Thousand Secrets*, by Barbara Wood; *I am Not a Serial Killer*, by Dan Wells; untitled memoir, by Bob Mould; *Children of the Mist*; by Paula Quinn; *Tutored*, by Allison Whittenberg; *Will You Take Me As I Am*, by Michelle Mercer. Other clients include: George Taber, Terry Kay, Scott Mebus, Jacqueline Kolosov, Jonathan Maberry, Tara Altebrando, Alex McAuley, Eva Nagorski, Greg Kot, Justine Musk, Alex McAuley, Nick Tasler, Ashley Kahn, Barbara De Angelis.

KNEERIM & WILLIAMS AT FISH & RICHARDSON

225 Franklin St., Boston MA 02110. (617)542-5070. Fax: (617)542-8906. E-mail: submissions@fr.com. Website: http://www.fr.com/practice. **Contact:** Cara Krenn. Represents 200 clients. 5% of clients are new/unpublished writers. Currently handles: nonfiction books 80%, novels 15%, movie scripts 5%.

- Prior to becoming an agent, Mr. Williams was a lawyer; Ms. Kneerim was a publisher and editor; Mr. Wasserman was an editor and journalist; Ms. Grosvenor was an editor.

Member Agents John Taylor Williams; Jill Kneerim; Steve Wasserman; Bretthe Bloom; Deborah C. Grosvenor.

Represents nonfiction books, novels. **Considers these nonfiction areas:** anthropology, biography, business, child, current affairs, government, health, history, language, memoirs, nature, popular culture, psychology, religion, science, sociology, sports, womens. **Considers these fiction areas:** historical, literary, mainstream. "This agency specializes in narrative nonfiction, history, science, business, women's issues, commercial and literary fiction, film, and television. We have 5 agents and 4 scouts in Boston, New York, Washington DC and Santa Fe." Actively seeking distinguished authors, experts, professionals, intellectuals, and serious writers. Does not want to receive blanket multiple submissions, genre fiction or original screenplays.

O→ "This agency specializes in narrative nonfiction, history, science, business, women's issues, commercial and literary fiction, film, and television. We have 5 agents and 4 scouts in Boston, New York, Washington DC and Santa Fe." Actively seeking distinguished authors, experts, professionals, intellectuals, and serious writers. Does not want to receive blanket multiple submissions, genre fiction or original screenplays.

How to Contact Submit query via e-mail only. No hard copies will be accepted. Submissions should contain a cover letter explaining your book and why you are qualified to write it, a two-page synopsis of the book, one sample chapter, and your c.v. or a history of your publications. Responds in 2 weeks to queries. Responds in 2 months to mss. Obtains most new clients through recommendations from others.

LINDA KONNER LITERARY AGENCY

10 W. 15th St., Suite 1918, New York NY 10011-6829. (212)691-3419. E-mail: ldkonner@cs.com. **Contact:** Linda Konner. Member of AAR. Signatory of WGA. Other memberships include ASJA. Represents 85 clients. 30-35% of clients are new/unpublished writers. Currently handles: nonfiction books 100%.

Represents nonfiction books. **Considers these nonfiction areas:** biography (celebrity only), gay, health, diet/nutrition/fitness, how to, money, personal finance, popular culture, psychology, pop psychology, self help, women's issues; African American and Latino issues; business; parenting; relationships. This agency specializes in health, self-help, and how-to books. Authors/co-authors must be top experts in their field with a substantial media platform.

O→ This agency specializes in health, self-help, and how-to books. Authors/co-authors must be top experts in their field with a substantial media platform.

How to Contact Query with SASE, synopsis, author bio, sufficient return postage. Prefers to read materials exclusively for 2 weeks. Accepts simultaneous submissions. Obtains most new clients through recommendations from others, occasional solicitation among established authors/journalists.

Terms Agent receives 15% commission on domestic sales. Agent receives 25% commission on foreign sales. Offers written contract. Charges one-time fee for domestic expenses; additional expenses may be incurred for foreign sales.

Recent Sales *A Baby at Last!* by Zev Rosenwaks, M.D., Marc Goldstein, M.D., with Mark Fuerst (S&S); *To Friend or Not to Friend*, by Andrea Bonnior, Ph.D. (Tom Dunne books/SMP); *The Winner's Brain*, by Jeff Brown, Mark Fenske, Liz Neporent, and the editors of Harvard Health Publications (Perseus); *Work Smart, Play Hard: Build a Million-Dollar Business Before You're 30*, by Nick Friedman, Omar Soliman, with Daylle Schwartz (Three Rivers Press/RH).

Writers Conferences ASJA Writers Conference, Harvard Medical School's "Publishing Books, Memoirs, and Other Creative Nonfiction" Annual Conference.

ELAINE KOSTER LITERARY AGENCY, LLC

55 Central Park W., Suite 6, New York NY 10023. (212)362-9488. Fax: (212)712-0164. **Contact:** Elaine Koster, Stephanie Lehmann, Ellen Twaddell. Member of AAR. Other memberships include MWA, Author's Guild, Women's Media Group. Represents 40 clients. 10% of clients are new/unpublished writers. Currently handles: nonfiction books 10%, novels 90%.

- Prior to opening her agency in 1998, Ms. Koster was president and publisher of Dutton-NAL, part of the Penguin Group.

Represents nonfiction books, novels. **Considers these nonfiction areas:** biography, business, child, cooking, current affairs, ethnic, health, history, how to, money, nature, popular culture, psychology, self help, spirituality, womens. **Considers these fiction areas:** ethnic, feminist, historical, literary, mainstream, mystery, regional, thriller, chick lit. This agency specializes in quality fiction and nonfiction. Does not want to receive juvenile, screenplays, or science fiction.

O→ This agency specializes in quality fiction and nonfiction. Does not want to receive juvenile, screenplays, or science fiction.

How to Contact Query with SASE. Prefers to read materials exclusively. Responds in 3 weeks to queries.

Responds in 1 month to mss. Obtains most new clients through recommendations from others.
Terms Agent receives 15% commission on domestic sales. Bills back specific expenses incurred doing business for a client.
Recent Sales *The Lost and Forgotten Languages* of Shanhai, by Ruiyan Xu (St. Martin's Press); Untitled new novel by David Ebershoff (Random House).
Tips "We prefer exclusive submissions. Don't e-mail or fax submissions. Please include biographical information and publishing history."

KRAAS LITERARY AGENCY

E-mail: irenekraas@sbcglobal.net. Website: www.kraasliteraryagency.com. **Contact:** Irene Kraas. Represents 35 clients. 75% of clients are new/unpublished writers. Currently handles: nonfiction books 2%, novels 98%.
Member Agents Irene Kraas, principal.
Represents novels. **Considers these fiction areas:** literary, thriller, young. This agency is interested in working with published writers, but that does not mean self-published writers. "Actively seeking psychological thrillers, medical thrillers, some literary fiction and young adult. With each of these areas, I want something new. No Da Vinci Code or Harry Potter ripoffs. I am especially not interested in storylines that include the Mafia or government. Not interested in personal stories of growth, stories about generation hangups and stories about drugs, incest, etc." Does not want to receive short stories, plays or poetry. This agency no longer represents adult fantasy or science fiction.

O⁻ This agency is interested in working with published writers, but that does not mean self-published writers. "Actively seeking psychological thrillers, medical thrillers, some literary fiction and young adult. With each of these areas, I want something new. No Da Vinci Code or Harry Potter ripoffs. I am especially not interested in storylines that include the Mafia or government. Not interested in personal stories of growth, stories about generation hangups and stories about drugs, incest, etc." Does not want to receive short stories, plays or poetry. This agency no longer represents adult fantasy or science fiction.

How to Contact Query and e-mail the first 10 pages of a completed ms. Requires exclusive read on mss. Accepts simultaneous submissions.
Terms Offers written contract.
Tips "I am interested in material - in any genre - that is truly, truly unique."

BERT P. KRAGES

6665 SW Hampton St., Suite 200, Portland OR 97223. (503)597-2525. E-mail: krages@onemain.com. Website: www.krages.com. **Contact:** Bert Krages. Represents 10 clients. 80% of clients are new/unpublished writers. Currently handles: nonfiction books 95%, scholarly books 5%.

- Mr. Krages is also an attorney.

Represents nonfiction books. **Considers these nonfiction areas:** agriculture horticulture, animals, anthropology, art, biography, business, child, computers, current affairs, education, ethnic, health, history, memoirs, military, nature, psychology, science, self help, sociology. "I handle a small number of literary clients and concentrate on trade nonfiction (science, history)." No fiction submissions until further notified - check the Web site.

O⁻ "I handle a small number of literary clients and concentrate on trade nonfiction (science, history)." No fiction submissions until further notified - check the Web site.

How to Contact Keep queries to one page - nonfiction only. E-mail submissions preferred. Accepts simultaneous submissions. Responds in 1-6 weeks to queries. Obtains most new clients through solicitations.
Terms Agent receives 15% commission on domestic sales. Agent receives 20% commission on foreign sales. Offers written contract, binding for 1 year; 60-day notice must be given to terminate contract. Charges for photocopying and postage only if the book is placed.
Tips Read at least 2 books on how to prepare book proposals before sending material. An extremely well-prepared proposal will make your material stand out.

STUART KRICHEVSKY LITERARY AGENCY, INC.

381 Park Ave. S., Suite 914, New York NY 10016. (212)725-5288. Fax: (212)725-5275. E-mail: query@skagency.com. Website: www.skagency.com. Member of AAR.
Member Agents Stuart Krichevsky; Shana Cohen (science fiction, fantasy); Kathryne Wick.
Represents nonfiction books, novels.
How to Contact Submit query, synopsis, 1 sample page via e-mail (no attachments). Snail mail queries also acceptable. Obtains most new clients through recommendations from others, solicitations.

EDITE KROLL LITERARY AGENCY, INC.

20 Cross St., Saco ME 04072. (207)283-8797. Fax: (207)283-8799. E-mail: ekroll@maine.rr.com. **Contact:** Edite Kroll. Represents 45 clients. 20% of clients are new/unpublished writers. Currently handles: nonfiction books 40%, novels 5%, juvenile books 40%, scholarly books 5%, other.

- Prior to opening her agency, Ms. Kroll served as a book editor and translator.

Represents nonfiction books, novels, very selective, juvenile, scholarly. **Considers these nonfiction areas:** juvenile, selectively, biography, current affairs, ethnic, gay, government, health, no diet books, humor, memoirs, selectively, popular culture, psychology, religion, selectively, self help, selectively, womens, issue-oriented nonfiction. **Considers these fiction areas:** juvenile, literary, picture books, young adult, middle grade, adult. "We represent writers and writer-artists of both adult and children's books. We have a special focus on international feminist writers, women writers and artists who write their own books (including children's and humor books)." Actively seeking artists who write their own books and international feminists who write in English. Does not want to receive genre (mysteries, thrillers, diet, cookery, etc.), photography books, coffee table books, romance or commercial fiction.

- "We represent writers and writer-artists of both adult and children's books. We have a special focus on international feminist writers, women writers and artists who write their own books (including children's and humor books)." Actively seeking artists who write their own books and international feminists who write in English. Does not want to receive genre (mysteries, thrillers, diet, cookery, etc.), photography books, coffee table books, romance or commercial fiction.

How to Contact Query with SASE. Submit outline/proposal, synopsis, 1-2 sample chapters, author bio, entire ms if sending picture book..No phone queries. Responds in 2-4 weeks to queries. Responds in 4-8 weeks to mss. Obtains most new clients through recommendations from others.

Terms Agent receives 15% commission on domestic sales. Agent receives 20% commission on foreign sales. Offers written contract; 30-day notice must be given to terminate contract. Charges clients for photocopying and legal fees with prior approval from writer.

Recent Sales Sold 12 domestic/30 foreign titles in the last year. This agency prefers not to share information on specific sales. Clients include Shel Silverstein estate, Suzy Becker, Geoffrey Hayes, Henrik Drescher, Charlotte Kasl, Gloria Skurzynski, Fatema Mernissa.

Tips "Please do your research so you won't send me books/proposals I specifically excluded."

KT LITERARY, LLC

9249 S. Broadway, #200-543, Highlands Ranch CO 80129. (720)344-4728. Fax: (720)344-4728. E-mail: queries@ktliterary.com. Website: www.ktliterary.com. **Contact:** Kate Schafer Testerman. Other memberships include SCBWI. Represents 20 clients. 60% of clients are new/unpublished writers. Currently handles: nonfiction books 5%, novels 5%, juvenile books 90%.

- Prior to her current position, Ms. Schafer was an agent with Janklow & Nesbit.

Represents nonfiction books, novels, juvenile books. **Considers these nonfiction areas:** popular culture. **Considers these fiction areas:** adventure, fantasy, historical, juvenile, romance, young adult. "I'm bringing my years of experience in the New York publishing scene, as well as my lifelong love of reading, to a vibrant area for writers, proving that great work can be found, and sold, from anywhere." "Actively seeking brilliant, funny, original middle grade and young adult fiction, both literary and commercial; witty women's fiction (chick lit); and pop-culture, narrative nonfiction. Quirky is good." Does not want picture books, serious nonfiction, and adult literary fiction.

- "I'm bringing my years of experience in the New York publishing scene, as well as my lifelong love of reading, to a vibrant area for writers, proving that great work can be found, and sold, from anywhere." "Actively seeking brilliant, funny, original middle grade and young adult fiction, both literary and commercial; witty women's fiction (chick lit); and pop-culture, narrative nonfiction. Quirky is good." Does not want picture books, serious nonfiction, and adult literary fiction.

How to Contact Query with SASE. Submit author bio, 2-3 sample pages.Absolutely no attachments. Paste text in e-mail body. E-mail queries only. Responds in 2 weeks to queries. Responds in 1 month to mss. Obtains most new clients through recommendations from others, solicitations, conferences.

Terms Agent receives 15% commission on domestic sales. Agent receives 20% commission on foreign sales. Offers written contract; 30-day notice must be given to terminate contract.

Writers Conferences Various SCBWI conferences, BookExpo.

Tips "If we like your query, we'll ask for (more). Continuing advice is offered regularly on my blog 'Ask Daphne', which can be accessed from my Web site."

KT PUBLIC RELATIONS & LITERARY SERVICES

1905 Cricklewood Cove, Fogelsville PA 18051. (610)395-6298. Fax: (610)395-6299. Website: www.ktpublicrelations.com. **Contact:** Jon Tienstra. Represents 12 clients. 75% of clients are new/unpublished writers. Currently handles: nonfiction books 50%, novels 50%.

- Prior to becoming an agent, Kae Tienstra was publicity director for Rodale, Inc. for 13 years and then founded her own publicity agency; Mr. Tienstra joined the firm in 1995 with varied corporate experience and a master's degree in library science.

Member Agents Kae Tienstra (health, parenting, psychology, how-to, crafts, foods/nutrition, beauty, women's fiction, general fiction); Jon Tienstra (nature/environment, history, cooking/foods/nutrition, war/military, automotive, health/medicine, gardening, general fiction, science fiction/contemporary fantasy, popular fiction).

Represents nonfiction books, novels. **Considers these nonfiction areas:** agriculture horticulture, crafts, animals, child, cooking, health, history, how to, military, nature, popular culture, psychology, science, self help, interior design/decorating. **Considers these fiction areas:** adventure, detective, family, fantasy, contemporary - no swords or dragons, historical, literary, mainstream, mystery, romance, science, thriller. "We have worked with a variety of authors and publishers over the years and have learned what individual publishers are looking for in terms of new acquisitions. We are both mad about books and authors and we look forward to finding publishing success for all our clients. Specializes in parenting, history, cooking/foods/nutrition, crafts, beauty, war, health/medicine, psychology, how-to, gardening, science fiction, fantasy, women's fiction, and popular fiction." Does not want to see unprofessional material.

"We have worked with a variety of authors and publishers over the years and have learned what individual publishers are looking for in terms of new acquisitions. We are both mad about books and authors and we look forward to finding publishing success for all our clients. Specializes in parenting, history, cooking/foods/nutrition, crafts, beauty, war, health/medicine, psychology, how-to, gardening, science fiction, fantasy, women's fiction, and popular fiction." Does not want to see unprofessional material.

How to Contact Query with SASE. Prefers snail mail queries. Will accept e-mail queries. Responds in 3 months to chapters; 6-9 months for mss. Accepts simultaneous submissions. Responds in 2 weeks to queries.

Terms Agent receives 15% commission on domestic sales. Agent receives 20% commission on foreign sales. Offers written contract. Charges clients for long-distance phone calls, fax, postage, photocopying (only when incurred). No advance payment for these out-of-pocket expenses.

ALBERT LaFARGE LITERARY AGENCY

Fax: (270)512-5179. E-mail: office@thelafargeagency.com. Website: www.thelafargeagency.com. **Contact:** Albert LaFarge. Represents 24 clients. 50% of clients are new/unpublished writers. Currently handles: nonfiction books 90%, novels 10%.

- Prior to becoming an agent, Mr. LaFarge was an editor.

Represents nonfiction books, novels. **Considers these nonfiction areas:** art, biography, current affairs, health, history, memoirs, music, nature, photography, psychology, sports. **Considers these fiction areas:** literary. This agency specializes in helping clients to develop nonfiction.

This agency specializes in helping clients to develop nonfiction.

How to Contact Query with SASE. Submit outline and sample chapters. Obtains most new clients through recommendations from others.

Terms Agent receives 15% commission on domestic sales. Agent receives 20% commission on foreign sales. Offers written contract. Charges for photocopying.

THE LA LITERARY AGENCY

P.O. Box 46370, Los Angeles CA 90046. (323)654-5288. E-mail: laliteraryag@mac.com. **Contact:** Ann Cashman, Eric Lasher.

- Prior to becoming an agent, Mr. Lasher worked in publishing in New York and Los Angeles.

Represents nonfiction books, novels. **Considers these nonfiction areas:** animals, anthropology, art, biography, business, child, cooking, current affairs, ethnic, government, health, history, how to, nature, popular culture, psychology, science, self help, sociology, sports, true crime, womens, narrative nonfiction. **Considers these fiction areas:** adventure, detective, family, feminist, historical, literary, mainstream, sports, thriller.

How to Contact Query with outline, 1 sample chapter. No fax or e-mail queries.

Recent Sales *Full Bloom: The Art and Life of Georgia O'Keeffe*, by Hunter Druhojowska-Philp (Norton); *And the Walls Came Tumbling Down*, by H. Caldwell (Scribner); *Italian Slow & Savory*, by Joyce Goldstein (Chronicle); *A Field Guide to Chocolate Chip Cookies*, by Dede Wilson (Harvard Common Press); *Teen Knitting Club* (Artisan); *The Framingham Heart Study*, by Dr. Daniel Levy (Knopf).

PETER LAMPACK AGENCY, INC.

551 Fifth Ave., Suite 1613, New York NY 10176-0187. (212)687-9106. Fax: (212)687-9109. E-mail: alampack@verizon.net. **Contact:** Andrew Lampack. Represents 50 clients. 10% of clients are new/unpublished writers. Currently handles: nonfiction books 20%, novels 80%.

Member Agents Peter Lampack (president); Rema Delanyan (foreign rights); Andrew Lampack (new writers).

Represents nonfiction books, novels. **Considers these fiction areas:** adventure, detective, family, literary, mainstream, mystery, thriller, contemporary relationships. "This agency specializes in commercial fiction and nonfiction by recognized experts." Actively seeking literary and commercial fiction, thrillers, mysteries, suspense, and psychological thrillers. Does not want to receive horror, romance, science fiction, westerns, historical literary fiction or academic material.

- "This agency specializes in commercial fiction and nonfiction by recognized experts." Actively seeking literary and commercial fiction, thrillers, mysteries, suspense, and psychological thrillers. Does not want to receive horror, romance, science fiction, westerns, historical literary fiction or academic material.

How to Contact Query via e-mail. *No unsolicited mss.* Responds within 2 months to queries. Obtains most new clients through referrals made by clients.

Terms Agent receives 15% commission on domestic sales. Agent receives 20% commission on foreign sales.

Recent Sales *Spartan Gold*, by Clive Cussler with Grant Blackwood; *The Wrecker*, by Clive Cussler with Justin Scott; *Medusa*, by Clive Cussler and Paul Kemprecos; *Corsair*, by Clive Cussler with Jack Dubrul; *Summertime*, by J.M. Coetzee; *Dreaming in French*, by Megan McAndrew; *Time Pirate*, by Ted Bell.

Writers Conferences BookExpo America; Mystery Writers of America.

Tips "Submit only your best work for consideration. Have a very specific agenda of goals you wish your prospective agent to accomplish for you. Provide the agent with a comprehensive statement of your credentials - educational and professional accomplishments."

LAURA LANGLIE, LITERARY AGENT

239 Carroll St., Garden Apartment, Brooklyn NY 11231. (718)855-8102. Fax: (718)855-4450. E-mail: laura@lauralanglie.com. **Contact:** Laura Langlie. Represents 25 clients. 50% of clients are new/unpublished writers. Currently handles: nonfiction books 15%, novels 58%, story collections 2%, juvenile books 25%.

- Prior to opening her agency, Ms. Langlie worked in publishing for 7 years and as an agent at Kidde, Hoyt & Picard for 6 years.

Represents nonfiction books, novels, short story collections, novellas, juvenile. **Considers these nonfiction areas:** animals, not how-to, biography, current affairs, ethnic, government, history, humor, memoirs, nature, popular culture, psychology, film, womens, history of medicine and science; language/literature. **Considers these fiction areas:** detective, ethnic, feminist, historical, humor, juvenile, literary, mystery, romance, thriller, young, mainstream. "I'm very involved with and committed to my clients. I also employ a publicist to work with all my clients to make the most of each book's publication. Most of my clients come to me via recommendations from other agents, clients and editors. I've met very few at conferences. I've often sought out writers for projects, and I still find new clients via the traditional query letter." Does not want to receive children's picture books, science fiction, poetry, men's adventure or erotica.

- "I'm very involved with and committed to my clients. I also employ a publicist to work with all my clients to make the most of each book's publication. Most of my clients come to me via recommendations from other agents, clients and editors. I've met very few at conferences. I've often sought out writers for projects, and I still find new clients via the traditional query letter." Does not want to receive children's picture books, science fiction, poetry, men's adventure or erotica.

How to Contact Query with SASE. Accepts queries via fax. Accepts simultaneous submissions. Responds in 1 week to queries. Responds in 1 month to mss. Obtains most new clients through recommendations, submissions.

Terms Agent receives 15% commission on domestic sales. Agent receives 20% commission on foreign sales. No written contract.

Recent Sales Sold 20 titles in the last year. *Ash*, by Malinda Lo (Little, Brown); *Airhead* series, by Meg Cabot (Scholastic); *Girls Acting Catty*, by Leslie Margolis (Bloomsbury). Other clients include Emily Arsenault, Renee Ashley, Mignon F. Ballard, Jessica Benson, Joan Druett, Jack El-Hai, Sarah Elliott, Dan Begley, Robin Hathaway, Melanie Lynne Hauser, Mary Hogan, Lauren Lipton, Jonathan Neale, Delia Ray, Cheryl L. Reed, Jennifer Sturman, Meg Tilly.

Tips Be complete, forthright and clear in your communications. Do your research as to what a particular agent represents.

LANGTONS INTERNATIONAL AGENCY

240 West 35th St., Suite 500, New York NY 10001. (212)929-1937. E-mail: langtonsinternational@gmail.com. Website: www.langtonsinternational.com. **Contact:** Linda Langton.

- Prior to becoming an agent, Ms. Langton was a co-founding director and publisher of the international publishing company, The Ink Group.

Represents nonfiction books, novels. **Considers these nonfiction areas:** biography, health, history, how-to, politics, self-help, true crime. **Considers these fiction areas:** literary, political thrillers, young adult and middle grade books."Langtons International Agency is a multi-media literary and licensing agency specializing in nonfiction, thrillers and children's books as well as the the visual world of photography, illustrative art, gift books, calendars, greeting cards, posters and other related products."

O→ "Langtons International Agency is a multi-media literary and licensing agency specializing in nonfiction, thrillers and children's books as well as the the visual world of photography, illustrative art, gift books, calendars, greeting cards, posters and other related products."

How to Contact Query with SASE. Submit outline/proposal, synopsis, publishing history, author bio. Only published authors should query this agency Accepts simultaneous submissions.

Recent Sales *Talking With Jean-Paul Sartre: Conversations and Debates*, by Professor John Gerassi (Yale University Press); *The Obama Presidency and the Politics of Redemption*, by Professor Stanley Renshon (Routledge Press); *I Would See a Girl Walking*, by Diana Montane and Kathy Kelly (Berkley Books); *Begin 1913-1992*, by Avi Shilon (Yale University Press); *This Borrowed Earth*, by Robert Emmet Hernan (Palgrave McMillan); *The Perfect Square*, by Nancy Heinzen (Temple Uni Press).

MICHAEL LARSEN/ELIZABETH POMADA, LITERARY AGENTS

1029 Jones St., San Francisco CA 94109-5023. (415)673-0939. E-mail: larsenpoma@aol.com. Website: www.larsen-pomada.com. **Contact:** Mike Larsen, Elizabeth Pomada, Laurie McLean. Member of AAR. Other memberships include Authors Guild, ASJA, PEN, WNBA, California Writers Club, National Speakers Association. Represents 100 clients. 40-45% of clients are new/unpublished writers. Currently handles: nonfiction books 70%, novels 30%.

- Prior to opening their agency, Mr. Larsen and Ms. Pomada were promotion executives for major publishing houses. Mr. Larsen worked for Morrow, Bantam and Pyramid (now part of Berkley); Ms. Pomada worked at Holt, David McKay and The Dial Press. Mr. Larsen is the author of the third editions of *How to Write a Book Proposal* and *How to Get a Literary Agent* as well as the coauthor of *Guerilla Marketing for Writers: 100 Weapons for Selling Your Work*, which will be republished in September 2009.

Represents Considers these nonfiction areas: anthropology, art, biography, business, current affairs, ethnic, film, foods, gay, government, health, history, humor, memoirs, money, music, nature, , popular culture, psychology, science, sociology, sports, travel, true crime, futurism. **Considers these fiction areas:** contemporary, glitz, adventure, detective, ethnic, experimental, family, fantasy, feminist, gay, historical, humor, literary, mainstream, mystery, religious, romance, contemporary, gothic, historical, chick lit. We have diverse tastes. We look for fresh voices and new ideas. We handle literary, commercial and genre fiction, and the full range of nonfiction books. Actively seeking commercial, genre and literary fiction. Does not want to receive children's books, plays, short stories, screenplays, pornography, poetry or stories of abuse.

O→ We have diverse tastes. We look for fresh voices and new ideas. We handle literary, commercial and genre fiction, and the full range of nonfiction books. Actively seeking commercial, genre and literary fiction. Does not want to receive children's books, plays, short stories, screenplays, pornography, poetry or stories of abuse.

How to Contact Query with SASE. Responds in 8 weeks to pages or submissions.

Terms Agent receives 15% commission on domestic sales. Agent receives 20% (30% for Asia) commission on foreign sales. May charge for printing, postage for multiple submissions, foreign mail, foreign phone calls, galleys, books, legal fees.

Recent Sales Sold at least 15 titles in the last year. *Crash Into Me*, by Jill Sorenson (Bantam); *Scalpel: Surgery as a Path to Spiritual Transformation for Patients and Physicians*, by Allan Hamilton, M.D. (Tarcher/Penguin); *The Solemn Lantern Maker*, by Merlinda Bobis (Delta); *Bitten to Death*, the fourth book in an urban fantasy series by J.D. Rardin (Laurie McKean), (Orbit/Grand Central).

Writers Conferences This agency organizes the annual San Francisco Writers' Conference (www.sfwriters.org).

Tips "We love helping writers get the rewards and recognition they deserve. If you can write books that meet the needs of the marketplace and you can promote your books, now is the best time ever to be a writer. We must find new writers to make a living, so we are very eager to hear from new writers whose work will interest large houses, and nonfiction writers who can promote their books. For a list of recent sales, helpful info, and three ways to make yourself irresistible to any publisher, please visit our Web site."

THE STEVE LAUBE AGENCY

5025 N. Central Ave., #635, Phoenix AZ 85012. (602)336-8910. E-mail: krichards@stevelaube.com. Website: www.stevelaube.com. **Contact:** Steve Laube. Other memberships include CBA. Represents 60+ clients. 5% of clients are new/unpublished writers. Currently handles: nonfiction books 48%, novels 48%, novella 2%, scholarly books 2%.

- Prior to becoming an agent, Mr. Laube worked 11 years as a Christian bookseller and 11 years as editorial director of nonfiction with Bethany House Publishers.

Represents nonfiction books, novels. **Considers these nonfiction areas:** religion. **Considers these fiction areas:** religious. We primarily serve the Christian market (CBA). Actively seeking Christian fiction and religious nonfiction. Does not want to receive children's picture books, poetry or cookbooks.

- We primarily serve the Christian market (CBA). Actively seeking Christian fiction and religious nonfiction. Does not want to receive children's picture books, poetry or cookbooks.

How to Contact Submit proposal package, outline, 3 sample chapters, SASE. .No e-mail submissions. Consult Web site for guidelines. Accepts simultaneous submissions. Responds in 6-8 weeks to queries. Obtains most new clients through recommendations from others, solicitations, conferences.

Terms Agent receives 15% commission on domestic sales. Agent receives 20% commission on foreign sales. Offers written contract; 30-day notice must be given to terminate contract.

Recent Sales Sold 80 titles in the last year. *Day With a Perfect Stranger*, by David Gregory (Kelly's Filmworks). Other clients include Deborah Raney, Bright Media, Allison Bottke, H. Norman Wright, Ellie Kay, Jack Cavanaugh, Karen Ball, Tracey Bateman, Susan May Warren, Lisa Bergren, John Rosemond, David Gregory, Cindy Woodsmall, Karol Ladd, Judith Pella, Michael Phillips, Margaret Daley, William Lane Craig, Vicki Hinze, Tosca Lee, Ginny Aiken.

Writers Conferences Mount Hermon Christian Writers' Conference; American Christian Fiction Writers' Conference.

LAUNCHBOOKS LITERARY AGENCY

566 Sweet Pea Place, Encinitas CA 92024. (760)944-9909. E-mail: david@launchbooks.com. Website: www.launchbooks.com. **Contact:** David Fugate. Represents 45 clients. 35% of clients are new/unpublished writers. Currently handles: nonfiction books 95%, multimedia 5%.

- Prior to his current position, Mr. Fugate was hired by the Margret McBride Agency to handle its submissions. In 1994, he moved to Waterside Productions, Inc., where he was an agent for 11 years and successfully represented more than 600 book titles before leaving to form LaunchBooks in 2005.

Represents nonfiction books, novels, textbooks. **Considers these nonfiction areas:** anthropology, biography, business, child, computers, cooking, current affairs, education, ethnic, government, health, history, how to, humor, memoirs, military, money, music, nature, popular culture, science, sociology, sports, true crime. Actively seeking a wide variety of nonfiction, including business, technology, adventure, popular culture, science, creative nonfiction, current events, history, politics, reference, memoirs, health, how-to, lifestyle, parenting and more.

- Actively seeking a wide variety of nonfiction, including business, technology, adventure, popular culture, science, creative nonfiction, current events, history, politics, reference, memoirs, health, how-to, lifestyle, parenting and more.

How to Contact Query with SASE. Submit outline/proposal, synopsis, 1 sample chapters, author bio. Accepts simultaneous submissions. Responds in 1 week to queries. Responds in 4 weeks to mss. Obtains most new clients through recommendations from others, solicitations.

Terms Agent receives 15% commission on domestic sales. Agent receives 25% commission on foreign sales. Offers written contract; 30-day notice must be given to terminate contract. Charges occur very seldom and typically only if the author specifically requests overnight or something of that nature. This agency's agreement limits any charges to $50 unless the author gives a written consent.

Recent Sales *$20 per Gallon*, by Christopher Steiner (Grand Central); *Kingpin*, by Kevin Poulsen (Crown); *The History of Our Future*, by Alexis Madrigal (Da Capo); *The Revenge of Everyday Things*, by Robert Vamosi (Basic Books); *SLOW: Life in a Tuscan Town*, by Douglas Gayeton (Welcome Books); *A Brief Guide to World Domination*, by Chris Guillebeau (Perigee); *The Impossible Dream: What Barack Obama Means to Black America*, by Jon Jeter & Robert Pierre (John Wiley & Sons).

LAZEAR GROUP, INC.

431 Second St., Suite 300, Hudson WI 54016. (715)531-0012. Fax: (715)531-0016. Website: www.lazear.com. **Contact:** Editorial Board. 20% of clients are new/unpublished writers. Currently handles: juvenile books 5%, other commercial fiction and nonfiction.

- The Lazear Group opened a New York office in September 1997.

Member Agents Jonathon Lazear; Christi Cardenas; Darrick Kline; Nate Roen; Anne Blackstone.

Represents nonfiction books, novels, juvenile. **Considers these nonfiction areas:** agriculture horticulture, americana, interior, juvenile, newage, young, animals, anthropology, art, biography, child, computers, cooking, creative, current affairs, ethnic, gardening, gay, government, health, history, how to, humor, language, memoirs, military, money, multicultural, music, nature, philosophy, photography, popular culture, psychology, recreation, regional, religion, science, self help, sex, sociology, software, spirituality, sports, film, travel, true crime, womens, creative nonfiction. **Considers these fiction areas:** newage, psychic, adventure, confession, detective, ethnic, family, fantasy, feminist, gay, gothic, hi lo, historical, humor, juvenile, literary, mainstream, military, multicultural, multimedia, mystery, occult, picture books, plays, poetry, poetry trans, religious, romance, science, short, spiritual, sports, thriller, translation, western, young, womens. Actively seeking new voices in commercial fiction and nonfiction. It's all about the writing, no matter the subject matter. Does not want to receive short stories, poetry, scripts and/or screenplays.

- Actively seeking new voices in commercial fiction and nonfiction. It's all about the writing, no matter the subject matter. Does not want to receive short stories, poetry, scripts and/or screenplays.

How to Contact Query with SASE. Submit outline/proposal, author bio, 1-2 page synopsis, 5-7 page sample.Query first. The agency will respond if interested. Include SASE for snail mail queries. Responds in 4 weeks to queries. Responds in 3 weeks to mss. Obtains most new clients through recommendations from others, solicitations.

Terms Agent receives 15% commission on domestic sales. Agent receives 20% commission on foreign sales. Offers written contract. Charges clients for photocopying, international express mail, bound galleys, books used for subsidiary rights sales. No fees charged if book is not sold.

Tips The writer should first view himself as a salesperson in order to obtain an agent. Sell yourself, your idea, your concept. Do your homework. Notice what is in the marketplace. Be sophisticated about the arena in which you are writing. Please note that we also have a New York office, but the primary office remains in Hudson, Wis., for the receipt of any material.

SARAH LAZIN BOOKS

126 Fifth Ave., Suite 300, New York NY 10011. (212)989-5757. Fax: (212)989-1393. Member of AAR. Represents 75+ clients. Currently handles: nonfiction books 80%, novels 20%.

Member Agents Sarah Lazin; Rebecca Ferreira.

Represents nonfiction books, novels. **Considers these nonfiction areas:** biography, ethnic, gay, history, memoirs, music, popular culture, religious, "We also work with companies who package their books, and handle some photography."

How to Contact Query with SASE. No e-mail queries.

Terms Agent receives 15% commission on domestic sales. Agent receives 20% commission on foreign sales.

SUSANNA LEA ASSOCIATES

28, rue Bonaparte, 75006 Paris France. E-mail: us-submissions@susannalea.com; uk-submissions@susannalea.com. Website: www.susannaleaassociates.com. **Contact:** Submissions Department. 331 West 20th Street, New York, NY 10011

Represents nonfiction books, novels. "We pride ourselves in keeping our list small: We prefer to focus our energies on a limited number of projects rather than spreading our energies thin. The company is currently developing new international projects: always selective, yet broad in their reach, they all remain faithful to the slogan, 'Published in Europe, Read by the World.'" Does not want to receive poetry, plays, screenplays, science fiction, educational text books, short stories or illustrated works.

- "We pride ourselves in keeping our list small: We prefer to focus our energies on a limited number of projects rather than spreading our energies thin. The company is currently developing new international projects: always selective, yet broad in their reach, they all remain faithful to the slogan, 'Published in Europe, Read by the World.'" Does not want to receive poetry, plays, screenplays, science fiction, educational text books, short stories or illustrated works.

How to Contact Send a query letter, brief synopsis, the first three chapters and/or proposal to this agency via e-mail.

Tips "Your query letter should be concise and include any pertinent information about yourself, relevant writing history, etc."

THE NED LEAVITT AGENCY

70 Wooster St., Suite 4F, New York NY 10012. (212)334-0999. Website: www.nedleavittagency.com. **Contact:** Ned Leavitt. Member of AAR. Represents 40+ clients.

Member Agents Ned Leavitt, founder and agent; Britta Alexander, agent; Jill Beckman, editorial assistant.

Represents nonfiction books, novels. "We are small in size, but intensely dedicated to our authors and to supporting excellent and unique writing."

- "We are small in size, but intensely dedicated to our authors and to supporting excellent and unique writing."

How to Contact This agency now only takes queries/submissions through referred clients. Do *not* cold query.

Tips "Look online for this agency's recently changed submission guidelines."

ROBERT LECKER AGENCY

4055 Melrose Ave., Montreal QC H4A 2S5 Canada. (514)830-4818. Fax: (514)483-1644. E-mail: leckerlink@aol.com. Website: www.leckeragency.com. **Contact:** Robert Lecker.Represents 20 clients. 20% of clients are new/unpublished writers. Currently handles: nonfiction books 80%, novels 10%, scholarly books 10%.

- Prior to becoming an agent, Mr. Lecker was the co-founder and publisher of ECW Press and professor of English literature at McGill University. He has 30 years of experience in book and magazine publishing.

Member Agents Robert Lecker (popular culture, music); Mary Williams (travel, food, popular science).

Represents nonfiction books, novels, scholarly, syndicated material. **Considers these nonfiction areas:** biography, cooking, ethnic, how to, language, music, popular culture, science, film. **Considers these fiction areas:** adventure, detective, erotica, literary, mainstream, mystery, thriller. RLA specializes in books about popular culture, popular science, music, entertainment, food and travel. The agency responds to articulate, innovative proposals within 2 weeks. Actively seeking original book mss only after receipt of outlines and proposals.

O→ RLA specializes in books about popular culture, popular science, music, entertainment, food and travel. The agency responds to articulate, innovative proposals within 2 weeks. Actively seeking original book mss only after receipt of outlines and proposals.

How to Contact Query first. Only responds to queries of interest. Discards the rest. Accepts simultaneous submissions. Responds in 2 weeks to queries. Responds in 1 month to mss. Obtains most new clients through recommendations from others, conferences, interest in Web site.

Terms Agent receives 15% commission on domestic sales. Agent receives 15-20% commission on foreign sales. Offers written contract, binding for 1 year; 6-month notice must be given to terminate contract.

LESCHER & LESCHER, LTD.

346 E. 84th St., New York NY 10028. (212)396-1999. Fax: (212)396-1991. **Contact:** Carolyn Larson. Member of AAR. Represents 150 clients. Currently handles: nonfiction books 80%, novels 20%.

Represents nonfiction books, novels. **Considers these nonfiction areas:** current affairs, history, memoirs, popular culture, biography; cookbooks/wines; law; contemporary issues; narrative nonfiction. **Considers these fiction areas:** literary, mystery, commercial. Does not want to receive screenplays, science fiction or romance.

O→ Does not want to receive screenplays, science fiction or romance.

How to Contact Query with SASE. Obtains most new clients through recommendations from others.

Terms Agent receives 15% commission on domestic sales. Agent receives 10% commission on foreign sales.

LEVINE GREENBERG LITERARY AGENCY, INC.

307 Seventh Ave., Suite 2407, New York NY 10001. (212)337-0934. Fax: (212)337-0948. Website: www.levinegreenberg.com. Member of AAR. Represents 250 clients. 33% % of clients are new/unpublished writers. Currently handles: nonfiction books 70%, novels 30%.

- Prior to opening his agency, Mr. Levine served as vice president of the Bank Street College of Education.

Member Agents James Levine, Daniel Greenberg, Stephanie Kip Rostan, Lindsay Edgecombe, Danielle Svetcov, Elizabeth Fisher, Victoria Skurnick.

Represents nonfiction books, novels. **Considers these nonfiction areas:** New Age, animals, art, biography, business, child, computers, cooking, gardening, gay, health, money, nature, religion, science, self help, sociology, spirituality, sports, womens. **Considers these fiction areas:** literary, mainstream, mystery, thriller, psychological, womens. This agency specializes in business, psychology, parenting, health/medicine, narrative nonfiction, spirituality, religion, women's issues, and commercial fiction.

O→ This agency specializes in business, psychology, parenting, health/medicine, narrative nonfiction, spirituality, religion, women's issues, and commercial fiction.

How to Contact See Web site for full submission procedure. Obtains most new clients through recommendations from others.

Terms Agent receives 15% commission on domestic sales. Agent receives 20% commission on foreign sales. Offers written contract. Charges clients for out-of-pocket expenses—telephone, fax, postage, photocopying—directly connected to the project.

Writers Conferences ASJA Writers' Conference.

Tips "We focus on editorial development, business representation, and publicity and marketing strategy."

PAUL S. LEVINE LITERARY AGENCY

1054 Superba Ave., Venice CA 90291-3940. (310)450-6711. Fax: (310)450-0181. E-mail: paul@paulslevinelit.com. Website: www.paulslevinelit.com. **Contact:** Paul S. Levine. Other memberships include the State Bar of California. Represents over 100 clients. 75% of clients are new/unpublished writers. Currently handles: nonfiction books 60%, novels 10%, movie scripts 10%, TV scripts 5%, juvenile books 5%.

Member Agents Paul S. Levine (children's and young adult fiction and nonfiction, adult fiction and nonfiction except sci-fi, fantasy, and horror); Loren R. Grossman (archaeology, art/photography/

architecture, gardening, education, health, medicine, science).

Represents nonfiction books, novels, episodic, movie, TV, feature, TV movie, sitcom, animation, documentary, miniseries, syndicated material, reality show. **Considers these nonfiction areas:** art, biography, business, computers, cooking, crafts, current affairs, education, ethnic, film, gay, government, health, history, humor, language, memoirs, military, money, music, nature, New Age, photography, popular culture, psychology, science, sociology, sports, true crime, creative nonfiction,. **Considers these fiction areas:** glitz, adventure, comic, confession, detective, erotica, ethnic, experimental, family, feminist, gay, historical, humor, literary, mainstream, mystery, regional, religious, romance, sports, thriller, western. Does not want to receive science fiction, fantasy, or horror.

- Does not want to receive science fiction, fantasy, or horror.

How to Contact Query with SASE. Accepts simultaneous submissions. Responds in 1 day to queries. Responds in 6-8 weeks to mss. Obtains most new clients through conferences, referrals, listings on various websites and in directories.

Terms Agent receives 15% commission on domestic sales. Offers written contract. Charges for postage and actual, out-of-pocket costs only.

Recent Sales Sold 10 books in the last year and 5 script projects. *Apocalypse Never*, by Tad Daley (Rutgers University Press); movie rights to *Vampire High*, by Douglas Rees (1492 Productions); *Silver*, by Steven Savile (Variance Publishing); *Romancing the Runway*, by Linda Hudson-Smith (Harlequin). Other clients include David Seidman, Patricia Santos, Carol Jones.

Writers Conferences Willamette Writers Conference; San Francisco Writers Conference; Santa Barbara Writers Conference and many others.

Tips "Write good, sellable books."

ROBERT LIEBERMAN ASSOCIATES

400 Nelson Rd., Ithaca NY 14850-9440. (607)273-8801. Fax: (801)749-9682. E-mail: rhl10@cornell.edu. Website: www.people.cornell.edu/pages/rhl10. **Contact:** Robert Lieberman. Represents 30 clients. 50% of clients are new/unpublished writers. Currently handles: nonfiction books 20%.

Represents nonfiction books, trade, scholarly, college-level textbooks. **Considers these nonfiction areas:** agriculture horticulture, anthropology, art, business, computers, education, health, memoirs, by authors with high public recognition, money, music, nature, psychology, science, sociology, film. This agency only accepts nonfiction ideas and specializes in university/college-level textbooks, CD-ROM/ software for the university/college-level textbook market, and popular trade books in math, engineering, economics, and other subjects. Does not want to receive any fiction, self-help, or screenplays.

- This agency only accepts nonfiction ideas and specializes in university/college-level textbooks, CD-ROM/software for the university/college-level textbook market, and popular trade books in math, engineering, economics, and other subjects. Does not want to receive any fiction, self-help, or screenplays.

How to Contact Prefers to read materials exclusively. Responds in 2 weeks to queries. Responds in 1 month to mss. Obtains most new clients through referrals.

Terms Agent receives 15% commission on domestic sales. Agent receives 20% commission on foreign sales. Offers written contract; 1-month notice must be given to terminate contract. Fees are sometimes charged to clients for shipping and when special reviewers are required.

Tips "The trade books we handle are by authors who are highly recognized in their fields of expertise. Our client list includes Nobel Prize winners and others with high name recognition, either by the public or within a given area of expertise."

LIMELIGHT MANAGEMENT

33 Newman St., London W1T 1PY England. (44)(207)637-2529. E-mail: mary@limelightmanagement.com; Submissions@limelightmanagement.com. Website: www.limelightmanagement.com. **Contact:** Fiona Lindsay.Other memberships include AAA. Represents 70 clients. Currently handles: nonfiction books 100%, multimedia.

- Prior to becoming an agent, Ms. Lindsay was a public relations manager at the Dorchester and was working on her law degree.

Represents nonfiction books. **Considers these nonfiction areas:** crafts, interior, newage, art, cooking, gardening, agriculture/horticulture, health, nature, photography, self help, sports, travel. "We are celebrity agents for TV celebrities, broadcasters, writers, journalists, celebrity speakers and media personalities, after dinner speakers, motivational speakers, celebrity chefs, TV presenters and TV chefs." This agency will consider women's fiction, as well.

- "We are celebrity agents for TV celebrities, broadcasters, writers, journalists, celebrity speakers and media personalities, after dinner speakers, motivational speakers, celebrity chefs, TV presenters and TV chefs." This agency will consider women's fiction, as well.

How to Contact Prefers to read materials exclusively. Query with SASE/IRC via e-mail. Agents will be in contact if they want to see more. No attachments to e-mails. Responds in 1 week to queries. Obtains most new clients through recommendations from others.

Terms Agent receives 15% commission on domestic sales. Agent receives 20% commission on foreign sales. Offers written contract; 2-month notice must be given to terminate contract.

LINDSTROM LITERARY MANAGEMENT, LLC

871 N. Greenbrier St., Arlington VA 22205. Fax: (703)527-7624. E-mail: submissions@lindstromliterary.com. Website: www.lindstromliterary.com. **Contact:** Kristin Lindstrom.Other memberships include Author's Guild. Represents 9 clients. 30% of clients are new/unpublished writers. Currently handles: nonfiction books 30%, novels 70%.

- Prior to her current position, Ms. Lindstrom was an editor of a monthly magazine in the energy industry, and an independent marketing and publicity consultant.

Represents nonfiction books, novels. **Considers these nonfiction areas:** animals, biography, business, current affairs, history, memoirs, popular culture, science, true crime. **Considers these fiction areas:** adventure, detective, erotica, mainstream, mystery, religious, thriller, womens. "In 2006, I decided to add my more specific promotion/publicity skills to the mix in order to support the marketing efforts of my published clients." Actively seeking commercial fiction and narrative nonfiction. Does not want to receive juvenile or children's books.

⊶ "In 2006, I decided to add my more specific promotion/publicity skills to the mix in order to support the marketing efforts of my published clients." Actively seeking commercial fiction and narrative nonfiction. Does not want to receive juvenile or children's books.

How to Contact Query via e-mail only. Submit author bio, synopsis and first four chapters if submitting fiction..For nonfiction, send the first 4 chapters, synopsis, proposal, outline and mission statement Accepts simultaneous submissions. Responds in 6 weeks to queries. Responds in 8 weeks to requested mss. Obtains most new clients through recommendations from others, solicitations.

Terms Agent receives 15% commission on domestic sales. Agent receives 20% commission on performance rights and foreign sales. Offers written contract. This agency charges for postage, UPS, copies and other basic office expenses.

Recent Sales Two book deal with Broadway Books for veterinarian Dr. Nick Trout; two new novels from Cathy Holton to Ballantine; two new mystery series for Juliet Blackwell.

Tips "Do your homework on accepted practices; make sure you know what kind of book the agent handles."

LINN PRENTIS LITERARY

155 East 116th St., #2F, New York NY 10029. Fax: (212)875-5565. E-mail: Linn@linnprentis.com. **Contact:** Linn Prentis, Acacia Stevens. Represents 18-20 clients. 25% of clients are new/unpublished writers. Currently handles: nonfiction books 5%, novels 65%, story collections 7%, novella 10%, juvenile books 10%, scholarly books 3%.

- Prior to becoming an agent, Ms. Prentis was a nonfiction writer and editor, primarily in magazines. She also worked in book promotion in New York. Ms. Prentis then worked for and later ran the Virginia Kidd Agency. She is known particularly for her assistance with manuscript development."

Represents nonfiction books, novels, short story collections, novellas, from authors whose novels I already represent, juvenile, for older juveniles, scholarly, anthology. **Considers these nonfiction areas:** juvenile, animals, art, biography, current affairs, education, ethnic, government, how to, humor, language, memoirs, music, photography, popular culture, sociology, womens. **Considers these fiction areas:** adventure, ethnic, fantasy, feminist, gay, glitz, historical, horror, humor, juvenile, lesbian, literary, mainstream, mystery, thriller. Because of the Virginia Kidd connection and the clients I brought with me at the start, I have a special interest in sci-fi and fantasy, but, really, fiction is what interests me. As for my nonfiction projects, they are books I just couldn't resist. Actively seeking hard science fiction, family saga, mystery, memoir, mainstream, literary, women's. Does not want to "receive books for little kids."

⊶ Because of the Virginia Kidd connection and the clients I brought with me at the start, I have a special interest in sci-fi and fantasy, but, really, fiction is what interests me. As for my nonfiction projects, they are books I just couldn't resist. Actively seeking hard science fiction, family saga, mystery, memoir, mainstream, literary, women's. Does not want to "receive books for little kids."

How to Contact Query with SASE. Submit synopsis. No phone or fax queries. Snail mail is best. Accepts simultaneous submissions. Obtains most new clients through recommendations from others, solicitations.

Terms Agent receives 15% commission on domestic sales. Agent receives 20% commission on foreign sales. Offers written contract; 60-day notice must be given to terminate contract.

Recent Sales Sold 15 titles in the last year. *The Sons of Heaven, the Empress of Mars, and The House of the Stag,* by Kage Baker (Tor); the last has also been sold to Dabel Brothers to be published as a comic book/graphic novel; *Indigo Springs* and a sequel, by A.M. Dellamonica (Tor); Wayne Arthurson's debut mystery plus a second series book; *Bone Crossed* and *Cry Wolf* for *New York Times* #1 bestselling author

Patricia Briggs (Ace/Penguin). "The latter is the start of a new series."
Tips Consider query letters and synopses as writing assignments. Spell names correctly.

WENDY LIPKIND AGENCY

120 E. 81st St., New York NY 10028. (212)628-9653. Fax: (212)585-1306. E-mail: lipkindag@aol.com. **Contact:** Wendy Lipkind. Member of AAR. Represents 50 clients. Currently handles: nonfiction books 100%.
Represents nonfiction books. **Considers these nonfiction areas:** biography, current affairs, health, history, science, womens, social history; narrative nonfiction. This agency specializes in adult nonfiction.

O→ This agency specializes in adult nonfiction.

How to Contact Prefers to read materials exclusively. Accepts e-mail queries only (no attachments). Obtains most new clients through recommendations from others.
Terms Agent receives 15% commission on domestic sales. Agent receives 20% commission on foreign sales. Sometimes offers written contract. Charges clients for foreign postage, messenger service, photocopying, transatlantic calls, faxes.
Recent Sales Sold 10 titles in the last year. *Lost at School*, by Ross Greene (Scribner); *Professional Wedding Cakes*, by Toba Garrett (Wiley); *One Small Step*, by Robert Mauner (Workman); *In the Land of Invisible Women*, by Dr. Qanta Amhed (Sourcebooks).
Tips Send intelligent query letter first. Let me know if you've submitted to other agents.

LIPPINCOTT MASSIE MCQUILKIN

27 West 20th Street, Suite 305, New York NY 10011. Fax: (212)352-2059. E-mail: info@lmqlit.com. Website: www.lmqlit.com. **Contact:** Rachel Vogel. Represents 90 clients. 30% of clients are new/unpublished writers. Currently handles: nonfiction books 40%, novels 40%, story collections 10%, scholarly books 5%, poetry 5%.
Member Agents Maria Massie (fiction, memoir, cultural criticism); Will Lippincott (politics, current affairs, history); Rob McQuilkin (fiction, history, psychology, sociology, graphic material); Jason Anthony (pop culture, memoir, true crime, and general psychology).
Represents nonfiction books, novels, short story collections, scholarly, graphic novels. **Considers these nonfiction areas:** animals, anthropology, art, biography, business, child, current affairs, ethnic, gay, government, health, history, language, memoirs, military, money, music, nature, popular culture, psychology, religion, science, self help, sociology, film, true crime, womens. **Considers these fiction areas:** adventure, comic, confession, family, feminist, gay, historical, humor, literary, mainstream, regional. "LMQ focuses on bringing new voices in literary and commercial fiction to the market, as well as popularizing the ideas and arguments of scholars in the fields of history, psychology, sociology, political science, and current affairs. Actively seeking fiction writers who already have credits in magazines and quarterlies, as well as nonfiction writers who already have a media platform or some kind of a university affiliation." Does not want to receive romance, genre fiction or children's material.

O→ "LMQ focuses on bringing new voices in literary and commercial fiction to the market, as well as popularizing the ideas and arguments of scholars in the fields of history, psychology, sociology, political science, and current affairs. Actively seeking fiction writers who already have credits in magazines and quarterlies, as well as nonfiction writers who already have a media platform or some kind of a university affiliation." Does not want to receive romance, genre fiction or children's material.

How to Contact "We accepts electronic queries only. Only send additional materials if requested." Accepts simultaneous submissions. Responds in 1 week to queries. Responds in 1 month to mss. Obtains most new clients through recommendations from others, solicitations, conferences.
Terms Agent receives 15% commission on domestic sales. Agent receives 20% commission on foreign sales. Offers written contract; 30-day notice must be given to terminate contract. Only charges for reasonable business expenses upon successful sale.
Recent Sales Clients include: Peter Ho Davies, Kim Addonizio, Don Lee, Natasha Trethewey, Anatol Lieven, Sir Michael Marmot, Anne Carson, Liza Ward, David Sirota, Anne Marie Slaughter, Marina Belozerskaya, Kate Walbert.

LITERARY AGENCY FOR SOUTHERN AUTHORS

2123 Paris Metz Road, Chattanooga TN 37421. E-mail: southernlitagent@aol.com. **Contact:** Lantz Powell.Represents 20 clients. 60% of clients are new/unpublished writers. Currently handles: nonfiction books 50%, novels 50%.

- Prior to becoming an agent, Mr. Powell was in sales and contract negotiation.

Represents nonfiction books, novels, juvenile, for ages 14 and up. **Considers these nonfiction areas:** crafts, interior, newage, art, biography, business, current affairs, education, ethnic, government, history, how to, humor, language, military, photography, popular culture, religion, self help, true crime. **Considers these fiction areas:** cartoon, comic books, humor, literary, mainstream, regional, religious, satire, young adult. "We focus on authors that live in the Southern United States. We have the ability to translate and explain complexities of publishing for the Southern author." "Actively seeking quality projects by authors with a vision of where they want to be in 10 years and a plan of how to get there." Does not want to receive unfinished, unedited projects that do not follow the standard presentation conventions of the trade. No romance.

O→ "We focus on authors that live in the Southern United States. We have the ability to translate and explain complexities of publishing for the Southern author." "Actively seeking quality projects by authors with a vision of where they want to be in 10 years and a plan of how to get there." Does not want to receive unfinished, unedited projects that do not follow the standard presentation conventions of the trade. No romance.

How to Contact Query via e-mail first and include a synopsis. Accepts simultaneous submissions. Responds in 2-3 days to queries. Responds in 1 week to mss. Obtains most new clients through recommendations from others.

Terms Agent receives 15% commission on domestic sales. Agent receives 25% commission on foreign sales. Offers written contract. "We charge when a publisher wants a hard copy overnight or the like. The client always knows this beforehand."

Recent Sales Sold 10+ titles in the last year. List of other clients and books sold will be available to authors pre-signing, but is not for public knowledge.

Writers Conferences Conference for Southern Literature; Tennessee Book Fair.

Tips "If you are an unpublished author, join a writers group, even if it is on the Internet. You need good honest feedback. Don't send a manuscript that has not been read by at least five people. Don't send a manuscript cold to any agent without first asking if they want it. Try to meet the agent face to face before signing. Make sure the fit is right."

LITERARY AND CREATIVE ARTISTS, INC.

3543 Albemarle St. NW, Washington DC 20008-4213. (202)362-4688. Fax: (202)362-8875. E-mail: lca9643@lcadc.com. Website: www.lcadc.com. **Contact:** Muriel Nellis. Member of AAR. Other memberships include Authors Guild, American Bar Association. Represents 75 clients. Currently handles: nonfiction books 70%, novels 30%.

Member Agents Muriel Nellis; Jane Roberts.

Represents nonfiction books, novels. **Considers these nonfiction areas:** biography, business, cooking, government, health, how to, memoirs, philosophy, human drama; lifestyle.

How to Contact Currently only accepting submissions by established authors. Responds in 3 months to queries.

Terms Agent receives 15% commission on domestic sales. Agent receives 20% commission on foreign sales. Agent receives 25% commission on film sales. Charges clients for long-distance phone/fax, photocopying, shipping.

Tips While we prefer published writers, publishing credits are not required if the proposed work has great merit.

THE LITERARY GROUP INTERNATIONAL

51 E. 25th St., Suite 401, New York NY 10010. (212)274-1616. Fax: (212)274-9876. E-mail: fweimann@theliterarygroup.com. Website: www.theliterarygroup.com. **Contact:** Frank Weimann. 65% of clients are new/unpublished writers. Currently handles: nonfiction books 50%, other 50% fiction.

Member Agents Frank Weimann; acquisitions editor Jaimee Garbacik.

Represents nonfiction books, novels, graphic novels. **Considers these nonfiction areas:** animals, anthropology, biography, business, child guidance, crafts, creative nonfiction, current affairs, education, ethnic, film, government, health, history, humor, juvenile nonfiction, language, memoirs, military, multicultural, music, nature, popular culture, politics, psychology, religious, science, self-help, sociology, sports, travel, true crime, women's issues, women's studies. **Considers these fiction areas:** adventure, contemporary issues, detective, ethnic, experimental, family saga, fantasy, feminist, historical, horror, humor, literary, multicultural, mystery, psychic, romance, sports, thriller, young adult, regional, graphic novels. This agency specializes in nonfiction (memoir, military, history, biography, sports, how-to).

O→ This agency specializes in nonfiction (memoir, military, history, biography, sports, how-to).

How to Contact Query with SASE. Prefers to read materials exclusively. Only responds if interested. Obtains most new clients through referrals, writers' conferences, query letters.

Terms Agent receives 15% commission on domestic sales. Agent receives 20% commission on foreign sales. Offers written contract; 30-day notice must be given to terminate contract.

Recent Sales *One From the Hart*, by Stefanie Powers with Richard Buskin (Pocket Books); *Sacred Trust, Deadly Betrayal,* by Keith Anderson (Berkley); *Gotti Confidential*, by Victoria Gotti (Pocket Books); Anna Sui's illustrated memoir (Chronicle Books); *Mania*, by Craig Larsen (Kensington); *Everything Explained Through Flowcharts*, by Doogie Horner (HarperCollins); *Bitch*, by Lisa Taddeo (TOR); film rights for *Falling Out of Fashion*, by Karen Yampolsky to Hilary Swank and Molly Smith for 2S Films.

Writers Conferences San Diego State University Writers' Conference; Maui Writers' Conference; Agents and Editors Conference; NAHJ Convention in Puerto Rico, among others.

LITERARY MANAGEMENT GROUP, INC.

(615)812-4445. E-mail: brucebarbour@literarymanagementgroup.com; brb@brucebarbour.com. Website: www.literarymanagementgroup.com; www.brucebarbour.com. **Contact:** Bruce Barbour.

- Prior to becoming an agent, Mr. Barbour held executive positions at several publishing houses, including Revell, Barbour Books, Thomas Nelson, and Random House.

Represents nonfiction books, novels. **Considers these nonfiction areas:** biography, Christian living; spiritual growth; women's and men's issues; prayer; devotional; meditational; Bible study; marriage; business; family/parenting. Does not want to receive gift books, poetry, children's books, short stories, or juvenile/young adult fiction. No unsolicited mss or proposals from unpublished authors.

⊶ Does not want to receive gift books, poetry, children's books, short stories, or juvenile/young adult fiction. No unsolicited mss or proposals from unpublished authors.

How to Contact Query with SASE. E-mail proposal as an attachment.
Terms Agent receives 15% commission on domestic sales.

LITERARY SERVICES, INC.

P.O. Box 888, Barnegat NJ 08005. (609)698-7162. Fax: (609)698-7163. E-mail: john@LiteraryServicesInc.com. Website: www.LiteraryServicesInc.com. **Contact:** John Willig. Other memberships include Author's Guild. Represents 85 clients. 25% of clients are new/unpublished writers. Currently handles: nonfiction books 100%.

Member Agents John Willig (business, personal growth, narratives, history, health); Cynthia Zigmund (personal finance, investments, entreprenuership).

Represents nonfiction books. **Considers these nonfiction areas:** art, biography, business, cooking, crafts, health, history, how-to, humor, language, money, New Age, popular culture, psychology, science, sports, true crime. "Our publishing experience and 'inside' knowledge of how companies and editors really work sets us apart from many agencies; our specialties are noted above, but we are open to unique presentations in all nonfiction topic areas." Actively seeking business, work/life topics, story-driven narratives. Does not want to receive fiction, children's books, science fiction, religion or memoirs.

⊶ "Our publishing experience and 'inside' knowledge of how companies and editors really work sets us apart from many agencies; our specialties are noted above, but we are open to unique presentations in all nonfiction topic areas." Actively seeking business, work/life topics, story-driven narratives. Does not want to receive fiction, children's books, science fiction, religion or memoirs.

How to Contact Query with SASE. For starters, a one-page outline sent via e-mail is acceptable. See our Web site to learn more. Accepts simultaneous submissions. Responds in 2 weeks to queries. Responds in 4 weeks to mss. Obtains most new clients through recommendations from others, solicitations, conferences.

Terms Agent receives 15% commission on domestic sales. Agent receives 20% commission on foreign sales. Offers written contract. This agency charges fees for copying, postage, etc.

Recent Sales Sold 32 titles in the last year. *In Pursuit of Elegance* (Doubleday/Currency). A full list of new books are noted on the Web site.

Writers Conferences Author 101; Mega Book Marketing; Publicity Summit; Writer's Digest.

Tips "Be focused. In all likelihood, your work is not going to be of interest to 'a very broad audience' or 'every parent,' so I appreciate when writers put aside their passion and do some homework, i.e. positioning, special features and benefits of your work. Be a marketer. How have you tested your ideas and writing (beyond your inner circle of family and friends)? Have you received any key awards for your work or endorsements from influential persons in your field? What steps have you taken to increase your presence in the market?"

LJK LITERARY MANAGEMENT

708 Third Ave., 16th Floor, New York NY 10018. (212)221-8797. Fax: (212)221-8722. E-mail: submissions@ljkliterary.com. Website: www.ljkliterary.com. Represents 20+ clients.

- Larry Kirschbaum is the former head of Time Warner Book group; Jud Laghi worked for ICM; Susanna Einstein worked for Maria B. Campbell Associates; Meg Thompson worked for Bill Clinton and Charlie Rose before joining Larry in starting LJK; Lisa Leshne co-founded The Prague Post.

Member Agents Larry Kirshbaum; Susanna Einstein (contemporary fiction, literary fiction, romance, suspense, historical fiction, middle grade, young adult, crime fiction, narrative nonfiction, memoir and biography); Jud Laghi (celebrity, pop culture, humor, journalism), Meg Thompson (new media, narrative nonfiction, politics, pop culture, humor); Lisa Leshne (nonfiction, memoirs, literary and popular fiction, business, politics, pop culture).

Represents nonfiction books, novels. We are not considering picture books or poetry collections.

- We are not considering picture books or poetry collections.

How to Contact Send query letter in the body of an e-mail to submissions@ljkliterary.com with 25-page sample (fiction) or proposal (nonfiction) as an attachment; if sending a paper query, include SASE. E-mail is preferred. No fax queries. Response time is about 8 weeks. Responds in 8 weeks to queries. Responds in 8 weeks to mss.

Recent Sales *Think Big and Kick Ass*, by Donald Trump and Bill Zanker; *The Book of Love*, by Kathleen McGowan; *The Christmas Pearl*, by Dorothea Benton Frank; *The Hidden Man*, by David Ellis; *Maphead*, by Ken Jennings; *Grandma's Dead*, by Ben Schwartz and Amanda McCall; *Found II*, by Davy Rothbart; *Amberville*, by Tim Davys; *Moses Never Closes*, by Jenny Wingfield; *Daily Routines*, by Mason Currey.

Tips "All submissions will receive a response from us if they adhere to our submission guidelines. Please do not contact us to inquire about your submission unless 8 weeks have passed."

JULIA LORD LITERARY MANAGEMENT

38 W. Ninth St., #4, New York NY 10011. (212)995-2333. Fax: (212)995-2332. E-mail: julialordliterary@nyc.rr.com. Member of AAR.

Member Agents Julia Lord, owner.

Represents Considers these nonfiction areas: biography, history, humor, nature, science, sports, travel, and adventure, African-American; lifestyle; narrative nonfiction. **Considers these fiction areas:** adventure, historical, literary, mainstream.

How to Contact Query with SASE or via e-mail. Obtains most new clients through recommendations from others, solicitations.

STERLING LORD LITERISTIC, INC.

65 Bleecker St., 12th Floor, New York NY 10012. (212)780-6050. Fax: (212)780-6095. E-mail: info@sll.com. Website: www.sll.com. Member of AAR. Signatory of WGA. Represents 600 clients. Currently handles: nonfiction books 50%, novels 50%.

Member Agents Sterling Lord; Peter Matson; Phillippa Brophy (represents journalists, nonfiction writers and novelists, and is most interested in current events, memoir, science, politics, biography, and women's issues); Chris Calhoun; Claudia Cross (a broad range of fiction and nonfiction, from literary fiction to commercial women's fiction and romance novels, to cookbooks, lifestyle titles, memoirs, serious nonfiction on religious and spiritual topics, and books for the CBA marketplace); Rebecca Friedman (memoir, reportorial nonfiction, history, current events, literary, international and commerical fiction); Robert Guinsler (literary and commercial fiction, journalism, narrative nonfiction with an emphasis on pop culture, science and current events, memoirs and biographies); Laurie Liss (commercial and literary fiction and nonfiction whose perspectives are well developed and unique); Judy Heiblum (fiction and non-fiction writers, looking for distinctive voices that challenge the reader, emotionally or intellectually. She works with journalists, academics, memoirists, and essayists, and is particularly interested in books that explore the intersections of science, culture, history and philosophy. In addition, she is always looking for writers of literary fiction with fresh, uncompromising voices); Neeti Madan (memoir, journalism, history, pop culture, health, lifestyle, women's issues, multicultural books and virtually any intelligent writing on intriguing topics. Neeti is looking for smart, well-written commercial novels, as well as compelling and provocative literary works); George Nicholson (writers and illustrators for children); Marcy Posner (commercial women's fiction, historical fiction, and mystery to biography, history, health, and lifestyle); Paul Rodeen (picture books by artists that both write and illustrate, but he is actively seeking writers of fiction and nonfiction for young adult and middle grade readers; different address: 3501 N. Southport #497, Chicago, IL 60657); Jim Rutman; Charlotte Sheedy; Ira Silverberg; Douglas Stewart (literary fiction, narrative nonfiction, and young adult fiction).

Represents nonfiction books, novels.

How to Contact Query with SASE by snail mail. Include synopsis of the work, a brief proposal or the first three chapters of the manuscript, and brief bio or resume. Does not respond to unsolicited e-mail queries. Responds in 1 month to mss. Obtains most new clients through recommendations from others.

Terms Agent receives 15% commission on domestic sales. Agent receives 20% commission on foreign sales. Offers written contract. Charges clients for photocopying.

NANCY LOVE LITERARY AGENCY

250 E. 65th St., New York NY 10065-6614. (212)980-3499. Fax: (212)308-6405. E-mail: nloveag@aol.com. **Contact:** Nancy Love.Member of AAR. Represents 60-80 clients. 25% of clients are new/unpublished writers. Currently handles: nonfiction books 100%.

- This agency is not taking on any new fiction writers at this time.

Represents nonfiction books. **Considers these nonfiction areas:** biography, cooking, current affairs, ethnic, government, health, history, how-to, nature, popular culture, psychology, science, sociology, spirituality, travel, women's issues. This agency specializes in adult nonfiction. Actively seeking narrative nonfiction.

This agency specializes in adult nonfiction. Actively seeking narrative nonfiction.

How to Contact Query with SASE. No fax queries. Accepts simultaneous submissions. Responds in 3 weeks to queries. Responds in 6 weeks to mss. Obtains most new clients through recommendations from others, solicitations.

Terms Agent receives 15% commission on domestic sales. Agent receives 20% commission on foreign sales. Offers written contract. Charges clients for photocopying if it runs more than $20.

Recent Sales New book on Middle East, by Stephen Kinzer (Henry Holt); *The Ten Stupidest Mistakes Men Make When Facing Divorce*, by Joseph E. Cordell, Esq. (Crown); *Brazil on the Rise*, by Larry Rohter (Macmillan).

Tips "Nonfiction authors and/or collaborators must be an authority in their subject area and have a platform. Send an SASE if you want a response."

LOWENSTEIN-YOST ASSOCIATES

121 W. 27th St., Suite 601, New York NY 10001. (212)206-1630. Fax: (212)727-0280. Website: www.lowensteinyost.com. **Contact:** Barbara Lowenstein or Nancy Yost. Member of AAR. Represents 150 clients. 20% of clients are new/unpublished writers. Currently handles: nonfiction books 60%, novels 40%.

Member Agents Barbara Lowenstein, president (nonfiction interests include narrative nonfiction, health, money, finance, travel, multicultural, popular culture and memoir; fiction interests include literary fiction and women's fiction); Nancy Yost, vice president (mainstream/contemporary fiction, mystery, suspense, contemporary/historical romance, thriller, women's fiction); Norman Kurz, business affairs; Zoe Fishman, foreign rights (young adult, literary fiction, narrative nonfiction); Natanya Wheeler (narrative nonfiction, literary fiction, historical, women's fiction, birds).

Represents nonfiction books, novels. **Considers these nonfiction areas:** animals, anthropology, biography, business, child, current affairs, education, ethnic, government, health, history, how to, language, memoirs, money, multicultural, nature, popular culture, psychology, self help, sociology, travel, womens, music; narrative nonfiction; science; film. **Considers these fiction areas:** detective, erotica, ethnic, feminist, historical, literary, mainstream, mystery, romance, contemporary, historical, regency, thriller, womens, fantasy, young adult. This agency specializes in health, business, creative nonfiction, literary fiction and commercial fiction—especially suspense, crime and women's issues. We are a full-service agency, handling domestic and foreign rights, film rights and audio rights to all of our books.

This agency specializes in health, business, creative nonfiction, literary fiction and commercial fiction—especially suspense, crime and women's issues. We are a full-service agency, handling domestic and foreign rights, film rights and audio rights to all of our books.

How to Contact Query with SASE or via electronic form on each agent's page. Submit to only one agent. Prefers to read materials exclusively. For fiction, send outline and first chapter. *No unsolicited mss.* Responds in 4 weeks to queries. Obtains most new clients through recommendations from others, solicitations, conferences.

Terms Agent receives 15% commission on domestic sales. Agent receives 20% commission on foreign sales. Offers written contract. Charges for large photocopy batches, messenger service, international postage.

Writers Conferences Malice Domestic

Tips Know the genre you are working in and read! Also, please see our Web site for details on which agent to query for your project.

ANDREW LOWNIE LITERARY AGENCY, LTD.

36 Great Smith St., London SW1P 3BU England. (44)(207)222-7574. Fax: (44)(207)222-7576. E-mail: lownie@globalnet.co.uk. Website: www.andrewlownie.co.uk. **Contact:** Andrew Lownie.Other memberships include AAA. Represents 130 clients. 20% of clients are new/unpublished writers. Currently handles: nonfiction books 90%, novels 10%.

- Prior to becoming an agent, Mr. Lownie was a journalist, bookseller, publisher, author of 12 books and director of the Curtis Brown Agency.

Represents nonfiction books. **Considers these nonfiction areas:** biography, current affairs, government, history, memoirs, military, popular culture, true crime. "This agent has wide publishing experience, extensive journalistic contacts, and a specialty in showbiz/celebrity memoir." Showbiz memoirs, narrative histories, and biographies. No poetry, short stories, children's fiction, academic or scripts.

"This agent has wide publishing experience, extensive journalistic contacts, and a specialty in showbiz/celebrity memoir." Showbiz memoirs, narrative histories, and biographies. No poetry, short stories, children's fiction, academic or scripts.

How to Contact Query with SASE and/or IRC. Submit outline, 1 sample chapter. Accepts simultaneous submissions. Responds in 1 week to queries. Responds in 1 month to mss. Obtains most new clients through recommendations from others.

Terms Agent receives 15% commission on domestic sales. Agent receives 15% commission on foreign sales. Offers written contract; 30-day notice must be given to terminate contract.

Recent Sales Sold 50 titles in the last year. *Avenging Justice*, by David Stafford (Time Warner); *Shadow of Solomon*, by Laurence Gardner; David Hasselhoff's autobiography. Other clients include Norma Major, Guy Bellamy, Joyce Cary estate, Lawrence James, Juliet Barker, Patrick McNee, Sir John Mills, Peter Evans, Desmond Seward, Laurence Gardner, Richard Rudgley, Timothy Good, Tom Levine.

LYONS LITERARY, LLC

27 West 20th St., Suite 10003, New York NY 10011. (212)255-5472. Fax: (212)851-8405. E-mail: info@lyonsliterary.com. Website: www.lyonsliterary.com. **Contact:** Jonathan Lyons. Member of AAR. Other memberships include The Author's Guild, American Bar Association, New York State Bar Associaton, New York State Intellectual Property Law Section. Represents 37 clients. 15% of clients are new/unpublished writers. Currently handles: nonfiction books 60%, novels 40%.

Represents nonfiction books, novels. **Considers these nonfiction areas:** crafts, animals, biography, cooking, current affairs, ethnic, gay, government, health, history, how to, humor, memoirs, military, money, multicultural, nature, popular culture, psychology, science, sociology, sports, translation, travel, true crime, womens. **Considers these fiction areas:** psychic, detective, fantasy, feminist, gay, historical, humor, literary, mainstream, mystery, regional, science, sports, thriller, womens, chick lit. "With my legal expertise and experience selling domestic and foreign language book rights, paperback reprint rights, audio rights, film/TV rights and permissions, I am able to provide substantive and personal guidance to my clients in all areas relating to their projects. In addition, with the advent of new publishing technology, Lyons Literary, LLC is situated to address the changing nature of the industry while concurrently handling authors' more traditional needs."

- "With my legal expertise and experience selling domestic and foreign language book rights, paperback reprint rights, audio rights, film/TV rights and permissions, I am able to provide substantive and personal guidance to my clients in all areas relating to their projects. In addition, with the advent of new publishing technology, Lyons Literary, LLC is situated to address the changing nature of the industry while concurrently handling authors' more traditional needs."

How to Contact Only accepts queries through online submission form. Accepts simultaneous submissions. Responds in 8 weeks to queries. Responds in 12 weeks to mss. Obtains most new clients through recommendations from others.

Terms Agent receives 15% commission on domestic sales. Agent receives 20% commission on foreign sales. Offers written contract.

Writers Conferences Agents and Editors Conference.

Tips "Please submit electronic queries through our Web site submission form."

DONALD MAASS LITERARY AGENCY

121 W. 27th St., Suite 801, New York NY 10001. (212)727-8383. E-mail: info@maassagency.com. Website: www.maassagency.com. Member of AAR. Other memberships include SFWA, MWA, RWA. Represents more than 100 clients. 5%% of clients are new/unpublished writers. Currently handles: novels 100%.

- Prior to opening his agency, Mr. Maass served as an editor at Dell Publishing (New York) and as a reader at Gollancz (London). He also served as the president of AAR.

Member Agents Donald Maass (mainstream, literary, mystery/suspense, science fiction).

Represents novels. **Considers these nonfiction areas:** narrative nonfiction. **Considers these fiction areas:** psychic, detective, fantasy, historical, horror, literary, mainstream, mystery, romance, historical, paranormal, time travel, science, thriller, womens. This agency specializes in commercial fiction, especially science fiction, fantasy, mystery and suspense. Actively seeking to expand in literary fiction and women's fiction. Does not want to receive nonfiction, picture books, prescriptive nonfiction, or poetry.

- This agency specializes in commercial fiction, especially science fiction, fantasy, mystery and suspense. Actively seeking to expand in literary fiction and women's fiction. Does not want to receive nonfiction, picture books, prescriptive nonfiction, or poetry.

How to Contact Query with SASE. Returns material only with SASE. Accepts simultaneous submissions. Responds in 2 weeks to queries. Responds in 3 months to mss.

Terms Agent receives 15% commission on domestic sales. Agent receives 20% commission on foreign sales.

Recent Sales *Codex Alera 5: Princep's Fury*, by Jim Butcher (Ace); *Fonseca 6: Bright Futures*, by Stuart Kaimsky (Forge): *Fathom*, by Cherie Priest (Tor); *Gospel Girls 3: Be Strong and Curvaceous*, by Shelly Adina (Faith Words); *Ariane 1: Peacekeeper*, by Laura Reeve (Roc); *Execution Dock*, by Anne Perry (Random House).

Writers Conferences Donald Maass: World Science Fiction Convention; Frankfurt Book Fair; Pacific Northwest Writers Conference; Bouchercon. Jennifer Jackson: World Science Fiction Convention; RWA National Conference.

Tips "We are fiction specialists, also noted for our innovative approach to career planning. Few new clients are accepted, but interested authors should query with a SASE. Works with subagents in all principle foreign countries and Hollywood. No prescriptive nonfiction, picture books or poetry will be considered."

MACGREGOR LITERARY

2373 N.W. 185th Ave., Suite 165, Hillsboro OR 97214. (503)277-8308. E-mail: submissions@macgregorliterary.com. Website: www.macgregorliterary.com. **Contact:** Chip MacGregor Signatory of WGA. Represents 40 clients. 10% of clients are new/unpublished writers. Currently handles: nonfiction books 40%, novels 60%.

- Prior to his current position, Mr. MacGregor was the senior agent with Alive Communications. Most recently, he was associate publisher for Time-Warner Book Group's Faith Division, and helped put together their Center Street imprint.

Represents nonfiction books, novels. **Considers these nonfiction areas:** business, current affairs, history, how to, humor, popular culture, religion, self help, sports, marriage, parenting. **Considers these fiction areas:** detective, historical, mainstream, mystery, religious, romance, thriller, women's/chick lit."My specialty has been in career planning with authors—finding commercial ideas, then helping authors bring them to market, and in the midst of that assisting the authors as they get firmly established in their writing careers. I'm probably best known for my work with Christian books over the years, but I've done a fair amount of general market projects as well." Actively seeking authors with a Christian worldview and a growing platform. Does not want to receive fantasy, sci-fi, children's books, poetry or screenplays.

"My specialty has been in career planning with authors—finding commercial ideas, then helping authors bring them to market, and in the midst of that assisting the authors as they get firmly established in their writing careers. I'm probably best known for my work with Christian books over the years, but I've done a fair amount of general market projects as well." Actively seeking authors with a Christian worldview and a growing platform. Does not want to receive fantasy, sci-fi, children's books, poetry or screenplays.

How to Contact Query with SASE. Accepts simultaneous submissions. Responds in 3 weeks to queries. Obtains most new clients through recommendations from others.

Terms Agent receives 15% commission on domestic sales. Agent receives 15% commission on foreign sales. Offers written contract; 30-day notice must be given to terminate contract. Charges for exceptional fees after receiving authors' permission.

Writers Conferences Blue Ridge Christian Writers' Conference; Write to Publish.

Tips "Seriously consider attending a good writers' conference. It will give you the chance to be face-to-face with people in the industry. Also, if you're a novelist, consider joining one of the national writers' organizations. The American Christian Fiction Writers (ACFW) is a wonderful group for new as well as established writers. And if you're a Christian writer of any kind, check into The Writers View, an online writing group. All of these have proven helpful to writers."

GILLIAN MACKENZIE AGENCY

E-mail: query@gillianmackenzieagency.com. Website: www.gillianmackenzieagency.com. **Contact:** Gillian MacKenzie.

- Prior to her current position, Ms. MacKenzie was vice president of Jane Startz Productions, Inc. She began her literary career at Curtis Brown.

Represents nonfiction books, juvenile. Actively seeking adult nonfiction and select children's titles.

Actively seeking adult nonfiction and select children's titles.

How to Contact Query via e-mail only. Obtains most new clients through recommendations from others, solicitations.

Recent Sales *Eight Pieces of Empire*, by Lawrence Scott Sheets (Crown); *The Last Single Woman in America*, by Cindy Guidry (Dutton); *The Go Pop series*, by Bob Staake (LB Kids).

RICIA MAINHARDT AGENCY (RMA)

612 Argyle Road, #L5, Brooklyn NY 11230. (718)434-1893. Fax: (718)434-2157. E-mail: ricia@ricia.com. Website: www.ricia.com. **Contact:** Ricia Mainhardt Represents 10 clients. 50% of clients are new/unpublished writers. Currently handles: nonfiction books 40%, novella 50%, juvenile books 10%.

Represents nonfiction books, novels, juvenile. **Considers these fiction areas:** glitz, psychic, adventure, confession, detective, erotica, ethnic, family, fantasy, feminist, gay, historical, horror, humor, juvenile, literary, mainstream, mystery, regional, romance, science, sports, thriller, western, young, womens. "We are a small boutique agency that provides hands-on service and attention to clients." Actively seeking adult and young adult fiction, nonfiction, picture books for early readers. Does not want to receive poetry, children's books or screenplays.

"We are a small boutique agency that provides hands-on service and attention to clients." Actively seeking adult and young adult fiction, nonfiction, picture books for early readers. Does not want to receive poetry, children's books or screenplays.

How to Contact Query with SASE or by e-mail. See guidelines on website depending on type of ms. No attachments or diskettes. Accepts simultaneous submissions. Responds in 1 month to queries. Responds in 4 months to mss. Obtains most new clients through recommendations from others, solicitations.

Terms Agent receives 15% commission on domestic sales. Offers written contract; 90-day notice must be given to terminate contract.

Writers Conferences Science Fiction Worldcon; Lunacon.

Tips "Be professional; be patient. It takes a long time for me to evaluate all the submissions that come through the door. Pestering phone calls and e-mails are not appreciated. Write the best book you can in your own style and keep an active narrative voice."

KIRSTEN MANGES LITERARY AGENCY

115 West 29th St., Third Floor, New York NY 10001. E-mail: kirsten@mangeslit.com. Website: www.mangeslit.com. **Contact:** Kirsten Manges.

- Prior to her current position, Ms. Manges was an agent at Curtis Brown.

Represents nonfiction books, novels. **Considers these nonfiction areas:** cooking, history, memoirs, multicultural, psychology, science, spirituality, sports, travel, womens, journalism, narrative. **Considers these fiction areas:** womens, commercial, chick lit. "This agency has a focus on women's issues. Actively seeking high quality fiction and nonfiction. I'm looking for strong credentials, an original point of view and excellent writing skills. With fiction, I'm looking for well written commercial novels, as well as compelling and provocative literary works."

> This agency has a focus on women's issues. Actively seeking high quality fiction and nonfiction. I'm looking for strong credentials, an original point of view and excellent writing skills. With fiction, I'm looking for well written commercial novels, as well as compelling and provocative literary works.

How to Contact Query with SASE. Obtains most new clients through recommendations from others, solicitations.

CAROL MANN AGENCY

55 Fifth Ave., New York NY 10003. (212)206-5635. Fax: (212)675-4809. E-mail: will@carolmannagency.com. Website: www.carolmannagency.com/. **Contact:** Nicole Bergstrom. Member of AAR. Represents roughly 200 clients. 15% of clients are new/unpublished writers. Currently handles: nonfiction books 90%, novels 10%.

Member Agents Carol Mann (health/medical, religion, spirituality, self-help, parenting, narrative nonfiction); Laura Yorke; Nicole Bergstrom; Urvashi Chakravarty.

Represents nonfiction books, novels. **Considers these nonfiction areas:** anthropology, art, biography, business, child, current affairs, ethnic, government, health, history, money, popular culture, psychology, self help, sociology, sports, womens, music. **Considers these fiction areas:** literary, commercial. This agency specializes in current affairs, self-help, popular culture, psychology, parenting, and history. Does not want to receive genre fiction (romance, mystery, etc.).

> This agency specializes in current affairs, self-help, popular culture, psychology, parenting, and history. Does not want to receive genre fiction (romance, mystery, etc.).

How to Contact Keep initial query/contact to no more than two pages. Responds in 4 weeks to queries.

Terms Agent receives 15% commission on domestic sales. Agent receives 20% commission on foreign sales. Offers written contract.

SARAH MANSON LITERARY AGENT

6 Totnes Walk, London N2 0AD United Kingdom. (44)(208)442-0396. E-mail: info@sarahmanson.com. Website: www.sarahmanson.com. **Contact:** Sarah Manson. Currently handles: juvenile books 100%.

- Prior to opening her agency, Ms. Manson worked in academic and children's publishing for 10 years and was a chartered school librarian for 8 years.

Represents This agency specializes in fiction for children and young adults. No picture books. Does not want to receive submissions from writers outside the United Kingdom and the Republic of Ireland.

> This agency specializes in fiction for children and young adults. No picture books. Does not want to receive submissions from writers outside the United Kingdom and the Republic of Ireland.

How to Contact See Web site for full submission guidelines.

Terms Agent receives 10% commission on domestic sales. Agent receives 20% commission on foreign sales. Offers written contract, binding for 1-month.

MANUS & ASSOCIATES LITERARY AGENCY, INC.

425 Sherman Ave., Suite 200, Palo Alto CA 94306. (650)470-5151. Fax: (650)470-5159. E-mail: manuslit@

manuslit.com. Website: www.manuslit.com. **Contact:** Jillian Manus, Jandy Nelson, Penny Nelson. Member of AAR. Represents 75 clients. 30% of clients are new/unpublished writers. Currently handles: nonfiction books 70%, novels 30%.

- Prior to becoming an agent, Ms. Manus was associate publisher of two national magazines and director of development at Warner Bros. and Universal Studios; she has been a literary agent for 20 years.

Member Agents Jandy Nelson, jandy@manuslit.com (self-help, health, memoirs, narrative nonfiction, women's fiction, literary fiction, multicultural fiction, thrillers); Jillian Manus, jillian@manuslit.com (political, memoirs, self-help, history, sports, women's issues, Latin fiction and nonfiction, thrillers); Penny Nelson, penny@manuslit.com (memoirs, self-help, sports, nonfiction); Dena Fischer (literary fiction, mainstream/commercial fiction, chick lit, women's fiction, historical fiction, ethnic/cultural fiction, narrative nonfiction, parenting, relationships, pop culture, health, sociology, psychology).

Represents nonfiction books, novels. **Considers these nonfiction areas:** biography, business, child, current affairs, ethnic, health, how to, memoirs, money, nature, popular culture, psychology, science, self help, womens, Gen X and Gen Y issues; creative nonfiction. **Considers these fiction areas:** literary, mainstream, multicultural, mystery, thriller, womens, quirky/edgy fiction. "Our agency is unique in the way that we not only sell the material, but we edit, develop concepts, and participate in the marketing effort. We specialize in large, conceptual fiction and nonfiction, and always value a project that can be sold in the TV/feature film market." Actively seeking high-concept thrillers, commercial literary fiction, women's fiction, celebrity biographies, memoirs, multicultural fiction, popular health, women's empowerment and mysteries. No horror, romance, science fiction, fantasy, Western, young adult, children's, poetry, cookbooks or magazine articles.

"Our agency is unique in the way that we not only sell the material, but we edit, develop concepts, and participate in the marketing effort. We specialize in large, conceptual fiction and nonfiction, and always value a project that can be sold in the TV/feature film market." Actively seeking high-concept thrillers, commercial literary fiction, women's fiction, celebrity biographies, memoirs, multicultural fiction, popular health, women's empowerment and mysteries. No horror, romance, science fiction, fantasy, Western, young adult, children's, poetry, cookbooks or magazine articles.

How to Contact Query with SASE. If requested, submit outline, 2-3 sample chapters. All queries should be sent to the California office. Accepts simultaneous submissions. Responds in 3 months to queries. Responds in 3 months to mss. Obtains most new clients through recommendations from others, solicitations, conferences.

Terms Agent receives 15% commission on domestic sales. Agent receives 20-25% commission on foreign sales. Offers written contract, binding for 2 years; 60-day notice must be given to terminate contract. Charges for photocopying and postage/UPS.

Recent Sales *Nothing Down for the 2000s* and *Multiple streams of Income for the 2000s*, by Robert Allen; *Missed Fortune 101*, by Doug Andrew; *Cracking the Millionaire Code*, by Mark Victor Hansen and Robert Allen; *Stress Free for Good*, by Dr. Fred Luskin and Dr. Ken Pelletier; *The Mercy of Thin Air*, by Ronlyn Domangue; *The Fine Art of Small Talk*, by Debra Fine; *Bone Men of Bonares*, by Terry Tamoff.

Writers Conferences Maui Writers' Conference; San Diego State University Writers' Conference; Willamette Writers' Conference; BookExpo America; MEGA Book Marketing University.

Tips "Research agents using a variety of sources."

MARCH TENTH, INC.

4 Myrtle St., Haworth NJ 07641-1740. (201)387-6551. Fax: (201)387-6552. E-mail: hchoron@aol.com; schoron@aol.com. Website: www.marchtenthinc.com. **Contact:** Harry Choron, vice president. Represents 40 clients. 30% of clients are new/unpublished writers. Currently handles: nonfiction books 100%.

Represents nonfiction books. **Considers these nonfiction areas:** biography, current affairs, health, history, humor, language, music, popular culture, film. "We prefer to work with published/established writers." Does not want to receive children's or young adult novels, plays, screenplays or poetry.

"We prefer to work with published/established writers." Does not want to receive children's or young adult novels, plays, screenplays or poetry.

How to Contact Query with SASE. Include your proposal, a short bio, and contact information. Accepts simultaneous submissions. Responds in 1 month to queries.

Terms Agent receives 15% commission on domestic sales. Agent receives 20% commission on foreign sales. Agent receives 20% commission on film sales. Charges clients for postage, photocopying, overseas phone expenses. Does not require expense money upfront.

THE DENISE MARCIL LITERARY AGENCY, INC.

156 Fifth Ave., Suite 625, New York NY 10010. (212)337-3402. Fax: (212)727-2688. Website: www.DeniseMarcilAgency.com. **Contact:** Denise Marcil, Anne Marie O'Farrell. Member of AAR.

- Prior to opening her agency, Ms. Marcil served as an editorial assistant with Avon Books and as an assistant editor with Simon & Schuster.

Member Agents Denise Marcil (women's commercial fiction, thrillers, suspense, popular reference, how-to, self-help, health, business, and parenting.

Represents *This agency is currently not taking on new authors.*

O→ *This agency is currently not taking on new authors.*

Terms Agent receives 15% commission on domestic sales. Agent receives 20% commission on foreign sales. Offers written contract, binding for 2 years. Charges $100/year for postage, photocopying, long-distance calls, etc.

Recent Sales *Home in Carolina*, by Sherryl Woods; *Prime Time Health*, by William Sears, M.D. and Martha Sears, R.N.; *The Autism Book*, by Robert W. Sears, M.D.; *The Yellow House*, by Patricia Falvey; *The 10-Minute Total Body Breakthrough*, by Sean Foy.

THE MARSH AGENCY, LTD

50 Albemarle Street, London England W1S 4BD United Kingdom. (44)(207)399-2800. Fax: (44)(207)399-2801. Website: www.marsh-agency.co.uk. Estab. 1994.

Member Agents Paul Marsh (agent), Geraldine Cook (agent), Jessica Woollard (agent), Caroline Hardman (agent), Piers Russell-Cobb (agent).

Represents nonfiction books, novels. "This agency was founded as an international rights specialist for literary agents and publishers in the United Kingdom, the U.S., Canada and New Zealand, for whom we sell foreign rights on a commission basis. We work directly with publishers in all the major territories and in the majority of the smaller ones; sometimes in conjunction with local representatives." Actively seeking crime novels.

O→ "This agency was founded as an international rights specialist for literary agents and publishers in the United Kingdom, the U.S., Canada and New Zealand, for whom we sell foreign rights on a commission basis. We work directly with publishers in all the major territories and in the majority of the smaller ones; sometimes in conjunction with local representatives." Actively seeking crime novels.

How to Contact Query with SASE. Obtains most new clients through recommendations from others, solicitations.

Recent Sales A full list of clients and sales is available online.

Tips "Use this agency's online form to send a generic e-mail message."

THE EVAN MARSHALL AGENCY

Six Tristam Place, Pine Brook NJ 07058-9445. (973)882-1122. Fax: (973)882-3099. E-mail: evanmarshall@optonline.net. **Contact:** Evan Marshall Member of AAR. Other memberships include MWA, Sisters in Crime. Currently handles: novels 100%.

Represents novels. **Considers these fiction areas:** adventure, erotica, ethnic, historical, horror, humor, literary, mainstream, mystery, religious, romance, contemporary, gothic, historical, regency, science, western.

How to Contact Query first with SASE; do not enclose material. No e-mail queries. Responds in 1 week to queries. Responds in 3 months to mss. Obtains most new clients through recommendations from others.

Terms Agent receives 15% commission on domestic sales. Agent receives 20% commission on foreign sales. Offers written contract.

Recent Sales *Breakneck*, by Erica Spindler (St. Martin's Press); *The Last Time I Was Me*, by Cathy Lamb (Kensington); *If He's Wicked*, by Hannah Howell (Zebra).

THE MARTELL AGENCY

1350 Avenue of the Americas, Suite 1205, New York NY 10019. Fax: (212)317-2676. E-mail: afmartell@aol.com. **Contact:** Alice Martell.

Represents nonfiction books, novels. **Considers these nonfiction areas:** business, health, fitness, history, memoirs, multicultural, psychology, self help, womens. **Considers these fiction areas:** mystery, thriller, womens, suspense, commercial.

How to Contact Query with SASE. Submit sample chapters. Submit via snail mail. No e-mail or fax queries.

Recent Sales *Peddling Peril: The Secret Nuclear Arms Trade*, by David Albright and Joel Wit (Five Press); *America's Women: Four Hundred Years of Dolls, Drudges, Helpmates, and Heroines*, by Gail Collins (William Morrow). Other clients include Serena Bass, Thomas E. Ricks, Janice Erlbaum, David Cay Johnston, Mark Derr, Barbara Rolls, Ph.D.

MARTIN LITERARY MANAGEMENT

17328 Ventura Blvd., Suite 138, Encino (LA) CA 91316. E-mail: sharlene@martinliterarymanagement.

com. Website: www.MartinLiteraryManagement.com. **Contact:** Sharlene Martin Ginny's address: 2511 West Schaumburg Road, No. 217, Schaumburg, IL 60184 (312) 480-5754 Member of AAR. 75% of clients are new/unpublished writers.

- Prior to becoming an agent, Ms. Martin worked in film/TV production and acquisitions.

Member Agents Sharlene Martin (nonfiction); Ginny Weissman (writers with a developed platform and a book that fits the Mind, Body, Spirit genre, including health, spirituality, religion, diet, exercise, psychology, relationships, and metaphysics).

Represents nonfiction books. **Considers these nonfiction areas:** biography, business, child, current affairs, health, history, how to, humor, memoirs, popular culture, psychology, religion, self help, true crime, womens. This agency has strong ties to film/TV. Actively seeking nonfiction that is highly commercial and that can be adapted to film. "We are being inundated with queries and submissions that are wrongfully being submitted to us, which only results in more frustrated for the writers. Under no circumstances do we accept fiction, screenplays, children's books, or poetry."

O→ This agency has strong ties to film/TV. Actively seeking nonfiction that is highly commercial and that can be adapted to film. "We are being inundated with queries and submissions that are wrongfully being submitted to us, which only results in more frustrated for the writers. Under no circumstances do we accept fiction, screenplays, children's books, or poetry."

How to Contact Query via e-mail with MS Word only. No attachments on queries; place letter in body of e-mail. Accepts simultaneous submissions. Responds in 1 week to queries. Responds in 3-4 weeks to mss. Obtains most new clients through recommendations from others.

Terms Agent receives 15% commission on domestic sales. Agent receives 25% commission on foreign sales. Offers written contract, binding for 1 year; 1-month notice must be given to terminate contract. Charges author for postage and copying if material is not sent electronically. 99 percent of materials are sent electronically to minimize charges to author for postage and copying.

Recent Sales *Publish Your Nonfiction Book*, by Sharlene Martin and Anthony Flacco (Writer's Digest); *Prince of Darkness--Richard Perle: The Kingdom, The Power, and the End of Empire in America*; by Alan Weisman (Union Square Press/Sterling); *Truth at Last: The Real Story of James Earl Ray*, by John Larry Ray with Lyndon Barsten (Lyons Press). Sales are updated weekly on website.

Tips "Have a strong platform for nonfiction. Please don't call. I welcome e-mail. I'm very responsive when I'm interested in a query and work hard to get my clients materials in the best possible shape before submissions. Do your homework prior to submission and only submit your best efforts. Please review our Web site carefully to make sure we're a good match for your work."

MAX AND CO., A LITERARY AGENCY AND SOCIAL CLUB

115 Hosea Ave., Cincinnati OH 45220. (201)704-2483. E-mail: mmurphy@maxlit.com. Website: www.maxliterary.org. **Contact:** Michael Murphy.

- Prior to his current position, Mr. Murphy was with Queen Literary Agency. He has been in book publishing since 1981. His first 13 years were with Random House, where he was a vice president. Later, he ran William Morrow as their publisher, up until the company's acquisition & merger into HarperCollins.

Represents Considers these nonfiction areas: humor, memoirs, narrative nonfiction. **Considers these fiction areas:** literary. Actively seeking narrative nonfiction, memoir, literary fiction, humor, and visual books. Does not want to receive genre fiction nor YA and children's books.

O→ Actively seeking narrative nonfiction, memoir, literary fiction, humor, and visual books. Does not want to receive genre fiction nor YA and children's books.

How to Contact Submit via e-mail attachment only.

MARGRET MCBRIDE LITERARY AGENCY

7744 Fay Ave., Suite 201, La Jolla CA 92037. (858)454-1550. Fax: (858)454-2156. E-mail: staff@mcbridelit.com. Website: www.mcbrideliterary.com. **Contact:** Michael Daley, submissions manager. Member of AAR. Other memberships include Authors Guild. Represents 55 clients.

- Prior to opening her agency, Ms. McBride worked at Random House, Ballantine Books, and Warner Books.

Represents nonfiction books, novels. **Considers these nonfiction areas:** biography, business, cooking, current affairs, ethnic, government, health, history, how to, money, music, popular culture, psychology, science, self help, sociology, womens, style. **Considers these fiction areas:** adventure, detective, ethnic, historical, humor, literary, mainstream, mystery, thriller, western. This agency specializes in mainstream fiction and nonfiction. Does not want to receive screenplays, romance, poetry, or children's/young adult.

O→ This agency specializes in mainstream fiction and nonfiction. Does not want to receive screenplays, romance, poetry, or children's/young adult.

How to Contact Query with synopsis, bio, SASE. No e-mail or fax queries. Accepts simultaneous submissions. Responds in 4-6 weeks to queries. Responds in 6-8 weeks to mss.

Terms Agent receives 15% commission on domestic sales. Agent receives 25% commission on foreign

sales. Charges for overnight delivery and photocopying.

THE MCCARTHY AGENCY, LLC

7 Allen St., Rumson NJ 07660. Phone/Fax: (732)741-3065. E-mail: mccarthylit@aol.com. **Contact:** Shawna McCarthy. Member of AAR. Currently handles: nonfiction books 25%, novels 75%.

Member Agents Shawna McCarthy (New Jersey address); Nahvae Frost (Brooklyn address).

Represents nonfiction books, novels. **Considers these nonfiction areas:** biography, history, philosophy, science. **Considers these fiction areas:** fantasy, juvenile, mystery, romance, science, womens.

How to Contact Query via e-mail. Accepts simultaneous submissions.

McCARTHY CREATIVE SERVICES

625 Main St., Suite 834, New York NY 10044-0035. (212)832-3428. Fax: (212)829-9610. E-mail: PaulMccarthy@McCarthyCreative.com. Website: www.McCarthyCreative.com. **Contact:** Paul D. McCarthy.Other memberships include The Authors Guild, American Society of Journalists & Authors, National Book Critics Circle, Authors League of America. Represents 5 clients. 0% of clients are new/unpublished writers. Currently handles: nonfiction books 95%, novels 5%.

- Prior to his current position, Mr. McCarthy was a professional writer, literary agent at the Scott Meredith Literary Agency, senior editor at publishing companies (Simon & Schuster, HarperCollins and Doubleday) and a public speaker. Learn much more about Mr. McCarthy by visiting his Web site.

Member Agents Paul D. McCarthy.

Represents nonfiction books, novels. **Considers these nonfiction areas:** animals, anthropology, art, biography, business, child, current affairs, education, ethnic, gay, government, health, history, how to, humor, language, memoirs, military, money, music, nature, popular culture, psychology, religion, science, self help, sociology, sports, translation, true crime, womens. **Considers these fiction areas:** glitz, adventure, confession, detective, erotica, ethnic, family, fantasy, feminist, gay, historical, horror, humor, literary, mainstream, mystery, regional, romance, science, sports, thriller, western, young, womens. "I deliberately founded my company to be unlimited in its range. That's what I offer, and the world has responded. My agency was founded so that I could maximize and build on the value of my combined experience for my authors and other clients, in all of my capacities and more. I think it's *very* important for authors to know that because I'm so exclusive as an agent, I may not be able to offer representation on the basis of the manuscript they submit. However, if they decide to invest in their book and lifetime career as authors, by engaging my professional, near-unique editorial services, there is the possibility that at the end of the process, when they've achieved the very best, most salable and competitive book they can write, I may see sufficient potential in the book and their next books, that I do offer to be their agent. Representation is never guaranteed." Established authors of serious and popular nonfiction, who want the value of being one of MCS's very exclusive authors who receive special attention, and of being represented by a literary agent who brings such a rich diversity and depth of publishing/creative/professorial experience, and distinguished reputation. No first novels. "Novels by established novelists will be considered very selectively."

O→ "I deliberately founded my company to be unlimited in its range. That's what I offer, and the world has responded. My agency was founded so that I could maximize and build on the value of my combined experience for my authors and other clients, in all of my capacities and more. I think it's *very* important for authors to know that because I'm so exclusive as an agent, I may not be able to offer representation on the basis of the manuscript they submit. However, if they decide to invest in their book and lifetime career as authors, by engaging my professional, near-unique editorial services, there is the possibility that at the end of the process, when they've achieved the very best, most salable and competitive book they can write, I may see sufficient potential in the book and their next books, that I do offer to be their agent. Representation is never guaranteed." Established authors of serious and popular nonfiction, who want the value of being one of MCS's very exclusive authors who receive special attention, and of being represented by a literary agent who brings such a rich diversity and depth of publishing/creative/professorial experience, and distinguished reputation. No first novels. "Novels by established novelists will be considered very selectively."

How to Contact Submit outline, one chapter (either first or best).E-queries only. Responds in 3-4 weeks to queries. Obtains most new clients through recommendations from others.

Terms Agent receives 15% commission on domestic sales. Agent receives 20% commission on foreign sales. Offers written contract; 30-day notice must be given to terminate contract. "All reading done in deciding whether or not to offer representation is free. Editorial services are available. Mailing and postage expenses that incurred on the author's behalf are always approved by them in advance."

Tips "Always keep in mind that your query letter/proposal is only one of hundreds and thousands that are competing for the agent's attention. Therefore, your presentation of your book and yourself as author has to be immediate, intense, compelling, and concise. Make the query letter one-page, and after short, introductory paragraph, write a 150-word KEYNOTE description of your manuscript."

ANNE MCDERMID & ASSOCIATES, LTD

83 Willcocks St., Toronto ON M5S 1C9 Canada. (416)324-8845. Fax: (416)324-8870. E-mail: info@mcdermidagency.com. Website: www.mcdermidagency.com. **Contact:** Anne McDermid. Represents 60 + clients.

Member Agents Lise Henderson, Anne McDermid.

Represents nonfiction books, novels. **Considers these nonfiction areas:** biography, history, memoirs, science, travel, true crime. Does not want to receive children's writing, self-help, business or computer books, gardening and cookery, fantasy, science fiction or romance.

- Does not want to receive children's writing, self-help, business or computer books, gardening and cookery, fantasy, science fiction or romance.

How to Contact Query via e-mail or mail with a brief bio, description, and first 5 pages of project only. Obtains most new clients through recommendations from others.

MCINTOSH & OTIS

353 Lexington Ave., 15th Floor, New York NY 10016. E-mail: info@mcintoshandotis.com. Website: www.mcintoshandotis.net/. Member of AAR.

Member Agents Eugene H. Winick; Elizabeth Winick (literary fiction, women's fiction, historical fiction, and mystery/suspense, along with narrative nonfiction, spiritual/self-help, history and current affairs. Elizabeth represents numerous New York T); Edward Necarsulmer IV; Rebecca Strauss (nonfiction, literary and commercial fiction, women's fiction, memoirs, and pop culture); Cate Martin; Ina Winick (psychology, self-help, and mystery/suspense); Ian Polonsky (Film/TV/Stage/Radio).

Represents nonfiction books, novels, movie, feature.

How to Contact Send a query, synopsis, two sample chapters, and SASE by regular mail. For nonfiction, include bio and outline. For screenplays, send a query letter, synopsis, and SASE by regular mail. Does not accept e-mail queries. Responds in 8 weeks to queries.

Tips "Please send a query letter, synopsis, two sample chapters, and SASE by regular mail. For nonfiction, please include a biography and outline as well. For screenplays, please send a query letter, synopsis, and SASE by regular mail. No phone calls please."

SALLY HILL MCMILLAN & ASSOCIATES, INC.

429 E. Kingston Ave., Charlotte NC 28203. (704)334-0897. Fax: (704)334-1897.
Contact: Sally Hill McMillan. Member of AAR.

Represents "We are not seeking new clients at this time. Agency specializes in Southern fiction, women's fiction, mystery and practical nonfiction."

- "We are not seeking new clients at this time. Agency specializes in Southern fiction, women's fiction, mystery and practical nonfiction."

How to Contact *No unsolicited submissions.*

MENDEL MEDIA GROUP, LLC

115 West 30th St., Suite 800, New York NY 10001. (646)239-9896. Fax: (212)685-4717. E-mail: scott@mendelmedia.com. Website: www.mendelmedia.com. Member of AAR. Represents 40-60 clients.

- Prior to becoming an agent, Mr. Mendel was an academic. "I taught American literature, Yiddish, Jewish studies, and literary theory at the University of Chicago and the University of Illinois at Chicago while working on my PhD in English. I also worked as a freelance technical writer and as the managing editor of a healthcare magazine. In 1998, I began working for the late Jane Jordan Browne, a long-time agent in the book publishing world."

Represents nonfiction books, novels, scholarly, with potential for broad/popular appeal. **Considers these nonfiction areas:** americana, animals, anthropology, art, biography, business, child, cooking, current affairs, education, ethnic, gardening, gay, government, health, history, how to, humor, language, memoirs, military, money, multicultural, music, nature, philosophy, popular culture, psychology, recreation, regional, religion, science, self help, sex, sociology, software, spirituality, sports, true crime, womens, Jewish topics; creative nonfiction. **Considers these fiction areas:** contemporary, glitz, adventure, detective, erotica, ethnic, feminist, gay, historical, humor, juvenile, literary, mainstream, mystery, picture books, religious, romance, sports, thriller, young, Jewish fiction. "I am interested in major works of history, current affairs, biography, business, politics, economics, science, major memoirs, narrative nonfiction, and other sorts of general nonfiction." Actively seeking new, major or definitive work on a subject of broad interest, or a controversial, but authoritative, new book on a subject that affects many people's lives." I also represent more light-hearted nonfiction projects, such as gift or novelty books, when they suit the market particularly well." Does not want "queries about projects written years ago that were unsuccessfully shopped to a long list of trade publishers by either the author or another agent. I am specifically not interested in reading short, category romances (regency, time travel, paranormal, etc.), horror novels, supernatural stories, poetry, original plays, or film scripts."

- "I am interested in major works of history, current affairs, biography, business, politics, economics, science, major memoirs, narrative nonfiction, and other sorts of general nonfiction." Actively seeking new, major or definitive work on a subject of broad interest, or a controversial, but authoritative, new book on a subject that affects many people's lives." I also represent more light-hearted nonfiction projects, such as gift or novelty books, when they suit the market particularly well." Does not want "queries about projects written years ago that were unsuccessfully shopped to a long list of trade publishers by either the author or another agent. I am specifically not interested in reading short, category romances (regency, time travel, paranormal, etc.), horror novels, supernatural stories, poetry, original plays, or film scripts."

How to Contact Query with SASE. Do not e-mail or fax queries. For nonfiction, include a complete, fully-edited book proposal with sample chapters. For fiction, include a complete synopsis and no more than 20 pages of sample text. Responds in 2 weeks to queries. Responds in 4-6 weeks to mss. Obtains most new clients through recommendations from others.

Terms Agent receives 15% commission on domestic sales. Agent receives 20% commission on foreign sales. Charges clients for ms duplication, expedited delivery services (when necessary), any overseas shipping, telephone calls/faxes necessary for marketing the author's foreign rights.

Writers Conferences BookExpo America; Frankfurt Book Fair; London Book Fair; RWA National Conference; Modern Language Association Convention; Jerusalem Book Fair.

Tips "While I am not interested in being flattered by a prospective client, it does matter to me that she knows why she is writing to me in the first place. Is one of my clients a colleague of hers? Has she read a book by one of my clients that led her to believe I might be interested in her work? Authors of descriptive nonfiction should have real credentials and expertise in their subject areas, either as academics, journalists, or policy experts, and authors of prescriptive nonfiction should have legitimate expertise and considerable experience communicating their ideas in seminars and workshops, in a successful business, through the media, etc."

MENZA-BARRON AGENCY

511 Avenue of the Americas, #51, New York NY 10011. (212)889-6850. **Contact:** Claudia Menza, Manie Barron. Member of AAR. Represents 100 clients. 50% of clients are new/unpublished writers.

Represents nonfiction books, novels, photographic books, especially interested in African-American material. **Considers these nonfiction areas:** current affairs, education, ethnic, especially African-American, health, history, multicultural, music, photography, psychology, film. This agency specializes editorial assistance and African-American fiction and nonfiction.

⊶ This agency specializes editorial assistance and African-American fiction and nonfiction.

How to Contact Query with SASE. Responds in 2-4 weeks to queries. Responds in 2-4 months to mss.

Terms Agent receives 15% commission on domestic sales. Agent receives 20% (if co-agent is used) commission on foreign sales. Agent receives 20% commission on film sales. Offers written contract.

SCOTT MEREDITH LITERARY AGENCY

200 W. 57th St., Suite 904, New York NY 10019. (646)274-1970. Fax: (212)977-5997. E-mail: aklebanoff@rosettabooks.com; info@scottmeredith.com. Website: www.scottmeredith.com. **Contact:** Arthur Klebanoff, CEO.Adheres to the AAR canon of ethics. Represents 20 clients. 0% of clients are new/unpublished writers. Currently handles: nonfiction books 90%, novels 5%, textbooks 5%.

- Prior to becoming an agent, Mr. Klebanoff was a lawyer.

Represents nonfiction books, textbooks. This agency's specialty lies in category nonfiction publishing programs. Actively seeking category leading nonfiction. Does not want to receive first fiction projects.

⊶ This agency's specialty lies in category nonfiction publishing programs. Actively seeking category leading nonfiction. Does not want to receive first fiction projects.

How to Contact Query with SASE. Submit proposal package, author bio. Accepts simultaneous submissions. Responds in 1 week to queries. Responds in 2 weeks to mss. Obtains most new clients through recommendations from others.

Terms Agent receives 15% commission on domestic sales. Agent receives 25% commission on foreign sales. Offers written contract.

Recent Sales *The Conscience of a Liberal*, by Paul Krugman; *The King of Oil: The Secret Lives of Marc Rich*, by Daniel Ammann; *Ten*, by Sheila Lukins; *Peterson Field Guide to Birds of North America*.

DORIS S. MICHAELS LITERARY AGENCY, INC.

1841 Broadway, Suite 903, New York NY 10023. (212)265-9474. Fax: (212)265-9480. E-mail: query@dsmagency.com. Website: www.dsmagency.com. **Contact:** Doris S. Michaels, president.Member of AAR. Other memberships include WNBA.

Represents novels. **Considers these fiction areas:** literary, with commercial appeal and strong screen potential.

How to Contact Query by e-mail; see submission guidelines on Web site. Obtains most new clients through recommendations from others, conferences.

Terms Agent receives 15% commission on domestic sales. Agent receives 20% commission on foreign sales. Offers written contract, binding for 1 year; 1-month notice must be given to terminate contract. Charges clients for office expenses, not to exceed $150 without written permission.
Writers Conferences BookExpo America; Frankfurt Book Fair; London Book Fair; Maui Writers Conference.

MARTHA MILLARD LITERARY AGENCY

420 Central Park West, #5H, New York NY 10025. (212)787-1030. **Contact:** Martha Millard.Member of AAR. Other memberships include SFWA. Represents 50 clients. Currently handles: nonfiction books 25%, novels 65%, story collections 10%.

- Prior to becoming an agent, Ms. Millard worked in editorial departments of several publishers and was vice president at another agency for more than four years.

Represents nonfiction books, novels. **Considers these nonfiction areas:** juvenile, New Age, art, biography, business, child, cooking, current affairs, education, ethnic, health, history, how to, memoirs, money, music, photography, popular culture, psychology, self help, film, true crime, womens. **Considers these fiction areas:** fantasy, mystery, romance, science.
How to Contact No unsolicited queries. **Referrals only**. Obtains most new clients through recommendations from others.
Terms Agent receives 15% commission on domestic sales. Agent receives 20% commission on foreign sales. Offers written contract.

PATRICIA MOOSBRUGGER LITERARY AGENCY

2720 Decker Ave. NW, Albuquerque NM 87107. (505)345-9297. E-mail: pm@pmagency.net. Website: www.pmagency.net. **Contact:** Patricia Moosbrugger. Member of AAR.
Represents nonfiction books.
How to Contact Query with SASE.

HOWARD MORHAIM LITERARY AGENCY

30 Pierrepont St., Brooklyn NY 11201. (718)222-8400. Fax: (718)222-5056. Website: www.morhaimliterary.com/. Member of AAR.
Member Agents Howard Morhaim, Kate McKean, Brandi Bowles, Katie Menick.
Represents Actively seeking fiction, nonfiction and young-adult novels.
O┳ Actively seeking fiction, nonfiction and young-adult novels.
How to Contact Query via e-mail with cover letter and three sample chapters. See each agent's listing for specifics.

HENRY MORRISON, INC.

105 S. Bedford Road, Suite 306A, Mt. Kisco NY 10549. (914)666-3500. Fax: (914)241-7846. **Contact:** Henry Morrison. Signatory of WGA. Represents 53 clients. 5% of clients are new/unpublished writers. Currently handles: nonfiction books 5%, novels 95%.
Represents nonfiction books, novels. **Considers these nonfiction areas:** anthropology, biography, government, history. **Considers these fiction areas:** adventure, detective, family, historical.
How to Contact Query with SASE. Responds in 2 weeks to queries. Responds in 3 months to mss. Obtains most new clients through recommendations from others.
Terms Agent receives 15% commission on domestic sales. Agent receives 25% commission on foreign sales. Charges clients for ms copies, bound galleys, finished books for submissions to publishers, movie producers and foreign publishers.

MORTIMER LITERARY AGENCY

52645 Paui Road, Aguanga CA 92536. (951)763-2600. E-mail: kmortimer@mortimerliterary.com. Website: www.mortimerliterary.com. **Contact:** Kelly L. Mortimer. Other memberships include American Christian Fiction Writers. Represents 15 clients. 70% of clients are new/unpublished writers. Currently handles: nonfiction books 5%, novels 90%, juvenile books 5%.

- Prior to becoming an agent, Ms. Mortimer was a freelance writer and the CFO of Microvector, Inc. She has a degree in contract law, and was nominated for the ACGW Agent of the Year award.

Represents nonfiction books, novels, novellas, juvenile, young adult and middle grade. **Considers these nonfiction areas:** religion, self help, relationship advice, finance. **Considers these fiction areas:** adventure, detective, historical, mainstream, mystery, religious, romance, thriller, young, middle grade. "I keep a short client list to give my writers personal attention. I edit my clients' manuscripts as necessary. I send manuscripts out to pre-selected editors in a timely fashion, and send my clients monthly reports. I am not seeking new clients now, but will be in the future."
O┳ "I keep a short client list to give my writers personal attention. I edit my clients' manuscripts as

necessary. I send manuscripts out to pre-selected editors in a timely fashion, and send my clients monthly reports. I am not seeking new clients now, but will be in the future."

How to Contact Only accepting new clients through conferences or contests. Accepts simultaneous submissions. Responds in 4 months to mss. Obtains most new clients through recommendations from others, solicitations, conferences.

Terms Agent receives 15% commission on domestic sales. Agent receives 20% commission on foreign sales. Offers written contract. "I charge for postage - only the amount I pay and it comes out of the author's advance. The writer provides me with copies of their manuscripts."

Writers Conferences RWA, ACFW.

Tips "Follow submission guidelines on the Web site, submit your best work and don't query unless your manuscript is finished. Don't send material or mss that I haven't requested."

DEE MURA LITERARY

269 West Shore Drive, Massapequa NY 11758-8225. (516)795-1616. Fax: (516)795-8797. E-mail: query@deemuraliterary.com. **Contact:** Dee Mura, Karen Roberts, Bobbie Sokol, David Brozain. Signatory of WGA. 50% of clients are new/unpublished writers.

- Prior to opening her agency, Ms. Mura was a public relations executive with a roster of film and entertainment clients and worked in editorial for major weekly news magazines.

Represents Considers these nonfiction areas: animals, anthropology, biography, business, child guidance, computers, current affairs, education, ethnic, finance, gay, government, health, history, how-to, humor, juvenile nonfiction, law, lesbian, medicine, memoirs, military, money, nature, personal improvement, politics, science, self-help, sociology, sports, technology, travel, true crime, women's issues, women's studies. **Considers these fiction areas:** action, adventure, contemporary issues, crime, detective, ethnic, experimental, family saga, fantasy, feminist, gay, glitz, historical, humor, juvenile, lesbian, literary, mainstream, military, mystery, psychic, regional, romance, science fiction, sports, thriller, westerns, young adult, political. **Considers these script areas:** action, cartoon, comedy, contemporary, detective, (and espionage), family, fantasy, feminist, gay/lesbian, glitz, historical, horror, juvenile, mainstream, mystery, psychic, romantic comedy, romantic drama, science, sports, teen, thriller, western. "Some of us have special interests and some of us encourage you to share your passion and work with us." Does not want to receive "ideas for sitcoms, novels, films, etc., or queries without SASEs."

O→ "Some of us have special interests and some of us encourage you to share your passion and work with us." Does not want to receive "ideas for sitcoms, novels, films, etc., or queries without SASEs."

How to Contact Query with SASE. Accepts e-mail queries (no attachments). If via e-mail, please include the type of query and your genre in the subject line. If via regular mail, you may include the first few chapters, outline, or proposal. No fax queries. Accepts simultaneous submissions. Only responds if interested; responds as soon as possible. Obtains most new clients through recommendations from others, queries.

Terms Agent receives 15% commission on domestic sales. Agent receives 20% commission on foreign sales. Offers written contract. Charges clients for photocopying, mailing expenses, overseas/long distance phone calls/faxes.

Recent Sales Sold more than 40 titles and 35 scripts in the last year.

Tips "Please include a paragraph on your background, even if you have no literary background, and a brief synopsis of the project."

ERIN MURPHY LITERARY AGENCY

2700 Woodlands Village, #300-458, Flagstaff AZ 86001-7172. (928)525-2056. Fax: (928)525-2480. **Contact:** Erin Murphy.

Represents "This agency only represents children's books. We do not accept unsolicited manuscripts or queries. We consider new clients by referral or personal contact only."

O→ "This agency only represents children's books. We do not accept unsolicited manuscripts or queries. We consider new clients by referral or personal contact only."

MUSE LITERARY MANAGEMENT

189 Waverly Place, #4, New York NY 10014. (212)925-3721. E-mail: museliterarymgmt@aol.com. Website: www.museliterary.com/. **Contact:** Deborah Carter. Associations: AWP, NAWE, International Thriller Writers, Historical Novel Society, Associations of Booksellers for Children, The Authors Guild, National Writers Union, and American Folklore Society. Represents 5 clients. 80% of clients are new/unpublished writers.

- Prior to starting her agency, Ms. Carter trained with an AAR literary agent and worked in the music business and as a talent scout for record companies in artist management. She has a BA in English and music from Washington Square University College at NYU.

Represents novels, short story collections, poetry books. **Considers these nonfiction areas:** narrative nonfiction (no prescriptive nonfiction), children's. **Considers these fiction areas:** adventure, detective, juvenile, mystery, picture books, suspense, thriller, young adult, espionage; middle-grade novels; literary short story collections, literary fiction with popular appeal,. Specializes in manuscript development, the sale and administration of print, performance, and foreign rights to literary works, and post-publication publicity and appearances. Actively seeking "writers with formal training who bring compelling voices and a unique outlook to their manuscripts. Those who submit should be receptive to editorial feedback and willing to revise during the submission provess in order to remain competitive. " Does not want "manuscripts that have been worked over by book doctors (collaborative projects ok, but writers must have chops); category romance, chick lit, sci-fi, fantasy, horror, stories about cats and dogs, vampires or serial killers, fiction or nonfiction with religious or spiritual subject matter."

O→ Specializes in manuscript development, the sale and administration of print, performance, and foreign rights to literary works, and post-publication publicity and appearances. Actively seeking "writers with formal training who bring compelling voices and a unique outlook to their manuscripts. Those who submit should be receptive to editorial feedback and willing to revise during the submission provess in order to remain competitive. " Does not want "manuscripts that have been worked over by book doctors (collaborative projects ok, but writers must have chops); category romance, chick lit, sci-fi, fantasy, horror, stories about cats and dogs, vampires or serial killers, fiction or nonfiction with religious or spiritual subject matter."

How to Contact Query with SASE. Query via e-mail (no attachments). Discards unwanted queries. Responds in 2 weeks to queries. Responds in 2-3 weeks to mss. Obtains most new clients through recommendations from others, conferences.

Terms Agent receives 15% commission on domestic sales. Agent receives 20% commission on foreign sales. One-year contract offered when writer and agent agree that the manuscript is ready for submission; manuscripts in development are not bound by contract. Sometimes charges for postage and photocopying. All expenses are preapproved by the client.

JEAN V. NAGGAR LITERARY AGENCY, INC.

216 E. 75th St., Suite 1E, New York NY 10021. (212)794-1082. E-mail: jvnla@jvnla.com. Website: www.jvnla.com. **Contact:** Jean Naggar. Member of AAR. Other memberships include PEN, Women's Media Group, Women's Forum. Represents 80 clients. 20% of clients are new/unpublished writers. Currently handles: nonfiction books 35%, novels 45%, juvenile books 15%, scholarly books 5%.

- Ms. Naggar has served as president of AAR.

Member Agents Jean Naggar (mainstream fiction, nonfiction); Jennifer Weltz, director (subsidiary rights, children's books); Alice Tasman, senior agent (commercial and literary fiction, thrillers, narrative nonfiction); Jessica Regel, agent (young adult fiction and nonfiction).

Represents nonfiction books, novels. **Considers these nonfiction areas:** juvenile, New Age, biography, child, current affairs, government, health, history, memoirs, psychology, religion, self help, sociology, travel, womens. **Considers these fiction areas:** psychic, adventure, detective, ethnic, family, feminist, historical, literary, mainstream, mystery, thriller. This agency specializes in mainstream fiction and nonfiction and literary fiction with commercial potential.

O→ This agency specializes in mainstream fiction and nonfiction and literary fiction with commercial potential.

How to Contact Query via e-mail. Prefers to read materials exclusively. No fax queries. Responds in 1 day to queries. Responds in 2 months to mss. Obtains most new clients through recommendations from others.

Terms Agent receives 15% commission on domestic sales. Agent receives 20% commission on foreign sales. Offers written contract. Charges for overseas mailing, messenger services, book purchases, long-distance telephone, photocopying--all deductible from royalties received.

Recent Sales *Night Navigation*, by Ginnah Howard; *After Hours At the Almost Home*, by Tara Yelen; *An Entirely Synthetic Fish: A Biography of Rainbow Trout*, by Anders Halverson; *The Patron Saint of Butterflies*, by Cecilia Galante, *Wondrous Strange*, by Lesley Livingston, *6 Sick Hipsters*, by Rayo Casablanca, *The Last Bridge*, by Teri Coyne; *Gypsy Goodbye*, by Nancy Springer, *Commuters*, by Emily Tedrowe; *The Language of Secrets*, by Dianne Dixon, *Smiling to Freedom*, by Martin Benoit Stiles; *The Tale of Halcyon Crane*, by Wendy Webb, *Fugitive*, by Phillip Margolin; *BlackBerry Girl*, by Aidan Donnelley Rowley; *Wild girls*, by Pat Murphy.

Writers Conferences Willamette Writers Conference; Pacific Northwest Writers Conference; Bread Loaf Writers Conference; Marymount Manhattan Writers Conference; SEAK Medical & Legal Fiction Writing Conference.

Tips "Use a professional presentation. Because of the avalanche of unsolicited queries that flood the agency every week, we have had to modify our policy. We will now only guarantee to read and respond to queries from writers who come recommended by someone we know. Our areas are general fiction and nonfiction--no children's books by unpublished writers, no multimedia, no screenplays, no formula fiction, and no mysteries by unpublished writers. We recommend patience and fortitude: the courage to be true to your own vision, the fortitude to finish a novel and polish it again and again before sending it out, and the patience to accept rejection gracefully and wait for the stars to align themselves appropriately for success."

NANCY COFFEY LITERARY & MEDIA REPRESENTATION

240 W. 35th St., Suite 500, New York NY 10001. Fax: (212)279-0927. **Contact:** Nancy Coffey. Member of AAR. Currently handles: nonfiction books 5%, novels 90%, juvenile books 5%.

Member Agents Nancy Coffey; Joanna Stampfel-Volpe.

Represents nonfiction books, novels, juvenile, young adult, from cutting edge material to fantasy. **Considers these fiction areas:** family, fantasy, military, espionage, mystery, romance, science, thriller, young, womens.

How to Contact Query with SASE.

NAPPALAND LITERARY AGENCY

A Division of Nappaland Communications, Inc., P.O. Box 1674, Loveland CO 80539-1674. Fax: (970)635-9869. E-mail: Literary@nappaland.com. Website: www.NappalandLiterary.com. **Contact:** Mike Nappa, senior agent. Represents 8 clients. 0% of clients are new/unpublished writers. Currently handles: nonfiction books 45%, novels 50%, scholarly books 5%.

- Prior to becoming an agent, Mr. Nappa served as an acquisition editor for three major Christian publishing houses.

Represents nonfiction books, novels. **Considers these nonfiction areas:** child, current affairs, popular culture, religion, womens. **Considers these fiction areas:** adventure, detective, literary, mainstream, religious, thriller. This agency will not consider any new authors unless they come with a recommendation from a current Nappaland client. All queries without such a recommendation are immediately rejected. "Interested in thoughtful, vivid, nonfiction works on religious and cultural themes. Also, fast-paced, well-crafted fiction (suspense, literary, women's) that reads like a work of art. Established authors only; broad promotional platform preferred." Does not want to receive children's books, movie or television scripts, textbooks, short stories, stage plays or poetry.

O→ This agency will not consider any new authors unless they come with a recommendation from a current Nappaland client. All queries without such a recommendation are immediately rejected. "Interested in thoughtful, vivid, nonfiction works on religious and cultural themes. Also, fast-paced, well-crafted fiction (suspense, literary, women's) that reads like a work of art. Established authors only; broad promotional platform preferred." Does not want to receive children's books, movie or television scripts, textbooks, short stories, stage plays or poetry.

How to Contact Query with SASE. Submit author bio. Include the name of the person referring you to us. Do *not* send entire proposal unless requested. Send query and bio only. E-queries preferred and given first priority. No attachments please. Accepts simultaneous submissions. Responds in 1 month to queries. Responds in 3 months to mss.

Terms Agent receives 15% commission on domestic sales. Agent receives 20% commission on foreign sales. Offers written contract; 30-day notice must be given to terminate contract.

Recent Sales *Perspectives on Family Ministry*, by Dr. Timothy Paul Jones (B&H Publishing Group); *Drift*, by Sharon Carter Rogers (Howard Books/Simon & Schuster); *Lunch Box Laughs*, by Tony Nappa (Standard Publishing).

Writers Conferences Colorado Christian Writers' Conference in Estes Park.

THE NASHVILLE AGENCY

P.O. Box 110909, Nashville TN 37222. (615)263-4143. Fax: (866)333-8663. E-mail: info@nashvilleagency.com; submissions@nashvilleagency.com. Website: www.nashvilleagency.com. **Contact:** Taylor Joseph. Represents 18 clients. 50% of clients are new/unpublished writers. Currently handles: nonfiction books 40%, novels 15%, novella 5%, juvenile books 40%.

Member Agents Tim Grable (business books); Jonathan Clements (nonfiction, juvenile); Taylor Joseph (fiction, novels, memoirs).

Represents nonfiction books, novels, novellas, juvenile, scholarly, movie, documentary. **Considers these nonfiction areas:** crafts, juvenile, biography, business, child, cooking, current affairs, education, history, how to, humor, memoirs, military, music, popular culture, religion, self help, sports, true crime, womens. **Considers these fiction areas:** adventure, fantasy, historical, humor, juvenile, literary, mainstream, mystery, regional, religious, thriller, young, womens. **Considers these script areas:** action, contemporary. "Our agency looks not as much for specific genres or stylings. Rather, we look for far-reaching potentials (i.e., brands, properties) to branch outside a token specific market." Actively seeking novels, nonfiction, religious/spiritual material. Does not want to receive poetry, stage plays or textbooks.

O→ "Our agency looks not as much for specific genres or stylings. Rather, we look for far-reaching potentials (i.e., brands, properties) to branch outside a token specific market." Actively seeking novels, nonfiction, religious/spiritual material. Does not want to receive poetry, stage plays or textbooks.

How to Contact Query via e-mail or by mail with SASE. No fax queries. Submit proposal package, synopsis, publishing history, author bio, Description of how your relationship with The Nashville Agency was initiated. Accepts simultaneous submissions. Responds in 3 weeks to queries. Responds in 3 months to mss. Obtains most new clients through recommendations from others.

Terms Agent receives 15% commission on domestic sales. Agent receives 20% commission on foreign sales. Offers written contract, binding for 5 years; 30-day notice must be given to terminate contract. This agency charges for standard office fees.

Recent Sales This agency prefers not to share information on specific sales.

Writers Conferences Blue Ridge Writers' Conference.

NELSON LITERARY AGENCY

1732 Wazee St., Suite 207, Denver CO 80202. (303)292-2805. E-mail: query@nelsonagency.com. Website: www.nelsonagency.com. **Contact:** Kristin Nelson. Member of AAR.

- Prior to opening her own agency, Ms. Nelson worked as a literary scout and subrights agent for agent Jody Rein.

Represents novels, select nonfiction. **Considers these nonfiction areas:** memoirs. **Considers these fiction areas:** literary, romance, includes fantasy with romantic elements, science fiction, fantasy, young adult, womens, chick lit (includes mysteries); commercial/mainstream. NLA specializes in representing commercial fiction and high caliber literary fiction. Actively seeking Latina writers who tackle contemporary issues in a modern voice (think *Dirty Girls Social Club*). Does not want short story collections, mysteries (except chick lit), thrillers, Christian, horror, or children's picture books.

- NLA specializes in representing commercial fiction and high caliber literary fiction. Actively seeking Latina writers who tackle contemporary issues in a modern voice (think *Dirty Girls Social Club*). Does not want short story collections, mysteries (except chick lit), thrillers, Christian, horror, or children's picture books.

How to Contact Query by e-mail only.

Recent Sales New York Times Bestselling author of *I'd Tell You I Love You, But Then I'd Have to Kill You*, Ally Carter's fourth novel in the Gallagher Girls series; *Hester* (historical fiction), by Paula Reed, *Proof by Seduction* (debut romance), by Courtney Milan, *Soulless* (fantasy debut), by Gail Carriger, *The Shifter* (debut children's fantasy), by Janice Hardy, *Real Life & Liars* (debut women's fiction), by Kristina Riggle, *Hotel on the Corner of Bitter and Sweet* (debut literary fiction), by Jamie Ford.

NINE MUSES AND APOLLO, INC.

525 Broadway, Suite 201, New York NY 10012. (212)431-2665. **Contact:** Ling Lucas. Represents 50 clients. 10% of clients are new/unpublished writers. Currently handles: nonfiction books 100%.

- Prior to her current position, Ms. Lucas served as vice president, sales/marketing director and associate publisher of Warner Books.

Represents nonfiction books. This agency specializes in nonfiction. Does not want to receive children's or young adult material.

- This agency specializes in nonfiction. Does not want to receive children's or young adult material.

How to Contact Submit outline, 2 sample chapters, SASE. .Prefers to read materials exclusively.

Terms Agent receives 15% commission on domestic sales. Agent receives 20-25% commission on foreign sales. Offers written contract. Charges clients for photocopying, postage.

Tips "Your outline should already be well developed, cogent, and reveal clarity of thought about the general structure and direction of your project."

NORTHERN LIGHTS LITERARY SERVICES, LLC

11248 N. Boyer Rd., Sandpoint ID 83864. (888)558-4354. Fax: (208)265-1948. E-mail: agent@northernlightsls.com. Website: www.northernlightsls.com. **Contact:** Sammie Justesen. Represents 25 clients. 35% of clients are new/unpublished writers. Currently handles: nonfiction books 90%, novels 10%.

Member Agents Sammie Justesen (fiction and nonfiction); Vorris Dee Justesen (business and current affairs).

Represents nonfiction books, novels. **Considers these nonfiction areas:** crafts, newage, animals, biography, business, child, cooking, current affairs, ethnic, health, how to, memoirs, nature, popular culture, psychology, religion, self help, sports, true crime, womens. **Considers these fiction areas:** glitz, psychic, adventure, detective, ethnic, family, feminist, historical, mainstream, mystery, regional, religious, romance, thriller, womens. "Our goal is to provide personalized service to clients and create a bond that will endure throughout the writer's career. We seriously consider each query we receive and will accept hardworking new authors who are willing to develop their talents and skills. We enjoy working with healthcare professionals and writers who clearly understand their market and have a platform." Actively seeking general nonfiction—especially if the writer has a platform. Does not want to receive fantasy, horror, erotica, children's books, screenplays, poetry or short stories.

"Our goal is to provide personalized service to clients and create a bond that will endure throughout the writer's career. We seriously consider each query we receive and will accept hardworking new authors who are willing to develop their talents and skills. We enjoy working with healthcare professionals and writers who clearly understand their market and have a platform." Actively seeking general nonfiction—especially if the writer has a platform. Does not want to receive fantasy, horror, erotica, children's books, screenplays, poetry or short stories.

How to Contact Query with SASE. Submit outline/proposal, synopsis, 3 sample chapters, author bio.E-queries preferred. No phone queries. All queries considered, but the agency only replies if interested. Accepts simultaneous submissions. Responds in 2 months to queries. Responds in 2 months to mss. Obtains most new clients through solicitations, conferences.

Terms Agent receives 15% commission on domestic sales. Agent receives 20% commission on foreign sales. Offers written contract; 30-day notice must be given to terminate contract.

Recent Sales *Intuitive Parenting*, by Debra Snyder, Ph.D. (Beyond Words); *The Confidence Trap,* by Russ Harris (Penguin); *The Never Cold Call Again Toolkit,* by Frank Rumbauskas, Jr. (Wiley); *Thank You for Firing Me*, by Candace Reed and Kitty Martini (Sterling); *The Wal-Mart Cure: Ten Lifesaving Supplements for Under $10* (Sourcebooks).

Tips "If you're fortunate enough to find an agent who answers your query and asks for a printed manuscript, always include a letter and cover page containing your name, physical address, e-mail address and phone number. Be professional!"

HAROLD OBER ASSOCIATES

425 Madison Ave., New York NY 10017. (212)759-8600. Fax: (212)759-9428. Website: www.haroldober.com. **Contact:** Craig Tenney. Member of AAR. Represents 250 clients. 10% of clients are new/unpublished writers. Currently handles: nonfiction books 35%, novels 50%, juvenile books 15%.

- Mr. Elwell was previously with Elwell & Weiser.

Member Agents Phyllis Westberg; Pamela Malpas; Craig Tenney (few new clients, mostly Ober backlist); Jake Elwell.

Represents nonfiction books, novels, juvenile. "We consider all subjects/genres of fiction and nonfiction."

"We consider all subjects/genres of fiction and nonfiction."

How to Contact Submit concise query letter addressed to a specific agent with the first five pages of the manuscript or proposal and SASE. Responds as promptly as possible. Obtains most new clients through recommendations from others.

Terms Agent receives 15% commission on domestic sales. Agent receives 20% commission on foreign sales. Charges clients for photocopying and express mail/package services.

OBJECTIVE ENTERTAINMENT

265 Canal St., Suite 603 B, New York NY 10013. (212)431-5454. Fax: (917)464.6394. E-mail: ej@objectiveent.com. Website: www.objectiveent.com. **Contact:** Elizabeth Joté.

Member Agents Jarred Weisfeld; Ian Kleinert, IK@objectiveent.com; Brendan Deneen. Brendan@objectiveent.com (novelists and screenwriters for publishing & film/television, as well as producing select feature film and television projects); Fred Borden, Fred@objectiveent.com (fiction and nonfiction related to Middle Eastern politics, sports - especially mixed martial arts - popular culture, and film); Elizabeth Jote, ej@objectiveent.com (commercial fiction (women's fiction, lad lit, thrillers, mysteries, young adult, urban fiction and multicultural books, narrative non-fiction, pop culture, current events, lifestyle books and graphic novels).

Represents nonfiction books, novels, movie, tv, feature.

How to Contact Query via e-mail. Send query only unless more information or materials are requested.

FIFI OSCARD AGENCY, INC.

110 W. 40th St., 21st Floor, New York NY 10018. (212)764-1100. Fax: (212)840-5019. E-mail: agency@fifioscard.com. Website: www.fifioscard.com. **Contact:** Literary Department. Signatory of WGA.

Member Agents Peter Sawyer; Carmen La Via; Kevin McShane; Carolyn French.

Represents nonfiction books, novels, stage plays. **Considers these nonfiction areas:** business, finance, history, religion, science, sports, womens, African American; biography; body/mind/spirit; health; lifestyle; cookbooks.

How to Contact Query through online submission form preferred, though snail mail queries are acceptable. *No unsolicited mss.* Responds in 2 weeks to queries.

Terms Agent receives 15% commission on domestic sales. Agent receives 20% commission on foreign sales. Agent receives 10% commission on film sales. Charges clients for photocopying expenses.

PARAVIEW, INC.

40 Florence Circle, Bracey VA 23919. Phone/Fax: (434)636-4138. E-mail: lhagan@paraview.com. Website: www.paraview.com. **Contact:** Lisa Hagan. Represents 75 clients. 15% of clients are new/unpublished writers. Currently handles: nonfiction books 100%.

Represents nonfiction books. **Considers these nonfiction areas:** agriculture horticulture, newage, animals, anthropology, art, biography, business, cooking, current affairs, education, ethnic, gay, government, health, history, how to, humor, language, memoirs, military, money, multicultural, nature, philosophy, popular culture, psychology, recreation, regional, religion, science, self help, sex, sociology, spirituality, travel, true crime, womens, Americana; creative nonfiction. This agency specializes in business, science, gay/lesbian, spiritual, New Age, and self-help nonfiction.

O→ This agency specializes in business, science, gay/lesbian, spiritual, New Age, and self-help nonfiction.

How to Contact Submit query, synopsis, author bio via e-mail. Responds in 1 month to queries. Responds in 3 months to mss. Obtains most new clients through Recommendations from editors and current clients.

Terms Agent receives 15% commission on domestic sales. Agent receives 20% commission on foreign sales.

Writers Conferences BookExpo America; London Book Fair; E3--Electronic Entertainment Exposition.

Tips "New writers should have their work edited, critiqued, and carefully reworked prior to submission. First contact should be via e-mail."

PARK LITERARY GROUP, LLC

270 Lafayette St., Suite 1504, New York NY 10012. (212)691-3500. Fax: (212)691-3540. Website: www.parkliterary.com.

- Prior to their current positions, Ms. Park and Ms. O'Keefe were literary agents at Sanford J. Greenburger Associates. Prior to 1994, she was a practicing attorney.

Member Agents Theresa Park (plot-driven fiction and serious nonfiction); Abigail Koons (quirky, edgy and commercial fiction, as well as superb thrillers and mysteries; adventure and travel narrative nonfiction, exceptional memoirs, popular science, history, politics and art).

Represents nonfiction books, novels. The Park Literary Group represents fiction and nonfiction with a boutique approach: an emphasis on servicing a relatively small number of clients, with the highest professional standards and focused personal attention. Does not want to receive poetry or screenplays.

O→ The Park Literary Group represents fiction and nonfiction with a boutique approach: an emphasis on servicing a relatively small number of clients, with the highest professional standards and focused personal attention. Does not want to receive poetry or screenplays.

How to Contact Query with SASE. Submit synopsis, 1-3 sample chapters, SASE. Send all submissions through the mail. Responds in 4-6 weeks to queries.

THE RICHARD PARKS AGENCY

Box 693, Salem NY 12865. (518)854-9466. Fax: (518)854-9466. E-mail: rp@richardparksagency.com. Website: www.richardparksagency.com. **Contact:** Richard Parks. Member of AAR. Currently handles: nonfiction books 55%, novels 40%, story collections 5%.

Represents nonfiction books, novels. **Considers these nonfiction areas:** crafts, animals, anthropology, art, biography, business, child, cooking, current affairs, ethnic, gardening, gay, government, health, history, how to, humor, language, memoirs, military, money, music, nature, popular culture, psychology, science, self help, sociology, film, travel, womens. Actively seeking nonfiction. Considers fiction by referral only. Does not want to receive unsolicited material.

O→ Actively seeking nonfiction. Considers fiction by referral only. Does not want to receive unsolicited material.

How to Contact Query with SASE. Other Responds in 2 weeks to queries. Obtains most new clients through recommendations/referrals.

Terms Agent receives 15% commission on domestic sales. Agent receives 20% commission on foreign sales. Charges clients for photocopying or any unusual expense incurred at the writer's request.

KATHI J. PATON LITERARY AGENCY

P.O. Box 2240 Radio City Station, New York NY 10101. (212)265-6586. E-mail: kjplitbiz@optonline.net. **Contact:** Kathi Paton. Currently handles: nonfiction books 85%, novels 15%.

Represents nonfiction books, novels, short story collections, book-based film rights. **Considers these nonfiction areas:** business, child, humor, money, personal investing, nature, psychology, religion, personal investing.**Considers these fiction areas:** literary, mainstream, multicultural, short stories. This agency specializes in adult nonfiction.

O→ This agency specializes in adult nonfiction.

How to Contact Accepts e-mail queries only. Accepts simultaneous submissions. Obtains most new clients through recommendations from current clients.

Terms Agent receives 15% commission on domestic sales. Agent receives 20% commission on foreign sales. Offers written contract. Charges clients for photocopying.

Writers Conferences Attends major regional panels, seminars and conferences.

PAVILION LITERARY MANAGEMENT

660 Massachusetts Ave., Suite 4, Boston MA 02118. (617)792-5218. E-mail: query@pavilionliterary.com; jeff@pavilionliterary.com. Website: www.pavilionliterary.com. **Contact:** Jeff Kellogg.

- Prior to his current position, Mr. Kellogg was a literary agent with The Stuart Agency, and an acquiring editor with HarperCollins.

Represents nonfiction books, novels, memoir. **Considers these nonfiction areas:** biography, computers, health, history, military, multicultural, nature, psychology, science, sports, travel, neuroscience, medicine, physics/astrophysics. **Considers these fiction areas:** adventure, fantasy, juvenile, mystery, thriller, general fiction, genre-blending fiction. "We are presently accepting fiction submissions only from previously published authors and/or by client referral. Nonfiction projects, specifically narrative nonfiction and cutting-edge popular science from experts in their respective fields, are most welcome."

"We are presently accepting fiction submissions only from previously published authors and/or by client referral. Nonfiction projects, specifically narrative nonfiction and cutting-edge popular science from experts in their respective fields, are most welcome."

How to Contact Query first by e-mail (no attachments). Your subject line should specify fiction or nonfiction and include the title of the work. If submitting nonfiction, include a book proposal (no longer than 75 pages), with sample chapters.

PEARSON, MORRIS & BELT

3000 Connecticut Ave., NW, Suite 317, Washington DC 20008. (202)723-6088. E-mail: dpm@morrisbelt.com; llb@morrisbelt.com. Website: www.morrisbelt.com.

- Prior to their current positions, Ms. Belt and Ms. Morris were agents with Adler & Robin Books, Inc.

Member Agents Laura Belt (nonfiction and computer books); Djana Pearson Morris (fiction, nonfiction, and computer books. Her favorite subjects are self-help, narrative nonfiction, African-American fiction and nonfiction, health and fitness, women's fiction, technology and parenting).

Represents nonfiction books, novels, computer books. This agency specializes in nonfiction, computer books and exceptional fiction. Does not want to receive poetry, children's literature or screenplays. Regarding fiction, this agency does not accept science fiction, thrillers or mysteries.

This agency specializes in nonfiction, computer books and exceptional fiction. Does not want to receive poetry, children's literature or screenplays. Regarding fiction, this agency does not accept science fiction, thrillers or mysteries.

How to Contact Query with SASE. Submit proposal (nonfiction); detailed synopsis and 2-3 sample chapters (fiction). Only query with a finished ms. Accepts e-mail queries but no attachments. Responds in 6-8 weeks to queries. Obtains most new clients through recommendations from others, solicitations.

Tips "Many of our books come from ideas and proposals we generate in-house. We retain a proprietary interest in and control of all ideas we create and proposals we write."

PELHAM LITERARY AGENCY

2451 Royal St. James Drive, El Cajon CA 92019-4408. (619)447-4468. E-mail: jmeals@pelhamliterary.com. Website: pelhamliterary.com. **Contact:** Jim Meals. Currently handles: nonfiction books 10%, novels 90%.

- Before becoming agents, both Mr. Pelham and Mr. Meals were writers.

Member Agents Howard Pelham; Jim Meals.

Represents nonfiction books, novels. "Every manuscript that comes to our agency receives a careful reading and assessment. When a writer submits a promising manuscript, we work extensively with the author until the work is ready for marketing."

"Every manuscript that comes to our agency receives a careful reading and assessment. When a writer submits a promising manuscript, we work extensively with the author until the work is ready for marketing."

How to Contact Query by mail or e-mail first; do not send unsolicited mss.

Terms Agent receives 15% commission on domestic sales. Offers written contract. Charges for photocopying and postage.

Tips "Only phone if it's necessary."

L. PERKINS ASSOCIATES

5800 Arlington Ave., Riverdale NY 10471. (718)543-5344. Fax: (718)543-5354. E-mail: lperkinsagency@yahoo.com. **Contact:** Lori Perkins, Amy Stout (jrlperkinsagency@yahoo.com). Member of AAR.

Represents 90 clients. 10% of clients are new/unpublished writers.

- Ms. Perkins has been an agent for 20 years. She is also the author of *The Insider's Guide to Getting an Agent* (Writer's Digest Books), as well as three other nonfiction books. She has also edited two anthologies.

Represents nonfiction books, novels. **Considers these nonfiction areas:** popular culture. **Considers these fiction areas:** erotica, fantasy, horror, literary, dark, science. Most of Ms. Perkins' clients write both fiction and nonfiction. This combination keeps my clients publishing for years. I am also a published author, so I know what it takes to write a good book. Actively seeking a Latino *Gone With the Wind* and *Waiting to Exhale*, and urban ethnic horror. Does not want to receive anything outside of the above categories (westerns, romance, etc.).

Most of Ms. Perkins' clients write both fiction and nonfiction. This combination keeps my clients publishing for years. I am also a published author, so I know what it takes to write a good book. Actively seeking a Latino *Gone With the Wind* and *Waiting to Exhale*, and urban ethnic horror. Does not want to receive anything outside of the above categories (westerns, romance, etc.).

How to Contact Query with SASE. Accepts simultaneous submissions. Responds in 12 weeks to queries. Responds in 3-6 months to mss. Obtains most new clients through recommendations from others, solicitations, conferences.

Terms Agent receives 15% commission on domestic sales. Agent receives 20% commission on foreign sales. No written contract. Charges clients for photocopying.

Writers Conferences San Diego State University Writers' Conference; NECON; BookExpo America; World Fantasy Convention.

Tips Research your field and contact professional writers' organizations to see who is looking for what. Finish your novel before querying agents. Read my book, *An Insider's Guide to Getting an Agent*, to get a sense of how agents operate. Read agent blogs - litsoup.blogspot.com and missnark.blogspot.com.

PFD NEW YORK

34-43 Russell St., London WC2B 5HA United Kingdom. (917)256-0707. Fax: (212)685-9635. Website: www.pfdny.com. **Contact:** Submissions Department.

- Prior to his current position, Mr. Reiter worked at IMG; Ms. Pagnamenta was with the Wylie Agency.

Member Agents Zoe Pagnamenta (U.S. authors), ajump@pfdgroup.com; Mark Reiter (U.S. authors), mreiter@pfdgroup.com.

Represents nonfiction books, novels, short story collections, if the author has other written works, poetry. This agency has offices in New York as well as the United Kingdom.

This agency has offices in New York as well as the United Kingdom.

How to Contact Query with SASE. Submit proposal package, synopsis, 2-3 sample chapters, publishing history, author bio, cover letter.Submit via snail mail. See online submission guidelines for more information. Responds in 1 month to queries. Obtains most new clients through recommendations from others, solicitations.

ALISON J. PICARD, LITERARY AGENT

P.O. Box 2000, Cotuit MA 02635. Phone/Fax: (508)477-7192. E-mail: ajpicard@aol.com. **Contact:** Alison Picard.Represents 48 clients. 30% of clients are new/unpublished writers. Currently handles: nonfiction books 40%, novels 40%, juvenile books 20%.

- Prior to becoming an agent, Ms. Picard was an assistant at a literary agency in New York.

Represents nonfiction books, novels, juvenile. **Considers these nonfiction areas:** juvenile, newage, young, animals, biography, business, child, cooking, current affairs, education, ethnic, gay, government, health, history, how to, humor, memoirs, military, money, multicultural, nature, popular culture, psychology, religion, science, self help, travel, true crime, womens. **Considers these fiction areas:** contemporary, glitz, newage, psychic, adventure, detective, erotica, ethnic, family, feminist, gay, historical, horror, humor, juvenile, literary, mainstream, multicultural, mystery, picture books, romance, sports, thriller, young. "Many of my clients have come to me from big agencies, where they felt overlooked or ignored. I communicate freely with my clients and offer a lot of career advice, suggestions for revising manuscripts, etc. If I believe in a project, I will submit it to a dozen or more publishers, unlike some agents who give up after four or five rejections." No science fiction/fantasy, Western, poetry, plays or articles.

"Many of my clients have come to me from big agencies, where they felt overlooked or ignored. I communicate freely with my clients and offer a lot of career advice, suggestions for revising manuscripts, etc. If I believe in a project, I will submit it to a dozen or more publishers, unlike some agents who give up after four or five rejections." No science fiction/fantasy, Western, poetry, plays or articles.

How to Contact Query with SASE. Accepts simultaneous submissions. Responds in 2 weeks to queries. Responds in 4 months to mss. Obtains most new clients through recommendations from others, solicitations.

Terms Agent receives 15% commission on domestic sales. Agent receives 20% commission on foreign sales. Offers written contract, binding for 1 year; 1-week notice must be given to terminate contract.
Recent Sales *Zitface*, by Emily Ormand (Marshall Cavendish); *Totally Together*, by Stephanie O'Dea (Running Press); *The Ultimate Slow Cooker Cookbook*, by Stephanie O'Dea (Hyperion); *Two Untitled Cookbooks*, by Erin Chase (St. Martin's Press); *A Journal of the Flood Year*, by David Ely (Portobello Books -- United Kingdom, L'Ancora -- Italy); *A Mighty Wall*, by John Foley (Llewellyn/Flux); *Jelly's Gold*, by David Housewright (St. Martin's Press).
Tips "Please don't send material without sending a query first via mail or e-mail. I don't accept phone or fax queries. Always enclose an SASE with a query."

PINDER LANE & GARON-BROOKE ASSOCIATES, LTD.

159 W. 53rd St., Suite 14C, New York NY 10019. Member of AAR. Signatory of WGA.
Member Agents Robert Thixton, pinderl@rcn.com; Dick Duane, pinderl@rcn.com.
Represents This agency specializes in mainstream fiction and nonfiction. Does not want to receive screenplays, TV series teleplays, or dramatic plays.

- ⊶ This agency specializes in mainstream fiction and nonfiction. Does not want to receive screenplays, TV series teleplays, or dramatic plays.

How to Contact Query with SASE. *No unsolicited mss.* Obtains most new clients through referrals.
Terms Agent receives 15% commission on domestic sales. Agent receives 30% commission on foreign sales. Offers written contract.

PIPPIN PROPERTIES, INC.

155 E. 38th St., Suite 2H, New York NY 10016. (212)338-9310. Fax: (212)338-9579. E-mail: info@pippinproperties.com. Website: www.pippinproperties.com. **Contact:** Holly McGhee. Represents 40 clients. Currently handles: juvenile books 100%.

- Prior to becoming an agent, Ms. McGhee was an editor for 7 years and in book marketing for 4 years. Prior to becoming an agent, Ms. van Beek worked in children's book editorial for 4 years.

Member Agents Holly McGhee; Emily van Beek; Samantha Cosentino.
Represents juvenile. "We are strictly a children's literary agency devoted to the management of authors and artists in all media. We are small and discerning in choosing our clientele." Actively seeking middle-grade and young-adult novels.

- ⊶ "We are strictly a children's literary agency devoted to the management of authors and artists in all media. We are small and discerning in choosing our clientele." Actively seeking middle-grade and young-adult novels.

How to Contact Query via e-mail. Include a synopsis of the work(s), your background and/or publishing history, and anything else you think is relevant. Accepts simultaneous submissions. Responds in 3 weeks to queries if interested. Responds in 10 weeks to mss. Obtains most new clients through recommendations from others.
Terms Agent receives 15% commission on domestic sales. Agent receives 25% commission on foreign sales. Offers written contract; 30-day notice must be given to terminate contract. Charges for color copying and UPS/FedEx.
Tips "Please do not start calling after sending a submission."

ALICKA PISTEK LITERARY AGENCY, LLC

302A W. 12th St., #124, New York NY 10014. Website: www.apliterary.com. **Contact:** Alicka Pistek. Represents 15 clients. 50% of clients are new/unpublished writers. Currently handles: nonfiction books 60%, novels 40%.

- Prior to opening her agency, Ms. Pistek worked at ICM and as an agent at Nicholas Ellison, Inc.

Represents nonfiction books, novels. **Considers these nonfiction areas:** animals, anthropology, biography, child, current affairs, government, health, history, how to, language, memoirs, military, money, nature, psychology, science, self help, travel, creative nonfiction. **Considers these fiction areas:** detective, ethnic, family, historical, literary, mainstream, mystery, romance, thriller. Does not want to receive fantasy, science fiction or Western's.

- ⊶ Does not want to receive fantasy, science fiction or Western's.

How to Contact Send e-query to info@apliterary.com. Include name, address, e-mail, and phone number, title, wordcount, genre of book, a brief synopsis, and relevant biographical information. Accepts simultaneous submissions. Responds in 2 months to queries. Will only respond if interested. Responds in 8 weeks to mss.
Terms Agent receives 15% commission on domestic sales. Agent receives 20% commission on foreign sales. Offers written contract. This agency charges for photocopying more than 40 pages and international postage.
Tips "Be sure you are familiar with the genre you are writing in and learn standard procedures for submitting your work. A good query will go a long way."

HELEN F. PRATT INC.

1165 Fifth Ave., New York NY 10029. (212)722-5081. Fax: (212)722-8569. E-mail: hfpratt@verizon.net. **Contact:** Helen F. Pratt. Member of AAR. Currently handles: other 100% illutsrated books and nonfiction.

Member Agents Helen Pratt (illustrated books, fashion/decorative design nonfiction).

Represents nonfiction books, illustrated books.

How to Contact Query with SASE. Include illustrations if possible.

AARON M. PRIEST LITERARY AGENCY

708 Third Ave., 23rd Floor, New York NY 10017-4103. (212)818-0344. Fax: (212)573-9417. Website: www.aaronpriest.com. Member of AAR. Currently handles: nonfiction books 25%, novels 75%.

Member Agents Aaron Priest, querypriest@aaronpriest.com (thrillers, commercial fiction, biographies); Lisa Erbach Vance, queryvance@aaronpriest.com (general fiction, international fiction, thrillers, upmarket women's fiction, historical fiction, narrative nonfiction, memoir); Lucy Childs, querychilds@aaronpriest.com (literary and commercial fiction, memoir, edgy women's fiction); Nicole Kenealy, querykenealy@aaronpriest.com (young adult fiction, narrative nonfiction, how-to, political, and pop-culture, literary and commercial fiction, specifically dealing with social and cultural issues).

Represents Does not want to receive poetry, screenplays or sci-fi.

- Does not want to receive poetry, screenplays or sci-fi.

How to Contact Query one of the agents using the appropriate e-mail. "Please do not submit to more than one agent at this agency. We urge you to check our website and consider each agent's emphasis before submitting. Your query letter should be about one page long and describe your work as well as your background. You may also paste the first chapter of your work in the body of the e-mail. Do not send attachments." Accepts simultaneous submissions. Responds in 3 weeks, only if interested.

Terms Agent receives 15% commission on domestic sales. This agency charges for photocopying and postage expenses.

Recent Sales *Divine Justice*, by David Baldacci, *The White Mary*, by Kira Salak, *Long Lost*, by Harlan Coben, *An Accidental Light*, by Elizabeth Diamond, *Trust No One*, by Gregg Hurwitz, *Power Down*, by Ben Coes.

PROSPECT AGENCY LLC

285 Fifth Ave., PMB 445, Brooklyn NY 11215. (718)788-3217. E-mail: esk@prospectagency.com. Website: www.prospectagency.com. **Contact:** Emily Sylvan Kim. Represents 15 clients. 50% of clients are new/unpublished writers. Currently handles: novels 66%, juvenile books 33%.

- Prior to starting her agency, Ms. Kim briefly attended law school and worked for another literary agency.

Member Agents Emily Sylvan Kim; Becca Stumpf (adult and YA literary, mainstream fiction; nonfiction interests include narrative nonfiction, journalistic perspectives, fashion, film studies, travel, art, and informed analysis of cultural phenomena. She has a special interest in aging in America and environmental issues); Rachel Orr (fiction and nonfiction, particularly picture books, beginning readers, chapter books, middle-grade, YA novels).

Represents nonfiction books, novels, juvenile. **Considers these nonfiction areas:** art, biography, history, juvenile nonfiction, law, memoirs, popular culture, politics, science, travel, prescriptive guides. **Considers these fiction areas:** adventure, detective, erotica, ethnic, family, juvenile, literary, mainstream, mystery, picture books, romance, science, thriller, western, young. "We are currently looking for the next generation of writers to shape the literary landscape. Our clients receive professional and knowledgeable representation. We are committed to offering skilled editorial advice and advocating our clients in the marketplace." Actively seeking romance, literary fiction, and young adult submissions. Does not want to receive poetry, short stories, textbooks, or most nonfiction.

- "We are currently looking for the next generation of writers to shape the literary landscape. Our clients receive professional and knowledgeable representation. We are committed to offering skilled editorial advice and advocating our clients in the marketplace." Actively seeking romance, literary fiction, and young adult submissions. Does not want to receive poetry, short stories, textbooks, or most nonfiction.

How to Contact Upload outline and 3 sample chapters to the Web site. Accepts simultaneous submissions. Responds in 3 weeks to queries. Responds in 1 month to mss. Obtains most new clients through recommendations from others, conferences, unsolicited mss.

Terms Agent receives 15% commission on domestic sales. Agent receives 20% commission on foreign sales. Offers written contract.

Recent Sales *BADD*, by Tim Tharp (Knopf); *Six*, by Elizabeth Batten-Carew (St. Martin's); *Rocky Road*, by Rose Kent (Knopf); *Mating Game*, by Janice Maynard (NAL); *Golden Delicious*, by Aaron Hawkins (Houghton Mifflin Harcourt); *Damaged*, by Pamela Callow (Mira); *Seduced by Shadows*, by Jessica Slade (NAL), *Identity of Ultraviolet*, by Jake Bell (Scholastic); *Quackenstein*, by Sudipta Bardhan-Quallen

(Abrams); *Betraying Season*, by Marissa Doyle (Holt); *Sex on the Beach*, by Susan Lyons (Berkley), more.
Writers Conferences "Please see our website for a complete list of attended conferences."

SUSAN ANN PROTTER, LITERARY AGENT

320 Central Park West, Suite 12E, New York NY 10025. Website: SusanAnnProtter.com. **Contact:** Susan Protter. Member of AAR. Other memberships include Authors Guild.

- Prior to opening her agency, Ms. Protter was associate director of subsidiary rights at Harper & Row Publishers.

Represents Writers must have a book-length project or ms that is ready to sell. Actively seeking for a limited number of quality new clients writing mysteries, health, science and medical. Nonfiction must be by authors with a platform and be new and original concepts by established professionals. Does not want westerns, romance, children's books, young adult novels, screenplays, plays, poetry, Star Wars, or Star Trek.

O→ Writers must have a book-length project or ms that is ready to sell. Actively seeking for a limited number of quality new clients writing mysteries, health, science and medical. Nonfiction must be by authors with a platform and be new and original concepts by established professionals. Does not want westerns, romance, children's books, young adult novels, screenplays, plays, poetry, Star Wars, or Star Trek.

How to Contact Query by snail mail are preferable; include SASE.
Terms Charges 15% commission on all sales.

PSALTIS LITERARY

Post Office: Park West Finance, P.O. Box 20736, New York NY 10025. E-mail: psaltsis@mpsaltisliterary.com. Website: www.mpsaltis.com/psaltisliterary.htm. **Contact:** Michael Psaltis. Member of AAR. Represents 30-40 clients.
Represents nonfiction books, novels. **Considers these nonfiction areas:** biography, business, cooking, health, history, memoirs, popular culture, psychology, science. **Considers these fiction areas:** mainstream.
How to Contact Query only by e-mail. Unrequested manuscripts will not be read. Responds only to queries of interest.
Terms Agent receives 15% commission on domestic sales. Agent receives 20% commission on foreign sales. Offers written contract.

P.S Literary Agency

520 Kerr St., #20033, Oakville ON L6K 3C7 Canada. E-mail: query@psliterary.com. Website: www.psliterary.com. **Contact:** Curtis Russell. Represents 8 clients. 25% of clients are new/unpublished writers. Currently handles: nonfiction books 50%, novels 50%.
Represents nonfiction books, novels, juvenile. **Considers these nonfiction areas:** biography, business, child, cooking, current affairs, government, health, how to, humor, memoirs, military, money, nature, popular culture, science, self help, sports, true crime, womens. **Considers these fiction areas:** adventure, detective, erotica, ethnic, family, historical, horror, humor, juvenile, literary, mainstream, mystery, picture books, romance, sports, thriller, young, womens. "What makes our agency distinct: We take on a small number of clients per year in order to provide focused, hands-on representation. We pride ourselves in providing industry leading client service." Does not want to receive poetry or screenplays.

O→ "What makes our agency distinct: We take on a small number of clients per year in order to provide focused, hands-on representation. We pride ourselves in providing industry leading client service." Does not want to receive poetry or screenplays.

How to Contact Query via mail or e-mail. Prefers e-mail. Submit synopsis, author bio. Accepts simultaneous submissions. Responds in 6 weeks to queries. Responds in 6 weeks to mss. Obtains most new clients through solicitations.
Terms Agent receives 15% commission on domestic sales. Agent receives 25% commission on foreign sales. Offers written contract; 30-day notice must be given to terminate contract. "This agency charges for postage/messenger services only if a project is sold."
Tips "Please review our Web site for the most up-to-date submission guidelines."

JOANNA PULCINI LITERARY MANAGEMENT

E-mail: info@jplm.com. Website: www.jplm.com. **Contact:** Joanna Pulcini.
Represents "JPLM is not accepting submissions at this time; however, I do encourage those seeking representation to read the 'Advice to Writers' essay on our Web site for some guidance on finding an agent."

O→ "JPLM is not accepting submissions at this time; however, I do encourage those seeking representation to read the 'Advice to Writers' essay on our Web site for some guidance on finding an agent."

How to Contact Do not query this agency until they open their client list.

THE QUADRIVIUM GROUP

7512 Dr. Phillips Boulevard, Suite #50-229, Orlando FL 32819. (407)516-1857. E-mail: SteveBlount@TheQuadriviumGroup.com. Website: www.thequadriviumgroup.com. **Contact:** Steve Blount. Represents 20-30 clients.

Represents "This agency specializes in Christian titles." "Open to a limited number of unpublished authors (with credentials, platform, compelling story/idea), and to new clients (mostly by referral). General agent. Handles Christian and general nonfiction and fiction for all ages, gift books, crossover books."

- "This agency specializes in Christian titles." "Open to a limited number of unpublished authors (with credentials, platform, compelling story/idea), and to new clients (mostly by referral). General agent. Handles Christian and general nonfiction and fiction for all ages, gift books, crossover books."

How to Contact Query with SASE.

Tips "Recognized in the Industry. Other services offered: consulting on book sales and distribution."

QUEEN LITERARY AGENCY

850 Seventh Ave., Suite 704, New York NY 10019. (212)974-8333. Fax: (212)974-8347. Website: www.queenliterary.com. **Contact:** Lisa Queen.

- Prior to her current position, Ms. Queen was a former publishing executive and most recently head of IMG Worldwide's literary division.

Represents nonfiction books, novels. Ms. Queen's specialties: While our agency represents a wide range of nonfiction titles, we have a particular interest in business books, food writing, science and popular psychology, as well as books by well-known chefs, radio and television personalities and sports figures.

- Ms. Queen's specialties: While our agency represents a wide range of nonfiction titles, we have a particular interest in business books, food writing, science and popular psychology, as well as books by well-known chefs, radio and television personalities and sports figures.

How to Contact Query with SASE.

Recent Sales *The Female Brain*, by Louann Brizendine; *Does the Noise in My Head Bother You?* by Steven Tyler; *What I Cannot Change*, by LeAnn Rimes and Darrell Brown.

QUICKSILVER BOOKS: LITERARY AGENTS

508 Central Park Ave., #5101, Scarsdale NY 10583. Phone/Fax: (914)722-4664. E-mail: quickbooks@optonline.net. Website: www.quicksilverbooks.com. **Contact:** Bob Silverstein. Represents 50 clients. 50% of clients are new/unpublished writers. Currently handles: nonfiction books 75%, novels 25%.

- Prior to opening his agency, Mr. Silverstein served as senior editor at Bantam Books and Dell Books/Delacorte Press.

Represents nonfiction books, novels. **Considers these nonfiction areas:** newage, anthropology, biography, business, child, cooking, current affairs, ethnic, health, history, how to, language, memoirs, nature, popular culture, psychology, religion, science, self help, sociology, sports, true crime, womens. **Considers these fiction areas:** glitz, adventure, mystery, thriller. This agency specializes in literary and commercial mainstream fiction and nonfiction, especially psychology, New Age, holistic healing, consciousness, ecology, environment, spirituality, reference, self-help, cookbooks and narrative nonfiction. Does not want to receive science fiction, pornography, poetry or single-spaced mss.

- This agency specializes in literary and commercial mainstream fiction and nonfiction, especially psychology, New Age, holistic healing, consciousness, ecology, environment, spirituality, reference, self-help, cookbooks and narrative nonfiction. Does not want to receive science fiction, pornography, poetry or single-spaced mss.

How to Contact Query with SASE. Authors are expected to supply SASE for return of ms and for query letter responses. Accepts simultaneous submissions. Responds in 2 weeks to queries. Responds in 1 month to mss. Obtains most new clients through recommendations, listings in sourcebooks, solicitations, workshop participation.

Terms Agent receives 15% commission on domestic sales. Agent receives 20% commission on foreign sales. Offers written contract.

Recent Sales *Simply Mexican*, by Lourdes Castro (Ten Speed Press); *Indian Vegan Cooking*, by Madhu Gadia (Perigee/Penguin); *Selling Luxury*, by Robin Lent & Genevieve Tour (Wiley); *Get the Job You Want, Even When No One's Hiring*, by Ford R. Myers (Wiley); *Matrix Meditations*, by Victor & Kooch Daniels (Inner Traditions Bear & Co.)

Writers Conferences National Writers Union.

Tips "Write what you know. Write from the heart. Publishers print, authors sell."

SUSAN RABINER LITERARY AGENCY, INC., THE

315 W. 39th St., Suite 1501, New York NY 10018. (212)279-0316. Fax: (212)279-0932. E-mail: susan@rabiner.net. Website: www.rabinerlit.com. **Contact:** Susan Rabiner.

- Prior to becoming an agent, Ms. Rabiner was editorial director of Basic Books. She is also the co-author of *Thinking Like Your Editor: How to Write Great Serious Nonfiction and Get it Published* (W.W. Norton).

Member Agents Susan Rabiner; Sydelle Kramer; Helena Schwarz; Holly Bemiss. See the Web site for individual agent e-mails.

Represents nonfiction books, novels, textbooks. **Considers these nonfiction areas:** biography, business, education, government, health, history, philosophy, psychology, religion, science, sociology, sports, biography, law/politics. "Representing narrative nonfiction and big-idea books - work that illuminates the past and the present." "I look for well-researched, topical books written by fully credentialed academics, journalists, and recognized public intellectuals with the power to stimulate public debate on a broad range of issues including the state of our economy, political discourse, history, science, and the arts."

O→ "Representing narrative nonfiction and big-idea books - work that illuminates the past and the present." "I look for well-researched, topical books written by fully credentialed academics, journalists, and recognized public intellectuals with the power to stimulate public debate on a broad range of issues including the state of our economy, political discourse, history, science, and the arts."

How to Contact Query by e-mail only, with cover letter and proposal for nonfiction. Accepts simultaneous submissions. Responds in 3 weeks to queries. Obtains most new clients through recommendations from others.

Terms Agent receives 15% commission on domestic sales. Agent receives 20% commission on foreign sales. Offers written contract; 1-month notice must be given to terminate contract.

LYNNE RABINOFF AGENCY

72-11 Austin St., No. 201, Forest Hills NY 11375. (718)459-6894. E-mail: Lynne@lynnerabinoff.com. **Contact:** Lynne Rabinoff.Represents 50 clients. 50% of clients are new/unpublished writers. Currently handles: nonfiction books 99%, novels 1%.

- Prior to becoming an agent, Ms. Rabinoff was in publishing and dealt with foreign rights.

Represents nonfiction books. **Considers these nonfiction areas:** anthropology, biography, business, current affairs, ethnic, government, history, memoirs, military, popular culture, psychology, religion, science, womens. "This agency specializes in history, political issues, current affairs and religion."

O→ "This agency specializes in history, political issues, current affairs and religion."

How to Contact Query with SASE. Submit proposal package, synopsis, 1 sample chapters, author bio. Responds in 3 weeks to queries. Responds in 1 month to mss. Obtains most new clients through recommendations from others.

Terms Agent receives 15% commission on domestic sales. Agent receives 20% commission on foreign sales. Offers written contract; 60-day notice must be given to terminate contract. This agency charges for postage.

Recent Sales *The Confrontation*, by Walid Phares (Palgrave); *Flying Solo*, by Robert Vaughn (Thomas Dunne); *Thugs*, by Micah Halpern (Thomas Nelson); *Size Sexy*, by Stella Ellis (Adams Media); *Cruel and Usual*, by Nonie Darwish (Thomas Nelson); *Now they Call Me Infidel*, by Nonie Darwish (Sentinel/Penguin); *34 Days*, by Avid Issacharoff (Palgrave).

RAINES & RAINES

103 Kenyon Road, Medusa NY 12120. (518)239-8311. Fax: (518)239-6029. **Contact:** Theron Raines (member of AAR); Joan Raines; Keith Korman.Represents 100 clients.

Represents nonfiction books, novels. **Considers these fiction areas:** adventure, detective, fantasy, historical, mystery, picture books, science, thriller, western.

How to Contact Query with SASE. Responds in 2 weeks to queries.

Terms Agent receives 15% commission on domestic sales. Agent receives 20% commission on foreign sales. Charges for photocopying.

RED SOFA LITERARY

2163 Grand Avenue, #2, St. Paul MN 55105. (651)224-6670. E-mail: dawn@redsofaliterary.com. Website: www.redsofaliterary.com. **Contact:** Dawn Frederick, Agent and Owner. Represents 10 clients. 50% of clients are new/unpublished writers. Currently handles: nonfiction books 97%, novels 2%, story collections 1%.

- Prior to her current position, Ms. Frederick spent five years at Sebastian Literary Agency.

Represents nonfiction books. **Considers these nonfiction areas:** crafts, animals, anthropology, cooking, current affairs, ethnic, gay, government, health, history, humor, popular culture, sociology, true crime,

womens.
How to Contact Query with SASE. Submit proposal package, synopsis, 3 sample chapters, author bio. Accepts simultaneous submissions. Responds in 3 weeks to queries. Responds in 6 weeks to mss. Obtains most new clients through recommendations from others, solicitations.
Terms Agent receives 15% commission on domestic sales. Agent receives 20% commission on foreign sales. Offers written contract. May charge a one-time $100 fee for partial reimbursement of postage and phone expenses incurred if the advance is below $15,000.
Writers Conferences SDSU Writers' Conference.
Tips "Truly research us. Don't just e-mail or snail mail blast us w/ your book idea. We receive so many, that it can become tedious reading queries we'd never represent to begin with. Look at the websites, guides like this one, online directories and more, before assuming every literary agent is wanting your book idea. Each agent has a vision of what he/she wants to represent, we're waiting for those specific book ideas to come our direction."

THE REDWOOD AGENCY

4300 SW 34th Avenue, Portland OR 97239. (503)219-9019. E-mail: info@redwoodagency.com. Website: www.redwoodagency.com. **Contact:** Catherine Fowler, founder. Adheres to AAR canon of ethics. Currently handles: nonfiction books 100%.

- Prior to becoming an agent, Ms. Fowler was an editor, subsidiary rights director and associate publisher for Doubleday, Simon & Schuster and Random House for her 20 years in NY Publishing. Content exec for web startups Excite and WebMD.

Represents nonfiction books, novels. **Considers these nonfiction areas:** business, cooking, health, humor, memoirs, nature, popular culture, psychology, self help, womens, narrative, parenting, aging, reference, lifestyle, cultural technology. **Considers these fiction areas:** literary, mainstream, suspense, women's, quirky. Along with our love of books and publishing, we have the desire and commitment to work with fun, interesting and creative people, to do so with respect and professionalism, but also with a sense of humor. Actively seeking high-quality, nonfiction works created for the general consumer market, as well as projects with the potential to become book series. Does not want to receive fiction. Do not send packages that require signature for delivery.

- Along with our love of books and publishing, we have the desire and commitment to work with fun, interesting and creative people, to do so with respect and professionalism, but also with a sense of humor. Actively seeking high-quality, nonfiction works created for the general consumer market, as well as projects with the potential to become book series. Does not want to receive fiction. Do not send packages that require signature for delivery.

How to Contact Query via e-mail only. Obtains most new clients through recommendations from others, solicitations.
Terms Offers written contract. Charges for copying and delivery charges, if any, as specified in author/agency agreement.

RED WRITING HOOD INK

2075 Attala Road 1990, Kosciusko MS 39090. (662)674-0636. Fax: (662)796-3095. E-mail: rwhi@bellsouth.net. Website: www.redwritinghoodink.net. **Contact:** Sheri Ables.Other memberships include adheres to AAR canon. Currently handles: nonfiction books 100%.

- Prior to her current position, Ms. Ables was an agent of the Williams Agency. In addition, she worked for an agency in Oregon from 1996-1997. Collectively, the staff of RWHI has more than 25 years experience in the publishing industry.

Member Agents Sheri Ables, agent; Terri Dunlap, literary assistant (terri@redwritinghoodink.net).
Represents nonfiction books. Biography, Children's, Crime & Thrillers, Entertainment, General Fiction, Health, History, Inspirationa, Mystery/Suspense, Romantic Fiction, General nonfiction, Self-help

- Biography, Children's, Crime & Thrillers, Entertainment, General Fiction, Health, History, Inspirationa, Mystery/Suspense, Romantic Fiction, General nonfiction, Self-help

How to Contact Send cover letter and 2-page synopsis only to e-mail. If mailing, include SASE.
Terms Agent receives 15% commission on domestic sales. Agent receives 20% commission on foreign sales.
Tips Writers: View submission guidelines prior to making contact.

HELEN REES LITERARY AGENCY

376 North St., Boston MA 02113-2013. (617)227-9014. Fax: (617)227-8762. E-mail: reesagency@reesagency.com. **Contact:** Joan Mazmanian, Ann Collette, Helen Rees, Lorin Rees. Member of AAR. Other memberships include PEN. Represents more than 100 clients. 50% of clients are new/unpublished writers. Currently handles: nonfiction books 60%, novels 40%.
Member Agents Ann Collette (literary fiction, women's studies, health, biography, history).
Represents nonfiction books, novels. **Considers these nonfiction areas:** biography, business, current

affairs, government, health, history, money, womens. **Considers these fiction areas:** historical, literary, mainstream, mystery, thriller.

How to Contact Query with SASE, outline, 2 sample chapters. No unsolicited e-mail submissions. No multiple submissions. Responds in 3-4 weeks to queries. Obtains most new clients through recommendations from others, conferences, submissions.

Terms Agent receives 15% commission on domestic sales. Agent receives 20% commission on foreign sales.

Recent Sales Sold more than 35 titles in the last year. *Get your Shipt Together*, by Capt. D. Michael Abrashoff; *Overpromise and Overdeliver*, by Rick Berrara; *Opacity*, by Joel Kurtzman; *America the Broke*, by Gerald Swanson; *Murder at the B-School*, by Jeffrey Cruikshank; *Bone Factory*, by Steven Sidor; *Father Said*, by Hal Sirowitz; *Winning*, by Jack Welch; *The Case for Israel*, by Alan Dershowitz; *As the Future Catches You*, by Juan Enriquez; *Blood Makes the Grass Grow Green*, by Johnny Rico; *DVD Movie Guide*, by Mick Martin and Marsha Porter; *Words that Work*, by Frank Luntz; *Stirring It Up*, by Gary Hirshberg; *Hot Spots*, by Martin Fletcher; *Andy Grove: The Life and Times of an American*, by Richard Tedlow; *Girls Most Likely To*, by Poonam Sharma.

REGAL LITERARY AGENCY

1140 Broadway, Penthouse, New York NY 10001. (212)684-7900. Fax: (212)684-7906. E-mail: info@regal-literary.com. Website: www.regal-literary.com. **Contact:** Barbara Marshall. Estab. 2002. Member of AAR. Represents 70 clients. 20% of clients are new/unpublished writers. Currently handles: nonfiction books 49%, novels 49%, poetry 2%.

- Prior to becoming agents, Mr. Regal was a musician; Ms. Reed was a magazine editor; Mr. Hoffman worked in the publishing industry in London.

Member Agents Joseph Regal (literary fiction, science, history, memoir); Bess Reed (literary fiction, narrative nonfiction, self-help); Lauren Pearson (literary fiction, commercial fiction, memoir, narrative nonfiction, thrillers, mysteries); Markus Hoffmann (foreign rights manager, literary fiction, mysteries, thrillers, international fiction, science, music). Michael Psaltis of Psaltis Literary also works with Regal Literary agents to form the Culinary Cooperative - a joint-venture agency dedicated to food writing, cookbooks, and all things related to cooking. Recent sales include *The Reverse Diet* (John Wiley & Sons).

Represents nonfiction books, novels, short story collections, novellas. **Considers these nonfiction areas:** anthropology, art, biography, business, cooking, current affairs, ethnic, gay, history, humor, language, memoirs, military, music, nature, photography, popular culture, psychology, religion, science, sports, translation, womens. **Considers these fiction areas:** comic, detective, ethnic, historical, literary, mystery, thriller, contemporary. "We have discovered more than a dozen successful literary novelists in the last 5 years. We are small, but are extraordinarily responsive to our writers. We are more like managers than agents, with an eye toward every aspect of our writers' careers, including publicity and other media." Actively seeking literary fiction and narrative nonfiction. Does not want romance, science fiction, horror, or screenplays.

- O→ We have discovered more than a dozen successful literary novelists in the last 5 years. We are small, but are extraordinarily responsive to our writers. We are more like managers than agents, with an eye toward every aspect of our writers' careers, including publicity and other media. Actively seeking literary fiction and narrative nonfiction. Does not want romance, science fiction, horror, or screenplays.

How to Contact Query with SASE. No phone calls. Submissions should consist of a one-page query letter detailing the book in question as well as the qualifications of the author. For fiction, submissions may also include the first ten pages of the novel or one short story from a collection. "We do not consider romance, science fiction, poetry, or screenplays. Accepts simultaneous submissions." Responds in 2-3 weeks to queries. Responds in 4-12 weeks to mss. Obtains most new clients through recommendations from others, unsolicited submissions.

Terms Agent receives 15% commission on domestic sales. Agent receives 20% commission on foreign sales. No written contract. Charges clients for typical/major office expenses, such as photocopying and foreign postage. No reading fees.

JODY REIN BOOKS, INC.

7741 S. Ash Ct., Centennial CO 80122. (303)694-4430. Fax: (303)694-0687. Website: www.jodyreinbooks.com. **Contact:** Winnefred Dollar. false Other memberships include Authors' Guild. Currently handles: nonfiction books 70%, novels 30%.

- Prior to opening her agency, Ms. Rein worked for 13 years as an acquisitions editor for Contemporary Books and as executive editor for Bantam/Doubleday/Dell and Morrow/Avon.

Represents nonfiction books, novels. **Considers these nonfiction areas:** business, child, current affairs, ethnic, government, history, humor, music, nature, popular culture, psychology, science, sociology, film, womens. **Considers these fiction areas:** literary, mainstream. This agency is no longer actively seeking clients.

O¬ This agency is no longer actively seeking clients.

Terms Agent receives 15% commission on domestic sales. Agent receives 25% commission on foreign sales. Agent receives 20% commission on film sales. Offers written contract. Charges clients for express mail, overseas expenses, photocopying mss.

Recent Sales *How to Remodel a Man*, by Bruce Cameron (St. Martin's Press); *8 Simple Rules for Dating My Teenage Daughter*, by Bruce Cameron (ABC/Disney); *Unbound*, by Dean King (Little, Brown); *Halfway to Heaven*, by Mark Obmascik (The Free Press); *The Rhino with Glue-On Shoes*, by Dr. Lucy Spelman (Random House); *When She Flew*, by Jennie Shortridge (NAL).

Tips "Do your homework before submitting. Make sure you have a marketable topic and the credentials to write about it. We want well-written books on fresh and original nonfiction topics that have broad appeal, as well as novels written by authors who have spent years developing their craft. Authors must be well established in their fields and have strong media experience."

THE AMY RENNERT AGENCY

98 Main St., #302, Tiburon CA 94920. E-mail: queries@amyrennert.com. Website: www.amyrennert.net. **Contact:** Amy Rennert.

Represents nonfiction books, novels. **Considers these nonfiction areas:** biography, health, history, memoirs, sports, lifestyle, narrative nonfiction. **Considers these fiction areas:** literary, mystery. "The Amy Rennert Agency specializes in books that matter. We provide career management for established and first-time authors, and our breadth of experience in many genres enables us to meet the needs of a diverse clientele."

O¬ "The Amy Rennert Agency specializes in books that matter. We provide career management for established and first-time authors, and our breadth of experience in many genres enables us to meet the needs of a diverse clientele."

How to Contact Query via e-mail or mail. For nonfiction, send cover letter and attach a Word file with proposal/first chapter. For fiction, send cover letter and attach file with 10-20 pages.

Tips "Due to the high volume of submissions, it is not possible to respond to each and every one. Please understand that we are only able to respond to queries that we feel may be a good fit with our agency."

JODIE RHODES LITERARY AGENCY

8840 Villa La Jolla Drive, Suite 315, La Jolla CA 92037-1957. **Contact:** Jodie Rhodes, president. Member of AAR. Represents 74 clients. 60% of clients are new/unpublished writers. Currently handles: nonfiction books 45%, novels 35%, juvenile books 20%.

- Prior to opening her agency, Ms. Rhodes was a university-level creative writing teacher, workshop director, published novelist, and vice president/media director at the N.W. Ayer Advertising Agency.

Member Agents Jodie Rhodes; Clark McCutcheon (fiction); Bob McCarter (nonfiction).

Represents nonfiction books, novels. **Considers these nonfiction areas:** biography, child, ethnic, government, health, history, memoirs, military, science, womens. **Considers these fiction areas:** ethnic, family, historical, literary, mainstream, mystery, thriller, young, womens. "Actively seeking witty, sophisticated women's books about career ambitions and relationships; edgy/trendy YA and teen books; narrative nonfiction on groundbreaking scientific discoveries, politics, economics, military and important current affairs by prominent scientists and academic professors." Does not want to receive erotica, horror, fantasy, romance, science fiction, religious/inspirational, or children's books (does accept young adult/teen).

O¬ "Actively seeking witty, sophisticated women's books about career ambitions and relationships; edgy/trendy YA and teen books; narrative nonfiction on groundbreaking scientific discoveries, politics, economics, military and important current affairs by prominent scientists and academic professors." Does not want to receive erotica, horror, fantasy, romance, science fiction, religious/inspirational, or children's books (does accept young adult/teen).

How to Contact Query with brief synopsis, first 30-50 pages, SASE. Do not call. Do not send complete ms unless requested. This agency does not return unrequested material weighing a pound or more that requires special postage. Include e-mail address with query. Accepts simultaneous submissions. Responds in 3 weeks to queries. Obtains most new clients through recommendations from others, agent sourcebooks.

Terms Agent receives 15% commission on domestic sales. Agent receives 20% commission on foreign sales. Offers written contract; 1-month notice must be given to terminate contract. Charges clients for fax, photocopying, phone calls, postage. Charges are itemized and approved by writers upfront.

Recent Sales Sold 42 titles in the last year. *The Ring*, by Kavita Daswani (HarperCollins); *Train to Trieste*, by Domnica Radulescu (Knopf); *A Year With Cats and Dogs*, by Margaret Hawkins (Permanent Press); *Silence and Silhouettes*, by Ryan Smithson (HarperCollins); *Internal Affairs*, by Constance Dial (Permanent Press); *How Math Rules the World*, by James Stein (HarperCollins); Diagnosis of Love, by

Maggie Martin (Bantam); Lies, Damn Lies, and Science, by Sherry Seethaler (Prentice Hall); Freaked, by Jeanne Dutton (HarperCollins); The Five Second Rule, by Anne Maczulak (Perseus Books); The Intelligence Wars, by Stephen O'Hern (Prometheus); Seducing the Spirits, by Louise Young (The Permanent Press), and more.

Tips "Think your book out before you write it. Do your research, know your subject matter intimately, and write vivid specifics, not bland generalities. Care deeply about your book. Don't imitate other writers. Find your own voice. We never take on a book we don't believe in, and we go the extra mile for our writers. We welcome talented, new writers."

JONNE RICCI LITERARY AGENCY

P.O. Box 13410, Palm Desert CA 92255. Website: jonnericciliteraryagency.net/. **Contact:** Jonne Ricci. Other memberships include Better Business Bureau of Southland (California), Follows AAR guidelines. Currently handles: novels, juvenile books.

Represents "We represent authors who have special writing skills and want to see their books published. We encourage first time writers to contact us. Our Agency is committed to finding new talent and we don't charge fees for reading or evaluating material. We urge you to learn more about our Agency. Explore our Webscape and see if your work fits with us."

- "Our agency represents writers of literary fiction. We are most interested in Crime, Mystery, Romance, Westerns, Thrillers and Adventure. We also specialize in Christian themes. If you feel your work fits with us, please send (in hard copy only, no submissions via e-mail) a query with Synopsis (3 pages or less) and the first few chapters (30 pages or less), all of which should be doubled spaced. SASE."

RICHARDS LITERARY AGENCY

P.O. Box 31-240, Milford, North Shore City 0741 New Zealand (64)(9)410-0209. E-mail: rla.richards@clear.net.nz. **Contact:** Ray Richards. Other memberships include NZALA. Represents 100 clients. 20% of clients are new/unpublished writers. Currently handles: nonfiction books 20%, novels 15%, story collections 5%, juvenile books 40%, scholarly books 5%, other 15% movie rights.

- Prior to opening his agency, Mr. Richards was a book publisher, managing director and vice chairman.

Represents We offer a high quality of experience, acceptances and client relationships.

- Does not want to receive short stories, articles or poetry.

How to Contact Submit outline/proposal.Do not send full ms until requested. Responds in 1 week to queries. Responds in 1 month to mss. Obtains most new clients through referrals.

Terms Agent receives 15% commission on domestic sales. Agent receives 20% commission on foreign sales. Offers written contract. Charges clients for overseas postage and photocopying.

Tips "We first need a full book proposal, outline of 2-10 pages, author statement of experience and published works."

ANGELA RINALDI LITERARY AGENCY

P.O. Box 7877, Beverly Hills CA 90212-7877. (310)842-7665. Fax: (310)837-8143. E-mail: amr@rinaldiliterary.com. Website: www.rinaldiliterary.com. **Contact:** Angela Rinaldi. Member of AAR. Represents 50 clients. Currently handles: nonfiction books 50%, novels 50%.

- Prior to opening her agency, Ms. Rinaldi was an editor at NAL/Signet, Pocket Books and Bantam, and the manager of book development for *The Los Angeles Times*.

Represents nonfiction books, novels, TV and motion picture rights (for clients only). **Considers these nonfiction areas:** biography, business, health, money, self help, true crime, womens, books by journalists and academics. **Considers these fiction areas:** literary, commercial. Actively seeking commercial and literary fiction. Does not want to receive scripts, poetry, category romances, children's books, Western's, science fiction/fantasy, technothrillers or cookbooks.

- Actively seeking commercial and literary fiction. Does not want to receive scripts, poetry, category romances, children's books, Western's, science fiction/fantasy, technothrillers or cookbooks.

How to Contact For fiction, send first 3 chapters, brief synopsis, SASE. For nonfiction, query with SASE or send outline/proposal, SASE. Do not send certified or metered mail. Brief e-mail inquiries are OK (no attachments). Other Responds in 6 weeks to queries.

Terms Agent receives 15% commission on domestic sales. Agent receives 20% commission on foreign sales. Offers written contract. Charges clients for photocopying.

ANN RITTENBERG LITERARY AGENCY, INC.

30 Bond St., New York NY 10012. (212)684-6936. Fax: (212)684-6929. Website: www.rittlit.com. **Contact:** Ann Rittenberg, president and Penn Whaling. Member of AAR. Currently handles: nonfiction books 50%, novels 50%.

Represents nonfiction books, novels. **Considers these nonfiction areas:** biography, history, social/cultural, memoirs, womens. **Considers these fiction areas:** literary. This agent specializes in literary fiction and literary nonfiction. Does not want to receive Screenplays, genre fiction, Poetry, Self-help.

- This agent specializes in literary fiction and literary nonfiction. Does not want to receive Screenplays, genre fiction, Poetry, Self-help.

How to Contact Query with SASE. Submit outline, 3 sample chapters, SASE. .Query via snail mail *only*. Accepts simultaneous submissions. Responds in 6 weeks to queries. Responds in 2 months to mss. Obtains most new clients through referrals from established writers and editors.

Terms Agent receives 15% commission on domestic sales. Agent receives 20% commission on foreign sales. Offers written contract. This agency charges clients for photocopying only.

Recent Sales *The Given Day*, by Dennis Lehane; *House and Home*, by Kathleen McCleary; *My Cat Hates You*, by Jim Edgar; *Three Weeks to Say Goodbye*, by CJ Box; and *Daughter of Kura*, by Debra Austin.

RIVERSIDE LITERARY AGENCY

41 Simon Keets Road, Leyden MA 01337. (413)772-0067. Fax: (413)772-0969. E-mail: rivlit@sover.net. **Contact:** Susan Lee Cohen. Member of AAR. Represents 40 clients. 20% of clients are new/unpublished writers.

Represents nonfiction cultural/social interests, religious/inspirational, spirituality, women's issues

How to Contact Query with SASE. Accepts simultaneous submissions. Responds in 2 weeks to queries. Obtains most new clients through referrals.

Terms Agent receives 15% commission on domestic sales. Offers written contract. Charges clients for foreign postage, photocopying large mss, express mail deliveries, etc.

LESLIE RIVERS, INTERNATIONAL (LRI)

P.O. Box 940772, Houston TX 77094-7772. (281)493–5822. Fax: (281)493–5835. E-mail: LRivers@LeslieRivers.com. Website: www.leslierivers.com. **Contact:** Judith Bruni. Other memberships include adheres to AAR's canon of ethics. Represents 20 clients. 80% of clients are new/unpublished writers. Currently handles: nonfiction books 10%, novels 90%.

- Prior to becoming agents, members were in marketing, sales, project management, customer satisfaction, writers, and publishing assistants.

Member Agents Judith Bruni, literary agent and founder; Mark Bruni, consulting editor.

Represents novels. "LRI collaborates with creative professionals and offers a customized, boutique service, based on the client's individual requirements. LRI maintains flexible hours to accommodate specific client needs. Its primary focus since 2005 is a high-end, no-fee based literary agency for authors. LRI provides quality service, feedback, and recommendations at no charge, which include readings, proofreading, editing--including content editing, analysis, feedback, and recommendations. Send only your finest work." Actively seeking fiction/novels only -- all subgenres. Does not want to receive children's books or poetry.

- "LRI collaborates with creative professionals and offers a customized, boutique service, based on the client's individual requirements. LRI maintains flexible hours to accommodate specific client needs. Its primary focus since 2005 is a high-end, no-fee based literary agency for authors. LRI provides quality service, feedback, and recommendations at no charge, which include readings, proofreading, editing--including content editing, analysis, feedback, and recommendations. Send only your finest work." Actively seeking fiction/novels only -- all subgenres. Does not want to receive children's books or poetry.

How to Contact Query via e-mail with Microsoft Word attachment. Submit synopsis, author bio, 3 chapters or 50 pages, whichever is longer. Prefers an exclusive read, but will consider simultaneous queries. Responds in 1-2 months to queries. Responds in 3 months to mss. Obtains most new clients through recommendations from others, solicitations.

Terms Agent receives 15% commission on domestic sales. Agent receives 25% commission on foreign sales. Offers written contract; 90-day notice must be given to terminate contract. This agency charges for postage, printing, copying, etc. If no sale is made, no charges are enforced.

Recent Sales *Secrets of Blood and Sand*, by Leona Wisoker (Mercury Retrograde Press). Other clients include Brinn Colenda, Don Armijo, Dwight Edwards, Edward Anthony Gibbons, Fletcher F. Cockrell, Fred Stawitz, Jerry Stefaniak, Kathy Keller, Leona Wisoker, Linda Sonna, Mark Bruni, Michael Eldridge, Michael Gemignani, Norma Chandler, RH Miller, Rhiannon Lynn, Scott Shepherd, Skott Darlow.

RLR ASSOCIATES, LTD.

Literary Department, 7 W. 51st St., New York NY 10019. (212)541-8641. Fax: (212)262-7084. E-mail: sgould@rlrassociates.net. Website: www.rlrliterary.net. **Contact:** Scott Gould. Member of AAR. Represents 50 clients. 25% of clients are new/unpublished writers. Currently handles: nonfiction books 70%, novels 25%, story collections 5%.

Represents nonfiction books, novels, short story collections, scholarly. **Considers these nonfiction areas:** interior, animals, anthropology, art, biography, business, child, cooking, current affairs, education, ethnic, gay, government, health, history, humor, language, memoirs, money, multicultural, music, nature, photography, popular culture, psychology, religion, science, self help, sociology, sports, translation, travel, true crime, womens. **Considers these fiction areas:** adventure, comic, detective, ethnic, experimental, family, feminist, gay, historical, horror, humor, literary, mainstream, multicultural, mystery, sports, thriller. "We provide a lot of editorial assistance to our clients and have connections." Actively seeking fiction, current affairs, history, art, popular culture, health and business. Does not want to receive screenplays.

O→ "We provide a lot of editorial assistance to our clients and have connections." Actively seeking fiction, current affairs, history, art, popular culture, health and business. Does not want to receive screenplays.

How to Contact Query by either e-mail or mail. Accepts simultaneous submissions. Responds in 4-8 weeks to queries. Obtains most new clients through recommendations from others.

Terms Agent receives 15% commission on domestic sales. Agent receives 20% commission on foreign sales. Offers written contract.

Recent Sales Clients include Shelby Foote, The Grief Recovery Institute, Don Wade, Don Zimmer, The Knot.com, David Plowden, PGA of America, Danny Peary, George Kalinsky, Peter Hyman, Daniel Parker, Lee Miller, Elise Miller, Nina Planck, Karyn Bosnak, Christopher Pike, Gerald Carbone, Jason Lethcoe, Andy Crouch.

Tips "Please check out our Web site for more details on our agency."

B.J. ROBBINS LITERARY AGENCY

5130 Bellaire Ave., North Hollywood CA 91607-2908. (818)760-6602. E-mail: robbinsliterary@aol.com. **Contact:** (Ms.) B.J. Robbins. Member of AAR. Represents 40 clients. 50% of clients are new/unpublished writers. Currently handles: nonfiction books 50%, novels 50%.

Represents nonfiction books, novels. **Considers these nonfiction areas:** biography, current affairs, ethnic, health, how-to, humor, memoirs, music, popular culture, psychology, self help, sociology, sports, film, travel, true crime, womens. **Considers these fiction areas:** detective, ethnic, literary, mainstream, mystery, sports, thriller.

How to Contact Query with SASE. Submit outline/proposal, 3 sample chapters, SASE. .Accepts e-mail queries (no attachments). Accepts simultaneous submissions. Responds in 2-6 weeks to queries. Responds in 6-8 weeks to mss. Obtains most new clients through conferences, referrals.

Terms Agent receives 15% commission on domestic sales. Agent receives 20% commission on foreign sales. Offers written contract; 3-month notice must be given to terminate contract. This agency charges clients for postage and photocopying (only after sale of ms).

Recent Sales Sold 15 titles in the last year. *Getting Stoned With Savages*, by J. Maarten Troost (Broadway); *Hot Water*, by Kathryn Jordan (Berkley); *Between the Bridge and the River*, by Craig Ferguson (Chronicle); *I'm Proud of You*, by Tim Madigan (Gotham); *Man of the House*, by Chris Erskine (Rodale); *Bird of Another heaven*, by James D. Houston (Knopf); *Tomorrow They Will Kiss*, by Eduardo Santiago (Little, Brown); *A Terrible Glory*, by James Donovan (Little, Brown); *The Writing on My Forehead*, by Nafisa Haji (Morrow); *Seen the Glory*, by John Hough Jr. (Simon & Schuster); *Lost on Planet China*, by J. Maarten Troost (Broadway).

Writers Conferences Squaw Valley Writers Workshop; San Diego State University Writers' Conference.

THE ROBBINS OFFICE, INC.

405 Park Ave., New York NY 10022. (212)223-0720. Fax: (212)223-2535. Website: www.robbinsoffice.com. **Contact:** Kathy P. Robbins, owner.

Member Agents Kathy P. Robbins; David Halpern.

Represents nonfiction books, novels. **Considers these nonfiction areas:** hitory, poliitics, journalism, regional interest, memoirs. This agency specializes in selling serious nonfiction as well as commercial and literary fiction.

O→ This agency specializes in selling serious nonfiction as well as commercial and literary fiction.

How to Contact Accepts submissions by referral only.

Terms Agent receives 15% commission on domestic sales. Agent receives 15% commission on foreign sales. Agent receives 15% commission on film sales. Bills back specific expenses incurred in doing business for a client.

ROGERS, COLERIDGE & WHITE

20 Powis Mews, London England W11 1JN United Kingdom. (44)(207)221-3717. Fax: (44)(207)229-9084. E-mail: info@rcwlitagency.co.uk. Website: www.rcwlitagency.co.uk. **Contact:** David Miller, agent. Estab. 1987.

- Prior to opening the agency, Ms. Rogers was an agent with Peter Janson-Smith; Ms. Coleridge worked at Sidgwick & Jackson, Chatto & Windus, and Anthony Sheil Associates; Ms. White was an editor and rights director for Simon & Schuster; Mr. Straus worked at Hodder and Stoughton,

Hamish Hamilton, and Macmillan; Mr. Miller worked as Ms. Rogers' assistant and was treasurer of the AAA; Ms. Waldie worked with Carole Smith.

Member Agents Deborah Rogers; Gill Coleridge; Pat White (illustrated and children's books); Peter Straus; David Miller; Zoe Waldie (fiction, biography, current affairs, narrative history); Laurence Laluyaux (foreign rights); Stephen Edwards (foreign rights).

Represents nonfiction books, novels, juvenile. **Considers these nonfiction areas:** cooking, current affairs, history, narrative, humor, sports, biography. Does not want to receive plays, screenplays, technical books or educational books.

O- Does not want to receive plays, screenplays, technical books or educational books.

How to Contact Submit synopsis, proposal, sample chapters, bio, SAE by mail. Submissions should include a covering letter telling us about yourself and the background to the book. In the case of fiction they should consist of the first 3 chapters or approximately the first 50 pages of the work to a natural break, and a brief synopsis. Non-fiction submissions should take the form of a proposal up to 20 pages in length explaining what the work is about and why you are best placed to write it. Material should be printed out in 12 point font, in double-spacing and on one side only of A4 paper. We cannot acknowledge receipt of material and nor can we accept responsibility for anything you send us, so please retain a copy of material submitted. Material will be returned only if sent with an adequately stamped and sized SASE; if return postage is not provided the material will be recycled. We do not accept email submissions unless by prior arrangement with individual agents. We will try to respond within 6-8 weeks of receipt of your material, but please appreciate that this isn't always possible as we must give priority to the authors we already represent. Please note that we do not represent scripts for theatre, film or television. Responds in 6-8 weeks to queries. Obtains most new clients through recommendations from others, solicitations, conferences.

Terms Agent receives 15% commission on domestic sales. Agent receives 20% commission on foreign sales. Offers written contract.

LINDA ROGHAAR LITERARY AGENCY, LLC

133 High Point Drive, Amherst MA 01002. (413)256-1921. Fax: (413)256-2636. E-mail: contact@lindaroghaar.com. Website: www.lindaroghaar.com. **Contact:** Linda L. Roghaar. Represents 50 clients. 10% of clients are new/unpublished writers. Currently handles: nonfiction books 100%.

- Prior to opening her agency, Ms. Roghaar worked in retail bookselling for 5 years and as a publishers' sales rep for 15 years.

Represents nonfiction books. **Considers these nonfiction areas:** animals, anthropology, biography, education, history, nature, popular culture, religion, self help, womens.

How to Contact Query with SASE. Accepts simultaneous submissions. Responds in 2 months to queries. Responds in 4 months to mss.

Terms Agent receives 15% commission on domestic sales. Agent receives negotiable commission on foreign sales. Offers written contract.

Recent Sales *Poetry as Spiritual Practice*, by Robert McDowell (Free Press); *Growing Up Dead*, by Peter Conners (DaCapo/Perseus); *Free-Range Knitter*, by Stephanie Pearl-McPhee (Andrews McMeel); *Starting from Scratch*, by Pam Johnson Bennett (Penguin); *The Ewe and I*, by Franklin Habit (Interweave); *Handmade Home*, by Amanda Soule (Shambhala); *Vintage Knits*, by Debbie Brisson (aka Stitchy McYarnpants) and Carolyn Sheridan (Wiley).

THE ROSENBERG GROUP

23 Lincoln Ave., Marblehead MA 01945. (781)990-1341. Fax: (781)990-1344. Website: www.rosenberggroup.com. **Contact:** Barbara Collins Rosenberg. Member of AAR. Other memberships include recognized agent of the RWA.Represents 25 clients. 15% of clients are new/unpublished writers. Currently handles: nonfiction books 30%, novels 30%, scholarly books 10%, other 30% college textbooks.

- Prior to becoming an agent, Ms. Rosenberg was a senior editor for Harcourt.

Represents nonfiction books, novels, textbooks, college textbooks only. **Considers these nonfiction areas:** current affairs, popular culture, psychology, sports, womens, women's health; food/wine/beverages. **Considers these fiction areas:** romance, womens. Ms. Rosenberg is well-versed in the romance market (both category and single title). She is a frequent speaker at romance conferences. Actively seeking romance category or single title in contemporary romantic suspense, and the historical subgenres. Does not want to receive inspirational or spiritual romances.

O- Ms. Rosenberg is well-versed in the romance market (both category and single title). She is a frequent speaker at romance conferences. Actively seeking romance category or single title in contemporary romantic suspense, and the historical subgenres. Does not want to receive inspirational or spiritual romances.

How to Contact Query with SASE. No e-mail or fax queries; will not respond. Responds in 2 weeks to queries. Responds in 4-6 weeks to mss. Obtains most new clients through recommendations from others, solicitations, conferences.

Terms Agent receives 15% commission on domestic sales. Agent receives 15% commission on foreign

sales. Offers written contract; 1-month notice must be given to terminate contract. Charges maximum of $350/year for postage and photocopying.
Recent Sales Sold 24 titles in the last year.
Writers Conferences RWA National Conference; BookExpo America.

RITA ROSENKRANZ LITERARY AGENCY

440 West End Ave., Suite 15D, New York NY 10024-5358. (212)873-6333. **Contact:** Rita Rosenkranz. Member of AAR. Represents 35 clients. 30% of clients are new/unpublished writers. Currently handles: nonfiction books 99%, novels 1%.

- Prior to opening her agency, Ms. Rosenkranz worked as an editor in major New York publishing houses.

Represents nonfiction books. **Considers these nonfiction areas:** animals, anthropology, art, autobiography, biography, business, child guidance, computers, cooking, crafts, cultural interests, current affairs, dance, decorating, economics, ethnic, film, gay, government, health, history, hobbies, how-to, humor, inspirational, interior design, language, law, lesbian, literature, medicine, military, money, music, nature, parenting, personal improvement, photography, popular culture, politics, psychology, religious, satire, science, self-help, sports, technology, theater, war, women's issues, women's studies. "This agency focuses on adult nonfiction, stresses strong editorial development and refinement before submitting to publishers, and brainstorms ideas with authors." Actively seeks authors who are well paired with their subject, either for professional or personal reasons.

O→ "This agency focuses on adult nonfiction, stresses strong editorial development and refinement before submitting to publishers, and brainstorms ideas with authors." Actively seeksauthors who are well paired with their subject, either for professional or personal reasons.

How to Contact Send query letter only (no proposal) via regular mail or e-mail. Submit proposal package with SASE only on request. No fax queries. Accepts simultaneous submissions. Responds in 2 weeks to queries. Obtains most new clients through directory listings, solicitations, conferences, word of mouth.
Terms Agent receives 15% commission on domestic sales. Agent receives 20% commission on foreign sales. Offers written contract, binding for 3 years; 3-month written notice must be given to terminate contract. Charges clients for photocopying. Makes referrals to editing services.
Recent Sales Sold 35 titles in the last year. *Get Known Before the Book Deal: Use Your Personal Strengths to Grow an Author Platform*, by Christina Katz (Writer's Digest Books); *29 Gifts*, by Cami Walker (DaCapo Press); *See Me After Class: Experienced Teachers Share the Lessons They Learned the Hard Way* (Kaplan); *Twenty Strengths Adoptive Parents Need to Succeed*, by Sherrie Eldridge (Bantam Dell); *Lifelines: The Black Book of Proverbs*, by Askhari Johnson Hodari and Yvonne McCalla Sobers (Broadway Books); *Encyclopedia of Jewish Food*, by Gil Marks (Wiley).
Tips "Identify the current competition for your project to make sure the project is valid. A strong cover letter is very important."

⊕ MERCEDES ROS LITERARY AGENCY

Castell 38, 08329 Teia, Barcelona Spain. (34)(93)540-1353. Fax: (34)(93)540-1346. E-mail: info@mercedesros.com. Website: www.mercedesros.com. **Contact:** Mercedes Ros.
Member Agents Mercedes Ros; Mercé Segarra.
Represents juvenile. "Gemser Publications publishes nonfiction and religious illustrated books for the 0-7 age group. Our products, basically aimed to convey concepts, habits, attitudes and values that are close to the child's environment, always adopt an open mentality in a globalized world. We combine excellent quality with competitive prices and good texts and beautiful illustrations to educate and inspire our young readers."

O→ "Gemser Publications publishes nonfiction and religious illustrated books for the 0-7 age group. Our products, basically aimed to convey concepts, habits, attitudes and values that are close to the child's environment, always adopt an open mentality in a globalized world. We combine excellent quality with competitive prices and good texts and beautiful illustrations to educate and inspire our young readers."

How to Contact Accepts submissions by e-mail or on disc.
Writers Conferences Frankfurt Book Fair; London Book Fair; Bologna Book Fair; BookExpo of America; Tokyo Book Fair; Beijing International Book Fair; Frankfurt Book Fair 2007.
Tips Try to read or look at as many books a publisher has published before sending in your material, to get a feel for their list and whether your manuscript, idea or style of illustration is likely to fit.

ANDY ROSS LITERARY AGENCY

767 Santa Ray Ave, Oakland CA 94610. (510)525-0685. E-mail: andyrossagency@hotmail.com. Website: www.andyrossagency.com. **Contact:** Andy Ross. Represents 20 clients. 20% of clients are new/unpublished writers. Currently handles: nonfiction books 100%.
Represents nonfiction books, scholarly. **Considers these nonfiction areas:** anthropology, biography,

child, current affairs, education, ethnic, government, history, language, military, nature, popular culture, psychology, science, sociology. "This agency specializes in general nonfiction, politics and current events, history, biography, journalism and contemporary culture." Actively seeking narrative nonfiction. Does not want to receive personal memoir, fiction, poetry, juvenile books.

- "This agency specializes in general nonfiction, politics and current events, history, biography, journalism and contemporary culture." Actively seeking narrative nonfiction. Does not want to receive personal memoir, fiction, poetry, juvenile books.

How to Contact Query via e-mail only. Accepts simultaneous submissions. Responds in 1 week to queries.

Terms Agent receives 15% commission on domestic sales. Agent receives 20% commission on foreign sales through a sub-agent. Offers written contract.

THE GAIL ROSS LITERARY AGENCY

1666 Connecticut Ave. NW, #500, Washington DC 20009. (202)328-3282. Fax: (202)328-9162. E-mail: jennifer@gailross.com. Website: www.gailross.com. **Contact:** Jennifer Manguera. Member of AAR. Represents 200 clients. 75% of clients are new/unpublished writers. Currently handles: nonfiction books 95%.

Represents nonfiction books. **Considers these nonfiction areas:** anthropology, biography, business, education, ethnic, gay, government, health, money, nature, psychology, science, sociology, sports, true crime. **Considers these fiction areas:** occasional commercial fiction.

- "This agency specializes in adult trade nonfiction." sci-fi, fantasy, romance, or children's books

How to Contact Query with SASE. No email. Accepts simultaneous submissions. Responds in 4-6 weeks to queries. Obtains most new clients through recommendations from others.

Terms Agent receives 15% commission on domestic sales. Agent receives 25% commission on foreign sales. Charges for office expenses.

CAROL SUSAN ROTH, LITERARY & CREATIVE

P.O. Box 620337, Woodside CA 94062. (650)323-3795. E-mail: carol@authorsbest.com. Website: www.authorsbest.com. **Contact:** Carol Susan Roth. Represents 50 clients. 15% of clients are new/unpublished writers. Currently handles: nonfiction books 100%.

- Prior to becoming an agent, Ms. Roth was trained as a psychotherapist and worked as a motivational coach, conference producer, and promoter for best-selling authors (e.g., Scott Peck, Bernie Siegal, John Gray) and the 1987 Heart of Business conference (the first business and spirituality conference).

Represents nonfiction books. **Considers these nonfiction areas:** business, health, wellness, history, humor, money, personal finance/investing, popular culture, religion, science, self help, spirituality, Buddhism, yoga, humor, real estate, entrepreneurship, beauty, social action, wellness. This agency specializes in health, science, pop culture, spirituality, personal growth, personal finance, entrepreneurship and business. Actively seeking previously published, media saavy journalists, authors, and experts with an established audience in pop culture, history, the sciences, health, spirituality, personal growth, and business. Does not want to receive fiction or children's books.

- This agency specializes in health, science, pop culture, spirituality, personal growth, personal finance, entrepreneurship and business. Actively seeking previously published, media saavy journalists, authors, and experts with an established audience in pop culture, history, the sciences, health, spirituality, personal growth, and business. Does not want to receive fiction or children's books.

How to Contact Submit proposal package, media kit, promotional video, SASE. . Accepts simultaneous submissions. Responds in 2 days to queries. Obtains most new clients through recommendations from others, solicitations.

Terms Agent receives 15% commission on domestic sales. Agent receives 15% commission on foreign sales. Offers written contract, binding for 3 years (only for work with the acquiring publisher); 60-day notice must be given to terminate contract. This agency asks the client to provide postage (FedEx airbills) and do copying. Refers to book doctor for proposal development and publicity service on request.

Recent Sales Sold 17 titles in the last year. *The Immortals* and *Confessions of an Alien Hunter*, by Seth Shostak; *How Life Begins*, by David Beamer; *The Magic Dictionary*, by Craig Conley; *Way of the Fertile Soul*, by Randine Lewis; *Teachings of the Adventure Rabbi*, by Rabbi jamie Korngold; *Seven Stories That Rocked the World*, by Patrick Hunt; *Ten Discoveries That Rewrote History*, by Patrick Hunt, *Snooze or Lose!*, by Helene Emsellem.

Writers Conferences Stanford Professional Publishing Course, MEGA Book Marketing University, Maui Writers Conference, Jack London Writers' Conference, San Francisco Writers' Conference.

Tips "Have charisma, content, and credentials--solve an old problem in a new way. I prefer experts with an Internet blog presence as well as extensive teaching and speaking experience."

THE ROTHMAN BRECHER AGENCY

9250 Wilshire Blvd., Penthouse, Beverly Hills CA 90212. (310)247-9898. E-mail: reception@rothmanbrecher.com. **Contact:** Andrea Kavoosi. Signatory of WGA.

Represents movie, tv, feature.

JANE ROTROSEN AGENCY LLC

318 E. 51st St., New York NY 10022. (212)593-4330. Fax: (212)935-6985. E-mail: lcohen@janerotrosen.com. Website: www.janerotrosen.com. Estab. 1974. Member of AAR. Other memberships include Authors Guild. Represents over 100 clients. Currently handles: nonfiction books 30%, novels 70%.

Member Agents Jane R. Berkey; Andrea Cirillo; Annelise Robey; Margaret Ruley; Christina Hogrebe; Peggy Gordijn, director of rights.

Represents nonfiction books, novels. **Considers these nonfiction areas:** biography, business, child, cooking, current affairs, health, how to, humor, money, nature, popular culture, psychology, self help, sports, true crime, womens. **Considers these fiction areas:** historical, mystery, romance, thriller, womens.

How to Contact Query with SASE. Responds in 2 weeks to writers who have been referred by a client or colleague. Responds in 2 months to mss. Obtains most new clients through recommendations from others.

Terms Agent receives 15% commission on domestic sales. Agent receives 20% commission on foreign sales. Offers written contract, binding for 3 years; 2-month notice must be given to terminate contract. Charges clients for photocopying, express mail, overseas postage, book purchase.

THE RUDY AGENCY

825 Wildlife Lane, Estes Park CO 80517. (970)577-8500. Fax: (970)577-8600. E-mail: mak@rudyagency.com. Website: www.rudyagency.com. **Contact:** Maryann Karinch. Other memberships include adheres to AAR canon of ethics. Represents 15 clients. 50% of clients are new/unpublished writers. Currently handles: nonfiction books 100%.

- Prior to becoming an agent, Ms. Karinch was, and continues to be, an author of nonfiction books - covering the subjects of health/medicine and human behavior. Prior to that, she was in public relations and marketing: areas of expertise she also applies in her practice as an agent.

Member Agents Maryann Karinch (nonfiction: health/medicine, culture/values, history, biography, memoir, science/technology, military/intelligence).

Represents nonfiction books, textbooks, with consumer appeal. **Considers these nonfiction areas:** anthropology, biography, business, child, computers, current affairs, education, ethnic, gay, government, health, history, how to, language, memoirs, military, money, music, nature, popular culture, psychology, science, self help, sociology, sports, true crime, womens. "We support authors from the proposal stage through promotion of the published work. We work in partnership with publishers to promote the published work and coach authors in their role in the marketing and public relations campaigns for the book." Actively seeking projects with social value, projects that open minds to new ideas and interesting lives, and projects that entertain through good storytelling. Does not want to receive poetry, children's/juvenile books, screenplays/plays, art/photo books, novels/novellas, religion books, and joke books or books that fit in to the impulse buy/gift book category.

- "We support authors from the proposal stage through promotion of the published work. We work in partnership with publishers to promote the published work and coach authors in their role in the marketing and public relations campaigns for the book." Actively seeking projects with social value, projects that open minds to new ideas and interesting lives, and projects that entertain through good storytelling. Does not want to receive poetry, children's/juvenile books, screenplays/plays, art/photo books, novels/novellas, religion books, and joke books or books that fit in to the impulse buy/gift book category.

How to Contact "Query us. If we like the query, we will invite a complete proposal. No phone queries." Accepts simultaneous submissions. Responds in 8 weeks to mss. Obtains most new clients through recommendations from others, solicitations.

Terms Agent receives 15% commission on domestic sales. Offers written contract, binding for 1 year.

Recent Sales Sold 11 titles in the last year. *Live from Jordan: Letters Home from My Journal Through the Middle East*, by Benjamin Orbach (Amacom); *Finding Center: Strategies to Build Strong Girls & Women*, by Maureen Mack (New Horizon Press); *Crossing Fifth Avenue to Bergdorf Goodman: An Insider's Account on the Rise of Luxury Retailing*, by Ira Neimark (SPI Books); *Hamas vs. Fatah: The Struggle for Palestine*, by Jonathan Schanzer (Palgrave Macmillan); *The New Rules of Etiquette and Entertaining*, by Curtrise Garner (Adams Media); *Comes the Darkness, Comes the Light*, by Vanessa Vega (Amacom); *Murder in Mayberry*, by Mary and Jack Branson (New Horizon Press); *Not My Turn to Die*, by Savo Heleta.

Writers Conferences BookExpo of America; industry events.

Tips "Present yourself professionally. I tell people all the time: Subscribe to *Writer's Digest* (I do), because you will get good advice about how to approach an agent."

MARLY RUSOFF & ASSOCIATES, INC.

P.O. Box 524, Bronxville NY 10708. (914)961-7939. E-mail: mra_queries@rusoffagency.com. Website: www.rusoffagency.com. **Contact:** Marly Rusoff.

- Prior to her current position, Ms. Rusoff held positions at Houghton Mifflin, Doubleday and William Morrow.

Member Agents Marly Rusoff.

Represents nonfiction books, novels. **Considers these nonfiction areas:** biography, business, health, history, memoirs, popular culture, psychology. **Considers these fiction areas:** historical, literary, commercial. "While we take delight in discovering new talent, we are particularly interested in helping established writers expand readership and develop their careers."

O⁻ "While we take delight in discovering new talent, we are particularly interested in helping established writers expand readership and develop their careers."

How to Contact Query with SASE. Submit synopsis, publishing history, author bio, contact information. For e-queries, include no attachments or pdf files. "We cannot read DOCXs." This agency only responds if interested. Responds to queries. Obtains most new clients through recommendations from others.

Recent Sales *The Thieves of Manhattan*, by Adam Langer (fiction, Spiegel & Grau); *The Kabul Beauty School*, by Deborah Rodriguez & Kristen Ohlson (memoir, Random House); *The Death of Santini*, by Pat Conroy (memoir, Nan Talese/Doubleday); *31 Bond Street*, by Ellen Horan (historical fiction, Harper); *My Name is Mary Sutter*, by Robin Oliveira (historical fiction, Viking); *Sweet Blasphemy*, by Elif Shafak (fiction). Other clients include: *Thrity Umrigar*, Elif Shafak, Arthur Phillips, Ron Rash, and Roland Merullo.

RUSSELL & VOLKENING

50 W. 29th St., #7E, New York NY 10001. (212)684-6050. Fax: (212)889-3026. **Contact:** Timothy Seldes (adult books), Jesseca Salky (adult, general fiction & nonfiction, memoirs), Carrie Hannigan (children's), Rosanna Bruno (adult, mysteries). Member of AAR. Represents 140 clients. 20% of clients are new/unpublished writers. Currently handles: nonfiction books 45%, novels 50%, story collections 3%, novella 2%.

Represents nonfiction books, novels, short story collections. **Considers these nonfiction areas:** anthropology, art, biography, business, cooking, current affairs, education, ethnic, gay, government, health, history, language, military, money, music, nature, photography, popular culture, psychology, science, sociology, sports, film, true crime, womens, creative nonfiction. **Considers these fiction areas:** adventure, detective, ethnic, literary, mainstream, mystery, picture books, sports, thriller. This agency specializes in literary fiction and narrative nonfiction. novels

O⁻ This agency specializes in literary fiction and narrative nonfiction. novels

How to Contact Query only with SASE to appropriate person. Responds in 4 weeks to queries.

Terms Agent receives 15% commission on domestic sales. Agent receives 20% commission on foreign sales. Charges clients for standard office expenses relating to the submission of materials.

Tips If the query is cogent, well written, well presented, and is the type of book we'd represent, we'll ask to see the manuscript. From there, it depends purely on the quality of the work.

REGINA RYAN PUBLISHING ENTERPRISES, INC.

251 Central Park W., 7D, New York NY 10024. (212)787-5589. E-mail: queryreginaryanbooks@rcn.com. **Contact:** Regina Ryan. Currently handles: nonfiction books 100%.

- Prior to becoming an agent, Ms. Ryan was an editor at Alfred A. Knopf, editor-in-chief of Macmillan Adult Trade, and a book producer.

Represents nonfiction books. **Considers these nonfiction areas:** gardening, government, history, psychology, travel, womens, narrative nonfiction; natural history (especially birds and birding); popular science; parenting; adventure; architecture, lifestyle.

How to Contact Query by e-mail or mail with SASE. No telephone queries. Does not accept queries for juvenile or fiction. Accepts simultaneous submissions. Tries to respond in 1 month to queries. Obtains most new clients through recommendations from others.

Terms Agent receives 15% commission on domestic sales. Agent receives 15% commission on foreign sales. Offers written contract. Charges clients for all out-of-pocket expenses (e.g., long distance calls, messengers, freight, copying) if it's more than just a nominal amount.

Recent Sales *Everything Changes: The Insider's Guide to Cancer in Your 20's and 30's*; *Gilded Mansions*, by Wayne Craven (WW Norton); *The Thinker's Thesaurus*, by Peter A. Meltzer (WW Norton); *What's Wrong With My Plant?* by David Deardorff, Ph.D and Kathryn Wadsworth (Timber Press); *Angel of Death Row: My Life as a Death Penalty Defense Lawyer*, by Andrea Lyon (Kaplan Publishing).

Tips "An analysis of why your proposed book is different and better than the competition is essential; a sample chapter is helpful."

THE SAGALYN AGENCY

4922 Fairmont Ave., Suite 200, Bethesda MD 20814. (301)718-6440. Fax: (301)718-6444. E-mail: query@sagalyn.com. Website: www.sagalyn.com. Member of AAR. Currently handles: nonfiction books 85%, novels 5%, scholarly books 10%.

Member Agents Raphael Sagalyn; Bridget Wagner, Shannon O'Neill.

Represents nonfiction books. **Considers these nonfiction areas:** biography, business, history, memoirs, popular culture, religion, science, journalism. Does not want to receive stage plays, screenplays, poetry, science fiction, fantasy, romance, children's books or young adult books.

- Does not want to receive stage plays, screenplays, poetry, science fiction, fantasy, romance, children's books or young adult books.

How to Contact Please send e-mail queries only (no attachments). Include 1 of these words in the subject line: query, submission, inquiry.

Tips "We receive 1,000-1,200 queries a year, which in turn lead to 2 or 3 new clients. Query via e-mail only. See our Web site for sales information and recent projects."

SALKIND LITERARY AGENCY

Part of Studio B, 734 Indiana St., Lawrence KS 66044. (913)538-7113. Fax: (516)706-2369. E-mail: neil@studiob.com. Website: www.salkindagency.com. **Contact:** Neil Salkind.Represents 100 clients. 25% of clients are new/unpublished writers. Currently handles: nonfiction books 60%, scholarly books 20%, textbooks 20%.

- Prior to becoming an agent, Mr. Salkind authored numerous trade and textbooks.

Represents nonfiction books, scholarly, textbooks. **Considers these nonfiction areas:** crafts, business, child, computers, cooking, education, ethnic, gay, health, how to, money, photography, popular culture, psychology, religion, science, self help, sports. "Actively seeking distinct nonfiction that takes risks and explores new ideas from authors who have, or can establish, a significant platform." Does not want "to receive book proposals based on ideas where potential authors have not yet researched what has been published."

- "Actively seeking distinct nonfiction that takes risks and explores new ideas from authors who have, or can establish, a significant platform." Does not want "to receive book proposals based on ideas where potential authors have not yet researched what has been published."

How to Contact Query with SASE. Submit publishing history, author bio. Responds in 1 week to queries. Responds in 1 week to mss. Obtains most new clients through recommendations from others.

Terms Agent receives 15% commission on domestic sales. Agent receives 15% commission on foreign sales.

Recent Sales Sold 120 titles in the last year. *Googlinaire*, by Anthony Boreilli (Wiley); *Clinical Psychology*, by Dean McKay (Blackwell); *The American Dream*, by Ralph Roberts (Kaplan); *Microsoft 2007 Exchange Admin Companion*, by Walter Glenn (Microsoft Press).

Tips "Present a unique idea based on a thorough knowledge of the market, be it a trade or textbook."

SALOMONSSON AGENCY

Svartensgatan 4, 116 20 Stockholm Sweden. E-mail: info@salomonssonagency.com. Website: www.salomonssonagency.com. **Contact:** Niclas Salomonsson. Currently handles: novels 100%.

Represents novels. "Salomonsson Agency is one of the leading literary agencies in Scandinavia. We focus on fiction from the Nordic countries."

- "Salomonsson Agency is one of the leading literary agencies in Scandinavia. We focus on fiction from the Nordic countries."

How to Contact This agency focuses on Scandinavian authors.

Recent Sales 9 book deal with Random House Canada regarding Liza Marklund; 2 book deal with HarperCollins US regarding Sissel-Jo Gazan; 8 book deal with Doubleday UK regarding Liza Marklund.

VICTORIA SANDERS & ASSOCIATES

241 Avenue of the Americas, Suite 11 H, New York NY 10014. (212)633-8811. Fax: (212)633-0525. E-mail: queriesvsa@hotmail.com. Website: www.victoriasanders.com. **Contact:** Victoria Sanders, Diane Dickensheid.Member of AAR. Signatory of WGA. Represents 135 clients. 25% of clients are new/unpublished writers. Currently handles: nonfiction books 30%, novels 70%.

Represents nonfiction books, novels. **Considers these nonfiction areas:** biography, current affairs, ethnic, gay, government, history, humor, language, music, popular culture, psychology, film, translation, womens. **Considers these fiction areas:** contemporary, adventure, ethnic, family, feminist, gay, literary, thriller.

How to Contact Query by e-mail only.

Terms Agent receives 15% commission on domestic sales. Agent receives 20% commission on foreign sales. Offers written contract. Charges for photocopying, messenger, express mail. If in excess of $100, client approval is required.

Recent Sales Sold 20+ titles in the last year.
Tips "Limit query to letter (no calls) and give it your best shot. A good query is going to get a good response."

SANDUM & ASSOCIATES

144 E. 84th St., New York NY 10028-2035. (212)737-2011. **Contact:** Howard E. Sandum.
Represents This agency specializes in general nonfiction and occasionally literary fiction.
- This agency specializes in general nonfiction and occasionally literary fiction.

How to Contact Query with synopsis, bio, SASE. Do not send full ms unless requested.
Terms Agent receives 15% commission on domestic sales. Charges clients for photocopying, air express, long-distance telephone/fax.

LENNART SANE AGENCY

Hollandareplan 9, S-374 34, Karlshamn Sweden. E-mail: info@lennartsaneagency.com. Website: www.lennartsaneagency.com. **Contact:** Lennart Sane.Represents 20+ clients.
Member Agents Lennart Sane, agent; Philip Sane, agent; Lina Hammarling, agent.
Represents nonfiction books, novels, juvenile. Lennart Sane Agency AB "represents the literary rights of authors, agents and publishers, in the markets of fiction, nonfiction, and film. "This European agency deals in a lot of translation rights, and North American authors are best *not* to query this agency without a strong referral."
- Lennart Sane Agency AB "represents the literary rights of authors, agents and publishers, in the markets of fiction, nonfiction, and film. "This European agency deals in a lot of translation rights, and North American authors are best *not* to query this agency without a strong referral.

How to Contact Query with SASE.

SCHIAVONE LITERARY AGENCY, INC.

236 Trails End, West Palm Beach FL 33413-2135. (561)966-9294. Fax: (561)966-9294. E-mail: profschia@aol.com. **Contact:** Dr. James Schiavone. CEO, corporate offices in Florida; Jennifer DuVall, president, New York office. New York office: 3671 Hudson Manor Terrace, No. 11H, Bronx, NY, 10463-1139, phone: (718)548-5332; fax: (718)548-5332; e-mail: jendu77@aol.com Other memberships include National Education Association. Represents 60+ clients. 2%% of clients are new/unpublished writers. Currently handles: nonfiction books 50%, novels 49%, textbooks 1%.
- Prior to opening his agency, Dr. Schiavone was a full professor of developmental skills at the City University of New York and author of 5 trade books and 3 textbooks. Jennifer DuVall has many years of combined experience in office management and agenting.

Represents nonfiction books, novels, juvenile, scholarly, textbooks. **Considers these nonfiction areas:** juvenile, animals, anthropology, biography, child, current affairs, education, ethnic, gay, government, health, history, how to, humor, language, military, nature, popular culture, psychology, science, self help, sociology, spirituality, mind and body, true crime. **Considers these fiction areas:** ethnic, family, historical, horror, humor, juvenile, literary, mainstream, science, young. This agency specializes in celebrity biography and autobiography and memoirs. Does not want to receive poetry.
- This agency specializes in celebrity biography and autobiography and memoirs. Does not want to receive poetry.

How to Contact Query with SASE. Do not send unsolicited materials or parcels requiring a signature. Send no e-attachments. Accepts simultaneous submissions. Responds in 2 weeks to queries. Responds in 6 weeks to mss. Obtains most new clients through recommendations from others, solicitations, conferences.
Terms Agent receives 15% commission on domestic sales. Agent receives 20% commission on foreign sales. Offers written contract. Charges clients for postage only.
Writers Conferences Key West Literary Seminar; South Florida Writers' Conference; Tallahassee Writers' Conference, Million Dollar Writers' Conference; Alaska Writers Conference.
Tips "We prefer to work with established authors published by major houses in New York. We will consider marketable proposals from new/previously unpublished writers."

HAROLD SCHMIDT LITERARY AGENCY

415 W. 23rd St., #6F, New York NY 10011. (212)727-7473. Fax: (212)807-6025. **Contact:** Harold Schmidt. Member of AAR. Represents 3 clients.
Represents novels. **Considers these fiction areas:** contemporary issues, gay, literary, multicultural, original fiction, likes offbeat/quirky, LGBT. Novels
- Novels

How to Contact Query with SASE. No email queries.

SUSAN SCHULMAN LITERARY AGENCY

454 West 44th St., New York NY 10036. (212)713-1633. Fax: (212)581-8830. E-mail: queries@schulmanagency.com. Website: www.schulmanagency.com. **Contact:** Susan Schulman.Member of AAR. Signatory of WGA. Other memberships include Dramatists Guild. 10% of clients are new/unpublished writers. Currently handles: nonfiction books 50%, novels 25%, juvenile books 15%, stage plays 10%.

Member Agents Linda Kiss, director of foreign rights; Katherine Stones, theater; Emily Uhry, submissions editor.

Represents Considers these nonfiction areas: anthropology, biography, business, child, cooking, current affairs, education, ethnic, gay, government, health, history, how to, language, memoirs, money, music, nature, popular culture, psychology, religion, self help, sociology, sports, true crime, womens. **Considers these fiction areas:** adventure, detective, feminist, historical, humor, juvenile, literary, mainstream, mystery, picture books, religious, young, womens. "We specialize in books for, by and about women and women's issues including nonfiction self-help books, fiction and theater projects. We also handle the film, television and allied rights for several agencies as well as foreign rights for several publishing houses." Actively seeking new nonfiction. Considers plays. Does not want to receive poetry, television scripts or concepts for television.

O→ "We specialize in books for, by and about women and women's issues including nonfiction self-help books, fiction and theater projects. We also handle the film, television and allied rights for several agencies as well as foreign rights for several publishing houses." Actively seeking new nonfiction. Considers plays. Does not want to receive poetry, television scripts or concepts for television.

How to Contact Query with SASE. Submit outline, synopsis, author bio, 3 sample chapters, SASE. Accepts simultaneous submissions. Responds in 6 weeks to queries. Responds in 6 weeks to mss. Obtains most new clients through recommendations from others, solicitations, conferences.

Terms Agent receives 15% commission on domestic sales. Agent receives 20% commission on foreign sales. Offers written contract; 30-day notice must be given to terminate contract.

Recent Sales Sold 50 titles in the last year; hundred of subsidiary rights deals.

Writers Conferences Geneva Writers' Conference (Switzerland); Columbus Writers' Conference; Skidmore Conference of the Independent Women's Writers Group.

Tips "Keep writing!"

THE SCIENCE FACTORY

2 Twyford Place, Devon EX 16 6AP United Kingdom. 44 (0) 207 193 7296. E-mail: info@sciencefactory.co.uk. Website: www.sciencefactory.co.uk. **Contact:** Peter Tallack.Estab. 2008.

- Prior to his current position, Mr. Tallack was with the UK agency Conville & Walsh.

Represents nonfiction books, novels. **Considers these nonfiction areas:** A diverse range of authors covering all areas of nonfiction, including history, biography, memoir, politics, current affairs and travel as well as science. **Considers these fiction areas:** Very rare, unless it is a thriller featuring scientists or a novel of ideas. "This agency specializes in representing authors aiming to satisfy the public's intellectual hunger for serious ideas. Experience of dealing directly in all markets, media and languages across the world." Actively seeking popular science nonfiction.

O→ "This agency specializes in representing authors aiming to satisfy the public's intellectual hunger for serious ideas. Experience of dealing directly in all markets, media and languages across the world." Actively seeking popular science nonfiction.

JONATHAN SCOTT, INC

933 West Van Buren, Suite 510, Chicago IL 60607. (847)557-2365. Fax: (847)557-8408. E-mail: jon@jonathanscott.us; scott@jonathanscott.us. Website: www.jonathanscott.us. **Contact:** Jon Malysiak, Scott Adlington.Represents 40 clients. 75% of clients are new/unpublished writers. Currently handles: nonfiction books 90%, novels 10%.

Member Agents Scott Adlington (narrative nonfiction, sports, health, wellness, fitness, environmental issues); Jon Malysiak (narrative nonfiction and fiction, current affairs, history, memoir, business).

Represents nonfiction books. **Considers these fiction areas:** No fiction."We are very hands-on with our authors in terms of working with them to develop their proposals and manuscripts. Since both of us come from publishing backgrounds—editorial and sales—we are able to give our authors a perspective of what goes on within the publishing house from initial consideration through the entire development, publication, marketing and sales processes." Categories of health/fitness, cooking, sports history, narrative non-fiction, memoir, parenting, general business, and travel essay, and all other non-fiction categories. We also represents books to be sold into film, television, and other subsidiary channels. To find out about literary representation, please contact Jon Malysiak, with a query email describing your book idea and/or a proposal.

O→ "We are very hands-on with our authors in terms of working with them to develop their proposals and manuscripts. Since both of us come from publishing backgrounds—editorial and sales—we are able to give our authors a perspective of what goes on within the publishing house from initial consideration through the entire development, publication, marketing and sales processes." Categories of health/fitness, cooking, sports history, narrative non-fiction, memoir, parenting, general business, and travel essay, and all other non-fiction categories. We also represents books to be sold into film, television, and other subsidiary channels. To find out about literary representation, please contact Jon Malysiak, with a query email describing your book idea and/or a proposal.

How to Contact We only accept electronic submissions. Query email describing your book idea and/or a proposal. Accepts simultaneous submissions. Responds in 1-2 weeks to queries. Responds in 4-6 weeks to mss. Obtains most new clients through recommendations from others, solicitations, contacting good authors for representation.

Terms Agent receives 15% commission on domestic sales. Agent receives 20% commission on foreign sales. Offers written contract; 30-day notice must be given to terminate contract.

Tips "Platform, platform, platform. We can't emphasize this enough. Without a strong national platform, it is nearly impossible to get the interest of a publisher. Also, be organized in your thoughts and your goals before contacting an agent. Think of the proposal as your business plan. What do you hope to achieve by publishing your book. How can your book change the world?"

Scovil Galen Ghosh Literary Agency, Inc.

276 Fifth Ave., Suite 708, New York NY 10001. (212)679-8686. Fax: (212)679-6710. E-mail: info@sgglit.com. Website: www.sgglit.com. **Contact:** Russell Galen. Member of AAR. Represents 300 clients. Currently handles: nonfiction books 60%, novels 40%.

Member Agents Jack Scovil, jackscovil@sgglit.com; Russell Galen, russellgalen@sgglit.com (novels that stretch the bounds of reality; strong, serious nonfiction books on almost any subject that teach something new; no books that are merely entertaining, such as diet or pop psych books; serious interests include science, history, journalism, biography, business, memoir, nature, politics, sports, contemporary culture, literary nonfiction, etc.); Anna Ghosh, annaghosh@sgglit.com (strong nonfiction proposals on all subjects as well as adult commercial and literary fiction by both unpublished and published authors; serious interests include investigative journalism, literary nonfiction, history, biography, memoir, popular culture, science, adventure, art, food, religion, psychology, alternative health, social issues, women's fiction, historical novels and literary fiction); Ann Behar, annbehar@sgglit.com (juvenile books for all ages).

Represents nonfiction books, novels.

How to Contact E-mail queries required. Accepts simultaneous submissions.

SCRIBBLERS HOUSE, LLC LITERARY AGENCY

P.O. Box 1007, Cooper Station, New York NY 10276-1007. (212)714-7744. E-mail: query@scribblershouse.net. Website: www.scribblershouse.net. **Contact:** Stedman Mays, Garrett Gambino. 25% of clients are new/unpublished writers.

Represents nonfiction books, novels, occasionally. **Considers these nonfiction areas:** business, health, history, how to, language, memoirs, popular culture, psychology, self help, sex, spirituality, diet/nutrition; the brain; personal finance; biography; politics; writing books; relationships; gender issues; parenting. **Considers these fiction areas:** historical, literary, womens, suspense; crime; thrillers.

How to Contact Query via e-mail. Put "nonfiction query" or "fiction query" in the subject line followed by the title of your project (send to our submissions email on our website). Do not send attachments or downloadable materials of any kind with query. We will request more materials if we are interested. Usually respond in 2 weeks to 2 months to email queries if we are interested (if we are not interested, we will not respond due to the overwhelming amount of queries we receive). We are only accepting email queries at the present time. Accepts simultaneous submissions.

Terms Agent receives 15% commission on domestic sales. Charges clients for postage, shipping and copying.

Tips "If you must send by snail mail, we will return material or respond to a U.S. Postal Service-accepted SASE. (No international coupons or outdated mail strips, please.) Presentation means a lot. A well-written query letter with a brief author bio and your credentials is important. For query letter models, go to the bookstore or online and look at the cover copy and flap copy on other books in your general area of interest. Emulate what's best. Have an idea of other notable books that will be perceived as being in the same vein as yours. Know what's fresh about your project and articulate it in as few words as possible. Consult our Web site for the most up-to-date information on submitting."

SCRIBE AGENCY, LLC

5508 Joylynne Dr., Madison WI 53716. E-mail: queries@scribeagency.com. Website: www.scribeagency.com. **Contact:** Kristopher O'Higgins. Represents 11 clients. 18% of clients are new/unpublished writers. Currently handles: novels 98%, story collections 2%.

- "We have 17 years of experience in publishing and have worked on both agency and editorial sides in the past, with marketing expertise to boot. We love books as much or more than anyone you know. Check our website to see what we're about and to make sure you jive with the Scribe vibe."

Member Agents Kristopher O'Higgins; Jesse Vogel.

Represents nonfiction books, novels, short story collections, novellas, anthologies. **Considers these nonfiction areas:** ethnic, gay, memoirs, popular culture, womens. **Considers these fiction areas:** detective, erotica, experimental, fantasy, feminist, gay, horror, humor, lesbian, literary, mainstream, mystery, psychic, thriller, science fiction,. Actively seeking excellent writers with ideas and stories to tell.

- Actively seeking excellent writers with ideas and stories to tell.

How to Contact E-queries only. See the Web site for submission info, as it may change. Responds in 3-4 weeks to queries. Responds in 5 months to mss.

Terms Agent receives 15% commission on domestic sales. Agent receives 20% commission on foreign sales. Offers written contract. Charges for postage and photocopying.

Recent Sales Sold 3 titles in the last year.

Writers Conferences BookExpo America; The Writer's Institute; Spring Writer's Festival; WisCon; Wisconsin Book Festival; World Fantasy Convention.

SEBASTIAN LITERARY AGENCY

1043 Grand Ave #557, St. Paul MN 55105. (952)471-9300. Fax: (952)314-4858. E-mail: laurie@sebastianagency.com. Website: www.sebastianagency.com. **Contact:** Laurie Harper. Author's Guild member. Represents 30 clients. 20% of clients are new/unpublished writers. Currently handles: nonfiction books.

- Prior to forming the agency, Laurie ran a small regional publishing company in San Francisco.

Represents nonfiction books. **Considers these nonfiction areas:** business, health, money, psychology, self help, sociology, womens. Takes on few new clients at this time. Actively seeking strong narrative nonfiction from authors with strong matching credentials and platform -- whether in the category of psychology, sociology, science, lifestyle, business, health, medicine, or women's issues. Does not want to receive memoir, biography, poetry, humor, relationship books.

- Takes on few new clients at this time. Actively seeking strong narrative nonfiction from authors with strong matching credentials and platform -- whether in the category of psychology, sociology, science, lifestyle, business, health, medicine, or women's issues. Does not want to receive memoir, biography, poetry, humor, relationship books.

How to Contact Query with SASE. Submit proposal package, outline, 3 sample chapters. Accepts simultaneous submissions. Responds in 3 weeks to queries. Obtains most new clients through recommendations from others.

Terms Agent receives 15% commission on domestic sales. Agent receives 20% commission on foreign sales. Offers written contract; 30-day notice must be given to terminate contract. Author is charged for copying of ms, if pre-authorized.

Recent Sales Sold 10 titles in the last year. *The Modern Mom's Guide to Dads*, by Hogan Hilling and Jesse Rutherford (Cumberland); *Customer Loyalty Guaranteed*, by Chip Bell and John Patterson (Adams); *More Than You Know*, by Michael Mauboussin (Columbia Univ).

SECRET AGENT MAN

P.O. Box 1078, Lake Forest CA 92609-1078. (949)698-6987. E-mail: scott@secretagentman.net. Website: www.secretagentman.net. **Contact:** Scott Mortenson.

Represents novels. **Considers these fiction areas:** detective, mystery, religious, thriller. Actively seeking selective mystery, thriller, suspense and detective fiction. Does not want to receive scripts or screenplays.

- Actively seeking selective mystery, thriller, suspense and detective fiction. Does not want to receive scripts or screenplays.

How to Contact Query with SASE. Query via e-mail or snail mail; include sample chapter(s), synopsis and/or outline. Prefers to read the real thing rather than a description of it. Obtains most new clients through recommendations from others, solicitations.

LYNN SELIGMAN, LITERARY AGENT

400 Highland Ave., Upper Montclair NJ 07043. (973)783-3631. **Contact:** Lynn Seligman. Other memberships include Women's Media Group. Represents 32 clients. 15% of clients are new/unpublished writers. Currently handles: nonfiction books 60%, novels 40%.

- Prior to opening her agency, Ms. Seligman worked in the subsidiary rights department of Doubleday and Simon & Schuster, and served as an agent with Julian Bach Literary Agency (which became IMG Literary Agency). Foreign rights are represented by Books Crossing Borders, Inc.

Represents nonfiction books, novels. **Considers these nonfiction areas:** interior, anthropology, art, biography, business, child, cooking, current affairs, education, ethnic, government, health, history, how to, humor, language, money, music, nature, photography, popular culture, psychology, science, self help, sociology, film, true crime, womens. **Considers these fiction areas:** detective, ethnic, fantasy, feminist, historical, horror, humor, literary, mainstream, mystery, romance, contemporary, gothic, historical, regency, science. "This agency specializes in general nonfiction and fiction. I also do illustrated and photography books and have represented several photographers for books."

- "This agency specializes in general nonfiction and fiction. I also do illustrated and photography books and have represented several photographers for books."

How to Contact Query with SASE. Prefers to read materials exclusively. Accepts simultaneous submissions. Responds in 2 weeks to queries. Responds in 2 months to mss. Obtains most new clients through referrals from other writers and editors.

Terms Agent receives 15% commission on domestic sales. Agent receives 25% commission on foreign sales. Charges clients for photocopying, unusual postage, express mail, telephone expenses (checks with author first).

Recent Sales Sold 15 titles in the last year. Lords of Vice series, by Barbara Pierce; Untitled series, by Deborah Leblanc.

SERENDIPITY LITERARY AGENCY, LLC

305 Gates Ave., Brooklyn NY 11216. (718)230-7689. Fax: (718)230-7829. E-mail: rbrooks@serendipitylit.com; info@serendipitylit.com. Website: www.serendipitylit.com. **Contact:** Regina Brooks. Represents 50 clients. 50% of clients are new/unpublished writers. Currently handles: nonfiction books 50%, other 50% fiction.

- Prior to becoming an agent, Ms. Brooks was an acquisitions editor for John Wiley & Sons, Inc. and McGraw-Hill Companies.

Member Agents Regina Brooks; Guichard Cadet (sports, pop culture, fiction, Caribbean writers).

Represents nonfiction books, novels, juvenile, scholarly, children's books. **Considers these nonfiction areas:** juvenile, newage, business, current affairs, education, ethnic, history, memoirs, money, multicultural, popular culture, psychology, religion, science, self help, sports, womens, health/medical; narrative; popular science, biography; politics; crafts/design; food/cooking; contemporary culture. **Considers these fiction areas:** adventure, confession, ethnic, historical, juvenile, literary, multicultural, picture books, thriller, suspense; mystery; romance. African-American nonfiction, commercial fiction, young adult novels with an urban flair and juvenile books. No stage plays, screenplays or poetry.

- African-American nonfiction, commercial fiction, young adult novels with an urban flair and juvenile books. No stage plays, screenplays or poetry.

How to Contact Prefers to read materials exclusively. For nonfiction, submit outline, 1 sample chapter, SASE. Write the field on the back of the envelope. See guidelines online. For adult fiction, please send a query letter that includes basic information that describes your project. Your query letter should include the title, premise, and length of the manuscript. See our guidelines onine. Write the genre of your book on the back of your envelope. Based on your initial query letter and synopsis, our office may request sample chapters, or your ms in its entirety. Responds in 2 months to queries. Responds in 3 months to mss. Obtains most new clients through conferences, referrals.

Terms Agent receives 15% commission on domestic sales. Agent receives 20% commission on foreign sales. Offers written contract; 2-month notice must be given to terminate contract. Charges clients for office fees, which are taken from any advance.

Tips "We are eagerly looking for young adult books. We also represent illustrators."

SEVENTH AVENUE LITERARY AGENCY

1663 West Seventh Ave., Vancouver British Columbia V6J 1S4 Canada. (604)734-3663. Fax: (604)734-8906. E-mail: info@seventhavenuelit.com. Website: www.seventhavenuelit.com. **Contact:** Robert Mackwood, director. Currently handles: nonfiction books 100%.

Represents nonfiction books. **Considers these nonfiction areas:** biography, business, computers, health, history, science, sports, travel, lifestyle. Seventh Avenue Literary Agency is one of Canada's largest and most venerable literary and personal management agencies. (The agency was originally called Contemporary Management.) Actively seeking nonfiction. Does not want to receive poetry, screenplays, children's books, young adult titles, or genre writing such as science fiction, fantasy or erotica.

- Seventh Avenue Literary Agency is one of Canada's largest and most venerable literary and personal management agencies. (The agency was originally called Contemporary Management.) Actively seeking nonfiction. Does not want to receive poetry, screenplays, children's books, young adult titles, or genre writing such as science fiction, fantasy or erotica.

How to Contact Query with SASE. Submit outline, synopsis, 1 (nonfiction) sample chapters, publishing history, author bio, table of contents with proposal or query. Send 1-2 chapters and submission history if sending fiction. No e-mail attachments. Provide full contact information. Obtains most new clients through recommendations from others, solicitations.

Tips "If you want your material returned, please include an SASE with adequate postage; otherwise, material will be recycled. (U.S. stamps are not adequate; they do not work in Canada.)"

THE SEYMOUR AGENCY

475 Miner St., Canton NY 13617. (315)386-1831. E-mail: marysue@twcny.rr.com. Website: www.theseymouragency.com. **Contact:** Mary Sue Seymour. Member of AAR. Signatory of WGA. Other memberships include RWA, Authors Guild. Represents 50 clients. 5% of clients are new/unpublished writers. Currently handles: nonfiction books 50%, other 50% fiction.

- Ms. Seymour is a retired New York State certified teacher.

Represents nonfiction books, novels. **Considers these nonfiction areas:** business, health, how-to, self help, Christian books; cookbooks; any well-written nonfiction that includes a proposal in standard format and 1 sample chapter. **Considers these fiction areas:** religious, Christian books, romance, any type.

How to Contact Query with SASE, synopsis, first 50 pages for romance. Accepts e-mail queries. Accepts simultaneous submissions. Responds in 1 month to queries. Responds in 3 months to mss.

Terms Agent receives 12-15% commission on domestic sales.

Recent Sales Don Reid of the Statler Brothers' second 2-book deal to Cook Communications Ministries; Amy Clipston's multi-book deal to Zondervan; Mary Elles' multi-book deal to Harvest House; Shelley Shepard Gray's multi-book deal to Harper One.

DENISE SHANNON LITERARY AGENCY, INC.

20 W. 22nd St., Suite 1603, New York NY 10010. (212)414-2911. Fax: (212)414-2930. E-mail: info@deniseshannonagency.com. Website: www.deniseshannonagency.com. **Contact:** Denise Shannon. Estab. 2002. Member of AAR.

- Prior to opening her agency, Ms. Shannon worked for 16 years with Georges Borchardt and International Creative Management.

Represents nonfiction books, novels. **Considers these nonfiction areas:** biography, business, health, narrative nonfiction; politics; journalism; social history. **Considers these fiction areas:** literary. "We are a boutique agency with a distinguished list of fiction and nonfiction authors."

O⊸ "We are a boutique agency with a distinguished list of fiction and nonfiction authors."

How to Contact Query by email to: submissions@deniseshannonagency.com, or mail with SASE. Submit query with description of project, bio, SASE. See guidelines online.

Tips "Please do not send queries regarding fiction projects until a complete manuscript is available for review. We request that you inform us if you are submitting material simultaneously to other agencies."

THE ROBERT E. SHEPARD AGENCY

1608 Dwight Way, Berkeley CA 94703-1804. (510)849-3999. E-mail: mail@shepardagency.com. Website: www.shepardagency.com. **Contact:** Robert Shepard. Other memberships include Authors Guild. Represents 70 clients. 15% of clients are new/unpublished writers. Currently handles: nonfiction books 90%, scholarly books 10%.

- Prior to opening his agency, Mr. Shepard was an editor and a sales and marketing manager in book publishing; he now writes, teaches courses for nonfiction authors, and speaks at many writers' conferences.

Represents nonfiction books, scholarly, appropriate for trade publishers. **Considers these nonfiction areas:** business, current affairs, gay, government, history, popular culture, psychology, sports, Judaica; narrative nonfiction; health; cultural issues; science for laypeople, parenting. This agency specializes in nonfiction, particularly key issues facing society and culture. Actively seeking works by experts recognized in their fields whether or not they're well-known to the general public, and books that offer fresh perspectives or new information even when the subject is familiar. Does not want to receive autobiographies, art books, memoir, spirituality or fiction.

O⊸ This agency specializes in nonfiction, particularly key issues facing society and culture. Actively seeking works by experts recognized in their fields whether or not they're well-known to the general public, and books that offer fresh perspectives or new information even when the subject is familiar. Does not want to receive autobiographies, art books, memoir, spirituality or fiction.

How to Contact Query with SASE. Accepts simultaneous submissions. Responds in 2-3 weeks to queries; 6 weeks to proposals or mss. Obtains most new clients through recommendations from others, solicitations.

Terms Agent receives 15% commission on domestic sales. Agent receives 20% commission on foreign sales. Offers written contract, binding for term of project or until canceled; 30-day notice must be given to terminate contract. Charges clients for phone/fax, photocopying, postage (if and when the project sells).

Recent Sales Sold 10 titles in the last year. *A Few Seconds of Panic*, by Stefan Fatsis (Penguin); *Big Boy Rules*, by Steve Fainaru (Da Capo Press); *The Fois Gras Wars*, by Mark Caro (Simon & Schuster).

Tips "We pay attention to detail. We believe in close working relationships between the author and agent, and in building better relationships between the author and editor. Please do your homework! There's no substitute for learning all you can about similar or directly competing books and presenting a well-reasoned competitive analysis in your proposal. Be sure to describe what's new and fresh about your work, why you are the best person to be writing on your subject, everything editors will need to know about your work, and how the book will serve the needs or interests of your intended readers. Don't work in a vacuum: Visit bookstores, talk to other writers about their experiences, and let the information you gather inform the work that you do as an author."

WENDY SHERMAN ASSOCIATES, INC.

450 Seventh Ave., Suite 2307, New York NY 10123. (212)279-9027. Fax: (212)279-8863. Website: www.wsherman.com. **Contact:** Wendy Sherman. Member of AAR. Represents 50 clients. 30% of clients are new/unpublished writers. Currently handles: nonfiction books 50%, novels 50%.

- Prior to opening the agency, Ms. Sherman worked for The Aaron Priest agency and served as vice president, executive director, associate publisher, subsidary rights director, and sales and marketing director in the publishing industry.

Member Agents Wendy Sherman; Michelle Brower.

Represents nonfiction books, novels. **Considers these nonfiction areas:** psychology, narrative; practical. **Considers these fiction areas:** literary, womens, suspense. "We specialize in developing new writers, as well as working with more established writers. My experience as a publisher has proven to be a great asset to my clients."

O‑ "We specialize in developing new writers, as well as working with more established writers. My experience as a publisher has proven to be a great asset to my clients."

How to Contact Query with SASE or send outline/proposal, 1 sample chapter. E-mail queries accepted by Ms. Brower only. Accepts simultaneous submissions. Responds in 1 month to queries. Obtains most new clients through recommendations from others.

Terms Agent receives 15% commission on domestic sales. Agent receives 20% commission on foreign sales. Offers written contract.

Recent Sales *The Measure of Brightness*, by Todd Johnson; *Supergirls Speak Out*, by Liz Funk; *Love in 90 Days*, by Diana Kirschner; *A Long Time Ago and Essentially*, by Brigid Pasulka; *Lunch in Paris*, by Elizabeth Bard; *Through the Eyes of a Cat*, by Michelle Nagelschneider.

Tips "The bottom line is: Do your homework. Be as well prepared as possible. Read the books that will help you present yourself and your work with polish. You want your submission to stand out."

ROSALIE SIEGEL, INTERNATIONAL LITERARY AGENCY, INC.

1 Abey Dr., Pennington NJ 08543. (609)737-1007. Fax: (609)737-3708. **Contact:** Rosalie Siegel. Member of AAR. Represents 35 clients. 10% of clients are new/unpublished writers. Currently handles: nonfiction books 45%, novels 45%, other 10% young adult books; short story collections for current clients.

How to Contact Obtains most new clients through referrals from writers and friends.

Terms Agent receives 15% commission on domestic sales. Agent receives 20% commission on foreign sales. Offers written contract; 2-month notice must be given to terminate contract. Charges clients for photocopying.

JEFFREY SIMMONS LITERARY AGENCY

15 Penn House, Mallory St., London NW8 8SX England. (44)(207)224-8917. E-mail: jasimmons@unicombox.co.uk. **Contact:** Jeffrey Simmons. Represents 43 clients. 40% of clients are new/unpublished writers. Currently handles: nonfiction books 65%, novels 35%.

- Prior to becoming an agent, Mr. Simmons was a publisher. He is also an author.

Represents nonfiction books, novels. **Considers these nonfiction areas:** biography, current affairs, government, history, language, memoirs, music, popular culture, sociology, sports, film, translation, true crime. **Considers these fiction areas:** adventure, confession, detective, family, literary, mainstream, mystery, thriller. "This agency seeks to handle good books and promising young writers. My long experience in publishing and as an author and ghostwriter means I can offer an excellent service all around, especially in terms of editorial experience where appropriate." Actively seeking quality fiction, biography, autobiography, showbiz, personality books, law, crime, politics, and world affairs. Does not want to receive science fiction, horror, fantasy, juvenile, academic books, or specialist subjects (e.g., cooking, gardening, religious).

O‑ "This agency seeks to handle good books and promising young writers. My long experience in publishing and as an author and ghostwriter means I can offer an excellent service all around, especially in terms of editorial experience where appropriate." Actively seeking quality fiction, biography, autobiography, showbiz, personality books, law, crime, politics, and world affairs. Does not want to receive science fiction, horror, fantasy, juvenile, academic books, or specialist subjects (e.g., cooking, gardening, religious).

How to Contact Submit sample chapter, outline/proposal, SASE (IRCs if necessary).Prefers to read materials exclusively. Responds in 1 week to queries. Responds in 1 month to mss. Obtains most new clients through recommendations from others, solicitations.

Terms Agent receives 10-15% commission on domestic sales. Agent receives 15% commission on foreign sales. Offers written contract, binding for lifetime of book in question or until it becomes out of print.

Tips "When contacting us with an outline/proposal, include a brief biographical note (listing any previous publications, with publishers and dates). Preferably tell us if the book has already been offered elsewhere."

BEVERLEY SLOPEN LITERARY AGENCY

131 Bloor St. W., Suite 711, Toronto ON M5S 1S3 Canada. (416)964-9598. Fax: (416)921-7726. E-mail: beverly@slopenagency.ca. Website: www.slopenagency.ca. **Contact:** Beverley Slopen. Represents 70 clients. 20% of clients are new/unpublished writers. Currently handles: nonfiction books 60%, novels 40%.

- Prior to opening her agency, Ms. Slopen worked in publishing and as a journalist.

Represents nonfiction books, novels, scholarly, textbooks, college. **Considers these nonfiction areas:** anthropology, biography, business, current affairs, psychology, sociology, true crime, womens. **Considers these fiction areas:** literary, mystery. "This agency has a strong bent toward Canadian writers." Actively seeking serious nonfiction that is accessible and appealing to the general reader. Does not want to receive fantasy, science fiction, or children's books.

O→ "This agency has a strong bent toward Canadian writers." Actively seeking serious nonfiction that is accessible and appealing to the general reader. Does not want to receive fantasy, science fiction, or children's books.

How to Contact Query with SAE and IRCs. Returns materials only with SASE (Canadian postage only). Accepts simultaneous submissions. Responds in 2 months to queries.

Terms Agent receives 15% commission on domestic sales. Agent receives 10% commission on foreign sales. Offers written contract, binding for 2 years; 3-month notice must be given to terminate contract.

Recent Sales *What They Wanted*, by Donna Morrissey (Penguin Canada); *The Age of Persuasion*, by Terry O'Reilly and Mike Tennant (Knopf Canada); *Prisoner of Tehran*, by Marina Nemat (Penguin Canada, Free Press US, John Murray UK); *Race to the Polar Sea*, by Ken McGoogan (HarperCollins Canada, Counterpoint US); *Transgression*, by James Nichol (HarperCollins US, McArthur Canada, Goldmann Germany); *Vermeer's Hat*, by Timothy Brook (HarperCollins Canada, Bloomsbury US); *Distantly Related to Freud*, by Ann Charney (Cormorant).

Tips "Please, no unsolicited manuscripts."

SLW LITERARY AGENCY

4100 Ridgeland Ave., Northbrook IL 60062. (847)509-0999. Fax: (847)509-0996. E-mail: shariwenk@gmail.com. **Contact:** Shari Wenk. Currently handles: nonfiction books 100%.

Represents nonfiction books. **Considers these nonfiction areas:** sports. "This agency specializes in representing books written by sports celebrities and sports writers."

O→ "This agency specializes in representing books written by sports celebrities and sports writers."

How to Contact Query via e-mail, but note the agency's specific specialty.

VALERIE SMITH, LITERARY AGENT

1746 Route 44/55, Modena NY 12548. **Contact:** Valerie Smith. Represents 17 clients. Currently handles: nonfiction books 2%, novels 75%, story collections 1%, juvenile books 20%, scholarly books 1%, textbooks 1%.

Represents nonfiction books, novels, juvenile, textbooks. **Considers these nonfiction areas:** agriculture horticulture, cooking, how to, self help. **Considers these fiction areas:** fantasy, historical, juvenile, literary, mainstream, mystery, science, young, women's/chick lit. "This is a small, personalized agency with a strong long-term commitment to clients interested in building careers. I have strong ties to science fiction, fantasy and young adult projects. I look for serious, productive writers whose work I can be passionate about." Does not want to receive unsolicited mss.

O→ "This is a small, personalized agency with a strong long-term commitment to clients interested in building careers. I have strong ties to science fiction, fantasy and young adult projects. I look for serious, productive writers whose work I can be passionate about." Does not want to receive unsolicited mss.

How to Contact Query with synopsis, bio, 3 sample chapters, SASE. Contact by snail mail only. Obtains most new clients through recommendations from others.

Terms Agent receives 15% commission on domestic sales. Agent receives 20% commission on foreign sales. Offers written contract; 6-week notice must be given to terminate contract.

ROBERT SMITH LITERARY AGENCY, LTD.

12 Bridge Wharf, 156 Caledonian Rd., London NI 9UU England. (44)(207)278-2444. Fax: (44)(207)833-5680. E-mail: robertsmith.literaryagency@virgin.net. **Contact:** Robert Smith. Other memberships include

AAA. Represents 40 clients. 10% of clients are new/unpublished writers. Currently handles: nonfiction books 80%, syndicated material 20%.

- Prior to becoming an agent, Mr. Smith was a book publisher.

Represents nonfiction books, syndicated material. **Considers these nonfiction areas:** biography, cooking, film, health, memoirs, music, popular culture, sports, true crime, entertainment. "This agency offers clients full management service in all media. Clients are not necessarily book authors. Our special expertise is in placing newspaper series internationally." Actively seeking autobiographies.

- "This agency offers clients full management service in all media. Clients are not necessarily book authors. Our special expertise is in placing newspaper series internationally." Actively seeking autobiographies.

How to Contact Submit outline/proposal, SASE (IRCs if necessary).Prefers to read materials exclusively. Responds in 2 weeks to queries. Obtains most new clients through recommendations from others, Direct approaches to prospective authors.

Terms Agent receives 15% commission on domestic sales. Agent receives 20% commission on foreign sales. Offers written contract, binding for 3 months; 3-month notice must be given to terminate contract. Charges clients for couriers, photocopying, overseas mailings of mss (subject to client authorization).

Recent Sales *Lawro*, by Mark Lawrenson (Penguin); *Enter the Dragon*, by Theo Paphitis (Orion); *Strong Women*, by Roberta Kray (Little, Brown); *Home From War*, by Martyn and Michelle Compton (Mainstream); *Diary of a Japanese P.O.W*, by John Baxter (Aurum Press); *A Different Kind of Courage*, by Gretel Wachtel and Claudia Strachan (Mainstream); *Drawing Fire*, by Len Smith (HarperCollins); *Mummy Doesn't Love You*, by Alexander Sinclair (Ebury Press); *Forgotten*, by Les Cummings (Macmillan); *Suffer the Little Children*, by Frances Reilly (Orion).

MICHAEL SNELL LITERARY AGENCY

P.O. Box 1206, Truro MA 02666-1206. (508)349-3718. **Contact:** Michael Snell. Represents 200 clients. 25% of clients are new/unpublished writers. Currently handles: nonfiction books 90%, novels 10%.

- Prior to opening his agency, Mr. Snell served as an editor at Wadsworth and Addison-Wesley for 13 years.

Member Agents Michael Snell (business, leadership, pets, sports).

Represents nonfiction books. **Considers these nonfiction areas:** agriculture horticulture, crafts, interior, newage, animals, pets, anthropology, art, business, child, computers, cooking, current affairs, education, ethnic, gardening, gay, government, health, history, how to, humor, language, military, money, music, nature, photography, popular culture, psychology, recreation, religion, science, self help, sex, spirituality, sports, fitness, film, travel, true crime, womens, creative nonfiction. This agency specializes in how-to, self-help, and all types of business and computer books, from low-level how-to to professional and reference. Especially interested in business, health, law, medicine, psychology, science, and women's issues. Actively seeking strong book proposals in any nonfiction area where a clear need exists for a new book--especially self-help and how-to books on all subjects, from business to personal well-being. Does not want to receive fiction, children's books, or complete mss (considers proposals only).

- This agency specializes in how-to, self-help, and all types of business and computer books, from low-level how-to to professional and reference. Especially interested in business, health, law, medicine, psychology, science, and women's issues. Actively seeking strong book proposals in any nonfiction area where a clear need exists for a new book--especially self-help and how-to books on all subjects, from business to personal well-being. Does not want to receive fiction, children's books, or complete mss (considers proposals only).

How to Contact Query with SASE. Prefers to read materials exclusively. Responds in 1 week to queries. Responds in 2 weeks to mss. Obtains most new clients through unsolicited mss, word of mouth, *Literary Market Place*, *Guide to Literary Agents*.

Terms Agent receives 15% commission on domestic sales. Agent receives 15% commission on foreign sales.

Recent Sales *How Did That Happen? Holding Other People Accountable for Results the Positive, Principled Way*, by Roger Connors and Tom Smith (Portfolio/Penguin); *Recovering the Lost River: Rewilding Salmon, Recivilizing Humans, Removing Dams*, by Steve Hawley (Beacon Press); *You, Him and Her: Coping With Infidelity in Your Marriage*, by Dr. Paul Coleman (Adams Media); *Strategic Customer Service*, by John Goodman (Amacom Books).

Tips "Send a maximum 1-page query with SASE. Brochure on 'How to Write a Book Proposal' is available on request with SASE. We suggest prospective clients read Michael Snell's book, *From Book Idea to Bestseller* (Prima 1997), or purchase a model proposal directly from the company."

SPECTRUM LITERARY AGENCY

320 Central Park W., Suite 1-D, New York NY 10025. Fax: (212)362-4562. Website: www.spectrumliteraryagency.com. **Contact:** Eleanor Wood, president. Estab. 1976. SFWA Represents 90 clients. Currently handles: nonfiction books 10%, novels 90%.

Member Agents Eleanor Wood, Justin Bell.

Represents nonfiction books, novels. **Considers these fiction areas:** fantasy, historical, mainstream, mystery, romance, science fiction.
How to Contact Query with SASE. Submit author bio, publishing credits. No unsolicited mss will be read. Snail mail queries **only**. Eleanor and Lucienne have different addresses - see the Web site for full info. Responds in 1-3 months to queries. Obtains most new clients through recommendations from authors.
Terms Agent receives 15% commission on domestic sales. Deducts for photocopying and book orders.
Tips "Spectrum's policy is to read only book-length manuscripts that we have specifically asked to see. Unsolicited manuscripts are not accepted. The letter should describe your book briefly and include publishing credits and background information or qualifications relating to your work, if any."

SPENCERHILL ASSOCIATES

P.O. Box 374, Chatham NY 12037. (518)392-9293. Fax: (518)392-9554. E-mail: ksolem@klsbooks.com; jennifer@klsbooks.com. **Contact:** Karen Solem or Jennifer Schober. Member of AAR. Represents 73 clients. 5% of clients are new/unpublished writers.

- Prior to becoming an agent, Ms. Solem was editor-in-chief at HarperCollins and an associate publisher.

Member Agents Karen Solem; Jennifer Schober.
Represents novels. **Considers these fiction areas:** detective, historical, literary, mainstream, religious, romance, thriller, young. "We handle mostly commercial women's fiction, historical novels, romance (historical, contemporary, paranormal, urban fantasy), thrillers, and mysteries. We also represent Christian fiction." No nonfiction, poetry, science fiction, children's picture books, or scripts.

O→ "We handle mostly commercial women's fiction, historical novels, romance (historical, contemporary, paranormal, urban fantasy), thrillers, and mysteries. We also represent Christian fiction." No nonfiction, poetry, science fiction, children's picture books, or scripts.

How to Contact Query jennifer@klsbooks.com with synopsis and first three chapters. E-queries preferred. Responds in 6-8 weeks to queries.
Terms Agent receives 15% commission on domestic sales. Agent receives 20% commission on foreign sales. Offers written contract; 3-month notice must be given to terminate contract.

THE SPIELER AGENCY

154 W. 57th St., Suite 135, New York NY 10019. E-mail: eric@spieleragency.com. **Contact:** Katya Balter. Represents 160 clients. 2% of clients are new/unpublished writers.

- Prior to opening his agency, Mr. Spieler was a magazine editor.

Member Agents Joe Spieler.
Represents nonfiction books, novels, children's books. **Considers these nonfiction areas:** biography, business, current affairs, film, gay, government, history, memoirs, money, music, nature, sociology, spirituality, travel. **Considers these fiction areas:** detective, feminist, gay, literary, mystery, children's books, Middle Grade and Young Adult novels.
How to Contact Accepts electronic submissions (spieleragency@spieleragency.com), or send query letter and sample chapters. Prefers to read materials exclusively. Returns materials only with SASE; otherwise materials are discarded when rejected. Accepts simultaneous submissions. Responds in 2 weeks to queries. Responds in 2 months to mss. Obtains most new clients through recommendations, listing in *Guide to Literary Agents.*
Terms Agent receives 15% commission on domestic sales. Charges clients for messenger bills, photocopying, postage.
Writers Conferences London Book Fair.
Tips "Check http://www.publishersmarketplace.com/members/spielerlit/."

PHILIP G. SPITZER LITERARY AGENCY, INC

50 Talmage Farm Ln., East Hampton NY 11937. (631)329-3650. Fax: (631)329-3651. E-mail: luc.hunt@spitzeragency.com. Website: www.spitzeragency.com. **Contact:** Luc Hunt. Member of AAR. Represents 60 clients. 10% of clients are new/unpublished writers. Currently handles: nonfiction books 35%, novels 65%.

- Prior to opening his agency, Mr. Spitzer served at New York University Press, McGraw-Hill, and the John Cushman Associates literary agency.

Represents nonfiction books, novels. **Considers these nonfiction areas:** Biography, History, Travel, Politics, Current Events. **Considers these fiction areas:** general fiction, detective, literary, mainstream, mystery, sports, thriller. This agency specializes in mystery/suspense, literary fiction, sports and general nonfiction (no how-to).

O→ This agency specializes in mystery/suspense, literary fiction, sports and general nonfiction (no how-to).

How to Contact Query with SASE. Responds in 1 week to queries. Responds in 6 weeks to mss. Obtains

most new clients through recommendations from others.
Terms Agent receives 15% commission on domestic sales. Agent receives 20% commission on foreign sales. Charges clients for photocopying.
Writers Conferences BookExpo America.

P. STATHONIKOS AGENCY

146 Springbluff Heights SW, Calgary Alberta T3H 5E5 Canada. (403)245-2087. Fax: (403)245-2087. E-mail: pastath@telus.net. **Contact:** Penny Stathonikos.

- Prior to becoming an agent, Ms. Stathonikos was a bookstore owner and publisher's representative for 10 years.

Represents nonfiction books, novels, juvenile. Children's literature, some young adult. Does not want to receive romance, fantasy, historical fiction, plays, movie scripts or poetry.

- Children's literature, some young adult. Does not want to receive romance, fantasy, historical fiction, plays, movie scripts or poetry.

How to Contact Query with SASE. Submit outline. Responds in 1 month to queries. Responds in 2 months to mss.
Terms Agent receives 10% commission on domestic sales. Agent receives 15% commission on foreign sales. Charges for postage, telephone, copying, etc.
Tips "Do your homework—read any of the Writer's Digest market books, join a writers' group and check out the local bookstore or library for similar books. Know who your competition is and why your book is different."

NANCY STAUFFER ASSOCIATES

P.O. Box 1203, 1540 Boston Post Road, Darien CT 06820. (203)202-2500. Fax: (203)655-3704. E-mail: StaufferAssoc@optonline.net. **Contact:** Nancy Stauffer Cahoon. Other memberships include Authors Guild. 5% of clients are new/unpublished writers. Currently handles: nonfiction books 15%, novels 85%.
Represents Considers these nonfiction areas: current affairs, ethnic, creative nonfiction (narrative). **Considers these fiction areas:** contemporary, literary, regional.
How to Contact Obtains most new clients through referrals from existing clients.
Terms Agent receives 15% commission on domestic sales. Agent receives 20% commission on foreign sales. Agent receives 15% commission on film sales.
Recent Sales *The Absolutely Diary of a Part-time Indian*, by Sherman Alexie; *West of Last Chance*, by Peter Brown and Kent Haruf.

STEELE-PERKINS LITERARY AGENCY

26 Island Ln., Canandaigua NY 14424. (585)396-9290. Fax: (585)396-3579. E-mail: pattiesp@aol.com. **Contact:** Pattie Steele-Perkins. Member of AAR. Other memberships include RWA. Currently handles: novels 100%.
Represents novels. **Considers these fiction areas:** romance, women's, All genres: category romance, romantic suspense, historical, contemporary, multi-cultural, and inspirational.
How to Contact Submit synopsis and one chapter via e-mail (no attachments) or snail mail. Snail mail submissions require SASE. Accepts simultaneous submissions. Responds in 6 weeks to queries. Obtains most new clients through recommendations from others, queries/solicitations.
Terms Agent receives 15% commission on domestic sales. Offers written contract, binding for 1 year; 1-month notice must be given to terminate contract.
Recent Sales Sold 130 titles last year. This agency prefers not to share specific sales information.
Writers Conferences RWA National Conference; BookExpo America; CBA Convention; Romance Slam Jam.
Tips "Be patient. E-mail rather than call. Make sure what you are sending is the best it can be."

STERNIG & BYRNE LITERARY AGENCY

2370 S. 107th St., Apt. #4, Milwaukee WI 53227-2036. (414)328-8034. Fax: (414)328-8034. E-mail: jackbyrne@hotmail.com. Website: www.sff.net/people/jackbyrne. **Contact:** Jack Byrne. Other memberships include SFWA, MWA. Represents 30 clients. 10% of clients are new/unpublished writers. Currently handles: nonfiction books 5%, novels 90%, juvenile books 5%.
Represents nonfiction books, novels, juvenile. **Considers these fiction areas:** fantasy, horror, mystery, science. Our client list is comfortably full and our current needs are therefore quite limited. Actively seeking science fiction/fantasy and mystery by established writers. Does not want to receive romance, poetry, textbooks, or highly specialized nonfiction.

- Our client list is comfortably full and our current needs are therefore quite limited. Actively seeking science fiction/fantasy and mystery by established writers. Does not want to receive romance, poetry, textbooks, or highly specialized nonfiction.

How to Contact Query with SASE. Prefers e-mail queries (no attachments); hard copy queries also acceptable. Responds in 3 weeks to queries. Responds in 3 months to mss.
Terms Agent receives 15% commission on domestic sales. Agent receives 20% commission on foreign sales. Offers written contract; 2-month notice must be given to terminate contract.
Tips "Don't send first drafts, have a professional presentation (including cover letter), and know your field. Read what's been done - good and bad."

STIMOLA LITERARY STUDIO, LLC

306 Chase Court, Edgewater NJ 07020. Phone/Fax: (201)945-9353. E-mail: info@stimolaliterarystudio.com. Website: www.stimolaliterarystudio.com. **Contact:** Rosemary B. Stimola. Member of AAR.
How to Contact Query via e-mail (no unsolicited attachments). Responds in 3 weeks to queries "we wish to pursue further." Responds in 2 months to requested mss. Obtains most new clients through referrals. Unsolicited submissions are still accepted.
Terms Agent receives 15% commission on domestic sales. Agent receives 20% (if subagents are employed) commission on foreign sales.
Recent Sales *The Hunger Games Trilogy*, by Suzanne Collins (Scholastic); *The Haunting of Charles Dickens*, by Lewis Buzbee (Feiwel & Friends); *Boys, Bears and a Serious Pair of Hiking Boots*, by Abby McDonald (Candlewick Press); *The Miles Betwee*n, by Mary E. Pearson (Holt); *Past Perfect*, by Siobhan Vivian (Scholastic, Push); *Amy & Roger Discover America*, by Morgan Matson (S&S); *Barbie, For Better or Worse*, by Tanya Lee Stone (Viking); *Felicity Rose and Cordelia Bean*, by Lisa Jahn-Clough (FSG); *The Flying Beaver Brothers*, by Maxwell Eaton III (Knopf).

STRACHAN LITERARY AGENCY

P.O. Box 2091, Annapolis MD 21404. E-mail: query@strachanlit.com. Website: www.strachanlit.com. **Contact:** Laura Strachan.

- Prior to becoming an agent, Ms. Strachan was (and still is) an attorney.

Represents nonfiction books, novels. **Considers these nonfiction areas:** interior, cooking, gardening, memoirs, photography, psychology, self help, travel, narrative, parenting, arts. **Considers these fiction areas:** literary, mystery, legal and pyschological thrillers, children's. "This agency specializes in literary fiction and narrative nonfiction." Actively seeking new, fresh voices.

- "This agency specializes in literary fiction and narrative nonfiction." Actively seeking new, fresh voices.

How to Contact Query with cover letter outlining your professional experience and a brief synopsis. Prefers e-mail queries; send no e-mail attachments. No sample pages unless requested.
Recent Sales *The Golden Bristled Boar* (UVA Press); *Poser* (Walker)

ROBIN STRAUS AGENCY, INC.

229 E. 79th St., New York NY 10075. (212)472-3282. Fax: (212)472-3833. E-mail: info@robinstrausagency.com.Website: www.robinstrausagency.com/. **Contact:** Ms. Robin Straus. Member of AAR.

- Prior to becoming an agent, Robin Straus served as a subsidary rights manager at Random House and Doubleday and worked in editorial at Little, Brown.

Terms Agent receives 15% commission on domestic sales. Agent receives 20% commission on foreign sales. Offers written contract. Charges for photocopying, express mail services, messenger and foreign postage, etc. as incurred.

PAM STRICKLER AUTHOR MANAGEMENT

1 Water St., New Paltz NY 12561. (845)255-0061. E-mail: pam302mail-aaaqueries@yahoo.com. Website: www.pamstrickler.com. **Contact:** Pamela Dean Strickler. Member of AAR.

- Prior to opening her agency, Ms. Strickler was senior editor at Ballantine Books.

Represents novels. **Considers these fiction areas:** historical, romance, women's. Does not want to receive nonfiction or children's books.

- Does not want to receive nonfiction or children's books.

How to Contact Prefers e-mail queries.

REBECCA STRONG INTERNATIONAL LITERARY AGENCY

235 W. 108th St., #35, New York NY 10025. (212)865-1569. E-mail: info@rsila.com. Website: www.rsila.com. **Contact:** Rebecca Strong. Estab. 2004.

- Prior to opening her agency, Ms. Strong was an industry executive with experience editing and licensing in the US and UK. She has worked at Crown/Random House, Harmony/Random House, Bloomsbury, and Harvill.

Represents nonfiction books, novels. **Considers these nonfiction areas:** biography, business, health, history, memoirs, science, travel. "We are a consciously small agency selectively representing authors all over the world." Does not want to receive poetry, screenplays or any unsolicited mss.

- "We are a consciously small agency selectively representing authors all over the world." Does not want to receive poetry, screenplays or any unsolicited mss.

How to Contact Email submissions only; subject line should indicate "submission query"; include cover letter with proposal. For fiction, include 1-2 complete chapters only. Accepts simultaneous submissions. Responds in 6-8 weeks to queries. Obtains most new clients through recommendations from others, conferences.

Terms Agent receives 15% commission on domestic sales. Agent receives 20% commission on foreign sales. Offers written contract, binding for 10 years; 30-day notice must be given to terminate contract.

Tips "I represent writers with prior publishing experience only: journalists, magazine writers or writers of fiction who have been published in anthologies or literary magazines. There are exceptions to this guideline, but not many."

THE STROTHMAN AGENCY, LLC

narrative nonfiction and literary fiction, Six Beacon St., Suite 810, Boston MA 02108. (617)742-2011. Fax: (617)742-2014. Website: www.strothmanagency.com. **Contact:** Wendy Strothman, Dan O'Connell. Member of AAR. Other memberships include Authors' Guild. Represents 50 clients. Currently handles: nonfiction books 70%, novels 10%, scholarly books 20%.

- Prior to becoming an agent, Ms. Strothman was head of Beacon Press (1983-1995) and executive vice president of Houghton Mifflin's Trade & Reference Division (1996-2002).

Member Agents Wendy Strothman; Dan O'Connell.

Represents nonfiction books, novels, scholarly. **Considers these nonfiction areas:** current affairs, government, history, language, nature. **Considers these fiction areas:** literary. "Because we are highly selective in the clients we represent, we increase the value publishers place on our properties. We specialize in narrative nonfiction, memoir, history, science and nature, arts and culture, literary travel, current affairs, and some business. We have a highly selective practice in literary fiction and smart self-help. We are now opening our doors to more commercial fiction but ONLY from authors who have a platform. If you have a platform, please mention it in your query letter." "The Strothman Agency seeks out scholars, journalists, and other acknowledged and emerging experts in their fields. We are now actively looking for authors of well written young-adult fiction and nonfiction. Browse the Latest News to get an idea of the types of books that we represent. For more about what we're looking for, read Pitching an Agent: The Strothman Agency on the publishing website mediabistro.com." Does not want to receive commercial fiction, romance, science fiction or self-help.

- "Because we are highly selective in the clients we represent, we increase the value publishers place on our properties. We specialize in narrative nonfiction, memoir, history, science and nature, arts and culture, literary travel, current affairs, and some business. We have a highly selective practice in literary fiction and smart self-help. We are now opening our doors to more commercial fiction but ONLY from authors who have a platform. If you have a platform, please mention it in your query letter." "The Strothman Agency seeks out scholars, journalists, and other acknowledged and emerging experts in their fields. We are now actively looking for authors of well written young-adult fiction and nonfiction. Browse the Latest News to get an idea of the types of books that we represent. For more about what we're looking for, read Pitching an Agent: The Strothman Agency on the publishing website mediabistro.com." Does not want to receive commercial fiction, romance, science fiction or self-help.

How to Contact Open to email (strothmanagency@gmail.com) and postal submissions. See submission guidelines. Accepts simultaneous submissions. Responds in 4 weeks to queries. Responds in 6 weeks to mss. Obtains most new clients through recommendations from others.

Terms Agent receives 15% commission on domestic sales. Agent receives 20% commission on foreign sales. Offers written contract; 30-day notice must be given to terminate contract.

THE STUART AGENCY

fiction and nonfiction, 260 W. 52 St., #24C, New York NY 10019. (212)586-2711. Fax: (212)977-1488. Website: http://stuartagency.com. **Contact:** Andrew Stuart.

- Prior to his current position, Mr. Stuart was an agent with Literary Group International for five years. Prior to becoming an agent, he was an editor at Random House and Simon & Schuster.

Represents nonfiction books, novels. **Considers these nonfiction areas:** biography, ethnic, government, history, memoirs, multicultural, psychology, science, sports, narrative nonfiction. **Considers these fiction areas:** ethnic, literary.

How to Contact Query by email or mail with SASE. Do not send any materials besides query/SASE unless requested.

SUBIAS

One Union Square West, # 913, New York NY 10003. (212)445-1091. Fax: (212)898-0375. E-mail: mark@marksubias.com. **Contact:** Mark Subias. Represents 35 clients. Currently handles: stage plays 100%.

Represents stage plays. This agency is not currently representing movie scripts.

⊶ This agency is not currently representing movie scripts.

How to Contact Query with SASE.

EMMA SWEENEY AGENCY, LLC

245 East 80th St., Suite 7E, New York NY 10075. E-mail: queries@emmasweeneyagency.com; info@emmasweeneyagency.com. Website: www.emmasweeneyagency.com. **Contact:** Eva Talmadge. Member of AAR. Other memberships include Women's Media Group. Represents 50 clients. 5% of clients are new/unpublished writers. Currently handles: nonfiction books 30%, novels 70%.

- Prior to becoming an agent, Ms. Sweeney was a subsidiary rights assistant at William Morrow. Since 1990, she has been a literary agent, and was most recently an agent with Harold Ober Associates.

Member Agents Emma Sweeney, president; Eva Talmadge, rights manager; Justine Wenger, junior agent/assistant (justine@emmasweeneyagency.com).

Represents nonfiction books, novels. **Considers these nonfiction areas:** agriculture horticulture, animals, biography, cooking, memoirs. **Considers these fiction areas:** literary, mystery, thriller, womens. "We specialize in quality fiction and non-fiction. Our primary areas of interest include literary and women's fiction, mysteries and thrillers; science, history, biography, memoir, religious studies and the natural sciences." Does not want to receive romance and westerns or screenplays.

⊶ "We specialize in quality fiction and non-fiction. Our primary areas of interest include literary and women's fiction, mysteries and thrillers; science, history, biography, memoir, religious studies and the natural sciences." Does not want to receive romance and westerns or screenplays.

How to Contact Send query letter and first ten pages in body of e-mail (no attachments) to queries@emmasweeneyagency.com. No snail mail queries.

Terms Agent receives 15% commission on domestic sales. Agent receives 10% commission on foreign sales.

Writers Conferences Nebraska Writers' Conference; Words and Music Festival in New Orleans.

THE SWETKY AGENCY

2150 Balboa Way, No. 29, St. George UT 84770. E-mail: fayeswetky@amsaw.org. Website: www.amsaw.org/swetkyagency/index.html. **Contact:** Faye M. Swetky. Other memberships include American Society of Authors and Writers. Represents 40+ clients. 80% of clients are new/unpublished writers. Currently handles: nonfiction books 30%, novels 30%, movie scripts 20%, TV scripts 20%.

- Prior to becoming an agent, Ms. Swetky was an editor and corporate manager. She has also raised and raced thoroughbred horses.

Represents nonfiction books, novels, short story collections, juvenile, movie, TV, feature, MOW, sitcom, documentary. **Considers these script areas:** action, biography, cartoon, comedy, contemporary, detective, erotica, ethnic, experimental, family, fantasy, feminist, gay, glitz, historical, horror, juvenile, mainstream, multicultural, multimedia, mystery, psychic, regional, religious, romantic comedy, romantic drama, science, sports, teen, thriller, western. "We handle only book-length fiction and nonfiction and feature-length movie and television scripts. Please visit our Web site before submitting. All agency-related information is there, including a sample contract, e-mail submission forms, policies, clients, etc." Actively seeking young adult material. Do not send unprofessionally prepared mss and/or scripts.

⊶ "We handle only book-length fiction and nonfiction and feature-length movie and television scripts. Please visit our Web site before submitting. All agency-related information is there, including a sample contract, e-mail submission forms, policies, clients, etc." Actively seeking young adult material. Do not send unprofessionally prepared mss and/or scripts.

How to Contact See Web site for submission instructions. Accepts e-mail queries only. Accepts simultaneous submissions. Response time varies. Obtains most new clients through queries.

Terms Agent receives 15% commission on domestic sales. Agent receives 20% commission on foreign sales. Agent receives 20% commission on film sales. Offers written contract, binding for 6 months; 30-day notice must be given to terminate contract.

Recent Sales *Growing Fruit and Vegetables in Pots; Phony; Sha Daa; Not Working.*

Tips "Be professional. Have a professionally prepared product."

STEPHANIE TADE LITERARY AGENCY

P.O. Box 235, Durham PA 18039. (610)346-8667. **Contact:** Stephanie Tade.

- Prior to becoming an agent, Ms. Tade was an executive editor at Rodale Press. She was also an agent with the Jane Rotrosen Agency.

Member Agents Stephanie Tade, Dana Bacher.

Represents nonfiction books, novels. **Considers these nonfiction areas:** celebrity, health/fitness, history, medicine, relationships/dating, self-help, self-improvement, spirituality, womens issues. **Considers these fiction areas:** commercial, historical, romance, YA. novels

O→ novels

How to Contact Query by email or postal mail with SASE.

TALCOTT NOTCH LITERARY

276 Forest Road, Milford CT 06460. (203)877-1146. Fax: (203)876-9517. E-mail: editorial@talcottnotch.net. Website: www.talcottnotch.net. **Contact:** Gina Panettieri, president. Represents 35 clients. 25% of clients are new/unpublished writers. Currently handles: nonfiction books 25%, novels 55%, story collections 5%, juvenile books 10%, scholarly books 5%.

- Prior to becoming an agent, Ms. Panettieri was a freelance writer and editor.

Member Agents Gina Panettieri (nonfiction, mystery); Rachel Dowen (children's fiction, mystery).

Represents nonfiction books, novels, juvenile, scholarly, textbooks. **Considers these nonfiction areas:** agriculture horticulture, animals, anthropology, art, biography, business, child, computers, cooking, current affairs, education, ethnic, gay, government, health, history, how to, memoirs, military, money, music, nature, popular culture, psychology, science, self help, sociology, sports, true crime, womens, New Age/metaphysics, interior design/decorating, juvenile nonfiction. **Considers these fiction areas:** adventure, detective, juvenile, mystery, thriller, young.

How to Contact Query via e-mail (preferred) or with SASE. Accepts simultaneous submissions. Responds in 1 week to queries. Responds in 4-6 weeks to mss.

Terms Agent receives 15% commission on domestic sales. Agent receives 20% commission on foreign sales. Offers written contract, binding for 1 year.

Recent Sales Sold 36 titles in the last year. *Made Here, Baby!* by Bruce Wolk (Amacom); *Breaking the Co-Sleeping Habit,* by Dr. Valerie Levine (Adams Media); *DeadTown,* by Nancy Holzner (Berkley); *Living With Someone With Bipolar Disorder,* by Dr. Bruce Cohen and Chelsea Lowe (Wiley); *The Legacy Family,* by Douglas Freeman and Lee Hausner (Palgrave-Macmillan); *Sleeping in the House of Murder,* by Ron Franscell (Fair Winds), *The Welcoming Kitchen: Completely Allergen-Free Recipes,* by Kim Lutz and Megan Hart (Sterling); *Cookie: A History from Animal Crackers to Zwieback,* by Brette Sember (University Press of Florida). Other clients include Rick Morris, Linda Matias, Erik Lawrence, Dr. Leslie Young, Moira McCarthy, Rabbi Ben Kamin, Stan Wenck, Connie Hansen, Dagmara Scalise, Sandra Dark, Sheri Amsel, Dawn-Michelle Baude, Eric Groves, Sr., Drs. Phil and Nancy Hall, Dr. Karyn Purvis, Dr. David Cross, and Wendy Lyons Sunshine.

Tips "Present your book or project effectively in your query. Don't include links to a Web page rather than a traditional query, and take the time to prepare a thorough but brief synopsis of the material. Make the effort to prepare a thoughtful analysis of comparison titles. How is your work different, yet would appeal to those same readers?"

N TDP LITERARY AGENCY & NOTARY

612 Ziegler Ave, Suite 16, Linden NJ 07036. (908)205-2793. Fax: (801)443-8968. E-mail: tdpliteraryagency@yahoo.com. Website: tdp-literaryagency.tripod.com/. **Contact:** Kye D. McKenzie. Represents 15 clients. 50% of clients are new/unpublished writers. Currently handles: nonfiction books 25%, novels 75%.

How to Contact Query via e-mail only per guidelines on website. Include one-paragraph synopsis, one-paragraph bio, up to one sample chapter. No attachments. Responds in 4-6 weeks to queries. Responds in 6-8 weeks to mss. Obtains most clients through recommendations from others, solicitations, conferences.

Terms Agent receives 15% commission on domestic sales. Agent receives 20% commission on foreign sales. Offers written contract; 30-day notice must be given to terminate contract. This agency charges for postage and photocopying. Author is consulted before any charges are incurred.

Recent Sales *It's In the Rhythm,* by Sammie Ward (Genesis Press).

PATRICIA TEAL LITERARY AGENCY

2036 Vista Del Rosa, Fullerton CA 92831-1336. Phone/Fax: (714)738-8333. **Contact:** Patricia Teal. Member of AAR. Other memberships include RWA, Authors Guild. Represents 20 clients. Currently handles: nonfiction books 10%, other 90% fiction .

Represents nonfiction books, novels. **Considers these nonfiction areas:** animals, biography, child, health, how to, psychology, self help, true crime, womens. **Considers these fiction areas:** glitz, mainstream, mystery, romance (contemporary, historical). This agency specializes in women's fiction, commercial how-to, and self-help nonfiction. Does not want to receive poetry, short stories, articles, science fiction, fantasy, or regency romance.

O→ This agency specializes in women's fiction, commercial how-to, and self-help nonfiction. Does not want to receive poetry, short stories, articles, science fiction, fantasy, or regency romance.

How to Contact Published authors only may query with SASE. Accepts simultaneous submissions. Responds in 10 days to queries. Responds in 6 weeks to mss. Obtains most new clients through conferences, recommendations from authors and editors.

Terms Agent receives 10-15% commission on domestic sales. Agent receives 20% commission on foreign sales. Offers written contract, binding for 1 year. Charges clients for ms copies.

Recent Sales Sold 30 titles in the last year. *Texas Rose*, by Marie Ferrarella (Silhouette); *Watch Your Language*, by Sterling Johnson (St. Martin's Press); *The Black Sheep's Baby*, by Kathleen Creighton (Silhouette); *Man With a Message*, by Muriel Jensen (Harlequin).

Writers Conferences RWA Conferences; Asilomar; BookExpo America; Bouchercon; Maui Writers Conference.

Tips "Include SASE with all correspondence. I am taking on published authors only."

TESSLER LITERARY AGENCY, LLC

27 W. 20th St., Suite 1003, New York NY 10011. (212)242-0466. Fax: (212)242-2366. Website: www.tessleragency.com. **Contact:** Michelle Tessler. Member of AAR.

- Prior to forming her own agency, Ms. Tessler worked at Carlisle & Co. (now a part of Inkwell Management). She has also worked at the William Morris Agency and the Elaine Markson Literary Agency.

Represents nonfiction books. **Considers these nonfiction areas:** business, history, memoirs, popular culture, psychology, travel. "The Tessler Agency is a full-service boutique agency that represents writers of literary fiction and high quality nonfiction in the following categories: popular science, reportage, memoir, history, biography, psychology, business and travel."

- "The Tessler Agency is a full-service boutique agency that represents writers of literary fiction and high quality nonfiction in the following categories: popular science, reportage, memoir, history, biography, psychology, business and travel."

How to Contact Submit query through Web site only.

THE TFS LITERARY AGENCY

P.O. Box 46-031, Lower Hutt 5044 New Zealand. E-mail: tfs@elseware.co.nz. Website: www.elseware.co.nz. **Contact:** Chris Else, Barbara Else. Other memberships include NZALA.

Represents Seeks general fiction, nonfiction, and children's books from New Zealand authors only. No poetry, individual short stories, or articles.

- Seeks general fiction, nonfiction, and children's books from New Zealand authors only. No poetry, individual short stories, or articles.

How to Contact Send query and brief author bio via e-mail.

THREE SEAS LITERARY AGENCY

P.O. Box 8571, Madison WI 53708. (608)221-4306. E-mail: queries@threeseaslit.com. Website: www.threeseaslit.com. **Contact:** Michelle Grajkowski, Cori Deyoe. Estab. 2000. Other memberships include RWA, Chicago Women in Publishing. Represents 40 clients. 10% of clients are new/unpublished writers. Currently handles: nonfiction books 5%, novels 80%, juvenile books 15%.

- Prior to becoming an agent, Ms. Grajkowski worked in both sales and purchasing for a medical facility. She has a degree in journalism from the University of Wisconsin-Madison. Prior to joining the agency in 2006, Ms. Deyoe was a multi-published author. She is excited to be part of the agency and is actively building her client list.

Member Agents Michelle Grajkowski; Cori Deyoe (cori@threeseaslit.com).

Represents nonfiction books, novels, juvenile, scholarly. 3 Seas focuses on romance (including category, historical, regency, Western, romantic suspense, paranormal), women's fiction, mysteries, nonfiction, young adult and children's stories. "Currently, we are looking for fantastic authors with a voice of their own. More specifically, we love any type of romance (historical, contemporary, romantic suspense, paranormal, chick lit, inspirations and fantasy) and young adult and middle-grade fiction as well as mysteries, thrillers and select nonfiction titles." No poetry, screenplays or novellas.

- 3 Seas focuses on romance (including category, historical, regency, Western, romantic suspense, paranormal), women's fiction, mysteries, nonfiction, young adult and children's stories. "Currently, we are looking for fantastic authors with a voice of their own. More specifically, we love any type of romance (historical, contemporary, romantic suspense, paranormal, chick lit, inspirations and fantasy) and young adult and middle-grade fiction as well as mysteries, thrillers and select nonfiction titles." No poetry, screenplays or novellas.

How to Contact E-mail queries only. For fiction titles, query with first chapter and synopsis embedded in the e-mail. for nonfiction, query with complete proposal attached. For picture books, query with complete text. Illustrations are not necessary. Accepts simultaneous submissions. Responds in 1 month to queries. Responds in 3 months to partials. Obtains most new clients through recommendations from others, conferences.

Terms Agent receives 15% commission on domestic sales. Agent receives 20% commission on foreign sales. Offers written contract.

Recent Sales *Steamed*, by Katie MacAlister, along with the next books in her Aisling Grey and Dark Ones paranormal romance series (NAL); Kerrelyn Spars' next paranormal romance (Avon), *The Winter*

King and the next books in her *Lord of the Fading Land* series by C.L. Wilson (Leisure). Other sales include titles by Anna DeStefano, Laura Marie Altom, Cathy McDavid and Trish Milburn, Winnie Griggs and Carla Capsha, Winnie Griggs and Lisa Mondello, *Heartbreak River*, Tricia Mills (Razorbill); *Hate List*, by Jennifer Brown (Little, Brown); Nancy Robards Thompson and Kristi Gold, *With Violets*, by Elizabeth Robard (HarperCollins).

ANN TOBIAS: A LITERARY AGENCY FOR CHILDREN'S BOOKS

520 E. 84th St., Apt. 4L, New York NY 10028. E-mail: AnnTobias84@hotmail.com. **Contact:** Ann Tobias. Represents 25 clients. 10% of clients are new/unpublished writers. Currently handles: juvenile books 100%.

- Prior to opening her agency, Ms. Tobias worked as a children's book editor at Harper, William Morrow and Scholastic.

Represents juvenile. **Considers these nonfiction areas:** juvenile. **Considers these fiction areas:** picture books, poetry, for children, young, illustrated mss; mid-level novels. This agency specializes in books for children.

O→ This agency specializes in books for children.

How to Contact For all age groups and genres: Send a one-page letter of inquiry accompanied by a one-page writing sample, double-spaced. No attachments will be opened. Other Responds in 2 months to mss. Obtains most new clients through recommendations from editors.

Terms Agent receives 15% commission on domestic sales. Agent receives 20% commission on foreign sales. No written contract. This agency charges clients for photocopying, overnight mail, foreign postage, foreign telephone.

Tips "Read at least 200 children's books in the age group and genre in which you hope to be published. Follow this by reading another 100 children's books in other age groups and genres so you will have a feel for the field as a whole."

TRANSATLANTIC LITERARY AGENCY

72 Glengowan Road, Toronto Ontario M4N 1G4 Canada. E-mail: info@tla1.com. Website: www.tla1.com. **Contact:** Lynn Bennett. Represents 250 clients. 10% of clients are new/unpublished writers. Currently handles: nonfiction books 30%, novels 15%, juvenile books 50%, textbooks 5%.

Member Agents Lynn Bennett, Lynn@tla1.com, (juvenile and young adult fiction); Shaun Bradley, Shaun@tla1.com (literary fiction and narrative nonfiction); Marie Campbell, Marie@tla1.com (literary juvenile and young adult fiction); Andrea Cascardi, Andrea@tla1.com (literary juvenile and young adult fiction); Samantha Haywood, Sam@tla1.com (literary fiction, narrative nonfiction and graphic novels); Don Sedgwick, Don@tla1.com (literary fiction and narrative nonfiction).

Represents nonfiction books, novels, juvenile. **Considers these nonfiction areas:** biography, business, current affairs, nature. **Considers these fiction areas:** juvenile, literary, mainstream. "In both children's and adult literature, we market directly into the United States, the United Kingdom and Canada." Actively seeking literary children's and adult fiction, nonfiction. Does not want to receive picture books, poetry, screenplays or stage plays.

O→ In both children's and adult literature, we market directly into the United States, the United Kingdom and Canada. Actively seeking literary children's and adult fiction, nonfiction. Does not want to receive picture books, poetry, screenplays or stage plays.

How to Contact Submit E-query query with synopsis, 2 sample chapters, bio. Always refer to the Web site as guidelines will change. Responds in 2 weeks to queries. Obtains most new clients through recommendations from others.

Terms Agent receives 15% commission on domestic sales. Agent receives 20% commission on foreign sales. Offers written contract; 45-day notice must be given to terminate contract. This agency charges for photocopying and postage when it exceeds $100.

Recent Sales Sold 250 titles in the last year.

S©OTT TREIMEL NY

434 Lafayette St., New York NY 10003. (212)505-8353. Website: ScottTreimelNY.blogspot.com; www.ScottTreimelNY.com. **Contact:** John M. Cusick. Member of AAR. Other memberships include Authors Guild, SCBWI. 10% of clients are new/unpublished writers. Currently handles: other 100% junvenile/teen books.

- Prior to becoming an agent, Mr. Treimel was an assistant to Marilyn E. Marlow at Curtis Brown, a rights agent for Scholastic, a book packager and rights agent for United Feature Syndicate, a freelance editor, a rights consultant for HarperCollins Children's Books, and the founding director of Warner Bros. Worldwide Publishing.

Represents nonfiction books, novels, juvenile, children's, picture books, young adult. This agency specializes in tightly focused segments of the trade and institutional markets. Career clients.

O→ This agency specializes in tightly focused segments of the trade and institutional markets. Career clients.

How to Contact Submissions accepted only via Web site.

Terms Agent receives 15% commission on domestic sales. Agent receives 20% commission on foreign sales. Offers verbal or written contract. Charges clients for photocopying, express postage, messengers, and books needed to sell foreign, film and other rights.

Recent Sales *The Hunchback Assignments*, by Arthur Slade (Random House, HarperCollins Canada; HarperCollins Australia); *Shotgun Serenade*, by Gail Giles (Little, Brown); *Laundry Day*, by Maurie Manning (Clarion); *The P.S. Brothers*, by Maribeth Boelts (Harcourt); *The First Five Fourths*, by Pat Hughes (Viking); *Old Robert and the Troubadour Cats*, by Barbara Joosse (Philomel); *Ends*, by David Ward (Abrams); *Dear Canada*, by Barbara Haworth-Attard (Scholastic); *Soccer Dreams*, by Maribeth Boelts (Candlewick); *Lucky Me*, by Richard Scrimger (Tundra); *Play, Louie, Play*, by Muriel Harris Weinstein (Bloomsbury).

Writers Conferences SCBWI NY, NJ, PA, Bologna; The New School; Southwest Writers' Conference; Pikes Peak Writers' Conference.

TRIADA U.S. LITERARY AGENCY, INC.

P.O. Box 561, Sewickley PA 15143. (412)401-3376. E-mail: uwe@triadaus.com. Website: www.triadaus.com. **Contact:** Dr. Uwe Stender. Represents 65 clients. 25% of clients are new/unpublished writers.

Member Agents Rebecca Post.

Represents fiction, nonfiction. **Considers these nonfiction areas:** biography, business, education, memoirs, popular culture, science, sports, advice, relationships, health, cooking, lifestyle. **Considers these fiction areas:** adventure, detective, ethnic, historical, horror, juvenile, literary, mainstream, mystery, occult, romance, women's, young adult. "We are looking for great writing and story platforms. Our response time is fairly unique. We recognize that neither we nor the authors have time to waste, so we guarantee a 5-day response time. We usually respond within 24 hours." Actively looking for both fiction and nonfiction in all areas. De-emphasizing fiction, although great writing will always be considered.

O→ "We are looking for great writing and story platforms. Our response time is fairly unique. We recognize that neither we nor the authors have time to waste, so we guarantee a 5-day response time. We usually respond within 24 hours. " Actively looking for both fiction and nonfiction in all areas. De-emphasizing fiction, although great writing will always be considered.

How to Contact E-mail queries preferred; otherwise query with SASE. Accepts simultaneous submissions. Responds in 1-5 weeks to queries. Responds in 2-6 weeks to mss. Obtains most new clients through recommendations from others, conferences.

Terms Agent receives 15% commission on domestic sales. Agent receives 20% commission on foreign sales. Offers written contract; 30-day notice must be given to terminate contract.

Recent Sales *Covert*, by Bob Delaney & Dave Scheiber (Sterling); *86'd*, by Dan Fante (Harper Perennial); *Everything I'm Not Made Me Everything I Am*, by Jeff Johnson (Smiley Books).

Tips "I comment on all requested manuscripts that I reject."

TRIDENT MEDIA GROUP

41 Madison Ave., 36th Floor, New York NY 10010. (212)262-4810. Website: www.tridentmediagroup.com. **Contact:** Ellen Levine. Member of AAR.

Member Agents Kimberly Whalen, whalen.assistant@tridentmediagroup (commercial fiction and nonfiction, women's fiction, suspense, paranormal and pop culture); Jenny Bent, jbent@tridentmediagroup.com (humor, literary fiction, women's commercial fiction, narrative nonfiction, biography, health, how-to); Eileen Cope, ecope@tridentmediagroup.comnarrative nonfiction, history, biography, pop culture, health, literary fiction and short story collections); Scott Miller, smiller@tridentmediagroup.com (thrillers, crime, mystery, young adult, children's, narrative nonfiction, current events, military, memoir, literary fiction, graphic novels, pop culture); Paul Fedorko, pfedorko@tridentmediagroup.com (commercial fiction, mysteries, thrillers, romantic suspense, business, sports, celebrity and pop culture); Alex Glass (aglass@tridentmediagroup, thrillers, literary fiction, crime, middle grade, pop culture, young adult, humor and narrative nonfiction); Melissa Flashman, mflashman@tridentmediagroup.com (narrative nonfiction, serious nonfiction, pop culture, lifstyle); Alyssa Henkin, ahenkin@tridentmediagroup.com (juvenile, children's, YA).

Represents nonfiction books, novels, short story collections, juvenile. **Considers these nonfiction areas:** young, biography, current affairs, government, humor, memoirs, military, multicultural, popular culture, true crime, womens. **Considers these fiction areas:** detective, humor, juvenile, literary, military, multicultural, mystery, short, thriller, young, womens. Actively seeking new or established authors in a variety of fiction and nonfiction genres.

O→ Actively seeking new or established authors in a variety of fiction and nonfiction genres.

How to Contact Query with SASE or via e-mail. Check Web site for more details.

Tips "If you have any questions, please check FAQ page before emailing us."

THE RICHARD R. VALCOURT AGENCY, INC.

1735 York Ave., #35-A, New York NY 10128. (212)570-2340. **Contact:** Richard R. Valcourt, president. 20% of clients are new/unpublished writers. Currently handles: nonfiction books 100%.

- Prior to opening his agency, Mr. Valcourt was a journalist, editor, and college political science instructor. He is also editor-in-chief of the *International Journal of Intelligence* and consulting faculty member at American Military University in West Virginia.

Represents scholarly. "Not accepting new clients at this time. This agency specializes in intelligence and other national security affairs. Represents exclusively academics, journalists, and professionals in the categories listed."

O→ "Not accepting new clients at this time. This agency specializes in intelligence and other national security affairs. Represents exclusively academics, journalists, and professionals in the categories listed."

How to Contact Prefers to read materials exclusively. No e-mail queries. Responds in 1 week to queries. Responds in 1 month to mss. Obtains most new clients through recommendations from others.

Terms Agent receives 15% commission on domestic sales. Agent receives 20% commission on foreign sales. Offers written contract. Charges clients for excessive photocopying, express mail, overseas telephone expenses.

VAN DIEST LITERARY AGENCY

Mainly nonfiction, some select fiction with a unique and timely message enhanced through fiction., P.O. Box 1482, Sisters OR 97759. Website: http://christianliteraryagency.com/contact.html.

Member Agents David Van Diest, Sarah Van Diest.

Represents Christian books. "We are actively looking to discover and bring to market a few authors with fresh perspectives on timely subjects."

O→ Christian books. "We are actively looking to discover and bring to market a few authors with fresh perspectives on timely subjects."

How to Contact "Before submitting a proposal or manuscript, we ask that you submit an online query found on the Contact Us page. We will contact you if we would like to receive a full proposal."

VANGUARD LITERARY AGENCY

81 E. Jefryn Blvd., Suite E,, Deer Park NY 11729. (718)710-3662. Fax: (917)591-7088. E-mail: sandylu@vanguardliterary.com; sandy@lperkinsagency.com. Website: www.vanguardliterary.com. **Contact:** Sandy Lu.Represents 15 clients. 60% of clients are new/unpublished writers. Currently handles: nonfiction books 20%, novels 80%.

- Prior to becoming an agent, Ms. Lu held managerial positions in commercial theater. "Ms. Lu is also an associate agent at the L. Perkins Agency. Please only send queries to one of her e-mail addresses."

Represents nonfiction books, novels, short story collections, novellas. **Considers these nonfiction areas:** anthropology, biography, cooking, ethnic, gay, history, memoirs, music, popular culture, psychology, science, sociology, translation, true crime, womens. **Considers these fiction areas:** adventure, confession, detective, ethnic, historical, horror, humor, literary, mainstream, mystery, regional, thriller, womens, (no chick lit). "Very few agents in the business still edit their clients' manuscripts, especially when it comes to fiction. Vanguard Literary Agency is different. I care about the quality of my clients' works and will not send anything out to publishers without personally going through each page first to ensure that when the manuscript is sent out, it is in the best possible shape." Actively seeking literary and commercial fiction with a unique voice. Does not want to receive movie or TV scripts, stage plays or poetry; unwanted fiction genres include science fiction/fantasy, Western, YA, children's; unwanted nonfiction genres include self-help, how-to, parenting, sports, dating/relationship, military/war, religion/spirituality, New Age, gift books.

O→ "Very few agents in the business still edit their clients' manuscripts, especially when it comes to fiction. Vanguard Literary Agency is different. I care about the quality of my clients' works and will not send anything out to publishers without personally going through each page first to ensure that when the manuscript is sent out, it is in the best possible shape." Actively seeking literary and commercial fiction with a unique voice. Does not want to receive movie or TV scripts, stage plays or poetry; unwanted fiction genres include science fiction/fantasy, Western, YA, children's; unwanted nonfiction genres include self-help, how-to, parenting, sports, dating/relationship, military/war, religion/spirituality, New Age, gift books.

How to Contact Only accepts e-mail queries. No fax queries. Accepts simultaneous submissions. Responds in 2 weeks to queries. Responds in 6-8 weeks to mss. Obtains most new clients through recommendations from others, solicitations, conferences.

Terms Agent receives 15% commission on domestic sales. Agent receives 20% commission on foreign sales. Offers written contract, binding for 1 year; 30-day notice must be given to terminate contract. This agency charges for photocopying and postage, and discusses larger costs (in excess of $100) with

authors prior to charging.
Tips "Do your research. Do not query an agent for a genre he or she does not represent. Personalize your query letter. Start with an interesting hook. Learn how to write a succinct yet interesting synopsis or proposal."

VENTURE LITERARY

8895 Towne Centre Drive, Suite 105, #141, San Diego CA 92122. (619)807-1887. Fax: (772)365-8321. E-mail: submissions@ventureliterary.com. Website: www.ventureliterary.com. **Contact:** Frank R. Scatoni.Represents 50 clients. 40% of clients are new/unpublished writers. Currently handles: nonfiction books 80%, novels 20%.

- Prior to becoming an agent, Mr. Scatoni worked as an editor at Simon & Schuster.

Member Agents Frank R. Scatoni (general nonfiction, biography, memoir, narrative nonfiction, sports, serious nonfiction, graphic novels, narratives).
Represents nonfiction books, novels, graphic novels, narratives. **Considers these nonfiction areas:** anthropology, biography, business, current affairs, ethnic, government, history, memoirs, military, money, multicultural, music, nature, popular culture, psychology, science, sports, true crime. **Considers these fiction areas:** adventure, detective, literary, mainstream, mystery, sports, thriller, womens. Specializes in nonfiction, sports, biography, gambling and nonfiction narratives. Actively seeking nonfiction, graphic novels and narratives.

O→ Specializes in nonfiction, sports, biography, gambling and nonfiction narratives. Actively seeking nonfiction, graphic novels and narratives.

How to Contact Considers e-mail queries only. *No unsolicited mss* and no snail mail whatsoever. See Web site for complete submission guidelines. Obtains most new clients through recommendations from others.
Terms Agent receives 15% commission on domestic sales. Agent receives 20% commission on foreign sales. Offers written contract.
Recent Sales *The 9/11 Report: A Graphic Adaptation*, by Sid Jacobson and Ernie Colon (FSG); *Having a Baby*, by Cindy Margolis (Perigee/Penguin); *Phil Gordon's Little Blue Book*, by Phil Gordon (Simon & Schuster); *Atomic America*, by Todd Tucker (Free Press); *War as They Knew It*, by Michael Rosenberg (Grand Central); *Game Day*, by Craig James (Wiley); *The Blueprint*, by Christopher Price (Thomas Dunne Books).

VERITAS LITERARY AGENCY

601 Van Ness Ave., Opera Plaza, Suite E, San Francisco CA 94102. Website: www.veritasliterary.com. **Contact:** Katherine Boyle. Member of AAR. Other memberships include Author's Guild.
Represents nonfiction books, novels. **Considers these nonfiction areas:** current affairs, government, memoirs, popular culture, womens, narrative nonfiction, art and music biography, natural history, health and wellness, psychology, serious religion (no New Age) and popular science. Does not want to receive romance, sci-fi, poetry or children's books.

O→ Does not want to receive romance, sci-fi, poetry or children's books.

How to Contact Query with SASE. This agency prefers a short query letter with no attachments.

BETH VESEL LITERARY AGENCY

80 Fifth Ave., Suite 1101, New York NY 10011. (212)924-4252. E-mail: mlindley@bvlit.com. **Contact:** Julia Masnik, assistant. Represents 65 clients. 10% of clients are new/unpublished writers. Currently handles: nonfiction books 75%, novels 10%, story collections 5%, scholarly books 10%.

- Prior to becoming an agent, Ms. Vesel was a poet and a journalist.

Represents nonfiction books, novels. **Considers these nonfiction areas:** biography, business, ethnic, health, how to, memoirs, psychology, self help, true crime, womens, cultural criticism. **Considers these fiction areas:** detective, literary, Francophone novels. "My specialties include serious nonfiction, psychology, cultural criticism, memoir, and women's issues." Actively seeking cultural criticism, literary psychological thrillers, and sophisticated memoirs. No uninspired psychology or run-of-the-mill first novels.

O→ "My specialties include serious nonfiction, psychology, cultural criticism, memoir, and women's issues." Actively seeking cultural criticism, literary psychological thrillers, and sophisticated memoirs. No uninspired psychology or run-of-the-mill first novels.

How to Contact Query with SASE. Accepts simultaneous submissions. Responds in 2 weeks to queries. Responds in 1 month to mss. Obtains most new clients through referrals, reading good magazines, contacting professionals with ideas.
Terms Agent receives 15% commission on domestic sales. Agent receives 20% commission on foreign sales. Offers written contract.
Recent Sales Sold 10 titles in the last year. *Life with Pop*, by Janis Spring, Ph.D (Avery); *American Scandal*, by Laura Kipnis (Metropolitan); *Bird in Hand*, by Christina Baker Kline (William Morrow); *Reimagining the South*, by Tracy Thompson (Simon & Schuster); *Are Fathers Necessary*, by Raul Raeburn

(Simon & Schuster); *Blind Date*, by Virginia Vitzhum (Workman); *Bipolar Breakthrough*, by Ron Fieve (Rodale).
Writers Conferences Squaw Valley Writers Workshop, Iowa Summer Writing Festival.
Tips "Try to find out if you fit on a particular agent's list by looking at his/her books and comparing yours. You can almost always find who represents a book by looking at the acknowledgements."

RALPH VICINANZA, LTD.

303 W. 18th St., New York NY 10011. (212)924-7090. Fax: (212)691-9644. Member of AAR.
Member Agents Ralph M. Vicinanza; Chris Lotts; Chris Schelling, Matthew Mahoney.
How to Contact This agency takes on new clients by professional recommendation only.
Terms Agent receives 15% commission on domestic sales. Agent receives 20% commission on foreign sales.

WADE & DOHERTY LITERARY AGENCY

33 Cormorant Lodge, Thomas Moore St., London E1W 1AU England. (44)(207)488-4171. Fax: (44)(207)488-4172. E-mail: bd@rwla.com. Website: www.rwla.com. **Contact:** Robin Wade. Estab. 2001.

- Prior to opening his agency, Mr. Wade was an author; Ms. Doherty worked as a production assistant, editor and editorial director.

Member Agents Robin Wade, Broo Doherty.
Represents fiction and nonfiction, including children's books. We are young and dynamic, and actively seek new writers across the literary spectrum. Does not want to receive poetry, plays or short stories.

O→ We are young and dynamic, and actively seek new writers across the literary spectrum. Does not want to receive poetry, plays or short stories.

How to Contact Submit synopsis (1-6 pages), bio, first 10,000 words via e-mail (Word or pdf documents only). If sending by post, include SASE or IRC. Responds in 1 week to queries. Responds in 1 month to mss.
Terms Agent receives 10% commission on domestic sales. Agent receives 20% commission on foreign sales. Offers written contract; 1-month notice must be given to terminate contract.
Tips "We seek manuscripts that are well written, with strong characters and an original narrative voice. Our absolute priority is giving the best possible service to the authors we choose to represent, as well as maintaining routine friendly contact with them as we help develop their careers."

MARY JACK WALD ASSOCIATES, INC.

fiction, 111 E. 14th St., New York NY 10003. **Contact:** Danis Sher. Member of AAR. Other memberships include Authors Guild, SCBWI. Represents 35 clients. 5% of clients are new/unpublished writers.
Member Agents Mary Jack Wald; Danis Sher; Alvin Wald, Sharon Shavers Gayle.
Represents nonfiction books, novels, short story collections, novellas, juvenile, clients' movie/TV scripts. **Considers these nonfiction areas:** juvenile, biography, current affairs, ethnic, history, language, music, nature, photography, sociology, film, translation, true crime. **Considers these fiction areas:** contemporary, glitz, adventure, detective, ethnic, experimental, family, feminist, gay, historical, juvenile, literary, mainstream, mystery, picture books, thriller, young adults, satire. This agency specializes in literary works, adult and juvenile works. novels

O→ This agency specializes in literary works, adult and juvenile works. novels

How to Contact Submit, will request more if interested. Query with SASE.
Terms Agent receives 15% commission on domestic sales. Agent receives 15-30% commission on foreign sales. Offers written contract, binding for 1 year.

WALES LITERARY AGENCY, INC.

P.O. Box 9428, Seattle WA 98109-0428. (206)284-7114. E-mail: waleslit@waleslit.com. Website: www.waleslit.com. **Contact:** Elizabeth Wales, Neal Swain. Member of AAR. Other memberships include Book Publishers' Northwest, Pacific Northwest Booksellers Association, PEN. Represents 65 clients. 10% of clients are new/unpublished writers. Currently handles: nonfiction books 60%, novels 40%.

- Prior to becoming an agent, Ms. Wales worked at Oxford University Press and Viking Penguin.

Member Agents Elizabeth Wales; Neal Swain.
Represents This agency specializes in narrative nonfiction and quality mainstream and literary fiction. Does not handle screenplays, children's literature, genre fiction, or most category nonfiction.

O→ This agency specializes in narrative nonfiction and quality mainstream and literary fiction. Does not handle screenplays, children's literature, genre fiction, or most category nonfiction.

How to Contact Query with cover letter, SASE. No phone or fax queries. Prefers regular mail queries, but accepts 1-page e-mail queries with no attachments. Accepts simultaneous submissions. Responds in 3 weeks to queries. Responds in 6 weeks to mss.
Terms Agent receives 15% commission on domestic sales. Agent receives 20% commission on foreign sales.

Recent Sales *Unterzakhn: a graphic novel*, by Leela Corman (Schocken/Pantheon, 2010); *Wisdom of the Last Farmer*, by David Mas Masumoto (Free Press, 2009); *Crow Planet*, by Lyanda Lynn Haupt (Little, Brown, 2009); *Flotsametrics and the Floating World*, by Curtis Ebbesmeyer and Eric Scigliano (Smithsonian/HarperCollins, 2009).
Writers Conferences Pacific Northwest Writers Conference; Willamette Writers Conference.
Tips "We are especially interested in work that espouses a progressive cultural or political view, projects a new voice, or simply shares an important, compelling story. We also encourage writers living in the Pacific Northwest, West Coast, Alaska, and Pacific Rim countries, and writers from historically underrepresented groups, such as gay and lesbian writers and writers of color, to submit work (but does not discourage writers outside these areas). Most importantly, whether in fiction or nonfiction, the agency is looking for talented storytellers."

CHRISTINA WARD LITERARY AGENCY

PO Box 7144, Lowell MA 01852. (978)656-8389. E-mail: christinawardlit@mac.com.
Represents nonfiction books, novels. **Considers these nonfiction areas:** biography, health, history, medicine, memoirs, nature, psychology, science, literary nonfiction, including narrative nonfiction. **Considers these fiction areas:** literary, mystery, suspense, thriller.

JOHN A. WARE LITERARY AGENCY

392 Central Park W., New York NY 10025-5801. (212)866-4733. Fax: (212)866-4734. **Contact:** John Ware. Represents 60 clients. 40%% of clients are new/unpublished writers. Currently handles: nonfiction books 75%, novels 25%.

- Prior to opening his agency, Mr. Ware served as a literary agent with James Brown Associates/Curtis Brown, Ltd., and as an editor for Doubleday & Co.

Represents nonfiction books, novels. **Considers these nonfiction areas:** anthropology, biography, current affairs, health, academic credentials required, history, oral history, Americana, folklore, language, music, nature, popular culture, psychology, academic credentials required, science, sports, true crime, womens, social commentary. **Considers these fiction areas:** detective, mystery, thriller, accessible literary noncategory fiction. Does not want personal memoirs.
O→ Does not want personal memoirs.
How to Contact Query with SASE. Send a letter only. Other Responds in 2 weeks to queries.
Terms Agent receives 15% commission on domestic sales. Agent receives 20% commission on foreign sales. Agent receives 15% commission on film sales. Charges clients for messenger service and photocopying.
Recent Sales *Where Men Win Glory: The Odyssey of Pat Tillman*, by John Krakauer (Doubleday); *Abundance of Valor* (military history), by Will Irwin (Random House); *Velva Jean Learns to Drive* (novel), by Jennifer Niven (Plume); *The Art of the Game* (basketball), by Chris Ballard (Sports Illustrated/Simon & Schuster); *The Aquanet Diaries: Big Hair, Big Dreams, Small Town* (high school memoir), by Jennifer Niven (Simon Spotlight Entertainment); *Spent: A Memoir of Shopaholism*, by Avis Cardella (Little, Brown); *To Kill a Page: A Memoir of Becoming Literate*, by Travis Hugh Culley (Random House); *The Pledge (of Allegiance)*, by Jeffrey Jones and Peter Mayer (thomas Dunne/St. Martin's Press).
Tips "Writers must have appropriate credentials for authorship of proposal (nonfiction) or manuscript (fiction); no publishing track record required. I am open to good writing and interesting ideas by new or veteran writers."

WATERSIDE PRODUCTIONS, INC.

computer & technology books, 2376 Oxford Ave., Cardiff-by-the-Sea CA 92007. (760)632-9190. Fax: (760)632-9295. Website: www.waterside.com. Estab. 1982.
Member Agents Bill Gladstone; Margot Maley Hutchison; Carole McClendon; William E. Brown; Lawrence Jackel; Ming Russell; Devra Ann Jacobs.
Represents nonfiction books. **Considers these nonfiction areas:** art, biography, business, child, computers, ethnic, health, how to, humor, money, nature, popular culture, psychology, sociology, sports, cookbooks, technology, natural health, medical, real estate, travel, parenting, lifestyles and more. Specializes in computer books, how-to, business, and health titles.
O→ Specializes in computer books, how-to, business, and health titles.
How to Contact Query via mail or online form. Phone queries are not accepted. Obtains most new clients through referrals from established client and publisher list.
Tips "For new writers, a quality proposal and a strong knowledge of the market you're writing for goes a long way toward helping us turn you into a published author. We like to see a strong author platform. Two foreign rights agents on staff, Neil Gudovitz; Kimberly Valentini, help us with overseas sales."

WATKINS LOOMIS AGENCY, INC.

literary, contemporary, young adult fiction, biography, moir, essay, political journalism, & travel., 133 E.

35th St., Suite 1, New York NY 10016. (212)532-0080. Fax: (212)889-0506. Website: www.watkinsloomis.com/. Estab. 1980. Represents 50 clients.

Member Agents Gloria Loomis, president.

Represents nonfiction books, novels, short story collections. **Considers these nonfiction areas:** biography, current affairs, ethnic, history, nature, popular culture, science, investigative journalism. **Considers these fiction areas:** literary. This agency specializes in literary fiction and nonfiction.

O→ This agency specializes in literary fiction and nonfiction.

How to Contact *No unsolicited mss.* This agency does not guarantee a response to queries.

Terms Agent receives 15% commission on domestic sales. Agent receives 20% commission on foreign sales.

WAXMAN LITERARY AGENCY, INC.

"Representing fiction and non-fiction authors with powerful stories.", 80 Fifth Ave., Suite 1101, New York NY 10011. Website: www.waxmanagency.com. **Contact:** Scott Waxman. Represents 60 clients. 50% of clients are new/unpublished writers. Currently handles: nonfiction books 80%, novels 20%.

- Prior to opening his agency, Mr. Waxman was an editor at HarperCollins.

Member Agents Scott Waxman (all categories of nonfiction, commercial fiction); Byrd Leavell; Farley Chase; Holly Root.

Represents nonfiction books, novels. **Considers these nonfiction areas:** prescriptive nonfiction. **Considers these fiction areas:** literary, romance, contemporary, young adult, womens, commercial, narrative, historical, humor, pop culture, biography, memoir, sports, celebrity. "We're looking for serious journalists and novelists with published works."

O→ "We're looking for serious journalists and novelists with published works."

How to Contact All unsolicited mss returned unopened. Query through Web site. Accepts simultaneous submissions. Responds in 6 weeks to queries. Responds in 8 weeks to mss. Obtains most new clients through recommendations from others, solicitations, conferences.

Terms Agent receives 15% commission on domestic sales. Agent receives 10% commission on foreign sales. Offers written contract; 2-month notice must be given to terminate contract.

IRENE WEBB LITERARY

822 Bishop's Lodge Road, Santa Fe NM 87501. E-mail: webblit@gmail.com. Website: www.irenewebb.com. **Contact:** Irene Webb.

Represents nonfiction books, novels. **Considers these nonfiction areas:** memoirs, popular culture, sports, true stories. **Considers these fiction areas:** mystery, thriller, young adult, middle grade, literary and commercial fiction. "Irene Webb Literary is known as one of the top boutique agencies selling books to film and TV. We have close relationships with top film producers and talent in Hollywood. Does not want to receive unsolicited manuscripts or screenplays."

O→ Irene Webb Literary is known as one of the top boutique agencies selling books to film and TV. We have close relationships with top film producers and talent in Hollywood. Does not want to receive unsolicited manuscripts or screenplays.

How to Contact Query via e-mail only. Obtains most new clients through recommendations from others, solicitations.

Recent Sales *Secrets of a Soap Opera Diva*, by Victoria Rowell (Atria); *Now I Can See the Moon*, by Elaine Hall (Harper Studio); *Dead Write*, by Sheila Low (NAL); *East to the Dawn*, by Susan Butler (Fox Studio for the Amelia Earhardt Story starring Hilary Swank).

THE WENDY WEIL AGENCY, INC.

232 Madison Ave., Suite 1300, New York NY 10016. (212)685-0030. Fax: (212)685-0765. E-mail: wweil@wendyweil.com. Website: www.wendyweil.com. Estab. 1987. Member of AAR. Currently handles: nonfiction books 20%, novels 80%.

Member Agents Wendy Weil (commercial fiction, women's fiction, family saga, historical fiction, short stories); Emily Forland; Emma Patterson.

Represents nonfiction books, novels. "The Wendy Weil Agency, Inc. represents fiction and non-fiction for the trade market. We work with literary and commercial fiction, mystery/thriller, memoir, narrative non-fiction, journalism, history, current affairs, books on health, science, popular culture, lifestyle, social activism, and art history. It is a full-service literary agency that handles around 100 authors, among them Pulitzer Prize winners, National Book Award winners, New York Times bestsellers." Does not want to receive screenplays or textbooks.

O→ "The Wendy Weil Agency, Inc. represents fiction and non-fiction for the trade market. We work with literary and commercial fiction, mystery/thriller, memoir, narrative non-fiction, journalism, history, current affairs, books on health, science, popular culture, lifestyle, social activism, and art history. It is a full-service literary agency that handles around 100 authors, among them Pulitzer Prize winners, National Book Award winners, New York Times bestsellers." Does not want to receive screenplays or textbooks.

How to Contact Accepts queries by regular mail and email, however, we cannot guarantee a response to electronic queries. Query letters should be no more than 2 pages, which should include a bit about yourself and an overview of your project. If you'd like, you're welcome to include a separate synopsis along with your query. For queries via regular mail, please be sure to include a SASE for our reply. Snail mail queries are preferred. 4-6 weeks. Obtains most new clients through recommendations from others, solicitations.

CHERRY WEINER LITERARY AGENCY

28 Kipling Way, Manalapan NJ 07726-3711. (732)446-2096. Fax: (732)792-0506. E-mail: cherry8486@aol.com. **Contact:** Cherry Weiner. Represents 40 clients. 10% of clients are new/unpublished writers. Currently handles: nonfiction books 10-20%, novels 80-90%.

Represents nonfiction books, novels. **Considers these nonfiction areas:** self help. **Considers these fiction areas:** contemporary, psychic, adventure, detective, family, fantasy, historical, mainstream, mystery, romance, science, thriller, western. This agency is currently not accepting new clients except by referral or by personal contact at writers' conferences. Specializes in fantasy, science fiction, Western's, mysteries (both contemporary and historical), historical novels, Native-American works, mainstream and all genre romances.

- This agency is currently not accepting new clients except by referral or by personal contact at writers' conferences. Specializes in fantasy, science fiction, Western's, mysteries (both contemporary and historical), historical novels, Native-American works, mainstream and all genre romances.

How to Contact Query with SASE. Prefers to read materials exclusively. Responds in 1 week to queries. Responds in 2 months to mss.

Terms Agent receives 15% commission on domestic sales. Agent receives 15% commission on foreign sales. Offers written contract. Charges clients for extra copies of mss, first-class postage for author's copies of books, express mail for important documents/mss.

Recent Sales Sold 56 titles in the last year. This agency prefers not to share information on specific sales.

Tips "Meet agents and publishers at conferences. Establish a relationship, then get in touch with them and remind them of the meeting and conference."

THE WEINGEL-FIDEL AGENCY

310 E. 46th St., 21E, New York NY 10017. (212)599-2959. **Contact:** Loretta Weingel-Fidel. Currently handles: nonfiction books 75%, novels 25%.

- Prior to opening her agency, Ms. Weingel-Fidel was a psychoeducational diagnostician.

Represents nonfiction books, novels. **Considers these nonfiction areas:** art, biography, memoirs, music, psychology, science, sociology, womens, investigative journalism. **Considers these fiction areas:** literary, mainstream. This agency specializes in commercial and literary fiction and nonfiction. Actively seeking investigative journalism. Does not want to receive genre fiction, self-help, science fiction, or fantasy.

- This agency specializes in commercial and literary fiction and nonfiction. Actively seeking investigative journalism. Does not want to receive genre fiction, self-help, science fiction, or fantasy.

How to Contact Accepts writers by referral only. *No unsolicited mss.*

Terms Agent receives 15% commission on domestic sales. Agent receives 20% commission on foreign sales. Offers written contract, binding for 1 year with automatic renewal. Bills sent back to clients are all reasonable expenses, such as UPS, express mail, photocopying, etc.

Tips "A very small, selective list enables me to work very closely with my clients to develop and nurture talent. I only take on projects and writers about which I am extremely enthusiastic."

TED WEINSTEIN LITERARY MANAGEMENT

307 Seventh Ave., Suite 2407, Dept. GLA, New York NY 10001. Website: www.twliterary.com. **Contact:** Ted Weinstein. Member of AAR. Represents 75 clients. 50% of clients are new/unpublished writers. Currently handles: nonfiction books 100%.

Represents Considers these nonfiction areas: biography, business, current affairs, government, health, history, popular culture, science, self help, travel, true crime, lifestyle, narrative journalism, popular science.

How to Contact Please visit website for detailed guidelines before submitting. E-mail queries **only**. Other Responds in 3 weeks to queries.

Terms Agent receives 15% commission on domestic sales. Agent receives 20% commission on foreign sales. Agent receives 20% commission on film sales. Offers written contract, binding for 1 year. Charges clients for photocopying and express shipping.

Tips "Send e-queries only. See the Web site for guidelines."

LARRY WEISSMAN LITERARY, LLC

526 8th St., #2R, Brooklyn NY **Contact:** Larry Weissman.Represents 35 clients. Currently handles: nonfiction books 80%, novels 10%, story collections 10%.

Represents nonfiction books, novels, short story collections. **Considers these fiction areas:** literary. "Very interested in established journalists with bold voices. He's interested in anything to do with food. Fiction has to feel "vital" and short stories are accepted, but only if you can sell him on an idea for a novel as well." Nonfiction, including food & lifestyle, politics, pop culture, narrative, cultural/social issues, journalism. No genre fiction, poetry or children's.

- "Very interested in established journalists with bold voices. He's interested in anything to do with food. Fiction has to feel "vital" and short stories are accepted, but only if you can sell him on an idea for a novel as well." Nonfiction, including food & lifestyle, politics, pop culture, narrative, cultural/social issues, journalism. No genre fiction, poetry or children's.

How to Contact Send e-queries only.

Terms Agent receives 15% commission on domestic sales. Agent receives 20% commission on foreign sales.

WESTWOOD CREATIVE ARTISTS, LTD.

94 Harbord St., Toronto Ontario M5S 1G6 Canada. (416)964-3302. Fax: (416)975-9209. E-mail: wca_office@wcaltd.com. Website: www.wcaltd.com. Represents 350+ clients.

Member Agents Deborah Wood, book-to-film agent; Ahston Westwood, book-to-film agent; Linda McKnight, literary agent; Jackie Kaiser, literary agent; Hilary McMahon, literary agent; Bruce Westwood, literary agent; John Pearce, literary agent; Natasha Daneman, subsidiary rights director; Michael Levine, film & TV agent; Chris Casuccio, administrative assistant.

How to Contact Query with SASE. Use a referral to break into this agency. Accepts simultaneous submissions.

Recent Sales A Biography of Richard Nixon, by Conrad Black (Public Affairs); *The New Cold War: Revolutions; Rigged Elections and Pipeline Politics in the Former Soviet Union*, by Mark MacKinnon (Carroll & Graf).

WHIMSY LITERARY AGENCY, LLC

New York/Los Angeles E-mail: whimsynyc@aol.com. **Contact:** Jackie Meyer.Other memberships include Center for Independent Publishing Advisory Board. Represents 30 clients. 20% of clients are new/unpublished writers. Currently handles: nonfiction books 100%.

- Prior to becoming an agent, Ms. Meyer was with Warner Books for 19 years; Ms. Vezeris and Ms. Legette have 30 years experience at various book publishers.

Member Agents Jackie Meyer; Olga Vezeris (fiction and nonfiction); Nansci LeGette, senior associate in LA.

Represents nonfiction books. **Considers these nonfiction areas:** agriculture, art, biography, business, child guidance, cooking, education, health, history, horticulture, how-to, humor, interior design, memoirs, money, New Age, popular culture, psychology, religious, self-help, true crime, women's issues, women's studies. **Considers these fiction areas:** mainstream, religious, thriller, womens. "Whimsy looks for projects that are concept and platform driven. We seek books that educate, inspire and entertain." Actively seeking experts in their field with good platforms.

- "Whimsy looks for projects that are concept and platform driven. We seek books that educate, inspire and entertain." Actively seeking experts in their field with good platforms.

How to Contact Send a query letter via e-mail. Send a synopsis, bio, platform and proposal. No snail mail submissions. Responds "quickly, but only if interested" to queries. Obtains most new clients through recommendations from others, solicitations.

Terms Agent receives 15% commission on domestic sales. Agent receives 20% commission on foreign sales. Offers written contract. Charges for posting and photocopying.

AUDREY R. WOLF LITERARY AGENCY

2510 Virginia Ave. NW, #702N, Washington DC 20037. **Contact:** Audrey Wolf. Member of AAR.

How to Contact Query with SASE.

WOLFSON LITERARY AGENCY

P.O. Box 266, New York NY 10276. E-mail: query@wolfsonliterary.com. Website: www.wolfsonliterary.com/. **Contact:** Michelle Wolfson. Adheres to AAR canon of ethics. Currently handles: nonfiction books 70%, novels 30%.

- Prior to forming her own agency, Michelle spent two years with Artists & Artisans, Inc. and two years with Ralph Vicinanza, Ltd.

Represents nonfiction books, novels. **Considers these nonfiction areas:** business, health, humor, memoirs, popular culture. **Considers these fiction areas:** mainstream, mystery, romance, thriller. Actively seeking commercial fiction, mainstream, mysteries, thrillers, suspense, women's fiction, romance, YA, practical nonfiction (particularly of interest to women), advice, medical, pop culture, humor, business.

- Actively seeking commercial fiction, mainstream, mysteries, thrillers, suspense, women's fiction, romance, YA, practical nonfiction (particularly of interest to women), advice, medical, pop culture, humor, business.

How to Contact Query with SASE. E-queries only! Accepts simultaneous submissions. Responds in 4 weeks to queries. Responds in 3 months to mss. Obtains most new clients through recommendations from others, solicitations.

Terms Agent receives 15% commission on domestic sales. Agent receives 25% commission on foreign sales. Offers written contract; 30-day notice must be given to terminate contract.

Writers Conferences SDSU Writers' Conference; New Jersey Romance Writers of America Writers' Conference; American Independent Writers Conference in Washington DC.

Tips "Be persistent."

WOLGEMUTH & ASSOCIATES, INC

8600 Crestgate Circle, Orlando FL 32819. (407)909-9445. Fax: (407)909-9446. E-mail: ewolgemuth@wolgemuthandassociates.com. **Contact:** Erik Wolgemuth. Member of AAR. Represents 60 clients. 10% of clients are new/unpublished writers. Currently handles: nonfiction books 90%, novella 2%, juvenile books 5%, multimedia 3%.

- "We have been in the publishing business since 1976, having been a marketing executive at a number of houses, a publisher, an author, and a founder and owner of a publishing company."

Member Agents Robert D. Wolgemuth; Andrew D. Wolgemuth; Erik S. Wolgemuth.

Represents Material used by Christian families. "We are not considering any new material at this time."

- "We are not considering any new material at this time."

Terms Agent receives 15% commission on domestic sales. Offers written contract, binding for 2-3 years; 30-day notice must be given to terminate contract.

WORDSERVE LITERARY GROUP

10152 S. Knoll Circle, Highlands Ranch CO 80130. (303)471-6675. Website: www.wordserveliterary.com. **Contact:** Greg Johnson; Rachelle Gardner. Represents 100 clients. 20% of clients are new/unpublished writers. Currently handles: nonfiction books 50%, novels 35%, juvenile books 10%, multimedia 5%.

- Prior to becoming an agent in 1994, Mr. Johnson was a magazine editor and freelance writer of more than 20 books and 200 articles.

Member Agents Greg Johnson; Rachelle Gardner.

Represents Considers these nonfiction areas: biography, child guidance, inspirational, memoirs, parenting, self-help. Materials with a faith-based angle.

- Materials with a faith-based angle.

How to Contact "Please go to www.wordserveliterary.com to review query policies. Accepts simultaneous submissions. Responds in 4 weeks to queries. Responds in 2 months to mss. Obtains most new clients through recommendations from others.

Terms Agent receives 15% commission on domestic sales. Agent receives 10-15% commission on foreign sales. Offers written contract; up to 60-day notice must be given to terminate contract.

Recent Sales Sold 1,500 titles in the last 15 years. *Redemption* series, by Karen Kingsbury (Tyndale); *Loving God Up Close*, by Calvin Miller (Warner Faith); *Christmas in My Heart*, by Joe Wheeler (Tyndale). Other clients include Doug Fields, Wanda Dyson, Catherine Martin, David Murrow, Leslie Haskin, Gilbert Morris, Robert Wise, Jim Burns, Wayne Cordeiro, Denise George, Susie Shellenberger, Tim Smith, Athol Dickson, Patty Kirk, John Shore, Marcus Bretherton, Rick Johnson.

Tips "We are looking for good proposals, great writing, and authors willing to market their books, as appropriate. Also, we're only looking for projects with a faith element bent. See the Web site before submitting."

WRITERS HOUSE

Fiction and non-fiction, for adults and juveniles., 21 W. 26th St., New York NY 10010. (212)685-2400. Fax: (212)685-1781. Website: www.writershouse.com. Estab. 1973. Member of AAR. Represents 440 clients. 50% of clients are new/unpublished writers. Currently handles: nonfiction books 25%, novels 40%, juvenile books 35%.

Member Agents Albert Zuckerman (major novels, thrillers, women's fiction, important nonfiction).

Represents nonfiction books, novels, juvenile. **Considers these nonfiction areas:** interior, juvenile, animals, art, biography, business, child, cooking, health, history, humor, military, money, music, nature, psychology, science, self help, film, true crime, womens. **Considers these fiction areas:** contemporary, newage, psychic, adventure, detective, erotica, ethnic, family, fantasy, feminist, gay, gothic, hi lo, historical, horror, humor, juvenile, literary, mainstream, military, multicultural, mystery, occult, picture books, regional, romance, science, short, spiritual, sports, thriller, translation, western, young, womens, cartoon. This agency specializes in all types of popular fiction and nonfiction. Does not want to receive scholarly, professional, poetry, plays, or screenplays.

O→ This agency specializes in all types of popular fiction and nonfiction. Does not want to receive scholarly, professional, poetry, plays, or screenplays.

How to Contact Query with SASE. Please send us a query letter of no more than 2 pages, which includes your credentials, an explanation of what makes your book unique and special, and a synopsis. (If submitting to Steven Malk or Lindsay Davis: Writers House, 3368 Governor Drive, #224F, San Diego, CA 92122). Responds in 6-8 weeks to queries. Obtains most new clients through recommendations from authors and editors.
Terms Agent receives 15% commission on domestic sales. Agent receives 20% commission on foreign sales. Offers written contract, binding for 1 year. Agency charges fees for copying mss/proposals and overseas airmail of books.
Tips "Do not send manuscripts. Write a compelling letter. If you do, we'll ask to see your work."

WRITERS' REPRESENTATIVES, LLC

116 W. 14th St., 11th Floor, New York NY 10011-7305. Fax: (212)620-0023. E-mail: transom@writersreps.com. Website: www.writersreps.com. Represents 130 clients. 10% of clients are new/unpublished writers. Currently handles: nonfiction books 90%, novels 10%.

- Prior to becoming an agent, Ms. Chu was a lawyer; Mr. Hartley worked at Simon & Schuster, Harper & Row, and Cornell University Press.

Member Agents Lynn Chu; Glen Hartley; Christine Hsu.
Represents nonfiction books, novels. **Considers these fiction areas:** literary. Serious nonfiction and quality fiction. No motion picture or television screenplays.

O→ Serious nonfiction and quality fiction. No motion picture or television screenplays.

How to Contact Query with SASE. Prefers to read materials exclusively. Considers simultaneous queries, but must be informed at time of submission.
Terms Agent receives 15% commission on domestic sales. Agent receives 20% commission on foreign sales.
Tips "Always include a SASE; it will ensure a response from the agent and the return of your submitted material."

THE WYLIE AGENCY

250 West 57th St., Suite 2114, New York NY 10107. (212)246-0069. Fax: (212)586-8953. E-mail: mail@wylieagency.com. Website: www.wylieagency.com. Overseas address: 17 Bedford Square, London WC1B 3JA, United Kingdom; mail@wylieagency.co.uk
Member Agents Andrew Wylie, Sarah Chalfant; Scott Moyers.
Represents nonfiction books, novels. High-profile and prolific authors. This agency is not currently accepting unsolicited submissions, so do not query unless you are asked.

O→ High-profile and prolific authors. "This agency is not currently accepting unsolicited submissions, so do not query unless you are asked."

How to Contact This agency does not currently take unsolicited queries/proposals.

WYLIE-MERRICK LITERARY AGENCY

1138 S. Webster St., Kokomo IN 46902-6357. (765)459-8258. Website: www.wylie-merrick.com. **Contact:** Robert Brown. Member of AAR. RWA Currently handles: nonfiction books 5%, novels 95%.

- Ms. Brown holds a master's degree in language education and is a writing and technology curriculum specialist.

Member Agents Sharene Martin-Browne (juvenile, picture books, young adult); Robert Brown.
Represents "Our clients are all professionals. We specialize only in highly commercial literature. Please note that we no longer represent children's picture books."

O→ "Our clients are all professionals. We specialize only in highly commercial literature. Please note that we no longer represent children's picture books."

How to Contact Correspond via e-mail only. No phone queries, please. Obtains new clients through e-mail queries, conferences, and client/editor/agent recommendations only.
Terms Agent receives 15% commission on domestic sales; 20% commission on foreign or dramatic rights sales. Offers written contract.
Recent Sales *Windless Summer and Damaged Goods*, by Heather Sharfeddin (Bantam Dell); *Shadow Lover*, by Lydia Parks (Harlequin Nocturne); *Animal Instinct*, by Lydia Parks (Kensington); *Devour Me*, by Lydia Parks (Kensington); *Texas Hold Him*, by Lisa Cooke (Dorchester); *Evil*, by Timothy Carter (Flux).
Tips "As the publishing industry is not static, please always check our Web site for our most updated needs lists. Also, we maintain an informative blog at www.wyliemerrick.blogspot.com. Both agents,

when time permits, can be found on Twitter and Facebook."

YATES & YATES

1100 Town & Country Road, Suite 1300, Orange CA 92868. Website: www.yates2.com. Represents 60 clients.

Represents nonfiction books, novels. **Considers these nonfiction areas:** business, current affairs, government, memoirs, religion. **Considers these fiction areas:** literary, regional, religious, thriller, womens.

Recent Sales *No More Mondays*, by Dan Miller (Doubleday Currency).

ZACHARY SHUSTER HARMSWORTH

"A full-service literary and entertainment agency," 1776 Broadway, Suite 1405, New York NY 10019. (212)765-6900. Fax: (212)765-6490. E-mail: kfleury@zshliterary.com. Website: www.zshliterary.com. **Contact:** Kathleen Fleury. Alternate address: 535 Boylston St., 11th Floor. (617)262-2400. Fax: (617)262-2468. Represents 125 clients. 20%% of clients are new/unpublished writers. Currently handles: nonfiction books 45%, novels 45%, story collections 5%, scholarly books 5%.

- Our principals include two former publishing and entertainment lawyers, a journalist, and an editor/agent. Lane Zachary was an editor at Random House before becoming an agent.

Member Agents Esmond Harmsworth (commercial mysteries, literary fiction, history, science, adventure, business); Todd Shuster (narrative and prescriptive nonfiction, biography, memoirs); Lane Zachary (biography, memoirs, literary fiction); Jennifer Gates (literary fiction, nonfiction). You can email any agent on the website online form.

Represents nonfiction books, novels. **Considers these nonfiction areas:** animals, biography, business, current affairs, gay, government, health, history, how to, language, memoirs, money, music, psychology, science, self help, sports, true crime, womens. **Considers these fiction areas:** detective, ethnic, feminist, gay, historical, literary, mainstream, mystery, thriller. This agency is still no longer accepting unsolicited work. Check the Web site for updated info.

O→ This agency is still no longer accepting unsolicited work. Check the Web site for updated info.

How to Contact Query with SASE. Obtains most new clients through recommendations from others.

Terms Agent receives 15% commission on domestic sales. Agent receives 20% commission on foreign sales. Offers written contract, binding for 1 work only; 30-day notice must be given to terminate contract.

KAREN GANTZ ZAHLER LITERARY MANAGEMENT AND ATTORNEY AT LAW

860 Fifth Ave., Suite 7J, New York NY 10065. (212)734-3619. E-mail: karen@karengantzlit.com. Website: www.karengantzlit.com. **Contact:** Karen Gantz Zahler. Currently handles: nonfiction books 95%, novels 5%, film, TV scripts.

- Prior to her current position, Ms. Gantz Zahler practiced law at two law firms, wrote two cookbooks, *Taste of New York* (Addison-Wesley) and *Superchefs* (John Wiley & Sons). She also participated in a Presidential Advisory Committee on Intellectual Property, U.S. Department of Commerce. She currently chairs Literary and Media Committee at Harmone Club NYC.

Represents nonfiction books, novels, very selective. "We are hired for two purposes, one as lawyers to negotiate publishing agreements, option agreements and other entertainment deals and two as literary agents to help in all aspects of the publishing field. Ms. Gantz is both a literary agent and a literary property lawyer. Thus, her firm involves themselves in all stages of a book's development, including the collaboration agreement with the writer, advice regarding the book proposal, presentations to the publisher, negotiations including the legal work for the publishing agreement and other rights to be negotiated, and work with the publisher and public relations firm so that the book gets the best possible media coverage. We do extensive manuscript reviews for a few." Actively seeking nonfiction. "We assist with speaking engagements and publicity."

O→ "We are hired for two purposes, one as lawyers to negotiate publishing agreements, option agreements and other entertainment deals and two as literary agents to help in all aspects of the publishing field. Ms. Gantz is both a literary agent and a literary property lawyer. Thus, her firm involves themselves in all stages of a book's development, including the collaboration agreement with the writer, advice regarding the book proposal, presentations to the publisher, negotiations including the legal work for the publishing agreement and other rights to be negotiated, and work with the publisher and public relations firm so that the book gets the best possible media coverage. We do extensive manuscript reviews for a few." Actively seeking nonfiction. "We assist with speaking engagements and publicity."

How to Contact Query with SASE. Include a summary. Check the Web site for complete submission information. Responds in 4 weeks to queries. Obtains most new clients through recommendations from others, solicitations.

Recent Sales *A Promise to Ourselves*, by Alec Baldwin (St. Martin's Press 2008); *Take the Lead, Lady! Kathleen Turner's Life Lessons*, by Kathleen Turner in collaboration with Gloria Feldt (Springboard Press

2007); *Tales of a Neo-Con*, by Benjamin Wattenberg (Tom Dunne 2008); *Beyond Control*, by Nancy Friday (Sourcebooks 2009); more sales can be found online.

Tips "Our dream client is someone who is a professional writer and a great listener. What writers can do to increase the likelihood of our retainer is to write an excellent summary and provide a great marketing plan for their proposal in an excellent presentation. Any typos or grammatical mistakes do not resonate well. If we want to review your project, we will ask you to send a copy by snail mail with an envelope and return postage enclosed. We don't call people unless we have something to report."

SUSAN ZECKENDORF ASSOC., INC.

171 W. 57th St., New York NY 10019. (212)245-2928. **Contact:** Susan Zeckendorf. Member of AAR. Represents 15 clients. 25% of clients are new/unpublished writers. Currently handles: nonfiction books 50%, novels 50%.

- Prior to opening her agency, Ms. Zeckendorf was a counseling psychologist.

Represents nonfiction books, novels. **Considers these nonfiction areas:** biography, health, history, music, psychology, sociology, womens. **Considers these fiction areas:** detective, ethnic, historical, literary, mainstream, mystery, thriller. Actively seeking mysteries, literary fiction, mainstream fiction, thrillers, social history, classical music, and biography. Does not want to receive science fiction, romance, or children's books.

- Actively seeking mysteries, literary fiction, mainstream fiction, thrillers, social history, classical music, and biography. Does not want to receive science fiction, romance, or children's books.

How to Contact Query with SASE. Accepts simultaneous submissions. Responds in 10 days to queries. Responds in 3 weeks to mss.

Terms Agent receives 15% commission on domestic sales. Agent receives 20% commission on foreign sales. Charges for photocopying and messenger services.

Writers Conferences Frontiers in Writing Conference; Oklahoma Festival of Books.

Tips "We are a small agency giving lots of individual attention. We respond quickly to submissions."

HELEN ZIMMERMANN LITERARY AGENCY

3 Emmy Lane, New Paltz NY 12561. (845)256-0977. Fax: (845)256-0979. E-mail: helen@zimmagency.com. Website: www.zimmermannliterary.com. **Contact:** Helen Zimmermann. Represents 25 clients. 50% of clients are new/unpublished writers. Currently handles: nonfiction books 80%, other 20% fiction.

- Prior to opening her agency, Ms. Zimmermann was the director of advertising and promotion at Random House and the events coordinator at an independent bookstore.

Represents nonfiction books, novels. **Considers these nonfiction areas:** animals, child, how to, humor, memoirs, nature, popular culture, sports. **Considers these fiction areas:** family, historical, literary, mystery. "As an agent who has experience at both a publishing house and a bookstore, I have a keen insight for viable projects. This experience also helps me ensure every client gets published well, through the whole process." Actively seeking memoirs, pop culture, women's issues and accessible literary fiction. Does not want to receive science fiction, poetry or romance.

- "As an agent who has experience at both a publishing house and a bookstore, I have a keen insight for viable projects. This experience also helps me ensure every client gets published well, through the whole process." Actively seeking memoirs, pop culture, women's issues and accessible literary fiction. Does not want to receive science fiction, poetry or romance.

How to Contact Accepts e-mail queries only. E-mail should include a short description of project and bio, whether it be fiction or nonfiction. Accepts simultaneous submissions. Responds in 2 weeks to queries. Responds in 1 month to mss. Obtains most new clients through recommendations from others, solicitations.

Terms Agent receives 15% commission on domestic sales. Offers written contract; 30-day notice must be given to terminate contract. Charges for photocopying and postage (reimbursed if project is sold).

Recent Sales *She Bets Her Life: Women and Gambling*, by Mary Sojourner (Seal Press); *Seeds: One Man's Quest to Preserve the Trees of America's Most Famous People*, by Rick Horan (HarperCollins); *Saddled*, by Susan Richards (Houghton Mifflin Harcourt); *Final Target*, by Steven Gore (HarperPerennial); *Liberated Body, Captive Mind: A WWII POW Memoir*, by Normal Bussel (Pegasus Books).

Writers Conferences BEA/Writer's Digest Books Writers' Conference, Portland, ME Writers Conference, Berkshire Writers and Readers Conference

RENEE ZUCKERBROT LITERARY AGENCY

115 West 29th St., Third Floor, New York NY 10001. (212)967-0072. Fax: (212)967-0073. E-mail: renee@rzagency.com. Website: rzagency.com. **Contact:** Renee Zuckerbrot. Represents 30 clients. Currently handles: novels, other 30% nonfiction and 70% fiction.

- Prior to becoming an agent, Ms. Zuckerbrot worked as an editor at Doubleday as well as in the editorial department at Putnam.

Represents nonfiction books, novels, short story collections. Literary fiction, short story collections, mysteries, thrillers, women's fiction, slipstream/speculative, narrative nonfiction (focusing on science, history and pop culture). No business books, self-help, spirituality or romance.

- O→ Literary fiction, short story collections, mysteries, thrillers, women's fiction, slipstream/speculative, narrative nonfiction (focusing on science, history and pop culture). No business books, self-help, spirituality or romance.

How to Contact Query by mail, e-mail. Include a description of your manuscript or proposal. Include your publishing history, if applicable. Include a brief personal bio. Include an SASE or an e-mail address.

Terms Agent receives 15% commission on domestic sales. Agent receives 25% commission on foreign sales.

Recent Sales *Pretty Monster*, by Kelly Link (Penguin); *Manhattan Primeval*, by Eric Sanderson (Abrams); *Everything Asian*, by Sung Woo (Dunne/St. Martin's); *The Dart League King*, by Keith Lee Morris (Tin House).

Conferences

Attending a writers' conference that includes agents gives you the opportunity to learn more about what agents do and to show an agent your work. Ideally, a conference should include a panel or two with a number of agents to give writers a sense of the variety of personalities and tastes of different agents.

Not all agents are alike: Some are more personable, and sometimes you simply click better with one agent versus another. When only one agent attends a conference, there is a tendency for every writer at that conference to think, "Ah, this is the agent I've been looking for!'' When the number of agents attending is larger, you have a wider group from which to choose, and you may have less competition for the agent's time.

Besides including panels of agents discussing what representation means and how to go about securing it, many of these gatherings also include time—either scheduled or impromptu—to meet briefly with an agent to discuss your work.

If they're impressed with what they see and hear about your work, they will invite you to submit a query, a proposal, a few sample chapters, or possibly your entire manuscript. Some conferences even arrange for agents to review manuscripts in advance and schedule one-on-one sessions during which you can receive specific feedback or advice regarding your work. Such meetings often cost a small fee, but the input you receive is usually worth the price.

Ask writers who attend conferences and they'll tell you that, at the very least, you'll walk away with new knowledge about the industry. At the very best, you'll receive an invitation to send an agent your material!

Many writers try to make it to at least one conference a year, but cost and location can count as much as subject matter when determining which one to attend. There are conferences in almost every state and province that can provide answers to your questions about writing and the publishing industry. Conferences also connect you with a community of other writers. Such connections help you learn about the pros and cons of different agents, and they can also give you a renewed sense of purpose and direction in your own writing.

SUBHEADS

Each listing is divided into subheads to make locating specific information easier. In the first section, you'll find contact information for conference contacts. You'll also learn conference dates, specific focus, and the average number of attendees. Finally, names of agents who will be speaking or have spoken in the past are listed along with details about their availability during the conference. Calling or e-mailing a conference director to verify the names of agents in attendance is always a good idea.

Costs: Looking at the price of events, plus room and board, may help writers on a tight budget narrow their choices.

Accommodations: Here conferences list overnight accommodations and travel information.

Often conferences held in hotels will reserve rooms at a discount rate and may provide a shuttle bus to and from the local airport.

Additional Information: This section includes information on conference-sponsored contests, individual meetings, the availability of brochures, and more.

Quick Reference Icons

At the beginning of some listings, you will find one or more of the following symbols:

N Conference new to this edition

Canadian conference

International conference

Find a pull-out bookmark with a key to symbols on the inside cover of this book.

AGENTS AND EDITORS CONFERENCE

Writers' League of Texas, 1501 W. Fifth St., Suite E-2, Austin TX 78703. (512)499-8914. Fax: (512)499-0441. E-mail: wlt@writersleague.org. Website: www.writersleague.org. Estab. 1982. Annual conference held in the summer. Conference duration: 3 days. Average attendance: 300. Provides writers with the opportunity to meet top literary agents and editors from New York and the West Coast. Topics include: finding and working with agents and publishers, writing and marketing fiction and nonfiction, dialogue, characterization, voice, research, basic and advanced fiction writing, the business of writing, and workshops for genres. Speakers have included Malaika Adero, Stacey Barney, Sha-Shana Crichton, Jessica Faust, Dena Fischer, Mickey Freiberg, Jill Grosjean, Anne Hawkins, Jim Hornfischer, Jennifer Joel, David Hale Smith and Elisabeth Weed.

Costs $309 member/$439 nonmember.

Accommodations 2009 event is at the Austin Sheraton Hotel, 701 East 11th St., Austin. Check back often for new information.

Additional Information June 26-28, 2009. Contests and awards programs are offered separately. Brochures are available upon request.

ALGONKIAN WRITER WORKSHOPS

2020 Pennsylvania Ave. NW, Suite 43, Washington DC 20006. (800)250-8290. E-mail: algonkian@webdelsol.com. Website: http://www.algonkianconferences.com/. Estab. 2001. "Conference duration: 5 days. Average attendance: 15/craft workshops; 60/pitch sessions. Workshops on fiction, short fiction, and poetry are held 12 times/year in various locations. Speakers have included Paige Wheeler, Elise Capron, Deborah Grosvenor and Kathleen Anderson. Agents will be speaking and available for meetings with attendees."

Costs Housing costs vary depending on the workshop's location.

Additional Information "These workshops are challenging and are not for those looking for praise. Guidelines and dates are available online or via e-mail."

AMERICAN CHRISTIAN WRITERS CONFERENCES

P.O. Box 110390, Nashville TN 37222-0390. (800)219-7483. Fax: (615)834-7736. E-mail: acwriters@aol.com. Website: www.acwriters.com. Estab. 1981. Conference duration: 2 days. Average attendance: 60. Annual conferences promoting all forms of Christian writing (fiction, nonfiction, scriptwriting). Conferences are held throughout the year in 36 US cities.

Costs Approximately $209, plus meals and accommodations.

Accommodations Special rates are available at the host hotel (usually a major chain like Holiday Inn).

Additional Information Send a SASE for conference brochures/guidelines.

AMERICAN INDEPENDENT WRITERS (AIW) SPRING WRITERS CONFERENCE

1001 Connecticut Ave. NW, Suite 701, Washington DC 20036. (202)775-5150. Fax: (202)775-5810. E-mail: info@aiwriters.org. Website: www.aiwriters.org. **Contact:** Taryn Carrino. Estab. 1975. Annual conference held in June. Average attendance: 350. Focuses on fiction, nonfiction, screenwriting, poetry, children's writing, and technical writing. Gives participants the chance to hear from and talk with dozens of experts on book and magazine publishing, as well as on the craft, tools, and business of writing. Speakers have included Erica Jong, John Barth, Kitty Kelley, Vanessa Leggett, Diana McLellan, Brian Lamb, and Stephen Hunter. New York and local agents attend the conference.

Additional Information See the Web site or send a SASE in mid-February for brochures/guidelines and fees information.

ANHINGA WRITERS' STUDIO WORKSHOPS

Gainesville Association for the Creative Arts, P.O. Box 357154, Gainesville FL 32635. (352) 379-8782. Fax: (352) 380-0018. E-mail: info@anhingawriters.org. Website: www.anhingawriters.org. Estab. 1997. *Formerly Writing the Region*. Annual conference held in July. 2009 dates: July 29-August 1. Conference duration: 4 days. Average attendance: 100. Conference concentrates on fiction, writing for children, poetry, nonfiction, drama, screenwriting, writing with humor, setting, character, and more. Held at the Hilton Hotel and Conference Center across from the University of Florida in Gainesville. Speakers have included Anne Hawking, Doris Booth, Sarah Bewley, Bill Maxwell, and Robert Fulton. Agent/editor appointments are available.

Costs Costs available online. Lower costs for half-day and one-day registration.

Accommodations Special rates are available at the Holiday Inn, University Center and the Residence Inn, Marriott.

ANTIOCH WRITERS' WORKSHOP

P.O. Box 494, Yellow Springs OH 45387. (937)475-7357. E-mail: info@antiochwritersworkshop.com. Website: www.antiochwritersworkshop.com. **Contact:** Sharon Short. Estab. 1986. Annual one-week

conference held in July. Average attendance: 80. Workshop focuses on poetry, scholarly nonfiction, literary fiction, mystery, memoir, and screenwriting. Workshop is located in the charming village of Yellow Springs, Ohio, on the edge of the Glen Helen Nature Preserve. Speakers have included Sue Grafton, Natalie Goldberg, Sena Jeter Naslund, Sigrid Nunez, Mary Kay Andrews and William Least Heat Moon. Agents will be speaking and available for meetings with attendees.
Costs $735, regular tuition; $675, alumni/locals.
Accommodations Accommodations are available at local hotels and in local homes.
Additional Information Optional ms critique is $75.

ASJA WRITERS CONFERENCE

American Society of Journalists and Authors, 1501 Broadway, Suite 302, New York NY 10036. (212)997-0947. Fax: (212)768-7414. E-mail: staff@asja.org; director@asja.org. Website: www.asja.org/wc. **Contact:** Alexandra Owens, exec. dir.. Estab. 1971. Annual conference held in April. Conference duration: 2 days. Average attendance: 600. Covers nonfiction and screenwriting. Held at the Grand Hyatt in New York. Speakers have included Dominick Dunne, James Brady, and Dana Sobel. Agents will be speaking at the event. Largest gathering of nonfiction freelance authors in the country.
Costs $200+, depending on when you sign up (includes lunch). Check website for updates.
Accommodations The hotel holding our conference always blocks out discounted rooms for attendees.
Additional Information Brochures available in February. Registration form is on the Web site. Inquire by e-mail or fax. Sign up for conference updates on website.

ASPEN SUMMER WORDS LITERARY FESTIVAL & WRITING RETREAT

Aspen Writers' Foundation, 110 E. Hallam St., #116, Aspen CO 81611. (970)925-3122. Fax: (970)925-5700. E-mail: info@aspenwriters.org. Website: www.aspenwriters.org. Estab. 1976. Annual conference held the fourth week of June. Conference duration: 5 days. Average attendance: 150 at writing retreat; 300+ at literary festival. Retreat for fiction, creative nonfiction, poetry, magazine writing, food writing, and literature. Festival includes author readings, craft talks, panel discussions with publishing industry insiders, professional consultations with editors and agents, and social gatherings. Retreat faculty members in 2007: Andrea Barzi, Katherine Fausset, Anjali Singh, Lisa Grubka, Amber Qureshi, Joshua Kendall, Keith Flynn, Robert Bausch, Amy Bloom, Percival Everett, Danzy Senna, Bharti Kirchner, Gary Ferguson, Dorianne Laux. Festival presenters include (in 2007): Ngugi Wa Thiong'o, Wole Soyinka, Chimamanda Ngozi Adichie, Alaa Al Aswany, Henry Louis Gates, Jr., Leila Aboulela, and many more!
Costs Check website each year for updates.
Accommodations Discount lodging at the conference site will be available. See updates each year.
Additional Information Workshops admission deadline is April 20 for the 2009 conference, or until all workshops are filled. Juried admissions for some workshops; writing sample required with application to juried workshops. Mss will be discussed during workshop. Literary festival and some retreat programs are open to the public on first-come, first-served basis; no mss required. Brochure, application and complete admissions information available on Web site, or request by phone, fax or e-mail. Include mailing address with all e-mail requests.

ASSOCIATED WRITING PROGRAMS ANNUAL CONFERENCE

Mail Stop 1E3, George Mason University, Fairfax VA 22030-4444. (703)993-4301. Fax: (703)993-4302. E-mail: conference@awpwriter.org. Website: www.awpwriter.org. Estab. 1992. Annual conference held between February and April. Average attendance: 5,000. The conference focuses on fiction, poetry, and creative writing and features 400 presentations--including readings, lectures, panel discussions and forums—plus hundreds of book signings, receptions, dances, and informal gatherings. In 2010, AWP will bring its annual conference and bookfair back to Denver, Colorado at the Hyatt Regency Denver & the Colorado Convention Center. Speakers have included Walter Mosley, Tim O'Brien, Denis Johnson, Tony Hoagland, Jane Hirshfield, Donald Hall, Naomi Shihab Nye, Chitra Divakaruni, B.H. Fairchild, and Marie Howe.
Costs See website.
Accommodations Offers overnight accommodations at a discounted rate. For 2010: $189 a night for a single/double occupancy room. Telephone for reservations: 1-800-233-1234. Website reservations: Hyatt's AWP webpage. To receive the special conference rate, contact the Hyatt Regency Denver directly and identify yourself as an AWP Conference attendee. You must make your reservations no later than Monday, March 15, 2010.

AUSTIN FILM FESTIVAL & CONFERENCE

1145 W 5th St., Suite 210, Austin TX 78703. (512)478-4795. Fax: (512)478-6205. Website: www.austinfilmfestival.com. **Contact:** Maya Perezz, conference director. Estab. 1994. Annual conference held in October. Conference duration: 4 days. Average attendance: 2,200. This festival is the first organization of its kind to focus on writers' unique creative contribution to the film and television industries. The conference takes place during the first four days of the festival. The event presents more than 75 panels, round tables and workshops that address various aspects of screenwriting and filmmaking. The Austin Film Festival is held in downtown Austin at the Driskill and Stephen F. Austin hotels. The AFF boasts a number of events and services for emerging and professional writers and filmmakers. Past participants include Robert Altman, Wes Anderson, James L. Brooks, Joel & Ethan Coen, Russell Crowe, Barry Levinson, Darren Star, Robert Duvall, Buck Henry, Dennis Hopper, Lawrence Kasdan, John Landis, Garry Shandling, Bryan Singer, Oliver Stone, Sandra Bullock, Harold Ramis, Danny Boyle, Judd Apatow, Horton Foote, and Owen Wilson.

Costs Approximately $300 for early bird entries(includes entrance to all panels, workshops, and roundtables during the 4-day conference, as well as all films during the 8-night film exhibitions and the opening and closing night parties). Go online for other offers.

Accommodations Discounted rates on hotel accommodations are available to attendees if the reservations are made through the Austin Film Festival office.

Additional Information The Austin Film Festival is considered one of the most accessible festivals, and Austin is the premier town for networking because when industry people are here, they are relaxed and friendly. The Austin Film Festival holds annual screenplay/teleplay and film competitions, as well as a Young Filmmakers Program. Check online for competition details and festival information. Inquire via e-mail or fax.

AUSTRALIAN POETRY FESTIVAL

2/370 Darling St., P.O. Box 91, Balmain NSW 2041 Australia. (61)(2)9818-5366. Fax: (61)(2)9818-5377. E-mail: info@poetsunion.com; martinlangford@bigpond.com. Website: www.poetsunion.com. Estab. 1998. Biennial conference held in September. The festival includes workshops, readings, and panel sessions.

BACKSPACE AGENT-AUTHOR SEMINAR

P.O. Box 454, Washington MI 48094-0454. (732)267-6449. Fax: (586)532-9652. E-mail: karendionne@bksp.org. Website: www.bksp.org. Estab. 2006. 2009 conference is over and was a success. Main conference duration: 1 day. Average attendance: 100. Annual seminar held in November. Panels and workshops designed to educate and assist authors in search of a literary agent to represent their work. Only agents will be in program. Past speakers have included Scott Hoffman, Dan Lazar, Scott Miller, Michael Bourret, Katherine Fausset, Jennifer DeChiara, Sharlene Martin and Paul Cirone.

Costs $165.

Additional Information The Backspace Agent-Author Seminar offers plenty of face time with attending agents. This casual, no-pressure seminar is a terrific opportunity to network, ask questions, talk about your work informally and listen from the people who make their lives selling books.

BACKSPACE WRITERS CONFERENCE

P.O. Box 454, Washington MI 48094-0454. (732)267-6449. Fax: (586)532-9652. E-mail: chrisg@bksp.org. Website: www.backspacewritersconference.com. Estab. 2005. The 2010 conference will be held in New York City in May. Conference duration: 2 days. Average attendance: 150. Conference focuses on all genres of fiction and nonfiction. Offers query letter workshop, writing workshop, and panels with agents, editors, marketing experts, and authors. Speakers have included Pulitzer-Prize-winning playwright Douglas Wright, Michael Cader, David Morrell, Lee Child, Gayle Lynds, Ron McLarty, C. Michael Curtis, Jeff Kleinman, Richard Curtis, Noah Lukeman, Jenny Bent, Dan Lazar and Kristin Nelson.

Costs $355 for Backspace members, $395 for non-members (includes 2-day, 2-track program and refreshments on both days, as well as a cocktail reception).

Additional Information This is a high-quality conference, with much of the program geared toward agented and published authors. Afternoon mixers each day afford plenty of networking opportunities. Go online for brochure, or request information via fax or e-mail.

BALTIMORE WRITERS' CONFERENCE

PRWR Program, LInthicum Hall 218K, Towson University, 8000 York Rd., Towson MD 21252. (410)704-5196. E-mail: prwr@towson.edu. Website: www.towson.edu/writersconference. Estab. 1994. "Annual conference held in November. Nov. 14 for 2009 at Townson University's University Union. Conference duration: 1 day. Average attendance: 150-200. Covers all areas of writing and getting published. Held at Towson University. Session topics include fiction, non-fiction, poetry, magazine and journals, agents and publishers. Sign up the day of the conference for quick critiques to improve your stories, essays, and poems." KEYNOTE SPEAKER for 2009 is Mark Bowden. Mark Bowden is the author of the books *Black Hawk Down* and *The Best Game Ever: Giants vs. Colts, 1958.*

Costs $75-95 (includes all-day conference, lunch and reception). Student special rate of $35 before Oct. 17, $50 thereafter.

Accommodations Hotels are close by, if required.

Additional Information Writers may register through the BWA Web site. Send inquiries via e-mail.

BAY AREA WRITER'S LEAGUE ANNUAL CONFERENCE

P.O. Box 580007, Houston TX 77058. E-mail: info@bawl.org. Website: www.bawl.org. The Bay Area Writer's League, known locally as BAWL, has returned to its two-day format with this past year's Writers Conference, which was called "Texas Writers Rock." The Conference was held at the Univ. of Houston Clear Lake, in the Bayou Building. Writers, Dayna Steele and Tammy Kling were Keynote speakers. Workshops were held during the conference on such topics as Author Organization, Memoir Journaling, Scriptwriting Techniques, What's New in the Publishing World, Websites for Authors, Keeping a Writers Notebook, Poetry, and many others. The Conference fee was $125, all inclusive. Past speakers have included Robin T. Popp (author), Leslie Kriewaldt (Barnes & Noble), Brian Klems (*Writer's Digest*), and Margie Lawson (author).
Costs $50/members; $65/nonmembers.

BIG SUR WRITING WORKSHOPS

Henry Miller Library, Highway One, Big Sur CA 93920. Phone/Fax: (831)667-2574. E-mail: magnus@henrymiller.org. Website: www.henrymiller.org/CWW. Annual workshops held in December (Dec. 4-6, 2009) for children's/young adult writing and in March for adult fiction and nonfiction.
Accommodations See location online at website. It has changed.

BLACK WRITERS REUNION & CONFERENCE

BWRC/Pentouch, P.O. Box 542711, Grand Prairie TX 75054-2711. E-mail: bwrc@blackwriters.org. Website: www.blackwriters.org. Estab. 2000. Annual conference held in August. Conference focuses on the craft of writing, publishing, fiction, poetry, romance, Christian fiction, playwriting, and screenwriting. Agent/editor critiques and pitch sessions are also offered. Speakers have included Vincent Alexandria, Venise Berry, Mondella Jones, Shana Murph, and Kat Smith.
Costs $225/full conference (includes workshops, breakfast buffet, luncheon); $100/day for workshops only.
Accommodations Offers $75/night rate at the Raddison Hotel & Suites in Dallas.
Additional Information The next Black Writers Reunion & Conference is scheduled to be held in Las Vegas, Nevada, June 18-19, 2009. Advance registration is now closed. Walk-up registration will open at the hotel on Thursday, June 18, at 10:30 a.m. at walk-up registration rates.

BLOODY WORDS

64 Shaver Ave., Toronto ON M9B 3T5 Canada. E-mail: carosoles@rogers.com; cheryl@freedmanandsister.com; amummenhoff@rogers.com; info@bloodywords.com. Website: www.bloodywords.com. **Contact:** Caro Soles. Estab. 1999. Annual conference held in June. 2009 dates: June 6-8. Conference duration: 3 days. Average attendance: 250. Focuses on mystery fiction and aims to provide a showcase for Canadian mystery writers and readers, as well as provide writing information to aspiring writers. We will present 3 tracks of programming: Just the Facts, where everyone from coroners to toxicologists to tactical police units present how things are done in the real works; and What's the Story - where panelists discuss subjects of interest to readers; and the Mystery Cafe, where 12 authors read and discuss their work. Bloody Words is Canada's oldest and largest gathering of mystery readers and authors. The conference has become *the* June event to look forward to for people who enjoy genre conventions.
Costs $125+ (Canadian). $115 (US). Includes banquet. If paying by mail, send to Caro Soles, 12 Roundwood Ct., Toronto, ON, M1W 1Z2, Canada.
Accommodations A special rate will be available at The Downtown Hilton Hotel in Toronto, Ontario.
Additional Information Registration is available online. Send inquiries via e-mail.

BLUE RIDGE MOUNTAIN CHRISTIAN WRITERS CONFERENCE

No public address available, E-mail: ylehman@bellsouth.net. Website: www.lifeway.com/christianwriters. Annual conference held in May. Conference duration: Sunday through lunch on Thursday. Average attendance: 400. A training and networking event for both seasoned and aspiring writers that allows attendees to interact with editors, agents, professional writers, and readers. Workshops and continuing classes in a variety of creative categories are also offered.
Costs 2009: $375 (includes sessions and a banquet). See website for next year's costs.
Accommodations $54-84, depending on room size, at the LifeWay Ridgecrest Conference Center near Asheville, North Carolina.
Additional Information The event also features a contest for unpublished writers and ms critiques prior to the conference.

BOOKEXPO AMERICA/WRITER'S DIGEST BOOKS WRITERS CONFERENCE

4700 E. Galbraith Rd., Cincinnati OH 45236. (513)531-2690. Fax: (513)891-7185. E-mail: publicity@fwpubs.com. Website: www.writersdigest.com/bea. Estab. 2003. Annual conference held in May the day before BookExpo America starts. The conference is at the same location as BEA. Average attendance: 500+. The conference offers instruction on the craft of writing, as well as advice for submitting work to publications, publishing houses, and agents. We provide breakout sessions on these topics, including expert advice from industry professionals, and offer workshops on fiction and nonfiction. We also provide agents to whom attendees can pitch their work. The conference is part of the BookExpo America trade show. Registration for the conference does not allow you access to the trade show. Speakers have included Jodi Picoult, Jerry Jenkins, Steve Almond, John Warner, Donald Maass, Noah Lukeman and Jennifer Gilmore. The conference finishes with a large Agent Pitch Slam, with up to 60 agents and editors taking pitches from writers. The slam is the largest of its kind. The conference portion of the week is sponsored by F+W Media. Annual

BOUCHERCON

World Mystery Convention, Bouchercon 2009 c/o The Mystery Company, 233 Second Ave. SW, Carmel IN 46032. E-mail: registration@bouchercon2009.com. Website: www.bouchercon.com. Estab. 1970. Annual convention held in late September/early October. The 40th Bouchercon World Mystery Convention will be held in Indianapolis, Indiana, October 15 - 18, 2009. Expecting 2,000. Co-chairs: Jim Huang, Mike Bursaw. Average attendance: 1,500. Focus is on mystery, suspense, thriller, and true crime novels. Speakers have included Lawrence Block, Jeremiah Healy, James Lee Burke, Ruth Rendell, Ian Rankin, Michael Connelly, Eileen Dreyer, and Earl Emerson. Agents will be speaking and available for informal meetings with attendees.

Costs $150 registration fee. Visit registration page.

Accommodations See online for hotel info. Attendees must make their own transportation arrangements.

Additional Information "This will be the first time that a Bouchercon will include sessions specifically for younger readers and their families. Read more on Children's Program page. During each session, attendees normally have 3-5 choices of programs to choose from. Types of programs include panel discussions on specific aspects of the genre, lectures, classes, demonstrations, book discussion groups, interviews, and more."

BREAD LOAF WRITERS' CONFERENCE

Middlebury College, Middlebury VT 05753. (802)443-5286. Fax: (802)443-2087. E-mail: ncargill@middlebury.edu. Website: www.middlebury.edu/blwc. Estab. 1926. Annual conference held in late August. Conference duration: 11 days. Average attendance: 230. Offers workshops for fiction, nonfiction, and poetry. Agents, editors, publicists, and grant specialists will be in attendance.

Costs $2,345 (includes tuition, housing).

Accommodations Bread Loaf Campus in Ripton, Vermont.

Additional Information 2009 Conference Dates: Wednesday, August 12 - Sunday, August 23. "Please note that all application deadlines for the 2009 session have now passed."

BRISBANE WRITERS FESTIVAL

P.O. Box 3453, 12 Merivale St., South Brisbane QLD 4101 Australia. (61)(7)3255-0254. Fax: (61)(7)3255-0362. E-mail: info@brisbanewritersfestival.com.au. Website: www.brisbanewritersfestival.com.au. **Contact:** Jane O'Hara, Artistic Director. Annual festival held in September. This event draws on local, national, and international guests for an eclectic mix of panels, discussions, debates, launches and interviews.

BYRON BAY WRITERS FESTIVAL

Northern Rivers Writers' Centre, P.O. Box 1846, 69 Johnson St., Byron Bay NSW 2481 Australia. 040755-2441. E-mail: jeni@nrwc.org.au. Website: www.byronbaywritersfestival.com. **Contact:** Jeni Caffin, dir.. Estab. 1997. Annual festival held the first weekend in August at Becton's Byron Bay Beach Resort. Conference duration: 3 days. Celebrate and reflect with over 100 of the finest writers from Australia and overseas. Workshops, panel discussions, and poetry readings will also be offered. The Byron Bay Writers Festival is organised by the staff and Committee of the Northern Rivers Writers' Centre, a member based organisation receiving core funding from Arts NSW.

Costs See costs online under Tickets. Early bird, NRWC members and students, kids.

Additional Information "2009 Festival dates are 7-9 August and discounted Early Bird 3 day passes are now on sale at our website or through Jetset Byron Bay on 02 6685 6262."

BYU WRITING AND ILLUSTRATING FOR YOUNG READERS WORKSHOP

348 HCEB, Brigham Young University, Provo UT 84602. (801)422-2568. E-mail: cw348@byu.edu. Website: wfyr.byu.edu. Estab. 2000. Annual workshop held in June 2010. Conference duration: 5 days. Average attendance: 100. "Learn how to write/illustrate and publish in the children's and young adult fiction and nonfiction markets. Beginning and advanced writers/illustrators are tutored in a small-group setting by published authors/artists and receive instruction from editors, a major publishing house

representative and a literary agent." Held at Brigham Young University's Harmon Conference Center. Speakers have included Edward Necarsulmer, Stephen Fraiser, Krista Marino, and Margaret Miller.
Costs Costs available online.
Accommodations A block of rooms is reserved at the Super 8 Motel and Marriott Courtyard at BYU conference discounted price.
Additional Information Guidelines and registration are on the Web site.

CALIFORNIA CRIME WRITERS CONFERENCE

cosponsored by Sisters in Crime/Los Angeles and the Southern California Chapter of Mystery Writers of America, No public address available, E-mail: sistersincrimela@yahoo.com. Website: www.sistersincrimela.com. Estab. 1995. Annual conference held in June. (2009 conference will be at the Hilton Pasadena, 168 S. Los Robles Ave., Pasadena, on the weekend of June 13 and 14, 2009. The keynote speakers will be Robert Crais, author of *The Watchman* and *L.A. Requiem*, and Laurie R. King, who brings us *A Grave Talent* and *Folly* as well as the Mary Russell series.) Average attendance: 150. Conference on mystery and crime writing. Offers craft and forensic sessions, a keynote speaker, a luncheon speaker, author and agent panels, and book signings.
Additional Information Conference information is available on the Web site.

CANBERRA READERS & WRITERS FESTIVAL

ACT Writers Centre, Gorman House, Ainslie Avenue, Braddon ACT 2612 Australia. (61)(2)6262-9191. E-mail: admin@actwriters.org.au. Website: www.actwriters.org.au. Annual conference held in late August. Local, national, and international writers will give readings, participate in workshops, and sign books.
Costs Most events are free and open to the public.
Additional Information This year's festival is July 10-12, 2009. Seminars: **Working with your publisher**; **Words Change Worlds**; **Readers, Critics, Writers**. See programs online.

CHATTANOOGA FESTIVAL OF WRITERS

Arts & Education Council, 3069 S. Broad St., Suite 2, Chattanooga TN 37408. (423)267-1218. Fax: (423)267-1018. E-mail: info@artsedcouncil.org. Website: www.artsedcouncil.org/page/chattanooga-festival-of-writers. Estab. 2006. Biennial conference held in late March. Conference duration: 2 days. Average attendance: 250. This conference covers fiction, nonfiction, drama and poetry through workshops and keynote. Held in downtown Chattanooga. Speakers have included Suzette Francis, Richard Bausch, David Magee, Philip Gerard, Elizabeth Kostova and Robert Morgan.
Costs $65-175 (depending on attendees participation in workshops, luncheon and dinner).
Additional Information Held during the off years of the AEC Conference on Southern Literature, the 2nd biennial Chattanooga Festival of Writers was March 28 and 29, 2008.

CHRISTOPHER NEWPORT UNIVERSITY WRITERS' CONFERENCE & WRITING CONTEST

1 University Place, Center for Community Learning, Newport News VA 23606-2988. (757)594-7938. Fax: (757)594-8736. E-mail: challiday@cnu.edu. Website: writers.cnu.edu/. Estab. 1981. Conference held in March. This is a working conference. Presentations made by editors, agents, fiction writers, poets and more. Breakout sessions in fiction, nonfiction, poetry, juvenile fiction and publishing. Previous panels included Publishing, Proposal Writing, Internet Research. Brings together published and aspiring authors.
Accommodations Provides list of area hotels.
Additional Information Save the date: 29th Annual Writers' Conference & Writing Contest, March 12-13, 2010. Explore your love of writing by joining us for this annual event that brings together published and aspiring authors. Full contest info will be available online.

CLARION SOUTH WRITERS WORKSHOPS

Fantastic Queensland, Inc., P.O. Box 1394, Toowong QLD 4101 Australia. E-mail: info@clarionsouth.org. Website: www.clarionsouth.org. Six-week workshop held in January for writers preparing for a professional career in speculative fiction, science fiction, fantasy, or horror. Each week, a different professional writer/editor conducts the workshop; mornings are devoted to critiquing stories and afternoons/evening/weekends are for individual writing, private conferences, and social activities. Participants produce new work and receive feedback on structure, style, and substance. Writers must apply to the workshop by submitting up to 6,000 words of their fiction.
Costs Check online (includes tuition and accommodations). Scholarships, bursaries, and other forms of financial aid are available.
Accommodations Griffith University, Nathan Campus dorms.
Additional Information "Clarion South runs every 2 years in Brisbane, Australia and is the most intensive

professional development program for speculative fiction writers in the southern hemisphere. The next workshop will run January- February 2011."

CLARION WEST WRITERS' WORKSHOP

340 15th Ave. E, Suite 350, Seattle WA 98112-5156. (206)322-9083. E-mail: info@clarionwest.org. Website: www.clarionwest.org. Clarion West is an intensive 6-week workshop for writers preparing for professional careers in science fiction and fantasy, held annually in Seattle, Washington, USA. Usually goes from late June through early July. Conference duration: 6 weeks. Average attendance: 18. Held near the University of Washington. Deadline for applications is March 1. Agents are invited to speak to attendees. This year's workshop will be held from June 21 - July 31, 2009.

Costs $3200 (for tuition, housing, most meals). $100 discount if application received prior to March 1. Limited scholarships are available based on financial need.

Additional Information "This is a critique-based workshop. Students are encouraged to write a story every week; the critique of student material produced at the workshop forms the principal activity of the workshop. Students and instructors critique mss as a group. Students must submit 20-30 pages of ms to qualify for admission. Conference guidelines are available for a SASE. Visit the Web site for updates and complete details."

CLARKSVILLE WRITERS CONFERENCE

1123 Madison St., Clarksville TN 37040. (931)645-2317. E-mail: corneliuswinn@bellsouth.net. Website: www.artsandheritage.us/writers/. Annual conference held in the summer. The conference features a variety of presentations on fiction, nonfiction and more. Our keynote speaker for 2009 will be John Egerton. Others attending: Darnell Arnoult, Earl S. Braggs, Christopher Burawa, Susan Gregg Gilmore, James & Lynda O'Connor, Katharine Sands, George Singleton, Bernis Terhune, p.m. terrell. Our presentations and workshops are valuable to writers and interesting to readers. This fun, affordable, and talent-laden conference is presented at Austin Peay State University and the Clarksville Country Club. Annual

Costs Costs available online; prices vary depending on how long attendees stay and if they attend the banquet dinner.

Accommodations Hotel specials provided every year. For 2009, discounted lodging package at Riverview Inn, a luxury hotel located in historic downtown Clarksville, is available for Clarksville Writers' Conference participants only. Call toll-free at 1-877-487-4837 to make reservations. Pay $74.00 per night plus tax, running July 10-12, 2008 (breakfast included). www.theriverviewinn.com

Additional Information "Clarksville Writers Conference 2009 information is being updated as it becomes available. Please check back frequently for updates. The Fifth Annual Clarksville Writers' Conference is July 22 - 25, 2009."

DESERT DREAMS

Phoenix Desert Rose Chapter No. 60, PO Box 27407, Tempe AZ 85285. (866)267-2249. E-mail: info@desertroserwa.org; desertdreams@desertroserwa.org. Website: www.desertroserwa.org. Estab. 1986. Conference held every other April. Conference duration: 3 days. Average attendance: 250. Covers marketing, fiction, screenwriting, and research. Keynote speakers: New York Times Bestselling Author Linda Lael Miller and Brad Schreiber VP of Storytech (The Writer's Journey with Chris Vogler).

Costs $218 + (includes meals, seminars, appointments with agents/editors).

Accommodations Discounted rates for attendees is negotiated at the Crowne Plaza San Marcos Resort in Chandler, Ariz.

Additional Information Send inquiries via e-mail. Visit Web site for updates and complete details.

DINGLE WRITING COURSES

Ballintlea, Ventry Co Kerry Ireland. Phone/Fax: (353)(66)915-9815. E-mail: info@dinglewritingcourses.ie. Website: http://www.dinglewritingcourses.ie. Estab. 1996. Workshops held in September and October. Average attendance: 14. Creative writing weekends for fiction, poetry, memoir, novel, starting to write, etc. Our courses take place over a weekend in a purpose-built residential centre at Inch on the Dingle peninsula. They are designed to meet the needs of everyone with an interest in writing. All our tutors are well-known writers, with experience tutoring at all levels. See courses and tutors online at website.

Costs 420-445 euros. Some bursaries are available from county arts officers.

Accommodations Provides overnight accommodations.

Additional Information Some workshops require material to be submitted in advance. Accepts inquiries by e-mail, phone, and fax.

EAST OF EDEN WRITERS CONFERENCE

P.O. Box 3254, Santa Clara CA 95055. E-mail: vp@southbaywriters.com; pres@southbaywriters.com. Website: www.southbaywriters.com. Estab. 2000. Biannual conference held in September. Average attendance: 300. Writers of all levels are welcome. Pitch-sessions to agents and publishers are available, as are meetings with authors and editors. Workshops address the craft and the business of writing. Location: Salinas, CA - Steinbeck Country.

Costs Costs vary. The full conference (Friday and Saturday) is approximately $250; Saturday only is approximately $175. The fee includes meals, workshops and pitch/meeting sessions. Optional events extra.

Accommodations Negotiated rates at local hotels - $85 per night, give or take.

Additional Information The East of Eden conference is run by writers/volunteers from the California Writers Club, South Bay Branch. The Salinas Community Center's Sherwood Hall has been reserved for September 24-26, 2010 for the next conference. For details, please visit our Web site or send an SASE.

EAST TEXAS CHRISTIAN WRITERS CONFERENCE

The School of Humanities, Dr. Jerry L. Summers, Dean, Scarborough Hall, East Texas Baptist Univ., 1209 N. Grove, Marshall TX 75670. (903)923-2269. E-mail: jhopkins@etbu.edu. Website: www.etbu.edu/News/CWC. Estab. 2002. Average attendance: 60. Conference offers: contact, conversation, and exchange of ideas with other aspiring writers; outstanding presentations and workshop experiences with established authors; potential publishing and writing opportunities; networking with other writers with related interests; promotion of both craft and faith; and consultations with agents, editors, and publishers. Speakers have included Mike and Susan Farris, Denny Boultinghouse, Pamela Dowd, and Mary Lou Redding.

Costs Visit Web site.

Accommodations Visit Web site for a list of local hotels offering a discounted rate.

Additional Information Next one will be held April 9-10, 2010.

FALL WRITERS' SEMINAR

Council for the Written Word, P.O. Box 298, Franklin TN 37065. (615)591-2947. E-mail: info-fallseminar@cww-writers.org. Website: www.asouthernjournal.com/cww. Annual conference held in September. The Sept. 12, 2009 session is named *The Unbridled Pen*. "Michael Martone will slice & dice your work in his interactive 'Cross-Sectional Workshop' revealing what comprises the best of titles, first lines, closing paragraphs, as well as narrative, plot, structure, and other elements of strong writing. Peggy Godfrey will discuss breathing 'geothermal' life into your prose & poetry in her workshop, 'Turning Experience Into Descriptive Prose & Poetry/the Author's Voice.' She will also discuss translating the passion & meaning of your work when reading to an audience."

Costs Fee is $73 ($65 postmarked by June 30, 2009). Covers pre-event reception, workshop, continental breakfast & lunch during workshop.

Additional Information Pre-event Reception held at Landmark Bookshop; workshop held at Christ UMC, 508 Franklin Rd., Franklin, TN.

FESTIVAL OF FAITH AND WRITING

Department of English, Fine Arts Center, Calvin College, 1795 Knollcrest Circle SE, Grand Rapids MI 49546. (616)526-6770. E-mail: ffw@calvin.edu. Website: www.calvin.edu/academic/engl/festival.htm. Estab. 1990. Biennial festival held in April. Conference duration: 3 days. The festival brings together writers, editors, publishers, musicians, artists, and readers to discuss and celebrate insightful writing that explores issues of faith. Focuses on fiction, nonfiction, memoir, poetry, drama, children's, young adult, academic, film, and songwriting. Past speakers have included Joyce Carol Oates, Salman Rushdie, Patricia Hampl, Thomas Lynch, Leif Enger, Marilynne Robinson and Jacqueline Woodson. Agents and editors attend the festival.

Costs Estimated at $170; $85/students (includes all sessions, but does not include meals, lodging, or evening concerts).

Accommodations Shuttles are available to and from local hotels. Shuttles are also available for overflow parking lots. A list of hotels with special rates for conference attendees is available on the festival Web site. High school and college students can arrange on-campus lodging by e-mail.

Additional Information Online registration opens in October. Accepts inquiries by e-mail, phone, and fax.

FESTIVAL OF WORDS

217 Main St. N., Moose Jaw SK S6J 0W1 Canada. (306)691-0557. Fax: (306)693-2994. E-mail: word.festival@sasktel.net. Website: www.festivalofwords.com. Estab. 1997. Annual festival held in July. 2009 dates: July 16-19. Conference duration: 4 days. Average attendance: 1,500.

Accommodations A list of motels, hotels, campgrounds, and bed and breakfasts is provided upon request.

Additional Information "Our festival is an ideal place for people who love words to mingle, promote their books, and meet their fans. Brochures are available; send inquiries via e-mail or fax."

FLATHEAD RIVER WRITERS CONFERENCE

P.O. Box 7711, Kalispeil MT 59904-7711. E-mail: answers@authorsoftheflathead.org. Website: www.authorsoftheflathead.org. Estab. 1990. Annual conference held in early mid-October. Average attendance: 100. We provide several small, intense 3-day workshops before the general weekend conference. Workshops, panel discussions, and speakers focus on novels, nonfiction, screenwriting, short stories, magazine articles, and the writing industry. Formerly held at the Grouse Mountain Lodge in Whitefish, Montana. Past speakers have included Sam Pinkus, Randy Wayne White, Donald Maass, Ann Rule, Cricket Pechstein, Marcela Landres, Amy Rennert, Ben Mikaelsen, Esmond Harmsworth, Linda McFall, and Ron Carlson. Agents will be speaking and available for meetings with attendees.

Accommodations Rooms are available at a discounted ratet. Whitefish is a resort town, so less expensive lodging can be arranged.

Additional Information "Our 19th Annual Flathead River Writers' Conference will be reduced in scope and duration. It will be a one-day conference on October 3, 2009 at Flathead Valley Community College and will be free for paid-up members of Authors of the Flathead. It is our hope that by doing this we can relieve some of the pressures on your pocketbooks and still make it possible for us to get together this year-- affordably. We will soon announcing the agenda for our conference and the particulars. Watch our website for details. Here are some added decisions/details: The conference will be by reservation only. Go online to sign up. Send inquiries via e-mail."

FLORIDA CHRISTIAN WRITERS CONFERENCE

2344 Armour Ct., Titusville FL 32780. (321)269-5831. Fax: (321)264-0037. E-mail: billiewilson@cfl.rr.com. Website: www.flwriters.org. Estab. 1988. Annual conference held in March. Conference duration: 4 days. Average attendance: 275. Covers fiction, nonfiction, magazine writing, marketing, Internet writing, greeting cards, and more. Conference is held at the Christian Retreat Center in Brandenton, Florida.

Costs $575 (includes tuition, meals).

Accommodations "We provide a shuttle from the Orlando airport. $725/double occupancy; $950/single occupancy."

Additional Information "Each writer may submit 2 works for critique. We have specialists in every area of writing. Brochures/guidelines are available online or for a SASE."

FLORIDA SUNCOAST WRITERS' CONFERENCE

University of South Florida, Continuing Education, 4202 E. Fowler Ave., NEC16, Tampa FL 33620-6758. (813)974-2403. Fax: (813)974-5421. E-mail: dcistaff@admin.usf.edu. Website: english.cas.usf.edu/fswc. Estab. 1970. Annual conference held in February. Conference duration: 3 days. Average attendance: 400. Conference covers poetry, short stories, fiction, nonfiction, science fiction, detective, travel writing, drama, TV scripts, photojournalism, and juvenile. Also features panels with agents and editors. We do not focus on any one particular aspect of the writing profession, but instead offer a variety of writing-related topics. The conference is held on the picturesque university campus fronting the bay in St. Petersburg, Floriday. Speakers have included Lad P.D. James, William Styron, John Updike, Joyce Carol Oates, Francine Prose, Frank McCourt, David Guterson, Jane Smiley, Augusten Burroughs, Billy Collins, and Heather Sellers.

Costs See updates.

Accommodations Special rates are available at area motels. All information is contained in our brochure.

Additional Information Participants may submit work for critiquing (costs $50). Inquire via e-mail or fax.

FRONTIERS IN WRITING

7221 Stagecoach Trail, Amarillo TX 79124. (806)383-4351. E-mail: fiw2006@hotmail.com; panhandleprowriters@yahoo.com. Website: www.panhandleprowriters.org. Estab. 1920. Annual conference held in June. Conference duration: 2 days. Average attendance: 125. Covers screenwriting, children's writing, nonfiction, poetry, and fiction (mystery, romance, mainstream, science fiction, fantasy). Speakers have included Devorah Cutler Rubenstein and Scott Rubenstein (editor/broker for screenplays), Andrew Brown (children's literary agent), Elsa Hurley (literary agent), and Hillary Sears (Kensington Books).

Costs Constantly updating website.

Accommodations Special room rates are available.

Additional Information Sponsors a contest. Guidelines available online or for a SASE.

FUN IN THE SUN

P.O. Box 550562, Fort Lauderdale FL 33355. E-mail: frw_registration@yahoo.com. Website: www.frwriters.org. Estab. 1986. Biannual conference held in February. Features intensive workshops on the craft of writing taught by an array of published authors; a marketing and publicity boot camp;

an open-to-the-public book signing for all attending published authors; one-on-one editor/agent pitch sessions; and special events.
Costs See website for updates, depending on membership status and registration date.
Additional Information "Ours is the longest-running conference of any RWA chapter. Brochures/registration are available online, by e-mail, or for a SASE."

GENEVA WRITERS CONFERENCE

Geneva Writers Group, Switzerland. E-mail: info@GenevaWritersGroup.org. Website: www.genevawritersgroup.org/conference.html. Estab. 2002. Conference held in Geneva, Switzerland. Conference duration: 2 days. Past speakers and presenters have included Thomas E. Kennedy, Nahid Rachlin, Jeremy Sheldon, Kwame Kwei Armah, Philip Graham, Mimi Schwartz, Susan Tiberghien, Jo Shapcott, Wallis Wilde Menozzi, David Applefield, Laura Longrigg, Bill Newlin, Zeki Ergas, D-L Nelson, Sylvia Petter, Alistair Scott Annual

THE GLEN WORKSHOP

Image, 3307 Third Avenue W., Seattle WA 98119. (206)281-2988. Fax: (206)281-2335. E-mail: glenworkshop@imagejournal.org; jmullins@imagejournal.org. Website: www.imagejournal.org/glen. Estab. 1991. Annual workshop held in August. Conference duration: 1 week. Workshop focuses on fiction, poetry, spiritual writing, playwriting, screenwriting, songwriting, and mixed media. Writing classes combine general instruction and discussion with the workshop experience, in which each individual's works are read and discussed critically. Held at St. John's College in Santa Fe, New Mexico. Faculty has included Scott Cairns, Jeanine Hathaway, Bret Lott, Paula Huston, Arlene Hutton, David Denny, Barry Moser, Barry Krammes, Ginger Geyer, and Pierce Pettis. The Glen Workshop combines an intensive learning experience with a lively festival of the arts. It takes place in the stark, dramatic beauty of the Sangre de Cristo mountains and within easy reach of the rich cultural, artistic, and spiritual traditions of northern New Mexico. Lodging and meals are included with registration at affordable rates. A low-cost "commuter" rate is also available for those who wish to camp, stay with friends, or otherwise find their own food and lodging. The next Glen Workshop will take place July 26 through August 2, 2009. The theme for the week will be "Fully Human." Faculty, speakers, and more here.
Costs See costs online. A limited number of partial scholarships are available.
Accommodations Offers dorm rooms, dorm suites, and apartments.
Additional Information 'Like *Image*, the Glen is grounded in a Christian perspective, but its tone is informal and hospitable to all spiritual wayfarers. Depending on the teacher, participants may need to submit workshop material prior to arrival (usually 10-25 pages)."

GLORIETA CHRISTIAN WRITERS CONFERENCE

CLASServices, Inc., 3311 Candelaria NE, Suite 1, Albuquerque NM 87107-1952. (800)433-6633. Fax: (505)899-9282. E-mail: info@classervices.com. Website: www.glorietacwc.com. Estab. 1997. Annual conference held in October. Conference duration: Wednesday afternoon through Sunday lunch. Average attendance: 350. Includes programs for all types of writing. Agents, editors, and professional writers will be speaking and available for meetings with attendees. Annual.
Costs For costs, see Web site. Critiques are available for an additional charge.
Accommodations Hotel rooms are available at the LifeWay Glorieta Conference Center. Santa Fe Shuttle offers service from the Albuquerque or Santa Fe airports to the conference center. Hotel rates vary. "We suggest you make airline and rental car reservations early due to other events in the area."
Additional Information Brochures are available April 1. Inquire via e-mail, phone, or fax, or visit the Web site.

GOTHAM WRITERS' WORKSHOP

WritingClasses.com, 555 Eighth Ave., Suite 1402, New York NY 10018. (212)974-8377. Fax: (212)307-6325. E-mail: dana@write.org. Website: www.writingclasses.com. Estab. 1993. Online classes are held throughout the year. There are four terms of NYC classes, beginning in January, April, June/July, and September/October. Offers craft-oriented creative writing courses in general creative writing, fiction writing, screenwriting, nonfiction writing, article writing, stand-up comedy writing, humor writing, memoir writing, novel writing, children's book writing, playwriting, poetry, songwriting, mystery writing, science fiction writing, romance writing, television writing, article writing, travel writing, business writing and classes on freelancing, selling your screenplay, hot to blog, nonfiction book proposal, and getting published. Also, Gotham Writers' Workshop offers a teen program, private instruction, mentoring program, and classes on selling your work. Classes are held at various schools in New York City as well as online at www.writingclasses.com. Agents and editors participate in some workshops.
Costs $395/10-week workshops; $125 for the four-week online selling seminars and 1-day intensive courses; $295 for 6-week creative writing and business writing classes.

THE GREAT AMERICAN PITCHFEST & SCREENWRITING CONFERENCE

Twilight Pictures, 12400 Ventura Blvd. #735, Studio City CA 91604. (877)255-2528. E-mail: info@pitchfest.com. Website: pitchfest.com/index.shtml. Conference duration: 3 days. "Our companies are all carefully screened, and only the most credible companies in the industry are invited to hear pitches. They may include: agents, managers, distributors and sales agents, Hollywood production companies, Canadian production companies, international production companies, advertisers and agencies, funding organizations, broadcasters and networks, studio representatives." Annual.

Costs Prices varies, depending on everything that an attendee wants to take part in. See online.

Accommodations All activities will be held at the Burbank Marriott Hotel & Convention Center, 2500 N. Hollywood Way, Burbank, CA 91505.

Additional Information June 12-14, 2009.

GREAT LAKES WRITER'S WORKSHOP

Alverno College, 3400 S. 43rd St., P.O. Box 343922, Milwaukee WI 53234-3922. (414)382-6176. Fax: (414)382-6088. Website: www.alverno.edu. Estab. 1985. Annual workshop held in June. Average attendance: 100. Workshop focuses on a variety of subjects, including fiction, writing for magazines, freelance writing, writing for children, poetry, marketing, etc. Participants may select individual workshops or opt to attend the entire weekend session. The workshop is held at Alverno College in Milwaukee, Wisconsin.

Costs In the past, the entire program cost $115 (early bird) (includes breakfast and lunch with the keynote author). June 27, 2009 workshop now $129. Deadline to register is June 23, 2009.

Accommodations Attendees must make their own travel arrangements. Accommodations are available on campus; rooms are in residence halls. There are also hotels in the surrounding area.

Additional Information View brochure online or send SASE after March. Send inquiries via fax.

GREEN LAKE CHRISTIAN WRITERS CONFERENCE

W2511 State Road 23, Green Lake Conference Center, Green Lake WI 54941-9599. (920)294-3323. E-mail: janwhite@glcc.org. Website: www.glcc.org. Estab. 1948. August 23-28, 2009. Conference duration: 1 week. Attendees may be well-published or beginners, may write for secular and/or Christian markets. Leaders are experienced writing teachers. Attendees can spend 11.5 contact hours in the workshop of their choice: fiction, nonfiction, poetry, inspirational/devotional. Seminars include specific skills: marketing, humor, songwriting, writing for children, self-publishing, writing for churches, interviewing, memoir writing, the magazine market. Evening: panels of experts will answer questions. Social and leisure activities included. GLCC is in south central WI, has 1,000 acres, 2.5 miles of shoreline on Wisconsin's deepest lake, and offers a resort setting.

Additional Information Brochure and scholarship info from website or contact Jan White (920-294-7327). To register, call 920-294-3323.

GREEN MOUNTAIN WRITERS CONFERENCE

47 Hazel St., Rutland VT 05701. (802)236-6133. E-mail: ydaley@sbcglobal.net. Website: www.vermontwriters.com. Estab. 1999. Annual conference held in the summer; 2009 dates are July 27-31. Covers fiction, creative nonfiction, poetry, journalism, nature writing, essay, memoir, personal narrative, and biography. Held at an old dance pavillion on on a remote pond in Tinmouth, Vermont. Speakers have included Joan Connor, Yvonne Daley, David Huddle, David Budbill, Jeffrey Lent, Verandah Porche, Tom Smith, and Chuck Clarino.

Costs $500 before July 1; $525 after July 1. Partial scholarships are available.

Accommodations "We have made arrangements with a major hotel in nearby Rutland and 2 area bed and breakfast inns for special accommodations and rates for conference participants. You must make your own reservations."

[N] GULF COAST WRITERS CONFERENCE

P.O. Box 35038, Panama City FL 32412. (850)639-4848. E-mail: MichaelLister@mchsi.com. Website: www.gulfcoastwritersconference.com/. Estab. 1999. Annual conference held in September in Panama City, Fla. Conference duration: 2 days. Average attendance: 100+. This conference is deliberately small and writer-centric with an affordable attedance price. Speakers include writers, editors and agents. Cricket Pechstein Freeman of the August Agency is often in attendance. The 2009 keynote speaker is mystery writer Michael Connelly.

HARRIETTE AUSTIN WRITERS CONFERENCE

Georgia Center for Continuing Education, The University of Georgia, Athens GA 30602-3603. Website: harrietteaustin.org/default.aspx. Annual conference held in July. Sessions cover fiction, poetry, freelance writing, computers, how to get an agent, working with editors, and more. Editors and agents will be speaking. Ms critiques and one-on-one meetings with an evaluator are available for $50.

Costs Cost information available online.
Accommodations Accomodations at the Georgia Center Hotel (georgiacenter.uga.edu).

HAWAII WRITERS CONFERENCE

P.O. Box 1118, Kihei HI 96753. (808)879-0061. Fax: (808)879-6233. E-mail: writers@hawaiiwriters.org. Website: https://www.hawaiiwriters.org/conference.php. Estab. 1993. Formerly the Maui Writers Conference. Annual conference held at the end of August or beginning of September (Labor Day weekend). Conference duration: 4 days. Average attendance: 600. Covers fiction, nonfiction, poetry, screenwriting, children's/young adult writing, horror, mystery, romance, science fiction, and journalism. Though previously held in Maui, the conference moved to Honolulu in 2008. Speakers have included Kimberley Cameron (Reece Halsey North), Susan Crawford (Crawford Literary Agency), Jillian Manus (Manus & Associates), Jenny Bent (Trident Media Group), Catherine Fowler (Redwood Agency), James D. Hornfischer (Hornfischer Literary Management), and Debra Goldstein (The Creative Culture). Annual
Costs $600-1,000. See the Web site for full information.
Additional Information "We offer a comprehensive view of the business of publishing, with more than 1,500 consultation slots with industry agents, editors, and screenwriting professionals, as well as workshops and sessions covering writing instruction. Consider attending the MWC Writers Retreat immediately preceding the conference. Write, call, or visit our Web site for current updates and full details on all of our upcoming programs."

HEART TALK

Women's Center for Ministry, Western Seminary, 5511 SE Hawthorne Blvd., Portland OR 97215-3367. (503)517-1931 or (800)517-1800, ext. 1931. Fax: (503)517-1889. E-mail: western@westernseminary.edu; kstein@westernseminary.edu. Website: www.westernseminary.edu/women. Estab. 1998. Biannual conference held in March. Conference alternates between writing one year and speaking the next. Provides inspiration and techniques for writing fiction, nonfiction, children's books, websites, blogs, etc. Editors/publicists available for one-on-one consultations. Past speakers have included Robin Jones Gunn, Deborah Hestrom-Page, Patricia Rushford, Sally Stuart, and many more. 2010 speaker's conference with Carol Kent and SpeakUp with Confidence team; 2011 next writer's conference.
Additional Information 2011 next writer's conference. Conference information is available by e-mail, phone, fax, or online.

HEDGEBROOK

2197 Millman Road, Langley WA 98260. (360)321-4786. Fax: (360)321-2171. E-mail: info@hedgebrook.org; kimberto@hedgebrook.org. Website: www.hedgebrook.org. **Contact:** Vito Zingarelli, residency director. Estab. 1988. "Hedgebrook is a retreat for women writers on Whidbey Island on 48 beautiful acres, near Seattle, where writers of diverse cultural backgrounds working in all genres, published or not, come from around the globe to write, rejuvenate, and be in community with each other. Writers stay in one of 6 handcrafted cottages for two to six weeks at no cost to the writer." Guidelines: women writers, ages 18 and up, unpublished; women of color encouraged to apply. Application procedure: application, project description, work sample and 425 fee; download appication from website beginning June 2009. Submission deadline: September 25, 2009.
Additional Information Go online for more information.

HIGHLAND SUMMER CONFERENCE

Box 7014, Radford University, Radford VA 24142-7014. (540)831-5366. Fax: (540)831-5951. E-mail: dcochran7@radford.edu; jasbury@radford.edu. Website: www.radford.edu/~arsc. Estab. 1978. Annual conference held in June. 2009 date: June 8-19. Conference duration: 2 weeks. Average attendance: 25. Covers fiction, nonfiction, poetry, and screenwriting. This year's Highland Summer Conference will be conducted the first week by Crystal Wilkinson, who is the author of *Water Street* **and** *Blackberries, Blackberries.* The second week of the Conference will be conducted by author Cathy Smith Bowers, whose works include *The Love that Ended Yesterday in Texas, A Book of Minutes, and Traveling in Time of Danger. Special evening readings by Sharyn McCrumb and Jim Minick. Go to website for more information.*
Costs The cost is based on current Radford tuition for 3 credit hours, plus an additional conference fee. On-campus meals and housing are available at additional cost. In 2007, conference tuition was $717/in-state undergraduates, $1,686/for out-of-state undergraduates, $780/in-state graduates, and $1,434/out-of-state graduates.
Accommodations "We do not have special rate arrangements with local hotels. We do offer accommodations on the Radford University campus in a recently refurbished residence hall. The 2005 cost was $26-36/night."
Additional Information Conference leaders typically critique work done during the 2-week conference, but do not ask to have any writing submitted prior to the conference. Conference brochures/guidelines

are available in March for a SASE. Inquire via e-mail or fax.

HIGHLIGHTS FOUNDATION FOUNDERS WORKSHOPS

814 Court St., Honesdale PA 18437. (570)253-1172. Fax: (570)253-0179. E-mail: contact@highlightsfoundation.org. Website: www.highlightsfoundation.org. Estab. 2000. Conference duration: 3-7 days. Average attendance: limited to 10-14. Genre specific workshops and retreats on children's writing: fiction, nonfiction, poetry, promotions. "Our goal is to improve, over time, the quality of literature for children by educating future generations of children's authors." Highlights Founders' home in Boyds Mills, PA. Faculty/speakers in 2003 included Joy Cowley, Patricia Lee Gauch, Carolyn Yoder, Andrea Early, Stephen Swinburne, Juanita Havill, Sandy Asher, Eileen Spinelli, Rich Wallace, Neil Waldman, Kent L. Brown, Jr. and Peter Jacobi. Workshops held seasonally in March, April, May, June, September, October, November.

Costs 2009 costs ranged from $795-1195, including meals, lodging, materials, and much more.

Accommodations Coordinates pickup at local airport. Offers overnight accommodations. Participants stay in guest cabins on the wooded grounds surrounding Highlights Founders' home adjacent to the house/conference center.

Additional Information Some workshops require pre-workshop assignment. Brochure available for SASE, by e-mail, on website, by phone, by fax. Accepts inquiries by phone, fax, e-mail, SASE. Editors attend conference. "Applications will be reviewed and accepted on a first-come, first-served basis, applicants must demonstrate specific experience in writing area of workshop they are applying for - writing samples are required for many of the workshops."

HIGHLIGHTS FOUNDATION WRITERS WORKSHOP AT CHAUTAUQUA

814 Court St., Honesdale PA 18431. (570)253-1192. Fax: (570)253-0179. E-mail: contact@highlightsfoundation.org. Website: www.highlightsfoundation.org. Estab. 1985. Annual conference held July 17-24, 2010. Average attendance: 100. Workshops are geared toward those who write for children at the beginner, intermediate, and advanced levels. Offers seminars, small group workshops, and one-on-one sessions with authors, editors, illustrators, critics, and publishers. Workshop site is the picturesque community of Chautauqua, New York. Speakers have included Bruce Coville, Candace Fleming, Linda Sue Park, Jane Yolen, Patricia Gauch, Jerry Spinelli, Eileen Spinelli, Joy Cowley and Pam Munoz Ryan.

Costs $2,400 (includes all meals, conference supplies, gate pass to Chautauqua Institution).

Accommodations We coordinate ground transportation to and from airports, trains, and bus stations in the Erie, Pennsylvania and Jamestown/Buffalo, New York area. We also coordinate accommodations for conference attendees.

Additional Information "We offer the opportunity for attendees to submit a manuscript for review at the conference. Workshop brochures/guidelines are available upon request."

HOFSTRA UNIVERSITY SUMMER WRITING WORKSHOPS

University College for Continuing Education, 250 Hofstra University, Hempstead NY 11549-2500. (516)463-5993. Fax: (516)463-4833. E-mail: uccelibarts@hofstra.edu. Website: www.hofstra.edu/ucce/summerwriting. Estab. 1972. Annual conference held in mid-July. 2009: July 6-17 ($550). Conference duration: 2 weeks. Average attendance: 65. Conference offers workshops in short fiction, nonfiction, poetry, and occasionally other genres such as screenplay writing or writing for children. Site is the university campus on Long Island, 25 miles from New York City. Speakers have inluded Oscar Hijuelos, Robert Olen Butler, Hilma and Meg Wolitzer, Budd Schulberg, Cynthia Ozick, and Rebecca Wolff.

Costs Check Web site for current fees. Credit is available for undergraduate and graduate students. Continental breakfast daily; tution also includes the cost of the banquet. All workshops include critiquing. Each participant is given one-on-one time for a half hour with a workshop leader. More details will be available in March. Accepts inquiries via fax and e-mail.

Accommodations Free bus operates between Hempstead Train Station and campus for those commuting from New York City on the Long Island Rail Road. Dormitory rooms are available.

Additional Information Students entering grades 9-12 can now be part of the Summer Writers Program with a special section for high school students. Through exercises and readings, students will learn how to use their creative impulses to improve their fiction, poetry and plays and learn how to create cleaner and clearer essays. During this intensive 2-week course, students will experiment with memoir, poetry, oral history, dramatic form and the short story, and study how to use character, plot, point of view and language.

HOLLYWOOD PITCH FESTIVAL

Fade In Magazine, 287 S. Robertson Blvd., #467, Beverly Hills CA 90211. (800)646-3896. E-mail: inquiries@fadeinonline.com. Website: hollywoodpitchfestival.com/. Estab. 1996. 2009: August 1 & 2, at Bergamot Station, Santa Monica, CA. Register online or Call To Register (800) 646-3896. Conference duration: Two days. This is a pitch event that provides non-stop pitch meetings over a two-day period

- with 200 of Hollywood's top buyers/representatives under one roof. HPF only has one class - a pitch class taught by a professional A-list filmmaker on Saturday morning, and it is optional. Each attendeewill received by e-mail a list of the companies/industry representatives attending, what each company is currently looking to produce (i.e., genre, budget), along with each company's credits. We also post a genre list at each event for cross-reference." Annual.

Costs Our ticket prices are flat fees that cover each attendee's entire weekend (including food and drink). There are no other extra, added costs (i.e., no per pitch meeting fees) involved (unless you're adding hotel rooms).

IDAHO WRITERS LEAGUE WRITERS' CONFERENCE

P.O. Box 492, Kootenai, ID 83840. (208)290-8749. E-mail: president@idahowritersleague.com. Website: www.idahowritersleague.com/Conference.html. Estab. 1940. Annual floating conference. Next conference: The Twin Falls Chapter will host the 2009 League Conference. Dates are beginning Thursday, September 24, 2009 for registration. The workshops will run Friday, September 25 and Saturday, September 26, 2009. The conference will be at the Red Lion Canyon Springs Hotel and Convention Center in Twin Falls. "As we receive information on the conference schedule, presenters, and other related information, we will add them to our Web page. Average attendance: 80+. We have such writers as magazine freelance and children's book author, Kelly Milner Halls; and author of the 2006 Christian Women's Fiction Book of the Year, Nikki Arana."

Costs Cost: $125. Check for updates on cost.

Additional Information "Check out our website at www.idahowritersleague.com."

IMAGINATION WRITERS WORKSHOP AND CONFERENCE

Cleveland State University, English Department, 2121 Euclid Ave., Cleveland OH 44115. (216)687-4522. Fax: (216)687-6943. E-mail: imagination@csuohio.edu. Website: www.csuohio.edu/imagination/. Estab. 1990. Annual conference is held in late June/early July. Conference duration: 6 days. Average attendance: 60. Program includes intensive workshops, panels, lectures on poetry, fiction, creative nonfiction, playwriting, and the business of writing by noted authors, editors and agents. Held at Trinity Commons, an award-winning urban renovation and ideal conference center adjacent to the CSU campus. Available both not-for-credit and for university credit.

Additional Information This year the conference will be held Tuesday Evening, July 7, through Sunday Afternoon, July 12, 2009. Application deadline: May 20.

INDIANA UNIVERSITY WRITERS' CONFERENCE

464 Ballantine Hall, Bloomington IN 47405. (812)855-1877. E-mail: writecon@indiana.edu. Website: www.indiana.edu/~writecon. Estab. 1940. Annual conference held in June. 2009: June 14-19. The Indiana University Writers' Conference, now in its 69th year, invites prominent writers who are equally skilled and involved teachers. Participants in the week-long conference join faculty-led workshops (fiction, poetry, and creative nonfiction), take classes, engage in one-on-one consultation with authors, and attend a variety of readings and social events. Previous speakers have included Raymond Carver, Mark Doty, Robert Olen Butler, Aimee Bender, Li-Young Lee, and Brenda Hillman.

Costs Costs available online.

Additional Information In order to be accepted in a workshop, the writer must submit the work they would like critiqued. Work is evaluated before the applicant is accepted. Go online or send a SASE for guidelines.

INTERNATIONAL MUSEUM PUBLISHING SEMINAR

University of Chicago, Graham School of General Studies, 1427 E. 60th St., Chicago IL 60637. (773)702-1682. Fax: (773)702-6814. E-mail: s-medlock@uchicago.edu. Website: grahamschool.uchicago.edu. Estab. 1988. Biennial conference. Conference duration: 2 1/2 days. Average attendance: 250. Primarily covers nonfiction, writing, and editing in museums. Recent themes have included selecting an attractive books cover, artful strategies for cutting costs, digital imaging, a survival guide, and more. The conference moves to a new city each year and is co-sponsored by the university with different museums.

Costs $600-650

Accommodations See Web site for hotel options.

Additional Information Send a SASE in January for brochure/guidelines. Inquire via e-mail or fax.

IN THE COMPANY OF WRITERS, WEBINARS AND TELESEMINARS

1071 Steeple Run, Lawrenceville GA 30043. (678)407-0703. Fax: (678)407-9917. E-mail: info@inthecompanyofwriters.com. Website: www.inthecompanyofwriters.com. Estab. 2006. Weekly and monthly classes via teleseminars and webinars starting in February (six-week, 12-hour class). Sessions range from two hours to six weeks. Learn from the nation's top experts, covering all genres and aspects of the writing life for inspiration, information, publication, marketing and more. Presented via telephone, online media and e-books. There's no traveling, no hotels and no expensive meals out.

Presenters include Dr. Brian J. Corrigan, Bobbie Christmas, mystery writer Fran Stewart, memoirist Sara Harrell Banks, poet Collin Kelley.
Costs Varies; the cost is free to some and can be up to $247 for others depending on subject and duration.
Additional Information "Join online in order to receive our FREE E-Lert Newsletter bringing you updates on courses, writing tips, and information, including markets, contests."

IOWA SUMMER WRITING FESTIVAL

C215 Seashore Hall, University of Iowa, Iowa City IA 52242. (319)335-4160. Fax: (319)335-4743. E-mail: iswfestival@uiowa.edu. Website: www.uiowa.edu/~iswfest. Estab. 1987. Annual festival held in June and July. Conference duration: Workshops are 1 week or a weekend. Average attendance: Limited to 12 people/class, with over 1,500 participants throughout the summer. We offer courses across the genres: novel, short story, poetry, essay, memoir, humor, travel, playwriting, screenwriting, writing for children, and women's writing. Held at the University of Iowa campus. Speakers have included Marvin Bell, Lan Samantha Chang, John Dalton, Hope Edelman, Katie Ford, Patricia Foster, Bret Anthony Johnston, Barbara Robinette Moss, among others.
Costs $500-525/week; $250/weekend workshop. Housing and meals are separate. See registration info online.
Accommodations Iowa House: $75/night; Sheraton: $88/night (rates subject to change).
Additional Information Brochures are available in February. Inquire via e-mail or fax.

IWWG EARLY SPRING IN CALIFORNIA CONFERENCE

International Women's Writing Guild, P.O. Box 810, Gracie Station, New York NY 10028-0082. (212)737-7536. Fax: (212)737-9469. E-mail: iwwg@iwwg.org. Website: www.iwwg.org. Estab. 1982. Annual conference held the second week in March. Average attendance: 50. Conference promotes creative writing, personal growth, and voice. Site is a redwood forest mountain retreat in Santa Cruz, California.
Costs $350/members; $380/nonmembers for weekend program with room and board; $125 for weekend program without room and board.
Accommodations All participants stay at the conference site or may commute.
Additional Information Brochures/guidelines are available online or for a SASE. Inquire via e-mail or fax.

IWWG Meet the Agents/Meet the Authors plus One Day Writing Workshop

c/o International Women's Writing Guild, P.O. Box 810, Gracie Station, New York NY 10028-0082. (212)737-7536. Fax: (212)737-9469. E-mail: iwwg@iwwg.org. Website: www.iwwg.org. Estab. 1980. Workshops are held the second weekend in April and October. Average attendance: 200. Workshops promote creative writing and professional success. A 1-day writing workshop is offered on Saturday. Sunday morning includes a discussion with up to 10 recently published IWWG authors and a book fair during lunch. On Sunday afternoon, up to 10 literary agents introduce themselves, and then members of the audience speak to the agents they wish to meet. Many as-yet-unpublished works have found publication in this manner. Speakers have included Meredith Bernstein, Rita Rosenkranz, and Jeff Herman.
Costs $130/members for the weekend; $160/nonmembers for the weekend; $90/100 for Saturday; $80/105 for Sunday.
Additional Information Information (including accommdations) is provided in a brochure. Inquire via fax or e-mail.

JACKSON HOLE WRITERS CONFERENCE

PO Box 1974, Jackson WY 83001. (307)413-3332. E-mail: tim@jacksonholewritersconference.com. Website: jacksonholewritersconference.com/. Estab. 1991. Annual conference held in June. For 2009: June 25-28. Conference duration: 4 days. Average attendance: 70. Covers fiction and creative nonfiction and offers ms critiques from authors, agents, and editors. Agents in attendance will take pitches from writers. Paid manuscript critique programs are available.
Costs $360-390
Additional Information Held at the Center for the Arts in Jackson, Wyoming.

JAMES RIVER WRITERS CONFERENCE

P.O. Box 25067, Richmond VA 23260. (804)474-3575. E-mail: fallconference@jamesriverwriters.com. Website: www.jamesriverwriters.com. Estab. 2003. Annual conference held in October. For 2009: Oct. 9-10. Average attendance: 250. The conference is held at the Library of Virginia, located in downtown Richmond. Some events planned include panel discussions on freelancing, historical fiction, how to create dialogue, and nonfiction. Speakers discuss the craft and profession of writing and publishing and present many genres--from fiction, nonfiction, and screenwriting, to poetry, children's literature, and

science fiction. New York agents, bestselling authors, and major publishers usually attend.
Costs $150 (early bird) for 2 days of speakers, panels/discussions, an agent meeting (if available), and a continental breakfast and box lunch on both days. Parking is not included.
Accommodations Overnight accommodation information is available on the Web site. A block of hotel rooms is also reserved at the Holiday Inn Central, located near downtown.
Additional Information Brochures/guidelines are available online or for a SASE. Send inquiries via e-mail.

KARITOS CHRISTIAN ARTS CONFERENCE

1122 Brentwood Ln., Wheaton IL 60189. (847)925-8018. E-mail: bob@karitos.com. Website: www.karitos.com. Estab. 1996. Annual conference held each summer. 2009: July 16-18. Average attendance: 300-400. Karitos is a celebration and teaching weekend for Christian artists and writers. Writing Division will focus on teaching the craft of writing, beginning and advanced, fiction and nonfiction. Site for this year's conference is Living Waters Community Church in the Chicago suburb of Bolingbrook, Faculty has included Lori Davis, John DeJarlais, Eva Marie Everson, Lin Johnson, Patricia Hickman, Elma Photikarm, Rajendra Pillai, Jane Rubietta, Travis Thrasher and Chris Wave.
Costs See website for costs.

KEENE STATE COLLEGE WRITERS CONFERENCE

Continuing Education and Extended Studies, 229 Main St., Keene, NH 03435-2605, (603)358-2290. Fax: (603)358-2569. Website: www.keene.edu/conted/writerconf/. 2009 dates: July 26-August 1. Conference duration: one week. Whether your interest lies in fiction, nonfiction, poetry or all three, this summer conference will help writers with their work. There are daily workshops, writings sessions, individual meetings, craft talks, readings, informal after-hours gatherings, and, above all, time to write. Annual.
Costs Approximately $990. Additional costs for college credit, room, meals.
Additional Information Please register early. Space is limited.

KENYON REVIEW WRITERS WORKSHOP

The Kenyon Review, Kenyon College, Gambier OH 43022. (740)427-5207. Fax: (740)427-5417. E-mail: reacha@kenyon.edu. Website: www.kenyonreview.org. Estab. 1990. Annual 8-day workshop held in June. Participants apply in poetry, fiction, or creative nonfiction, and then participate in intensive daily workshops which focus on the generation and revision of significant new work. Held on the campus of Kenyon College in the rural village of Gambier, Ohio. Workshop leaders have included David Baker, Ron Carlson, Rebecca McClanahan, Rosanna Warren and Nancy Zafris.
Costs $1,995 (includes tuition, housing, meals).
Accommodations Participants stay in Kenyon College student housing.

KEY WEST LITERARY SEMINAR

718 Love Ln., Key West FL 33040 (December-April). (888)293-9291. E-mail: mail@kwls.org. Website: www.keywestliteraryseminar.org. 16 Prayer Ridge Rd., Fairview NC 28730 (May-November). Annual conference held in January. 2010: Jan. 7-10 at San Carlos Institute. See website for topics. 2010 conference is a celebration of 60 years of American poetry.
Costs $495/seminar; $450/writers workshop (Jan. 10-14, 2010).
Accommodations A list of nearby lodging establishments is made available.

N KILLALOE HEDGE-SCHOOL OF WRITING

4 Riverview, Ballina, Killaloe Co. Clare Ireland. (353)(61)375-217. Fax: (353)(61)375-487. Website: www.killaloe.ie/khs. Estab. 1999. Conference duration: 2 days. Holds workshops on 6 different topics.
Costs €235/course.
Accommodations There is a list of hotels and bed and breakfasts on the Web site.

KILLER NASHVILLE

P.O. Box 680686, Franklin TN 37068-0686. (615)599-4032. E-mail: contact@killernashville.com. Website: www.killernashville.com. Estab. 2006. Annual conference held in August. Next conference: Aug. 14-16, 2009. Conference duration: 3 days. Average attendance: 180+. Conference designed for writers and fans of mysteries and thrillers, including fiction and nonfiction authors, playwrights, and screenwriters. There are many opportunities for authors to sign books. Authors/panelists have included Michael Connelly, Bill Bass, J.A. Jance, Carol Higgins Clark, Hallie Ephron, Chris Grabenstein, Rhonda Pollero, P.J. Parrish, Reed Farrel Coleman, Kathryn Wall, Mary Saums, Don Bruns, Bill Moody, Richard Helms, Brad Strickland and Steven Womack. Literary agents and acquisitions editors attend and take pitches from writers. The conference is sponsored by American Blackguard, Barnes and Noble, Mystery Writers of America, Sisters in Crime and the Nashville Scene, among others. Representatives from the FBI,TBI, ATF, police department and sheriff's department present on law enforcement procedures to the general public.

LA JOLLA WRITERS CONFERENCE

P.O. Box 178122, San Diego CA 92177. (858)467-1978. Fax: (858)467-1971. E-mail: jkuritz@san.rr.com. Website: www.lajollawritersconference.com. Estab. 2001. Annual conference held in October/November. Conference duration: 3 days. Average attendance: 200. In addition to covering nearly every genre, we also take particular pride in educating our attendees on the business aspect of the book industry by having agents, editors, publishers, publicists, and distributors teach classes. Our conference offers 2 types of classes: lecture sessions that run for 50 minutes, and workshops that run for 110 minutes. Each block period is dedicated to either workshop or lecture-style classes. During each block period, there will be 6-8 classes on various topics from which you can choose to attend. For most workshop classes, you are encouraged to bring written work for review. Literary agents from The Andrea Brown Literary Agency, The Dijkstra Agency, The McBride Agency and Full Circle Literary Group have participated in the past.

Costs Costs are available online.

Accommodations We arrange a discounted rate with the hotel that hosts the conference. Please refer to the Web site.

Additional Information "Our conference is completely non-commercial. Our goal is to foster a true learning environment. As such, our faculty is chosen based on their expertise and willingness to make themselves completely available to the attendees. Brochures are online; send inquiries via e-mail or fax."

LAS VEGAS WRITERS CONFERENCE

Henderson Writers Group, 614 Mosswood Drive, Henderson NV 89015. (702)564-2488. E-mail: info@lasvegaswritersconference.com. Website: www.lasvegaswritersconference.com/. Annual conference just outside of Las Vegas. Conference duration: 3 days. Average attendance: 140. Join writing professionals, agents, industry experts and your colleagues for four days in Las Vegas, NV, as they share their knowledge on all aspects of the writer's craft. One of the great charms of the Las Vegas Writer's Conference is its intimacy. Registration is limited to 140 attendees so there's always plenty of one-on-one time with the faculty. While there are formal pitch sessions, panels, workshops, and seminars, the faculty is also available throughout the conference for informal discussions and advice. Plus, you're bound to meet a few new friends, too. Workshops, seminars and expert panels will take you through writing in many genres including fiction, creative nonfiction, screenwriting, poetry, journalism and business and technical writing. There will be many Q&A panels for you to ask the experts all your questions. Annual.

Accommodations Sam's Town Hotel and Gambling Hall.

LEAGUE OF UTAH WRITERS ANNUAL CONFERENCE AND ROUNDUP

P.O. Box 18430, Kearns UT 84118. Website: www.luwrite.com. Estab. 1935. Annual conference held in September. (2009: Sept. 18-19, Heber Valley, UT) Conference duration: 2 days. Offers up to 16 workshops, a keynote speaker, and an awards banquet. Speakers cover subjects from generating ideas, to writing a novel, to working with a publisher.

Additional Information This conference is held in a different site in Utah each year. See the Web site for updated information.

N LIGONIER VALLEY WRITERS CONFERENCE

P.O. Box B, Ligonier PA 15658. (724)593-7294. E-mail: jgallagher@LHTC.net. Website: www.lvwonline. Annual conference held last weekend in July. 2009: July 18, 2009. Details will be posted on their site: lvwonline. Readings, seminars, and workshops cover nonfiction, fiction, children's, poetry, creative nonfiction, playwriting, screenwriting, memoir, travel, historical, fantasy, science fiction, romance, journaling, nature, horror, plot development, and editing. Speakers have included Julia Kasdorf, Paola Corso, Randall Silvis, David Walton, Hilary Masters, Amanda Lynch, and Kathleen George.

Costs See costs for members/nonmembers at lvwonline.

Accommodations A special rate is available at the Ramada Inn of Ligonier.

Additional Information Attendees can submit up to 20 pages for a critique.

LOVE IS MURDER

E-mail: hanleyliz@wideopenwest.com. Website: www.loveismurder.net. Annual conference held in February for readers, writers, and fans of mystery, suspense, thriller, romantic suspense, dark fiction, and true crime. Published authors provide ms critiques; editors/agents participate in pitch sessions. Attorneys, criminal justice experts, forensic scientists, and physicians also attend.

Additional Information Sponsors Reader's Choice Awards for best first novel, historical novel, series, crime-related nonfiction, private investigator/police procedural, paranormal/science fiction/horror, traditional/amateur sleuth, suspense thriller, romance/fantasy, and short story.

THE MACDOWELL COLONY

100 High St., Peterborough NH 03458. (603)924-3886. Fax: (603)924-9142. E-mail: admissions@macdowellcolony.org. Website: www.macdowellcolony.org. Estab. 1907. Open to writers, playwrights, composers, visual artists, film/video artists, interdisciplinary artists and architects. Applicants send information and work samples for review by a panel of experts in each discipline. See application guidelines for details.

Costs Financial assistance is available for participants of the residency, based on need. There are no residency fees.

MAGNA CUM MURDER

The Mid America Crime Writing Festival, The E.B. and Bertha C. Ball Center, Ball State University, Muncie IN 47306. (765)285-8975. Fax: (765)747-9566. E-mail: magnacummurder@yahoo.com; kennisonk@aol.com. Website: www.magnacummurder.com. Estab. 1994. Annual conference held in October. Average attendance: 350. Festival for readers and writers of crime writing. Held in the Horizon Convention Center and Historic Hotel Roberts. Dozens of mystery writers are in attendance and there are presentations from agents, editors and professional writers. The Web site has the full list of attending speakers.

Costs Check website for updates.

MALICE DOMESTIC

PO Box 8007, Gaithersburg MD 20898-8007. Fax: (301)432-7391. E-mail: malicechair@malicedomestic.org. Website: www.malicedomestic.org/. Estab. 1989. 2010 dates: April 30 - May 2, 2010. The conference is for mystery writers of all kinds and always held in the Washington, DC regional area. The conference includes authors and literary agents.

Costs See website for additional information.

MANHATTANVILLE SUMMER WRITERS' WEEK

2900 Purchase St., Purchase NY 10577-0940. (914)323-5239. Fax: (914)694-0348. E-mail: gps@mville.edu; dowdr@mville.edu. Website: www.mville.edu. Estab. 1983. Annual conference held in late June. 2009: June 22-26. Conference duration: 5 days. Average attendance: 100. Workshops are offered in fiction, nonfiction, personal narrative, poetry, children's/young adult, and literature/playwriting. Held at a suburban college campus 30 miles from New York City. Workshop sessions are held in a 19th century Norman castle, which serves as the college's administration building. Speakers have included Brian Morton, Valerie Martin, Ann Jones, Mark Matousek, Major Jackson, Linda Oatman High, Jeffrey Sweet, Alice Quinn (*The New Yorker*), Georgia Jelatis Hoke (MacIntosh & Otis), Paul Cirone (Aaron Priest Literary Agency), and Emily Saladino (Writer's House). Agents will be speaking and available for meetings with attendees.

Costs $650/noncredit (includes all workshops, craft seminars, readings, keynote lecture); $1,040/2 graduate credits. Participants may purchase meals in the college cafeteria or cafe.

Accommodations A list of hotels in the area is available upon request. Overnight accommodations are also available in the college residence halls.

Additional Information Brochures are available online or for a SASE at the end of February. Inquire via e-mail or fax.

[N] [C] MARITIME WRITERS' WORKSHOP

UNB Art Centre, Box 4400, Fredericton NB E3B 5A3 Canada. (506)452-6360. E-mail: rhona.sawlor@unb.ca. Website: www.unb.ca/extend/writers. **Contact:** Allison Howells. Estab. 1976. Annual workshop held in July. Average attendance: 50. Offers workshops in 4 areas: fiction, poetry, nonfiction, and writing for children. Site is the University of New Brunswick, Fredericton campus.

Costs $115 per workshop, or $460 for the week.

Accommodations $725/single occupancy; $705/double occupancy. Meals are included.

Additional Information Participants must submit 10-20 manuscript pages for workshop discussions. Brochures are available after March (no SASE necessary). Accepts inquiries via e-mail.

MARYMOUNT MANHATTAN COLLEGE WRITERS' CONFERENCE

Marymount Manhattan College, 221 E. 71st St., New York NY 10021. (212)774-4810. E-mail: lfrumkes@mmm.edu. Estab. 1993. Annual conference held in June. 2009 keynote speakers: Joseph O'Neill (Netherland), Christopher Reich (Rules of Deception), Peter Scoblic (Managing Editor, *The New Republic*). Conference duration: 1 day. Average attendance: 200. We present workshops on several different writing genres and panels on fiction and nonfiction, literary agents, memoir and more. Over 60 distinguished authors, agents, and publicists attend. Keynote speakers have included Lewis Lapham and Joyce Carol Oates.

Costs $165 before June 1; $185 after June 1 (includes lunch, reception).

MAUMEE VALLEY FREELANCE WRITERS' CONFERENCE

Lourdes College, Franciscan Center, 6832 Convent Blvd., Sylvania OH 43560. (800)878-3210, ext. 3707. E-mail: gburke@lourdes.edu. Website: www.maumeevalleywritersconference.com/. Estab. 1997. Annual conference held in May. Sessions include: Freelance Writing for Magazines, Jumpstart your Stalled Novel, Personal Essays, and Asking the Right Questions: the Art of the Interview. Speakers have included Craig Holden, Matt Betts, Russ Franzen, Benjamin Gleisser, Nicole Hunter, and Jack Lessenberry. Agents and editors participate in the conference.
Costs $99 (includes lunch); $49/students; $30/ms critique.

MENDOCINO COAST WRITERS CONFERENCE

1211 Del Mar Dr., Fort Bragg CA 95437. (707)962-2600, ext. 2167. E-mail: info@mcwc.org. Website: www.mcwc.org. Estab. 1988. Annual conference held in August. Average attendance: 90. Provides workshops for fiction, nonfiction, scriptwriting, children's, mystery, and writing for social change. Held at a small community college campus on the northern Pacific Coast. Speakers have included Jandy Nelson, Paul Levine, Sally Werner, John Lescroart, and Maxine Schur. Agents will be speaking and available for meetings with attendees.
Costs $450+ (includes panels, meals, 2 socials with guest readers, 1 public event, 1 day intensive in 1 subject and 2 days of several short sessions).
Accommodations Information on overnight accommodations and shared rides from the San Francisco Airport is made available.
Additional Information Emphasis is on writers who are also good teachers. Brochures are online or available with a SASE after January. Send inquiries via e-mail.

MIDWEST WRITERS WORKSHOP

Department of Journalism, Ball State University, 2800 Bethel Ave., Muncie IN 47306. (765)282-1055. Fax: (765)285-5997. E-mail: info@midwestwriters.org. Website: www.midwestwriters.org. **Contact:** Jama Bigger, registrar. Estab. 1974. Annual workshop held last weekend in July. Conference duration: 3 days. Covers fiction, nonfiction, poetry, writing for children, how to find an agent, memoirs, Internet marketing and more. Speakers have included best selling authors, literary agents, and editors.
Costs $100-295; $25/ms evaluation

MONTROSE CHRISTIAN WRITERS' CONFERENCE

5 Locust St., Montrose PA 18801. (570)278-1001 or (800)598-5030. Fax: (570)278-3061. E-mail: mbc@montrosebible.org. Website: www.montrosebible.org. Estab. 1990. Annual conference held in July. Offers workshops, editorial appointments, and professional critiques. We try to meet a cross-section of writing needs, for beginners and advanced, covering fiction, poetry, and writing for children. It is small enough to allow personal interaction between attendees and faculty. Speakers have included William Petersen, Mona Hodgson, Jim Fletcher, and Terri Gibbs.
Costs $150/tuition; $35/critique for 2008.
Accommodations Housing and meals are available on site.

MOUNT HERMON CHRISTIAN WRITERS CONFERENCE

37 Conference Drive, Mount Hermon CA 95041. E-mail: info@mounthermon.org. Website: www.mounthermon.org/writers. Estab. 1970. Annual conference held in the spring. 2008 dates were March 14-16. Average attendance: 450. We are a broad-ranging conference for all areas of Christian writing, including fiction, children's, poetry, nonfiction, magazines, books, inspirational and devotional writing, educational curriculum and radio and TV scriptwriting. This is a working, how-to conference, with many workshops within the conference involving on-site writing assignments. The conference is sponsored by and held at the 440-acre Mount Hermon Christian Conference Center near San Jose, California, in the heart of the coastal redwoods. The faculty-to-student ratio is about 1 to 6. The bulk of our more than 60 faculty members are editors and publisher representatives from major Christian publishing houses nationwide. Speakers have included T. Davis Bunn, Debbie Macomber, Jerry Jenkins, Bill Butterworth, Dick Foth and others.
Accommodations Registrants stay in hotel-style accommodations. Meals are buffet style, with faculty joining registrants.
Additional Information "The residential nature of our conference makes this a unique setting for one-on-one interaction with faculty/staff. There is also a decided inspirational flavor to the conference, and general sessions with well-known speakers are a highlight. Registrants may submit 2 works for critique in advance of the conference, then have personal interviews with critiquers during the conference. Brochures/guidelines are available December 1. All conference information is now online only. Send inquiries via e-mail or fax. Tapes of past conferences are also available."

MUSE AND THE MARKETPLACE

160 Boylston St., 4th Floor, Boston MA 02116. (617)695.0075. E-mail: info@grubstreet.org. Website: www.grubstreet.org. The conferences are held in the late spring, such as early May. Conference duration: 2 days. Average attendance: 400. Dozens of agents are in attendance to meet writers and take pitches. Previous keynote speakers include Jonathan Franzen. The conferences has workshops on all aspects of writing. Annual.

Costs Approx. $250-400 depending on if you're a Member or Non-Members (includes 6 workshop sessions and 2 Hour of Power sessions with options for the Manuscript Mart and a Five-Star lunch with authors, editors and agents). Other passes are available for Saturday only and Sunday only guests.

NASHVILLE SCREENWRITERS CONFERENCE

(615)254-2049. Website: nashscreen.com/nsc/. This is a three-day conference dedicated to those who write for the screen. "Nashville is a city that celebrates its writers and its creative community, and every writer wants to have a choice of avenues to increase their potential for success. In this memorable weekend, conference participants will have the opportunity to attend various writing panels led by working professionals and participate in several special events." Annual.

NATCHEZ LITERARY AND CINEMA CELEBRATION

P.O. Box 1307, Natchez MS 39121-1307. (601)446-1208. Fax: (601)446-1214. E-mail: carolyn.smith@colin.edu. Website: www.colin.edu/NLCC. Estab. 1990. Annual conference held in February. Conference duration: 5 days. Conference focuses on all literature, including film scripts. Each year's conference deals with some general aspect of Southern history. Speakers have included Eudora Welty, Margaret Walker Alexander, William Styron, Willie Morris, Ellen Douglas, Ernest Gaines, Elizabeth Spencer, Nikki Giovanni, Myrlie Evers-Williams, and Maya Angelou.

NATIONAL WRITERS ASSOCIATION FOUNDATION CONFERENCE

P.O. Box 4187, Parker CO 80134. (303)841-0246. Fax: (303)841-2607. E-mail: natlwritersassn@hotmail.com. Website: www.nationalwriters.com. Estab. 1926. Annual conference held the second week of June in Denver. Conference duration: 1 day. Average attendance: 100. Focuses on general writing and marketing.

Costs Approximately $100

Additional Information Awards for previous contests will be presented at the conference. Brochures/guidelines are online, or send a SASE.

NATIONAL YOUNG WRITERS FESTIVAL

3/231 King St., Newcastle NSW 2300 Australia. (61)(2)4927-1475. Fax: (61)(2)4927-0470. E-mail: submissions.nywf@gmail.com. Website: www.youngwritersfestival.org. Estab. 1998. Annual festival held in September/October. Conference duration: 5 days. "Poets, editors, comic creators, spoken word artists, script writers, journalists, and all-and-sundry 'friends of the word' gather for workshops, discussions, performances, and collaborations. The National Young Writers' Festival is part of a coalition of festivals called This Is Not Art that occurs over the same 5 days in Newcastle and offers a vibrant and unique mix of experimental and independent arts and media events.

Costs All sessions are free of charge.

NATJA ANNUAL CONFERENCE & MARKETPLACE

North American Travel Journalists Association, 531 Main St., #902, El Segundo CA 90245. (310)836-8712. Fax: (310)836-8769. E-mail: chelsea@natja.org ; elizabeth@natja.org. Website: www.natja.org/conference. Estab. 2003. Annual conference held in May or June. Conference duration: 3 days. Average attendance: 250. Provides professional development for travel journalists and gives them the chance to market themselves to destinations and cultivate relationships to further their careers. Previous speakers have included Lisa Lenoir (*Chicago Sun-Times*), Steve Millburg (*Coastal Living*) and Peter Yesawich. The dates and location of this event change each year, so checking the Web site is the best way to go. Annual.

Accommodations Different destinations host the conference each year, all at hotels with conference centers.

Additional Information E-mail, call, or go online for more information.

NEBRASKA SUMMER WRITERS' CONFERENCE

Department of English, University of Nebraska, Lincoln NE 68588-0333. (402)472-1834. E-mail: nswc@unl.edu. Website: www.nswc.org. Annual conference held in June. Conference duration: 1 week. Faculty include Sara Gruen, Ron Hansen, Li-Young Lee, Sean Doolittle, Lee Martin, Dorianne Laux, Jim Shepard, Judith Kitchen, Joe Mackall, Hilda Raz, William Kloefkorn, agent Sonia Pabley, Timothy Schaffert, Brent Spencer, Stan Sanvel Rubin, agent Emma Sweeney, Jane Von Mehren (vice president,

Random House). An agent is usually in attendance to take pitches.
Costs Costs available online.

NECON

Northeastern Writers Conference, 330 Olney St., Seekonk MA 02771. (508)557-1218. E-mail: daniel.booth77@gmail.com. Website: www.campnecon.com. Estab. 1980. Annual conference typically held in July. Conference duration: Four days. Average attendance: 200. The conference is dedicated to those who write fiction. Held at Roger Williams University in Bristol, RI. Themes vary from year to year. Agents attend the workshop each year. Annual
Costs $350-450. This includes meals and lodging.
Accommodations Attendees stay on campus in the dorm rooms. This housing cost is in the registration fee.
Additional Information Shuttle service provided to the convention site as well as the airport and train station. We are a very laid back, relaxed convention. However, work is accomplished each year and it's a good opportunity to network.

NETWO WRITERS ROUNDUP

Northeast Texas Writers Organization, P.O. Box 411, Winfield TX 75493. (903)856-6724. E-mail: netwomail@netwo.org. Website: www.netwo.org. Estab. 1987. Annual conference held in April. Conference duration: 2 days. Presenters include agents, writers, editors, and publishers. Agents in attendance will take pitches from writers. The conference features a writing contest, pitch sessions, critiques from professionals, as well as dozens of workshops and presentations.
Costs $60+ (discount offered for early registration).
Additional Information Conference is co-sponsored by the Texas Commission on the Arts. See Web site for current updates.

NEW-CUE WRITERS' CONFERENCE & WORKSHOP IN HONOR OF RACHEL CARSON

New-Cue, Inc., Methodist College, Clark Hall, 5300 Ramsey St., Fayetteville NC 28311. (845)630-7047 or (910)630-7046. Fax: (910)630-7221. E-mail: info@new-cue.org. Website: www.new-cue.org. Estab. 1999. Biannual conference held in June. Next one will be in 2010. Conference duration: 4 days. Average attendance: 100. This interdisciplinary event will be a blend of scholarly presentations, readings, informal discussions, and writing workshops. Held at The Spruce Point Inn in Boothbay Harbor, Maine. Speakers have included Lawrence Buell, Bill McKibben, Carl Safina and Linda Lear.
Costs Registration costs include sessions, meals and keynote reception.
Accommodations Special rates are available for participants at the Spruce Point Inn. Transportation and area information is available through the Boothbay Harbor Chamber of Commerce.

NEW JERSEY ROMANCE WRITERS PUT YOUR HEART IN A BOOK CONFERENCE

P.O. Box 513, Plainsboro NJ 08536. E-mail: njrwconfchair@yahoo.com; njrw@njromance writers.org. Website: www.njromancewriters.org. Estab. 1984. Annual conference held in October. Average attendance: 500. Workshops are offered on various topics for all writers of romance, from beginner to multi-published. Speakers have included Nora Roberts, Kathleen Woodiwiss, Patricia Gaffney, Jill Barnett and Kay Hooper. Appointments are offered with editors/agents. Annual
Accommodations Special rate available for conference attendees at the Sheraton at Woodbridge Place Hotel in Iselin, New Jersey.
Additional Information Conference brochures, guidelines, and membership information are available for SASE. Massive bookfair is open to the public with authors signing copies of their books.

THE NEW LETTERS WEEKEND WRITERS CONFERENCE

University of Missouri-Kansas City, 5101 Rockhill Rd., Kansas City MO 64110-2499. (816)235-1168. Fax: (816)235-2611. E-mail: newletters@umkc.edu. Website: www.newletters.org. **Contact:** Betsey Beasley. Estab. 1970s (as The Longboat Key Writers Conference). Annual conference held in late June. Conference duration: 3 days. Average attendance: 60. The conference brings together talented writers in many genres for seminars, readings, workshops, and individual conferences. The emphasis is on craft and the creative process in poetry, fiction, screenwriting, playwriting, and journalism, but the program also deals with matters of psychology, publications, and marketing. The conference is appropriate for both advanced and beginning writers. The conference meets at the university's beautiful Diastole Conference Center. Two- and 3-credit hour options are available by special permission from the Director Robert Stewart.
Costs Participants may choose to attend as a noncredit student or they may attend for 1 hour of college credit from the University of Missouri-Kansas City. Conference registration includes Friday evening reception and keynote speaker, Saturday and Sunday continental breakfast and lunch.

Accommodations Registrants are responsible for their own transportation, but information on area accomodations is available.
Additional Information Those registering for college credit are required to submit a ms in advance. Ms reading and critique are included in the credit fee. Those attending the conference for noncredit also have the option of having their ms critiqued for an additional fee. Brochures are available for a SASE after March. Accepts inquiries by e-mail and fax.

NEW ZEALAND POST WRITERS AND READERS WEEK

New Zealand International Arts Festival, P.O. Box 10-113, Level 2, Anvil House, 138-140 Wakefield St., Wellington New Zealand. (64)(4)473-0149. Fax: (64)(4)471-1164. E-mail: nzfestival@festival.co.nz. Website: www.nzfestival.telecom.co.nz. Biennial festival held in March. 2010: Feb. 26-Mar. 21. Conference duration: 5 days. Focuses on fiction, poetry, and serious nonfiction. Participants are selected by a committee of writers and other book professionals. Held at the Embassy Theatre.
Costs Tickets range from $13-50.
Additional Information Sign up for newsletter online.

NIMROD AWARDS CELEBRATION & WRITING WORKSHOP

University of Tulsa, 800 S. Tucker Drive., Tulsa OK 74104-3189. (918)631-3080. Fax: (918)631-3033. E-mail: nimrod@utulsa.edu. Website: www.utulsa.edu/nimrod. Estab. 1978. Annual conference held in October. Conference duration: 1 day. Offers one-on-one editing sessions, readings, panel discussions, and master classes in fiction, poetry, nonfiction, memoir, and fantasy writing. Speakers have included Myla Goldberg, B.H. Fairchild, Colleen McElroy, Gina Ochsner, Kelly Link, Rilla Askew, Matthew Galkin, and A.D. Coleman.
Additional Information Full conference details are online in August.

NORTH CAROLINA WRITERS' NETWORK FALL CONFERENCE

P.O. Box 954, Carrboro NC 27510-0954. (919)967-9540. Fax: (919)929-0535. E-mail: mail@ncwriters.org. Website: www.ncwriters.org. Estab. 1985. "Annual conference held in November in Research Traingle Park (Durham, North Carolina). Average attendance: 450. This organization hosts two conferences: one in the spring and one in the fall. Each conference is a weekend full of workshops, panels, book signings, and readings (including open mic). There will be a keynote speaker, along with sessions on a variety of genres, including fiction, poetry, creative nonfiction, journalism, children's book writing, screenwriting, and playwriting. We also offer craft, editing, and marketing classes. We hold the event at a conference center with hotel rooms available. Speakers have included Donald Maass, Noah Lukeman, Joe Regal, Jeff Kleinman, and Evan Marshall. Some agents will teach classes and some are available for meetings with attendees."
Costs Approximately $250 (includes 2 meals).
Accommodations Special rates are available at the Sheraton Hotel, but conferees must make their own reservations.
Additional Information Brochures/guidelines are available online or by sending your street address to mail@ncwriters.org. You can also register online.

NORTHERN COLORADO WRITERS CONFERENCE

108 East Monroe Dr., Fort Collins CO 80525. (970)556-0908. E-mail: kerrie@ncwc.biz. Website: www.ncwc.biz/. Estab. 2006. Annual conference held in the spring in Colorado. Conference duration: 2 days. The conference features a variety of speakers, agents and editors. There are workshops and presentations on fiction, nonfiction, screenwriting, staying inspired, and more. Previous agents who have attended and taken pitches from wirters include Jessica Regel, Kristen Nelson, Rachelle Gardner, Andrea Brown, Jessica Faust, Jon Sternfeld, and Jeffrey McGraw. Each conference features more than 30 workshops from which to choose from. Annual
Costs $200-300, depending on what package the attendee selects.
Accommodations The conference is hosted at the Fort Collins Hilton, where rooms are available at a special rate.

NORWESCON

P.O. Box 68547, Seattle WA 98168-9986. (206)270-7850. Fax: (520)244-0142. E-mail: info@norwescon.org. Website: www.norwescon.org. Estab. 1978. Annual conference held in April. (Norwescon 33 will be held April 1-4, 2010.) Average attendance: 2,800. General multitrack convention focusing on science fiction and fantasy literature with wide coverage of other media. Tracks cover science, socio-cultural, literary, publishing, editing, writing, art, and other media of a science fiction/fantasy orientation. Agents will be speaking and available for meetings with attendees.
Accommodations Conference is held at the Seatec Doubletree Hotel.
Additional Information Brochures are available online or for a SASE. Send inquiries via e-mail.

ODYSSEY FANTASY WRITING WORKSHOP

P.O. Box 75, Mont Vernon NH 03057. E-mail: jcavelos@sff.net. Website: www.odysseyworkshop.org. Estab. 1996. Annual workshop held in June (through July). Conference duration: 6 weeks. Average attendance: 16. A workshop for fantasy, science fiction, and horror writers that combines an intensive learning and writing experience with in-depth feedback on students' mss. Held on the campus of Saint Anselm College in Manchester, New Hampshire. Speakers have included George R.R. Martin, Elizabeth Hand, Jane Yolen, Harlan Ellison, Melissa Scott and Dan Simmons.

Costs $1,900/tuition; $700-1,400/on-campus apartment; approximately $550/on-campus meals. Scholarships are available.

Additional Information Prospective students must include a 15-page writing sample with their application. Accepts inquiries by SASE, e-mail, fax and phone. Application deadline April 8.

OKLAHOMA WRITERS' FEDERATION CONFERENCE

1213 E. 9th, Sand Springs OK 74063. (918)519-6707. Fax: (918)519-6707. E-mail: conferenceinfo@owfi.org; rangerjudy@cox.net. Website: www.owfi.org. Estab. 1968. Annual conference held in May. Average attendance: 500. Features writers, editors, agents, and informative programs to help authors write well and get published. Editor/agent appointments are available. Speaker have included Daniel Lazar (Writer's House), Robyn Russell (Amy Rennert Agency), Bryan Painter (*The Oklahoman*), and Mike Sanders (Alpha Books).

Costs $60-200 depending on if attendee partakes in dinners and sessions, as well as the attendee's registration date.

Accommodations Embassy Suites Hotel in Oklahoma City (within walking distance of the airport).

Additional Information We have a writing contest with 27 categories that pay cash prizes.

OPEN WRITING WORKSHOPS

Creative Writing Program, Deptartment of English, Bowling Green State University, Bowling Green OH 43403. (419)372-6864. Fax: (419)372-6805. E-mail: masween@bgnet.bgsu.edu. Website: www.bgsu.edu/departments/creative-writing/wshop.html. **Contact:** Mary Ann Sweeney. Estab. 1999. Annual workshops held in the Spring and Fall. Conference duration: 1 day. Average attendance: 10-20/workshop. Intensive manuscript-based workshops designed for fiction writers and poets of all levels of experience who are working in a variety of genres. Writers in the workshops share their work in a professional studio setting and receive commentary on works in progress from published writers and editors.

Additional Information Participants need to submit workshop material prior to conference.

OUTDOOR WRITERS ASSOCIATION OF AMERICA ANNUAL CONFERENCE

158 Lower Georges Valley Rd., Spring Mills PA 16875. (814)364-9557. Fax: (814)364-9558. E-mail: eking@owaa.org. Website: www.owaa.org. Estab. 1927. Annual conference held in June. (Held June 13-16, 2009 in Grand Rapids.) Conference duration: 4 days. Sessions concentrate on outdoor topics for all forms of media. Held in Lake Charles, Louisianna. Speakers have included Jill Adler, Eric Chaney, Todd Smith, Risa Weinreb-Wyatt, Bob Marshall, and Kathleen Kudlinski.

Costs See website.

Accommodations A block of rooms is held at a special rate.

OZARK CREATIVE WRITERS CONFERENCE

ETSU-Box 23115, Johnson City TN 37614. (423)439-6024. E-mail: ozarkcreativewriters@earthlink.net. Website: www.ozarkcreativewriters.org. Estab. 1975. Annual conference held the second weekend in October, in Eureka Springs, AR. Includes programs for all types of writing. Speakers have included Dan Slater (Penguin Putnam), Stephan Harrigan (novelist/screenwriter), and Christopher Vogler. At least one literary agent is in attendance each year to take pitches.

Costs Approximately $150.

Accommodations Special rates are available at the Inn of the Ozarks in Eureka Springs, Arkansas.

Additional Information The conference has a friendly atmosphere and conference speakers are available. Many speakers return to the conference for the companionship of writers and speakers. Brochures are available for a SASE.

PARIS WRITERS WORKSHOP

WICE, 7, Cité Falguiére, Paris 75015 France. (33)(14)566-7550. Fax: (33)(14)065-9653. E-mail: pww@wice-paris.org. Website: www.wice-paris.org. Estab. 1987. Annual conference held in July. Conference duration: 1 week. Average attendance: 12/section. Each participant chooses one workshop section - creative nonfiction, novel, poetry, or short story - which meets for a total of 15 classroom hours. Writers in residence have included Vivian Gornick, Lynne Sharon Schwartz, Liam Rector, Ellen Sussman, and Katharine Weber. Located in the heart of Paris, the site consists of 4 classrooms, a resource center/library, and a private terrace.

Costs See website for more information
Accommodations Hotel information is on the Web site.

WILLIAM PATERSON UNIVERSITY SPRING WRITER'S CONFERENCE

English Department, Atrium 232, 300 Pompton Rd., Wayne NJ 07470. (973)720-3067. Fax: (973)720-2189. E-mail: parrasj@wpunj.edu. Website: http://euphrates.wpunj.edu/writersconference. Annual conference held in April. Conference duration: 1 day. Average attendance: 100-125. Panels address topics such as writing from life, getting your work in print, poetry, playwriting, fiction, and creative nonfiction. Sessions are led by William Paterson faculty members and distinguished writers and editors of verse and prose. Speakers have included Alison Lurie and Edward Hower.
Costs $50 (includes lunch).

PENNWRITERS ANNUAL CONFERENCE

E-mail: conferenceco@pennwriters.org. Website: www.pennwriters.org. Estab. 1987. Annual conference held the third weekend of May. Conference duration: 3 days. Average attendance: 120. Offers agent and editor panel and workshops on marketing, fiction, romance, networking, and more. Speakers have included Evan Marshall, Nancy Martin, Evan Fogelman, Cherry Weiner, and Karen Solen. Agents will be speaking and available for meetings with attendees.
Costs $150+ (includes all workshops and panels, as well as any editor or agent appointments). There is an additional charge for Friday's keynote dinner and Saturday night's dinner activity.
Accommodations We arrange a special rate with the hotel; details will be in our brochure.
Additional Information We are a multi-genre group encompassing the state of Pennsylvania and beyond. Brochures available in February for SASE. Send inquiries via e-mail or visit the Web site for current updates and details.

PHILADELPHIA WRITERS' CONFERENCE

121 Almatt Terrace, Philadelphia PA 19115-2745. E-mail: info@pwcwriters.org. Website: www.pwcwriters.org. Estab. 1949. Annual conference held in June. Conference duration: 3 days. Average attendance: 150+. Workshops cover short stories, poetry, travel, humor, magazine writing, science fiction, playwriting, memoir, juvenile, nonfiction, and fiction. Speakers have included Ginger Clark (Curtis Brown), Sara Crowe (Harvey Klinger), Samantha Mandor (Berkley), Nancy Springer, Susan Guill, Karen Rile, Gregory Frost, and John Volkmer. Editor/agent critiques are available.
Costs Costs available online.

PIKES PEAK WRITERS CONFERENCE

4164 Austin Bluffs Pkwy., #246, Colorado Springs CO 80918. (719)531-5723. E-mail: info@pikespeakwriters.com. Website: www.pikespeakwriters.com. Estab. 1993. Annual conference held in April Conference duration: 3 days. Average attendance: 400. Workshops, presentations, and panels focus on writing and publishing mainstream and genre fiction (romance, science fiction/fantasy, suspense/thrillers, action/adventure, mysteries, children's, young adult). Agents and editors are available for meetings with attendees on Saturday.
Costs $300-500 (includes all meals).
Accommodations Marriott Colorado Springs holds a block of rooms at a special rate for attendees until late March.
Additional Information Readings with critiques are available on Friday afternoon. Also offers a contest for unpublished writers; entrants need not attend the conference. Deadline: November 1. Registration and contest entry forms are online; brochures are available in January. Send inquiries via e-mail.

PIMA WRITERS' WORKSHOP

Pima College, 2202 W. Anklam Road, Tucson AZ 85709-0170. (520)206-6084. Fax: (520)206-6020. E-mail: mfiles@pima.edu. Website: www.pima.edu. **Contact:** Meg Files, director. Estab. 1988. Annual conference held in May. Conference duration: 3 days. Average attendance: 300. Covers fiction, nonfiction, poetry, and scriptwriting for beginner or experienced writers. The workshop offers sessions on writing short stories, novels, nonfiction articles and books, children's and juvenile stories, poetry, and screenplays. Sessions are held in the Center for the Arts on Pima Community College's West campus. Speakers have included Larry McMurtry, Barbara Kingsolver, Jerome Stern, Connie Willis, Jack Heffron, Jeff Herman, and Robert Morgan. Agents will be speaking and available for meetings with attendees.
Costs $80 (can include ms critique). Participants may attend for college credit, in which case fees are $117 for Arizona residents and $340 for out-of-state residents. Meals and accommodations are not included.
Accommodations Information on local accommodations is made available. Special workshop rates are available at a specified motel close to the workshop site (about $70/night).
Additional Information The workshop atmosphere is casual, friendly, and supportive, and guest authors

are very accessible. Readings and panel discussions are offered, as well as talks and manuscript sessions. Participants may have up to 20 pages critiqued by the author of their choice. Mss must be submitted 3 weeks before the workshop. Conference brochure/guidelines available for SASE. Accepts inquiries by e-mail.

PNWA SUMMER WRITERS CONFERENCE

PMB 2717, 1420 NW Gilman Blvd., Issaquah WA 98027. (425)673-2665. E-mail: pnwa@pnwa.org. Website: www.pnwa.org. Estab. 1955. All conferences are held in July. Conference duration: 4 days. Average attendance: 400. Attendees have the chance to meet agents and editors, learn craft from authors and uncover marketing secrets. Speakers have included J.A. Jance, Sheree Bykofsky, Kimberley Cameron, Jennie Dunham, Donald Maass, Jandy Nelson, Robert Dugoni and Terry Brooks. Annual

Costs For cost and additional information, please see the Web site.

Accommodations The conference is held at the Hilton Seattle Airport & Conference Center.

Additional Information "PNWA also holds an annual literary contest every February with more than $12,000 in prize money. Finalists' manuscripts are then available to agents and editors at our summer conference. Visit the Web site for further details."

PORT TOWNSEND WRITERS' CONFERENCE

Box 1158, Port Townsend WA 98368. (360)385-3102. Fax: (360)385-2470. E-mail: info@centrum.org. Website: www.centrum.org/writing. Estab. 1974. Annual conference held in mid-July. Average attendance: 180. Conference promotes poetry, fiction, and creative nonfiction and features many of the nation's leading writers. All conference housing and activities are located at beautiful Fort Worden State Park, a historic fort overlooking the Strait of Juan de Fuca, with expansive views of the Olympic and Cascade mountain ranges.

Costs See website for cost and accommodation information.

Additional Information The conference focus is on the craft of writing and the writing life, not on marketing. Guidelines/registration are available online or for SASE.

ROBERT QUACKENBUSH'S CHILDREN'S BOOK WRITING & ILLUSTRATING WORKSHOP

460 E. 79th St., New York NY 10075-1443. (212)744-3822. Fax: (212)861-2761. E-mail: rqstudios@aol.com. Website: www.rquackenbush.com. Estab. 1982. Annual workshop held during the second week in July. Conference duration: 4 days. Average attendance: Enrollment limited to 10. Workshops promote writing and illustrating books for children and are geared toward beginners and professionals. Generally focuses on picture books, easy-to-read books, and early chapter books. Held at the Manhattan studio of Robert Quackenbush, author and illustrator of more than 200 books for children. All classes led by Robert Quackenbush.

Costs $750 tuition covers all the costs of the workshop, but does not include housing and meals. A $100 nonrefundable deposit is required with the $650 balance due two weeks prior to attendance.

Accommodations A list of recommended hotels and restaurants is sent upon receipt of deposit.

READERS & WRITERS HOLIDAY CONFERENCE

Central Ohio Fiction Writers, P.O. Box 1981, Westerville OH 43086-1981. E-mail: mollygbg@columbus.rr.com. Website: www.cofw.org. Estab. 1991. Annual conference held in October. The conference is designed to address the needs of writers in all genres of fiction. It explores fiction-writing trends and discusses the business and craft of writing.

Accommodations Attendees are given discounted hotel accommodations.

Additional Information See website for location, costs, and other information.

REMEMBER THE MAGIC

International Women's Writing Guild, P.O. Box 810, Gracie Station, New York NY 10028-0082. (212)737-7536. Fax: (212)737-9469. E-mail: iwwg@iwwg.org. Website: www.iwwg.org. Estab. 1978. Annual conference held in June. Average attendance: 400. Conference to promote creative writing and personal growth, professional know-how and contacts, and networking. Site is the campus of Skidmore College in Saratoga Springs, New York (near Albany). Approximately 65 workshops are offered each day. Conferees have the freedom to make their own schedule.

Costs $1,085 single/$945 double for members; $1,130 single/$990 double for nonmembers. These fees include the 7-day program and room and board for the week. Rates for a 5-day stay and a weekend stay, as well as commuter rates, are also available.

Additional Information Conference brochures/guidelines are available online or for a SASE. Inquire via e-mail or fax.

RETREAT FROM HARSH REALITY

Mid-Michigan RWA Chapter, 6845 Forest Way, Harbor Springs MI 49740. E-mail: retreat@midmichiganrwa.org. Website: www.midmichiganrwa.org/retreat.html. Estab. 1985. Annual conference held in April Average attendance: 50. Conference focusing on romance and fiction writing. Speakers have included Rosanne Bittner, Debra Dixon, Bettina Krahn, Ruth Ryan Langan, Elizabeth Bevarly, Julie Kistler, Merline Lovelace, and Elizabeth Grayson.

ROCKY MOUNTAIN FICTION WRITERS COLORADO GOLD

Rocky Mountain Fiction Writers, P.O. Box 545, Englewood CO 80151. E-mail: conference@rmfw.org. Website: www.rmfw.org/default.aspx. Estab. 1983. Annual conference held in September/October. Conference duration: 3 days. Average attendance: 250. Themes include general novel-length fiction, genre fiction, contemporary romance, mystery, science fiction/fantasy, mainstream, and history. Speakers have included Terry Brooks, Dorothy Cannell, Patricia Gardner Evans, Diane Mott Davidson, Constance O'Day, Connie Willis, Clarissa Pinkola Estes, Michael Palmer, Jennifer Unter, Margaret Marr, Ashley Krass, and Andren Barzvi. Approximately 4 editors and 5 agents attend annually.

Costs Costs available online.

Accommodations Special rates will be available at a nearby hotel.

Additional Information Editor-conducted workshops are limited to 10 participants for critique, with auditing available.

ROMANCE WRITERS OF AMERICA NATIONAL CONFERENCE

16000 Stuebner Airline Rd., Suite 140, Spring TX 77379. (832)717-5200. Fax: (832)717-5201. Website: www.rwanational.com. Estab. 1981. Annual conference held in July. Average attendance: 2,000. More than 100 workshops on writing, researching, and the business side of being a working writer. Publishing professionals attend and accept appointments. The keynote speaker is a renowned romance writer. Held at the Hyatt Regency in Dallas.

Costs $340-550 depending on your membership status as well as when you register.

Additional Information Annual RTA awards are presented for romance authors. Annual Golden Heart awards are presented for unpublished writers.

ROMANTIC TIMES CONVENTION

55 Bergen St., Brooklyn NY 11201. (718)237-1097 or (800)989-8816, ext. 12. Fax: (718)624-2526. E-mail: jocarol@rtconvention.com. Website: www.rtconvention.com. Annual conference held in April. Features 125 workshops, agent and editor appointments, a book fair, and more.

Costs See website for pricing and other information.

ROPEWALK WRITERS' RETREAT

University of Southern Indiana, 8600 University Blvd., Evansville IN 47712. (812)464-1863. E-mail: ropewalk@usi.edu; lcleek@usi.edu. Website: www.ropewalk.org. Estab. 1989. Annual conference held in June. Conference duration: 1 week. The retreat gives participants an opportunity to attend workshops and to confer privately with one of 4 or 5 prominent writers. Held at the historic New Harmony Inn and Conference Center in Indiana. Faculty members have included Stephen Dobyns, Heather McHugh, Ellen Bryant Voigt, Susan Neville, and Bob Shacochis.

Costs $645 (includes workshops, individual conference, readings, receptions, meals); 10% discount for Indiana residents. Scholarships are available.

Accommodations A block of rooms is reserved at the New Harmony Inn ($96-606) and at The Barn Abbey ($25/night).

SAGE HILL WRITING EXPERIENCE

Box 1731, Saskatoon SK S7K 2Z4 Canada. Phone/Fax: (306)652-7395. E-mail: sage.hill@sasktel.net. Website: www.sagehillwriting.ca. Annual workshops held in late July/August and May. Conference duration: 10-14 days. Average attendance: 40/summer program; 8/spring program. Sage Hill Writing Experience offers a special working and learning opportunity to writers at different stages of development. Top-quality instruction, low instructor-student ratio, and the beautiful Sage Hill setting offer conditions ideal for the pursuit of excellence in the arts of fiction, poetry and playwriting. The Sage Hill location features individual accommodations, in-room writing areas, lounges, meeting rooms, healthy meals, walking woods, and vistas in several directions. Classes being held (may vary from year to year) include: Introduction to Writing Fiction & Poetry, Fiction Workshop,; Writing Young Adult Fiction Workshop, Poetry Workshop, Poetry Colloquium, Fiction Colloquium, Novel Colloquium, Playwriting Lab, Fall Poetry Colloquium, and Spring Poetry Colloquium. Speakers have included Nicole Brossard, Steven Galloway, Robert Currie, Jeanette Lynes, Karen Solie and Colleen Murphy.

Costs Summer program: $1,095 (includes instruction, accommodation, meals). Fall Poetry Colloquium: $1,375. Scholarships and bursaries are available.

Accommodations Located at Lumsden, 45 kilometers outside Regina.
Additional Information For Introduction to Creative Writing, send a 5-page sample of your writing or a statement of your interest in creative writing and a list of courses taken. For workshop and colloquium programs, send a résumé of your writing career and a 12-page sample of your work, plus 5 pages of published work. Guidelines are available for SASE. Inquire via e-mail or fax.

SANDHILLS WRITERS CONFERENCE

Augusta State University, Department of Communications and Professional Writing, 2500 Walton Way, Augusta GA 30904-2200. E-mail: akellman@aug.edu. Website: www.sandhills.aug.edu. Annual conference held the fourth weekend in March. Covers fiction, poetry, children's literature, nonfiction, plays, and songwriting. Located on the campus of Augusta State University in Georgia. Agents and editors will be speaking at the event.
Accommodations Several hotels are located near the university.

SAN DIEGO STATE UNIVERSITY WRITERS' CONFERENCE

SDSU College of Extended Studies, 5250 Campanile Dr., San Diego State University, San Diego CA 92182-1920. (619)594-2517. Fax: (619)594-8566. E-mail: jgreene@mail.sdsu.edu; rbrown2@mail.sdsu.edu. Website: www.ces.sdsu.edu/writers. Estab. 1984. Annual conference held in January/February. 2010 dates: Jan. 29-31. Conference duration: 2 days. Average attendance: 375. Covers fiction, nonfiction, scriptwriting and e-books. Held at the Doubletree Hotel in Mission Valley. Each year the conference offers a variety of workshops for the beginner and advanced writers. This conference allows the individual writer to choose which workshop best suits his/her needs. In addition to the workshops, editor reading appointments and agent/editor consultation appointments are provided so attendees may meet with editors and agents one-on-one to discuss specific questions. A reception is offered Saturday immediately following the workshops, offering attendees the opportunity to socialize with the faculty in a relaxed atmosphere. Last year, approximately 60 faculty members attended.
Costs Approximately $365-485 (2010 costs will be published with a fall update of the Web site).
Accommodations Doubletree Hotel (800)222-TREE. Attendees must make their own travel arrangements.

SANDY COVE CHRISTIAN WRITERS CONFERENCE

Sandy Cove Ministries, 60 Sandy Cove Rd., North East MD 21901. (410)287-5433. Fax: (410)287-3196. E-mail: info@sandycove.org. Website: www.sandycove.org. Estab. 1991. Annual conference held the first week in October. Conference duration: 4 days. Average attendance: 200. There are major workshops in fiction, article writing, and nonfiction books for beginner and advanced writers. The conference has plans to add tracks in screenwriting and musical lyrics. Workshops offer a wide variety of hands-on writing instruction in many genres. While Sandy Cove has a strong emphasis on available markets in Christian publishing, all writers are more than welcome. Speakers have included Francine Rivers, Lisa Bergen, Ken Petersen (Tyndale House), Linda Tomblin (*Guideposts*), and Karen Ball (Zondervan).
Costs Call for rates.
Accommodations Sandy Cove is a full-service conference center located on the Chesepeake Bay. All the facilities are first class, with suites, single rooms, and double rooms available.
Additional Information "Conference brochures/guidelines are available. Visit the Web site for exact conference dates."

SAN FRANCISCO WRITERS CONFERENCE

1029 Jones St., San Francisco CA 94109. (415)673-0939. Fax: (415)673-0367. E-mail: sfwriterscon@aol.com. Website: www.sfwriters.org. **Contact:** Michael Larsen, director. Estab. 2003. Annual conference held President's Day weekend in February. Average attendance: 400+. Top authors, respected literary agents, and major publishing houses are at the event so attendees can make face-to-face contact with all the right people. Writers of nonfiction, fiction, poetry, and specialty writing (children's books, cookbooks, travel, etc.) will all benefit from the event. There are important sessions on marketing, self-publishing, technology, and trends in the publishing industry. Plus, there's an optional 3-hour session called Speed Dating for Agents where attendees can meet with 20+ agents. Speakers have included Jennifer Crusie, Richard Paul Evans, Lalita Tademy, Jamie Raab, Mary Roach, Jane Smiley, Debbie Macomber, Firoozeh Dumas, Zilpha Keatley Snyder. More than 20 agents and editors participate each year, many of whom will be available for meetings with attendees.
Costs $600+ with price breaks for early registration (includes all sessions/workshops/keynotes, Speed Dating with Editors, opening gala at the Top of the Mark, 2 continental breakfasts, 2 lunches). Optional Speed Dating for Agents is $50.
Accommodations The Intercontinental Mark Hopkins Hotel is a historic landmark at the top of Nob Hill in San Francisco. Elegant rooms and first-class service are offered to attendees at the rate of $139/night. The hotel is located so that everyone arriving at the Oakland or San Francisco airport can take BART to

either the Embarcadero or Powell Street exits, then walk or take a cable car or taxi directly to the hotel.
Additional Information "Present yourself in a professional manner and the contact you will make will be invaluable to your writing career. Brochures and registration are online."

SANTA BARBARA WRITERS CONFERENCE

P.O. Box 6627, Santa Barbara CA 93160. (805)964-0367. E-mail: info@sbwriters.com. Website: www.sbwriters.com. Estab. 1973. Annual conference held in June. Average attendance: 450. Covers poetry, fiction, nonfiction, journalism, playwriting, screenwriting, travel writing, young adult, children's literature, chick lit, humor, and marketing. Speakers have included Kenneth Atchity, Michael Larsen, Elizabeth Pomada, Bonnie Nadell, Stuart Miller, Angela Rinaldi, Katherine Sands, Don Congdon, Mike Hamilburg, Sandra Dijkstra, Paul Fedorko, Andrea Brown and Deborah Grosvenor. Agents appear on a panel, plus there will be an agents and editors day when writers can pitch their projects in one-on-one meetings.
Accommodations Fess Parker's Doubletree Resort.
Additional Information Individual critiques are also available. Submit 1 ms of no more than 3,000 words in advance (include SASE). Competitions with awards are sponsored as part of the conference. E-mail or call for brochure and registration forms.

SANTA FE WRITERS CONFERENCE

Southwest Literary Center, 826 Camino de Monte Rey, A3, Santa Fe NM 87505. (505)577-1125. Fax: (505)982-7125. E-mail: litcenter@recursos.org. Website: www.santafewritersconference.com. **Contact:** Ellen Bradbury, director. Estab. 1985. Annual conference held in June. Conference duration: 5 days. Average attendance: 50. Conference offering intimate workshops in fiction, poetry, and creative nonfiction. Speakers have included Lee K. Abbott, Alice Adams, Lucille Adler, Francisco Alarcon, Agha Shahid Ali, Rudolfo Anaya, Max Apple, Jimmy Santiago Baca, Madison Smartt Bell, Marvin Bell, Molly Bendall, Elizabeth Benedict, Roo Borson, Robert Boswell, Kate Braverman, Mei-Mei Berssenbrugge, Ron Carlson, Denise Chavez, Lisa D. Chavez, Alan Cheuse, Ted Conover, Robert Creeley, C. Michael Curtis, Jon Davis, Percival Everett, Jennifer Foerster, Richard Ford, Judith Freeman, Samantha Gillison, Natalie Goldberg, Jorie Graham, Lee Gutkind, Elizabeth Hardwick, Robert Hass, Ehud Havazelet, Elizabeth Hightower, Tony Hillerman, Brenda Hillman, Tony Hoagland, Garrett Hongo, Lewis Hyde, Mark Irwin, Charles Johnson, Diane Johnson, Teresa Jordan, Donald Justice, Laura Kasischke, Pagan Kennedy, Brian Kiteley, William Kittredge, Carolyn Kizer, Verlyn Klinkenborg, Karla Kuban, Mark Levine, Alison Lurie, Tony Mares, Kevin McIlvoy, Christopher Merrill, Jane Miller, Mary Jane Moffat, Carol Moldow, N. Scott Momaday, David Morrell, Antonya Nelson, Susan Neville, John Nichols, Sharon Niederman, Naomi Shahib Nye, Grace Paley, Ann Patchett, Margaret Sayers Peden, Michael Pettit, Robert Pinsky, Melissa Pritchard, Annie Proulx, Ron Querry, Judy Reeves, Katrina Roberts, Janet Rodney, Pattiann Rogers, Suzanna Ruta, David St. John, Scott Sanders, Bob Shacochis, Julie Shigekuni, John Skoyles, Carol Houck Smith, Gibbs M. Smith, Roberta Smoodin, Marcia Southwick, Kathleen Spivack, Gerald Stern, Robert Stone, Arthur Sze, Elizabeth Tallent, Nathaniel Tarn, James Thomas, Frederick Turner, Leslie Ullman, David Wagoner, Larry Watson, Rob Wilder, Eleanor Wilner, Diane Williams, Kimberly Witherspoon, Charles Wright, Dean Young, Norman Zollinger.
Costs $575+.
Accommodations A special rate is offered at a nearby hotel.
Additional Information Brochure are available online or by e-mail, fax, or phone.

SCBWI SOUTHERN BREEZE FALL CONFERENCE

P.O. Box 26282, Birmingham AL 35260. E-mail: jskittinger@bellsouth.net. Website: www.southern-breeze.org. Estab. 1992. Annual conference held on the third Saturday in October (2009: Oct. 17). Conference duration: 1 day. Geared toward the production and support of quality children's literature. Offers approximately 28 workshops on craft and the business of writing, including a basic workshop for those new to the children's field. Manuscript and portfoli critiques are offered. Agents and editors participate in the conference. Speakers include editors, agents, art directors, authors and illustrators.
Accommodations We have a room block with a conference rate. The conference is held at a nearby school.

SCENE OF THE CRIME CONFERENCE

Kansas Writers Association, P.O. Box 2236, Wichita KS 67201. (316) 618-0449; (316)208-6961. E-mail: info@kwawriters.org. Website: www.kwawriters.org/sceneofthecrime.htm. Biennual conference held in April. Features agent/editor consultations, mixer, banquet and two days of speaker sessions with detectives, government agents, CSI professionals, editors, agents and authors. A full list of each year's speakers is available to see in full on the Web site. Annual
Accommodations Wichita Airport Hilton.

THE SCHOOL FOR WRITERS SUMMER WORKSHOP

The Humber School for Writers, Humber Institute of Technology & Advanced Learning, 3199 Lake Shore Blvd. W., Toronto ON M8V 1K8 Canada. (416)675-6622. E-mail: antanas.sileika@humber.ca; hilary.higgins@humber.ca. Website: www.creativeandperformingarts.humber.ca/content/writers.html. Annual workshop held second week in July. Conference duration: 1 week. Average attendance: 100. New writers from around the world gather to study with faculty members to work on their novel, short stories, poetry, or creative nonfiction. Agents and editors participate in conference. Include a work-in-progress with your registration. Faculty has included Martin Amis, David Mitchell, Rachel Kuschner, Peter Carey, Roddy Doyle, Tim O'Brien, Andrea Levy, Barry Unsworth, Edward Albee, Ha Jin, Mavis Gallant, Bruce Jay Friedman, Isabel Huggan, Alistair MacLeod, Lisa Moore, Kim Moritsugu, Francine Prose, Paul Quarrington, Olive Senior, and D.M. Thomas.

Costs $949/Canadian residents before June 12; $1,469/non-Canadian residents before June 12; $999/ Canadian residents after June 12; $1,519/non-Canadian residents after June 12 (includes panels, classes, lunch). Scholarships are available.

Accommodations $480/week for a modest college dorm room. Nearby hotels are also available.

Additional Information Accepts inquiries by e-mail, phone, and fax.

THE SCREENWRITING CONFERENCE IN SANTA FE, LLC

P.O. Box 29762, Santa Fe NM 87592. (866)424-1501. Fax: (505)424-8207. E-mail: writeon@scsfe.com. Website: www.scsfe.com. Estab. 1999. "SCSFe was the first screenwriting conference in the world." Annual conference held the week following Memorial Day. Average attendance: 175. The conference is divided into 2 componants: The Screenwriting Symposium, designed to teach the art and craft of screenwriting, and The Hollywood Connection, which speaks to the business aspects of screenwriting. Held at The Lodge in Santa Fe.

Costs $695 for The Screenwriting Symposium; $245 for The Hollywood Connection. Early discounts are available. Includes 9 hours of in-depth classroom instruction, over 2 dozen seminars, panel discussions, a screenplay competition, academy labs for advanced screenwriters, live scene readings, and social events.

SCREENWRITING EXPO

6404 Hollywood Blvd., Suite 415, Los Angeles CA 90028. E-mail: info@creativescreenwriting.com. Website: www.screenwritingexpo.com/. Conference duration: 3-4 days. The Screenwriting Expo is produced by Creative Screenwriting Magazine. The expo is a large conference and trade show for writers. Speaker lists frequently include A-list screenwriters and academy award winners. Recent special guests include William Goldman (*All the President's Men*), David Koepp (*Spider-Man*) and Paul Haggis (*Crash*).

SEAK FICTION WRITING FOR PHYSICIANS CONFERENCE

P.O. Box 729, Falmouth MA 02541. (508)548-7023. Fax: (508)540-8304. E-mail: mail@seak.com. Website: www.seak.com. Annual conferences held on Cape Cod. The medical seminar is taught by *New York Times* bestselling authors Michael Palmer, MD and Tess Gerritsen, MD. Session topics include writing fiction that sells, screenwriting, writing riveting dialogue, creating memorable characters, getting your first novel published, and more. Agents will be speaking and available for one-on-one meetings.

SEWANEE WRITERS' CONFERENCE

735 University Ave., 123 Gailor Hall, Stamlor Center, Sewanee TN 37383-1000. (931)598-1141. E-mail: cpeters@sewanee.edu. Website: www.sewaneewriters.org. **Contact:** Cheri B. Peters, Creative Writing Programs Manager.. Estab. 1990. Annual conference held in the second half of July. Conference duration: 12 days. Average attendance: 144. "We offer genre-based workshops in fiction, poetry, and playwriting. The conference uses the facilities of Sewanee: The University of the South. The university is a collection of ivy-covered Gothic-style buildings located on the Cumberland Plateau in mid-Tennessee. Editors, publishers, and agents structure their own presentations, but there is always opportunity for questions from the audience." 2009 faculty included fiction writers Richard Bausch, Tony Earley, Diane Johnson, Randall Kenan, Jill McCorkle, Alice McDermott, Erin McGraw, and Steve Yarbrough; poets Daniel Anderson, Claudia Emerson, Debora Greger, Andrew Hudgins, William Logan, Alan Shapiro, Dave Smith, and Greg Willimson; and playwrights Lee Blessing and Dan O'Brien. Visiting agents include Gail Hochman and Georges Borchardt. A score of writing professionals will visit.

Costs $1,700 (includes tuition, board, single room, sports and fitness center access).

Accommodations Participants are housed in single rooms in university dormitories. Bathrooms are shared by small groups. Motel or B&B housing is available, but not abundantly so.

Additional Information "Complimentary chartered bus service is available from the Nashville Airport to Sewanee and back on the first and last days of the conference. We offer each participant (excepting auditors) the opportunity for a private manuscript conference with a member of the faculty. These manuscripts are due 1 month before the conference begins. Brochures/guidelines are free. The conference provides a limited number of fellowships and scholarships; these are awarded on a competitive basis."

SOCIETY OF CHILDREN'S BOOK WRITERS & ILLUSTRATORS ANNUAL SUMMER CONFERENCE ON WRITING AND ILLUSTRATING FOR CHILDREN

8271 Beverly Blvd., Los Angeles CA 90048-4515. (323)782-1010. Fax: (323)782-1892. E-mail: scbwi@scbwi.org. Website: www.scbwi.org. Estab. 1972. Annual conference held in early August. Conference duration: 4 days. Average attendance: 1,000. Held at the Century Plaza Hotel in Los Angeles. Speakers have included Andrea Brown, Steven Malk , Scott Treimel, Ashley Bryan, Bruce Coville, Karen Hesse, Harry Mazer, Lucia Monfried, and Russell Freedman. Agents will be speaking and sometimes participate in ms critiques.

Costs Approximately $400 (does not include hotel room).

Accommodations Information on overnight accommodations is made available.

Additional Information Ms and illustration critiques are available. Brochure/guidelines are available in June online or for SASE.

SOUTH CAROLINA WRITERS WORKSHOP

P.O. Box 7104, Columbia SC 29202. (803)413-5810. E-mail: conference@myscww.org. Website: www.myscww.org/. Estab. 1991. Annual conference in October held at the Hilton Myrtle Beach Resort in Myrtle Beach, SC. Conference duration: 3 days. The conference features critique sessions, open mic readings, presentations from agents and editors and more. The conference features more than 50 different workshops for writers to choose from, dealing with all subjects of writing craft, writing business, getting an agent and more. Agents will be in attendance.

SOUTH COAST WRITERS CONFERENCE

Southwestern Oregon Community College, P.O. Box 590, 29392 Ellensburg Avenue, Gold Beach OR 97444. (541)247-2741. Fax: (541)247-6247. E-mail: scwc@socc.edu. Website: www.socc.edu/scwriters. Estab. 1996. Annual conference held President's Day weekend in February. Conference duration: 2 days. Covers fiction, historical, poetry, children's, nature, and marketing. Larry Brooks is the next scheduled keynote speaker and presenters include Shinan Barclay, Jim Coffee, Linda Crew, Roger Dorband, Jayel Gibson, Phil Hann, Rachel Ellen Koski, Bonnie Leon, John Noland, Joanna Rose and J.D. Tynan.

Additional Information See website for cost and additional details.

SOUTHEASTERN WRITERS WORKSHOP

P.O. Box 82115, Athens GA 30608. E-mail: info@southeasternwriters.com. Website: www.southeasternwriters.com. Estab. 1975. Held annually the third week in June at Epworth-by-the-Sea, St. Simons Island, Georgia. Conference duration: 4 days. Average attendance: Limited to 100 students. Classes are offered in all areas of writing, including fiction, poetry, nonfiction, inspirational, juvenile, specialty writing, and others. The faculty is comprised of some of the most successful authors from throughout the southeast and the country. Agent-in-Residence is available to meet with participants. Up to 3 free ms evaluations and critique sessions are also available to participants if mss are submitted by the deadline.

Costs Costs change each year. See the Web site.

Additional Information Multiple contests with cash prizes are open to participants. Registration brochure is available in March--e-mail or send a SASE. Full information, including registration material, is on the Web site.

SOUTHERN CALIFORNIA WRITERS' CONFERENCE

1010 University Ave., #54, San Diego CA 92103. (619)303-8185. Fax: (619)303-7428. E-mail: wewrite@writersconference.com. Website: www.writersconference.com. Estab. 1986. Annual conference held in February in San Diego and in September in Los Angeles. The conference is also held periodically in Palm Springs (dates to be announced). Conference duration: 3 days. Average attendance: 250. Covers fiction and nonfiction, with a particular emphasis on reading and critiquing conferees' manuscripts. Offers extensive reading and critiquing workshops by working writers, plus over 3 dozen daytime workshops and late-night sessions that run until 3-4 a.m. Agents will be speaking and available for meetings with attendees.

Additional Information Brochures are available online or for SAE. Inquire via e-mail or fax.

SOUTHERN LIGHTS CONFERENCE

First Coast Roance Writers, P.O. Box 32456, Jacksonville FL 32237. (352)687-3902. E-mail: conference@firstcoastromancewriters.com. Website: www.firstcoastromancewriters.com. Estab. 1995. Annual conference held in late March/early April. Conference duration: 2 days. Offers workshops, author panels, industry expert sessions, editor/agent appointments, and a keynote address. Speakers have included

Joan Johston, Steven K. Brown, Tracy Montoya, Kristy Dykes, and Caren Johnson (Firebrand Literary).

SOUTHWEST WRITERS CONFERENCE MINI-CONFERENCE SERIES

3721 Morris St. NE, Suite A, Albuquerque NM 87111. (505)265-9485. E-mail: swwriters@juno.com. Website: www.southwestwriters.org. Estab. 1983. Annual mini-conferences held throughout the year. Average attendance: 50. Speakers include writers, editors, agents, publicists, and producers. All areas of writing, including screenwriting and poetry, are represented.

Costs Fee includes conference sessions and lunch.

Accommodations Usually have official airline and hotel discount rates.

Additional Information Sponsors a contest judged by authors, editors from major publishers, and agents from New York, Los Angeles, etc. There are 16 categories. Deadline: May 1; late deadline May 15. Entry fee ranges from $20-60. There are quarterly contests with various themes - $10 entry fee. See Web site for details. Brochures/guidelines are available online or for a SASE. Inquire via e-mail or phone. A one-on-one appointment may be set up at the conference with the editor or agent of your choice on a first-registered, first-served basis.

SPACE COAST WRITERS GUILD ANNUAL CONFERENCE

No public address available, (321)956-7193. E-mail: scwg-jm@cfl.rr.com. Website: www.scwg.org/conference.asp. Annual conference held in January along the east coast of central Florida. Conference duration: 2 days. Average attendance: 150+. This conference is hosted each winter in Florida and features a variety of presenters on all topics writing. Critiques are available for a price, and agents in attendance will take pitches from writers. Previous presenters have included Davis Bunn (writer), Ellen Pepus (agent), Miriam Hees (editor), Lauren Mosko (editor), Lucienne Diver (agent) and many many more. Annual

Accommodations The conference is hosted on a beachside hotel, where rooms are available.

SPRINGFED WRITING RETREAT

P.O. Box 304, Royal Oak MI 48068-0304. (248)589-3913. Fax: (248)589-9981. E-mail: johndlamb@ameritech.net. Website: www.springfed.org. Estab. 1999. Annual conference held in October. Average attendance: 75. "Focus includes fiction, poetry, screenwriting and nonfiction." Past faculty included Billy Collins, Michael Moore, Jonathan Rand, Jacquelyn Mitchard, Jane Hamilton, Thomas Lux, Joyce Maynard, Jack Driscoll, Dorianne Laux, and Cornelius Eady.

Costs $625, $560 (3 days, 2 nights, all meals included). $360 non-lodging.

Accommodations The Birchwood Inn, Harbor Spring, MI. "Attendees stay in comfortable rooms, and seminars are held in conference rooms with fieldstone fireplaces and dining area." Shuttle rides from Traverse City Airport or Pellston Airport. Offers overnight accommodations. Provides list of area lodging options.

Additional Information "Optional: Attendees may submit 3 poems or 5 pages of prose for conference with a staff member. Brochures available mid-June by e-mail, on Web site, or by phone. Accepts inquiries by SASE, e-mail, phone."

SPRING WRITER'S FESTIVAL

University of Wisconsin-Milwaukee, School of Continuing Education, 161 W. Wisconsin Ave., Suite 6000, Milwaukee WI 53203. (414)227-3311. Fax: (414)227-3146. E-mail: sce@uwm.edu. Website: www3.uwm.edu/sce. Annual conference held in April. Features readings, craft workshops, panels, ms reviews, preconference intensive workshops, and pitch sessions with literary agents. Speakers have included Joanna MacKenzie, Alec Yoshio MacDonald, A. Manette Ansay, Liam Callanan, C.J. Hribal, and Kelly James-Enger.

Costs See website for more information on cost and accommodations.

SPRING WRITERS' WORKSHOP

Council for the Written Word, P.O. Box 298, Franklin TN 37065. (615)591-7516. E-mail: publicity@cww-writers.org. Website: www.cww-writers.org. Annual workshop held in March. An intensive, half-day event with instruction and hands-on experience in a specific genre.

SQUAW VALLEY COMMUNITY OF WRITERS WORKSHOP

P.O. Box 1416, Nevada City CA 95959-1416. (530)470-8440. E-mail: info@squawvalleywriters.org. Website: www.squawvalleywriters.org/writers_ws.htm. Estab. 1969. Annual conference held the first full week in August. Conference duration: 1 week. Average attendance: 124. Covers fiction, nonfiction, and memoir. Held in Squaw Valley, California--the site of the 1960 Winter Olympics. The workshops are held in a ski lodge at the foot of this spectacular ski area. Literary agent speakers have recently included Betsy Amster, Julie Barer, Michael Carlisle, Elyse Cheney, Mary Evans, Christy Fletcher, Theresa Park, B.J. Robbins and Peter Steinberg. Agents will be speaking and available for meetings with attendees.

Costs $750 (includes tuition, dinners). Housing is extra.
Accommodations Single room: $550/week; double room: $350/week per person; multiple room: $210/week per person. The airport shuttle is available for an additional cost.
Additional Information Brochures are available online or for a SASE in March. Send inquiries via e-mail.

STEAMBOAT SPRINGS WRITERS CONFERENCE

Steamboat Springs Arts Council, P.O. Box 774284, Steamboat Springs CO 80477. (970)879-8079. E-mail: info@steamboatwriters.com. Website: www.steamboatwriters.com. **Contact:** Susan de Wardt. Estab. 1982. Annual conference held in mid-July. Conference duration: 1 day. Average attendance: approximately 35. Attendance is limited. Featured areas of instruction change each year. Held at the restored train depot. Speakers have included Carl Brandt, Jim Fergus, Avi, Robert Greer, Renate Wood, Connie Willis, Margaret Coel and Kent Nelson.
Costs $50 prior to May 21; $60 after May 21 (includes seminars, catered lunch). A pre-conference dinner is also available.
Additional Information Brochures are available in April for a SASE. Send inquiries via e-mail.

STELLARCON

Box 4, Brown Annex, Elliott University Center, UNCG, Greensboro NC 27412. (336)294-8041. E-mail: info@stellarcon.org. Website: www.stellarcon.org. Estab. 1976. Annual conference held in March. Average attendance: 500. Conference focuses on general science fiction, fantasy, horror with an emphasis on literature, and comics. Held at the Radisson Hotel in High Point, North Carolina.

STONECOAST WRITERS' CONFERENCE

University of Southern Maine, P.O. Box 9300, Portland ME 04104. (207)228.8393. Website: www.usm.maine.edu/summer/stonecoastwc/. **Contact:** Justin Tussing. Estab. 1979. Annual conference held in mid-July. Conference duration: 10 days. Average attendance: 90-100. Concentrates on fiction, poetry, popular fiction, and creative nonfiction. Held at Wolfe's Neck on Casco Bay in Freeport, Maine. Speakers have included Christian Barter, Brian Turner, Chun Yu, Margo Jefferson, Mike Kimball, and Jack Neary.
Costs See website for tuition and cost of accommodations.

STONY BROOK SOUTHAMPTON SCREENWRITING CONFERENCE

Stony Brook Southampton, 239 Montauk Highway, Southampton NY 11968. (631)632-5030. E-mail: southamptonwriters@notes.cc.sunysb.edu. Website: www.sunysb.edu/writers/screenwriting/. The Southampton Screenwriting Conference welcomes new and advanced screenwriters, as well as all writers interested in using the language of film to tell a story. The five-day residential Conference will inform, inspire, challenge, and further participants' understanding of the art of the screenplay and the individual writing process. Our unique program of workshops, seminars, panel presentations, and screenings will encourage and motivate attendees under the professional guidance of accomplished screenwriters, educators, and script analysts. Annual
Costs $1,000+.
Additional Information Space is limited.

SUNSHINE COAST FESTIVAL OF THE WRITTEN ARTS

Box 2299, Sechelt BC V0N 3A0 Canada. (604)885-9631 or (800)565-9631. Fax: (604)885-3967. E-mail: info@writersfestival.ca. Website: www.writersfestival.ca. Estab. 1983. Annual festival held in August. Conference duration: 3 1/2 days. Average attendance: 3,500. The festival does not have a theme. Instead, it showcases 25 or more Canadian writers in a variety of genres each year. Held at the Rockwood Centre. Speakers have included Jane Urquhart, Sholagh Rogers, David Watmough, Zsuzsi Gartner, Gail Bowen, Charlotte Gray, Bill Richardson, P.K. Page, Richard B. Wright, Madeleine Thien, Ronald Wright, Michael Kusugak, and Bob McDonald.
Accommodations A list of hotels is available.
Additional Information The festival runs contests during the event. Prizes are books donated by publishers. Brochures/guidelines are available. Visit the Web site for current updates and details.

SURREY INERNATIONAL WRITERS' CONFERENCE

10707 146th St., Surrey BC V3R 1T5 Canada. (640)589-2221. Fax: (604)589-9286. Website: www.siwc.ca. Estab. 1992. Annual conference held in October. Conference duration: 3 days. Average attendance: 600. Conference for fiction, nonfiction, scriptwriting, and poetry. Held at the Sheraton Guildford Hotel. Speakers have included Donald Maass, Meredith Bernstein, Charlotte Gusay, Denise Marcil, Anne Sheldon, Diana Gabaldon, and Michael Vidor. Agents will be speaking and available for one-on-one meetings with attendees.
Costs See Web site for full cost information and list of upcoming speakers for the next year.

Accommodations Attendees must make their own hotel and transportation arrangements.

SYDNEY WRITERS' FESTIVAL

10 Hickson Rd., The Rocks NSW 2000 Australia. (61)(2)9252-7729. Fax: (61)(2)9252-7735. E-mail: info@swf.org.au. Website: www.swf.org.au. Estab. 1997. Annual festival held in May. The event celebrates books, reading, ideas, writers, and writing.
Costs Over 70% of events are free.

TAOS SUMMER WRITERS' CONFERENCE

Department of English Language and Literature, MSC 03 2170, University of New Mexico, Albuquerque NM 87131-0001. (505)277-5572. Fax: (505)277-2950. E-mail: taosconf@unm.edu. Website: www.unm.edu/~taosconf. Estab. 1999. Annual conference held in July. Conference duration: 7 days. Offers workshops in novel writing, short story writing, screenwriting, poetry, creative nonfiction, travel writing, historical fiction, memoir, and revision. Participants may also schedule a consultation with a visiting agent/editor.
Costs $325/weekend; $625/week; discounted tuition rate of $275/weekend workshop with weeklong workshop or master class registration.
Accommodations $69-109/night at the Sagebrush Inn; $89/night at Comfort Suites.

THRILLERFEST

PO Box 311, Eureka CA 95502. E-mail: infocentral@thrillerwriters.org. Website: www.thrillerwriters.org/thrillerfest/. **Contact:** Shirley Kennett. Estab. 2006. 2010 conference: July 7-10 in Manhattan. Conference duration: 4. Average attendance: 700. Conference "dedicated to writing the thriller and promoting the enjoyment of reading thrillers." Speakers have included David Morrell, Sandra Brown, Eric Van Lustbader, David Baldacci, Brad Meltzer, Steve Martini, R.L. Stine, Katherine Neville, Robin Cook, Andrew Gross, Kathy Reichs, Brad Thor, Clive Cussler, James Patterson, Donald Maass, and Al Zuckerman. Two days of the conference is CraftFest, where the focus is on writing craft, and two days is ThrillerFest, which showcases the author-fan relationship. Also featured are an Awards Banquet, and AgentFest, a unique event where authors can pitch their work face-to-face to forty top agents in one afternoon. There is also AgentFest, where authors can pitch their work to agents in attendance. Annual
Costs Price will vary from $200 to $1,000 dollars depending on which events are selected. Various package deals are available, and Early Bird pricing is offered beginning August 2009.
Accommodations Grand Hyatt in New York City.

TMCC WRITERS' CONFERENCE

5270 Neil Road, #216, Reno NV 89502. (775)829-9010. Fax: (775)829-9032. E-mail: wdce@tmcc.edu. Website: wdce.tmcc.edu. Estab. 1991. Annual conference held in April. Average attendance: 125. Focuses on fiction, poetry, and memoir, plus an assortment of other forms of writing, such as screenwriting, thrillers, mysteries, and nonfiction. There is always an array of speakers and presenters with impressive literary credentials, including agents and editors. Speakers have included Dorothy Allison, Karen Joy Fowler, James D. Houston, James N. Frey, Gary Short, Jane Hirschfield, Dorrianne Laux, Kim Addonizio, Amy Rennert, and Laurie Fox.
Costs $99 for a full-day seminar; $15 for 15 minute one-on-one appointment with an agent or editor.
Accommodations The Nugget offers a special rate and shuttle service to the Reno/Tahoe International Airport, which is less than 20 minutes away.
Additional Information "The conference is open to all writers, regardless of their level of experience. Brochures are available online and mailed in the fall. Send inquiries via e-mail."

UCLA EXTENSION WRITERS' PROGRAM

10995 Le Conte Ave., #440, Los Angeles CA 90024. (310)825-9415 or (800)388-UCLA. Fax: (310)206-7382. E-mail: writers@uclaextension.edu. Website: www.uclaextension.org/writers. Estab. 1891. "As America's largest and most comprehensive continuing education creative writing and screenwriting program, the UCLA Extension Writers' Program welcomes and trains writers at all levels of development whose aspirations range from personal enrichment to professional publication and production. Taught by an instructor corps of 250 professional writers, the Writers' Program curriculum features 530 annual open-enrollment courses onsite and online in novel writing, short fiction, personal essay, memoir, poetry, playwriting, writing for the youth market, publishing, feature film writing, and television writing, and is designed to accommodate your individual writing needs, ambitions, and lifestyle. Special programs and services include certificate programs in creative writing, feature film writing, and television writing; a four-day Writers Studio which attracts a national and international audience; nine-month master classes in novel writing and feature film writing; an online screenwriting mentorship program; one-on-one script and manuscript consultation services; literary and screenplay competitions; advisors who help you determine how best to achieve your personal writing goals; and free annual public events such as Writers Faire and Publication Party which allow you to extend

your writing education and network with the literary and entertainment communities."
Costs Depends on length of the course.
Accommodations Students make their own arrangements. Out-of-town students are encouraged to take online courses.
Additional Information Some advanced-level classes have ms submittal requirements; see the UCLA Extension catalog or see website.

UNIVERSITY OF NORTH DAKOTA WRITERS CONFERENCE

Department of English, 110 Merrifield Hall, 276 Centennial Drive, Stop 7209, Grand Forks ND 58202. (701)777-3321. E-mail: english@und.edu. Website: www.undwritersconference.org. Estab. 1970. Annual conference held in March. Offers panels, readings, and films focused around a specific theme. Almost all events take place in the UND Memorial Union, which has a variety of small rooms and a 1,000-seat main hall. Future speakers include Stuart Dybek, Mary Gaitskill, Li-Young Lee, Timothy Liu, Leslie Adrienne Miller, Michelle Richmond, Miller Williams and Anne Harris.
Costs All events are free and open to the public. Donations accepted.

UNIVERSITY OF WISCONSIN AT MADISON WRITERS INSTITUTE

21 N. Park St., Madison WI 53715-1218. (608)262-3447. Website: www.dcs.wisc.edu/lsa. Estab. 1990. Annual conference held in April. (The 2010 conference is set for April 23-25, 2010.) Average attendance: 200. Conference on fiction and nonfiction held at the University of Wisconsin at Madison. Guest speakers are published authors, editors, and agents.
Costs Approximately $245 for the weekend; $145 per day; critiques and pitch meetings extra.
Accommodations Information on accommodations is sent with registration confirmation.
Additional Information Critiques are available. Go online for conference brochure.

VIRGINIA FESTIVAL OF THE BOOK

Virginia Foundation for the Humanities, 145 Ednam Dr., Charlottesville VA 22903. (434)924-6890. Fax: (434)296-4714. E-mail: vabook@virginia.edu. Website: www.vabook.org. Estab. 1995. Annual festival held in March. 2010 dates: March 17-21. Average attendance: 26,000. Festival held to celebrate books and promote reading and literacy.

WESLEYAN WRITERS CONFERENCE

Wesleyan University, 294 High St., Room 207, Middletown CT 06459. (860)685-3604. Fax: (860)685-2441. E-mail: agreene@wesleyan.edu. Website: www.wesleyan.edu/writers. Estab. 1956. Annual conference held the third week of June. Average attendance: 100. Focuses on the novel, fiction techniques, short stories, poetry, screenwriting, nonfiction, literary journalism, memoir, mixed media work and publishing. The conference is held on the campus of Wesleyan University, in the hills overlooking the Connecticut River. Features a faculty of award-winning writers, seminars and readings of new fiction, poetry, nonfiction and mixed media forms - as well as guest lectures on a range of topics including publishing. Both new and experienced writers are welcome. Participants may attend seminars in all genres. Speakers have included Esmond Harmsworth (Zachary Schuster Agency), Daniel Mandel (Sanford J. Greenburger Associaties), Dorian Karchmar, Amy Williams (ICM and Collins McCormick), Mary Sue Rucci (Simon & Schuster), Denise Roy (Simon & Schuster), John Kulka (Harvard University Press), Julie Barer (Barer Literary) and many others. Agents will be speaking and available for meetings with attendees. Participants are often successful in finding agents and publishers for their mss. Wesleyan participants are also frequently featured in the anthology *Best New American Voices*.
Accommodations Meals are provided on campus. Lodging is available on campus or in town.
Additional Information Ms critiques are available, but not required. Scholarships and teaching fellowships are available, including the Joan Jakobson Awards for fiction writers and poets; and the Jon Davidoff Scholarships for nonfiction writers and journalists. Inquire via e-mail, fax, or phone.

WESTERN RESERVE WRITERS' CONFERENCE

Lakeland Community College, 7700 Clocktower Dr., Kirtland OH 44060-5198. (440)525-7116 or (800)589-8520. E-mail: deencr@aol.com. Website: www.deannaadams.com. Estab. 1983. Biannual conference held in March and September. Average attendance: 120. Conference covers fiction, nonfiction, business of writing, children's writing, science fiction/fantasy, women's fiction, mysteries, poetry, short stories, etc. Classes take place on a community college campus. Editors and agents will be available for meetings with attendees. Biannual
Costs $69 for March mini-conference (half day); $95 for September all-day conference, including lunch. There is an additional fee for agent consultations.
Additional Information Presenters are veterans in their particular genres. There will be a prestigious keynote speaker at the September conference. Check Web site 6 weeks prior to the event for guidelines and updates. Send inquiries via e-mail.

WHIDBEY ISLAND WRITERS' CONFERENCE

Whidbey Island Writers' Association, P.O. Box 1289, Langley WA 98260. (360)331-6714. E-mail: wiwa@whidbey.com. Website: http://writeonwhidbey.org. Annual conference held in February/March. Conference duration: 2 days. Average attendance: 250. Annual conference, located near Seattle, combines pre-conference workshops, signature fireside chats, professional instruction and island hospitality to encourage and inspire writers. Check out this year's upcoming talent on our Web site. Covers fiction, nonfiction, screenwriting, writing for children, poetry, travel, and nature writing. Class sessions include Dialogue That Delivers and Putting the Character Back in Character. Held at a conference hall, with break-out fireside chats held in local homes near the sea. Past speakers included Elizabeth George, Maureen Murdock, Steve Berry, M.J. Rose, Katharine Sands, Doris Booth, Eva Shaw, Stephanie Elizondo Griest.

Costs See website for costs and early registration deadlines.

Additional Information Brochures are available online or for a SASE. Send inquiries via e-mail.

WILDACRES WRITERS WORKSHOP

233 S. Elm St., Greensboro NC 27401. (336)370-9188. E-mail: judihill@aol.com. Website: www.wildacres.com. Estab. 1985. Annual workshop held in July. Conference duration: 1 week. Average attendance: 90. Workshop focuses on novel, short story, flash fiction, poetry, and creative nonfiction. Held at a retreat center in the Blue Ridge Mountains of North Carolina. Speakers have included Gail Adams, Rand Cooper, Philip Gerard, Luke Whisnant, and Janice Fuller.

Costs See website for pricing.

Additional Information Include a 1-page writing sample with your registration. See the Web site for information.

WILLAMETTE WRITERS CONFERENCE

9045 SW Barbur, Suite 5-A, Portland OR 97219. (503)452-1592. Fax: (503)452-0372. E-mail: wilwrite@willamettewriters.com. Website: www.willamettewriters.com. Estab. 1968. Annual conference held in August. Average attendance: 600. "Williamette Writers is open to all writers, and we plan our conference accordingly. We offer workshops on all aspects of fiction, nonfiction, marketing, the creative process, etc. Also, we invite top-notch inspirational speakers for keynote addresses. We always include at least 1 agent or editor panel and offer a variety of topics of interest to screenwriters and fiction and nonfiction writers." Speakers have included Laura Rennert, Kim Cameron, Paul Levine, Angela Rinaldi, Robert Tabian, Joshua Bilmes and Elise Capron. Agents will be speaking and available for meetings with attendees.

Costs Pricing schedule available online.

Accommodations If necessary, arrangements can be made on an individual basis. Special rates may be available.

Additional Information Brochure/guidelines are available for a catalog-sized SASE.

WINTER & SUMMER FISHTRAP

Fishtrap, Inc., P.O. Box 38, 400 Grant St., Enterprise OR 97828. (503)426-3623. Fax: (503)426-9075. E-mail: rich@fishtrap.org. Website: www.fishtrap.org. Estab. 1988. Annual gatherings held in February and July. Fishtrap gatherings are about writing and the West (there is a theme for each conference). They are about ideas more than the mechanics and logistics of writing/publishing. Workshops are not ms reviews, but rather writing sessions. Fishtrap events meet at Wallowa Lake Lodge in Joseph, Oregon. Previous faculty has included Donald Snow, Suan Power, Aimee Pham, Judith Barrington, Laurie Lewis (songwriter), and Michael Wiegers (Copper Canyon). Agents and editors occasionally participate in conference.

Costs See website for pricing and details on accommodations.

Additional Information Five fellowships are given annually for Summer Fishtrap. Submit 8 pages of poetry or 2,500 words of prose (no name on ms) by February 6. Entries are judged by a workshop instructor. Inquire via e-mail or phone.

WINTER POETRY & PROSE GETAWAY IN CAPE MAY

No public address available, (609)823-5076. E-mail: info@wintergetaway.com. Website: www.wintergetaway.com. Estab. 1994. Annual workshop held in January. Conference duration: 4 days. Offers workshops on short stories, memoirs, creative nonfiction, children's writing, novel, drama, poetry and photography. Classes are small, so each person receives individual attention for the new writing or work-in-progress that they are focusing on. Held at the Grand Hotel on the oceanfront in historic Cape May, New Jersey. Speakers have included Stephen Dunn (recipient of the 2001 Pulitzer Prize for poetry), Christian Bauman, Kurt Brown, Catherine Doty, Douglas Goetsch, James Richardson, Robbie Clipper Sethi and many more.

WISCONSIN BOOK FESTIVAL

222 S. Bedford St., Suite F, Madison WI 53703. (608)262-0706. Fax: (608)263-7970. E-mail: alison@wisconsinbookfestival.org. Website: www.wisconsinbookfestival.org. Estab. 2002. Annual festival held in October. Conference duration: 5 days. The festival features readings, lectures, book discussions, writing workshops, live interviews, children's events, and more. Speakers have included Michael Cunningham, Grace Paley, TC Boyle, Marjane Satrapi, Phillip Gourevitch, Myla Goldberg, Audrey Niffenegger, Harvey Pekar, Billy Collins, Tim O'Brien and Isabel Allende.

Costs All festival events are free.

WISCONSIN REGIONAL WRITERS' ASSOCIATION CONFERENCES

No public address available, E-mail: vpresident@wrwa.net. Website: www.wrwa.net. Estab. 1948. Annual conferences are held in May and September. Conference duration: 1-2 days. Provides presentations for all genres, including fiction, nonfiction, scriptwriting, and poetry. Presenters include authors, agents, editors, and publishers. Speakers have included Jack Byrne, Michelle Grajkowski, Benjamin Leroy, Richard Lederer, and Philip Martin.

Additional Information Go online for brochure or make inquiries via e-mail or with SASE.

THE WOMEN WRITERS CONFERENCE

232 E. Maxwell St., Lexington KY 40506. (859)257-2874. E-mail: wwk.info@gmail.com. Website: www.thewomenwritersconference.org. Estab. 1979. The conference switches months and dates each year. Programming is presented in a festival atmosphere and includes small-group workshops, panel discussions, master classes, readings, film screenings, and performances. Presenters include Sara Vowell, Patricia Smith, Hayden Herrera, Diane Gilliam Fisher, Jawole Willa Jo Zollar and the Urban Bush Woman, Sonia Sanchez, Heather Raffo, Mabel Maney, Phoebe Gloeckner, Lauren Weinstein, Kim Ganter, Jane Vandenburgh, and Alex Beauchamp. Annual

Additional Information Visit the Web site to register and get more information.

WOMEN WRITING THE WEST

8547 Araphoe Rd., Box J-541, Greenwodd Village CO 80112-1436. E-mail: wwwadmin@lohseworks.com. Website: www.womenwritingthewest.org. Annual conference held in September. Covers research, writing techniques, multiple genres, marketing/promotion, and more. Agents and editors will be speaking and available for one-on-one meetings with attendees. Conference location changes each year.

Accommodations See website for location and accommodation details.

WORDS & MUSIC

624 Pirates Alley, New Orleans LA 70116. (504)586-1609. Fax: (504)522-9725. E-mail: info@wordsandmusic.org. Website: www.wordsandmusic.org. Estab. 1997. Annual conference held the first week in November. Conference duration: 5 days. Average attendance: 300. Presenters include authors, agents, editors and publishers. Past speakers included agents Deborah Grosvenor, Judith Weber, Stuart Bernstein, Nat Sobel, Jeff Kleinman, Emma Sweeney, Liza Dawson and Michael Murphy; editors Lauren Marino, Webster Younce, Ann Patty, Will Murphy, Jofie Ferrari-Adler, Elizabeth Stein; critics Marie Arana, Jonathan Yardley, and Michael Dirda; fiction writers Oscar Hijuelos, Robert Olen Butler, Shirley Ann Grau, Mayra Montero, Ana Castillo, H.G. Carrillo. Agents and editors critique manuscripts in advance; meet with them one-on-one during the conference.

Costs See website for a costs and additional information on accommodations.

Accommodations Hotel Monteleone in New Orleans.

WRANGLING WITH WRITING

Society of Southwestern Authors, P.O. Box 30355, Tucson AZ 85751-0355. (520)546-9382. Fax: (520)751-7877. E-mail: Carol Costa (Ccstarlit@aol.com). Website: www.ssa-az.org/conference.htm. **Contact:** Carol Costa. Estab. 1972. Sept. 26-27, 2009. Conference duration: 2 days. Average attendance: 300. Conference offers 36 workshops covering all genres of writing, plus pre-scheduled one-on-one interviews with 30 agents, editors, and publishers representing major book houses and magazines. Speakers have included Ray Bradbury, Clive Cussler, Elmore Leonard, Ben Bova, Sam Swope, Richard Paul Evans, Bruce Holland Rogers and Billy Collins. Annual

Costs 2007 costs were $275/members; $350/nonmembers. Five meals included.

Additional Information Brochures/guidelines are available as of July 15 by e-mail address above. Two banquets will include editor and agent panels for all attendees, and Saturday evening winning plays from contestants will be presented.

WRITE! CANADA

The Word Guild, P.O. Box 487, Markham ON L3P 3R1 Canada. (905)294-6482. E-mail: events@thewordguild.com. Website: www.writecanada.org. Conference duration: 3 days. Annual conference for writers of all types and at all stages. Offers solid instruction, stimulating interaction, exciting challenges, and worshipful community.

WRITE ON THE SOUND WRITERS' CONFERENCE

Edmonds Arts Commission, 700 Main St., Edmonds WA 98020. (425)771-0228. Fax: (425)771-0253. E-mail: wots@ci.edmonds.wa.us. Website: www.ci.edmonds.wa.us/ArtsCommission/wots.stm. Estab. 1985. Annual conference held in October. Conference duration: 2.5 days. Average attendance: 200. Features over 30 presenters, a literary contest, ms critiques, a reception and book signing, onsite bookstore, and a variety of evening activities. Held at the Frances Anderson Center in Edmonds, just north of Seattle on the Puget Sound. Speakers have included Elizabeth George, Dan Hurley, Marcia Woodard, Holly Hughes, Greg Bear, Timothy Egan, Joe McHugh, Frances Wood, Garth Stein and Max Grover.

Costs See website for more information.

Additional Information Brochures are available Aug. 1. Accepts inquiries via phone, e-mail and fax.

WRITERS@WORK CONFERENCE

P.O. Box 540370, North Salt Lake UT 84054-0370. (801)292-9285. E-mail: lisa@writersatwork.org. Website: www.writersatwork.org. Estab. 1985. Annual conference held in June. Conference duration: 5 days. Average attendance: 250. Morning workshops (3-hours/day) focus on novel, advanced fiction, generative fiction, nonfiction, poetry, and young adult fiction. Afternoon sessions will include craft lectures, discussions, and directed interviews with authors, agents, and editors. In addition to the traditional, one-on-one manuscript consultations, there will be many opportunities to mingle informally with agents/editors. Held at Spiro Arts Community at Silver Star, Park City, Utah. Speakers have included Steve Almond, Bret Lott, Shannon Hale, Emily Forland (Wendy Weil Agency), Julie Culver (Folio Literary Management, Chuck Adams (Algonquin Press), and Mark A. Taylor (Juniper Press).

Costs See website for pricing informaiton.

Accommodations Onsite housing in luxury condos available. Can choose between 2, 3, or 4 bedroom suites. Secondary offer includes lower-priced condos a short walk away. Additional lodging and meal information is on the Web site.

WRITERS AT THE BEACH: SEAGLASS WRITERS CONFERENCE

Writers at the Beach, PO Box 1326, Rehoboth Beach DE 19971. (302)226-8210. E-mail: contactus@rehobothbeachwritersguild.com. Website: www.writersatthebeach.com/. Annual conference held in the spring. 2010 dates: March 26-28. Conference duration: 3 days. Annual conference on the Delaware coast featuring a variety of editors, agents and writers who present workshops on fiction writing, nonfiction writing and more. Manuscript readings are available, and a 'Meet the Authors' sessions takes place. The beachcoast conference is a great opportunity to learn and charge your batteries. Some proceeds from the conference go to charity.

Accommodations Held at the Atlantic Sands Hotel. See website for pricing, details, and to join mailing list.

WRITERS RETREAT WORKSHOP

E-mail: wrw04@netscape.net. Website: www.writersretreatworkshop.com. Estab. 1987. Annual workshop held in August. Conference duration: 10 days. Focuses on fiction and narrative nonfiction books in progress (all genres). This is an intensive learning experience for small groups of serious-minded writers. Founded by the late Gary Provost (one of the country's leading writing instructors) and his wife Gail (an award-winning author). The goal is for students to leave with a solid understanding of the marketplace, as well as the craft of writing a novel. Held at the Marydale Retreat Center in Erlanger, Kentucky (just south of Cincinnati, Ohio). Speakers have included Becky Motew, Donald Maass, Jennifer Crusie, Michael Palmer, Nancy Pickard, Elizabeth Lyon, Lauren Mosko (Writer's Digest Books), Adam Marsh (Reece Halsey North), and Peter H. McGuigan (Sanford J. Greenburger Literary Agency).

Costs $1,725 (includes meals, housing, consultations, materials). Scholarships are available.

WRITERS WORKSHOP IN SCIENCE FICTION

English Department/University of Kansas, Lawrence KS 66045-2115. (785)864-3380. Fax: (785)864-1159. E-mail: jgunn@ku.edu. Website: www.ku.edu/~sfcenter. Estab. 1985. Annual workshop held in late June/early July. Average attendance: 15. Conference for writing and marketing science fiction. Classes meet in university housing on the University of Kansas campus. Workshop sessions operate informally in a lounge. Speakers have included Frederik Pohl, Kij Johnson, James Gunn, and Chris McKitterick.

Costs See website for tuition rates, dormitory housing costs, and deadlines.

Accommodations Housing information is available. Several airport shuttle services offer reasonable transportation from the Kansas City International Airport to Lawrence.

Additional Information Admission to the workshop is by submission of an acceptable story. Two additional stories should be submitted by the middle of June. These 3 stories are distributed to other participants for critquing and are the basis for the first week of the workshop. One story is rewritten for the second week. Send SASE for brochure/guidelines. This workshop is intended for writers who have just started to sell their work or need that extra bit of understanding or skill to become a published writer.

WRITE-TO-PUBLISH CONFERENCE

WordPro Communication Services, 9118 W Elmwood Dr., #1G, Niles IL 60714-5820. (847)296-3964. Fax: (847)296-0754. E-mail: lin@writetopublish.com. Website: www.writetopublish.com. Estab. 1971. Annual conference held June 2-5, 2010. Conference duration: 4 days. Average attendance: 250. Conference on writing fiction, nonfiction, devotions, and magazine articles for the Christian market. Held at Wheaton College in Wheaton, Illinois. Speakers have included Dr. Dennis E. Hensley, agent Chip MacGregor, David Long (Bethany House), Carol Traver (Tyndale House), Dave Zimmerman (InterVarsity Press), Ed Gilbreath (Urban Ministries), Ken Peterson (WaterBrook Multnomah).
Costs $470 (includes all sessions, Saturday night banquet, 1 ms evaluation); $105/meals.
Accommodations Campus residence halls: $260/double; $340/single. A list of area hotels is also on the Web site.

WRITING FOR THE SOUL

Jerry B. Jenkins Christian Writers Guild, 5525 N. Union Blvd., Suite 200, Colorado Springs CO 80918. (866)495-5177. Fax: (719)495-5181. E-mail: paul@christianwritersguild.com. Website: www.christianwritersguild.com/conferences. **Contact:** Paul Finch, admissions manager. Annual conference held in February. Workshops and continuing classes cover fiction, nonfiction, magazine writing, children's books, and teen writing. Appointments with more than 30 agents, publishers, and editors are also available. The keynote speakers are nationally known, leading authors. The conference is hosted by Jerry B. Jenkins.
Costs $649/guild members; $799/nonmembers.
Accommodations $159/night at the Grand Hyatt in Denver.

WRITING TODAY

Birmingham-Southern College, Box 549066, Birmingham AL 35254. (205)226-4922. Fax: (205)226-4931. E-mail: agreen@bsc.edu. Website: www.writingtoday.org. Estab. 1978. Annual conference held during the second weekend in March. The 2010 dates and location have yet to be determined. Conference duration: 2 days. Average attendance: 300-350. Conference hosts approximately 18 workshops, lectures, and readings. We try to offer sessions in short fiction, novels, poetry, children's literature, magazine writing, songwriting, and general information of concern to aspiring writers, such as publishing, agents, markets, and research. The event is held on the Birmingham-Southern College campus in classrooms and lecture halls. Speakers have included Eudora Welty, Pat Conroy, Ernest Gaines, Ray Bradbury, Erskine Caldwell, John Barth, Galway Kinnell, Edward Albee, Horton Foote, and William Styron and other renowned writers.
Costs To be determined. Please check website or join mailing list for upcoming information.
Accommodations Attendees must arrange own transportation and accommodations.
Additional Information For an additional charge, poetry and short story critiques are offered for interested writers who request and send mss by the deadline. The conference also sponsors the Hackney Literary Competition Awards for poetry, short stories, and novels.

RESOURCES

Glossary

#10 Envelope. A standard, business-size envelope.

Acquisitions Editor. The person responsible for originating and/or acquiring new publishing projects.

Adaptation. The process of rewriting a composition (novel, story, film, article, play) into a form suitable for some other medium, such as TV or the stage.

Advance. Money a publisher pays a writer prior to book publication, usually paid in installments, such as one-half upon signing the contract and one-half upon delivery of the complete, satisfactory manuscript. An advance is paid against the royalty money to be earned by the book. Agents take their percentage off the top of the advance as well as from the royalties earned.

Adventure. A genre of fiction in which action is the key element, overshadowing characters, theme and setting.

Auction. Publishers sometimes bid for the acquisition of a book manuscript with excellent sales prospects. The bids are for the amount of the author's advance, guaranteed dollar amounts, advertising and promotional expenses, royalty percentage, etc. Auctions are conducted by agents.

Author's Copies. An author usually receives about 10 free copies of his hardcover book from the publisher; more from a paperback firm. He can obtain additional copies at a price that has been reduced by an author's discount (usually 40 percent of the retail price).

Autobiography. A book-length account of a person's entire life written by the subject himself.

Backlist. A publisher's list of books that were not published during the current season, but that are still in print.

Backstory. The history of what has happened before the action in your script takes place, affecting a character's current behavior.

Bible. The collected background information on all characters and story lines of all existing episodes, as well as projections of future plots.

Bio. A sentence or brief paragraph about the writer; includes work and educational experience.

Blurb. The copy on paperback book covers or hardcover book dust jackets, either promoting the book and the author or featuring testimonials from book reviewers or well-known people in the book's field. Also called flap copy or jacket copy.

Boilerplate. A standardized publishing contract. Most authors and agents make many changes on the boilerplate before accepting the contract.

Book Doctor. A freelance editor hired by a writer, agent or book editor who analyzes problems that exist in a book manuscript or proposal and offers solutions to those problems.

Book Packager. Someone who draws elements of a book together-from the initial concept to writing and marketing strategies-and then sells the book package to a book publisher and/or movie producer. Also known as book producer or book developer.

Bound Galleys. A prepublication-often paperbound-edition of a book, usually prepared from photocopies of the final galley proofs. Designed for promotional purposes, bound galleys serve as the first set of review copies to be mailed out. Also called bound proofs.

Category Fiction. A term used to include all types of fiction. See genre.

Clips. Samples, usually from newspapers or magazines, of your published work. Also called tearsheets.

Commercial Fiction. Novels designed to appeal to a broad audience. These are often broken down into categories such as western, mystery and romance. *See genre.*

Concept. A statement that summarizes a screenplay or teleplay-before the outline or treatment is written.

Confession. A first-person story in which the narrator is involved in an emotional situation that encourages sympathetic reader identification, concluding with the affirmation of a morally acceptable theme.

Contributor's Copies. Copies of the book sent to the author. The number of contributor's copies is often negotiated in the publishing contract.

Co-Publishing. Arrangement where author and publisher share publication costs and profits of a book. Also called co-operative publishing.

Copyediting. Editing of a manuscript for writing style, grammar, punctuation and factual accuracy.

Copyright. A means to protect an author's work.

Cover Letter. A brief letter that accompanies the manuscript being sent to an agent or publisher.

Coverage. A brief synopsis and analysis of a script provided by a reader to a buyer considering purchasing the work.

Creative Nonfiction. Type of writing where true stories are told by employing the techniques usually reserved for novelists and poets, such as scenes, dialogue and detailed descriptions. Also called literary journalism.

Critiquing Service. An editing service offered by some agents in which writers pay a fee for comments on the salability or other qualities of their manuscript. Sometimes the critique includes suggestions on how to improve the work. Fees vary, as does the quality of the critique.

Curriculum Vitae (CV). Short account of one's career or qualifications.

D Person. Development person; includes readers, story editors and creative executives who work in development and acquisition of properties for TV and film.

Deal Memo. The memorandum of agreement between a publisher and author that precedes the actual contract and includes important issues such as royalty, advance, rights, distribution and option clauses.

Development. The process in which writers present ideas to producers who oversee the developing script through various stages to finished product.

Division. An unincorporated branch of a company.

Docudrama. A fictional film rendition of recent news-making events or people.

Electronic Rights. Secondary or subsidiary rights dealing with electronic/multimedia formats (the Internet, CD-ROMs, electronic magazines).

Elements. Actors, directors and producers attached to a project to make an attractive package.

El-Hi. Elementary to high school. A term used to indicate reading or interest level.

Episodic Drama. An hour-long, continuing TV show, often shown at 10 p.m.

Erotica. A form of literature or film dealing with the sexual aspects of love. Erotic content ranges from subtle sexual innuendo to explicit descriptions of sexual acts.

Ethnic. Stories and novels whose central characters are African American, Native American, Italian American, Jewish, Appalachian or members of some other specific cultural group. Ethnic fiction usually deals with a protagonist caught between two conflicting ways of life: mainstream American culture and his ethnic heritage.

Evaluation Fees. Fees an agent may charge to evaluate material. The extent and quality of this evaluation varies, but comments usually concern the salability of the manuscript.

Exclusive. Offering a manuscript, usually for a set period of time, to just one agent and guaranteeing that agent is the only one looking at the manuscript.

Experimental. Type of fiction that focuses on style, structure, narrative technique, setting and strong characterization rather than plot. This form depends largely on the revelation of a character's inner being, which elicits an emotional response from the reader.

Family Saga. A story that chronicles the lives of a family or a number of related or interconnected families over a period of time.

Fantasy. Stories set in fanciful, invented worlds or in a legendary, mythic past that rely on outright invention or magic for conflict and setting.

Film Rights. May be sold or optioned by the agent/author to a person in the film industry, enabling the book to be made into a movie.

Floor Bid. If a publisher is very interested in a manuscript, he may offer to enter a floor bid when the book goes to auction. The publisher sits out of the auction, but agrees to take the book by topping the highest bid by an agreed-upon percentage (usually 10 percent).

Foreign Rights. Translation or reprint rights to be sold abroad.

Foreign Rights Agent. An agent who handles selling the rights to a country other than that of the first book agent. Usually an additional percentage (about 5 percent) will be added on to the first book agent's commission to cover the foreign rights agent.

Genre. Refers to either a general classification of writing, such as a novel, poem or short story, or to the categories within those classifications, such as problem novels or sonnets. Genre fiction is a term that covers various types of commercial novels, such as mystery, romance, Western, science fiction and horror.

Ghostwriting. A writer puts into literary form the words, ideas, or knowledge of another person under that person's name. Some agents offer this service; others pair ghostwriters with celebrities or experts.

Gothic. Novels characterized by historical settings and featuring young, beautiful women who win the favor of handsome, brooding heroes while simultaneously dealing with some life-threatening menace—either natural or supernatural.

Graphic Novel. Contains comic-like drawings and captions, but deals more with everyday events and issues than with superheroes.

High Concept. A story idea easily expressed in a quick, one-line description.

Hi-Lo. A type of fiction that offers a high level of interest for readers at a low reading level.

Historical. A story set in a recognizable period of history. In addition to telling the stories of ordinary people's lives, historical fiction may involve political or social events of the time.

Hook. Aspect of the work that sets it apart from others and draws in the reader/viewer.

Horror. A story that aims to evoke some combination of fear, fascination and revulsion in its readers—either through supernatural or psychological circumstances.

How-To. A book that offers the reader a description of how something can be accomplished. It includes both information and advice.

Imprint. The name applied to a publisher's specific line of books.

Independent Producers. Self-employed entrepreneurs who assemble scripts, actors, directors and financing for their film concepts.

IRC. International Reply Coupon. Buy at a post office to enclose with material sent outside the country to cover the cost of return postage. The recipient turns them in for stamps in their own country.

Joint Contract. A legal agreement between a publisher and two or more authors that establishes provisions for the division of royalties the book generates.

Juvenile. Category of children's writing that can be broken down into easy-to-read books (ages 7-9), which run 2,000-10,000 words, and middle-grade books (ages 8-12), which run 20,000-40,000 words.

Literary. A book where style and technique are often as important as subject matter. Also called serious fiction.

Logline. A one-line description of a plot as it might appear in *TV Guide*.

Mainstream Fiction. Fiction on subjects or trends that transcend popular novel categories like mystery or romance. Using conventional methods, this kind of fiction tells stories about people and their conflicts.

Marketing Fee. Fee charged by some agents to cover marketing expenses. It may be used to cover postage, telephone calls, faxes, photocopying or any other expense incurred in marketing a manuscript.

Mass Market Paperbacks. Softcover books, usually 4 × 7, on a popular subject directed at a general audience and sold in groceries, drugstores and bookstores.

Memoir. An author's commentary on the personalities and events that have significantly influenced one phase of his life.

MFTS. Made for TV series.

Midlist. Those titles on a publisher's list expected to have limited sales. Midlist books are mainstream, not literary, scholarly or genre, and are usually written by new or relatively unknown writers.

Miniseries. A limited dramatic series written for television, often based on a popular novel.

MOW. Movie of the week. A movie script written especially for television, usually seven acts with time for commercial breaks. Topics are often contemporary, sometimes controversial, fictional accounts. Also called a made-for-TV movie.

Multiple Contract. Book contract with an agreement for a future book(s).

Mystery. A form of narration in which one or more elements remain unknown or unexplained until the end of the story. Subgenres include: amateur sleuth, caper, cozy, heist, malice domestic, police procedural, etc.

Net Receipts. One method of royalty payment based on the amount of money a book publisher receives on the sale of the book after the booksellers' discounts, special sales discounts and returned copies.

Novelization. A novel created from the script of a popular movie and published in paperback. Also called a movie tie-in.

Novella. A short novel or long short story, usually 25,000-50,000 words. Also called a novelette.

Occult. Supernatural phenomena, including ghosts, ESP, astrology, demonic possession and witchcraft.

One-Time Rights. This right allows a short story or portions of a fiction or nonfiction book to be published again without violating the contract.

Option. Instead of buying a movie script outright, a producer buys the right to a script for a short period of time (usually six months to one year) for a small down payment. If the movie has not begun production and the producer does not wish to purchase the script at the end of the agreed time period, the rights revert back to the scriptwriter. Also called a script option.

Option Clause. A contract clause giving a publisher the right to publish an author's next book.

Outline. A summary of a book's content (up to 15 double-spaced pages); often in the form of chapter headings with a descriptive sentence or two under each one to show the scope of the book. A script's outline is a scene-by-scene narrative description of the story (10-15 pages for a ½-hour teleplay; 15-25 pages for 1-hour; 25-40 pages for 90 minutes; 40-60 pages for a 2-hour feature film or teleplay).

Picture Book. A type of book aimed at ages 2-8 that tells the story partially or entirely with artwork, with up to 1,000 words. Agents interested in selling to publishers of these books often handle both artists and writers.

Pitch. The process where a writer meets with a producer and briefly outlines ideas that could be developed if the writer is hired to write a script for the project.

Platform. A writer's speaking experience, interview skills, Web site and other abilities which help form a following of potential buyers for his book.

Proofreading. Close reading and correction of a manuscript's typographical errors.

Property. Books or scripts forming the basis for a movie or TV project.

Proposal. An offer to an editor or publisher to write a specific work, usually a package consisting of an outline and sample chapters.

Prospectus. A preliminary written description of a book, usually one page in length.

Psychic/Supernatural. Fiction exploiting—or requiring as plot devices or themes—some contradictions of the commonplace natural world and materialist assumptions about it (including the traditional ghost story).

Query. A letter written to an agent or a potential market to elicit interest in a writer's work.

Reader. A person employed by an agent or buyer to go through the slush pile of manuscripts and scripts and select those worth considering.

Regional. A book faithful to a particular geographic region and its people, including behavior, customs, speech and history.

Release. A statement that your idea is original, has never been sold to anyone else, and that you are selling negotiated rights to the idea upon payment.

Remainders. Leftover copies of an out-of-print or slow-selling book purchased from the publisher at a reduced rate. Depending on the contract, a reduced royalty or no royalty is paid on remaindered books.

Reprint Rights. The right to republish a book after its initial printing.

Romance. A type of category fiction in which the love relationship between a man and a woman pervades the plot. The story is told from the viewpoint of the heroine, who meets a man (the hero), falls in love with him, encounters a conflict that hinders their relationship, and then resolves the conflict with a happy ending.

Royalties. A percentage of the retail price paid to the author for each copy of the book that is sold. Agents take their percentage from the royalties earned and from the advance.

SASE. Self-addressed, stamped envelope. It should be included with all correspondence.

Scholarly Books. Books written for an academic or research audience. These are usually heavily researched, technical, and often contain terms used only within a specific field.

Science Fiction. Literature involving elements of science and technology as a basis for conflict, or as the setting for a story.

Screenplay. Script for a film intended to be shown in theaters.

Script. Broad term covering teleplay, screenplay or stage play. Sometimes used as a shortened version of the word manuscript when referring to books.

Serial Rights. The right for a newspaper or magazine to publish sections of a manuscript.

Simultaneous Submission. Sending the same manuscript to several agents or publishers at the same time.

Sitcom. Situation comedy. Episodic comedy script for a television series. The term comes from the characters dealing with various situations with humorous results.

Slice of Life. A type of short story, novel, play or film that takes a strong thematic approach, depending less on plot than on vivid detail in describing the setting and/or environment, and the environment's effect on characters involved in it.

Slush Pile. A stack of unsolicited submissions in the office of an editor, agent or publisher.

Spec Script. A script written on speculation without confirmation of a sale.

Standard Commission. The commission an agent earns on the sales of a manuscript or script. For literary agents, the commission percentage (usually 10-20 percent) is taken from the advance and royalties paid to the writer. For script agents, the commission (usually 15-20 percent) is taken from script sales. If handling plays, agents take a percentage from the box office proceeds.

Subagent. An agent handling certain subsidiary rights, usually working in conjunction with the agent who handled the book rights. The percentage paid the book agent is increased to pay the subagent.

Subsidiary. An incorporated branch of a company or conglomerate (e.g., Knopf Publishing Group is a subsidiary of Random House, Inc.).

Subsidiary Rights. All rights other than book publishing rights included in a book publishing contract, such as paperback rights, book club rights and movie rights. Part of an agent's job is to negotiate those rights and advise you on which to sell and which to keep.

Syndication Rights. The right for a station to rerun a sitcom or drama, even if the show originally appeared on a different network.

Synopsis. A brief summary of a story, novel or play. As a part of a book proposal, it is a comprehensive summary condensed in a page or page and a half, single-spaced. See *outline*.

Teleplay. Script for television.

Terms. Financial provisions agreed upon in a contract.

Textbook. Book used in a classroom at the elementary, high school or college level.

Thriller. A story intended to arouse feelings of excitement or suspense. Works in this genre are highly sensational, usually focusing on illegal activities, international espionage, sex and violence.

TOC. Table of Contents. A listing at the beginning of a book indicating chapter titles and their corresponding page numbers. It can also include brief chapter descriptions.

Trade Book. Either a hardcover or softcover book sold mainly in bookstores. The subject matter frequently concerns a special interest for a general audience.

Trade Paperback. A soft-bound volume, usually 5 × 8, published and designed for the general public; available mainly in bookstores.

Translation Rights. Sold to a foreign agent or foreign publisher.

Treatment. Synopsis of a television or film script (40-60 pages for a two-hour feature film or teleplay).

Unsolicited Manuscript. An unrequested manuscript sent to an editor, agent or publisher.

Westerns/Frontier. Stories set in the American West, almost always in the 19th century, generally between the antebellum period and the turn of the century.

Young Adult (YA). The general classification of books written for ages 12-17. They run 50,000-60,000 words and include category novels—adventure, sports, career, mysteries, romance, etc.

Literary Agents Specialties Index

This index is divided into fiction and nonfiction subject categories. To find an agent interested in the type of manuscript you've written, see the appropriate sections under the subject headings that best describe your work.

FICTION

Adventure

Comic Books

Confession

Contemporary

Detective

Erotica

Ethnic

Experimental

Family

Family Saga

Fantasy

Feminist

Gay

Glitz

Gothic

Historical

Specialties Index

Horror

Humor

Juvenile

Specialties Index

Literary

Mainstream

Military

Multicultural

Multimedia

Mystery

New Age

Picture Books

Psychic

Regional

Religious

Romance

Science

Science Fiction

Sports

Suspense

Thriller

Western

Women's

Young Juvenile

Young Adult

NONFICTION

Agriculture/Horticulture

Americana

Animals

Anthropology

Art

Biography

Business

Child

Computers

Cooking

Crafts

Current Affairs

Education

Ethnic

Film

Gardening

Gay

Government

Health

History

How To

Humor

Interior

Juvenile

Language

Law

Medicine

Memoirs

Military

Money

Multicultural

Music

Nature

New Age

Parenting

Philosophy

Photography

Politics

Popular Culture

Psychology

Recreation

Regional

Religion

Science

Specialties Index

Self Help

Sex

Sociology

Software

Spirituality

Sports

Technology

Translation

Travel

True Crime

Women's

Agents Index

C

D

E

H

I

J

K

S

T

U

V

W

Y

Z

General Index

C

D

E

General Index

J

K

L

M

General Index

Y

Z